Cheese Puffs

Ruby Matenko

CHEESE PUFFS

Dedication

To my mommy: no matter what age you could have had me, you have always been and will always be the best mommy ever. I love you the best in the world.

Prologue

I've been sitting in this hospital for what feels like years but has probably only been a couple of hours, having no idea if my dad is alive or not.

We came here straight from home. Mom was working on the final rewrite of the book she's been working on for so long, and since it's Dad's birthday, we were all going to go out for his birthday dinner once he got home from work. We were so excited to leave for the restaurant, we were just waiting for him to get home. He never did.

Mom came downstairs, saying she was almost done with her chapter, and she kept looking at her watch, because it was unlike Dad to be late getting home. She was worried he got held up in traffic. Which he did, in a way. Looking more and more disturbed, she asked me to fix my little sister's hair so that it would look nice for dinner.

"Josie, how about some nice braids for Dad's birthday?" I said to her, and she immediately sat in front of me. She always loves when I braid her hair.

As I was finishing up the braided pigtails, I heard Mom on the phone upstairs. "What?!? Where?!?" she shrieked, and then she rushed downstairs, grabbing us and her car keys and crying to us that Dad had been in a car accident, a really bad one.

I honestly don't remember how we got to the hospital, I just remember running to the car and noticing one of Josie's braids was unraveling because I hadn't been able to tie the bottom of it when Mom got the call. I kept thinking I needed to fix it, but I also felt like I couldn't move or speak or do anything but stay frozen.

Now we're at the hospital. The intensive care unit's waiting room, to be exact. It's busy and loud. I've never been to such a hectic place. There are people being wheeled around in wheelchairs and on gurneys, each one with an injury worse than the last. Some look dead. I keep my eyes down and hold Josie's hand as she sits on my mom's lap. We haven't said a word to each other since we got here. It's like we're all paralyzed.

Suddenly, a doctor calls out, "Is anyone here for Thomas Davis?" Mom jumps up, and we follow him over to a less busy section. Josie walks in front of me, I see that her braid is completely unraveled now. I really should have tied it before we left for the hospital.

Once we get to the secluded area, I see that the doctor has an odd expression on his face. My heart thuds. *He'll be okay. He's my dad. He'll be okay. He has to be.*

"Mrs. Davis?" the doctor says. My mom nods, stares at him, looking for answers, looking for *good* answers. He looks at all of us, then puts his hand on Mom's shoulder. "I'm so sorry...it was a really bad car crash...he didn't make it..."

After hearing that, the world starts to spin and everything is a blur and Mom falls to the floor and people rush in and Josie is screaming...

And just like that, my world crashes into a million pieces.

Chapter 1: Life as We Know It, Gone

AROUND TWO YEARS LATER

"Okay, Mom!" I call back to my mom after she reminds me to watch Josie, then she rushes out the door for work, and I go to set the kitchen table for me and Josie.

"Josie, food!" I call out to my little sister, who's now ten years old and not so little anymore. I can hear her blasting dance music upstairs as I dish out microwave tacos on my plate, and then on her plate. As usual, it's a pretty busy, stressful night around here in my house. It's been this way since my dad died. My mom works three jobs to compensate for the loss of Dad's income, while I babysit Josie pretty much every night. Our family was put into a state of dysfunction after he was gone. But I'm used to it, at this point.

But I guess just because you're used to something doesn't make it okay.

The phone rings, I wipe off my hands and rush to pick it up. "Hello?" I ask a little too loudly, brushing a long strand of blonde hair out of my mouth.

"Whoa, calm down, Mads, it's Leo," says my boyfriend.

"Sorry, I'm just trying to get my sister down to dinner, and then I have to do my homework, and I have *so* much editing to do for the paper, and then-"

"Okay, okay, deep breaths, Mads." He laughs. "Uh, I could come over when that's all done, if you want." I can tell he's smiling. "When will your mom be home?"

"Around midnight, but I don't know, let's just play it by ear. I'll get back to you after Josie goes to bed. Miss you."

He blows me a kiss through the phone and then hangs up. Shivers run down my back; even though we've been together for over a year, I still get excited to see him. I walk back to the kitchen, picking up some textbooks on the way, trying to clean up a bit. Our living room connects to the dining room, which connects to the kitchen. There's a huge gray couch in the living room, which matches the rug. Framed family photos are hung above the fireplace. The large, oak-wood dining table stands in the middle of the dining room. We haven't used it since my dad died, and it just *sits* there, as a constant reminder. Near the door to the kitchen,

3

there's a painting of a sunset on the wall. We got it in 2013, ten years after I was born, so it's been hanging there for five years now. I can't believe I'm only fifteen. I feel like I'm thirty, with all the things I have to do and take care of.

"Josie, get down here!" She never listens the first time.

Finally, she emerges, her dirty blonde hair messy all around her face. She devours the tacos and it makes me smile. I love knowing she's enjoying food I made for her. She's incredibly skinny, and has the fastest metabolism in the world, like me. Everyone thinks it's awesome to be so petite, but I don't like it at all. People have called me a "little twerp" and "bony bones" before, and I hate it. I actually have to work hard to gain weight. It's so embarrassing to me. I wish I had more of a "body" like other girls.

Before digging into my own food, I make a quick phone call to Janet. She's my assistant at the school newspaper, and I'm the editor-in-chief. I remind her that she needs to send me the editing for this week's edition so that I can review it before she sends it to be printed. I try to tell her calmly, because she's pretty much always in a bad or stressed out mood, and she tends to take it out on me. But I know that if I become a journalist one day, I'll have to deal with many people like Janet.

My school newspaper is called *The Redford Story.* I became editor-in-chief because of the killer story I wrote about the senior prom at our high school. For some reason, it all came together and I was able to word it so perfectly, and my English teacher was so impressed that she recommended me for the position.

It's always been my dream to be a journalist. Since I can remember, I've always loved to tell a story, and I've always loved watching the news. Mom told me I would always want to watch reporters on television, rather than Elmo on Sesame Street. I've done a lot of research about journalism as a career, and about various famous reporters, journalists, et cetera. I figured out which university I want to go to: Harvard. They have an amazing journalism program. So, I set my life plan, which is that I'm going to study journalism at Harvard, become a journalist, get married in my late twenties (hopefully to Leo), and then have three kids. Two girls, then a boy.

My mother encourages my love of journalism more than anything. In fact, she was going to be a published writer herself, but then, well...

The book she'd been working on for what seemed like forever needed just one more rewrite in order to be published. She actually already had a publisher who was interested, based on a draft she'd sent in. The publisher loved it, but said it needed a rewrite, and Mom was in the middle of working on it when Dad died. So not only did she lose her husband, but the career she'd been working for all those years never happened, because she just could never bring herself to go back to working on it after that. The association was too painful. Besides, she was left alone with two daughters and no money coming in, so she had to take on three jobs, and none of them were what she had dreamed of. She lost all her hopes and dreams in one horrible moment.

It's not something I like to talk about or to even think about.

And I would never tell her, but part of the reason I work at the newspaper is for her. She enjoys hearing about the stories I write and watching me work, in the same way a gardener would enjoy seeing her flowers grow.

After hanging up with Janet, I sit down to eat with Josie. "Did you finish your homework? Mom told me that you need to do that instead of playing on your iPad."

She nods, and I smile at her with relief, because she's not lying. I can usually tell when she's lying, she's not a great liar.

"Hey Maddie, could you ask Mom to let me go get ice cream after school tomorrow? This cool girl Hannah asked me to go tomorrow, and-"

"Josie, you're in fifth grade. I didn't get to go anywhere by myself or with friends until I was..." I stop, because I realize that there are a lot of things I've had to do earlier than most kids my age, like taking care of my sister all the time. So my argument isn't really going to get anywhere. Looking at her sad face, I promise her I'll discuss it with Mom. I feel like Josie, Mom, and I never talk directly, all three of us *together*. There's always either communication between me and Mom, Josie and Mom, or just Josie and me. Our family always talked to each other a lot better when my dad was still here.

"Clean up when you're done. I have lots of homework," I tell Josie, and then I put my dishes in the sink, and go upstairs to my room, stopping by the laundry room to put the clothes from the washing machine into the dryer. There's something about the laundry room that I find comforting. The detergent smell, the clothes and towels and linens being cleaned.

I love my bedroom, too. My mom went all "Laura Ashley," so I have pretty light blue walls with white flowers for the ceiling trim. It's been this way since I was a baby.

I go to my desk and take out my computer, getting ready to edit my English essay which is due tomorrow. Once a week, my English teacher, Mrs. Perry, gives us a one-paragraph assignment. They are always very philosophical questions.

Madison Davis
Period 6
10/04/2018

Question: Under what conditions does a person change?

My answer: Change happens when someone comes face-to-face with some sort of a challenge. Then, they know that they have to make a decision, or a choice. These choices change people drastically. It's like when the wind suddenly blows strongly and stirs everything up. Everything just randomly falls to the ground. Then the person is faced with many choices, and they have to make a decision about what to do with all the leaves. But change is always inevitable, no matter how the wind blows.

I know it probably needs a bit more work, but I think it's good enough, so I send it to my teacher. I laugh to myself, thinking about the fact that I just made a *choice* to send it to her when it might not be up to my usual quality of work. But, I'm facing a *challenge* right now to get all of my homework done. I still have math and French homework, and the editing for the newspaper article that Janet is sending me, and I have to watch Josie and put her to bed. And, well, I really want to see Leo tonight, too.

I hear Josie blasting her dance music again, and I yell at her to turn it down. It's so hard for me to concentrate with loud noise.

Once I'm done my homework, it's nearly ten. Josie's bedtime was an hour ago. She'd better not tell Mom I forgot to tell her when it was time for bed. I go into her room, which is basically an explosion of pink: the rug, the walls, the bed, even her clothes and shoes that clutter up the room, all pink. Okay, yes, there's a little purple, too. Her favorite jeans are purple.

She's scrolling on her iPad. "Brush your teeth and go to bed, Josie, okay?"

She nods, and I kiss her on her forehead the way Mom would have done, then I take her iPad, and shut the door. Mom doesn't want Josie to sleep with her iPad, because she's worried she'll just spend the whole night on it.

Once I hide the iPad in the pantry, I take out my cell phone and dial Leo's number. He sounds happy and excited, and he tells me he'll be over in ten minutes. I look down at my ratty white tee and stained gray sweatpants. No way am I wearing *this*.

I go into my room, shutting the door quietly so Josie won't wake up. I look inside my dresser drawers and take out a pair of short black shorts. *Should I?* Nah, I don't even think they'd look good on me, because I'm too skinny. I borrowed them from my best friend Molly, who's a normal size.

Instead, I slip on some black sweatpants that look okay, and I put on a red tank top that's a little revealing, but it's hot in the house and Mom says we can't use the air conditioning unless we really have to, because it's expensive. I'm so self-conscious about my body that I end up putting a black hoodie on top of my outfit. Before I have a chance to change my mind again, I hear the doorbell ring.

I hurry downstairs and open the door. Leo stands there, smiling. He's absolutely gorgeous, with thick brown hair and the most comforting light green eyes, a lanky yet muscular frame. He pulls me in for a long kiss. I love the way he kisses me, like he's inhaling me. I'm so glad that we get to be alone, since Mom will be at work till late.

Leo's been there for me since the first day of high school, so around a year and a half ago, when I tripped on the soccer field and got a bad cut on my chin. He called an ambulance and came with me to the hospital, and stayed with me when I had to get stitches. Afterwards, we went out for ice cream, and then he said I had to "get back on the horse," so we played a game of soccer, just the two of us. I had liked him for a while, but I don't think he really noticed me until that day, and then we became a couple. I love being with Leo. When I'm with him, it makes me forget about my dad's death and all the things that have happened to my family since.

We make our way up the stairs, turning left down the hallway, and I open my bedroom door.

Chapter 2: This Isn't Happening

AROUND TWO MONTHS LATER

After I get home from school, I collapse on the couch, exhausted; I can hardly keep my eyes open. I have so much homework, so much to do...but I'm *so tired*.

The next thing I know, I'm being shaken awake by Mom, her tired eyes and bottle-blonde hair filling my vision.

"Honey? I have to go to work now. I think you've been going to bed too late, so please get more sleep. I need you to not be too tired to watch your sister. You'll have to make dinner for both of you again, and please do your homework and make sure Josie does hers, okay?" Before I can even say anything, she rushes out the door.

I lazily get up and prepare some leftover pizza for me and Josie. Then Josie runs down the stairs, grabbing some slices before she runs out the front door. "Josie? Where are you going?" I scream, but then I sigh. She's probably just going to the library, which is only a couple blocks away, and it's usually okay with Mom as long as she's back soon enough.

And I'm too tired to run after her.

I'd better start on my math homework. I already didn't finish the assignment last night, because I was too tired. This isn't good. I can't let my grades slip. I feel like I'm always just trying to catch up these days.

I take my notes out and start, but my mind drifts, thinking of Leo. It's weird, but things have kind of cooled off between us. He's been busy with soccer (he's trying to get a soccer scholarship for college), and running the newspaper has been taking up a lot of my time. I really hope that we can plan something fun for winter break, like hot chocolate, cuddling and watching some of our favorite holiday movies by the fireplace, and then going outside and playing in the snow.

I don't know if we're even getting snow this year. Redford, the town I live in, only gets snow every few years. It's a small town in Northern California with less than twenty thousand people. The residential and community areas of the town are in the center, and the city-like areas are on the outside, so it's like a guarded circle, which makes me feel safe in a way.

I finish my math homework an hour later, and Josie comes back. I should have stopped her and asked her where she was going, and being too tired is not an excuse. Mom would be so upset with me. Luckily, Josie's back and she's fine. I realize that I forgot to eat my pizza, and it's been sitting on the counter for over an hour. I've been extremely forgetful lately, and I think it's just the stress about midterms coming up. I really need to start cracking down on studying.

I eat my pizza, though it's gross cold, and then I ask Josie where she went. She looks at her shoes and quietly says, "I went to get ice cream with Hannah. You know how we talked about it, like a little while ago?"

"Yeah, and I asked Mom a few times for you, and she said no. I told you that. So, you didn't listen to *either* of us," I say angrily. I hate when she doesn't listen to me. Even though I love her so much, it's already hard enough to have to always watch her. And I can't tell Mom when she does something she isn't supposed to, because then we will *both* get in trouble. Besides, Mom is always stressed out enough with all her jobs; filing papers for a business company in the morning, then her afternoon shift at the retail store, and at night, waitressing.

"I'm sorry," Josie says quietly, twisting her foot around nervously.

"Sorry isn't good enough. It was dangerous what you did. You need to be properly supervised to go out with friends at your age."

"Just please don't tell Mom."

"I won't, but I'm only not telling her because she's stressed with work. Now it's time to go up and get ready for bed." She trudges upstairs, changes, then brushes her teeth. I kiss her forehead and then take her iPad and hide it in the pantry, our usual routine, so she won't think I'm mad at her. I'm not really mad that she went for ice cream. I actually feel bad for her, since Mom's never home and she has to answer to me all the time. I just feel guilty for letting her go and not checking where. I'm going to try to get more sleep so I won't be as tired and I can take better care of her.

I go on my computer to finish editing a story for journalism, and then I begin my chemistry homework. We have to write a two-page report on this lab we did in class.

I yawn again. I'm just irritable and fed up with all the schoolwork I have to do, and I'm really, *really* tired. I just want to go to bed and sleep for the rest of my life.

A pang of worry thumps inside my stomach, and I try to push this gnawing feeling that I've been having aside. But I can't help it. I check the calendar hung above my desk, decorated with stars and sheep, looking to the date of my last period. I always put a little "P" on the day I get it. I look for the "P" and see that it's been a little over two months since my last period. *Two months.* I always get it right on time.

I shake my head. It's probably just the stress of everything. To take my mind off things, I decide to call Leo, but it goes right to his voicemail, so I leave a message. "Leo, uh, just wanted to say hi. Haven't seen you in a week. Call me, okay? I miss you."

I hang up and decide to put off my science homework until tomorrow. It isn't due till Friday, and so I have a couple days. I'm just too tired to even *think* right now.

Normally, I stay awake to hear Mom's key turn in the door at midnight because it makes me feel safe, but tonight, I fall asleep before ten-thirty.

But I still feel like I haven't slept a wink when I open my eyes, listening to my alarm going off. I hit "snooze" three times until Josie shakes me awake, backpack on, shoes tied. "Maddie, we're going to be late! You have to walk me to school!"

I look at the clock, rubbing sleep out of my eyes. Oh, shoot. It's a quarter to eight. We have to be in class *at* eight. We're usually out the door five minutes ago.

"Josie, go downstairs, finish up any breakfast you have left, and just give me five minutes, okay? Just five minutes! Go!"

I stand up, feeling a little dizzy. Maybe I'm getting sick? *Ugh,* I hate being sick. I go to the bathroom, splash water on my face, and brush my teeth, but then I promptly spit out the toothpaste. Yuck. Did Mom change the brand of toothpaste we use?

I check the label. Nope. It's the same mint I've always used. Maybe it's expired. Can toothpaste become expired? Whatever, I don't have time to think about this.

I rinse my mouth out with water, throw on a pair of jeans and a hoodie, and I hurry down the stairs to find Josie waiting by the door, an exasperated look on her face. "Okay, sorry, let's go!" I say.

I open the door and start down the street, feeling mist in the air. It's definitely getting colder out. The neighborhood streets I've grown up on are bustling with the usual weekday morning parents walking their kids to school. I love my neighborhood, the trees are so tall, the houses are a typical family suburban style. The air feels cold and smells fresh and clean today, and the grass is wet from dew.

Even with our quick walking, we have to run the last block to school. Josie runs into the elementary school, and just around the corner is my high school. I rush in, whizzing past the other kids to my locker, quickly jamming my books for my first two classes into my bag, and then running to math, my first period of the day. The bell rings just as I slide in my chair. Yes! I made it.

I feel *so* winded, though. It surprises me how tired and sick and awful I feel. I think I'm getting the flu. Normally, a little running would be nothing for me, as I'm pretty fit and active. I go for hikes with Leo all the time, I practice soccer with him, and sometimes, on nights when I'm not babysitting Josie, I'll go for a run. It makes sense that I have the flu; it is December, after all, and it seems like someone at my school is always sick, so viruses and all that go around.

But I still like my school. It's the typical public school; crappy cafeteria food, cheap metal lockers, linoleum floors, bad lighting. But it's very big, with a brick and stone exterior, and besides its clichéness, I don't mind it. I'm not popular, but I'm not *not* popular, if that makes any sense at all.

Mrs. Wu is writing equations on the board when I feel a sudden wave of nausea. I shake it off, trying to focus on the math problems. I've always had really bad emetophobia, a fear of throwing up, and so I'm just trying to ignore it. The feeling gets stronger though, so I ask Mrs. Wu if I can go to the bathroom. She nods, because we're in the middle of a break to catch up on the notes she's written so far, and I grab a hall pass. I know I'm going to throw up, but I hate throwing up. Maybe it's not the flu. It might be that fish Mom picked up for dinner a couple nights ago. My system doesn't work that well with fish. If it's the slightest bit undercooked, or if it has a bad piece in it, I get sick.

But why is it just hitting me now?

Maybe it's something else that's making me sick, though I don't know what.

But deep down, I think I kind of *do* know what.

I lean over the nearest toilet and throw up, but nothing really comes out. I didn't have breakfast today and the pizza from last night was digested a long time ago. I just retch over the toilet for a couple minutes, until the feeling passes. Then I splash my face with water, and look at myself in the mirror. My eyes are hazel and they sometimes change color and look a bit more green or brown or blue, depending on what I'm wearing or what my surroundings are. Right now, they just look worried. *What if all of this isn't just stress? What if it's what I don't want it to be?*

I walk back to math, return the hall pass, and try to catch up on the notes. We turn in our homework at the end of class, and she assigns three pages of math problems to do tonight. Each page in our textbook has thirty problems. I'll be up all night. I take a deep breath and jot it down in my agenda so I won't forget to do it.

I go over to the newspaper office next. I know we were supposed to have a meeting about the extra editing I need people to do and the new writers we're supposed to take on, but I forgot my notes at home. It took me so long to write them a couple nights ago. What a waste. I end up using Janet's notes. She always comes double-prepared, like she's planning on replacing me at any moment. She scowls at me. I smile in response, knowing it will annoy her, and she looks away.

After that, I have a free period, so I go to the library to start my math homework, then it's finally lunch time. I'm suddenly starving, no longer nauseous. But I forgot to make a sandwich. *Well, this is turning out to be one great day.*

I sit there for a moment, thinking about all my symptoms. The forgetfulness, the dizziness, the exhaustion, the nausea, and I decide I can't take worrying about this anymore, so I'm going to head to the pharmacy. I think about telling Molly, who's been my best friend since seventh grade, when on the first day of school, I got ink all over my elbow from a pen that leaked on my desk, and she helped me clean it up in the bathroom. It ended up looking like a bad bruise, but we became friends, nonetheless. But I decide I'd better wait and not tell her. Hopefully there will be nothing to even tell.

My heart rate speeds up as I head out of school, grabbing a bright purple "leaving" pass that we have to wear pinned to our clothes. We're allowed to leave campus for lunch, as long as we return before the bell rings, and we have to take a pass. Only freshmen are not allowed to leave for lunch, and it's exciting to be able to do it this year, as a sophomore. Last year, I'd look on enviously as I watched the upper grades leave and return with delicious, hot lunches, not gross, soggy ones from home, or having to eat the disgusting cafeteria food.

I walk to the pharmacy, passing the little houses with pretty flowers. The town center has a few blocks of shops, all decorated in pastel colors. The store owners are friendly and they always have a smile waiting for you. It's pretty ideal in some ways, because it's a very family-oriented town and it feels welcoming, but it can also be difficult because everybody knows your business, because it's such a small town.

My mom has always been really nice and friendly to the store owners, and she even became good friends with the woman who owns the hair salon, but after my dad died, she's so busy working all the time that she doesn't have a social life. I find it sad that, like my mother, *I'm* always so busy that I can't have that great of a social life.

There's a real chill in the air now, and it's obvious that winter is coming. I sigh. When it's cold, the shops and houses don't look as bright. Redford looks best in the sunlight. But I like living in this part of California. While I do get curious from time to time about Los Angeles and Hollywood and all the celebrities over there, I like being in this tucked-away little suburb. I'm not a major city girl, but I'm also not a total nature-obsessed, let's-go-camping girl. I think I fit somewhere in the middle.

As I enter the pharmacy, I try to snap myself out of my distractions and focus on what's *actually* happening. I scour the aisles for what I'm looking for, not wanting to ask the cashier for help. She knows me and my family.

My eyes land on a pregnancy test.

My lip quivers nervously. My head feels cloudy. This doesn't even feel *real*. But I need to take a test, because if it's positive, I obviously need to know.

Shame draws its awful lines all over my face as I go to the counter to pay for the test with Mom's debit card, because I don't have any cash on me. I think of that night with Leo. October fourth.

The cashier stares at me, clearly thinking, *Why is Madison Davis buying a pregnancy test?* She *knows* me. I come here for gum, hair ties, pads, and other things I need, all the time. I can't meet her eyes.

As soon as I pay, I rush home. It's just a couple of minutes from here. I head to my bathroom, tear open the pink box and read the instructions. I have no idea how to do this. But I do follow the instructions and pee on the stick, and then I wait. It says three minutes, so I set a timer on my phone. The whole time, I pray that I don't see a second line. I don't want to see that second line. It's impossible to even think of what I will do if I see the second line. If I'm...I can't even *think* of the word.

The three minutes feel like an hour. I look away from the stick, making sure the bathroom door is locked, even though I know no one will be home. Mom's at work and Josie's at school. Then the timer on my phone goes off. It's time. I look down. There are two lines. I rub my eyes. Maybe they're blurry? Nope. Two lines. *Two lines.*

I can't process it. It must be wrong. It *has* to be wrong. But deep down, I know it's *not* wrong, with how sick I've been feeling, my forgetfulness, my exhaustion, the calendar above my desk which shows I haven't had my period for *two months*.

I wrap the test in toilet paper and throw it in my bathroom trash can, all the way to the bottom, and then I walk out of my house, shaking.

Suddenly, my whole life as I pictured it goes through my mind. Graduating high school, Harvard, becoming a journalist, getting married, *then* having kids. Doing things *right*. But all of these things are suddenly thrown up in the air. The words swirl around me like wind and I can't think straight.

Maybe the test is wrong.

But I just know it, in my heart, that it's right.

How could I have let this happen to myself? What should I do now? Should I get an abortion? How do I even get an abortion? I mean, should I *keep* it? How would I even keep it? What are my other options? I need to think. I need to go to that place that I've heard about but that I never thought I would need to go to: Planned Parenthood.

I think of the last time that I walked into school without this burden, which was just about a couple hours ago. I was just a teenage girl. This morning, I woke up, and for all I knew, I was just a regular teenage girl, worried about being late for school, *and being late for my period!* How will I ever be the same again, now that I know I'm pregnant? There's a *baby* growing inside me. What makes me so sad is that I've always wanted to be a mother, I've always wanted a baby eventually, but not like *this*. Not *now*. When I'm an adult, when I'm older, having experienced more of life, not actually *creating* a life when I haven't even done the whole experiencing-my-own-life thing first.

How can I get rid of it? I have no idea. But how could I *keep* it? I'm only a sophomore in *high school*. And I was *finally* getting back on my feet since my dad died. Nothing's been perfect, especially with Mom working all the time, but we were at least in a routine. And now I ruined everything.

I'm such an *idiot*. I was too caught up in the moment to even think this would actually happen to me. I've heard stories about teen pregnancies. I've watched videos of teen parents online. I never thought this would happen to *me*. I've ruined *everything* no matter what, whatever decision I make, I will be changed by this, I know this already.

I'm going to have to talk to someone to help me figure out what to do. Mom? No way. But who, then? I remember one of these teen moms I watched on YouTube said she went to Planned Parenthood. Maybe I can go there. What a joke that I'm figuring this out from YouTube. But I can't deal with this right now, I have to go back to school.

I walk back, and when I enter the school, I feel like a totally different person.

I will never be the same again, no matter what choice I make.

Chapter 3: Too Much, Too Soon

I can hardly concentrate through the rest of my classes. The same thoughts just circle around my head over and over again, like cars on a racing track, and I just feel numb and in complete denial.

I know I need to make an appointment with Planned Parenthood. They can help me, I think, so I'll go right after school. I guess I'll have to use Mom's debit card again. It's strictly for emergencies, but I think this qualifies as a bit of an emergency.

Should Leo come with me? I mean, it's his baby, too. *Oh my God, it's Leo's baby, too.* But oh my God, how am I going to tell him? I want to cry, but I just can't muster up the tears. They don't come, for some reason. Even though I just found out, I already feel too drained to cry. But I have a feeling I'll be crying a lot later.

I get my books from my locker and then head over to Josie's school to pick her up. As we walk home, she chats about her day. Normally, I'd chime in, but I can't muster anything up. What am I supposed to tell her? *"I took a pregnancy test and there were two lines?"* Yeah, right. Once we're home, I fix her a quick snack, which she takes upstairs to eat while she does her homework.

After looking up Planned Parenthood's number online, I dial it, hiding in the hall closet downstairs so that Josie won't hear me.

"Hello, this is Planned Parenthood, how may I help you?" a cheery voice asks.

"Hi, um, my name's Madison. I need to make an appointment to talk to someone. I just found out I'm pregnant, and I'm only fifteen." My face feels hot. I can't believe I'm saying this. But the person on the other end doesn't seem surprised or judgmental, she's just straightforward and nice.

"Okay, please don't worry, and please know that you're not alone and we will help you. So, what time would you like to come in?"

"In an hour?" That should be enough time to get someone to watch Josie.

"Booking you for 4:30pm, is that okay?"

I say yes and hang up, then call Molly, as I know that she can probably come watch Josie. She says she'll be right over. I wish I could tell her what's going on. But she won't know what to do anymore than I do. We're both just teenage girls.

I'm so scared. I don't think I've ever felt this kind of stuff before.

Somehow, this is so different from when my dad died. I can't even really put it into words.

Molly arrives ten minutes later. She's so reliable. It's one of the reasons I'm best friends with her. She was really there for me when my dad died. She has sweet brown eyes and tons of freckles. When I open the door, I immediately notice she's wearing her auburn hair in braids, and I flinch. I *hate* braids. They'll always remind me of the day my Dad died, and Josie's unraveling braid. I remember thinking I just needed to tie it up, as if that would fix everything. Now I always associate them with something unlucky or bad happening, so I guess it's fitting that Molly wore them today.

I thank her for coming and give her a hug. She doesn't know how much I need that hug. I wonder if she'd still want to be my friend if she knew what was going on.

"What's wrong?" she asks. "You almost never need me to watch Josie."

"Yeah, I just have a ton of errands to run today and it's faster if I'm by myself and I want to make sure she isn't alone. I'll be back soon, though, I promise."

I use Uber to call a car, and once it pulls up to the curb, I get in. A woman is driving and when I tell her I need to go to Planned Parenthood, I can almost feel some sort of palpable judgement coming from her. I'm so ashamed.

I stare out the window. It's windy and there are tons of leaves spinning in the air. The drive is pretty much a blur, but I still try to focus on what's in front of me and not think too much. Red lights turn green. Yellow lights turn red. We pass by "Sunny," the breakfast place where my family used to go out for so many happy breakfasts, both before my dad died, and a few after. It's only open for breakfast, and I see the yellow, sunflower-decorated sign says "Closed."

We pass the toy store, and I look at the felt dolls in the front of the window. For some reason, I think of a baby, *my* baby, playing with those dolls. I can't believe *these* are my thoughts now, not thoughts of school or the newspaper or my friends or Leo.

We pull up, and I give her the cash and then go inside. I check in at the front and the woman tells me to go sit in the waiting room and someone will be with me shortly. A wide range of people are waiting, young and old, some that even look younger than me, if that's possible. I can't believe that I'm here, that I'm one of them.

How many weeks pregnant am I? I wonder, so I calculate from October fourth. Nine weeks. It's December twelfth, so I'm technically nine weeks and a day pregnant. I know I'm going to have to make a quick decision, no time to waste if I'm going to get an abortion. But I don't want to have to make a decision. I just want it to go away.

To pass the waiting time, I take out my phone and look up "week nine pregnancy symptoms." I find an article, and it confirms all of my symptoms and adds, "Only six months left to go!" with a picture of a cute baby and rubber duckies.

It also says online that breast tenderness and enlargement is a common pregnancy symptom. I hold up a book from my backpack to cover myself as I discreetly feel around my bra. Yep. My boobs definitely feel bigger than they were a couple weeks ago. I'm an A-cup, but now my bra feels really tight.

A nurse calls me back, takes my height and weight and blood pressure. I'm 5'3, so I've grown about an inch since my last check-up. But I'm shocked when I look at the scale. It says I weigh 104 pounds! I was only 98 at my last appointment! I sigh and slip my shoes back on, and then I go to give a urine sample as the nurse told me they have to confirm the pregnancy. Hope fills me. *Maybe that test at the drug store was wrong! Oh please, let that be the case,* I pray silently. After I pee and leave the sample in the bathroom, I head into an office, which is decorated with charts of the reproductive organs. A woman walks in with a clipboard and sits down across from me. She looks like she knows everything. At least one of us does.

"Hello, Madison, is it?" she asks, and I nod. "My name is Renee. First things first, I want you to know that everything we say here today is confidential. And your urine sample confirms that you're pregnant." Any hope I had drains out of me. "So I'm here to help you talk this through. First of all, how are you doing?"

"I don't know, honestly. It just...doesn't feel real. I...I don't know how I can make a decision about this, I can't bear the thought of giving up a baby, but...I'm only fifteen!" I feel like I'm about to cry. But the tears won't come. It's like I'm frozen.

"I know. And it's totally normal to feel this way in your situation. I want to go over your options so that you feel safe and also informed to make the decision that is right for you, okay?" I nod. Her voice is so calm and reassuring. I wish she could make the decision for me.

"Everyone faced with this has three options: keeping the baby, terminating the pregnancy, or having the baby and then giving it up for adoption. If you decide to terminate the pregnancy, sooner is better than later, as it only gets more complicated in terms of the procedure. If you were to keep the baby, the logistics of that are something that will take some time to figure out, but it's completely doable. As far as adoption, there are long waiting lists of people waiting to adopt, so that's always an option, too."

As she continues to talk, my mind becomes overwhelmed and I truly don't know what to think or say or do. I'm grateful that she's here to help me, but I know the decision will still have to be *mine*. *I* am responsible for this. *I* am responsible.

"It's good to ask yourself questions, such as, 'How is this going to affect me? Am I ready to go through a pregnancy? Childbirth? How will my decision change my life? How will it affect the people around me?'" She pauses. "Are you close to the father? Does he know yet?"

I shake my head. "He doesn't know. But we've been a little distant lately, I guess, not so close these days." I look down sadly. "We're just in high school. I mean, I can't tell him without laying out some sort of plan of *how* I'm going to tell him. I don't even know what words would come out of my mouth."

"Were you sexually active for a while before you conceived?"

I shake my head, looking away. "It was only one time."

"Were you using protection when you conceived?"

I want to throw up in disgust. I hate that word that she keeps using. *Conceived.* We were just two stupid high school kids. "No, um…we didn't." I want to pinch myself. I want to say that I didn't believe I could get pregnant from just one time having sex. That I didn't think in a million years it would happen to me. But I *did* know what could happen. We learned about it in school, I've seen it on YouTube, my mom told me how babies were made in middle school. I was careless and stupid, so maybe I deserve this.

"I was stupid," I blurt. "And I know this is all…wrong, but…I've always wanted to be a mom someday. Just…not *now*. Not like *this*. But I'm really…torn, I guess."

"Are you thinking of keeping it?" she asks gently.

"I don't know," I admit. "I really don't, but…when I think of separating myself from something growing *inside* of me, I just don't know if I could do that. It'll follow me the rest of my life, it'll always be there, it'll…" Finally, the tears come. I just start bawling, right there in her office, and she puts her arm around me comfortingly.

"Whatever you decide, it will be the right decision. You will make it work. Now, we need to do an ultrasound, to see what's going on in your uterus. This would happen whether or not you terminate or decide to continue the pregnancy. Come with me."

She takes me down the hall, into a room, where she gives me a paper cover up and tells me to undress from the waist down. After I've put the paper gown on, she comes back in with a technician, who tells me to lie down on the table and lift my shirt. She squirts a warm, sticky gel all over and moves a wand that feels like it's massaging me all over my lower stomach. Suddenly, on the little screen, I hear a fast thudding. The technician tells me that's the fetal heartbeat. *The heartbeat.* Then she points out a little scrunched-up thing that reminds me of a cheese puff, my favorite snack. I'm actually craving them right now, but I also feel nauseous. I can't believe that's a *baby.* It will become a person, just like me. *And I'm growing it.*

How can I get rid of it? I would be stopping that *heartbeat.* I shake my head slowly, a huge lump forming in my throat.

"I can't have an abortion. I can't do it. Not right now, not after just seeing that, I can't, I can't..." I say quietly, almost inaudibly. But I don't know how I can *keep* it. I'm way too young to have a baby.

Maybe the best thing to do is have it and give it up for adoption. That's better. I can do that, I think. I feel a little better even just thinking of that option. But still, something stirs in me. That cheese-puff-sized baby...it's *attached* to me. I'm *growing* that baby. It's *mine.* So how could I give it up in *any* way?

The technician finishes and wipes off my stomach. Renee comes back in and tells me I have time to think about it, and not to rush, that she can tell the decision isn't clear to me. She said a lot of people come in here and they know already for sure that they want to terminate. Those are the easy cases. She said mine is more complicated, because she can see I'm not sure, that I'm torn. She gives me her card and tells me that I can come back anytime, or I can even just call her. I just wish I could talk to my mom about this, and have her help me make a decision, but I don't think I can or if she would even want to talk to me about it and not be mad at me, and that just makes me feel so alone. I'm still going to need to tell her, though.

No matter what, my life has changed. I can't see myself living with myself if I get rid of it. Seeing that heartbeat...it made it so much more *real* for me. I can't be responsible for stopping that heartbeat. Maybe other people can get abortions, but I don't think I'm strong enough to get through that. But I'm too young to raise a baby. Maybe adoption is the answer. Maybe not. I need to think. It's going to be so hard to decide. I don't know what I'm going to do. But at least I know one thing.

I can't get rid of it.

Chapter 4: She Knows

Quietly, I slip inside the front door to my house when I see Mom storming up to me, dressed in her waitress uniform, about to go to work. *Uh-oh.*

"You have one job, Maddie. *One job.* To watch Josie. And you send Molly over to do it?" she asks, shaking her head.

"I'm sorry," I say, trying to keep things calm, still not knowing when or how I'm going to tell her about the baby. "I was-"

"Oh, don't even try to lie. I know what you've been doing." Her voice breaks a little, an odd expression immediately filling her face, and I know.

I know that somehow, she knows.

I know that I'm a horrible daughter and that I let her down.

"Mom..."

"How could you do this? How could you? Tell me, really, I want to understand! You used *my* debit card to buy a *pregnancy test*? The money I've been saving so you could go to *Harvard*? Get out of here!" she yells.

I've never seen my mother like this. Tears begin to trickle down my face. "I'm sorry, Mom! I just...please don't be mad!" I say, desperate.

"It's Leo you're having sex with, isn't it?" She scoffs angrily. "So you just *had* to have sex at *fifteen years old*, huh?!?"

I stay silent. "So, are you? Are you pregnant?!?" she yells. I can't look at her. I look away. "Madison, answer me!"

Somehow, I get the strength to nod, keeping my gaze planted on the floor. Then she lets out a scream. A scream like I haven't heard since we found out that Dad died. And then she runs out the front door, slamming it behind her.

I break down, crumpling into a ball on the floor. When I feel arms around me, I remember that Molly was there for all of it, waiting in the dining room. She heard everything. How humiliating, now she knows too.

"It's okay," she says, stroking my back. "It's okay." She repeats this a bunch of times until I stop crying, which is only because it's hard to breathe from crying so hard.

And then I remember: Molly's mother was a teen mother. She wasn't as young as I am, she was eighteen, but that's still a teen pregnancy. She's in her thirties now, they live a block away. Molly told me this on a sleepover when we were both really tired, that time in a sleepover where you tell everything and all your secrets to your friend.

The thought crosses my mind that I should ask Molly if I can come stay with them for a while. Mom doesn't want me here anymore and Josie will think I'm disgusting. She won't even watch people kissing in a movie. She always turns away. I shouldn't be here to be a bad influence for her.

"Molly, uh, do you think there's a chance your mom would let me stay with you guys for a little while? Just until things, you know, settle down, maybe?"

"Yeah, definitely. I mean, come over and talk to my mom. I just texted her, she wants to talk to you. Maybe we could...figure something out."

I shake my head, now having no idea what I'm doing. What am I thinking? I can't leave! Sure, it might be stressful around here since Dad died...but it's my *home*. And I still haven't even decided what to do about the pregnancy yet. My mind's like a ping-pong game right now, my heart pounds, completely overwhelmed by everything.

"Molly, you're really sweet, but I just need to sit here by myself and think for a bit, okay? I'll call you later, and maybe talk to your mom, just, thank you, but I just really need to be alone right now, okay?" I feel like I'm speaking in almost a frantic way, but thankfully, she nods, gives me another one of her amazing hugs, and leaves.

I sit there sobbing, hugging myself, my sleeves getting wet with my tears. I go upstairs to get some tissues, and on the way to my room, I pass Josie's door. I hear her dancing to her favorite dance music, and it just makes me cry even more.

I'm so scared. I can't even feel the baby, but I *know* it's inside me now, which is probably the most surreal thing in the entire world. Hearing that heartbeat was probably the weirdest thing that has ever happened to me.

I hear the door open again and I rush downstairs. It's Mom, and her face looks puffy and her eyes are red and swollen, she's obviously been crying.

She walks up to me. "I can't go to work before I say this to you. Before you know how I feel."

I shut my eyes, bracing myself, as more tears drip down my face.

"I am *so disappointed* that you've done this to yourself. I mean, I can't even *look* at you! How could you be so careless?!?"

My mother has never said anything like this to me. I shake my head back and forth, back and forth, sobbing, unable to believe this is real.

"Well, you need to go to Planned Parenthood and get an abortion!"

"No, Mom, I can't!" I say, my voice shaking with tears.

"What do you mean, you *can't*?!"

"I mean, I went to Planned Parenthood already, and I heard the heartbeat, and I saw...on the screen...I can't, I can't get rid of it! I might do adoption, but I can't do it, I just can't completely get rid of it..."

"Are you kidding me?!? Now you're going to *keep* it?!? Madison, are you crazy?!? You can't go through pregnancy at your age!"

"You've always said that...that children are the most precious thing! Why would I kill it?!? Why would you want me to get an abortion?!? You said that-"

"Oh, that's ridiculous! I meant when you were *older!* You're too young! You're in *school!* You'll ruin your life! You were going to be something! Be *someone!* And now your whole life is over!"

"But I didn't mean to!" I realize that I sound ridiculous. I sound *stupid.*

"That's what they all say! What a joke!" she roars. "I can't believe you! Oh my God, where is your father when I need him more than ever?! I mean, can you imagine what he'd think?!? He would be *so disappointed in you!*"

Now I feel like I've been stabbed in the chest. Hot tears sting my eyes and dribble down. "Mom, I need you! I-I *need* you, you're all I've got!"

"And I needed *you* to make good decisions! And you clearly didn't do that!"

My voice is raw from crying. "You know, I'm *sorry* that I made this mistake, but maybe it would've helped to have a mother who's *there!* You're *never* home! You're always at work! Do you even know how it feels to constantly be in charge of this house and of Josie? I mean, at least I had Leo! At least I had Leo to come over and-"

"*How dare you!* I work because of *you!* For you, and for your sister! I had no idea that your dad was going to die! I *have* to work to keep this house going, and you have to do your part! And your part is *not going off with some boy like a little slut and getting pregnant!* This was the last thing I needed after all I've been through! I lose my husband and then my daughter gets knocked up like some pathetic, disgusting *slut?!?*"

Her words are like knives through my heart. I can't listen anymore. I need to leave. *I need to leave.* I run upstairs and grab the duffel bag my dad used to take when he went on business trips. It's big, and my mom won't even remember he gave it to me for when I had overnights with my friends. It's hard to see through the tears, so I just grab a bunch of clothes, my toothbrush, my school books, some shoes.

Just as I'm about to leave, I stop in my tracks. There's one thing I really need to bring with me. It's something I've kept hidden that no one even knows about. It's the last can of shaving cream that my dad ever used. For a little while after he died, my mom kept things the way they were. It's like she was hoping he would come back. Then, one day, she just decided to throw everything out. I snuck the can of shaving cream before she saw it. I'm not sure why that was what I chose to save, but I'm so glad I did, because when I smell it, it's almost like he's here. It reminds me so much of him and it's so comforting to smell it, especially whenever I'm sad. I want it to last, so I only use a tiny bit of it, only when I really need to. I just put a tiny bit on my wrist, but it's enough to get the smell of him.

I put the can in the duffel bag, and then I rush back downstairs and out the door without looking over at Mom, calling Molly and telling her I'm coming over.

Chapter 5: Nothing Will Ever Be The Same Again

As I'm walking to her house, I see Molly walking towards me. She looks worried. She gives me a hug and we walk the rest of the way to her house together.

It's quiet until she says, "You know I'll support you no matter what you do, okay? And my mom wants to talk to you, too. We'll help you, really."

I nod. And then it hits me how starving I am. I can't remember the last thing I ate. It's making me nauseous to be so hungry and I don't want to ask for food after I'm already just bursting into their house like this, but I'm so hungry.

The streets are completely littered with leaves, blown around from wind. The air feels thicker and colder than it did this morning, and the houses seem quiet. Like they're waiting to see what's going to happen to me. I'm waiting, too. But it feels like this is happening to someone else, like I'm watching one of those bad movies aimed to convince teenagers like me to not do what I've done.

Across the street, a group of older kids from the high school walk the opposite way, giggling and talking. Will I ever be that happy again? I can't think that far ahead. I can't even imagine what *tomorrow* will be like. Mom's words fill my head as we walk. I'm still so stunned. She's never, ever yelled at me or said things like that to me before.

We approach Molly's house, which is a cute brick house with a yellow door and a large chimney. I can smell the fire from the fireplace inside. I've been here a million times, doing homework, hanging out, but walking into the house with Molly now feels like it's the first time I've been here. The house is cozy, warm, and inviting, with comfy brown furniture and cream-colored walls, dark wood floors. Pictures of Molly and her mom are framed on the walls. Colorful, chocolate-stained mugs are scattered in random places. Molly and her mom both like hot chocolate, but the smell of it right now makes me nauseous. I really need to eat.

Ms. Katz approaches, wearing a slightly stained white apron (whenever I'm over for dinner, she cooks a lot, and she's great at it), and jeans, with her light brown hair pulled back into a ponytail, a concerned but kind expression on her face.

"Oh, Madison, Molly told me," she says, and then presses me up against her. It's not my mom's touch, which I'm craving, but it still satisfies me to hug a mother.

Then I realize *I'm* going to be a mother to someone. But not if I give it up for adoption. But even then, I'll know I had a baby and it'll be out there, in the world.

"Listen, there's something important you should know. Even though it seems like your mother hates you right now, she doesn't. She's just very upset about what's going on with you right now, okay? You both need to take time to cool off, settle down, and figure things out. In the meantime, you're welcome to stay with us, for a day, a week, a month, whatever you need, really. I've got the space, and Molly would be thrilled. I'm going to call your mom right now, so she knows and to make sure she's okay with it."

"No! Don't call her! She'll start screaming!"

Ms. Katz shakes her head. "Listen, Madison, I know exactly what you're going through right now. I know what to say to your mom."

She heads off to the living room to call Mom. I tap my foot anxiously while Molly grabs us a bag of chips to eat. Ms. Katz walks back in about ten minutes later.

"She told me that she's fine with you staying, for now. She agrees it isn't good for you two to be screaming at each other, and she understands you haven't made any real decisions yet, but when you do, she wants to know what you decide to do. I'm going to make you something to eat, and then we'll talk, okay?"

She makes me a peanut butter and jam sandwich, and I gobble it up. Then she tells me to come sit in the living room, and we all go to the couch and sit down.

"First of all, have you decided what you want to do yet?"

"No, I...I went to Planned Parenthood, they told me my options. I heard the heartbeat. I can't believe it's a real baby growing inside of me. I really can't..." I start crying again, even harder than I did last time, and she hugs me. "I can't get rid of it." I shake my head. "But how can I keep it? I'm way too young. I mean, I'm thinking of having it and then just...giving it up for adoption."

"I considered that, too, when I found out I was pregnant with Molly. My mother wanted me to. It was a tough time. But there hasn't been one day since that I haven't felt that I made the right choice by keeping Molly." She hugs Molly, and Molly smiles.

I sigh. "It's just...when I think of adoption, it feels like the right choice, but at the same time, it doesn't. I mean, it's *my* baby. I'm *making* him or her. "

"It's a decision that only you can make. Everyone will have a different opinion, and most people would tell you to just abort, because of your age. But only you know what is really the right thing for you." She pauses. "How about the father? What does he want to do?"

"I haven't told him yet."

"Well, you'd better tell him soon. He has a right to know, but, you know, I don't know how he'll take it. Molly's father...he seemed like he'd stick around until she was born, when he ran off to get diapers and never came back. I laugh about it now, because things all worked out, but at the time, I was devastated. But it's been just me and Molly all these years, and we have an amazing relationship, don't we, honey?"

"Yeah. And I can't even imagine things being any different, or things with anyone else. I love you so much, Mom."

They hug again, and I smile as I watch them. But still, I can't picture doing this without Leo. After all, this happened because we were together, because of our...love. Well, kind of. I start hyperventilating again. What if I decide to keep it and he doesn't stay with me? Are we ready to be *parents?*

"But you do need to tell him soon," Dianne says. "Molly told me his name a little while ago, Leo Smith, right?"

"Leo Schmitz," I correct. "But what if I decide to give it up for adoption? Then why do I need to tell him? I mean, I know I'll need to tell him either way, but-"

"It all depends on your choice. In the end, it's your body, so it's ultimately up to you. But I'm going to help you through it, Madison. When I was pregnant with Molly, I always felt so alone, I wish I had someone there to help *me,* so I want to be there for you. It just feels like the right thing to do."

I smile tearfully. "Thank you."

"Now, it sounds like you're pretty sure you don't want to terminate the pregnancy." She frowns. "I always hated that they used the word 'terminate.' Anyway, whether you choose adoption or to keep the baby, you'll need an obstetrician. I'm going to make you an appointment with Dr. Lippincott. She was my doctor during *my* pregnancy with Molly. She's older now, but still practicing. You'll also need to get some prenatal vitamins. I'm going to run down to the pharmacy to get some."

"No, no," I say quickly. "I'll get prenatal vitamins for myself. Please don't worry about me, you've done enough already!" It occurs to me that if I'm keeping the baby, I'll have all kinds of expenses. I'll need to find a job right away. The funny thing is, I was going to try to get a part-time job after school, anyway, just to make a little spending money. Even if I didn't get pregnant. *Even if I didn't get pregnant.* Is there an alternate version of me still out there, who's just Madison? Not Madison who's pregnant at *fifteen?*

26

Ms. Katz sighs. "Please don't worry about me doing things for you. Like I said, I want to help. And don't worry. I've got the means to help."

Well, I know that's true. I know that she writes books, and she's pretty successful. I think she works from home and Molly says she's always on her computer, typing, writing, researching. I know she must make a lot of money to be able to afford this nice house and do everything on her own. I don't want to take advantage of her, but right now I don't see how I can't accept her offer. It's temporary, anyway. I'll stay here for a bit, make a decision, and then once I have a job, I can pay her back. I'll go home at some point. How can I not be with my mom and Josie through this? This all feels so weird. I just want to sleep. But I know I have to figure things out first.

Molly pipes up. "How does it feel, you know, to have a baby inside you? I mean, do you feel anything?"

"I can't really feel anything yet, but I feel sick and tired and just really out of it. It's like it isn't there but I know it is, do you know what I mean?"

Molly shakes her head, and we laugh, which feels good.

"But I have to figure this all out now. If I do keep it, how am I going to go to school with this now? How am I going to go to Harvard if I get in? Am I going to keep the baby? Is my mom ever going to..."

"Don't worry. Your mom will come around," Ms. Katz assures me. "It's funny how they use the expression 'coming around,' like there's this massive boulder to get around, which, metaphorically speaking, is kind of true. I mean, my mom was really angry, too, but then she came around the 'boulder,' and once she accepted it, she became an amazing grandmother to Molly." I nod, and I cling to the hope that Mom will come around, but then I think of our horrible fight, and it's all just too much right now.

"Madison, you need a good night's sleep. Trust me, things will be clearer in the morning after some rest. Let me get you set up."

Molly and I watch TV while Ms. Katz gets the guest room ready. I literally can't wait to go to sleep. The room is small, but cozy, and it has a small desk, dresser, and a twin bed made up with dark blue sheets. A snow globe with a cheerful snowman in it that reads on the bottom *"Holiday Greetings"* sits on the shelf above the desk. There's a window right above the bed, with white curtains.

"Thank you so much, Ms. Katz," I say, tearing up. "You don't know how much this means to me."

"You can call me Dianne, okay?" She rubs my shoulder. "It'll all be okay in the long run. None of us, not your mom, not me...we won't let anything bad happen to you."

"Okay, thank you. I'm really tired, so I think I'm going to go to bed. Tomorrow's Friday, so at least I can figure things out this weekend...but for now, I need sleep."

"Exactly, just get some rest."

I say goodnight and thank you to her and Molly. Thank God for them. They're really saving me right now. I unpack the few things I brought, then brush my teeth and get into bed. I can't even think right now, I need to sleep. I can't keep my eyes open.

The next thing I know, it's morning. I wake up at seven, and right away I can feel that weird tickle in my throat. I'm going to throw up. I run to the bathroom and vomit into the toilet, cringing right after. There's nothing I hate more than throwing up, but I feel so sick. I brush my teeth, trying to get rid of the horrible taste in my mouth.

I go into the kitchen and there's a plate of scrambled eggs and toast waiting for me. Dianne's just about to leave for a meeting with her agent, and she tells us to have a good day at school. For a moment, I can pretend everything is normal and this is just the morning after a sleepover with Molly, like we used to have, even though it's not.

On the way to school, Molly says her mom told her that if I keep it, I should tell my teachers soon, because she didn't tell her teachers when she was pregnant and it ended up being crazy when her stomach started getting bigger. I hadn't even thought of that yet. What will my *teachers* think? Could they lower my grades because of this?

Molly interrupts my thoughts by saying, "Do you feel any better?"

I shrug. "Kind of."

"Hey, so by the way, I'm sorry if my mom smothers you a little too much."

"Are you crazy? She's so nice. I wish I could do something for her, to..." I trail off, shocked to see Josie, being walked to school by an older woman. And Josie looks so happy. *Wow.* Mom *already* got someone to take my place? It feels like a punch to my gut, even though I'm relieved that someone is there for Josie.

A weird thought comes to mind. Maybe this baby is a chance to have a do-over. I've never had the greatest relationship with my mom, but now I get a chance to have a good relationship with *my* baby. That's one good reason for me to keep it, isn't it? But I should still be thinking about adoption. But I just don't know if I could go through this whole thing, be pregnant and get attached to the baby, and then just give it away. I wonder what my dad would say. He used to play with my dolls with me, when I would pretend my doll was pregnant. That's the thing. I've always wanted to have a baby, even when I was a little kid, I used to pretend I was a mother. But I'm too young right now.

I don't want to give the baby up. I don't want to stop its heartbeat, and I also don't want to give it to someone else. Still, I feel so mad at myself. I could erase this. I could go back to normal, I could pretend it never happened. *But I don't want to.*

When I walk inside the school, breathless, I realize how...different everything looks. Everyone's happy. Everyone isn't worrying about a baby and making money and pregnancy. They're thinking about school, clothes, homework, sports...*normal* teenage things. I'm no longer normal.

At the end of the day, I tell Molly I want to stop by the coffee shop and get an application. She comes with me and we walk into the cute little neighborhood coffee shop, "Roast and Drink." I imagine myself wearing the turquoise apron with a mug of coffee on the front that all the employees wear, and I smile.

Molly orders a hot chocolate for both of us and we sit at a table and I fill out the application and then hand it in. They pay $12 an hour. I wonder if it's enough.

Once Molly and I get back to her house, Dianne rushes up to me with a McDonalds bag that smells really good. "Cheeseburger, large fries, ketchup, Oreo McFlurry. I craved McDonald's all throughout my pregnancy with Molly. I know it's not the greatest to eat all the time, but once in a while, it's okay. Now is a good time to indulge." She winks and I thank her.

In my new room, I think of Mom. She's still at her afternoon shift at the retail store. She's probably just thinking about what a horrible daughter I am.

Or is she? Maybe it was crazy for me to leave so quickly. Maybe Mom regrets it. But she told me that she didn't want to even look at me. Among other things.

Then I hear a muffled argument through my closed door. "But, Mom! *I* wanted McDonalds!" Molly shouts angrily.

"I'm sorry, sweetheart, it's too unhealthy, okay? You can have a healthier snack with less calories. Now go do your homework, please."

Is Molly watching her weight? Come to think of it, I guess Molly's a *little* on the big side, but I never noticed it much. It's honestly just her thighs, but I think it's because they're muscular. I feel bad for her, but honestly, I'd rather have her body than mine.

Then emails ping into my computer. All of them are from my teachers, telling me that Dianne told them I was pregnant, that they all offer their support, and that they want to know if I'll be staying in school, which of course I will be. They sound supportive on email, but how do I know that they won't treat me differently now? I shake my head. Of *course* they'll treat me differently now. How could they not?

Then I check my debit card's account. I only have a hundred dollars. Mom used to pay me $20 each month for watching Josie, but now I don't think she'll do that anymore. I'll just use the money I get from my new job, if I get it.

I had so many plans for myself, I think sadly. Not only my ambitions for Harvard and being a journalist, but I wanted to have a normal, fun high school experience. Prom, homecoming, working at the newspaper, having a boyfriend and friends.

I start panicking again, so I decide to call Renee, from Planned Parenthood. I tell her that I'm still torn between keeping the baby and adoption. She tells me again that she could see from when I came in that I'm not like most of the other girls around my age that she sees come. She says again that the majority of them want to abort it right away. We talk a bit more about what would go into keeping the baby, but also what would happen if I gave it up for adoption. She tells me that if I'm not terminating it, then either way I have to go through the pregnancy. She tells me that one option is that I can proceed as if I'm going to keep it and try to work out the details and plan for everything financially, and with school, and then if it looks like I won't be able to make it work, I can choose to go with adoption. She tells me that either way, it will be okay, as long as I plan carefully and try to get help from those around me. She says I can always call her again, if I want to talk. I thank her for being so nice and helpful and I hang up, feeling a lot better.

I know that she said that having adoption as something to fall back on is a good idea, and it is, so I guess that maybe if I really can't do it, then I'll think about it.

But at least right now I have a plan, which is to try to see if I can make this work. Make keeping the baby work. I've always wanted to be a mother, more than anything. So even though it's way too soon, I'm going to give it my all to do this and help myself still accomplish everything *I* want, as well. Now I just have to figure out the many steps that I know I have to take to be the best young mother that I could possibly be.

♡　　　♡　　　♡　　　♡

To-Do List

- get prenatal vitamins at pharmacy
- ask Molly's mom about OB appointment
- tell Leo ASAP
- send e-mails to Mom + Josie
- STUDY FOR MID-TERMS!!
- finish history essay (10 pages)
- study for math test
- talk to school counselor?

☆ ask Janet to send me her stories
　 for editing
☆ organize layout for this week's newspaper
　 edition

- buy new jeans (bigger size)
- buy books on pregnancy / babies

EAT! GAIN WEIGHT!

9 weeks = 3 months
　　　　pregnant

→
scale

- apply to Roast and Drink?

☆ ask Janet to cover the winter dance

Chapter 6: Week Ten

"Your baby is as big as a prune," I read on my new favorite pregnancy website, called "Baby Size." Basically, it gives me the size of my baby each week. I'm ten weeks pregnant. It's Sunday morning, I should be working on my ten-page history paper (groan), but I'm so fascinated by these pregnancy websites.

I read a little more: tooth buds are now developing under the gums, and bones and cartilage are forming this week. I don't feel any of this happening, but it's weird knowing that it's happening inside me.

I'm still so exhausted and I'm also still pretty nauseous, not wanting to eat much, but getting nauseous when I don't eat for a while. It feels like I have the flu really bad.

Now, I take a prenatal vitamin, gulping it down with some water. *Ugh,* I hate swallowing pills, and I've never really had to until now.

I start on my history paper. So boring. While I work, I keep one hand on my belly the whole time. In a weird way, it keeps me calm, knowing a life is forming in there.

Dianne phoned my mother yesterday, and my mom said that she didn't want me to move back in yet because she knew we both still needed to cool off, and that I was in good hands, and besides, she was really busy with work, and Josie was covered for babysitting. After hearing that, I made a decision: I'm not planning to move back at all. Not in the near future, anyway. I need stability, and I need to stay in one place. I also don't know if my mom will ever be ready to have me back, with how angry and busy she is. So I'm going to stay with Molly and Dianne, if they're okay with me staying, until after I have the baby, and then hopefully I'll be stable enough to take this all into my own hands and move to my own apartment. That's the plan for now, anyway.

I look at my notes, and type and type and type for literally four hours. It's noon now. I sigh, submitting the paper online, I'm so glad it's done. I write an email to both Mom and Josie before I get off the computer.

To: tdavis31@gmail.com
From: maddieluvspizza@gmail.com

Hey Mom,

I'm sorry for what happened. I'm so sorry for getting pregnant. I'm sorry for everything. But I decided that I'm keeping the baby. I thought about adoption, and if I can't work things out, I might look into it a little more, but I'm trying my hardest to be able to keep it, and unless you want me back, I'm going to be at Molly's and Dianne's. I know how hard you worked for me to give me a good life and my best chance even after Dad died and everything, and I'm really sorry, I really am. I'm trying to get a job at a coffee shop and I am studying and staying in school and I'm going to take care of myself and the baby during the pregnancy. I'll be fine. Just try not to worry, okay? You can also take as much time as you need to think. I'm fine here with Dianne and Molly. But if you do want to talk, just email me. I hate that we fought but yeah, maybe I deserved it. But anyway, I love you and I should've told you and I'm sorry. I love you.

Love,
Maddie

To: josiejosie22@gmail.com
From: maddieluvspizza@gmail.com

Hi Josie,

It's Maddie, Josie. I'm sorry about not telling you about being pregnant, and I want to make sure that you know that I know what a bad influence I am to you, and that's why I left, not because I don't love you, okay? If you heard me yelling about always having to take care of you, it's not you that I'm angry about. It's just the situation. Anyway, I hope one day I can make it up to you and you can be proud of your big sister again. Take care of Mom. I really really miss you and I love you so much, and hopefully I'll see you sometime soon. I love you.

Love,
Maddie

I really hope they understand. And I really hope that they still love me.

I need to tell Leo. I'm stalling, this isn't good. He still hasn't called me all week, but I *need* to tell him. Soon.

But now all I can think of is when our relationship used to be sweet and innocent, a high school romance, nothing more. Now it got so much more complicated.

... August 2017...

"You can't beat me!" Leo shouted one sunny afternoon, when we were still just friends and playing soccer. I laughed, because I knew he was right, but I was giving it my all, anyway. My chin was still hurting from when I tripped over the soccer field when we first met, but at the time, I was just so attracted to him, and I think that distracted me from the pain.

I kicked the ball right into the goal, smiling triumphantly, impressing Leo.

He looked at me, surprised. "That was awesome!" he exclaimed, running up to me, giving me a spontaneous hug. Shivers ran down my arms as I felt his touch, but he pulled away before I could even fully enjoy it.

"Come on," he said, grinning. "Let's go walking."

He picked up his soccer ball and we began our way across the field at the park.

"So, you really like soccer, huh?" I asked.

"Yeah. I've been playing for years," he said. "I also love watching soccer."

"It's cool." Then, I admitted, "I'm not a *huge* sports person, but I think soccer's pretty fun."

"Really?" he asked, and I looked down, feeling shy. He was just so cute, the way he looked, the way he talked, everything about him. We bumped into each other playfully, and our fingers lightly brushed. I had liked him for a while, so I was really excited and I couldn't believe this was finally happening.

He looked at me, like he was silently asking, *Is this okay?* I nodded a little, hoping that soon we'd go on another date, maybe to get ice cream again.

He slipped his hand into mine. Then, after a few blissful moments, he yanked it away playfully. "Race you to the end of the field!"

"Oh, you're on!" I called, running and running, but he was sprinting so fast that he was already almost at the end. I was disappointed. I wanted to win the race, to impress him again, but I have to say, it was fun watching him run, it was like watching a gorgeous lion. That's honestly what he's always reminded me of: a lion.

...

Breaking into my memories of that day is the sound of Dianne on the phone, booking me for an appointment with Dr. Lippincott. I also hear Molly in her room, which is upstairs above mine. Her radio is blasting, just like Josie's always does. They both do their homework with music on, which is something I could never do, I need total silence. For a moment, I pretend I'm back at Mom's and Josie is dancing around to her music, as usual. Then I start to feel sad. I miss Josie so much.

But I really need to study right now. I open my math book and begin taking notes on the formulas, and then I hear a knock on the door. It's Dianne, with a burrito and a salad. She's really so nice to me. I don't know how I'll ever thank her.

I nibble on the lettuce, not that hungry. I used to love salads, but now the smell of a cucumber makes me want to throw up. I instantly put the salad down, but it's too late; I run to the bathroom and throw up. I can't stand all the nausea and throwing up, it's so disgusting that this comes with being pregnant. I wipe off my mouth and return to my studying, and then my phone rings loudly, and I groan. I can't study with so many interruptions!

"Hello?" I shout.

"Uh, is this Madison Davis?"

"Yes, who's this?"

"I'm calling from the Roast and Drink coffee shop. We reviewed your application and we'd like you to come in for an interview."

"Oh, wow, that's great!" I say, surprised. "When?"

"Anytime today would be great. Now is good, if you can."

"Okay, I'll be right there! Thank you for considering me, I'll be right there."

I rush over there, letting Dianne and Molly know I'm leaving. Once I'm there, the aroma of fresh coffee fills my nostrils. Luckily, the smell of coffee isn't one of the things that makes me nauseous. A guy named Johnny tells me he's the manager, and that he will be doing the interview. I follow him into the back room, which has a desk, a couple of chairs, and a ton of unopened coffee beans boxes. There's a turquoise coffee mug on the desk that reads "Roast and Drink," with their logo. This may sound stupid, but one of the reasons I wanted to work here is because I love their logo. I love the color and the cute little mug with steam coming out of it.

"Please take a seat," he tells me, and I sit on the chair across from him. "So, according to your application, you're in your sophomore year, is that correct?" I nod. "Could you tell me if you've ever had any barista experience?"

I shake my head. "I haven't, but I have some references on that application, like a couple families I used to babysit for. I was very skilled at cooking for them, and I'm very good at learning how to do new things."

"Alright. So now, why do you want this job, Ms. Davis?"

I bite my lip and clench my teeth. Maybe I should just tell him why, not come up with some fake answer. "I mean, uh, do you want the truth?" I ask quietly.

"Of course," he says, and I can tell he's curious to see what I'm going to say.

"I'm...pregnant."

I see the look of surprise on his face and I keep going. "I really need to earn some money and I've always loved this place, so it seems like a great place to work. I'll work really hard, you'll see. I'm really friendly, and I'd be good to the customers, really." I gulp. Maybe I shouldn't have been honest. What if he won't hire me now? I could have gotten a couple months in before I started showing I was pregnant. And by then, they would see what a good employee I am. But it's not like I can take the words back.

He actually looks a little touched, then he kind of laughs a nervous laugh. "Oh, wow, well, you certainly are young to be having a...you know, but I'm sure you already know this. Uh, could you please give me a minute? I'm going to make a call to my supervisor, see what she thinks about this."

He leaves to make the call and I sit there, fidgeting nervously as I wait. I realize that I *had* to be honest, because any job I get, I'll need to have for a while, so they need to know my situation, and if they don't want me, it's better to find out now.

He walks in a minute later, smiling. "Good news. She said yes. You seem very nice and genuine, so we're taking a chance, but you have to work hard, okay?"

I nod excitedly as he tells me the details: $12 an hour, and I'm taking the afternoon shifts, so I can come after school from four to eight. Perfect!

"Your first day will be tomorrow, you'll get a couple hours of training, and then you should be good to go. How does that all work for you?"

I squeal. "It all works, thank you so much! You'll see, I'll do a really good job!"

Johnny chuckles. "Well, alright then. We're looking forward to your first day."

"Not as much as I am!"

I rush home, excited to tell Dianne and Molly. They aren't there, so I go into my room, and when I glance at my phone, my good mood immediately disappears. I know I need to tell Leo. I just have to do it. But I realize I don't have the guts to tell him in person, so I decide to text him.

Maddie: Leo? Are you there? I really need to talk to you. Text me back, okay?

I freak out that I sent the text, so I put the phone down to take my mind off it, and I try to get back into studying for math, but then my phone dings.

Leo: Mads? Sorry I haven't called in a while LOL. What's up?

I start shaking, I'm so nervous. I take a deep breath and begin writing, tears starting to form in my eyes. A few minutes ago, he was just a teenage boy, but now...he's going to be a father. Maybe I shouldn't tell him. But I have to.

Maddie: I don't want you to get mad at me, but I have to tell you this.

Leo: Mads you're scaring me. What's wrong??

Maddie: Remember 10/04?

Leo: What's 10/04?

Maddie: When we had, you know...It.

Leo: Okay, yeah, what about it?

Maddie: I found this out last week and I guess I should have told you sooner.

Leo: What?! Madison I swear tell me now you're scaring me!

Maddie: I'm pregnant, Leo. It's yours. I'm sorry.

The three little dots appear, and then disappear. They appear, and then disappear again, but finally, I get a text back.

Leo: WTF?! Is this some kind of joke? That's impossible, sorry but you're full of shit Madison, just leave me alone.

Maddie: I'm telling the truth! I can take another pregnancy test to show you! Please Leo, I really need you right now.

I stare at the screen for five minutes straight, waiting for the three little dots to appear again. They don't.

Maddie: Leo? Are you there? Please please please write back.

He still doesn't write back, not even ten minutes later. *That's fine,* I try to tell myself. *That's just fine.*

I decide to go for a walk.

But what if Leo writes back, and what if there's bad WiFi on the street?

Stop thinking about Leo, I urge myself. He doesn't care. And he doesn't matter. Honestly, I sort of knew this would happen. How many guys would stick around in this situation? I hadn't been hearing from Leo even before this happened. And there I was going around thinking that he was special. I'm such an idiot.

I start down the street. Leaves are flying everywhere, the wind is so strong and so cold, biting my cheeks. Leo's house is three blocks away. Maybe he tried to respond? Maybe his phone died? *Maybe, maybe, maybe,* my mind taunts me. *You should just accept it for what it is. He's not coming back.*

I look out near the direction of school. I don't want to go tomorrow, I'll have to see Leo, playing soccer on the field. I can see him from my math classroom. I always picked a seat right by the window, so when class got boring, I could watch him, because he has P.E. when I have math.

I hope Leo doesn't tell his parents, but they're bound to find out, anyway, if they see me around town once my stomach gets big. Word will have gotten around at that point, too. But I don't want them to be involved. If Leo isn't going to answer, then *none* of them deserve to be involved.

I just can't believe that now everyone, from my mom to my best friend to my teachers to Leo's parents, will know we slept together. I'm so ashamed. But then when I think of the innocent growing baby inside me,

I feel ashamed for feeling ashamed. I'm a mess. If I ever write an autobiography one day, that's what I'll call it: "A Mess."

Once I'm home, I send the story that I've been working on to Janet so she can send it to the printer. Her personality reminds me of Paris Geller from the show *Gilmore Girls,* but she looks different, and she's definitely meaner. I've always loved that show. Rory Gilmore is kind of my inspiration, since she wants to be a journalist, too. I always thought I was like her. But the funny thing is, Lorelai was the teen mom; so now I guess I'm sort of more like *her.*

Anyway, I haven't told Janet about my pregnancy. She'll probably never speak to me again, which I don't mind. She's set on going to Princeton, so at least I won't have to see her at Harvard, if I even get in. Only around five students from our school go to the Ivy League schools each year, and that makes me nervous.

I think I'm in denial. Why am I thinking about Janet and *Gilmore Girls* when I should be thinking about Leo?

Dianne knocks. "Come in," I say miserably.

"What's wrong?" she asks, frowning.

"Leo's...he's not going to be involved, I guess," I say, my voice cracking.

She sits down on my bed and rubs my shoulder. "Oh, Madison." I can tell she doesn't really know what to say, and I don't blame her.

"I'm going to the school's library," I say. "It's open on Sunday afternoons."

I grab my books to study and leave the house, walking to the school, passing my house on the way. It looks dark inside. *Josie probably likes the new nanny more than me,* I think. The new nanny probably doesn't have homework to do, so she can *play* with Josie, unlike me, who was always too busy with everything else.

My nose stings, which it always does when I'm about to cry. I should make an appointment with the school counselor. I just can't believe I'm this young, having a baby. I'm fifteen, sixteen in February, so at least I'll be sixteen when the baby's born.

As I pass the local DMV, I remember my driving classes, which Mom paid for. They're on Saturdays, and I missed mine yesterday. I completely forgot. I guess I'll go next week.

There's actually a car waiting for me in our garage. It's my mom's old yellow Volkswagen Beetle. She took my dad's car when he died, and she was going to sell hers, but then she thought it made more sense to keep it for me for when I got my license. I wonder if she still has it waiting for me. Probably not.

Eventually, I get to the school, going into the library. I freeze once

I step inside. Lulu's here. She's not that popular in school, but she spreads rumors and makes anyone and everyone look bad. She's always been annoying, even back in elementary school, when she spread rumors about kids who couldn't afford the newest trendy items.

I instinctively cover my stomach, even though I'm not showing yet, of course. Lulu smirks at me. Maybe it's just my imagination.

A couple minutes later, as I'm adding stuff to my To-Do list, she walks over, flipping her glossy brown hair with attitude. "So you got knocked up, huh?" she asks in a fake-sympathetic voice.

"What? H-how do you know that?" I stutter. How could *anyone* know yet?

She shrugs. "I heard about it. Well, more like I *saw* it. I'm in Ms. Perry's English class? Yeah, well, she kind of left her pathetic email exchange with you, where you were telling her you were pregnant, on her computer when she left the classroom to print something. I took a peek."

"Uh, okay, well, could you please just leave me alone? I'm trying to study."

"Oh, no problem," she says fake sweetly. Oh, no. She's going to tell everybody, if she hasn't already. Hopefully it won't spread around the school as fast as I know it will.

I finish some assignments, review my midterms schedule, study my textbooks, and an hour later, I pack up my backpack. As I'm exiting the library, I stop. That picture posted to the bookshelf looks a lot like me.

I take a closer look. Sure enough, I see an image of my face pasted on a curvy model, with breasts busting out of her bikini, on top of Leo (a cut-out of him turned sideways, where he's smiling on the soccer field), I read the words.

Madison Davis. We all know her, right? Editor-in-chief of our newspaper. Impressive. Plans to go to Harvard. To marry Leo Schmitz. (That's right, Leo, she's ALL over you). Unfortunately, because she's the biggest slut in the school (no, make that the world), she got pregnant. Oopsies! Poor Madison! Washed up at 15, knocked up at 15. Hope you're reading this, Mads! Now everyone can know what a slut you are! (Oh, and by the way, I pasted your face on a *much* prettier body than yours, just thought you should know how UGLY you are - honestly, it's kind of a surprise that someone would want to knock YOU up, of all people!)

I sob so hard, I can hardly breathe. I yank the paper off the bookshelf, and stumble out of the library, throwing up into a bush. I bring my hand to my mouth, shaking, and run all the way to Molly's house.

The words echo in my head. *Slut. Slut. Slut.*

I'm *not* a slut! I'm stupid, but I'm not a slut. I didn't sleep with Leo until I knew him for over a year! And I only did it *once,* and I wasn't even sure I wanted to. I'm just an idiot. But maybe I'm a slut, too. I mean, my own mother called me one last week.

I run into the house and go straight to my room, throwing myself on my bed and burrowing up in the blankets, trying to cry quietly so Dianne and Molly don't hear me.

Dianne comes in. "Oh, no, Madison, what's wrong?"

"Just *stop!* Stop hiding it from me! I know, I'm a slut! I am! Stop acting like I'm deserving of something when I'm really *not!*"

"What happened?" she asks calmly. Molly walks downstairs with headphones on, sees me on my bed, and immediately takes them off.

"What's wrong, Mads?" she asks, concerned.

"Don't you *ever* call me Mads again! That's what Lulu called me!"

"Lulu? The loser girl who spreads rumors?" A knowing look appears on Molly's face. "Yeah. Remember when she spread that rumor about me secretly going to Wendy's every single day after school and ordering up? She's the biggest jerk alive."

"Who's Lulu?" Dianne asks. We fill her in, and she gets a stern look on her face as she turns to me. "What did she do to you?"

I hand them the paper and then put my face in my pillow. Then I feel Dianne's arms around me.

"We're going to report this to the principal."

"I want to rip that paper up," Molly snarls. "She's such a bitch."

"Molly, don't use names like that." Then she smirks. "Although she *does* deserve it. We need to have a good night together, to cheer Madison up. Let's order Chinese food. Molly, take my card and order it while I write an email to the principal about this."

Molly grabs me and gives me a huge hug. "None of that stuff is true. You have to believe it, because nothing is farther from the truth than what she said."

I force a weak smile at her, and then she goes off to order the food.

Even though I feel a little better, I still wonder if I'm being a little self-centered. Maybe I really should give this baby a better chance and put it up for adoption, even though it would kill me inside. I should stop being so selfish and sacrifice my feelings for my baby having a better life. I still don't think that I can do this.

A sad lump forms in my throat. I miss my mom and Josie, no matter how much Dianne and Molly are helping me and caring about me. I wanted my mom to be able to talk about this with me, to care.

And I wanted Leo to care. Like he *used* to care about me.

Despite my brain telling me not to, I remember our first kiss.

... September 2017...

"Die!" Leo and I shout at the same time, playing one of his favorite battle video games on his TV in his basement. He invited me over for dinner that night, so while his mom cooked, we were playing video games. Well, Leo was *teaching* me how to play them. I hadn't quite mastered the art of battling cars on a screen yet.

My blue metallic destroyer car exploded into flames on the screen. "Aw," I groaned. I wanted to win and impress Leo.

A gold medal popped up on Leo's screen and he stood up, doing a funny dance. "Yes! I won!" he shouted, and I pulled him back down to the couch, rolling my eyes and laughing.

"I hate video games! It's not my fault that the screen made flames show up and then my car went down!"

He smiled. "You're cute when you get worked up."

I dodged the compliment, mostly because I was shy, and although I wanted him to like me more than anything, I was still self-conscious. It had been a month since we had met, and we had been hanging out almost everyday, holding hands, kind of like friends, even though I wanted more.

I shrugged. "It's just a simulation, anyway."

"Yeah."

It was awkwardly silent at that point.

"Sooo..." he said.

"So," I said quickly.

I think I knew he was going to kiss me just a second before it happened. Suddenly, he touched my lips with his, and then he touched my shoulder, and I pulled him closer as my heart rate sped up. He pulled away after a couple amazing minutes. He smiled at me. I gazed into his eyes, light green, so sparkly and gorgeous.

"Dinner, kids!" his mother called.

"Until next time," he said charmingly, and then we went upstairs for dinner.

That was it. I had officially fallen for a guy that would leave me a little over a year later, and all because I was pregnant with *his* baby.

...

"Dinner, girls!" Dianne calls, interrupting my memory with Leo that's no longer a happy one to me after what he's done.

I shake my head. I wish my dad was here right now. Whenever I was bullied or going through something really hard, he always knew what to do; buy me a bag of cheese puffs, my very favorite snack, and watch old TV shows with me. But he isn't here anymore, so I have to be strong for myself, no matter how hard it is. I need to stop believing what other people say about me if I'm going to get through this.

And I have to stop considering adoption when what I really want is to keep the baby. I can't think of adoption as something I can fall back on. If what I want is to keep the baby, I have to work extremely hard and be extremely strong in almost every area possible if I want this to work. And not just for myself. Now I have someone *else* to work for, too, which is motivating me that much more.

10 weeks

To-Do List
- appointment with Dr. Lippincott on December 23rd 2pm
- talk to school counselor!!
- pick up paycheck on Friday from Roast and Drink

I GOT THE JOB!!! ☆ ☆ ☆ ☆

- keep studying for midterms
- buy more pregnancy/parenting books

☆ Birthday in... 2 months!! (February 18)

- look for sales on baby items
  (Babies R' Us New Year's Sale coming up)

- design graphics for this week's newspaper edition
- assemble everyone's stories into the new layout
- edit fundraiser story
- check with "features" editor about upcoming stories
- finish history assignment ☆ tell Leo

Screw Lulu   Adoption? look into agencies?

Chapter 7: Week Eleven

"Your baby is the size of a large strawberry," I read on my newly favorite pregnancy website. It also tells me that this week I'll be experiencing more nausea, breast tenderness, frequent urination, and fatigue, all of which are very true and have already been happening to me.

Good news! I'm finally on winter break, and I think I aced all of my midterms. I also made $240 this week, as I was able to work four hours every day after school. Of course, tax is taken off, something I never even knew about, but I'm learning. *And* my morning sickness has been easing up!

But something I'd been dreading happened at school this week: I ran into Leo. I was walking on the field during lunch because I had forgotten my sweater there. I was pretty happy because I felt like I had done really well on my English final. Then, he suddenly appeared and grabbed my hand, pulling me to a corner where no one was around. At first, I was happy, thinking maybe he had just needed time to think, and he was going to tell me he wanted me. And the baby. But that wasn't the case.

"Madison, are you insane?! I mean, what the *hell* is wrong with you?"

I started crying immediately. "Leo, it's not my fault! We did this *together*!"

"You don't understand. My parents were reading our texts, Madison! Do you know how angry they are?!? I mean, I'm planning to go to Stanford! To get a soccer scholarship! This *can't* happen. You need to get rid of it. Now."

"I can't do it. I won't do it! I'm having this baby! You need to step up and own up to *your* responsibility, too!" I screamed, sobbing.

"Shut up, just...*shut up*! I don't want *anything* to do with this! It's crazy for you to have it, but it's *your* choice. Not mine. I will *not* be a part of it. And don't you dare tell *anyone* we slept together! Too late for my parents, because they already know, but seriously, just stay away from me!"

Any hope I had left for him to come around was gone after that. I cried and cried and was a total mess all day after that. But then, I woke up the next day and realized that I don't want him in my life if he's going to be that way, no matter how much it hurts. I'm now also angry. So angry that I don't even want to think about Leo for one more second. I'm determined to forget about him, no matter how hard it'll be.

Word has started to get around, anyway, so Leo will be upset that everyone *will* know, even if he doesn't want them to. Lulu's note was seen by people who told other people, so now I'm just hoping that the *whole* school won't find out. The principal suspended Lulu for two days before winter break after Dianne told her. It serves her right, and the principal was really nice about the whole thing, so at least that's good.

It's Christmas in two days, and I'm kind of sad about it, as I remember what Mom and Josie and I used to do. We'd open presents first, then make banana-chocolate-chip pancakes, and then watch *Home Alone,* both the first and the second movie. For this Christmas, though, I have gifts ready for Dianne and Molly. I used my work money, but that's okay. I owe them both a lot more than a couple of gifts.

I've noticed something weird lately; every week, my bank account amount goes up $20. It's Mom, it has to be. It makes me want to cry that she is still helping me, even if she doesn't want to see me right now. I feel guilty using her money, so I just plan to use it for the baby and pay Mom back eventually. I miss her. Even though things weren't *great* before I found out I was pregnant, they were still okay. I miss my old life in general. Especially at this time of year, because we always made a big deal about Christmas. But honestly, I think I don't miss only my old life, I miss my *old* old life, the life where Dad was still here. And unfortunately, that's the life that I can never get back.

My first appointment with Dr. Lippincott is in half an hour. I meet Dianne and Molly at the front door, and Dianne drives us to the office. I think of the large strawberry growing inside of me and I'm really anxious to see it on screen. My heart starts beating excitedly, but also nervously.

We pull up and find a spot right next to the door. We check in, and get called back within two minutes. I like this doctor already! No wait times!

I give a urine sample, they weigh me, take some blood, and put me in an exam room and have me change from the waist down and put a sheet over my stomach and legs. Dr. Lippincott walks in, a bright smile on her face. She's an African-American woman with a head full of gorgeous curls.

"Hello, Madison! It's so nice to meet you!" she says, shaking my hand, then she turns to Dianne, "It's so nice to see you after all these years!" They hug and then she grins at Molly, pinching her cheeks. "And someone has grown into a beautiful young woman from just a little baby, I can see!" Molly smiles shyly.

Then Dr. Lippincott sits down at the ultrasound machine. "Now, we're going to do an ultrasound, see the baby's heart rate, and we can give you your due date. Then we'll meet in my office to go over everything, seeing as this is your official first appointment with me. Sound good?"

I nod, smiling at her. She's making me feel really comfortable, which I like.

She puts the ultrasound wand on my belly, and I hear that same thumping I heard a couple weeks ago. She shows me the baby on the screen. Then she zooms in, and I see the faintest outlines of facial features. I begin to tear up as I think of my mom. What was going through her head at *her* first ultrasound with me? Was she nervous? Scared? Happy? Excited? Was her mother with her, or my dad, or was she alone? I've never asked her any of these questions, and now I'd really like to know.

I look over at Molly and Dianne and they are both smiling and staring at the screen. Dianne comes to take my hand. I feel like crying the whole time and when the ultrasound is finished, I clean the gel off with a towel, Dr. Lippincott hands me a couple ultrasound pictures, and tells me to get dressed and meet her in her office.

"So, now's the time to tell me anything I should know about. Any chronic illnesses? Past surgeries? Allergies?"

"Nope, nope, and allergy-free!"

"Great! How old were you when you had your first menstrual period?"

"Twelve." I still remember the day I got it, November sixth. My mom and dad made me a *red velvet* cake, ha-ha.

"So, just confirming, you're fifteen, but you'll be sixteen when the baby is born." I nod as she takes notes. "Okay, let's discuss your diet. Since you're on the skinny side, you're going to need to put on a little extra weight."

"Yeah, I'm trying to eat lots of healthy but fattening foods. Dianne has been making me a lot of amazing meals." Dianne smiles at me.

"And how much sleep have you been getting?" Dr. Lippincott asks.

"I try to be in bed by eleven, and I wake up at around seven for school."

Fine, that's a lie. I've been going to bed a little later than that, but it's because of homework. Now that it's winter break, I can sleep and wake up whenever I want.

"Okay. And I want to tell you your due date. The ultrasound showed you're eleven weeks. So, when did you conceive?" she asks, like it's a perfectly normal question.

Trying to block out all embarrassment, I say, "The fourth of October." I'll always remember that day. That night. *October fourth.*

"And when was the first day of your last period?"

"October...first," I say, trying to remember the best I can.

She nods. "Sounds about right. Okay, let me calculate..." It takes her a minute, but then she laughs. "Looks like you're due on the fourth of July. Great date! Also, it's good because you won't be in school."

I'll be having a summer baby! A Fourth of July baby! That's cool! But, then again, I don't think all babies are born on their exact due dates.

At the end of the appointment, Dianne makes another one for four weeks later. On the way back to the car, Dianne says, "I know you've only been wearing one pair of jeans, judging by what's in the laundry machine, and I'm assuming they're the only pair that fit you, so I want to take you to the mall so that we can get you some new clothes that make you feel good, okay?"

"You don't have to do that," I say quickly.

"It's okay. Let's go."

Molly smiles at me shyly. "You know, this is fun, having you here. It's like having a twin sister," she says, and I laugh.

We pull up to the front of Streets Mall, a popular mall near here, named "Streets Mall" because it's on a street called "Streets Street." Kind of a funny name, and we all love it. Like, who thought of that name? The mall has restaurants on one side and shops on the other, with a huge three-level Bloomingdales' in the center. I miss when Mom and Josie and I would all go to the mall on Sundays for ice cream. We never bought much, but once in a while I'd save up my allowance and buy something for Josie, like a toy or some cute clothes or something.

Now, Dianne takes us into a boutique called "Fit," which sells jeans. I pick up some size two jeans and a couple shirts that might fit me better. Molly grabs some jeans, too, in a size six. Was she always bigger than me? I can't remember. We used to share clothes a lot, and we still do sometimes. I know Molly is sensitive about her weight because I overheard her the night we had McDonald's. But I would so much rather have her weight than mine. She looks healthy, and I've always looked way too skinny.

We head to the changing rooms, and I put on the dark jeans I picked and a baggier-than-usual top. I decide to buy this outfit and *only* this outfit. I really feel guilty that Dianne is going to spend more money on me, it isn't fair to her, I'm not her daughter. I know she said she has made a lot of money in her career, but that's money for her and Molly, not for me. She has already been so generous with me and I told her I would repay her and I will. Her wanting to buy me some clothes is really sweet, but it's another thing I will add to the list of things I need to repay her for. So, I'm just asking for these jeans and this top, and that's it.

Once we get home, Molly comes into my room. We haven't had

much time to actually talk and hang out, crazy as that might sound, as we're living in the same house now. While we talk, I start to paint my nails, while Molly tries new hairstyles.

"Do you want a boy or a girl?" Molly asks, as she braids her hair. I flinch when I first see she is making a braid, but then I try to block out the stupidity of my feelings. *It's just a hairstyle,* I tell myself. Will I ever get over this association?

Anyway, I'm afraid to admit it, but I do want a girl. I feel like a boy will remind me a lot of Leo, and I don't really want to look at the baby and think of Leo all the time. But if it's a boy, then obviously I'll still love it more than anything. It'll be a whole lot easier if it doesn't look like Leo, though. He's cute, but he's hurt me so much.

"As long as it's healthy, that's the main thing. I want a girl, but obviously it would be okay if it's a boy. And it's not like I can control it." I laugh.

"I would want a girl, too. Do you think all girls feel that way? Poor boys." We laugh and then Molly gets serious. "Do you think Leo will ever come back or want to be involved with you again?"

I try to fight back the tears. "I don't think so. I'm better off without him, though."

She smiles. "Yeah, you are! Hey, so what about the back-to-school winter dance? We went last year. Are we going this year?"

"I don't really know. I think I'll have to see how I feel. When is it?"

"The night after school starts up again, January eighth, I think."

I cap the nail polish, opening the window to get rid of that strong nail polish smell. Maybe it's not good for the baby, I hope it's okay, I need to read up on it.

"So, what's it like working at that coffee shop, is it fun?"

"Yeah, it's fun, and I like seeing everyone's orders. On Friday, I had to make a ton of plain black coffees. So boring." We like the sugary frappuccinos, so it's completely foreign to us to drink plain black coffee. Actually, I haven't been really wanting coffee that much lately, because I read online that it could be bad for the baby.

It makes me angry. I've had to change so much in my life, and Leo doesn't have to do anything. Thoughts like this keep popping into my mind. I can't believe that I never knew what a jerk he really was. And the thing is, he was still being nice to me until I told him I was pregnant. So, he was nice up until I was going through something that *he* should have been going through too. So unfair.

Dianne taps on my door and tells us it's time to go for dinner. We are going to Slurp, a new ramen noodle place, tonight. I'm starving and can't wait to eat. If I let myself go too long without eating, the nausea comes back, so I keep having little snacks. And I love ramen, so it's going to be good. On the way, we pass my house and I spot Mom getting in her Volvo, in her waitressing uniform, on her way to work.

"Dianne, um, has my mom called recently?"

"No. Sorry, Madison. But I'm sure she will soon. I know you guys will reconcile at some point. Right now, I feel guilty saying this, but I'm enjoying having you with me. I always wanted Molly to have a brother or sister, but I just never found the right guy to have it with. And I definitely wasn't going to do a second one on my own." She laughs.

We approach the funky restaurant with the neon sign reading "Slurp." We're supposed to order outside and then go in to be seated. I order the plain ramen bowl, with noodles and chicken, and the fried egg on top. Dianne makes me order extra vegetables with mine. I'm salivating, I can't wait to eat.

There are long wooden benches for seating, at huge tables, and the whole room is kind of steamy and it smells like ramen. As we are being seated, I spot Leo sitting at a table, in his soccer uniform, with his group of friends. He must have just come back from a soccer game, and they're all laughing and having a great time. My stomach drops, I don't want to see him. I realize I better get used to this, though, as our town is so small, people are always running into each other. Still, it hurts to see him, laughing and living it up without a care in the world. I see him glance at me, and then look away. I decide to ignore him and I sit facing away from him. I want to enjoy this meal.

The food arrives pretty quickly and it's as delicious as we hoped. Molly and I slurp so loud that we start laughing. Then, Molly suggests we go to the ice cream place next door for dessert, where they serve your ice cream on waffles. So good.

"I think that's enough food for you tonight," Dianne says, trying to lower her voice, but I hear her.

Molly frowns. I feel so bad for her, and I know her mom is just looking out for her, but it's really crazy, Molly isn't even fat. Maybe just a *bit* overweight, but more curvy than overweight, honestly.

Dianne changes the subject. "So, guys, I wanted to tell you that my brother Ian is coming to visit in May."

Molly immediately brightens. "Ian's coming? Yay!" She turns to me. "Oh my God, Maddie, you'll love him, he's the best. He's actually only eighteen, because when my mom had me, he was only three years old. He's away at University of Iowa right now, he's in his first year of college."

"Nice," I say, worried that with him there, they won't want me to stay, it will be too crowded. Maybe by then I'll be back with my mom. Or I'll try to find my own place before the baby's born, even though the plan was to move out *after* the baby is born.

"Yeah, it's funny having an uncle only three years older than you." Molly laughs. "He comes to visit and stay with us pretty much every summer."

As if reading my mind, Dianne turns to me. "So, Madison, have you been figuring things out lately? Like, the logistics of everything...?"

"You mean money and stuff? Yeah, well, now I have the job at Roast and Drink, and I think I'll keep working there. And I guess a lot of it just depends on whether or not Mom wants me to move back in." I frown. "But at the same time, I don't know if that would even be a good thing. I mean, I love Mom and Josie so much, but it was always so stressful to watch Josie while dealing with my own stuff at the same time, and-"

"Your mother works three jobs, right?" Dianne asks kindly.

"Yeah," I tell her, not wanting to get into it.

"Well, I just want you to know that you always have a place with us, for as long as you need, okay? Obviously, at some point, it would be better for you to go back to your mom, or to even be on your own, but you need to do it when the time is right for you. In the meantime, please don't stress about this. You looked stressed when I mentioned my brother. There's always going to be plenty of room for all of us, so don't worry."

She really must have read my mind. Was I that obvious? But nevertheless, I'm so relieved. I thank her and Molly gives me a hug, telling me to stop worrying so much.

As I'm falling asleep, I feel calmer. I'm proud of myself for not ruining my night just because I saw Leo. And I know there's still a lot I need to figure out, but right now I feel like I'll be able to handle it. It was a good day. I love it when that happens.

☆ Done with 1st trimester in 2 weeks!

To-Do List
- get new bra (bigger size)
- birthing classes?
        (too early)
- wrap Molly + Dianne's Christmas presents

4th of July = due date!

- START A BUDGET!! ⟶
- buy crib, diapers, wipes, clothes, toys?
        (do research on what I need to buy)
- make another appointment with Dr. Lippincott
  (ask Dianne to do it)
- do more research on pregnancy/babies

♡   ♡   ♡

♡ BPM

⟵ baby's heartbeat!

♡   ♡   ♡

    ♡   ♡

♡   ♡   ♡

Chapter 8: Week Twelve

"Your baby is as big as a lime," I read online. I can't believe that I'm on the last week of my third month, that I'm almost done with my first trimester, and that it's New Years' Eve tomorrow!

I've been feeling better, a lot of my nausea is gone. I'm still dizzy sometimes, but Dianne says it's normal. And I don't grimace from the taste of my toothpaste anymore, so my taste aversions are definitely going away.

Today's going to be fun. I'm driving out with Molly and Dianne to visit Molly's grandparents. They drive out to this area about an hour away, every year, right before New Years' Eve. I didn't know if I should come, but they insisted. I'm a little nervous to meet them. Will they just see me as an irresponsible, pregnant teenager, or will they sympathize, because it happened to Dianne, too? Even with her being a grandmother and all, Mrs. Katz is pretty young, I think she had Dianne when she was twenty-five and then Dianne had Molly when she was eighteen, so she's a really young grandmother. It makes me think of my own mom and how young a grandmother she will be. But will she want anything to do with her grandchild?

On the way to their house, I snack on some cheese puffs. They've been my biggest craving so far, but honestly, I *always* crave them, I craved them even before I was pregnant. Then I get an alert on my phone that I have a new email. It's from Josie.

To: maddieluvspizza@gmail.com
From: josiejosie22@gmail.com

Hey Maddie,
It's so sad here without you. The new nanny isn't very fun. She's strict and doesn't let me have my iPad as much as you did and she yells at me to do my homework. Also, she only gives me healthy snacks, none of the fun stuff we used to eat. Are you okay? Mom's been really sad, never smiling really. She's busy working more than ever but I can hear her crying at night. But she's also still mad, I can tell. I miss you and I'm sorry about the baby and everything. I wish I could see you.

Love,
Josie

I feel tears rush to my eyes. Josie and I have always loved each other so much. Especially after our dad died and we had to stick together. We're still close, I guess, but now...I mean, I feel bad, just leaving her like that. But hopefully I'll be back soon.

We pull up to a farm-style home. Potted plants line the brick stairs leading up to the wooden front door. This area we're in is called Flock Valley or something, it's more secluded than Redford, but still really homey. All of the houses look inviting, some older than others, some more modern. A kid whizzes down the street on his bike, his mother calling after him to not go so fast, which makes me smile.

Dianne's mom, Mrs. Katz, throws open the door and rushes out to hug Molly. She has graying hair, but other than that, she looks really young. Her face lights up when she sees all of us.

"My girls!" she says as they all hug. "Oh, and I have heard about you, Madison! It's very nice to meet you! How are you feeling?" She gives me a hug, too.

I smile. "Pretty good, thanks."

"Well, come on in!"

The house is beautiful, with traditional, ornate furniture and pretty vases displayed everywhere. I see a framed painted picture of Dianne over the big fireplace. She looks around my age in it. I wonder if it was painted before or after she had Molly.

Dianne's father walks in, says hello to everyone and goes to sit on the couch. He has a nice smile and a head full of gray hair. Dianne looks more like him, minus the gray hair.

I feel uncomfortable intruding on their family time as they catch up on what's been going on over the last year, so I just sit there quietly. After a little while, I ask where the bathroom is, I have to pee constantly these days. There are little fancy soaps in pretty soap dishes and a spray that I guess you're supposed to use if you go number two. At my house, all the soaps are half-used, and bunched together so we don't waste them. Something about the smell of the soap makes me want to throw up, and before I can even think about it, I projectile vomit right in the toilet. I nearly throw up again from the taste of it in my mouth. I hope this nausea will be over soon. Hopefully once my first trimester is over. I flush and use the spray to make the room smell better, and I rinse out my mouth, thankfully feeling better now.

When I come out of the bathroom, Molly is waiting for me.

"Sorry you have to be around my boring family," she says, rolling her eyes.

"No, everyone's really sweet."

"Are you sure? I feel bad. I'm sure they'll talk to you more when we eat."

During lunch, sure enough, they do talk to me, asking me about school, and I tell them about being editor-in-chief of the newspaper.

"How impressive!" Mrs. Katz exclaims. "Do you want to be a journalist when you grow up?"

I nod and then it occurs to me how ridiculous it sounds, like I'm sitting here pregnant and talking about what I want to be when I grow up. But being pregnant has already made me have to grow up much faster than I could ever have imagined.

"Yes. I really liked it once I started doing it. It's really interesting to tell stories in a certain journalistic format. I also wanted to do it for my mom, because, well..."

"Because of what?"

"She wanted to be a writer, and she was actually really close to finishing a book, but, um, something happened." I shake my head. "Anyway, I just love it. I'm planning to go to Harvard for their journalism program, and if I get in, I'll find an apartment near there for me to live in with the baby."

"Dianne went to UCLA and got a little apartment with baby Molly," Mrs. Katz tells me, smiling at them. "If you're strong and you're a hard worker, you can make good things happen even through a sticky situation."

"Madison's staying with us while her mom takes some time to cool off and think about the situation," Dianne explains. "It's very nice to have her in our house, but I've told her that her mother will come around eventually."

"I'm sure she will. If I did, anyone can." She laughs, and I feel relieved that they are talking to me, while Mrs. Katz continues to catch up with Dianne and Molly. Mr. Katz reads the newspaper the whole time. It's kind of funny and calming at the same time.

We stay about an hour after lunch and as we're about to leave, Mrs. Katz takes me aside and says, "One thing you might want to consider is making an appointment with an adoption agency. Since you seem like such an ambitious young girl, I don't know...it's just, it's always good to educate yourself about all your options."

I nod and she hugs me and everyone hugs again and we leave. In the car ride home, I'm preoccupied by what she said. Does she think I won't be able to do it? I was planning on keeping the baby, only using adoption as a back-up option, but now I have way more doubts about myself than I did before.

"We should totally stay up till midnight tomorrow to watch the ball drop on TV," Molly says.

"Yeah, I stay up until midnight every year, usually with Josie. My mom always liked to work as a caterer on New Years' because it paid really well, so Josie and I would stay up and make s'mores in the microwave, then pig out and watch the ball drop."

My smile turns into a yawn, I'm suddenly really tired, so I rest my head against the back of my seat and fall asleep.

When I wake up, it's dark out, and I'm still in the car. Dianne is in the front, typing away on her computer, balancing it on the steering wheel. Huh?

"Dianne?" I ask, rubbing my eyes. "What are you doing here? Why am I in the car, when did we get home?"

She smiles at me calmly. "A little while ago. But you were just sleeping so well that I figured I shouldn't disturb you. I didn't want you to be outside all by yourself, though, so I'm just writing out here so I can stay with you. Reminds me of when Molly was a baby, she would always fall asleep in the car and I would stay in the car with her until she woke up, because she needed the sleep, as all babies do."

I smile, thinking it's ironic how babies need their sleep and so do mothers making babies. Then we go inside, and I head up to my room and check my email. A new email from Josie pops up.

To: maddieluvspizza@gmail.com
From: josiejosie22@gmail.com

Maddie please come home!! I can't sleep without you here and New Years' Eve won't be any fun without you tomorrow. We have to make the s'mores! At least just come see me! Please!!!

Love,
Josie

I feel terrible, but I can't go home, I can't see Mom, not yet, anyway. But I do want to see Josie. I miss her so much. Her long hair that matches mine, her big smile, the cute round freckle in the middle of her nose. She must be home if she's sending me emails from her iPad, so maybe I could go see her now! Mom's at her waitressing job by now, so I'm safe.

I scribble a note down for Dianne and Molly, saying they don't have to worry about me for dinner and then I walk over to my house. I look inside the front window, the nanny is on the phone. Josie must be in her room. I go around the side of the house where I can see into Josie's room and a lot of the house. There's a big tree for privacy, but I know the exact spot to stand so no one sees me, but I can see them. Sure enough, she's in her bedroom on her iPad. I wave my arms, windmilling them to get her attention, until she finally sees me. Her eyes light up and she gives me a huge smile, I motion her to come outside. I watch her tip-toe down the stairs so that the nanny doesn't see her, and she quietly comes out the door. We sit behind the tree, and she gives me a huge hug and then looks at my stomach.

"You aren't pregnant," she says doubtfully.

I laugh. "Your stomach doesn't get big until a little later. Anyway, how are you?"

"Not happy, because you aren't there, but I'm fine, I guess."

I try not to cry. "You're so brave, Josie. You're doing really well, okay? I might come back soon, I just..." I bite my lip. "Are you mad at me?"

"No, Maddie! I was actually excited to be an auntie, but I would never admit that to Mom, she's so freaked out! Oh, can I please see the baby, do you have a picture from the doctor? I read that they can give you a picture."

I'm so happy, I was hoping she'd ask. I take out the ultrasound picture, and she grabs it, trying to figure it out. I point to the little area where the head is, and the eyes, et cetera. "Hi, baby," she breathes. Then she looks up at me. "Who's the daddy?"

I swallow and say, "Uh, Leo. But he's...he's not the actual daddy because he's not going to be there and be a dad like...like Dad was. It's complicated, and I don't think you can really understand it. You're too young."

She frowns. "But how-"

"Josie, when you're a bit older I'll explain it to you, but it's not something you should worry about, okay? All you need to know is that Leo isn't going to be there."

She bites her lip, like she's deep in thought. Then she eventually says, "Well, if he's not going to be a daddy even though he *is* a daddy, then I don't like him anymore."

I put my arm around her and tell her it's okay to feel that way and we should just think of happy things. Then, I kiss her on the top of her head. "I know you're being a good girl and helping Mom, right? Tell her I love her, okay? And tell her I know she needs time. And that I need time. But that I'm sorry. Now go back inside, it's cold. I love you so much and I really miss you. I'll try to come again really soon, I promise."

We hug and then she kisses my stomach and runs back inside, trying to do it quietly. Tears blur my vision. Right now, I wish that I could hit the rewind button, and go back and not have Dad die and not have me get pregnant. I feel like everything is wrong, not the way it should be.

As I walk back to Molly's, I squeeze my eyes shut and think of my poor Mom. How she had to give up her writing career so she could make enough money for me and Josie, all while struggling with losing her husband...and then I get pregnant and totally wreck Mom's life in a whole new way, like I was just adding a piece to the top of the awful tower, like a Jenga game, and then it just crashed.

When I get there, Dianne is sipping hot chocolate from one of her colorful mugs at the dining room table, looking a little angry. "What's wrong?" I ask nervously.

"Your dinner's cold, and it's not a good idea for you to skip a meal. You didn't even say where you would be. If you want to live here, you have to live by my rules. And one of my rules is that you aren't allowed to go out without telling me where you are. If something happens to you, what will your mother think of me?"

"I'm sorry. I...I won't do it again."

"I mean, honestly, Madison, do you even appreciate that you're staying here?"

"Oh my gosh, of course, Dianne! I think about it all the time, and I feel guilty-"

"Just please let me know where you're going next time." She sighs and then she goes upstairs with her computer.

I sit there at the table for a minute, listening to her start typing upstairs. Then I go to her room, where she's sitting on her computer, writing away. She looks at me, surprised to see me there, and I just go up to her and hug her.

"Thank you for everything, for letting me stay here, for all the meals and the good advice, and taking me to the doctor, and for staying in the car with me when I fell asleep, and-" The tears start flowing, I'm still emotional after seeing Josie and it's all just hitting me again. I don't want to fight with Dianne. She's been so nice to me.

"Oh, Madison, that's very sweet. You're welcome. But I truly am happy to help."

"And I'm sorry."

"I know, don't worry."

We hug for a minute and then I go downstairs, into my new room, and decide to write another email to Mom.

To: tdavis31@gmail.com
From: maddieluvspizza@gmail.com

Mom, hi. I know you've been paying me, so I just wanted to let you know that I'll be paying back every cent when I get enough money. I just had to tell you, I'm handling it. You don't even need to continue paying me. But just please know that I will be paying it all back. I love you, and thank you.

I needed to get that off my chest. I need her to know that I really appreciate it. Because I realized, Dianne didn't even know that I appreciated what she's doing for me. Maybe I just haven't been forward enough.

I change into my pajamas and get into bed. *Think calming thoughts,* I tell myself. Tomorrow's New Years' Eve. I'll stay up till midnight and have fun hanging out with Molly and Dianne, then I go back to school on the seventh, then the winter dance is on the eighth, am I really going to go?

So much for thinking calming thoughts.

It's weird. I feel lonely, even though I have all this amazing help from Molly and Dianne. Maybe it's because there's another person *inside* of me that's with me all the time. I have the baby *inside* me. But I haven't connected with it. I mean, I've sort of connected with it, it's the reason why I'm doing all of this, but even the fact that I call it "it," that feels weird.

I put my hand on my belly. "Hey," I say quietly. I try to think of a name to call it that doesn't sound as awful as "it." I've heard of people calling their babies things like "my little peanut." Suddenly, the name comes to me: "Cheese Puff!" It's been my biggest craving so far, and for my whole life, honestly. And right now, my baby is pretty much the actual size of a cheese puff! It's perfect!

"Cheese Puff is your name until I find out what a real name could be for you." Then I sigh, my smile disappearing. "I won't deny that you were a mistake. I don't know this for sure, but I think that maybe you're the best mistake that I've ever made. I'm really sorry about a lot of things, and..." A huge lump forms in my throat, and I feel like I'm going to cry again. It feels like all I ever do these days is cry.

"Anyway. I just wanted to say that I'm sorry. I mean, I'm not much. I'm just a fifteen year old girl in high school, but...I'm going to be a *mother* to you now, and that's just so crazy. But I'm going to try my hardest to give you your best life possible...I'm, uh, working out the details on what that will be. But one thing you should know is that I always wanted to be a mother. Always. So, you're earlier than I planned, but I wanted you one day, and I want you to know that."

I know it's too early to feel the baby kick, but I swear I just felt...*something* down there. Some sort of feeling, like a little flutter, like I'm connecting with Cheese Puff.

Happy tears well up in my eyes. "I'm really happy you're here," I whisper, rubbing my stomach lightly, and I fall asleep this way.

<>

The next day, as Dianne's calling me for dinner, my phone tells me that I have a voicemail. "I'll be there in a minute!" I call to Dianne, pressing "play."

-Voicemail- from 'Unknown'

Transcription:

Hello Madison, this is Mrs. Schmitz, Leo's mom. I know that you're pregnant and that you're, uh, keeping it.. I saw the texts on Leo's phone last week. I would like to talk to you about my involvement with the...baby, along with Mr. Schmitz, since we won't want to get lawyers involved to work out child support and all that, but...just please call me back and let's set up a time to meet. I would like to meet with your mother, too, okay? I'd appreciate it if you'd give me a call soon, so we can set a date and time to discuss things. Or I can always meet with just your mother, I understand why you might not want to talk to us, so...so just call me at (310) 110-6110. Okay, thank you. Bye.

Now tears are beginning to wet my eyes and my heart is thumping really hard. I didn't expect this at all. I just figured if Leo didn't want anything to do with me, neither would his parents. She sounded angry and nervous. I'm not sure what to do, because I really don't feel comfortable meeting with her alone, but I also don't feel comfortable meeting with her and my mom. I shake my head. I don't want to deal with this right now, it's New Year's Eve. I guess I'll think about what to do later.

After dinner, we watch some of the live broadcasts from New York. I've always loved the entertainment they have on New Year's Eve. But I guess I look worried, probably about Leo's mom's voicemail, because Dianne eyes me and then suddenly pauses the TV and says, "By the way, Madison, I just wanted to follow up with what we talked about last night. I'm sorry if I made it seem like I didn't think you appreciated what I'm doing for you. I know that you do, and you don't owe me anything. This is a pleasure for me, helping you. So don't think of me as someone you owe something to."

"But...but you've given me so much that you shouldn't have even had to."

"Madison, it's *nice* to have you here. I know it won't be forever, but

60

it's nice to have you here with Molly, it's like I have twin girls." She laughs. "I'm fortunate in that I have made a good living, doing something I love, and I'm happy to be able to afford to help in this kind of situation."

"Wait, so you're a writer, right?" She nods. "How did you get into that? I'm interested in writing, too, because I want to be a journalist."

Dianne smiles. "Well, as you know, I wasn't expecting to have to earn a living as young as I did. When Molly was a baby, I worked at a home cleaning service, then once she started preschool, I got a job at a pharmacy. It provided me with enough money to take care of us both. But eventually, I got bored." She laughs. "There was something I had always enjoyed and I wondered if I could make a living at it. That was writing. Horror writing, to be exact. It's kind of funny the way it came about. When I was pregnant with Molly, I watched a ton of horror movies. I think I was interested in them back then because I was so worried about being a pregnant teenager, and whatever the characters were going through was always a lot worse than my situation. So, I started really liking horror. Then, one day, I had an idea and I started writing, and well, it just flowed out of me. It's kind of ironic that it was the horror movies that I watched *because I was pregnant* that inspired me and helped me afford to give Molly a good life. Out of that scary situation, something really good happened. I've been very lucky to be able to earn a living doing what I love. More than anything, I love getting inside the character's heads and writing about their experiences."

"I like that, too. You know, to capture a story, to get inside someone's head."

"Molly told me you want to go to Harvard?" I nod. "Oh. I wanted to go to Princeton, for literature."

"But you didn't go there, right? You went to UCLA, your mom said."

"Yup. But while I had to give up Princeton, I still did work very hard to get everything I wanted without attending that university, and I got Molly and myself into this house and this life, and I did it all myself."

"Yes, you did, Mom. Now, come on, can we unpause the TV now?" Molly complains, and we laugh and go back to watching TV.

I love when Dianne talks about this kind of stuff with me. It really helps so much. She makes me feel like I can handle all of this, and that things will all be okay. I look around the cozy, warm house, the family photos and the colorful mugs everywhere, and I watch Molly cuddling up to Dianne on the couch, and I smile. Maybe I really will get this one day, with Cheese Puff.

12 weeks

To-Do List

- go to Babies R' US soon
- pick up paycheck on Friday from Roast and Drink

buy: ✱ EXERCISE!!
- new stretchy shirts   ✱ EAT MORE
- new notebooks for school   CALORIES!!
- cheese puffs!

☺ Hi! I'm a calorie!

⭐ NEW YEAR'S EVE

- email Josie? visit Josie?

⟵ my Cheese Puff   ♡ ♡ ♡

- find out the gender?

⭐ watch New Year's countdown
   with Molly + Dianne!

- start thinking about new-semester
  stories for the newspaper

- call Mrs. Schmitz back? call Mom about this?

        ♡   ♡
   ♡ Cheese Puff ♡
        ♡   ♡

Chapter 9: Week Thirteen

"Your baby is as big as a lemon," I read online. I'm trying to distract myself from the recent big news, which is that my mom met with Leo's parents. She called me this morning to tell me. I was shocked to hear from her, and at first I was so happy because I thought she was maybe finally coming around, but then she told me the reason she called was because she spoke to them. According to her, they were all angry at first but then they settled down, and Leo's father is a lawyer so he wanted to work out legal stuff for the baby. That freaked me out, but my mom said it was necessary and it would be mostly financial stuff, but we also had to figure out what visitation for the baby would be like for Leo's parents because they will want to have an option of knowing the baby, even if Leo doesn't. It's all so much to process and I can't stand thinking about it. Even though Mom and I didn't talk at all about *me,* we just talked about Leo's parents and the situation, it still made me happy to hear from her. I really miss her and I wish things could be different. She did ask how things were at Dianne's and she sounded a bit sad when I said they were good. I wish she would ask me to come home, but I don't think she wants me there right now. I think we'll just start fighting again. Still, I wish she'd asked me. Maybe she wishes *I* would ask to come home? I don't know. All I know is I don't want anymore stress or fighting and it's at least calm here with Molly and Dianne.

Anyway, I'm relieved that Mom is the one dealing with Leo's parents, although I don't really understand why they have to be involved at all. She said she will work things out with them, but it sounds like they will be contributing to some of the stuff for the baby, every month or year, or something. My mom said Leo has to be responsible eventually, but because he's only almost sixteen, his parents will be responsible for a little while. I don't know how much money it is or will be, or in what area of the baby's life it will be in, and I really don't care. I don't *want* their money. If Leo doesn't want anything to do with me or the baby, then I don't want anything from him. It will just remind me of him and all the sadness. But Mom says this is important and that child support is also a legal thing, so for the meantime, I'm just leaving it up to her and Leo's parents.

This week, I've been starting to get this weird discharge down there, something I've researched called *leukorrhea,* and it's normal and it's happening because of my increasing estrogen and blood flow to my pelvic area. It's sort of weird, but it's not too bad. I'm definitely not as tired as I've been the past few weeks, so that's good.

Tomorrow's the first day of the new semester, and I really don't want to go back. It was so nice to have a break. The only thing I'm looking forward to is working on the newspaper. I'm also going back to work at Roast and Drink tomorrow after school, so now I *really* have to see if I can balance work, school, and homework.

And the new-semester-winter dance is on Tuesday, and I'm just not feeling like I want to go. I keep gaining weight, which the doctor says is good, but my hips feel so huge now, and my stomach is definitely getting bigger. And, before all this happened, I had really wanted to go with Leo as my date.

I try to distract myself with the pregnancy info online. It says vocal cords are forming, wow, that's so cool. It also says the eyes are still shut. I wonder what color they'll end up being: hazel, like my own, or light green, like Leo's?

I feel like maybe I should actually do something today instead of just sitting around, so I find Molly in her room and ask her if she wants to go to the park for a walk. She says yes, so we get dressed and head out.

Stonewood Park is only a couple blocks away. It has tennis courts and an enormous playground. There's a little girl on the monkey bars and she's doing all kinds of tricks on them. Then, she slips and falls and her mother rushes over, picks her up and rushes back to her stroller, which has her other child, a baby, inside. She looks so stressed out. I can't even imagine how hard it would be to have two kids, and I don't even have *one* yet and it already seems like *that's* going to be so hard.

"I'm so scared."

"I know. Trust me, I mean, I seriously can't even imagine how you must feel," Molly says. Oh, God, did I just say that out loud? "But don't be scared," she adds. "I mean, you'll be a great mom."

"Thanks."

"And, if you think of it, you're my best friend, but you also feel like my sister now, so in a way, I'm the future aunt of your baby!"

We laugh, and it feels good to know how much she cares and how excited she seems. I do think of her as my sister, a lot of the time, especially now that we're living together. But it even felt that way before all this, because sometimes Dianne would let Molly sleep over with me and Josie, and we would all giggle together in my room, like all *three* of us were sisters.

We're quiet for a little bit, then I decide to ask her a question about something that's been bothering me since the night where Dianne got me McDonald's and she wouldn't let Molly have any.

"Hey, Molly? Are you...worried about your weight or something? I've overheard you and your mom, I don't know, talking about it, I guess?"

She doesn't answer me right away. I start to feel bad for even bringing it up. But then she says, "I'm a size six, which I know isn't the worst thing in the world, but it was kind of embarrassing when I was a bridesmaid at my mom's friend's wedding, and I couldn't fit into my dress that I'd gotten made a month earlier. I mean, maybe I had a growth spurt, I don't know, but I definitely gained a few pounds. Anyway, my mom says she struggled with being a little overweight when she was a kid and she doesn't want the same thing to happen to me. I just hate worrying about it, it really sucks."

"Yeah. I guess I can understand that. But you don't look overweight to me and you're beautiful, no matter what." I laugh. "It's hard to picture your mom overweight, though, she's so thin."

"Yeah. But I just wish I had to work to *gain* weight, like you. Then I could eat whatever I wanted, whenever I wanted!"

I roll my eyes. "No, you don't want that! It's the worst! A week after each of my yearly check-ups, when the doctor would say I needed to gain more weight, my mom would practically force food down my throat at all hours of the day. She got so nuts she'd make me have two pieces of toast with tons of butter after each meal, even if I was full to the max, and then I always wanted to throw up."

"That does suck," Molly says. "We have crazy parents, don't we?" We laugh. It always feels good to laugh with Molly, even when it's a serious matter.

She looks down. "I know you probably don't want to talk about it, but was it nice? With Leo, I mean. You never told me that you guys, well, you know, did it."

I try to push my sadness away. "Yeah. He was really sweet, it was...it was really great, yeah. He was...I mean, it was nice." Okay. What I'm saying *might* be a lie. He wasn't exactly considering my feelings when he wanted to have sex and I wasn't sure I even wanted to do it yet. So it wasn't all that great. But I don't want to admit that, because then I'll really look like a total loser.

"It's just weird, I mean, you never told me you were having sex."

"I wasn't having sex *all* the time. It was just one time, actually."

"I know, I believe you, I just didn't know that you lost your virginity, you know?"

"Yeah. I'm sorry, I should've told you, it was just-"

"Weird?"

"Yeah."

I feel like it's confession-o-rama over here with Molly, but my next question I've never really talked about with her, and the one I'm most curious about now, slips out. "Does it feel weird knowing you were a mistake?" I feel horrible the second I say it, because it sounds so bad out loud. "Sorry, I didn't mean to say 'mistake.' That's not really a great choice of words. I just mean, does it feel weird, like, that you weren't really planned, that you were the result of a teen pregnancy?"

She looks down. "It's okay that you said 'mistake.' It's the truth. But I don't know, I've never felt like my mom thought that way about me. But yeah, I guess it is weird to think about it that way." Suddenly she realizes. "Oh. Do you want to know because you want to know how your baby will feel about...*you?*"

I nod, my heart rate kicking up nervously.

"Well, it feels a little upsetting when you really think about it, and thinking of my mom with some guy I've never met, but...I don't think it's really that bad. I mean, not every pregnancy that wasn't a teen pregnancy was planned either. My mom always told me it made me special, and I believed it and I still do. I mean, I can't imagine not being born, you know?"

We laugh again, and I hug her, I'm just so grateful that she's so open and honest with me.

Then, out of the blue, a soccer ball rolls over and hits my feet, and a little boy comes running after it. "Sorry!" he says, and I kick it back to him, and he runs off with his friends. Of course, it makes me think of Leo, and then I can't help but picture my baby, possibly liking soccer one day. At some point, I'm going to have to feel better about whatever the baby does that reminds me of Leo. I hope that one day I won't hate him as much as I do right now.

We start walking back home. "Hey, so do you want me in the room when you give birth? I promise, I won't laugh," Molly says.

I smile. "Oh my God, would you be there? That would be amazing. I haven't really thought about who else I want in the room, though, and all that. But I'm actually kind of really nervous about that. You know, the whole labor and delivery thing. Do you think it'll really hurt?"

"I don't know. I mean, there's like over seven billion people in the world! If it hurt too much, not everyone would have babies, you know?"

I never thought about it like that, and it makes me feel better. "Yeah. I mean, our moms went through it!" We giggle, but then I stop, looking down, feeling sad, and I think Molly can tell.

"You miss your mom and Josie, huh?"

I try not to cry but this is a hard thing for me to talk about with Molly, especially because she and Dianne have been so nice to me. "More than anything. I mean, it was so weird leaving like that, but we had the most horrible fight that day, we both said such bad things to each other..."

Across the street I see a group of girls around Josie's age, all of them are wearing braids in their hair. It makes my stomach clench but I can't stop staring at them.

Molly frowns. "What's wrong, do you know those kids?"

"No, I just...I don't like wearing braids, or even *seeing* them on anyone."

"Why?"

"When I found out about my dad, I was braiding Josie's hair, and her braid, it got all ruined, and...it just makes me feel sick to my stomach to see braids. I can't control it, it just automatically happens when I see them. It's like they're bad luck or something."

"Oh. That really sucks. I didn't know that," she says, and then she stops and gives me a hug. We talked about so much today, so many different really personal things on just a walk to the park. It feels good, though. I thought Molly and I were close before, but I feel so much closer to her after all of this. I haven't been able to talk about a lot of these things with anyone else.

<>

The next morning, I dread going back to school. But I'm just going to try my best to do well and keep my grades high, and remind myself that I only have one semester till summer, which is also pretty much only one semester until I have Cheese Puff.

As I'm heading to my locker at school, I keep my head down self-consciously. People have been giving me looks since Lulu spread the news around. They look at my stomach and I'm sure they're wondering why there's nothing there yet. They probably think it's just a rumor, but no one has asked me. It's just something I've had to get used to. Once my stomach gets bigger and they realize it's true, I'm sure they will all think I'm a big slut and they'll feel sorry for me in a condescending way. It's embarrassing, but I'm getting used to it, and I wasn't friends with any of these people anyway. I'm just friends with Molly, some other girls that I never really see anymore because of the rumors, and this nice girl, Cheryl, but she's more friends with Molly than me.

I spin the dial and think of how much more mature I'm involuntarily getting. I just feel different. Like all these kids in the hallway aren't at all like me anymore, which I guess they truly aren't.

My friend Matthew is in my history class. I don't see him all the time because there are about thirty kids in the class, and people sit in different seats all the time. Matthew's really smart, funny and sweet, too.

He's pretty tall, with a nice smile and hair the same color as brown sugar. We've known each other since middle school, where we both signed up for the after school improv club, so we became friends doing that together. We have hung out a few times, and he's a good friend, but we haven't been as close since we came to the high school because we're both super busy with homework and things. Also, when I was with Leo, Leo didn't like me hanging out with other guys, even if they were just friends.

Today, Matthew is sitting behind me, which surprises me, because he hasn't done that in a while. "Hey," he says. "How are you? I was thinking about you over the holidays, we haven't really hung out in a while."

"I know, how's it going? It's nice to see you!"

"So, uh, I was wondering, do you want to go to the dance with me tomorrow? As friends, you know, to reconnect? We haven't really talked or anything for a while."

I'm shocked. But I don't think I should say yes. Even though it's probably impossible, there's a part of me that is thinking that Leo's planning a huge surprise for me. That he's going to use this dance as an opportunity to get back with me.

"Um, thanks, but I don't think I can. I might be going with someone else."

"Oh, okay." He looks hurt, but he smiles. "Maybe another time, then."

I nod and smile apologetically and then turn back to pay attention to the teacher.

After my study period, the bell rings for lunch, and I go find Molly in the cafeteria. "Save my seat, okay? I'm going to get lunch," I say and then I get in line, gathering together my crumpled up bills. I keep my tips from the coffee shop for buying lunch at school. Lots of singles, and they get all bunched together. I need to get more organized and get a proper wallet or something.

I feel like eating a burger and fries, but I'm trying to eat more healthy so I get the chicken breast with a side of broccoli, and then go to sit down with Molly. She smiles and says, "Hey, let's talk about the winter dance. I know you don't really want to go, but it'll be fun if we go together, so come on, okay?!"

I think about Matthew and his offer, and then I think of Leo. Wouldn't he have asked me by now? Or maybe he'll just surprise me at the dance. I mean, I really just see Matthew as a friend, so I don't want to lead him on, just in case he meant more than just as friends. Besides, he probably doesn't even know I'm pregnant, and even if he heard the rumor, he probably doesn't believe it. So I agree to go with Molly.

I take a bite of the broccoli, and suddenly my stomach lurches. Oh, no. It's making me really nauseous. *No, you are not going to throw up right now.* I try to swallow the broccoli down, not breathing in through my nose so I can't taste it. I know it's good for me and Cheese Puff to eat vegetables, but this is really making me feel sick.

I try to distract myself by looking around and I see a bunch of guys laughing in the corner of the cafeteria. Leo is one of them. He doesn't see me, so I can get a good look at him. He looks happy and carefree, just living his life, no problem. He's so good-looking, and I hate myself for even thinking that. He has no idea how much my life has changed, and it's obvious that he doesn't care. It hurts so much to see him. I don't want to be here right now.

Molly looks at where I'm looking. "Are you okay?" she asks.

I shake my head sadly, because I'm really *not* okay. I still remember everything about him, every single thing, from his soft brown hair, to his light green eyes, to the little scar on his eyebrow from tripping and cutting himself on the edge of a table when he was six, the square-shaped birthmark on his back.

"It's just so *hard.* I know it's so freakin' stupid, but I really did think that we'd be together forever."

"I get it," she says sympathetically. "Well, actually, that's so stupid for me to say. I *don't* get it, Mads. What you're going through must be so awful. I'm so sorry."

The sadness overwhelms me and I bury my face in my hands. I'm not crying, I just can't look at everyone right now. All the stupid hope I had drains out of me. I guess he *isn't* planning some big surprise for the dance.

"I loved him," I say, and now the tears fall. "I loved him so much, and I thought he loved me back, and I didn't think *this* would happen, you know?" I steal another quick glance at Leo and notice him looking at me, but when he sees me look over, he makes a face and quickly looks away.

I take another bite of my broccoli, but now I *really* feel nauseous. I manage to say to Molly in a shaky voice, "I've got to go to the bathroom," and then I race to the girls' bathroom, which thankfully is only one hall away from the cafeteria, and I lock myself into a stall and spew broccoli *everywhere.* That's it, I don't care how healthy broccoli is for me, I can't eat it, it makes me way too nauseous right now. I don't know if it was just the broccoli itself, or if it was Leo, but the combination…oh my God, there are little bits of broccoli all over the walls. This is the worst thing to throw up because there are so many little pieces. *Ew!* I use toilet paper to clean it up, and then I flush the toilet and come out and wash my hands.

When I go back to our table, I tell Molly that I lost my appetite, and so we throw our leftovers in the trash. I glance at Leo again, but he's busy having fun with his friends.

After lunch, I have English. This is my favorite class, and I love the posters that my teacher put up around the room. There's one that's my favorite. It says. "Hyphenated. Non-hyphenated. That's irony." It always cheers me up. I'll miss it when I go to junior year and I don't have her anymore and I can't look at that poster. I've always done so well in English, and my teacher loves that I'm editor-in-chief at the newspaper. I wonder what she thinks of me now that she knows I'm pregnant.

I manage to make it through the rest of the day, even though I'm feeling really tired. I have my shift at the coffee shop after school. I don't know how I'm going to get the energy to get through it. I would love to have a coffee, but I know it's not good for the baby.

I feel like the best part of working here is just observing the customers. A group of teen girls from another high school. A redhead who wears a necklace that I wish I owned. An older man who does a lot of writing on a computer has been here for all my shifts so far, and he seems so hopeful and into whatever he's writing. A single dad who always looks a little rushed comes here often, sometimes with his daughter, who always orders a hot chocolate with extra whipped cream. He reminds me of my dad, with his hazel eyes like my dad had, and like I have. How would I appear to someone like me, who people-watches? Pregnant teenager, scared, but still hopeful? I wonder.

I wonder so many things. Especially what my dad would think about all this. It's hard to think about. I mean, when we fought, my mom said he'd be disappointed in me, but I don't know. Would he really be disappointed? Or would he be there for me, trying to help in any way he could? I think that knowing my dad, my guess would be the latter.

<>

When the dance comes around, Molly and I get ready together. It's six-thirty (normally I'd be at work, but I changed shifts and I'm working Saturday instead this week), and Molly and I are having a ball, blasting music, getting ready.

I speak to my stomach. "Cheese Puff, it's your first school dance!"

"You call it 'Cheese Puff'?" Molly giggles.

"Yeah, I think it's cute," I say, a little embarrassed.

"It *is* cute," she says, and we laugh again, finishing up our makeup and hair.

We're about to leave, but first Dianne takes some pictures of us. In the car, she asks me if I want her to send some to my mom.

"Oh. Um, sure, if you don't think it will upset her."

"No, I don't think it will. I think she would be happy to see you happy."

Once we're there, we enter the school gym, where all the school's dances are held. The room has a blue light from a disco ball cast over it, and a fast, pop song blares through the room. Molly and I head to the dance floor, making each other laugh with funny dance moves. But then Matthew walks up, scowling at me. *Oh, no.*

He shakes his head. "So, you don't have another date. You came with Molly. You lied to me, that's really nice, Madison."

"Matthew, please. I didn't mean to lie, I did want to go with you, it's just...I'm kind of...going through a lot right now."

"What? What's wrong? I mean, you used to like hanging out with me."

"I know, I'm so sorry. But we can definitely try to hang out some other time, okay? Really. I miss you."

"Whatever."

"Please don't be mad. I swear, I do want to be friends with you!"

"I'm not mad, I'm just annoyed that you lied to me. *Friends* don't lie to each other," he says, shaking his head.

"You heard me, I'm going through a *lot* right now, okay?"

"What's going on?" he asks, sounding a little concerned now.

"Just...forget it. I'm fine, and I do want to be friends with you, and..."

It's awkward. Even I know it.

"Okay. I'm here if you want to talk, I guess," he says, shrugging. He's a nice guy.

I hurry back to Molly and try to figure out why he would be so upset. Does he...? No. He can't. We've been friends for so long, and only friends.

As if reading my mind, Molly says, "I think he likes you."

It's too overwhelming to think of this right now. I really just want to have a carefree night. As if on cue, the song *Shake It Off* by Taylor Swift comes on, and we start to dance.

Lemon
(baby size!)

13 weeks

To - Do List
- buy new pencils/pens for school
- pick up paycheck on Friday from Roast and Drink

♡   ♡   ♡   ♡ Cheese Puff ⟶

- call Mom again + ask about
  what's going on with Leo's parents

☆ NEW SEMESTER ☆
(2 1/2 years of high school left)

- do French + math homework during free period
- history report due January 21st
- study for science test next Wednesday
- edit stories for this week's newspaper
  edition
- ask Janet to send me her edited stories
  so I can edit them
- organize notes for journalism
- start working on English
  paper   (NEVER EAT   ☆ Dr. Lippincott
                  BROCCOLI   appointment
          ↑   AGAIN)   on January 20th
                                    at 5:30pm
                                  ☆ 30% discount on
LOTS TO DO!   diapers at Babies
get cracking!   ♡   R' Us next week!

                           ♡

                                    ♡

Chapter 10: Week Fourteen

"Your baby is as big as a navel orange," I read while eating some cheese puffs. I've always had an addiction to them, but since getting pregnant, it's worse than ever. I would eat them all day, everyday, if I could. Some pregnancy chat rooms that I've been reading say that craving salty food indicates a boy, but some say it means a girl. They also say citrus cravings mean a girl, but can also mean a boy. It's so funny because they all contradict each other so it's impossible to believe either, but it's fun to read about.

I'm in my fourth month, and my second trimester! And according to the articles online, it's a good trimester to be in, because I'm supposed to start feeling better, getting more energy. Except I'm also apparently going to start gaining a lot of weight this trimester, which makes me nervous, but I know it's necessary in order to grow a baby. So is eating. All these pregnancy websites tell me that I should be making time to eat substantial meals, and I do, it's just hard with school and work and everything else.

But I'm very excited, because there's "only" twenty-six weeks left of pregnancy. And I've gotten A-pluses on all my homework assignments, I've been editing stories for the paper like crazy, and Dianne set up my monthly appointments with Dr. Lippincott, so that's all set.

The only thing that's really bothering me right now is that my mom hasn't gotten back to me about what's happening with Leo's parents. While I do have a while before the baby is born to think about it, I know they're going to want to be involved, even if Leo isn't. My mom told me they said they want to be involved with their grandchild, no matter how it came about. I wonder if Mom feels the same way. She hasn't said anything about that. When we've talked, it's all been very business-like, about her dealing with Leo's parents, et cetera. She said they want to help financially, and I don't know why, but I really don't want their money, even though I know I sure could use it. I just want to do it myself. If Leo was a part of this, it would feel different. But he isn't a part of this, and so this is how I'm feeling right now.

Right now, I'm finishing up homework and I'm studying, and it isn't even noon yet! I love being productive. I'm also planning to go to Babies R' Us to shop for some supplies, since I picked up my work check and I have some money to spend on the baby. I've been doing some research, and I know what to buy.

I take an Uber to Babies R' Us and I get a nervous excitement just walking into the store. I can't believe I'm here to shop for my own baby. I choose some cute yellow clothes, and then some newborn diapers, gazing at the cute newborn in the picture, wondering if Cheese Puff will look like that. I also select more baby things, like linens and lotions, and because I've been collecting coupons for a while, I'm able to save a good amount of money!

It's kind of awkward seeing other mothers selecting things. They probably think I'm shopping for my mother, or for someone else. My stomach still isn't really showing yet. A heavily pregnant woman stares at me, and keeps looking at my stomach, as if trying to figure out if I could possibly be pregnant at my age.

Suddenly I lose interest in doing this shopping right now. I'll come back another time. When I get home, I put the things I bought under my bed, thinking of Josie, who used to hide her iPad under the bed so that I wouldn't take it from her.

Speaking of Josie, Mom and I kind of made a deal, communicating through Dianne. Whenever I'm not working or too busy with schoolwork, I'll let my Mom know and then I will be the one to watch Josie. It's so that Mom doesn't have to pay the nanny as much. I'm happy about this and can't wait to spend time with Josie again. Dianne says that it's a step in the right direction, and I agree.

Once I'm at my house, I go up to the window and wave my arms wildly until she notices me. She's writing something in a notebook, but she smiles the minute she sees me, pulls on her purple jacket, and leaves her room. I skip back to the front of my old house, which brings me a twinge of sadness in my chest that I don't really live here anymore. I peer into Mom's bedroom. The curtains aren't shut, and I can see the faint outline of the family pictures that she's always had hung on her wall.

Seeing her room, I realize how much I miss my mom. But of course, it makes sense. I mean, she's my *mom*.

Josie runs out the front door excitedly. We hug and then she looks at my stomach. "It looks a little bigger!"

I chuckle as we start down the street. "Come on. Let me buy you some ice cream. Where's the nanny?"

"She's not here now because Mom told her you were coming, but she eats all of our good bagged popcorn, which is so annoying," Josie groans. "Mom's still a mess, by the way. I know she misses you, even if she doesn't say it."

"So, hey. I had an idea," I start, changing the subject. I want this visit with Josie to be a good one, not a negative one. "Do you want to come to my next doctor's appointment? For the baby, I mean?"

Josie claps her hands excitedly. "That would be so great!"

"It's on the twentieth at 5:30. I'll pick you up. I know Mom will be between shifts, so..." I bite my lip.

"No. She's starting work earlier now. She says she needs more money, because now she has to pay the nanny. So you can come, she won't be there, don't worry."

I nod, trying to ignore my guilt. "Okay, then I'll pick you up at 5:30!"

We turn the corner and almost run into a big redwood tree. It's part of why the town was named *Red*ford, because there are so many of these trees. We laugh and go around it, and continue walking. Josie slips her hand into mine, and I smile happily.

"How's Molly?" she asks.

"She's good."

"How are you feeling?"

"Better. No more nausea in the mornings," I tell her. "Well, sometimes I have it. But I've been eating these things called Saltine crackers that poof my nausea away."

"What flavor of ice cream are you going to get?" she asks. "Not Saltine cracker flavor, I hope!"

I laugh. "I'll have to see."

After another block and more cute questions from Josie, we turn into Sweet Cream Ice Cream, our town's best ice cream parlor, and the bell tinkles as we push open the door. Josie examines the available flavors. "I'll have cotton candy, please."

"I'll have a double scoop, mint chip and bubble gum," I say. I pay and then we go outside to eat at the little pink tables with the pink chairs. There's warm heating lamps beside us, since it's winter, which makes me feel cozy.

"How's school?" I ask Josie.

"It's okay. I just miss you walking me to school."

"I miss it, too."

"Someone at school asked me if you were my sister."

"What do you mean?"

"Like, they said their older sibling or something who goes to the high school knows you're pregnant, and I guess now they know I'm your sister."

I frown, and what she just said now really upsets me. My one mistake has already affected so many people, even my little sister. I mean, I hope the kids don't start bullying *Josie* for what *I* did.

Luckily, Josie doesn't want to talk about that anymore, just about what she's learning in school. When we're done with our ice cream, I walk her home. The nanny is about to come, as I told Mom I only had an hour.

I'm glad that I get to watch Josie some of the time now. It feels normal, almost like old times. But it also feels like a hundred years since I've been with her.

When I get back home, Molly races past me, out the door. "If my mom asks where I am, I'm at the mall, bye!"

I catch a whiff of her cinnamon perfume and see her in her favorite jeans and a cute white top. Where's she going? I smile, wondering if she has a date.

I decide to go to my room and research a little about Harvard. I scroll down the pages of their website, looking at the admissions and faculty page, and my head hurts a little. I want to go there so badly, I really hope I get in, even though I will have a baby. It's the only university I want to go to. I know how cliché it is to want to go to Harvard, but it's such a great school, and it's always been my dream to go there and to be a part of their journalism program.

An hour later, Molly knocks on my door, and I swing it open to find her with a huge smile on her face. "You've got to tell me where you were!"

"Remember Jay Caulfield came up to us at the dance and offered to get us drinks?"

"Ha-ha, and I told you he was looking at you in that way..."

She giggles. "Ha-ha, you were right! Well, at the end of the night, when you went off to find my mom, he asked me if I wanted to go walking around Green Lane sometime. It's a pretty far walk, but it was really nice."

"Wait, so you went walking with him?"

"Yeah. We ended up getting some ice cream, too. It was fun! He paid, and he was so sweet about it."

"That's awesome! Do you think this'll turn into something? Ooh, is he going to be your boyfriend now?"

Molly smiles and playfully swats me. "I don't know. But he said he'd call me at eight tonight." She glances down at her clothes, worriedly. "Do you think my outfit was good enough?"

"Yes, don't worry, it's perfect, and you look gorgeous, as usual. Just be confident on the phone, you know, and see if he wants to hang out again."

I'm really happy for Molly. She's been rejected by guys so many times, for no reason. In eighth grade, she asked Michael Hernandez to the Valentine's Day dance. He turned her down cold. In freshman year, she asked Cody Valance to hang out and study with her after school, and he said no. We recited what she was going to say millions of times and I kept telling her it was his problem, she was too good for him. It's great that she finally found someone who likes her and sees how good she is as a catch. I hope Jay's nice to her, because it's what she deserves.

"Thanks, Mads. You're the best," she says, grinning, and leaves the room. I sigh. I remember when I was really excited about Leo. I feel weirdly...*wise* about relationships now, in a way that almost makes me uncomfortable. I wish I could still be naive and innocent, I don't want to be this negative about relationships, but I can't help it.

At dinner, Molly has a little smile on her face the whole time, and Dianne notices and asks her what's going on.

"Well, if you must know, I went out with Jay Caulfield this afternoon."

"Really? Well, well, well, look who's blushing!" she exclaims, smiling. "That's very nice! Did you guys kiss?"

"Mom!"

"Ooh, Jay," I say, joining in, teasing Molly by pretending to make out with myself, and she turns bright red again.

"Guys, stop it!" she shrieks, and we laugh and go back to eating.

At eight o' one, the phone rings, and Molly literally runs to get it. I laugh as she shushes me and picks up the phone. Dianne grins and goes upstairs with her computer.

I get to work on setting up some articles for the newspaper, to get them ready to send to Janet so she can send them for printing. I have been stalling telling Janet I'm pregnant, because I know she'll be totally judgmental and probably mean. I know I have to tell her, though, as I'm going to start showing soon and I'd rather have her hear it from me than the rest of the school. I decide to text her.

Maddie: Janet? You there? I have to tell you something.

Janet: I'm studying. What do you want?

Maddie: I need to tell you something.

Janet: What?

I take a deep breath and type.

Maddie: A little while ago I found out I was pregnant. Don't worry, I'll still be at school, and I'm handling it. But I just thought you should know.

Janet: WHAT? What the hell Madison?? I heard Lulu was telling everyone you were pregnant but we all thought it was another one of her rumors and lies. It's actually true??

Maddie: Yes, it's true. And I don't want to get into details, but I thought you should know.

Janet: I didn't even know you had a boyfriend! Whose is it?

Maddie: It's none of your business. Anyway, I told you, so, there.

Janet: We have so many stories coming up! You're not dropping out are you?? Oh my God, are you still going to be able to go to Harvard??

Maddie: I'm not dropping out. I'll be working as hard as I am now. I'm not having the baby till summer. I can still run the paper, seriously, and I'm going to Harvard if I can help it. I'm going to send you the articles for next week's edition, just send them to the printer, okay?

Janet: K, gotta go, bye.

Ugh. Well, that's pretty much what I figured her response would be. She's one of the most ambitious people I know, this is something that I can't imagine happening to her in a million years. Then again, I didn't think in a million years this would happen to *me*. But how is she going to consider me her *boss* anymore?

Molly bursts into my room. "Jay said he wanted to eat lunch with me tomorrow at school!"

"That's amazing, Molly!" Then, I fake-pout. "Who's going to sit with me at lunch tomorrow, then?"

"Cheryl," she suggests. "I'll tell her to meet you at our usual table! Oh, now I have to find an outfit for tomorrow!" She rushes back to her room, all giggly. I'm so happy for her, it makes me smile.

But I guess I lost my lunch buddy. At least Cheryl's nice. She's friends with both of us, but a little closer to Molly. She's really into fashion, and she's going to try to go to NYU for design, it's her dream school. I think Molly should go there, too, because it's a school of arts, and Molly's really creative. I wish Molly wanted to go to Harvard, so we could go together if we both got in, but she doesn't.

The next day, I go into the cafeteria, get my food, and then I see Cheryl waiting for me, thank goodness. I really don't want to sit alone these days.

"Hey Mads, come sit! Molly's on her hot lunch date with Jay!" Cheryl's obnoxious, but I still like her. I sit down and we start eating. She leans over and says sympathetically, "I know we haven't had a chance to talk lately, but I want you to know I'm here if you need anything."

"Thanks, Cheryl."

"Still going to try to go to Harvard?" It feels like that's always everyone's first question. Well, I guess I can understand why. Then Cheryl offers me a cherry tomato and I cringe.

Cherry tomatoes remind me of Leo. We always ate them together as a snack, we would share a bag of them. The memory hits me, even though I try to stop it.

... April 2018...

Leo and I were walking slowly down the street one sunny spring day, sharing a fresh basket of cherry tomatoes from the supermarket. There were three left. I took one. He took one.

We laughed and kissed. Then, I was about to ask him if he wanted the last one, but his hand was already in there, taking it for himself. I just stared at him, shocked as he just popped it in his mouth, without even offering it to me. It was so rude and at the time I thought it was unlike him. Little did I know.

"Has anyone ever accused you of being selfish?" I asked him, only half-joking.

"No, why?" he asked, chomping down on the tomato.

"Never mind," I said, laughing it off.

But maybe I shouldn't have just laughed it off. Because it was a moment that showed who he truly was. Instead of being a decent guy and offering me the last cherry tomato, he just took it for himself.

...

I realize Cheryl is staring at me. "Sorry, I didn't mean to bring up Harvard."

"No, it's fine, don't worry. It wasn't that, I was just thinking about something else. Anyway, yeah, I'm still going to try to get into Harvard like I was before."

We chat about things that we haven't caught up on, she gives me some good fashion advice on what I could do once my stomach starts to show. She can actually be nice and helpful at times, even though I still can't stop thinking about Leo and Harvard, which is just stressing me out more than ever now.

After lunch, I have journalism. I keep my head down when Janet walks in and am just trying to focus on working hard and getting the editing done, since the new edition is coming out this Monday. As I'm typing editing notes for one of our writers, our features writer, who's wearing braids, nudges one of our graphic designers, and whispers loudly, "I heard from Lulu that Madison's *pregnant*."

"I heard it, too, but she doesn't even look fat," the girl whispers back.

I feel sick seeing those braids. This just proves to me again that they're bad luck.

At the end of class when the bell rings, Janet takes my arm and takes me behind a row of lockers, glowering. "What is wrong with you?! I really want to know. I mean, why would you get pregnant? I unfortunately *need* you to be functional!"

"Janet, I don't have to answer to you! I'm still going to help with the paper, and, excuse me, *run the paper*, unlike *you*, and I'm still in school, okay? I'm planning on graduating, just like *you*! Just because I'm pregnant doesn't mean that-"

"Whatever. I'm just...well, shocked. That you let this happen to yourself."

She lets out a sound of disgust and walks down the hallway. I start walking towards my locker, with my head down, so I don't have to deal with anyone else. Then, I bump into someone. "Sorry," I say automatically, but then I look up to see it's Lulu, and I regret apologizing. She shoots me a fake smile, and I turn and walk the other way.

I hate being in school, I hate being around people who say these things about me. This whole day has just really sucked.

I'm excited for Molly, but I'm also jealous. She has exactly what I want, which is to be in a relationship. I loved having a boyfriend. Just having someone there who liked me and who I liked back, someone I could talk to in that way, someone to kiss.

After school, I go to my shift at Roast and Drink, and the whole time, the little voice in the back of my head says, *You're not going to have enough money for all your expenses. You have to get a higher-paying job.* I try to push it away.

One woman orders a macchiato with two extra pumps of coffee, which was Mom's usual order whenever we went out and she ordered coffee, and I start missing her again. I can't stand it, I can't catch a break from feeling awful, no matter what I'm doing. And I'm just so exhausted from dealing with this. I see why people my age shouldn't be having children. I knew it before, but now I *really* get it.

But you did this to yourself, that stupid voice says.

I trudge home after my shift is over and I sit down at the table where Dianne has left me some meatloaf and carrots. She's so sweet.

Thank God for her. But I'm so tired, I feel like I can't even lift the fork, though. I just want to go to bed, I don't even feel like eating.

Dianne comes in, takes one look at me, and asks, "Are you feeling alright, Madison?"

"Just tired. Thank you for dinner."

"I think you're working too hard. Maybe you should quit working at the coffee shop. You still have homework after this, right?"

"Yeah, but I'm fine," I say quietly. "And I *have* to work. If I don't work, I don't get money. I *need* money."

"If you willingly accepted help from Leo's parents, then you wouldn't need to work as hard. Your mom told me that they're trying to figure out the amounts of money you could receive each month or year, and in what area that would go towards. That money could really be a big help, and if you take initiative, you guys could resolve things faster. I think it might be a good idea. And-"

"I don't *want* their money!" Tears spring to my eyes. "I want to do this *myself.*"

"But throughout my whole pregnancy, it was so hard for me to manage everything. It was also very important for me to rest. I knew when I needed to focus on my priorities, which are health and wellness."

I nod, not really listening.

"Madison? Are you hearing me?"

"Dianne, please, just stop. It's stressing me out even more to hear how I have to rest, on top of everything else. I don't have time for rest. Has my mom called?"

She looks a little irritated. "I just said she did. Along with the thing with Leo's parents, she said if you can find time to watch Josie on Saturday, that would be appreciated. And I'm just trying to help."

"Thanks for your help." I feel awful that I'm being rude, but I'm just so tired. Thankfully, Dianne seems to understand, and she doesn't push it.

I manage to get through dinner without falling asleep, then I go to my room and open my chemistry textbook. I have to fill out all this stuff...and...I nearly fall asleep on the textbook. *No. Maddie. Focus. Chemistry equations. Stay awake.*

I almost want to laugh. I wish that I could take pregnancy and parenting classes in school instead of figuring out which combined chemicals create reactions. This stuff seems so meaningless to me now. I think it's because I've figured out by now that babies just don't mix well with high school.

26 weeks
left of
being pregnant!

To-Do List

- Dr. Lippincott appointment on January 20th at 5:30pm
  (pick Josie up)
- pick up paycheck on Friday from Roast and Drink
- $ work on budget $
- look for sales at Target/Babies R' Us
- go to Babies R' Us
- watch Josie after Babies R' Us

buy:
- cheese puffs
- tissues
- new bra : go to Victoria's Secret Target

- chemistry equations
  on page 105   too expensive →
- read 4 chapters
  + do summary on them
  for English
- math problems page 310
- conjugate new verbs
  for French
- ask Janet to
  write an editorial
  on the college
  fair
- finish editing new
  stories for this week's
  newspaper edition

- lotion
- bigger sweatpants
- Saltine crackers

Molly + Jay
K−I−S−S−I−N−G

Cheese
Puff
+
me

Chapter 11: Week Fifteen

"Your baby is as big as a pear," I read online on my pregnancy website. I also read that Cheese Puff is over four inches now! And only twenty-five weeks left! *Only.*

I have an appointment with Dr. Lippincott, so we're leaving in a few minutes. I'm so glad that Dr. Lippincott has office hours on Sundays, because I don't have to miss school. I've never heard of a doctor who works on Sundays, but I don't think she works on Fridays and Saturdays. She does deliveries, though, so I guess sometimes she has to work those days. It's not like the baby knows what day of the week it is, ha-ha.

I'm starting to look pregnant now, I look bloated, but now I know that the pear-sized baby inside of me is making me look that way, and it makes me both excited and nervous. Also, a lot of my fatigue and nausea is gone, it only happens once in a while, usually if I haven't eaten for a few hours, or if I didn't sleep well the night before. All in all, I'm feeling a lot better, way more energetic than I've been lately.

I change into a soft flannel button-down, so I can easily undo my shirt when they do the ultrasound. Then I slide my feet into sneakers. I've heard your feet can swell during pregnancy, but so far mine haven't.

Dianne, Molly, and I pull up to my house, and Josie is waiting on the front porch. She runs out excitedly. I'm so glad she's coming with us today. Everyone is excited to see each other and we catch up with Josie in the car ride over there. Once we get there, we sit in the waiting room, and I read a magazine about eating healthy food during pregnancy (turns out I've been eating way too many cheese puffs), and Josie jiggles her feet, giddy.

"What do you think the baby will look like now?" she asks eagerly.

"I don't know," I say, curious myself. Her excitement makes me think of Leo, and what it would be like if he and I were together and he was here with me for the ultrasound. I'm such a moron, even after he doesn't want anything to do with me, I *still* want him here. I start fantasizing about what would happen if he was here. If we were older, still together, and I was pregnant.

"Excited to see the baby?" Leo asks, holding my hand, smiling.

"Yeah, thanks for coming," I tell him. "I know you have to work, so…"

"I wouldn't miss viewing the baby for the world," he says, and gives me a kiss.

"Madison Davis?" A nurse calls my name, bringing me back to

reality. She takes my blood pressure, weighs me, has me pee in a cup in the bathroom to check my sugar levels and make sure I don't have a UTI, and *finally*, I get to relax on the examining bed and wait for Dr. Lippincott. I really want to ask her about amniocentesis, which I've read about. I know they say it's only women over thirty-five who need them, but I still worry. Obviously, I didn't get genetically tested for disorders or conditions that I could carry before I got pregnant, and I can't ask Leo to, so I'm worried that some unknown genetic condition will show up when the baby is born.

A couple minutes later, Dr. Lippincott walks in. "So great to see you, Madison! Hi everyone! And who is this cutie?" she asks, gesturing to Josie.

"She's my little sister, Josie."

"Well, very nice to meet you, Josie."

Josie looks down shyly. "Nice to meet you, too."

I pipe up. "Um, before the ultrasound, I wanted to ask you something."

"Yes, of course, you can ask me anything," she says kindly.

"Can I have amniocentesis? I want to do it today, because I heard about genetic conditions that can surface, and...do you think we could do it today?"

"No, Madison, that's for genetic problems that tend to surface when you're an *older* pregnant woman, which is called *advanced maternal age*, something you are the opposite of. So, there's no need. But we can get you a blood test to check for the more common genetic disorders, as you don't know if you're a carrier for things like Tay-Sachs, cystic fibrosis, et cetera. So, we will do that test at the end of the appointment. Now, let's see here..." She looks at my chart and is happy to see my weight is going up. Then she starts the ultrasound, Josie holds my hand, and Molly and Dianne watch from their chairs at the side of the room.

On the screen, I see a head, and then a semblance of a forming body. I tear up again. I can't believe that's what's inside me, and that *I'm* responsible for making it, that it's genuinely mine and will always be the one thing that always belongs to *me*. It's just so unbelievable.

"At your next appointment, we'll be able to look for gender, right now the baby's in a position where we can't see it. Everything looks great, though. Good work!" She pats my shoulder, and I let the tears fall, I'm so relieved everything is still okay. Josie is just staring at the screen, a huge smile of wonder on her face.

Dr. Lippincott notices Josie's face and says, "Isn't it beautiful? In all my years of practicing obstetrics, I still feel amazed whenever I see the developing baby."

I stare at the screen in complete awe. I wonder if it's a girl or boy. But more than that, I wonder what it'll *be*. A doctor? A lawyer? A writer? An actor? Who knows? All I know is that I hope it's healthy and happy. I want this baby to have such a good life, I just want my Cheese Puff to be happy.

Dianne passes me a tissue. I realize I'm really crying now. I feel sort of embarrassed for getting so emotional. I feel like I'm not allowed to be happy about this baby, because I'm really just an irresponsible teenager.

As if reading my mind, Dianne says, "I know exactly how you're feeling right now." She's always so comforting, it makes me appreciate her so much. I think of my mom and then I push the thoughts away, it's still too painful.

When it comes time for the blood test, I brace myself. I hate needles. The nurse finds a vein and sticks the sharp needle in. It stings as it takes my blood out. But who cares if I'm in pain? I just want my baby to be okay.

"This will be sent to the lab," the nurse says. "The results will come within the week. You're good to go."

Later that night, I curl up in bed and I start feeling really scared. What if something is wrong? What if Leo carried some horrible gene? What if *I* do? I touch my stomach, worried tears springing up in my eyes.

"I don't want you to have something wrong with you," I whisper. "I don't want something to be wrong. I want you to be healthy." My voice sounds throaty, and I cough to clear the mucus. I sniffle, and wipe my eyes with my hand. I want my mom. I also want my dad, and that just makes me sadder because I truly can't have him. Then I sense someone standing over me, and I turn around to see Dianne. I didn't even hear her come in.

She gives me a huge hug. "What's wrong, Madison? Tell me, what is it?"

"I'm really scared," I say shakily. "That something's wrong with the baby. And it's my fault if there is, I mean, I didn't get tested, Leo didn't get tested. I'm just now getting the blood test I was supposed to get before conceiving, but we obviously weren't planning to get pregnant. I didn't know what I was doing."

I pause to take a deep breath, because I'm crying so hard. She rubs my back.

"And I'm going to feel so awful if there *is* something wrong, because I don't want to get an abortion, I want my baby, but I want it to be okay. I'm really scared..." I trail off, sobbing.

"I know, Madison. I'm so sorry you're feeling this way, but I went through it, too. As far as something being wrong, *most* people don't get tested before conceiving, even happy couples who are planning to get pregnant. You'd be surprised at how few people go through that step. And, most of the time, the baby is just fine. The odds are in your favor, please don't worry. But I totally get it. I cried a lot, too. I remember I used to have to muffle my cries into this flimsy air mattress that I slept on at Molly's father's house, in the beginning. But everything was okay with Molly, and I'm sure it will be with your little baby, too. Now get some sleep, okay?"

After she leaves the room, I fall asleep, thinking about the things that *used* to scare me that all seem so stupid now.

... February 2018...

One night when I didn't have to babysit Josie, I was over at Leo's and he insisted on watching the movie Scream. I'm not one of those people who love horror movies, they really scare me.

"Don't be scared," Leo teased, but even though I was burying my head in the couch pillows, I could still hear the crazy murder sounds, and I screamed and knocked the popcorn all over the couch.

"Ugh, look what you did! You're such a scaredy-cat!" he teased again, and I peeked open my eyes. I started picking up the popcorn, eating it at the same time.

"I don't see how you like these movies," I said to Leo. "They just scare me."

He rolled his eyes. "Everything scares you, Madison. Your grades dropping from an A to an A minus, not writing the perfect story for journalism or not getting the articles printed in time, worrying that I'm mad at you..."

I threw a pillow at him, then he threw it back at me, and we started laughing as the popcorn went flying all over again, and then we started kissing, the horror sounds from the movie fading into the background.

...

The next day at work, I'm determined to use it as a distraction from how scared I am about getting the test results from the blood test. But I also get a surprise, because when I walk in, I see Matthew working there! At first, I thought he was a customer, but then I see he's wearing the "Roast and Drink" apron. He notices my apron, and starts laughing as I come behind the counter and get ready to serve customers.

"Mads! Oh, wow, you work here, too?"

"Yeah, I do," I say, still feeling a little embarrassed because of what happened at the dance.

"That's so awesome! My parents wanted me to get a part-time job and I've always loved this place. It's going to be so much fun working here with you. And honestly, I just want to forget what happened at the dance. I'm sorry I reacted weirdly, or whatever I did. Let's just start over, okay?"

I smile. "Yeah, okay, good." In between serving customers, we talk quietly to each other. The manager isn't here today, so we won't get in trouble for talking. I love that we're running the place ourselves today. It would be amazing if we could always do these shifts together. "So, when did you apply for the job?" I ask.

"A week ago. They said they already had someone, but they could use extra help for the latte swirls. I guess you can't do them." He winks and smiles mischievously. "Just kidding. I saw the notice that they were hiring. Johnny interviewed me and I started training this weekend, I'm going to work a lot of weekends."

"The funny thing is, it's true, I need to learn to do those latte swirls better. Everyone loves them. Maybe you can teach me, Mr. Big Shot Latte Swirler?" He laughs and agrees to teach me later, when there's a break in customers.

Then, he asks, "What's going on with Leo?" I hear a tinge of bitterness in his voice. "I think I heard that you guys broke up a little while ago?"

"How did you even know we were together?" I ask delicately. Should I tell him I'm pregnant? I mean, he's my friend, I will have to tell him eventually. I wonder if the rumors have made it to him, but if they had, I think he would have said something. And even if he's heard something, he probably thinks it isn't true, because my stomach isn't even big at all yet.

He shrugs, "Word travels, I guess."

"Yeah, well, it just, uh, didn't work out," I say. If only it were that simple.

But despite the sadness I'm still feeling about Leo, I'm glad that Matthew and I are talking again. It was extremely awkward at the dance. I want to forget about it and make a new start with him, like he said.

Matthew's shift ends before mine, and I'm glad because I realized he would probably want to walk me home and I would have to explain why I'm living with Molly. I'm not ready to tell him anything yet.

At dinner once I'm home, I tell Molly about Matthew working at the coffee shop. She tells me she thinks he got the job because he found out I worked there. She's half kidding, but it's funny, she always says she thinks he has a crush on me, even though I tell her we're just friends. Dianne listens to our conversation with an amused expression on her face.

"Does he know about the baby?" Molly asks.

"Not unless he heard the rumors and hasn't got the guts to ask me. But I do need to tell him, before I start really showing. I don't even know how I'll bring it up. It stresses me out to even think about." I change the subject, and ask Molly, "What's going on with you and *Jay*?"

"Ooh, the plot is rich and thick at the dinner table tonight!" Dianne says, and we all laugh together. It feels really nice to laugh after I've been so worried, waiting for the blood test results.

Just before bed, I get a text from Matthew, talking about our history teacher, who drones on in a monotone voice. We end up texting for a while, and it's like we just pick up right where we left off. I'm really glad he's a part of my life again. I hope Molly's wrong and he doesn't have a crush on me, because I really just want to be friends with him, and everything would be so complicated if he actually liked me. We've been friends our whole life. I want to keep it that way.

But I'm too tired to think about all this stuff, and before I know it, I'm sleeping. That's one thing I really like about being pregnant, it's so easy to fall asleep. After my dad died, I had trouble falling asleep for a long time. Now, it's just easy.

<>

On Wednesday, during my free period, I'm studying in the library, and my phone rings. I can't believe I forgot to turn the ringer off. The librarian glares at me. "Sorry," I whisper, rushing to get to the hallway to answer.

"Hello?"

"Hi, Madison?"

"Yes?"

"It's Dr. Lippincott. I wanted to tell you that I have the blood test results. Good news, you're not a carrier for any of the most common genetic abnormalities. An unremarkable result, just what I like to see." She chuckles.

"Unremarkable?" I ask.

She chuckles again. "That's a good thing. It just means it's a normal result, nothing out of the ordinary. Anyway, you can stop worrying about this now."

I start crying and I head to the bathroom as I start to notice people glancing at me. "I'm *so* happy! Thank you, Dr. Lippincott, thank you so much!"

I hang up and do a little dance, whispering, "Did you hear that, Cheese Puff? You're okay!"

A girl in the bathroom stares at me, but I ignore her. My baby's healthy, and to me, that's all that matters.

♡   ♡   ♡   15 weeks

♡

To-Do List
- Dr. Lippincott appointment today (pick up Josie)
  *ask about amniocentesis
- blood test results coming   ☆ 50% off
  this week   baby clothes
  ♡   at Target
- finish French paper   this week
- start outline for English essay
- study for science test
- history notes due Friday (5 pages)
- practice science presentation
- study for math test
- edit "entertainment" section stories for
  newspaper
- finish story on the new "arts" club + edit it
- study with Matthew?

☆ tell Janet to send   ☆ **START**
this week's newspaper   **BUDGET**
edition to be printed

☆ research about
how to apply
to Harvard for
when the time comes

♡   Cheese Puff
    is healthy!!!   ♡   ☆ pick up paycheck
on Friday from
Roast and Drink

Chapter 12: Week Sixteen

"Your baby is as big as an avocado," I read online as I sit at my desk, starting my math homework.

I haven't been doing so well. I can tell I'm gaining weight from the pregnancy, I see it in my stomach and my thighs. And I've been really stuffy lately, tons of nasal congestion, which I've heard is normal during pregnancy, but it's just really annoying.

I've also been having *so* much homework, and I know that I heard about having a lot of homework in high school, but now I feel like it's *really* starting to become crazy. I also researched more into applying to Harvard, and it just seems like...a lot. I mean, I'm not applying yet, of course, but I'm going to be so busy with the baby that I really want to be prepared to know how to do it when the time comes to apply, in senior year.

I've been freaking out a little about all of it, and so I decided to schedule an appointment with the local adoption agency. I keep thinking about what Dianne's mother told me, that it's a good idea "just to see." It's not that I can even imagine giving up Cheese Puff, at this point, but I feel like I need to know that this is an option, just in case. Things are so hard with school now, and I can't even imagine doing it with a newborn baby. It's just to see. That's all.

Mom called yesterday, and I thought she was just going to tell me more about what she's been talking about with Leo's parents, but she said she just wanted to say hi and see how I was doing. It really surprised me, but I was happy to hear from her. She said she knew that Josie had come to the appointment with me and that Josie told her the baby looked so cute. She said she feels conflicted about the whole thing still, but that she would like to see an ultrasound picture, if I had one. I said I would send her an email with the pictures. It was a bit awkward, but it really made me happy that we're even talking about it at all. We didn't really get into detail, I think we're both scared we will start fighting, but at least it's something.

She also said that she and Leo's parents are still figuring out financial stuff and that she is trusting them, as Leo's dad is a lawyer and they are actually nice people. She said they're really angry with Leo. I could tell that made her happy and that she feels like it justifies her being angry with me, too. Anyway, I secretly hope they don't end up making an agreement, because I don't want anything from Leo's parents, I don't want to have to deal with them at all.

I'm also starting to show a bit. When I wear one of my old tight shirts, it's like someone sliced off the top of a cupcake or a muffin and plopped it on my stomach. And I had to buy a new bra yesterday. It's a B-cup, one size larger than I usually wear. I feel like I have a totally different chest, which makes me feel kind of weird. It feels like *everything* grows when you're pregnant, which I guess it really does!

I'm really not looking forward to this appointment with the adoption agency, but   I decide to walk even though it's a bit far, so I can get some exercise and hopefully have a clear head when I get there. The building is smaller than I pictured it, and it just has a small sign at the front, "Anderson Adoption Agency." I have no idea who Anderson is, but I guess he owns it? Or she? This is all so confusing.

I enter and go to the desk at the front and check in. A few minutes later, a perky-looking woman wearing a bright yellow dress and such high heels that I can't even imagine how she walks in them, comes out and takes me to her office.

She has pictures all over the walls of what look like places she's gone on vacation. I wonder if she considers what she does as just a job, something she has to do to make money so she can go on vacation. Her job must be so stressful. She helps people make decisions about whether or not to keep their baby, or give it to someone else to raise it.

She explains all different things about adoption. That you can have open or closed adoptions, where you can either still see or know the baby, or not. I tell her that I think I'd want an open adoption. Then she talks about all the legal stuff, and shows me some pictures of happy couples with babies who have been adopted from their agency in the past. I can barely concentrate, because this all just feels so wrong to me.

I ask if Leo would have to give consent to the adoption, because it's a question that's been in my mind for a while. And she says that yes, at this agency, they do need consent from the father. That's when my head really fogs up. Leo won't want to agree to anything, he won't even want to have the conversation about it. He wanted me to abort it, he won't want to know his baby is out there all the time. I don't even know how I would ask him about this.

This whole thing just doesn't feel right at all. I already told everyone I'm keeping it. I've been planning to keep it. I *want* to keep it. At first, it felt like a really kind and selfless thing to do, giving up my baby to someone else who wants a baby but can't have one. Someone who could raise it and give it a better life than I could. But, that was when I first found out and when I was really shocked and didn't know what to do. Now that I've had some time to think about everything and even find a job, even though I know it's not much yet, it feels like I can actually figure it all out and make it work somehow. Even though it will be hard. And even though this woman is really nice and she's telling me what a wonderful thing adoption is. I just...I *want* to keep this baby.

I start crying and she asks me what I'm thinking but I can't even talk, I'm crying so hard. She reaches across the table and puts her hand on mine and tells me she knows how hard this is and that I don't have to make the decision now. She said a lot of people come to see her several times and that I'm welcome to come back to talk about it anytime. She did say it was better not to make a decision until I'm really sure, and that she's seen people be devastated by mothers like me who say they are going to give their baby to someone and then change their mind at the last minute. So, she says I need to really be sure.

I tell her that I need to think about everything and that maybe I'll come back another time, and she says that it's totally fine, and that I can call to make another appointment any time. She hands me a business card for their agency, and I leave.

On the long walk home, I keep crying on and off. I don't know how I'm going to make this work, and I'm scared, but I really just don't think I can go through with adoption. I want to be a mother, even though it's not the right time. I realize I'm already *so* attached to my little Cheese Puff, and I know how ridiculous that sounds. The only reason I considered adoption was that I thought I couldn't give the baby its best life, and because of what Dianne's mom said, saying that I should see all my options. And I know that keeping the baby might be ruining my chances of giving *myself* a good life. If I give the baby up, things go back to normal and I can apply to Harvard and try to be a journalist and do something good with my life. But for some reason, I don't think even then things would ever go back to normal again. It's too late. Things haven't been normal since my dad died, and now they're so far from normal, it's not even funny.

I think of Mom. She didn't have to go through this with us. She had a nice, happy pregnancy with both of us, and she got to experience it with my dad. She used to tell us about all the activities and crafts she used to do during her pregnancy, how excited she was, how *happy* she was. I can't believe I'll never have that. It brings an overwhelmingly sad feeling to my chest. I didn't wait, and I was stupid, and if I had waited, I could have probably gotten everything I wanted.

But it's too late now. The baby is *inside of me* right now. Like it says in the pregnancy books, it knows *my* voice and *my* sounds and *my* smells, and it will be moving and kicking and *I* will eventually feel it, which will make me even more attached to it. How can I go through all of this and then separate myself from it? I just can't do it.

When I get back, Dianne serves dinner. Molly seems upset, she just sits there looking down at her plate, dangling her fork.

"What's wrong, Molly Lolly Pop?" I ask her, using the name I used when we met in seventh grade. It's kind of babyish, but sometimes I use it.

"Nothing. It's just...I tried to talk to Jay multiple times today, and he just kept blowing me off, kind of ignoring me."

Dianne strokes her arm. "It's okay. He's probably just busy with school. Which you should be, too. Didn't you just tell me you had a huge math test tomorrow? Study for that after dinner, please."

"Maddie, where were you?" Molly asks, changing the subject and looking at me.

Lying, I say, "Oh, I just went out to Target. I wanted to see if there were any sales on things I need for the baby."

"Oh."

It's a little quiet now, which makes me uneasy. Molly looks at me again. "How do you get a guy to love you like you did with Leo?"

"Molly, come on, don't bring Leo into this," Dianne says.

"It's okay," I say to Molly. "You can ask me anything about Leo, or whatever."

Molly frowns, pushing her plate away. "I'm not hungry. I'm going up to study."

She gets up and walks off. "Let her go," Dianne says when I try to go after her. "She'll be okay. There are some things I would like to talk to you about, anyway. I know it's a little early, but we should start talking about what it'll be like for the birth."

"Okay. Like, what sort of things do we have to talk about?"

"The plan, who you want there, what you want to happen. If you want any kind of epidural or pain medication."

"Oh, I'm *definitely* getting an epidural," I say, laughing. "And I want you guys there, obviously, I mean, if you want to be there. And Josie." I bite my lip. "If Mom comes around, her, too. It's just weird to not talk to Mom in person these days."

"I know. I didn't talk to my mom through a lot of my pregnancy, either, I stayed at Molly's father's house. But I think it's easier for them after the baby's born, because they see their grandchild, and they see it's not so bad once there's a new person to love."

"That makes sense."

"And what about after the baby is born? At Slurp that night, you said you were looking for an apartment?"

"Yeah. You know those apartments near the high school? They're small but not that expensive and I always see an 'for rent' sign when I walk by."

"Well, good. You sound like you're thinking of the right things. You're smart, Madison. You're managing to figure out your baby and yourself all at the same time, which is very good." She pauses. "But I know you weren't running errands tonight. You're not the best liar, and I know when people lie. Where were you?"

I gulp. Will she understand? She might, she might not. But it *was* her mother who suggested I go there, in the first place. "I was, well, I went to that adoption agency that your mom suggested. I made an appointment and talked to someone. But I decided I don't want to do it, I just can't do it."

Dianne takes a breath. "Well, I'm glad you went, and I think it was a good suggestion even though my mother can be bossy at times. Though my mother loves me and Molly very much now, I think at the time, she wished I had given Molly up for adoption so I could go to Princeton. She was probably just pushing what she wanted for me onto you. Anyway, the point is that you have to decide what is right for *you*."

"I know. I decided I'm keeping the baby for sure, though, really."

She smiles knowingly. "I see so much of myself in you. I understand how you feel. Everything happens for a reason. Imagine if I hadn't kept Molly. You two might not have ever met. And now, I can be here for you and help you through this. I'm not sure if you understand how happy I am to be able to help you right now."

"Thank you, Dianne. I think I do understand a bit. Because now I think about what would happen if *my* baby grew up and had a friend who got pregnant and was in the same type of situation. I would want to help them, too. I mean, this is such a hard thing."

"I know it is, sweetie. I know."

Dianne is so sweet, but I feel guilty that she's down here with me talking about this when Molly is upstairs really upset about Jay. I also wish my *own* mother could be here, but I realize that she could never relate to me the way Dianne can right now.

I thank Dianne and then go up to talk to Molly, but I see she's already gone to sleep. I draw a little picture of a lollipop on some paper from her desk and then tuck it under the blanket next to her, hoping it will cheer her up when she sees it when she wakes up. It's been a long day and I can hardly wait to get into my *own* bed. Which I do. And then I fall asleep within three seconds.

<>

At school the next day, I hang out with Matthew at lunch, because Molly is busy talking to Jay. I look over at them and they seem to be having a good conversation, I really hope things are better with them. Matthew and I sit on the benches near the grassy area of the school yard and eat.

"Ready for work again after school today?" I ask.

"Yeah. And don't worry, I'm happy to step in to do the latte swirls."

"You're like my life-saver." I smile. It's nice to just sit and relax with Matthew and pretend I don't have a huge thing to tell him. I really don't know when I'm going to tell him about the pregnancy, but I'm dreading it and I'm also worried he won't want to be friends with me anymore.

"Hey, so do you still like acting?" he asks.

I laugh. "Not much. I mean, I liked improv, partly because I got to hang out with you there, but I'm really into journalism now. I want to go to Harvard, study journalism, and then, well, become a journalist."

"Oh, wow. That's really cool."

"How about you?"

"I really want to go to Yale. Don't laugh, but I used to love that show *Gilmore Girls*. I know that sounds really girly, but anyway, Rory went to Yale, and-"

"Are you kidding? I loved that show, too! And I bet you'll get into Yale. What do you want to study?"

"I was actually thinking of studying, well, theater. I love when we talk about Shakespeare in English class, I just love everything about acting and theatre and writing plays. I want to do all of it."

I smile. For some reason, just talking about this academic stuff, and college plans, it makes me really happy. Like it's all still possible. But I really want to tell Matthew about the baby. There's something about him that makes me feel so comfortable and even safe. I just don't feel like I can do it yet, though.

After school, as I'm walking home, I decide to walk by Leo's house. I've been going to the other side of the block to avoid going anywhere near there. But today, I just feel like I should stop being so afraid. Maybe it was my conversation with Matthew, I don't know, but I feel a little more confident about things.

I start walking past his house, but then someone brushes past me, and it's actually *Leo*! He's wearing his backpack, with his house key attached to it. I gave him a soccer ball decal to put on his keychain, and I notice he still has it.

He looks really pissed. "What are you doing outside my house?"

"I was just...walking home."

"Look, I don't want you hanging around outside my house, and I don't want you flaunting the baby when you start to show or any of that shit! I mean it when I say just *get out* of my life! You know, my parents hate me because of *you!*"

Tears come to my eyes. "Your parents are being way nicer than you are, they've been talking to my mom all the time, they're even going to pay me child support, did you know that? And then when you're eighteen, my mom says you'll have to, as well. It's your baby too, Leo. Whether you want it or not."

"I *don't* want it, you've got that right." He scoffs. "Child support, what a joke. Trust me, I'll find a way out of it. I don't want *anything* to do with you and that big mistake you're carrying around. Why on earth didn't you get an abortion? That's what any *normal* girl would do. I don't want to see you! Your face makes me sick."

He pushes past me, and goes into his house.

I just stand there staring, my vision blurry from the tears. I can't even believe what he just said to me, it all hurts so much. It's so unfair. *So unfair.* He doesn't understand that there's no way I could abort this baby and there's no way I could give it up. He just doesn't get it. And it's my decision and I don't want anything from him anyway. I just don't understand how he could be so mean to me after how *nice* he used to be to me. I mean, this happened because we were *together.* And it was his idea in the first place!

I start to run away from his house and the next thing I know, I'm on the ground. *Ugh,* I fell, and my knee is bleeding. I carry a little first aid kit in my backpack that my mom gave me when I started elementary school. I've hardly had to use it and so a lot of what's in there has been in there for almost ten years. It still has some of the little princess Band-Aids in it that she used to use on me, when I was little and obsessed with princesses. They're too small to cover this cut on my knee and it makes me cry harder to see them, and suddenly it all hits me again and I really miss my mom and my dad and all I want in the world is to go back to the days before my dad died.

I somehow manage to stop crying by the time I get to work. I'm just exhausted from all of this and I don't know how I'm going to get through my shift. At six o'clock, I take a bathroom break and when I look down, I see that there's *blood* in my underwear.

Oh, no, this isn't good! *What is happening?* What is this?! Is the baby okay? Should I go to the hospital? What am I saying, I *need* to go to the hospital! I'm hyperventilating. I need to calm down! But I can't! I'm freaking out!

I rush out of the bathroom and tell Matthew that I have to leave because of a family emergency, and I tell him to cover my shift. "Okay, but you know Johnny. He'll take away half your pay for the day."

"I don't care," I say, yanking off my apron and leaving.

I take an Uber home, I'm too scared to walk because of the bleeding. When I get inside, I rush over to Dianne and tell her I'm bleeding *down there*. I tell her that it's like a period, but kind of worse, and that I want to go to the hospital.

"How much blood?" she asks, and she sounds a bit worried so that makes *me* worry even more.

I make a circle with my thumb and index finger. "That much was on my underwear fifteen minutes ago!"

"Let's go see Dr. Lippincott. We don't need to go to the hospital unless she recommends it. Hopefully it's nothing, but we have to get you checked out."

Before we leave, I put a pad on, something I haven't done for so long. I realize I'm shaking, I just can't believe something might be wrong with my little Cheese Puff.

The nurse takes me in right away and she takes my blood pressure and tells me my pulse is high and that I should try to calm down. Then Dr. Lippincott comes in and we fill her in, I tell her about how I fell when I was running to work. I leave out the part about Leo and how horrible he was to me.

"Okay, no need to panic. A little bleeding can be normal sometimes. Let's take a look." She puts the gel on my stomach and does an ultrasound. I see little Cheese Puff on the screen and everything looks the same as last week, maybe even a little bigger. I don't see anything that makes me freak out, but then again, I don't know how to tell what's what on an ultrasound.

"Everything looks good, Madison. The baby is fine." Dianne takes my hand as the tears start rolling down my face again. Dr. Lippincott smiles calmly. "This could be related to when you fell. But besides that, did you have anything stressful happen to you today? You seem really stressed out."

I think of Leo. "I had a stressful encounter, I guess you could say."

"Well, I need to caution you to keep your stress levels down. I know it's hard, but it's not good for the baby. The fact that you fell might have caused a little nick in the placenta or something, which caused the bleeding, but the baby looks perfectly fine, so it should resolve."

I'm so relieved, I take a deep breath and sigh. I ask if she's sure and she repeats that she is. "But I need you to take it easy for the rest of this week, and that means a few days of bed rest. I don't want to risk any more bleeding, seeing as when you're a teenager, there are more risks to pregnancy complications. You can go back to school on Monday. But for now, you need to stay home and take it easy."

My heart rate kicks back up again. "But I have so many tests to take this week, and editing to do for the newspaper, and-"

"This stress isn't good for the baby, so if you want your baby to continue to thrive, you have to go on bed rest until Monday. You need the rest of this week and the weekend to take it easy. Is that clear?"

"Don't worry, I'll make sure she rests," Dianne says. "We'll let your teachers know, I can email them for you, I don't want you to get stressed out about it."

Dr. Lippincott smiles. "Things like this happen, it's pretty common. We're being cautious so nothing happens. I'm sorry you have to go through this, but you're on this journey and you have to accept that things will come up. It's all part of it."

As we leave, the thought occurs to me that this is Leo's revenge for me wanting to keep the baby. It all happened after what he said to me. All he wanted was for me to get an abortion. But I couldn't do it. I still wouldn't be able to do it, actually even more now. I guess I'm crazy and not *normal* like other girls, as he said.

In the car, Dianne asks me what happened and I tell her about Leo and what he said. Reliving it, I start crying again. All I do is cry. She puts her hand on my shoulder and says, "That must have been so hard. But I'm glad you told me about it." She pauses. "You know that Leo's reaction is not fair, but there's nothing you can do about how he feels, right? I mean, it would be wonderful if he felt differently, but he doesn't. He's a young teenage boy and he's scared, just like you. But you're right, what you said; this is something you did *together*. It's not your fault anymore than it is his. You have a right to keep the baby, just like he has a right to *not* want to have a baby. But he can't control what you do with *your* body. He should have thought of this before he had sex with you. This is not an original situation, it happens way more than you'd think. And while he might be right that most girls in your situation would choose to get an abortion, just because you won't doesn't mean you're crazy. You chose the hard path, but you're doing it for the right reasons. Not everyone is going to understand or agree with this. And I'm not going to lie to you, it's going to be really hard at times, maybe even harder than this. But if you know in your heart that you are doing what's best for you and your baby, then that's all that matters. You'll learn this more and more as you go along."

She's so wise, it's insane to me, and I realize how amazing it is that I have someone like her in my life, who's been through something almost exactly the same and who knows and understands what I'm going through. I wonder if I will ever be able to be calm and wise about everything, like her.

Suddenly, I feel an overwhelming urge to call my mom. I miss her so much. It started with the princess Band-Aids and now Dianne is acting like a mother would towards me. I *really* want my mom, even if it's babyish.

When we get home, Dianne tells me to just get into bed and she will bring me something to eat. I dial Mom's number and it goes to voicemail. She's probably at work. I leave a message.

"Hi, Mom. I just had some bleeding tonight, and I'm fine, but I have to be on bed rest for a few days. I just thought I should, well, tell you, I guess. I love you so much, and I wanted you to know that you can take as much time as you need until you're ready to talk to me, I just wanted to say this to you again, and, uh...okay, bye."

As I end the call, all I can hear are the words that Mom was saying to me that awful night she found out.

So you just had to have sex at fifteen years old, huh?!

I am so disappointed that you've done this to yourself.

You were going to be something! Be someone! And now your whole life is over!

Can you imagine what your father would think?!? He would be so disappointed in you!

I had to do my part after your dad died, and so did you! And your part was not going off with some boy like a little slut and getting pregnant!

I let her down so much, and after remembering all that stuff she said, it's even clearer how much I hurt her. But she's my *mom*. I need her. I really hope that one day she can forgive me and I hope I can prove to her that I'm responsible and that I'm able to do it all, take care of the baby and still have a career someday, and do something with my life. I'm going to just keep trying. That's all I can do.

And maybe it's part of growing up. Learning to accept the fact that there's going to be people who aren't going to want to be there, and there's nothing I can do about it. A lot of people aren't going to want to be involved. I'm a *teen mom*. It's *always* going to be a part of me: "Oh, you know that girl Madison Davis? Yeah, she's the one that got pregnant at fifteen. Crazy, right?"

Lots of people are still going to leave, probably even more than the people who have already. But at least I'll always have myself, and I'll also always have my Cheese Puff right there, too, and honestly? I think that may be all I need.

♡ ♡ ♡ ♡ (16 weeks)

(To - Do List)

-pick up paycheck on Friday from Roast and Drink
-finish math homework (pages 200 - 213)
-finish French essay
- go to driving class   ☆ appointment with
  on Saturday   Anderson Adoption
  * schedule driving test   Agency tonight
    for February 18
    (my birthday!!)
-figure out when to   (ad̶option)
 take childbirth classes?
- history paper
  5 pages double-spaced   ☆ sale on diapers at
  due Monday   Babies R' Us this
- Science lab report   weekend
  due Friday

☆ call newspaper meeting on what stories
  we are writing for this week's edition

-figure out budget!!   bed rest until
                              Monday

$ $ $ $

                              * get work from
                                teachers
          ←— Cheese   * call Johnny and
              Puff   tell him I'll be
         ♡   back at work on
    ♡   ♡   Monday

Chapter 13: Week Seventeen

"Your baby is as big as a large onion," I read, scrolling through my phone, lying in bed, burrowed under the covers. For the past few days, except for using the bathroom and showering, I've been in bed, doing schoolwork and working on some stories for journalism, researching the baby, things like that. But, tomorrow is Monday and I get to go back to school! I don't think I've ever been so excited for school in my entire life, ha-ha.

I'm in my first week of my fifth month of pregnancy, it's crazy how fast the time is going by. I almost cried of happiness when I read that the baby is starting to be able to hear my voice. It makes me want to talk to my little Cheese Puff even more. Every night, I try and say at least a few sentences before I fall asleep. I also sing a little song, even though my voice isn't the greatest. Hopefully, little Cheese Puff won't care. Unfortunately, I didn't inherit my dad's voice. He was the best at singing us bedtime songs, and sometimes he'd even make up his own.

I'm even more hungry than I've been for the past few weeks. I'm starving all the time, grabbing crackers and cheese to eat whenever I'm feeling hungry. I've been getting this annoying heartburn which gets worse at night time. It's really hard to sleep sometimes because of it, and I'm frustrated because I know I really need the sleep.

Now, I start on an English assignment on my computer, balancing the computer on a pillow in my bed. As I'm typing, Dianne comes in with a tray of my dinner. "Last tray-dinner!" she announces, and we laugh. But then Dianne gets a sparkle in her eyes. "You know what? Let's *all* have tray-dinners tonight!"

She goes back to the kitchen and after a few minutes, she and Molly come in with their own trays and they sit on my bed with me and we all eat together with our trays. It's really nice to have them here, for the first few days of bed rest, they ate in the dining room while I ate alone in my bedroom.

"How are you feeling?" Molly asks.

"Good," I say. "Tired, but good."

"I know you're going back to school and work tomorrow, but that doesn't mean that you shouldn't still be taking it easy, so I want you to keep doing calm breathing and not let yourself get stressed, okay?" Dianne says.

I nod. "I know, thank you." I turn to Molly. "So, what's going on with Jay?"

She smiles. "We've been going out a lot, he's not avoiding me anymore. He was just stressed with school, like Mom said. We're going out for dessert after dinner."

"That's great, Molly. I'm so happy it's working out!"

"Thanks!"

We finish our dinner together, then Molly goes out with Jay, and Dianne goes to do some writing. I can't wait to get out of this bed. It's funny because usually I can't wait to get into bed because I'm so tired, but after so many days of being cooped up in here, I just can't wait to be out in the real world again. I'm a bit nervous, but thankfully, the bleeding has stopped completely. I check every time I go to the bathroom.

I've been wondering what's going on with Leo's parents, since Mom hasn't mentioned it for a while. After I left her that message, she called back a bit later and asked me how I was doing, and we talked for a few minutes, but she didn't mention Leo's parents at all. I really am feeling more and more like I don't want anything to do with them or Leo. I wish I had been able to hide the whole thing from them. I don't want or need their money. I've already saved up some money and if I keep working steadily, it will be enough. I make around $240 a week, but I do spend some of it, so I really only save $200 a week.

But what if I'm wrong? Maybe it won't be enough. I need to sit down and figure it all out and give myself a budget to stick to. They keep mentioning this in the pregnancy books I've been reading.

At least I've started working out a plan for what happens after the birth. Cheese Puff will be born on July 4th, or around that time, so she or he will be nearly two months old by the time I go back to school on August 22nd. I'm going to look for apartments, hopefully find a cheap one to rent, and then my goal is to move in the week before school starts.

But what if I can't even find a good apartment for what I can afford? It's just so unnerving, how many things I have no control over. I guess I'll just have to wait and see what happens.

<>

"Someone's excited for school!" Molly says as we walk together and I keep pulling ahead, a big smile on my face. She laughs. "It's funny, you're so excited, and I wish we could go back and start the weekend all over again."

When I get to school, I go to my locker and get my books. Some people stare at me, as usual, still checking to see if the rumors are true. I've been wearing a baggy shirt, though, so it's impossible to see my stomach that isn't even very big yet. I'm so happy to be back here that I don't care what anyone thinks. In class, I feel really productive and my mind feels so much clearer than it has in a while.

At lunch, I sit with Molly. Before I had to take the week off, I had been sitting with Matthew, and Molly had been with Jay. It's nice to sit with Molly again. She's really an amazing friend, and even though we're living together right now, we don't get sick of each other.

"Hey, did I tell you that Jay and I are going for dinner tonight? He said he wanted to talk to me about something. He sounded very serious," Molly says, her eyes glowing.

"That's great! Maybe he really wants to become exclusive with you, to become more serious, you know?"

"What about you? Any potential love interests?" Molly asks playfully, and then she grimaces. "Sorry. That was really rude."

"Nah, it wasn't. And I don't have any, you know, 'potential love interests.' I don't even want people to know I'm pregnant, Molly, let alone a guy."

"Well, the baggy shirts aren't going to hide it forever. Your stomach is definitely getting bigger. Pretty soon, people are going to know for sure and it won't just be a rumor from crazy Lulu. You might as well reveal it, sooner rather than later."

"I guess you're right. Maybe I should just be confident about it! Who cares what they think?" But then I sigh, shaking my head. "But this shouldn't even...I mean, I shouldn't even have to tell everyone. This shouldn't even be *happening*. Why am I talking about it like it's a good thing?"

"I know, but in the end, it *will* be a good thing. Like my mom says, she wouldn't have had me if she hadn't made the choice to keep me. Seriously, Mads, you're awesome. You're doing so well throughout this whole thing. Stupid kids at this stupid school shouldn't affect that at all."

"Okay. Thanks. But sometimes I just feel a little... overwhelmed."

"I do, too. Even not being pregnant!" Molly says, and we giggle together.

"I'm also worried about Valentine's Day. I mean, before Leo, I don't even remember what I did!"

"I'll be your valentine!" she offers happily, and we laugh together. "Actually, no. I'm hoping Jay and I can do something fun together. Maybe he'll take me out to dinner."

"Yeah, that's cool," I say, feeling a quick pang of jealousy. It passes really quickly, though. I'm happy for her. She deserves to be treated like a princess.

"You have a shift at the coffee shop after school, right? I might come and do my homework there, and it'll be like we're hanging out." She laughs.

"Yeah, that would be really fun!" I say. "You can watch me work!"

After school, she walks over with me to work and I begin my shift while she takes the table nearest to the counter I'm working at, orders a frappuccino, and starts her homework. It's nice to have her here, but I have to admit, I feel a bit awkward when she watches me and Matthew working together. She still has the idea in her head that he likes me, which I don't *really* believe.

I'm tired again, and really hungry. Employees get a discount, so I put some money in the cash register and grab a bagel with cream cheese.

Molly comes up. "Another coffee, please! I'm starting to feel tired, and I need to be alert for dinner with Jay tonight, I'm leaving to meet him in an hour!"

I giggle and whip her up another one. She thanks me and goes back to her homework. But then she eventually leaves to go get ready. "See you at home later!"

"That's sweet that she comes to watch you work," Matthew says.

I turn to him and smile. "Yeah, she's really awesome."

"But why did she say that she'd see you at home later?"

I freeze. "Uh...oh...well, we have a sleepover planned to, um, study later, after she goes for dinner with her boyfriend."

"Oh, cool."

Phew, that was some quick thinking on my part.

Later that night, I hear the door slam really loud as I'm working on homework in my room. I come out of my room as Molly runs past me to her room, and I can see she has tears running down her face.

"What happened?" I ask, stopping her and pulling her into my room.

"He broke up with me!" she wails. "And I know we weren't together for very long, but it seemed like he wanted to go on a date, not *break up!*"

"Oh, God, Molly, I'm so sorry." Now I feel guilty. I was the one who was a little jealous of her having a boyfriend and me not having one. But I really *was* happy for her! I definitely didn't want him to break up with her!

"And he said it was because he started dating someone else and he didn't want to lie to me!" she cries.

I rub her back. "Well, at least he was honest. You wouldn't want to find out he doesn't want to be with you by catching him cheating, would you?"

"No," she says miserably, shaking her head. "But I asked who the girl was, and he said Beatrix Ross. Who's that?"

"Let's look her up on Instagram." I take my phone, looking her up. I don't actually have an Instagram account, I just look at what's on my feed since I don't have an active account. Her page pops up quickly. I see that other people at my school follow her, she's a sophomore. She has light blonde hair and green eyes, and a wide smile on every picture she's posted. She's pretty, but personally, I think Molly's prettier.

"She's so much prettier than I am," Molly cries.

"Actually, her hair has zero volume, unlike yours. And I happen to think her eyes are *too* green," I say, trying to reassure her.

"Look at her waist!" Molly exclaims sadly. "She's probably a size zero! No wonder he didn't want to be with me when he could have her instead!"

"Molly, are you serious right now? If he wants you for your body, then he isn't worth having as a boyfriend at all."

"This is the worst night of my life," she says, gulping down tears. "Thanks, Maddie I'm going to bed."

I sigh. I feel really bad for her. And I don't want to ever look at Jay again. Why does he want to be with someone else when he could be with someone as amazing as Molly? What a jerk. Are all guys like this? I mean, Leo left me, now Jay left Molly...I'm so sick of them.

I finish my homework and end up in bed by midnight, groaning, knowing I can only get six and a half hours of sleep at the most by now.

But I can't fall asleep right away, even though I'm exhausted. I just keep thinking of poor Molly, and then it makes me think of Leo and the time his friend was going through the same kind of thing.

... November 2017...

"I have to go," Leo said one night, after glancing quickly at his phone. We were having dinner together in my kitchen after Josie fell asleep.

"Why?" I asked. "Stay longer, we can watch TV! I'll even watch a horror movie with you if you want, ha-ha!"

"My friend Joe just broke up with his girlfriend. Actually, she broke up with him. He's really upset. I need to go hang out with him, he wants to kick some soccer balls around or something. Gotta go," he said, kissing me.

I liked that Leo was there for his friend and I thought it would be great to be the kind of couple that would always be there for our friends for break-ups. Of course, I was hoping that *we* would never be the ones to break up ourselves, but we did.

...

In the morning, I make it my mission to make Molly feel better. After getting ready, I sit with her at breakfast. She hasn't touched her plate.

"Come on, Molly, eggs are your favorite!" Dianne smiles at me trying to encourage her as she eats with us, too.

"I'm not hungry," Molly says, pushing her plate away.

"Okay, well, what do you want to do at lunch today, after we eat? Spy on Josie playing on her playground? Go walk around the whole school? Anything you want!"

"I don't care. Whatever you want."

On the way to school, it's clear that I can't get Molly into a better mood. She keeps her head down the whole time and doesn't laugh at any of my jokes.

We get to school, and I go to my locker and then head to my first class. Once I'm done with the notes and my teacher gives us all a quick break, I zone out and stare at my desk, completely caught up with my thoughts. I don't know what my problem is, but I find myself daydreaming about a life with Leo. I feel like I'm crazy.

I hang another stuffed monkey on the wall, glancing up at my Harvard diploma I hung on the wall in the baby's nursery. I want the baby to look at it and see what its mother has accomplished. Of course we hung Leo's Stanford diploma up on the wall, as well.

Leo comes in and wraps his arms around my waist. I smile, breathing him in. "I have to get to work," I say. "They're expecting me to record the news for today at the studio."

Leo turns to his phone. "Where do you want to make dinner reservations for your birthday?" he asks.

"That Italian restaurant a few blocks over, near the park," I tell him. I can't believe I'm turning twenty-seven! I wish I could freeze time! Things are so perfect.

I blink, coming back from my stupid, never-going-to-happen fantasy. I shake my head at myself. I'm just so stupid. My life isn't ever going to be that perfect, and I'm going to have to accept it.

At lunch, I meet Molly at our table. There's no lunch in front of her. I pay extra for a chicken salad and a bag of chips for her, but she just pushes them toward me.

"Molly, you have to eat something! You haven't eaten since yesterday!"

"Some people go weeks without eating."

"Yeah, and you aren't going to be one of them. You're being self-destructive!"

"Maybe if I don't eat, I'll be skinnier," she says, shrugging, like it's so simple.

"That's not healthy, Molly. Sorry, you can't do that!" I say, getting a little worried. But she just stares straight ahead. I push the salad towards her, giving up. "Fine, just eat this. You can't gain much weight from lettuce, chicken pieces, shredded carrots, and tomatoes."

She nibbles on the tomatoes but leaves the rest. I'm really worried now. She needs to eat. This is ridiculous. But it's not like I can force food down her throat, so I guess she'll eat once she's hungry enough.

At dinner with Dianne back at home, she tells me that it's just us tonight, because Molly said she's grabbing a bite to eat with Cheryl.

But it occurs to me that she's probably *not* going to eat. But I don't want to intrude on their personal lives, I don't want to get in the middle of things. Maybe Molly really *is* going to eat with Cheryl.

Still. I'm worried about her. I want to laugh at that, though. Pretty soon, I'll *always* have someone to be worried about: Cheese Puff. I might as well get used to worrying.

♡ cheese Puff can hear me!

(To-Do List)   17 weeks!!

buy:
- new shirts
- cheese puffs
- chocolate for Valentine's Day next week

- pick up paycheck on Friday from Roast and Drink
- start story on Valentine's Day for newspaper
- edit book reviews for newspaper
- finish story on the cheerleading team + edit!
- English chapters 17-20
- finish science lab report
- finish French paper
- HISTORY NOTES DUE TOMORROW
- answer English questions #1-10   ☆ visit Josie soon!

♡   ♡   ♡   ♡   ♡   ♡

- MAKE A BUDGET!
- figure out baby names for both boys and girls
- call Mom?

♡   ♡   ☆ make Molly eat!!
       ♡   ☆ buy candy gram for Molly for Valentine's Day next week

⟵ Cheese Puff! (boy or girl?)

♡
       ♡   ♡
  ♡
♡   ♡
       ♡

Chapter 14: Week Eighteen

"Your baby is as big as a cucumber," I read, surprised. That's pretty big! But it's understandable; I look insanely bloated, so I guess that means that Cheese Puff is getting bigger inside there!

I research just a little more: apparently, the genitals are now probably visible, so I could find out the gender. That makes my heart thud a little around my chest, nervously but also excitedly. Whatever I'm having now, boy or girl, is already formed in there. It's weird to think about, but it's also really cool. I don't know if I could be a girl mom or a boy mom. I mean, I think it would be really hard to raise both, and I want both for different reasons, so I'll just have to wait and see, because I've decided I don't want to find out the gender ahead of time. I want it to be a surprise. Maybe if I ever have another baby, then I'll have some sort of gender reveal party, but for this pregnancy, I want to be surprised.

One really, *really* cool thing is happening now: I think I can feel the baby. It feels exactly like I thought, like a baby literally kicking at me. It's slight right now, like a little flutter and some light jabs. It honestly feels like bubbles and gas, but last night, for example, I laid on my bed for thirty minutes with my hand on my stomach and just felt for it. It was really amazing. Little kicks that felt like gas, but then I realized it was probably the feet. Sometimes, it feels like a light punch. I wondered why I was feeling the kicks early on, and the websites said that skinny people tend to feel the kicks earlier and stronger. Now that the baby's kicking, sometimes I like to go to the kitchen and get a cold glass of water, because I learned that when I drink cold things, the baby is more active. Or if I drink orange juice, it will do the same thing. I think the sugar they say makes the baby more active. It's so odd and amazing, so mind-blowing and surreal that I'm able to grow this human being in my body. This is what I've wanted since I was a little kid. I still can't believe I'm *already* doing it.

Mom told me that Leo's parents wanted me to look at the different estimations they've been coming up with for how much they should provide me with for each month, and to compare it with what my monthly expenses are going to be, and I just told Mom that I'd rather not bother with them. She got a little angry, and said that if we didn't make a decision soon, we'd have to get lawyers involved, and that shut me up. I know Mom doesn't have enough money for that, and I don't want to go through a whole lawyer thing, anyway. She said that since Mr. Schmitz was a lawyer, the last thing that he wanted to do, too, was to get a lawyer, because he knows how complicated it can get and how everyone starts fighting. Mom says she trusts him and it's easier for her to just work things out with him so I'm letting them do that. I really don't want to think about it. If they gave me nothing, I would be fine with that.

Anyway, it's Sunday morning, and I'm finishing up homework and counting money, researching about the baby, my usual routine. Dianne said she wanted to go out for lunch with Molly and me in an hour, so I have to start getting ready soon.

I sit back in my chair and rub my back. I've been having this annoying back pain lately. It started around the time I had to go on that short bed rest, but Dianne assured me it was normal. She said it's because of my stretching uterus and ligaments. Oh, boy, if my back already hurts now, I can hardly imagine what it will feel like at the end of my pregnancy. I'm a little upset, because after I have the baby, I'm going to have a totally stretched-out body, and by that I mean that I'll never have those really good years of having a young body to flaunt. I never really cared about it before, but now I sort of do.

Once I'm finished with homework, I fold my checks from work back into my wallet that I'm going to deposit into my bank account soon, and then I get dressed, and then absentmindedly tie my hair into a braid. My fingers shake as I take it out. *What am I thinking?* I can't believe I just did that. I hope I didn't jinx myself.

We arrive at Dianne's favorite lunch spot near Green Lane, called "Sandwich." Obviously, they sell the most amazing sandwiches. There's a mint-colored awning and a matching door. People can eat inside or outside, and I've always loved the tables with pretty checkered tablecloths draped over them. There are sunflowers all around the patio area. I love the sunflowers here in Redford, they get so tall. One sunflower near the area where I used to live is taller than I am.

Molly looks very pale and tired as we sit down, and she doesn't even open her menu. A waitress walks up, and Dianne and I order, and then Molly starts to open her menu but then suddenly she turns even more pale and slumps forward onto the table.

"Oh my God, Molly!" I scream and Dianne rushes to lift her up, but her eyes are closed and Dianne can't wake her. "What happened?! Oh God, I don't know what's wrong! Madison, call 911! *Now!*"

My hands are shaking, and I can barely even dial the numbers on my cell phone. I manage to do it, and when they answer, I tell them where we are and what happened. Everyone at the restaurant is staring, some are offering to help, but there's nothing anyone can do, Molly's just sitting there, passed out.

But even though I'm really shocked, I think I might know why she fainted. She hasn't eaten pretty much anything for a *week*. I've seen her nibble on vegetables, but that's about it. I'm really scared, and I don't want her to have an eating disorder or something. Molly's always been so strong, and seeing her weak like this kills me.

The ambulance arrives and the paramedics come in and check her pulse and blood pressure and listen to her with a stethoscope. She starts to wake up, she looks confused when she sees the paramedics and everyone staring at her. Dianne says, "She just fainted, but I don't know what's wrong, she's never done that before, she hasn't been sick!"

The paramedics suggest taking Molly to the hospital to get checked out. She's awake now, but they want to make sure she's okay. I want to tell everyone that she hasn't been eating but I feel like Molly will get mad at me. We go in the ambulance with her, and when we arrive at the hospital, they get her into a room pretty quickly. They put a gown on Molly and she lies in the bed not saying anything, just looking tired and weak and sick. Dianne paces back and forth. It suddenly hits me that this is where we came when my dad died. *The same hospital. St. Redford's Hospital.* I try to block it out, I can't bear to think about it even for a second. Besides, I need to focus on Molly.

A doctor comes in and examines her and says they are going to do blood tests and give her some fluids. I quickly excuse myself to go to the bathroom and I stare at myself in the mirror. I can't believe I'm back here and now something is wrong with *Molly.* I look at my hair, remembering that I absentmindedly started braiding it this morning. *Oh my God, I really did jinx myself.* Or Molly. I know it's crazy to think like this, but I can't help it.

When I come back to the room, the nurse has just finished taking Molly's blood and Dianne tells me that Molly admitted that she hasn't been really eating much.

"I'm glad you finally admitted it, Molly," I say.

"Why didn't you tell me if you knew?" Dianne asks me, looking hurt.

"It's not her fault, I didn't want anyone to know and...I told Maddie not to say anything," Molly lies, but I guess she doesn't want me to get in trouble with Dianne. She's so sweet, even when she's sick. But still, I feel guilty for not saying anything to her mom, because her health was in danger.

I'm so worried for her. I just want her to be back to my happy, cheery best friend. But I'm just realizing now that maybe the whole thing with Jay is really upsetting her. I didn't know, I should have talked to her more. She kept saying the new girl Jay liked was skinnier than her. I should have realized that was why she was starving herself. I'm so angry at Jay, and at myself for not saying anything.

The doctor comes in after about an hour and he says that her blood tests show that she's malnourished and that her weight is perfect for someone her height, so she needs to eat. Then he hands Dianne a pamphlet about eating disorders and says it's very common in this age group and that she should be getting some help, someone to talk to, like a therapist, or a support group. I can't believe this is happening, but I'm glad it's out in the open.

They say Molly needs to have the rest of the fluids they are giving her through her arm, and then we can go home. Dianne asks if Molly wants to get McDonald's, and Molly smiles for the first time in a while. "Oh, so this is what it took for you to let me get McDonald's?" she says.

We all laugh, and everyone is so relieved she is okay, especially Molly, who I can tell got really freaked out by this. Hopefully, she won't do this again.

On the drive home, everyone is quiet. Tears well up in my eyes. I hate that my best friend felt this way, like she couldn't let herself eat. I also hate that I don't even know what that feels like. I don't want Molly to ever compare herself to other girls, especially ones that her ex is now dating. It makes me worry that she's been secretly comparing herself to me, because I've always been so freakishly skinny. I have to talk to her and find out, because it's really bugging me. She has to eat to *live.* It's scary what the doctor said about it being common for eating disorders to happen with this age.

I feel the tiniest kick in my stomach (or uterus, I guess), and it brings me just a little happiness in the midst of the awfulness. I place my hand on my stomach, enjoying the little kicking going on in there. It's like nothing I've ever felt before.

We go through the drive-thru at McDonald's and Molly orders a quarter pounder with cheese and a McFlurry. Dianne and I get hamburgers with fries and milkshakes. We decide to have another tray dinner together, this time on Molly's bed.

Molly eats most of it, but says she can't finish it all. Dianne says it's probably best for her to not stuff herself after she wasn't eating for so long. Then, she says, "Molly, I just wanted to say that if it's because of me, because I tried to limit your calories, I feel terrible. I didn't want you to think you needed to starve yourself. You're a beautiful young woman with a healthy weight. I just don't want you to go down a path which could lead to being overweight as it's hard once you get to that point to go back to being healthier. The most important thing is to eat healthy foods and well-balanced meals. That's all I was trying to teach you."

"It's not your fault, Mom," Molly says and she bursts into tears. "It's embarrassing to admit this, but...I wanted to be skinnier so Jay would like me again. He's started dating someone who's got the perfect body and she's much skinnier than I am. I thought maybe if I got skinny like her, he would take me back. It sounds so dumb now..."

"Oh sweetie, I know how that feels. But this is why I think it would be a good idea for you to speak to someone, like the doctor suggested. Would you want to try a support group or would you rather go to a therapist? There might even be a counselor at your school that I could sign you up for sessions with."

After Molly agrees to see the school counselor, Dianne clears the trays and goes downstairs. I tell Molly that Jay isn't worth it if he would break up with her because of something so superficial, and that she's beautiful and anyone can see that if they aren't blind. But I also tell her that he should also like her for her beautiful *mind*, and that she's so creative and just amazing in every area possible.

Molly nods slowly. "I'm sorry." She takes a deep breath. "Thank you."

"Also, I want to ask you something...you don't compare yourself to *me*, do you? Because I know I'm skinny, but I actually am *too* skinny. Or at least I was before I got pregnant. But it's not even good to be that skinny. I don't look good in anything, I have no curves. I just hope you weren't comparing yourself to me, too."

She looks down, like she's afraid to admit it. "Well...sometimes, yeah, I do. I mean, you've already had a serious boyfriend, you're already pregnant...and yeah, I know it's too early for you to be, but at least you had someone who was, um, *able* to get you pregnant, I guess is what I'm trying to say. Like, you know, you've already had..."

I shake my head, knowing what she's trying to say, getting a little upset. "Molly, you can't compare yourself to other people. Yeah, I had sex already, but look what happened because of it." We both look at my stomach and laugh. *What a crazy day this has been.*

Molly says she wants to sleep, so I leave and go downstairs. Dianne sees me in the hall and tells me to come into the kitchen, she says she wants to talk to me. "Madison, I don't know why you hadn't told me what was going on with Molly," she says.

"I didn't know she was *entirely* not eating," I say. "But anyway, I just figured it would be better to stay out of yours and Molly's business. I don't want to, you know, interfere with anything while I'm here."

"Sometimes you *have* to interfere, Madison. That was a situation where you should have told me. My job is to make sure Molly is safe and healthy. You'll understand pretty soon. If something happens to your baby, you just feel like you want to die."

I gulp. "I'm really sorry, seriously. If something else is ever going on with Molly, I'll definitely tell you, I promise."

"Thank you, Madison. I appreciate it. It's...it's been a rough day for all of us."

I want to tell her that she doesn't even know how hard it was for me to be at the hospital again. *The same place where my dad died.* I don't want to even think about it, let alone talk to Dianne about it. I just nod and tell her I have to study, and I go to my room.

I decide to study for my driver's test next week in bed, going over the packets and reviewing the street signs, but I can't even see the words because my eyes are blurry from the tears. I try to focus but I realize it's not going to happen. So I get my computer and decide to distract myself with something good, like looking on the Harvard website. There is a section on tips for applying and how it's important to have community service, experience in the area you're applying for, leadership roles, stellar grades, et cetera. My grades are good, I have around a 95% average, but who knows if that's even enough. My dad knew I wanted to go to Harvard and he used to tell me I was a shoe-in and that they would be lucky to have me. I wonder what he would say now. Thinking about him makes me think about the hospital earlier today, and that's it, I can't hold the tears in any longer, I start bawling.

I cry for a while and then I just can't stand being alone anymore so I go into Molly's room. She asks me what's wrong and I start crying again and then she starts crying and we both just sit there crying and telling each other all the things that are wrong with our lives. It's so ridiculous that we're not even sixteen and yet so much is wrong.

Then I feel a bunch of flutters in my stomach, it's like Cheese Puff is crying too. I feel like maybe the crying is upsetting her or him, which is the last thing I want. I put my hands on my stomach and Molly asks if the baby is kicking. I say yes and tell her to try to feel it. She keeps her hand on there for a minute. There's another flutter. Her eyes go really wide.

"Maddie, that's incredible!" she exclaims in a whisper. "Oh my God!"

"I know. Isn't it amazing?"

We stare at my stomach that looks like a muffin top, and then we start laughing. Then we spend the rest of the night stuffing our faces with ice cream and trying to feel for Cheese Puff's kicks. I'm so glad I have a best friend to share all of this with. I never wanted to lose her as a friend, and that was one of my worries when I found out I was pregnant. I'm so glad that she's still here.

<>

At school the next day, Matthew and I hang out at lunch while Molly goes to see the school's counselor about the weight and eating stuff. I like being with Matthew because we don't always have to talk, we can just sit and eat, or think or read a book, and it feels totally comfortable.

This Saturday is my last driving class before I sign up for the driver's test, which I hope I'll ace. Every Saturday I've been taking a few hours of driving lessons. I'm excited to get my license, although I'm not going to drive until I can get a car, which probably won't be for a zillion years, looking at my current financial situation.

I've been adding up my weekly expenses, trying to figure out how much money I will need. I usually spend around $50 a week right now, so I only save around $200 a week from work, so that's a little less than $800 coming in for the baby per month. Right now, I have $908.16 in my bank account. If I can get $800 each month until I stop working around two weeks before the baby's born, then I'll have around $4,000. It's not enough for everything.

I hate to even *think* it, but maybe money from Leo's parents wouldn't be so bad.

I feel awful for thinking that, it feels like I'm going against everything I want for myself and for Cheese Puff. And I am really going to try and find a job that pays more and that lets you bring your baby to work. I'll catch up on money and budget carefully, and I'll be able to pay my rent on time once I get an apartment. It'll take a lot of work, but if I do work hard, then I won't need any help, hopefully.

Even though I don't want Leo or his parents to help, it's because Leo has hurt me so much. He's made it clear that he thinks I should have aborted Cheese Puff. He doesn't want anything to do with us. But still, I shouldn't have to do this alone. If Leo did it with me, I wouldn't have to worry about jobs and money, because if Leo had wanted to stay with me, possibly marry me, and raise the baby with me, then things would be so much easier. We could have been parents *together*. Life would be so good right now if he had stuck around. But he didn't, and I have to stop daydreaming about it.

"Hello? Earth to Madison?"

I realize Matthew has been trying to talk to me but I've been so immersed in my own thoughts, I didn't hear him. "Sorry, what did you say?"

"I'm going to the bathroom, can you meet in the library in five minutes?"

We meet in the library, do some studying, and then I head to the guidance counselor's office. I didn't tell anybody, but after Dianne made Molly's appointment for the eating stuff, I realized I would maybe be able to go to the guidance counselor to talk about my own situation.

Mrs. Sherman has been the guidance counselor at the school for like twenty-five years. Her office smells like vanilla lotion, and she has a bunch of pictures on a bulletin board of her with her husband and her sons. I went to her last year when I was stressed about choosing my electives. She's really easy to talk to and she makes you feel comfortable. I don't know why I didn't think of talking to her before, but I guess what happened with Molly and the doctor's suggestion that she speak to someone made me realize I could do it, too. Some of my teachers have even come up to me and told me that I should go to her. School counselors can be really helpful, I think; after my dad died, in seventh grade, I went to my middle school counselor, and she really helped.

Once I'm in Mrs. Sherman's office, I tell her about everything that's going on, and she tells me that she knows because my teachers told her, but at the same time, she also just looks kind of shocked. Then I tell her that I can't seem to get rid of the fantasy that I'm going to end up with Leo, that he'll somehow come back or something, and I ask her if she has any tips for that, because it's really been taking up all my thoughts.

She says that she sometimes recommends that people write letters to express their thoughts. She said I don't even have to actually send it to Leo, but maybe if I wrote him a letter, getting all my thoughts down, it might help me get it out and get some closure. It sounds like a good idea, although it's nerve-wracking to think about giving Leo a letter with *everything* I've been thinking written down. So I'm not sure if I would give it to him, but she says the point of writing the letter is to just get it out of myself and not keep it inside. She says it doesn't even have to be a letter, it can be a journal or something like that. She says it's just the act of writing that can be so helpful. I think about how much I love writing for the newspaper, and how my mom and Dianne are both writers. I know there's something so satisfying about getting things down on the page. I think about all the thoughts I keep inside me, about my dad's death, for example. It would probably be good to write about that, too. I'm not sure I'm ready to do that now, but maybe someday. Journalism and writing are kind of interconnected, so maybe I could be just like my mom and Dianne and write a book someday.

The bell rings, and I have to leave for class. I wish I had more time with Mrs. Sherman, but she says I can come back anytime. I think I'm going to.

<>

A few days later, it was Valentine's Day. It ended up being a good day, even though I was dreading it because I'm not with Leo anymore. Molly and I got each other chocolates and candy, and my mom actually called to wish me a Happy Valentine's Day. I was surprised, but so happy to hear from her. Josie sent me a card that she made.

But I still found myself missing Leo and wondering what he was doing, like if he had another date. Obviously he'll get another girlfriend at some point, if he hasn't already, and I have no idea how I'll be able to deal with that.

I decided to write the letter that Mrs. Sherman recommended. I wrote it by hand, because somehow it felt like it would really help feel like I was getting everything out. I cried the whole time I wrote it, and my hand hurt from writing because I'm so used to doing everything on the computer.

Leo,

I know now that you don't want anything to do with me. Or your baby. I've given you tons of time and you've clearly proven that you are not going to own up to your part of what happened. But I wanted to tell you that I'm for sure keeping it. So this baby, yours and mine, that we made together, even though we didn't plan to, will always be out there. It will be in the world whether you like it or not. And you are always going to have a daughter or son that you won't even know. Even your parents want to be involved, but not you! I truly don't understand you at all. I guess I never did. I'm sure you're happy thinking about getting through college, getting a job, not struggling like I will be. I know it's my choice to keep it, but I can't even imagine not wanting to have something so beautiful and wonderful. I'm sure you'll eventually get married and you'll have kids that will be half-siblings to this baby, but they will never know because you won't tell them about her or him. But I can only hope that one day you'll realize what a rotten soul you have and will always have. But whatever. Just do whatever the hell you want. You're the one who's going to have to live with yourself, not me.

No longer yours,
Madison

I haven't given it to him yet. Part of me really wants him to know what I'm thinking and feeling and how hurt I am, but part of me just wants to avoid him completely. I read it over and I can't believe how much anger I have towards him, and how much more I could go on and on, but I guess I got tired of writing, my hand hurt too much.

I feel like if I don't give it to him, then it will still keep stewing inside of me, even though I've written it out. Before I can think about it any more, I put it in an envelope, walk to his house, and see that the curtains are shut and the car isn't in the garage, which means no one's home. Perfect.

I slide it under the door.

18
weeks

●

To-Do List

$240
− 18
$222
− 30
($192)

200
× 9
800
+3200
$4000

+ expenses?

●

0 ← Cheese Puff
kicking

- pick up paycheck on Friday from Roast and Drink
- French essay due tomorrow
- finish math homework   (FEED MOLLY)
- organize notes for history report
- finish editing stories for the front page of this
  week's newspaper edition
- edit Janet's story on the new art teacher
- ask Janet to send articles to be printed for newspaper
  on Friday
- science notes due Friday   ☆ study for
- science lab report due Monday   driver's test
                                         next week

$$ from Leo's   ☆ go to last driving
parents ?   class ever on
                         Saturday

- write a letter to Leo?
- make Valentine's Day cards   buy:
  for Molly + Dianne   - cheese puffs
- look into community   - new folder for math
  service?   - new markers

♡   ♡   ♡   ☆ cancel shift at
    ♡   ♡   Roast and Drink on
♡ Valentine's ♡   my birthday
       Day
♡ ♡   ♡   ♡   turning 16 next week!!
   ♡ ♡ ♡ ♡

● give the letter to Leo?

Chapter 15: Week Nineteen

"Your baby is as big as a mango," I read after school, scrolling quickly through the pregnancy website on my phone as I walk over to the DMV. It's my birthday, and I'm taking my driver's test today! I never would have thought that I would be nineteen weeks pregnant on my sixteenth birthday. Almost halfway through my pregnancy and yet halfway through my teenage years. It's so crazy.

My stomach is definitely looking bigger, and so are my breasts. I'm wearing my baggiest shirt and pants today, because I don't want the person at the DMV who tests me to judge me and maybe not pass me. There's no way they can see the bump the way I'm dressed.

I've been feeling Cheese Puff kicking even more now, and my back is still hurting. My legs have also started hurting a bit, and I think it's the extra weight I'm not used to. Dianne says it's all completely normal, but it's pretty uncomfortable. My nausea and fatigue are both completely gone, and I'm always hungry now, trying to sneak snacks in school.

Speaking of school, I've been changing in the bathroom for gym, obviously not wanting to get naked in front of the girls who will then see my growing stomach. But Lulu came up to me the other day and told me to stop hiding the fact that I was pregnant, that it was just so obvious. And it's true; my gym clothes can't hide my stomach like the baggy clothes I've been wearing can. I try to wear sweatshirts over the gym clothes and just tell my teacher I'm cold, but I'm really just trying to put off actually revealing my pregnancy to my entire school for as long as I possibly can.

Now, as I check in at the DMV, my heart is pounding. I'm really nervous to take the test, I *really* hope I pass. I approach the DMV, my heart jumping around nervously. Between my heart and Cheese Puff kicking, there's lots of action going on inside me!

A stern-looking woman approaches me and introduces herself as Quinta, my test examiner, and she tells me to follow her. She leads me to one of the cars in their lot and gestures for me to get into the driver's seat, then she gets in the passenger seat. I've been reviewing street signs and all my driver's informational packets that my driving instructors gave me for weeks now, and I'm ready! At least I hope I am.

She watches me as I adjust my mirrors and then put my seatbelt on, and I see her make note of it. This is part of what they instruct you to do when you first get in the car, and if you don't do it, you lose points, because it's important.

I start the car and she tells me to back up out of the lot and take a turn to the right onto Avenue Road, and I follow her instructions, trying to stay calm even though my heart is beating nearly out of my chest. I try to remember everything my instructor taught me to do in my driving lessons as she tells me to do things like switch lanes and make a left at a main intersection. I have to keep reminding myself to go the speed limit, because I feel like I keep going too slow. I'm also trying not to brake too hard, which is also something my instructor taught me when I did the lessons with her.

Quinta tells me I'm driving "nice and smooth," which makes me happy. Then I have to park behind a car, and I'm nervous, because my parking still needs some work, especially parallel parking. But I manage to do it, and after that we return to the DMV lot. We go inside, and she tells me to take a seat near the entrance, and then she goes to speak to someone I assume is her boss. They keep looking at me and I'm worried they aren't going to pass me, but I really think I did everything right so I don't know what the reason would be. Cheese Puff keeps kicking and I want to rub my stomach to calm Cheese Puff down, but I don't want to draw attention to my stomach, in case they use it against me and don't give me my license.

Just as I'm giving up hope and thinking they are going to say no, she calls me over to take my license picture! *Yay! I passed!* I'm beaming from ear to ear. I think this is one of the happiest pictures I've ever taken.

The woman who is going to take my picture first asks me for my name, height, and weight. I'm not sure which weight to put down, because it's temporary right now because I'm pregnant, so I just put my original weight, ninety-eight pounds. She doesn't seem to question it.

"Okay, almost done," the lady says. "We just need your address to go on the license and also for it to be mailed to you." I freeze. I don't know which address to give them, should it be Mom's? I mean, technically it's still my home, but will I ever live there again? I really don't know where I will be living, seeing as I'm planning to get my own apartment, so I just decide to say Mom's address. She then prints something out and folds it up and hands it to me. She says it's my temporary license until the card one comes in the mail. I'm so excited, I can't believe this is really happening. *I can drive!*

I had a plan to celebrate if I passed, and so when I leave, I go straight to the bus stop and then take a ride on the bus which goes through my old neighborhood to the park right near where my family used to live right before Josie was born. It's my favorite park in Redford. I used to go there all the time and sit on the bench. I have a lot of happy memories just sitting there, and that's what I wanted to do today.

I sit down on my favorite bench and take a moment to look around. The park is just as I remember it. I see the swing I fell off of and scraped my knee and hands when I was three. I remember Mom picking me up and hugging me when I was crying. I look at the first slide I ever slid on and I can picture my dad waiting to catch me at the bottom. They are such good memories, and even though I feel like crying because things are so different now, I want to be happy today. So I force myself to think happy thoughts, like how I should bring my Cheese Puff here when she or he is old enough.

This is the first birthday I've ever spent without Mom and Josie. It's the third birthday I've spent without my dad. My mom always got me practical presents, like clothes and things I needed, which is fine but it wasn't that exciting. But my dad would give me something that related to something we had done together, like once when we were at the mall, we passed a music shop and I pointed out how cool vintage record players were. Three months later, on my birthday, he remembered what I said and he bought me one. It made me feel so special, that he took the time to really listen to me. He called them "memory presents." I still have the record player, it's at Mom's, and even though it doesn't work anymore, I still love it. Looking at it makes me happy and sad at the same time. Kind of like how I feel about being pregnant and being sixteen and getting my driver's license, all at the same time.

I try to stay in a good mood, but I can't help it, and I start to cry. I don't want to be sad on my birthday, but I just can't help it. Especially thinking of my dad. I mean, he died on *his birthday*. It's so horrible, it's impossible to really even think about. And I want to know so many things, like, *what was the last thing he was thinking about before the car crashed into him? Was he thinking of us? Was he conscious for even a few seconds after he got into the accident?*

I realize that it was probably stupid of me to get my license on my birthday, as it was a car crash that killed my dad on his own birthday. I usually block it out, but I remember that they said the other driver was drunk, and that's why he went through an intersection and went into Dad's car. The counselor at school that I went to after he died was worried that I would always be afraid to be in a car, and that I would be scared to get my own license, because of what happened. She really helped me get over the fear, and even now, I'm not worried about it, because I know that I'm going to be careful.

Since my mind is on Dad right now, I'm starting to wonder what he'd have to say about all this. About me getting pregnant so young. I try to picture him and what he would say. He was always the cheerful one in our family. He would probably tell me to think about the good things.

So I start thinking about our old house, the one before the house Mom and Josie are in now. We had a small but very pretty house near this park. My parents bought it a year before I was born, and sold it once Mom got pregnant with Josie, because we needed more space. It was made mostly of brick, but it had light-colored wood panels and a blue door. Mom always said the door made her think of the sky. The house itself was small, but the yard was big, and Dad had a vegetable garden that he made, and he grew things like tomatoes, cucumbers, radishes, and carrots. He would also grow pumpkins sometime in the spring, he would plant the seeds and we would have our own pumpkins that we grew ourselves every year for Halloween. We also had a swing set, it was yellow and got a bit rusty and it squeaked. I would swing for hours. Mom would watch me from the window sometimes when she was writing on her computer.

It took her ten years to find the right idea for her book. *Ten years!* She used to love just typing up the first few pages of an idea on her computer, but she would never finish anything. But eventually, when I was around ten or eleven, she finally finished something. It was a five-hundred-page novel that she said was about life and love and things she'd learned.

It was such a huge deal for her, because she had never worked in an office or anything, and she didn't really have a career, she just wanted to write. She was hoping to become a successful author. She went to college, and she was an English major, but then when she married Dad, she had me almost right away, and she just put her dreams of being a writer away for a little while. My dad worked as a real estate broker, although he always said that it wasn't his passion to work in real estate. It was just to provide for us. He liked doing other things when he wasn't working, like cooking or baking or gardening or playing with me and Josie.

Now, I look at the playground where I used to play all the time, because when we lived in that house, we would always come here. It's winter now, so the roses aren't blooming, but I remember how gorgeous they are in the summer, and I remember being here one summer when I was around eight, and I was asking my mom if she could wear a perfume that smelled like the roses because they smelled so good, and I remember she laughed and told me I was so cute. I think my dad would be sad about what's happened with me and Mom.

As if trying to get me to stop being sad, Cheese Puff gives me a big kick. I laugh and pat my stomach. "Cheese Puff, it's Mommy's birthday," I say softly. "I can't wait for *your* birthday."

I sit a bit longer and then start to walk back to the bus stop. Suddenly, out of the blue, I hear someone calling my name and I turn to see Josie running up to me. Mom's following behind her. They must have remembered that I come here every year on my birthday. I'm so surprised, I just stand there.

"Happy birthday!" Josie squeals, and gives me a big hug.

"Happy birthday, Madison," Mom says, looking down, but then she looks up. "So, I assume you went to get your license, like you planned?"

I nod excitedly, and Josie hugs me again. Mom isn't smiling, but she doesn't look angry, she just seems very matter-of-fact. Then she hands me a key and looks over to the parked cars on the street. One of them is her old yellow Volkswagen. My heart jumps. *What's happening? I don't know what to think.*

"It's yours now," she says.

I can't believe she's still giving it to me. "You don't have to...I mean, I don't really think that I deserve it anymore-"

"This has nothing to do with anything other than me keeping a promise I made to you for your sixteenth birthday. It's from me and your father, we'd discussed this years ago. I'm honoring a promise to him, too. And just so you know, I had it checked out and the only thing it really needed was an oil change. It's still in good shape, and it's safe, which is the most important thing."

I start bawling again. Just her mentioning Dad and the fact that she's still doing this for me, after everything that's happened. "Thank you, Mom, thank you so much," I say. "You don't know how much this means to me that you're doing this."

She looks like she's about to cry, too, but then I see her stop herself and she clears her throat. "You're welcome," she says. "So, I think you should drive us all to Dianne's. I've already cleared it with her, you can park in her driveway or in the garage."

"Mom, I don't even know what to say, I don't even know how to thank you, I'm-"

"You can thank me by always driving safely and paying attention to the road. No phones, no distractions, none of that. Got it?"

I nod, and then I can't help myself, I go to give her a hug. For just a second, she hugs me back, and it feels like old times. I don't want to let go. Josie joins in the hug, and now she's crying too. It's sort of a bittersweet moment.

Mom breaks away from the hug first and looks down at my stomach. "I could feel a little bump, but you aren't really showing yet, are you?"

It feels really awkward, and I look down at my baggy clothes and I don't know what to say. She interrupts my thoughts and says that we should go, so we get in the car, me in the driver's seat. I drive really slowly, being super careful. I glance over at Mom a few times when we get to stoplights but she just stares straight ahead at the road. Josie keeps giggling from the back and saying that she can't believe I'm driving.

Then, out of the blue, a song comes on that almost makes me stop the car.

...July 2015...

We were on a summer road trip, driving to Sedona, Arizona. Mom had always wanted to go there, she had read about all the beauty of the rusty colored hills and mountains. We stopped at a gas station and Mom and Josie went into the store to get snacks while Dad was filling up the car with gas, and I stayed with him. I always loved being in the car with Dad while he got gas. We always made estimations as to how much it was going to cost, it was a fun game to see who got closer.

While it was filling up, he left the radio on and a song came on that made him smile. He said, "I love James Taylor. *Fire and Rain* is one of his best songs," and then he started singing along to it.

"Just yesterday morning, they let me know you were gone
Suzanne the plans they made put an end to you
I walked out this morning and I wrote down this song
I just can't remember who to send it to

I've seen fire and I've seen rain
I've seen sunny days that I thought would never end
I've seen lonely times when I could not find a friend
But I always thought that I'd see you again."

"It sounds like a great song," I said, and he explained that the lyrics were about a guy who lost somebody in a plane crash. I remember thinking how sad it was and I couldn't understand how he could like a song like that, even though it sounded nice.

"Your mother and I listened to it a lot before you were born. It's a sad subject but it's really beautiful. When you were born, it actually came on the radio we had in the hospital room! I always consider it a good-luck song for me."

...

I can't believe that song just started playing. It's like a sign from Dad. It's really weird, I haven't heard it in so long, I can't even remember when the last time was, and now the lyrics really make me sad. Dad thought it was good luck, but it's weird because it was about a plane crash, and he died in a *car* crash, and now here I am, driving for the first time with my new license. I really hope it's a sign that he thinks I'll be fine, and nothing bad will happen. I look over at Mom and she turns her head away and looks out her window. It's probably so hard for her to listen to.

It's not fair. *Why did he have to die?* If he was still alive, things would be so different now. Maybe I wouldn't be living with Dianne. Maybe Dad would have understood more than Mom. But then again, he wanted me to have a really good future, so he probably would have agreed with Mom. Then again, who knows if I would have even gotten pregnant if he had still been alive? Mom wouldn't have been working all the time, so I wouldn't have been left alone with Josie, and then maybe I wouldn't have been there with Leo that night.

I can't think about it right now. I have to concentrate on my driving. The song ends, and Mom sighs and I see she was crying because there are tears on her cheeks, but I don't say anything. I drop her and Josie off, it's sad saying goodbye today, and Josie hugs me really hard.

Once I'm back at Dianne's house, I park on the street out front, not sure if she wants me to go into the driveway, I'll have to ask her. When I get inside, it's dark, which is weird. I didn't know they were going out tonight.

"*SURPRISE!*" I hear a bunch of voices shouting, and suddenly the lights flick on, and I see Dianne, Molly, Matthew, Cheryl, and a couple of other girls from school.

I'm totally shocked and I feel speechless. "Oh my God, I...thank you guys so much!" Everyone laughs and Dianne brings out a beautiful vanilla cake with pink icing on the top which says, "Happy 16th, Madison!" They all sing "Happy Birthday" to me and tell me to make a wish and blow out the candles.

I feel like I want to cry, but I don't want to do it in front of everyone. But I feel a tear fall down my cheek, anyway. Stupid pregnancy hormones. All I ever do is cry! And I just realized that Matthew is here and I'm not wearing my jacket or my apron to cover up my stomach. *Shoot.* Hopefully, the baggy clothes that worked at the DMV will work here, too.

What should I wish for? So many wishes scatter around my head.

I wish for my Cheese Puff to be healthy and happy and to have a great life. I wish things will get better with my mom, that Jose and I can be close again, that Dad is somehow and he's proud of me, that I can pay Dianne and Molly back for everything they've done for me, that I'll meet another guy someday. But mainly, I wish that everyone will be proud of me one day. That one day I'll be thought of as a good mother, and not just as a teen mother.

I blow the candles out and everyone cheers and then we eat the delicious cake, which is rich and full of buttercream frosting. Then, suddenly, Mom and Josie walk through the front door. Oh, wow, they were invited, and they came! I'm so happy! Dianne greets them and gets them some cake and they hang out at the side, not really talking to anyone, but they seem okay.

Matthew comes up to me, smiling. "Happy birthday!" he says, and then he frowns. "And hey, why is the party at Molly's house?"

"Oh, well..." I try to come up with something quick. "My mom asked Molly's mom if we could do the party here. Because they're re-painting the walls at my house." I hate lying to Matthew, but I still haven't been ready to tell him. I know I have to do it soon.

"Time for presents! Everyone please come into the living room!" Dianne calls.

I open my presents, I get so many cute little things from Cheryl and the other girls, like a bracelet and a bag of candy and chocolate bars, and I end up crying *again*. Then Molly passes me *her* present. "I'll give you my card later," she whispers, and I nod.

I open it, and it's the most beautiful dress I've ever seen. It has tank top straps, and it's mostly black and white, but then it cascades down into a black and silver pattern with a black sash tied around the waist.

"It's so gorgeous, Molly," I breathe. "Thank you so much. I have to pay you back for this, it's too expensive, it's-"

"Don't worry about it. Happy birthday."

Matthew hands me his present. There's a little card on top that says, "Dear Madison, Happy Birthday! Hope you have a great year! - Matthew."

When I open it, it's a stack of three books. One is titled, "How to be a Successful Journalist." The next one reads, "Improv 101." The last one reads, "10 Ways to Get Good Grades." I laugh and so does everyone else.

"Thank you so much!" I say, hugging him. It feels nice, but I pull away, not wanting him to feel my stomach through the hug.

Afterwards, everyone is just sitting around talking and looking on their phones, and Mom takes me aside and hands me a little gift wrapped in tissue paper. I open it up and see it's a picture that was taken on my fifth birthday. I remember this picture from one of our photo albums, Mom must have taken it out. It was from my birthday party at a cool trampoline park. Mom was pregnant with Josie, her stomach was pretty big. She was holding me in her arms, and I was reaching down smiling and touching her stomach. What really stands out to me is that my hair was in braids. It's so weird to see this and have a *happy* association with braids.

Mom turns it over and shows me that she's written, "Happy Birthday, Madison. Love, Mom." on the back. My eyes tear up for the millionth time. "Thank you, Mom," I say. "Really. I love this picture."

I hug her and Dianne comes up to us and says, "Now this is what I like to see." We all laugh, a bit awkwardly. Josie breaks up the tension by coming up to me with a small gift wrapped in tissue paper.

"I have something for you, too!" she says, and I open it up to find a gorgeous dark red knitted scarf. I take it out and put it around my neck, it's so fuzzy and soft and warm. "I made it myself!" she exclaims.

"Are you serious, Josie? That's amazing!"

She smiles proudly. "The nanny taught me. I kept telling her I missed you, and she came up with the idea because it's like you were sort of there with me when I was making it for you. Do you like it?"

"Josie, are you kidding me? I love it!" I exclaim, and we hug each other tightly.

"I thought the color would look great against your blonde hair, and it does!"

"I'll wear it every day," I promise her.

"What about when it gets warmer out?"

"Even then."

Josie giggles, and Mom smiles for the first time since I can't even remember. People start to leave and before I know it, it's just me and Dianne and Molly again. It's really hard again to say goodbye to my mom and Josie. I wonder if I will ever be living with them again. I'm scared to push things, but I'm so happy that things seem a little better with Mom.

I thank Dianne and Molly for the party and tell them that I can't believe they managed to keep it as a surprise from me. Along with the dress, Dianne also got me some really nice maternity clothes, and it's perfect timing because I'm starting to show. Then Molly takes me upstairs into her room and gives me her card, which is beautiful, with hand-drawn flowers all over it.

Dear Madison,

Happy 16th! We talked about turning 16 so much when we were younger and now it's here! Well, not for me yet, but soon. You're the best friend any girl could ever have, and I want you to know that you are strong, beautiful, and amazing. I love you (in the most non-creepy way possible, ha-ha).

Love,
Your best friend, Molly Lolly Pop

I laugh and almost start crying again, but I don't have the energy, and besides, I think I've cried enough for twenty lifetimes. "Thank you so much, Molly," I say, hugging her tightly. "This is the best card I've ever gotten."

That night, I line up my presents and cards on my dresser. It all looks really nice. I put the picture Mom gave me right next to my bed on my nightstand, right next to the can of shaving cream that I keep on it, so I can look at both before I fall asleep, one thing from each of my parents. Maybe they will help me have good dreams. I read an article online that says when you find yourself feeling down or sad a lot, it's a good idea to think about all the things you're grateful for. I start thinking about all the good things that are in my life, right up to today with getting my license, and Mom and Josie being there, and of course Dianne and Molly, and all the friends who came to the party, and last but not least, my Cheese Puff. And then, one more thing hits me that I'm grateful for. And it's a big thing: I haven't thought about Leo *at all* today! Not even for a second, until now. This makes me so happy, it's the perfect end to an amazing birthday.

After eating a bag of cheese puffs, what I try to do now almost every night before I go to bed as a little routine, I get into bed and wrap my warm blankets around me, staring out of my window. A bird flies by. It's a really quiet, still night. I put my hand on my stomach and start to talk.

"Hey, Cheese Puff. I just wanted you to know that you made my birthday extra special. I could feel you with me the whole day, kicking away all the time. I hope you liked the cake I ate!" The thought of the baby eating whatever I eat makes me laugh, I don't know why I find it so funny. "In just about a year from now, we'll be waiting for your *first* birthday to come. It's hard to imagine you as a real baby because you're still so small inside me. But then after your first birthday, it'll be your second and third and fourth, and so on and so on, until one day you'll be as big as me." Tears spring to my eyes. "And *I* will have been the one responsible for all that. Isn't that crazy?"

Cheese Puff kicks, as if to say "yes."

<>

A few days later, Mom leaves me a voicemail while I'm at school telling me that my license has been delivered and to come home to pick it up. I'm really excited and I'm also happy she still calls it "home" for me. When I go to get it, she opens the door and hands it to me. She looks very serious but definitely not as sad or angry as she used to. "I want to talk with you soon, so I'll email you once I'm ready, okay?"

I nod, and then she looks out to where I parked her car, now *my* car, on the street. She asks if it's been driving okay and I tell her it has. She smiles and I smile back and go to leave. Just as I'm almost at my car, she calls out, "Madison?"

I turn back, and she says, "I'm proud of you."

I can't believe it for a second. *Is she really saying this to me?* Then, she says, "You know, for getting your license and for taking driving seriously, and for being careful."

Even though I realize I was hoping she meant she was proud of me for other things, like how I'm handling being pregnant, I'm so happy to hear her say this. All I want is for her to see that she can still be proud of me. I think this is a good start.

19 weeks!!

☆

☆ ☆ ☆

To-Do List

$4,000
- food
- diapers
- other stuff?
(approx.)
$3,200
(+ rent for
an apartment?)

$1,600/
month =
savings?

- pick up paycheck on
Friday from Roast and
Drink
- finish this week's
editing for newspaper
ASAP!!
- do French worksheets
- label geography map
- study for math test
- start history paper
- study English vocabulary
words

Bank Account = $1,002.16
✳ look up how to make
a budget

$
$
$
$
$

buy:
- cheese puffs
- diapers, wipes, baby clothes
- new pens + paper

- read the books that Matthew got me

← Cheese Puff!!!

IT'S MY
BIRTHDAY!!!

☆ driver's test 4pm
at the DMV
☆ go to park afterwards
♡
♡ ♡
♡
♡ ♡

☆ pick up driver's
license from
Mom's
☆ send Mom +
Josie thank-you
emails

♡
♡ ♡
♡ ♡ ♡

Chapter 16: Week Twenty

"Your baby is as big as a sweet potato," I read. Pretty sweet. What else is sweet? The fact that I'm *halfway through my pregnancy*!

It's Sunday February 24th today. Right now, I'm getting ready to go to my Level 2 Ultrasound 20-Week Anatomy Scan. It's supposedly a very big deal, and I'm excited for it. I'm also a bit nervous, because I don't want them to find something wrong.

I've been adding numbers all week, and looking for higher-paying jobs, and really trying hard to boost my grades up even more in school. I did it, though, and now all my grades (except for French) are above 94%.

Currently, I feel like I'm going to burst, because I have to pee so badly, but the specialist who is doing this ultrasound said to drink a lot so my bladder is full, so he can see better or something like that. I can't go to Dr. Lippincott for this, but the report is going to be sent to her, and I have a follow-up appointment with her after it.

I have to make sure to tell the specialist to not reveal the gender. It's so weird that he'll know what I'm having and that he won't tell me unless I ask.

Dianne, Molly, and I wait in the room, and I'm wearing one of the paper gowns they give you, opened to the front like they told me. Dianne looks at my stomach and says it's definitely getting bigger. Molly nods and I realize that I'm going to have to just stop hiding it at school, but I don't want to think about it right now.

The specialist comes in and introduces himself as Dr. Kerr. He says, "This scan is going to focus on the fetal anatomy. We just have to measure specific parts of the baby's body, and make sure everything's great, which it probably will be. And we will hopefully be able to give you some nice pictures at the end, too. First of all, do you know the gender?"

"No, and I was going to ask you not to tell me, thanks for reminding me."

We all laugh, and Molly and Dianne come closer so they can see the monitor screen as he starts to measure and point out the different parts of my sweet Cheese Puff. "This is the femur, it's the leg bone and it's the largest bone in the body. We measure it because it's a good indicator of whether the baby is growing properly."

"And is it the right size?" I ask nervously.

"Yes, it is," he says, and I breathe a sigh of relief.

He then goes onto measure the heart chambers and all kinds of other things that I would never have even thought about. I'm learning so much about how human beings are made, and it's amazing to me that I can be making this whole person without even doing anything other than living myself.

"Looks like the little one is sucking its thumb now," he says, and we look at what really does seem to be a baby sucking its thumb. Dr. Kerr presses a button and says he will give me a picture of that, and I see it print out at the side of the machine.

Molly takes it and hands it to me, and we look at it and I can't believe it. I think about how one day this will be a real baby that I actually hold in my arms, and it will sucks its thumb when it's *outside* of me. I stare at the picture while he finishes up the ultrasound, just wishing that things didn't have to be so complicated. That I could just have my sweet little baby and not have to worry about anything else. But unfortunately, that isn't life. I kiss the picture and say, "Hi, my little Cheese Puff."

"Cheese Puff?" Dr. Kerr says, and I tell him that's what I've been calling it because I've always loved cheese puffs and I've been craving them the whole pregnancy. He laughs and says, "That's one I've never heard before."

After the ultrasound, we go to Dr. Lippincott's office, which is in the same building, just two floors down. She has already seen the report as he sent it to her right away. She tells me everything looks good and healthy and that the baby is now almost six and a half inches! *Wow!*

She asks me about how I've been sleeping and eating, and about how I've been managing my stress since the bed rest. I tell her that I've been calmer and not letting myself get too stressed. I tell her about getting my driver's license and my mom coming to the party that Dianne and Molly had for me for my birthday. She's happy to hear this. I tell her I've also been doing tons of research and that I've typed the words "teen mom" into the search bar so much that it's kind of embarrassing how often I do it.

I also watched this movie called *Waitress.* It's about a woman who gets pregnant and the father isn't involved because he's abusive and she leaves him. She ends up raising the baby herself and it's a really happy story. She works at a pie shop and bakes the most amazing-looking pies. It was nice to watch, because it showed me I'm not alone. I'm going to try to watch some more movies like this because they make me feel like things will be okay. I know a movie isn't real life, but it still helps.

Dr. Lippincott's voice brings me back from thinking about the movie. "You do sound prepared, but I want you to know that the life of a teen mother isn't easy. And I'm not saying this to be discouraging, it's just the truth. We've been focusing a lot on the health of you and the baby but it's really important for you to be planning and prepared. You will have to work extremely hard to graduate high school, get into college, earn a living, et cetera."

"I know, believe me, I've been thinking about it all the time. Right now I work at a coffee shop to make money for the baby, but I'm planning on becoming a journalist one day, or maybe a reporter, after college. I'm figuring out how it can all work."

"Good," she says, and then she pauses. "Now, Dianne already told me this, but I just want to confirm...is the father involved?"

Tears start up in my eyes. "No, he's not."

How many more times am I going to have to say that to people?

"I'm so sorry. I know that this can be so hard," she says, touching my hand comfortingly. "But I know that you're a strong young woman and that you can do it yourself." She smiles thoughtfully. "You know, I still remember something from when I was growing up. My mom's best friend was a teen mom, and she would come over all the time for help. She went to night school for a while, and she eventually graduated and became an obstetrician, like me. It just showed me that you have to be strong and believe in yourself. And I know you have that in you. It's going to be okay. Focus on your goals. Let me confirm the next appointment with Dianne so you can leave."

"Your next appointment is on March 24th at five," Dianne informs me once I'm out of her office. "After that visit, you start seeing her every two weeks. Then, once you're in your final month, it's every week."

It's approaching so fast. The talk with Dr. Lippincott made me realize that I have so much to do in such a *short* amount of time, not that I didn't already know that.

Back at home, I go up to Molly's room to find her browsing for new clothes on her computer, earphones in. I'm so incredibly envious of her. All she has to worry about is clothes, school, boys...she's carefree. She gets to have a normal teenage life. I want that, too. I want all the things she has. I feel like a little kid thinking this, like I'm in sixth grade again, when everyone had these glow-in-the-dark sneakers and I would tell my mom, *"She* has them, and *she* has them."

What would Mom say now? I miss her. I miss living with her and talking to her and being around her. I want to talk to her so badly. She hasn't even called since my birthday last week. I thought maybe things were starting to change after she gave me the car and came to the party, but maybe she just did that as some sort of final send-off, so she didn't have to have anything that reminded her of me around anymore.

I tug the left earphone out of Molly's ear and she looks at me and asks, "What's wrong, Madison?"

"I just...I don't know. I thought the 20-week scan would be a good day. Instead I feel more depressed than ever. This baby shouldn't belong to me." My voice hardens. "I'm a horrible human being that screws everything up and that doesn't deserve it."

"Madison, stop. You were so happy, just a few hours ago!" she says. "I mean, who cares if you didn't have a baby when you're older? Who cares if you aren't leading the same boring life everyone else is?"

"Because you don't know how much I'm going to have to do." My voice breaks. "You don't know what I'm going to have to go through to give this baby a *halfway* decent life. And..." I pause because my head is pounding. "I've hardly started. I need a better job. I need to finish high school. I need to get into Harvard. It's my dream. I won't be able to live without my dream. But I also can't give up this baby. It's a part of me now, and it's up to me to raise it. And I *want* to raise it, but wanting to raise a baby and loving it isn't enough! I don't know how I'm going to do all the stuff I have to do!"

"Madison, come on, don't freak out, it's-"

"You don't get it, Molly! I envy your life! I *envy* it! I look at you and I wonder what *I* would be doing right now if I had just been more forceful telling Leo *no!*"

Molly's expression changes. "Oh, no, Madison..." She trails off, unsure of what to say, but I finish for her, holding my hands up in quotation marks.

"It's all going to be okay, Madison. Everything's going to turn out fine, Madison."

Molly looks at me with guilt and hurt at the same time.

"What if everything just won't? Huh?" I turn on my heel and clomp downstairs.

I feel so dumb and humiliated, even with my own best friend. I can't believe she knows what Leo and I did. I can't believe that soon *everyone's* going to be knowing.

I'm a failure in every way possible. What if I end up on the streets? What kind of person will everyone think I am? If I can't find a better job, if I can't afford anything for the baby, if I can't pay rent, if I don't get into any colleges? Everyone will think I'm lower than dirt! And what if Cheese Puff feels that way about me, too? I can even picture Cheese Puff blaming me for giving her or him such a horrible life, coming up to me one day and saying, *"Why did you put me into this mess?"*

I can't take it anymore, it's just too much and now I have a headache and I feel exhausted. I get into bed. My last thoughts before falling asleep are that I can't let it happen. I can't just let my life fall apart. I'll find a way to make things better. I need to go back to Mrs. Sherman and talk to her soon. She gave me good advice about the letter to Leo, and maybe she can help with this. But for now, I need sleep. Lots of it.

<>

In the morning, I feel like a weight has been placed over my eyelids. I feel hot and stuffy and sweaty. When Molly comes into my room to see where I am, I tell her that I'm not going to school because I think I'm sick, and I ask her to pick up my schoolwork for me, which she agrees to do.

After I sleep for another two hours, I feel slightly better. Truthfully, I don't think I'm actually sick. I think I'm just generally stuffy and tired. I work on school assignments and editing for the paper in bed, and then I email Mom to tell her I stayed home from school, just to update her, although I know she probably won't even care, which makes me so sad.

I feel a bit better later in the day, and so I go to work. Matthew asks why I wasn't at school earlier, and I tell him I was feeling sick.

"Glad you're feeling better," he says. "Hey, so have you read all the books I got you for your birthday?"

"Yeah, almost," I say. "I read the one about journalism, and I'm starting the improv one. I love them, Matthew. Thanks again."

He smiles and says he's glad, and I sigh. He's so sweet and kind to me, but I know that will probably change once I tell him. For a brief moment, I wonder how different things would be if Matthew was the one I was in love with and this was his baby. I bet he would have stuck around. But I wasn't attracted to Matthew. Apparently, I only like mean guys. What's my problem? Then again, I didn't know what a jerk Leo really was until this happened.

After work, I walk home, even though I know I could drive now that I have the car. But it feels good to exercise, and I don't want to have to pay for gas any more than I have to. I kind of wish I had driven, though, it's so cold. As the wind bites my face, I think of Leo, anger pulsing through my veins. I have to go through this all alone. It's half his fault. And here I am, covering his half and struggling to keep up with mine. Having to sacrifice so much of what I wanted for myself while he gets to do whatever he wants. It makes me want to scream. It makes me want to punch something. But there's nothing I can do except let it stew inside me. I guess writing the letter to him didn't really help.

Once I'm home, I see that I have a voicemail.

-Voicemail- from 'Mrs. Schmitz'

Hi Madison, it's Mrs. Schmitz, Leo's mom. I just wanted to tell you that I saw the letter you wrote to Leo. I made Leo read it with me and as I'm sure you can imagine, he didn't want to listen to any of it. Although I'm still not happy with this situation, I do acknowledge that it's 50% my son's responsibility. My husband and I want to do our part, and we are working things out with your mom, who is a very nice lady, by the way. We know what happened to your dad a few years back and we're very sorry. Although Leo doesn't want anything to do with the baby now, he might change his mind in the future. Regardless, my husband and I will want to know our grandchild, even if he or she wasn't born under ideal circumstances. We are fortunate that we have done well in our lives, and we would really appreciate it if you were more open to accepting the child support that we are going to be giving you. Hope you are doing well and taking care of yourself. Again, we apologize for our son's behavior. So, take care, bye.

I can't believe any of what she just said. I can't believe that she read what I wrote. I'm so embarrassed. I should never have just slid it under the door, what was I thinking? And I don't want their help! I don't want to accept it. I'm so glad she didn't expect me to call her back, I really don't want to deal with her at all.

I decide to send an email to Mom.

To: tdavis31@gmail.com
From: maddieluvspizza@gmail.com

Mom,
I just wanted to thank you for the car. I know that I already did, but really, words can't say how grateful I am. I am going to pay you back for it because I don't really deserve it. I don't have the money now, but I will. I know you said you want to talk, but I haven't heard from you. I understand how busy you are and you can take as much time as you need. Thank you for coming to my birthday, and for everything else, especially for working things out with Leo's parents when it isn't even your job to do it. Let me know when you want to talk, okay? I love you.

Maddie

I miss her so badly. I wonder if she even misses me.

Lying in bed that night, I talk to Cheese Puff as I touch my stomach. It's become a little routine that I do now before I fall asleep. "I was thinking about how many things I'd love to wish for you the other day," I say softly. "And it's funny, because when I was little, I used to pretend to be a fairy and make wishes on my dolls, and I'd pretend to be a mommy. You'll probably love to play pretend, too. Anyway...this is a situation where I wish I could play pretend, I guess."

I feel a tiny flutter in my stomach, as if Cheese Puff is listening. Well, maybe she or he is, I know babies can hear your voice in the womb.

"I wish I could pretend to be a fairy and just...*poof* you into having an amazing life. I wish I could devote every moment to you and have a perfect little family for you. I'm going to try my hardest to give you a semblance of that. And I think that everything will be worth it because I'll have you and you'll have me."

"And it's not like I *didn't* want this to happen. I just wanted it to happen later on. But just because it's sooner than I planned doesn't mean I can't make it work. And it doesn't mean that I don't want you to have everything the world has to offer. Because...there's just so much good out there. Okay, sure, there's a lot of bad people, but there are also so many good people, people that I can't wait for you to meet, and there are smiles and birthdays and cake and moons and stars, and...there's something really good that I just know you will love: *cheese puffs!*"

It makes me laugh to say that, and just saying all of this out loud makes me feel so much stronger than I did earlier. Like I can handle anything. And maybe, since I have not only myself but also Cheese Puff to think of, I really can.

20 weeks!

😊 = sweet potato = Cheese Puff!

To-Do List

$800 =
expenses?
or $600?

- pick up paycheck on Friday from Roast and Drink
- edit Janet's stories
- recruit new writers?
- finish story on the blood drive
- math test on Friday
- fill out English summary chart
- finish French essay

☆ Level 2
Ultrasound
20-week
Anatomy Scan
TODAY

☆ make sure to get pictures from ultrasound

☆ next appointment with Dr. Lippincott = March 24th 5pm

BOY or GIRL?

I need
more $$
too many
expenses
can't do it
bad mom
total
failure

- Send email to Mom: thank-you for the car + thank-you about Leo's parents
- keep reading "Improv 101"
- research Cheese Puff's stage right now
- research Harvard more?

buy:
- more baby diapers
- car key holder
- new math notebook
- cheese puffs!

☆ 30% off on diapers at Target next week

Chapter 17: Week Twenty-One

"Your baby is the size of a large banana," I read. Wow, Cheese Puff seems to be so much bigger every week. And I'm officially six months pregnant! I really *look* pregnant now. I've "popped," as they describe it on the websites, and even the baggiest sweatshirts I have aren't covering it anymore. There are still rumors circulating at school, but no one has said anything to my face. I hear them whispering and I see them looking at me. It's horrible, but I've had to just accept that this is the way it's going to be. I can't wait for the day when I already have the baby and I'm in college or wherever, and people don't see me being pregnant. Thankfully, I don't have any social media accounts, my mom would never let me do that, so no one's harassing me on there.

Matthew is the only one I care about, and I'm just praying that the rumors haven't gotten to him, even though it's inevitable that they probably have, but I've been hiding the pregnancy with jackets and my apron at work, so even if he's heard something, he probably doesn't believe it. I'm surprised he hasn't asked me about it, actually. I think that one night after work, I'll go out for dinner with him and tell him.

I have a few maternity shirts that Molly and Dianne gave me for my birthday, but I really have to get more soon. Just another expense of being pregnant!

Something else is happening that I actually like; my hair is growing fast, and it looks so voluminous, and my nails have never been longer, I have to cut them way more often than usual. I read online that it's a pregnancy symptom, having thick hair and nails and that they grow fast, it's one of the good symptoms.

I've also been getting these weird stretch marks on my lower abdomen. I showed them to Dianne and she said she got them, too, that they sometimes lighten up or go away after you have the baby. Not everyone gets them, but it's apparently genetic. I wish I could ask my mom if she had them.

Anyway, on a happier note, spring break is starting at the end of next week, and what my school calls the "spring dance" is on Friday. I don't know if I'm going to go, Molly might want to, but anyway, I'm excited for spring break.

Tonight, Dianne and Molly are both out. Molly is trying out for the dance club at our school, and Dianne has a meeting with her literary agent. I've been craving French fries like crazy, and there's a diner a few blocks away that has really good fries and they're only four dollars. I feel like I need a treat, I've been working really hard, so I decide to go get some.

I put on a jacket and start walking. It's windy and cold, so this time I decide to turn back and drive. I feel guilty that I have a car. Do I even deserve to have this privilege? I slide into the car, being careful not to bump my stomach against the steering wheel. It's definitely getting bigger, there's still a lot of space, but not as much as before.

Then something occurs to me. If I got this car fixed up, I bet I could sell it for around a thousand dollars. I can take the bus or even walk, because pretty much everything around Redford is in walkable distance. It would be sad, parting with the car because it was Mom's, but it would be for a good cause. For Cheese Puff. But would Mom want me to have money for the baby now more than she would want me to keep the car? I mean, I guess it's something to *consider*. I don't think Mom would want me to, though. And it's just a thought, anyway. I also realize it will probably be easier to take the baby places if I have a car.

I park in front of the diner, and look at the sign: "Home's Diner." It's such a comforting sign, a warm yellow, with red letters, and I love the name. I've been coming here since I was a little kid. The smell of their food wafts out onto the street, and it looks like a little warm glow in the middle of the dark night.

But just as I'm getting out of the car, I notice two people in a booth in the window. No, I can't be seeing that right.

But I am. It's Leo. With Dina Caldwell.
Dina Caldwell.

...October 4th, 2018...

"Dina Caldwell would have sex with me. She actually told me. But you, you, my girlfriend of over a *year*, won't do it? Come on, Madison, it'll be good."

...

I still remember how Leo's voice sounded when he said that. It's hard to admit it, but it's one of the main reasons I agreed to sleep with him that night. The night we conceived the baby in my stomach. He was trying to persuade me, and it worked. *How stupid am I, really?*

It's all so disgustingly perfect. He ended up getting together with *her*. Because after he got what he wanted from me, I was just old, used garbage that he couldn't wait to chuck so he could go off with *Dina*. A girl who doesn't even go to our school! She goes to a private school just outside of Redford, but she takes classes at our community center a lot, so I guess that's how he met her.

I crouch down in the car so no one can see me and I watch them as Leo pays and they leave. *Leo pays.* My heart sinks down to the bottom of my ribs. Dina's wearing white skinny jeans that hug her perfect curves. Of course she has the perfect body.

A hole opens up in me like I've never felt before.

Leo whispers in her ear, and she laughs hysterically and they kiss and then they get into the car in front of me. Leo's *driving?* Oh, yeah. I forgot. His birthday is on January fifth. So now he has his license and a car. I remember that I was going to take him to his favorite Mexican restaurant for his birthday. I had a whole evening planned, even though it was months away. That's how much *I* cared about him.

I'm horrified as I stare at them flirting, then kissing. *Is this really happening?*

I finally wrench my head away when I see him caressing her shoulders like he used to do to me. It always felt so good, so soft. It made me feel safe. What a joke.

Sobs overwhelm me, huge sobs that force me to take in a ton of air. I'm shaking and crying and there's snot coming out of my nose and I don't have a tissue but I don't even care.

I turn away because I want to leave and I need to stop crying to drive. I need to drive safely, so I wait until I can see clearly and then I drive off, passing his car, not looking. The second I'm home, I crumple into a ball on the floor, bawling.

So he's moved on. He gets to date girls that aren't me and do whatever he wants. *And not help me at all.* I was *so* wrong about him. What kind of moron was I that I didn't see it before? I was just way too caught up in how he made me feel like the most important person in the world to see it.

... June 2018...

One day, Leo and I were hiking. It was really hot outside so I was sweating and uncomfortable, but I was having a great time, because I was with Leo. Suddenly, I tripped over a branch and totally wiped out, landing on my hands, scraping my knees.

It hurt, but I got right back up, too embarrassed to ask Leo for help. I brushed myself off like it was nothing, and I took a sip of my water to hide that I was in pain.

He was standing there, staring at me. "That's what I love about you," he said, smiling. "You get right back up."

Thinking back, I wonder why he didn't help me up. All I could think about at the time was how gorgeous he was and how "lucky" I was to have him. Little did I know.

...

Now that I've seen him with Dina, I'm obsessed all over again. I can't stop thinking about him, I just can't. I want him here with me. I want the *old* him here, I miss him so much. I just want to go sit on the couch with him and have him stroke my shoulders and tell me that all he wants is to be with me and Cheese Puff.

But I can't have that. I will never have that.

On my bed, I touch my stomach lightly. "Leo's not going to be your father." I make myself say it. Yeah, sure, he will genetically, but a real father? No way. I'm glad his parents are stepping up, but he sure isn't. I hate him so much, with this new stabbing hatred that I've never felt before in my entire life, towards anyone I've ever known.

"He's not, he's not, he's not, HE'S NOT!" I work myself up to shouting, which makes me sob more. I reach for a tissue and blow my nose. It feels good to let it out.

After a while, I feel calmer. Sometimes crying helps me feel better. I hate when my emotions get too built-up inside me. I take the iron supplements Dianne gave me with some orange juice, and then I open a fresh bag of cheese puffs. I eat more of them than I probably should, but I need it tonight. I never did get my fries.

Then I take a shower and it feels good just letting the water wash over me, like I'm washing away all the negative feelings.

Before I fall asleep, I squirt a small amount of Dad's last can of shaving cream onto my wrist, just a tiny amount. I want it to last, I don't ever want it to run out. Thankfully, when I shake it, I can feel that it's still almost full. And the smell immediately makes me feel like he's close. I miss him so much. But thank God he never met Leo. He would be hating him right now, I know it. I bet he would think I was nuts to have been so in love with such a jerk.

I wish Dad was here right now to talk to. But the closest thing I have is the smell of him, so I fall asleep smelling the shaving cream on my wrist.

… January 2016…

One night, after I failed a math test for the first time in my life, in seventh grade, I brought it home because the teacher said I had to show it to my parents. The big red "F" on the front was so embarrassing. I couldn't believe I had done so badly, and I was terrified about their reaction.

Mom was busy writing, so I showed it to Dad. Instead of getting angry, he smiled. Even though I was already thirteen, he sat me in his lap like he did when I was little. I looked into his hazel eyes, the ones I inherited from him, and he stroked my hair comfortingly.

"It's okay," he said. "Everyone fails a test at some point." He laughed. "It's kind of a rite of passage."

"But aren't you mad?" I asked in a shaky voice.

"Madison, honey, you know all I want in life is for you to be happy. Grades are important, and I know you know that. I also know you can and will do better than this. It just means that you need to try a bit harder next time. That's all, sweetie."

Now I'm wondering if he would feel this way about me being pregnant at such a young age. This is more than just a failed test. And it's not like I can really just try a bit harder next time. This is a big deal. Would he be disappointed in me? He always told me he wanted me to be happy, and I'm not happy right now. Well, part of me is happy. And my goal is to be happy. But now I also have a new goal, and I think I'm beginning to understand how my dad felt. Because even though Cheese Puff is still just a tiny kicking…*thing,* in my stomach, all I will want is her or his happiness.

…

In the morning, I get dressed for school, putting on my most baggy, oversized sweatshirt. I check myself out in the mirror. There's just the faintest outline of my stomach, and I realize again that the baggy clothes aren't going to cover it much longer. I should stop being such a baby, get some more maternity clothes, and reveal my pregnancy to the school. Stop being a *baby.* How ironic.

On the way to school, I tell Molly about seeing Leo with another girl last night. She stops walking, shocked. Then she gives me a big hug and shakes her head angrily. "If I could punch him, I would. I can't believe all of what he's done to you."

"I cried a lot last night, like a *lot,* but…I guess he's just not worth all this. I mean, I've known this for a while now," I say, trying to actually feel what I'm saying. As we enter the school, I look around, really hoping not to run into him.

"Who was Leo with, if you don't mind me asking?"

"Dina Caldwell. She's from another school."

"I think I know who she is. She takes classes at the community center. Long black hair and freckles?" I nod and she says, "Well, he's the one missing out on you and that cute baby growing in your stomach." She looks at my stomach. "By the way, I think it's time for you to wear the maternity clothes my mom and I gave you."

I shush her. "What?" she whispers.

"I don't want people at school to...know yet."

"Um, Madison? A girl in my art class told me that she heard you were pregnant, and I had to sit there and pretend to be clueless. Trust me, I think people know! I mean, when you wear your gym clothes..."

"Really? It's obvious during gym?" I ask frantically.

"Well, yeah! Everyone knows, seriously, you just haven't confirmed it."

"I know, but how are they going to react? Once, you know, I confirm the rumors? I mean, it's a small town. *Everyone's* going to talk."

"They're *already* talking. And truthfully, they don't care! Sure, they might gossip for a *little* while, but all they really care about is themselves. You know who your true friends are. You don't need the ones who gossip behind your back."

I nod. It's true. "Well, I'm so happy you're my friend. All I need is you."

"Don't make me cry at school!" Molly says, and we laugh.

At work later that day, I'm thankful to have the turquoise apron because it helps cover my stomach, and even though I want to do it, I'm still stalling telling Matthew. I'm just *not ready.* It's been so much fun working with him, on top of our usual friendship, and I'm not ready to lose that yet. Even though I know what Molly said earlier is true, I think it might be different with Matthew. He'll be really upset, I just know it. Especially because I didn't tell him sooner.

"Ready to watch the master do yet another latte swirl?" Matthew jokes. I kind of half nod. I'm preoccupied with everything, and I didn't even really hear what he said. "Hey, what's wrong?" he asks.

"Nothing. Just a little stressed, you know, about schoolwork and stuff."

"My parents asked about you. They said they missed you coming over and rehearsing with me from our old acting days." He laughs. "Want to come over tonight after work?"

Oh, God, no. They'll for sure notice my stomach. I shake my head. "I can't."

"Why not?" He frowns. "Madison, is something wrong?"

"Can we go to Home's Diner after work, instead?" I ask suddenly. "I really have to talk to you about something, actually."

"Okay. Sure."

I can't believe I'm finally going to do it. But when he asked me to come over, I realized I can't wait anymore.

I want the shift to last forever, but the hours fly by, of course, and the next thing I know, we're at the diner, sitting across from each other. Luckily, it isn't busy and we managed to find a booth off to the side, where no one's around. No one from school is here, thank God.

I take a deep breath and say, "So, you know how I broke up with Leo?"

"Yeah, wasn't that a couple months ago? Oh, are you back together?"

"No, we aren't. Anyway..." My heart rate speeds up. I'm actually going to do this. It's going to be *out*. For real. "We broke up because..."

"Because what?"

Just say it, Madison. "Because I'm pregnant."

"What?"

"I'm pregnant." I close my eyes. I'm scared to even look at him. I hate saying these words. I wish I could just take them back.

"What? *What?*" he asks. I open my eyes, and he's staring at me, looking totally shocked and confused. I guess he really hadn't heard the rumors.

I nod, and then stand up and show him my belly. I can't believe I'm doing this. My heart's pounding and I feel like I'm going to cry. *What else is new?*

"Wow. *Wow.* I don't believe this, I-I don't even know what to say."

"It's okay," I say. "I'll understand if you hate me now or don't want anything to do with me. I get it. I'm sorry. I wanted to tell you sooner, but I was...scared."

"And you're having the baby? I mean, oh, I guess you are. Wow." He shakes his head. "I'm just...trying to understand this, get my head around this. Wow."

I sit there, looking down, listening to him, praying he still wants to stay friends with me. His words are swimming around my head and I can't focus. I knew this would be hard, but I didn't realize *how* hard.

"Madison?"

I realize he's been asking me something and I didn't hear. I look up.

"Are you okay? Now I'm worried about you. Is there anything I can do to help you?" he says in the nicest, sweetest voice that I think I've ever heard from a guy.

"Matthew, no," I say. "I'm okay. You're so sweet. I just want to be friends and not let this...affect our friendship. That's what I want. Is that...okay?"

"Are you crazy? This isn't something I would end our friendship over. I mean, I'm upset you didn't tell me, yeah. It's weird, you know, I actually heard a rumor at school that you were pregnant. But I totally thought it was a lie from one of those idiots like Lulu who's always starting rumors and things. But, wow. I guess it was true." He shakes his head. "I just can't believe Leo. I just can't believe he left you because you were pregnant with *his* baby. That's so unfair to you."

My eyes tear up. It's such a relief to me that he didn't start asking about school or money or my career, or anything like that. He just seems to care about how I'm *doing*. He's amazing. "Thank you."

"For what?"

"For not...running off or anything."

"Madison, you're my friend. I care about you."

"I know, and you're being so nice, I've just been so scared to tell you. I mean, I wish I'd known you'd react like this."

"Wait, is this why you didn't want to come see my parents?"

"Um, yeah. I don't want them to know. Not yet, anyway, I mean, they always liked me. I don't want that to change."

"Okay, I won't tell them, but at some point they'll find out." He smiles. "We're going to be friends for a long time, you and me."

He reaches for my hand, then stops. "I'm sorry. Maybe I shouldn't have-"

"It's alright," I say, smiling a little and I take his hand.

It feels awkward for a minute because we've been friends for so long and I don't think we've ever held hands. But I know he's trying to be comforting and I'm really so happy, I can't believe it. I didn't think it would go this well. I value his friendship so much and maybe it doesn't have to change just because I'm pregnant. I mean, true friends stay friends no matter what, right? Like Molly.

I realize I'm starving, and I'm excited to finally get the fries I've been craving. Matthew orders a burger, and we eat mostly not talking, but comfortable, just like always, when we didn't have to say anything and it wouldn't be awkward. It's almost like nothing has changed. I now wish I'd told him sooner.

When the waitress brings the bill, I try to pay, but he won't let me. He kind of jokes that I need to save money for the baby, and that I also need to really pay attention to the latte swirls so I can make them better myself and get better tips. I love that he's trying to joke and cheer me up.

I laugh and thank him, and then I tell him that I have to get back to Molly's. I tell him about the fight with my mom and how I'm living with Molly and her mom for now.

"Oh. So *that's* why you had your party there," he says.

"Are you mad that I didn't tell you sooner?"

"I wish you'd told me *everything* sooner, but I get why you wouldn't want to."

"I just didn't feel ready to until...tonight."

He nods. "It's okay. I get it."

We leave and he walks me back to Molly's, which is on the way to his house. We say goodnight and I stand there for a minute, outside, just thinking about what just happened.

When I get inside, Molly and Dianne are in the kitchen having hot chocolate. Dianne asks if I want one and I say yes, it'll help me stay up to do my homework and study. She makes the best hot chocolate, with whipped cream and chocolate shavings, and it's perfect to have right now when I'm already in such a good mood from how it went with Matthew.

We sit at the kitchen table and Dianne tells us some good news about her book. During the last half of spring break, she'll be in Los Angeles to meet with someone about potentially making one of her books into a movie. That's really exciting news! But she says that she wants to make sure Molly and I will be okay staying alone for a few days. We tell her it's totally fine and Molly and I laugh when Dianne says, "No parties!"

Later, when I'm changing into my pajamas, Molly comes into my room and stares at my stomach. "Wow, it really is popping out now. Seriously, Mads, you need to just let people see it at school. Like we were saying this morning, you-"

"I told Matthew."

"Oh wow, you did? Really?! How'd he take it?"

"He was actually...very supportive." Unexpected tears rush to my eyes. *Here we go, everything makes me cry.*

"Oh, Mads, that's amazing. I'm so happy to hear that," she says, and then she giggles. "I bet he wishes it was his!"

"I don't think so. But he was really nice, and he hates Leo, I can tell."

"Good."

"You know what?" I say suddenly. "I'm going to wear one of my maternity shirts to school tomorrow. The tight pink one that will show off my stomach. I'm not going to be afraid anymore. Your advice this morning was right. I'm doing it."

There. It's decided.

In the morning, I almost chicken out, but then I just do it. I put on the bright pink maternity shirt birthday present from Dianne. It totally shows off that I'm pregnant. I do my make up and hair today, and I try to look really good. I'm nervous, but I'm going to do it, and I want to look as good as I can so no one can feel sorry for me. I do one more thing before I leave, and it gives me the extra burst of confidence I need. I squirt a tiny bit of my dad's shaving cream on my wrist and rub it in, smelling it.

When I get to school, I take a deep breath, Molly wishes me luck and tells me it will be fine and that she's there for me. I walk down the hallway with my head up, not trying to hide with my books or backpack or clothes anymore.

I see what feels like a million eyes zero in on my stomach. Everyone is noticing, and whispering and I even hear people saying things like, "Oh my God, she *is* pregnant!" "That's why she hides in the bathroom to change for gym!" "Who do you think the father is?" "That's why she broke up with Leo!" "This happened to *her?*" "Oh, I would just die if that happened to *me.*" "Hasn't she heard of *birth control?*"

But I don't care anymore. Let them say what they want. I'm just trying to ignore them. I pretend there's music on and I'm listening to it, and then suddenly the song *Fire and Rain* starts going through my head. It's weird that this is the song my mind goes to, but it helps me tune out what's happening around me. And it's like my dad is here, whispering into my ear, "It's going to be okay."

← cheese puff - sized! ☆ 21 weeks ☆

To-Do List

Food: $200/month
Baby: $200/month
???
$17/hour job?

```
17      68
x4      x5
68     340
       x  4
      1360
      -200
      1160
      -160
    $1,000
not enough
```

$
$
$
$
♡

- pick up paycheck on Friday from Roast and Drink
- work on budget
- send Janet new layout for newspaper
- finish cover story on new clubs
- ask "features" editor to send me her edited pieces
- finish math homework
- label science diagram
- English essay due March 6th
- organize history notes
- study for French test
- memorize new English vocab words for test on Monday
- read chapters 4-6 in science textbook
- design graphics for this week's newspaper edition
- START THINKING OF BABY NAMES!!!!

☆ sell car??
   for $1,000?
   (think about it)

buy:
- cheese puffs
- another bottle of prenatal vitamins
- maternity clothes

☆ take iron supplement once a day

☆ finish the books Matthew got me!

☆ look for sales on baby items / maternity clothes!

♡ my ♡ Cheese Puff ♡

Chapter 18: Week Twenty-Two

"Your baby is as big as a red bell pepper," I see online. I also recently figured out that my Cheese Puff can detect "sunlight" now! I borrowed Molly's flashlight and shone it on my stomach for an hour last night, moving it around. It's so interesting how the baby moves close to wherever I shine the light. It was really peaceful, and it felt like Cheese Puff and I were actually hanging out.

I've felt my uterus bunching up and hardening a little, and I told Dianne and she thought it was something called Braxton Hicks, but she called Dr. Lippincott to make sure. She said the same thing, it's basically little practice contractions that the uterus does to get ready for when the baby comes. She said you can get them at any time throughout the pregnancy and that a lot of people don't feel them early on, but if you're skinny you might feel them earlier, just like the kicks. She said as long as they don't hurt and they're not really strong, they're normal and not a sign of labor. It kind of feels like when I've had my blood pressure taken at the doctor, but around my stomach.

Lately, when I stand up, sometimes I feel a little dizzy, sort of like I did in my first trimester. I did some research, and apparently my expanding uterus is putting pressure on my blood vessels, which is reducing blood flow and causing my dizziness. It's annoying, but at least I know it's normal. It said to keep drinking lots of water and that's what Dr. Lippincott says too, so I've just got to keep remembering to drink a lot. But then I have to pee a lot, which can be hard at school.

I've started taking a magnesium and calcium supplement along with my iron supplement, because Dianne says it will make the baby's bones and teeth stronger. It's crazy how many pills you have to take to ensure a healthy baby. But I know I need to, because I've read about people who take prenatal vitamins even before getting pregnant, to make sure their eggs are in good shape and that they have a lot of something called folic acid. Obviously, I wasn't doing that, so now I'm really trying to make sure I take everything I need so that the baby is as healthy and smart as it can be.

Since I basically confirmed the pregnancy at school, it's been really weird and awful. A lot of the kids literally part the way for me when I walk down the hallway, they act as if they're scared that they'll "catch" pregnancy from me, or something like that. Some people are being jerks, making rude remarks and leaving disgusting notes on my locker. And some of them are a little too interested in my pregnancy, and they just keep coming up and asking to touch my stomach. I keep thinking that if I had a baby when I was older, or the "right" age, then people would be congratulating me. Instead, it's the complete opposite.

Anyway, I've been taking long walks around the neighborhood when I'm finished with my homework, usually just before I go to bed, at eleven. It calms me down and I like to get some fresh air and exercise, and this seems to be the only free time I have these days.

Today is Wednesday March 13th, and I'm actually on my nightly walk right now. It's eleven at night, I'm done my homework, and I'm trying to push my tiredness away and get some exercise. I had to buy a new pair of sneakers because my feet are swelling up. Everything swells during pregnancy!

I look up at the moon, and then at my stomach. I think about astronauts who go to the moon. I wish I was there right now and didn't have to deal with all these jerks at school. Who knows, maybe Cheese Puff will one day do something amazing, like go to the moon? It's so weird to think that I'm creating a person that will be in the world and can do whatever it wants with its life, and I will always be its mother.

I've started thinking about names for both girls and boys...

Girls	Boys
Tabitha	Liam
Rachel	Chris
Mavis	Oliver
Melanie	
Chrissy	
Charlotte	

Every cute name for a boy that I can think of reminds me of Leo. Liam? He was Leo's soccer instructor. Chris? This guy he's friends with. Oliver? His best friend in fifth grade. I have to come up with more names.

I feel guilty thinking this, but I still don't think that my heart can handle having a boy. It will just make me think of Leo. I know I will love whatever I have, it's just hard to think about it now.

I also find myself wondering what the baby will end up looking like. Will the baby have my blonde hair, or Leo's brown hair? My hazel eyes or Leo's light green ones? My skinny, petite frame or Leo's strong, lanky one? Full, straight lips like me or upturned, thin ones like Leo's? Round eyes like me or oval-shaped eyes like Leo? A big forehead, like Leo has? A heart-shaped face, like me? It will probably be a mix of both of us. And even my parents and Leo's parents, I know from everything I'm reading about how it can all be passed down from other generations. I hope there's some of my dad in the baby. I'm so excited to find out what she or he looks like.

Looking at the moon and the stars calms me a lot, and I like to be out at night doing these walks. I feel like my head is clearest then. The stars are really twinkling brightly tonight. It reminds me of when I was little, and my parents used to drive us to an area near the water where we could see the stars really clearly because there was no light from the town distracting us. We would always find one star and then make a wish on it, saying the "Star Light, Star Bright" poem. I decide to do it tonight.

"Star light, Star bright, first Star I see tonight, I wish I may, I wish I might...have the wish I wish tonight..."

I wish for everything to be good again. For my mom and I to be able to talk and have a good relationship again. For me and Josie to see each other more. I wish for my baby to be healthy. I wish for my friendships to last. I wish for my dad to come back, even though I know that's not possible, but maybe somehow he can still see me wherever he is, if he's somewhere up in the sky like heaven. I wish for school to go well and for me to still be able to be a journalist and take care of Cheese Puff all at the same time. I wish for another guy to come into my life at some point. I wish for so many things, and then I end the wish the way we always did when I was little and our family did this together. I say, "Thank you, Star. Goodnight."

<>

At school the next day, I bump into Matthew on the way to sit with Molly at lunch. We say hi and he reminds me that if I ever need to talk or anything, he's there.

I bet he knows that most of the kids have been whispering about me.

"Game night tonight?" he asks before I go to the cafeteria. "My parents installed a ping-pong table in our basement. They won't be home, they're going for dinner, so it'll be just us. We can play ping-pong and other games! After dinner, come over!"

"Yeah, sure. That would be nice," I say, smiling, excited, glad he isn't making a big deal out of my pregnancy, glad that not everything has to be about it.

I can see Leo sitting with his friends at lunch. I'm sure he's heard a lot of the gossip and he probably hates that some of it is about *him,* too. I never confirmed to anyone that he's the father, but people have been saying it since they know we were dating for over a year.

After school, as I'm packing up my books from my locker, one of the boys in my gym class suddenly comes up and grabs me by the shoulders, then kisses me. I fumble around and push him away, and he starts laughing and I see a group of boys watching, snickering, as he goes back to them and says, "Yeah, she's a slut, alright."

I run off, feeling the tears coming. Why do these kids think it's fun to make fun of me? Do they not have hearts or brains? I would never *ever* do this to someone.

This puts me in a bad mood for the rest of the day, until I walk over to Matthew's, breathing in the cold night air. I keep my eyes shut as I walk past Leo's house. It used to remind me of love and warmth and comfort, but now it just looks like the evil villain's lair in a Disney movie.

I haven't been to Matthew's house in so long. We used to spend a lot of time in his basement and it feels good to be back. It's pretty big and there's a TV and a couch, also bookshelves and board games, and now he has a new ping-pong table.

"Whoa," I say, laughing. "It's so cool!"

"Let's play!" he says excitedly, and hands me a paddle. I'm not very good, I've hardly played this game before. I manage to get the ball off to the side so he can't get it, and he does the same to me the next turn, and he ends up winning 10-4.

"Whatever," I say, rolling my eyes and laughing. "That was fun, even though you beat me."

"Yeah, I like it, especially since I'm so good at it." He winks. "Monopoly?"

I nod and he pulls out the game board, setting it up, giving us each $1,500 (if only I could actually be handed that much money in real life) and dividing up the properties in the beginning, because it's a faster way to play.

I get Boardwalk and Park Place, and I manage to build hotels on them by the end of the game, but because Matthew built hotels on the reds and yellows, I eventually go bankrupt even after mortgaging everything I own and selling my hotels and houses on the pinks and oranges. Even though it's just a game, part of me can't help but wonder if this could happen to me in real life.

By mistake, I knock over the game pieces with my hand. I've become more and more clumsy these days, it must be the pregnancy. I start cleaning it up. "Sorry," I say quietly.

"Hey, we should play that game next." He goes to get the "Sorry" game box. I smile at him, but it's kind of a forced smile, and I think he notices.

"How are you doing?" he asks. "With the pregnancy and everything. We should, you know, talk about it...if you want."

"I'm...fine, I guess. I'm okay."

His eyebrows crease in concern. "You don't seem fine, and I'm *worried* about you, seriously. And I want to *help,* you know, if there's anything I can do."

I try to stop them, but the tears start to come. It's just that he's so *caring.* I can't imagine Leo or anyone saying this stuff to me. And I bet that some of it is pregnancy hormones making me cry, but it's also because he's just so nice to me.

He takes me over to the couch, and I just curl up and smush my face into the cushions. "Why don't you tell me what's going on, Madison? I'm happy to talk to you," he says softly, and I wonder if he really will understand why I'm crying.

"I'm sorry, Matthew...I'm so sorry," I choke out. "It's just...you're so sweet. Leo was such a jerk, he would never say nice stuff to me about the baby, ever, so I just didn't know how it felt, having someone want to be there for me."

I sob harder. He runs his hands through my hair, it feels so good.

"Leo is such a *jerk.* I could never stand that guy. How could he do something like this to you? He should realize he was lucky to have you at all." Suddenly, I notice his eyes look like they're tearing up.

"Oh my God, Matthew, why are *you* crying?"

"Because you're my friend, and I don't know how someone could do that to someone as...as...well, someone as amazing as you."

"I'm not amazing. I got myself pregnant."

"No, you *are* amazing. I just want to know that you're okay. That's seriously all that matters. I...don't like seeing you sad."

He goes to hug me and I just fall into his arms, crying. He hugs me for what seems like hours and I feel so safe, so taken care of. I can't believe he's saying this stuff to me. It feels so good, like nothing I've ever felt before...and...I just want to...

I look up at him and I think we both go for it at the same time. We start to kiss. I feel breathless. I pull away after a minute and ask him, whispering, "What does this...mean?"

He looks worried, shaking his head. "I'm sorry. I shouldn't have done that. It's just, you look so pretty, and I just want to make you feel better. Okay?"

155

I can't believe I haven't seen it for so long. I *like* him. My stomach starts dancing around. I like everything about him...I can't believe I never realized it before. I was so obsessed with Leo, I couldn't see that I had an amazing guy right in front of me the whole time.

"It's okay. I like doing this with you." I smile, my heart beating a little faster, and suddenly we're kissing again, and I'm so happy and surprised, I just can't believe that it's happening.

He pulls away for a moment. "Do you want to go to the spring dance with me tomorrow?"

"I'd love to."

"I'll pick you up at eight thirty at Molly's."

"Okay."

"Okay."

We kiss for a little while longer, and it feels so nice to just have innocent kisses and not have someone pressuring me to have sex with him. With Leo, it always felt like some sort of countdown until he'd want to do it. I just still can't believe what a moron I was with him. But I'm definitely smarter now.

Eventually it's getting late and Matthew's parents are supposed to come home, so I decide to leave. He walks me back to Molly's and we have a nice, long kiss goodbye in front of the house. Everyone is in their own room when I get inside, so I decide to wait until tomorrow to tell Molly.

As I'm falling asleep, I think about everything that happened. The bullying from the kids at school doesn't even bother me anymore, because now I have Matthew. It feels so right to be with him. This is the best night I've had for a really long time.

<>

Molly was so excited when I told her about Matthew. I think she must have said, "I told you so!" about a hundred times. She's fine with me going to the dance with Matthew, she says she's happy to third-wheel with us.

It's Friday night, and Molly and I are getting ready for the dance. I help her zip up her dark purple dress and she helps me into the dress she got me for my birthday. I twist my hair into braids because I want to leave them in for a bit so my hair will look wavy. The braids don't make me cringe *as* much, now I just try to think of the picture of me that Mom gave me, where I'm wearing braids and things were good and happy.

Molly puts some makeup on, and she looks great. "Jay would be nuts if he didn't want to get back with you after you look like this," I say, starting on my mascara. Quickly, I follow that up by saying, "But you are *not* dating him again after what he did to you."

She nods, putting on a second coat of clear lip gloss. "I won't, I swear. I'm completely over him. And you look great, too." Then she giggles.

"What?" I ask.

"Oh, it's just so funny. Like, I thought you and Matthew would really be perfect for each other, you know? And now you're together!"

"Yeah! I honestly can't believe I didn't see it before! I'm just so happy!"

I gaze at my figure in the mirror once I'm done with my makeup. The dress hugs my new curves and shows off my growing belly bump, but who cares? Not me, because everyone knows now! I'm going to push away my self-consciousness and have some fun. I'm so giddy at the thought of a *new* relationship, especially with someone as sweet as Matthew, and it's even better because we've known each other for so long.

Matthew comes to pick us up in his dad's car. "Your chauffeur awaits, ladies," he says, and we laugh as we get into the backseat.

I sigh happily. It's finally spring break! I get a whole week of peace and quiet, and hopefully dates with Matthew! I really want to do things like go out for ice cream, and see if he likes my favorite flavor, bubble gum.

Once we're inside, Molly says she's going to look for Cheryl and Matthew takes me onto the dance floor. It's a slow song, and he pulls me in close to him, smiling.

"There's something I have to tell you," he whispers into my ear. "I've...liked you for a while now." He turns bright red. "I didn't know if you knew."

I smile and kiss him. Molly was *so* right. But now it's not just him that likes me; I like him, too. A lot. "I know. And I feel the same way."

Then we start dancing to a fast song, Matthew shows off his funny dance moves, and I laugh. It's pretty crowded on the dance floor and someone bumps into me. I turn around and see that it's Leo. *Great.*

He stares at Matthew, who straightens up to look taller. Leo never liked Matthew, he hated our friendship, I think he was threatened by it. Matthew never liked Leo, either. Knowing what I know now, I guess he was jealous.

Leo gets a stupid look on his face and he says to me, "So you found someone who doesn't mind your nasty little secret?"

"Yes, that's right," Matthew says, stepping in for me. "Only we found *each other*. And I *know* I'll be better to her than you ever were."

"You wanted her for years," Leo scoffs. "You're just a sloppy second."

"Back off, Leo, your jealousy is showing."

"Jealous? Because you're with the little slut now? You can have her."

Then it all happens so fast. Leo deliberately knocks into Matthew's shoulder as he goes to walk off, but then Matthew grabs him and throws a hard punch right in the middle of his face. I see Leo's nose start to bleed, and he shouts "What is *wrong* with you, man?!?" and then he grabs Matthew by the shirt, trying to punch him back.

Oh, no, why did they have to get into this? "Stop!" I shriek. "Guys, *stop!*"

Matthew throws another punch aiming for Leo's arm, missing, and then suddenly the dance monitor walks up and pulls them apart. "Hey, hey, *hey*! What are you boys doing?!? Report to the office *immediately*! This is *unacceptable* behavior!" she yells, and Leo clutches his nose and they follow her. Everyone is staring behind us as we walk off. I'm shaking, I'm so freaked out by their behavior.

Molly rushes over. "Oh my God, what the hell?! What is wrong with Leo? And what's with Matthew? Why'd he punch him?"

I shake my head, following the boys and the monitor. Molly stays behind.

"Ma'am, Leo Schmitz started it," I say shakily, and Leo turns around, shooting me a glare so intense that I feel scared, so I stop talking, even though I want to make it clear that *Leo* started it. Matthew wouldn't just randomly punch someone.

We all enter the principal's office. Principal Barnes is really strict and she's going to come down hard on them, I know it. There are cameras all around the school and she's for sure seen everything.

Matthew and Leo plop down on the two chairs, and I take the couch in the back of her office, holding back my tears as best as I can.

Tight-lipped, Principal Barnes says, "I saw everything. You boys should be ashamed of yourselves. I've already called your parents."

She hands Leo some tissues for his bleeding nose. Matthew's face is red and he's breathing heavily. He shakes his head. "I couldn't let him sit there and bad-mouth Madison. I just couldn't."

Principal Barnes just sits staring at all of us. No one says anything and it's very uncomfortable. I guess we're waiting for their parents to show up.

Suddenly, Matthew's parents appear in the doorway, looking both concerned and angry. "Matthew, the principal called us," his father says, with anger pulsing behind his voice. "What on earth is going on? Why the hell would you punch a guy, Matthew?" They turn to me. "Madison, why are you-"

I see their eyes zero in on my growing stomach. I turn away. I can't do it, I can't look at their faces.

"I was defending Madison," Matthew says. "And I would do it again."

Leo's parents enter and then it all gets very intense. The principal explains to everyone what she saw and then replays the cameras for them. They are all shocked and the anger and disappointment on their faces is just unbearable for me to watch.

"Madison's pregnant, and Leo just left her," Matthew croaks. "He's been a total jerk to her and I couldn't just sit by silently anymore while he treated her like that. Madison and I are together now, and I wasn't going to let someone push her around."

"She's *pregnant* and you're *dating* her?!" his mother shrieks.

Principal Barnes waves her hand, stopping us. "Listen, this is not a discussion we need to have in my office. You guys need to all go and work it out amongst yourselves. But I can't allow this kind of violence in my school. There is never an excuse for violence, no matter what, I don't care who made what comment."

I see Leo smile, like he's won or something. I want to punch him now too.

"Matthew will be suspended from school for the first two days after spring break. He will not be allowed to make up any work he misses. I'm sorry, but this school has a no-tolerance policy for physical altercations."

Matthew's parents freak out and Matthew actually starts crying. My heart feels like it's going to break apart. Principal Barnes tells us all to leave. I try to defend Matthew but she won't let me talk. She says she feels sorry for me because I'm in the "condition" I'm in, which makes me feel even worse.

We all leave the office and as Leo goes down the hall with his parents, he turns and waves with a big smile on his face, and it takes everything in me not to run after him screaming.

And then I stand awkwardly with Matthew and his parents in the hallway.

"You two are together?" his father asks. We nod, tense.

"And she's pregnant?!?" his mom shrieks again, looking at me with a look I never wanted her to look at me with.

I start to cry again. "I have it all under control, I'm not going to do anything bad to Matthew, I'm-"

"I don't want to hear it!" his father bellows. "This is unacceptable. I can't believe it, actually. Madison, I thought better of you, I thought we knew you! Oh, your poor mother." He shakes his head. "No *way* are you dragging our son down with you. Sorry."

At this point, I'm crying so hard I start choking. Matthew goes to put his arm around me and his mother stops him. "Whatever this is, is *over*. Look at her," his mother says simply. "Mascara running down her face...she's just a mess." She turns to Matthew. "You aren't working at the coffee shop anymore. You can get a job somewhere else, because you're no longer going to be anywhere near Madison. And you two are officially broken up as of tonight."

"But, but..." I blubber. "We haven't even been together for a *day!* Just...just at least let me prove that I won't-"

"*No!* We are Matthew's parents, and *we* are going to make choices for him, seeing as he clearly has no idea about what goes on in the world! That girls who have sex at your age are attention-seeking whores who don't understand consequences!"

"I've owned up to everything I've done! I understand the consequences! Why are you yelling at me?!?" I cry, my voice scratchy, trying to stand up for myself. "This is not your place! You're not even my mother!"

"Exactly. I'm *Matthew's* mother. And as Matthew's mother, I'm not going to let him be subjected to someone like you anymore. I will never have any respect for someone that throws their life away." She turns to Matthew, who's crying a little, too. "Come on. We're going home."

They start down the hallway but Matthew stays planted right beside me. His father yells, *"Come on!"* and then he reluctantly follows his parents, but before he leaves through the doors, he turns to me, giving me those puppy-dog eyes, and I know that this is it for us, whatever "us" was. He isn't going to be able to stand up to his parents, and why should he? It would ruin his life. I'm not worth it.

I walk down the hallway in the other direction, away from all of them, and then I just crumple down to the floor. I have no energy, not even to cry. Molly comes rushing down the hall and says she's been looking everywhere for me. I tell her I want to go home. She helps me up and then leads me out. We have to walk now. Matthew was our ride home, and now he's *gone.*

"It's over," I say disbelievingly. "It barely started and now it's over. Matthew's parents hate me, and now I've not only lost him as a friend but as a *boyfriend,* and I wanted to be with him so badly."

"You don't want to be with him if he has a family like that," Molly says, trying to comfort me, but I'm inconsolable. "Leo's an asshole, but we already knew that!"

I limp a little as we walk, my one-inch heels are hurting my ankles. As we walk past Leo's house, rage surges through me, like electricity, but there's nothing I can do about it. I'm just a stupid wimp.

When we finally get home, I can barely wait to get into bed. I stare at myself in the mirror, looking at my mascara that's smudged all over my face from crying, thinking about what Matthew's mother said. It's all too sad. My whole life. This is what I turned into. And just less than twenty-four hours ago, I was happier and feeling more positive than I have in so long.

I don't want to think anymore. I get into bed, and I can feel little kicks. I'm surprised all of this didn't kill the baby, I mean, talk about stress. I feel guilty for getting so stressed and even for getting involved with Matthew. What was I thinking? Of course his parents reacted that way. It would never have worked. It will never work with anyone again. Leo ruined me for anyone else.

At least I'll have Cheese Puff. Sighing, I touch my stomach and look out the window. I talk quietly now, much calmer.

"I'm sorry, my little Cheese Puff." That's all I can think of to say tonight. I'm too tired to even cry anymore, I just fall asleep, hoping tomorrow will be a better day.

⬦ ← red bell pepper   ♡ 22 weeks ♡

⬤ ╔═══════════╗
    ║ To-Do List ║
    ╚═══════════╝

Rent Estimations	- pick up paycheck on Friday from Roast and Drink
	- finish French essay
	- start English essay
(Aug.)	- study for science test on Friday
$1,000	- finish summary on history notes
	- do math homework pages 400-406
(Sep.)	- read English chapters 7-9
$1,000	

Bank Account =
$2,221.94

buy:
- bell peppers!!
- cheese puffs!!
- iron + magnesium + calcium supplements

☆ game night with
   Matthew tonight

(Oct.)
$1,000

- ask Janet to cover the
  spring dance
- assemble book/movie reviews
  for new section of the
  newspaper
- start story on the
  history of Redford

☆ browse used
  cribs (go to
  Goodwill?)

(Nov.)
$1,000

(Dec.)
$1,000
= $5,000
(rent till
the end of
the year
for an
apartment?)

♡ SPRING
   BREAK ♡

Girls	Boys
Rachel	Liam
Mavis	Chris
Tabitha	Oliver
Melanie	
Chrissy	
Charlotte	

☆ Matthew picking me
   up at 8:30pm

☆ think of more
   names

screw Leo
screw Matthew's parents
I'm done
I ruin everything

Chapter 19: Week Twenty-Three

"Your baby is as big as a grapefruit," I read online. My stomach has probably grown, but it looks the same to me. It's hard to tell day-by-day. At least I don't have to face the kids at school this week, because of spring break.

I'm in the car with Dianne and Molly. We're on our way to Disneyland! Dianne wanted to kick off spring break with something fun for us, and also to cheer me up. Last week, the morning after the awful dance, I told Dianne and Molly what happened and what Matthew's parents said to me. Molly knew about the fight at the dance, obviously, but she didn't know what his parents had said. They were both really upset, but Dianne said that one day, I'll find a guy who will really love not only me, but also the baby. That his whole family will love all of us, and it won't matter whether I have a baby already or not. I know she was trying to make me feel better, and I don't know if it will ever happen, but I sure hope so. Many tissues and hugs later, I've made it through the week and I guess I'm feeling a little better about things.

Anyway, we're almost at Disneyland. It's around two hours from Redford, so we've been in the car for a while. We've also had to stop for me to pee a couple times. I'm so hungry all the time now that we had to stop at a drive-thru to get me a burger and fries. Dianne and Molly decided to indulge, too, because Dianne says on a day like today, a Disneyland day, "nothing counts," you can eat whatever you want and just enjoy it all. I haven't been to Disneyland since I was ten, so I'm excited. I'm also determined to use it to take my mind off everything.

"Woo-hoo, Disneyland!" Molly whoops as we enter the parking garage. It's always so crowded, I can't believe it, we have to drive around the parking garage for like ten minutes to even get to a spot. I remember the long escalator ride down and then the wait for the tram to take us to the actual entrance to the park. It's the only time I don't mind waiting for things like this, because I know how much fun we're going to have. The only thing is, there are a lot of rides I won't be able to go on this time, because I'm pregnant. But it'll still be fun.

Thankfully, it's not too hot and the lines aren't too long. We go through the "It's A Small World" ride three times. It's always been my favorite one, it's so colorful and vivid and I love seeing all the different places in the world. The music almost makes me cry this time, I hope that Cheese Puff can hear it from the womb.

We walk through Cinderella's castle, then go on the teacups and the Dumbo flying ride, and then we do the Winnie the Pooh ride a few

163

times. I keep thinking about how amazing it'll be to bring Cheese Puff here one day.

Dianne gets us cotton candy, popcorn, hotdogs, and she buys us Minnie Mouse ears. She takes a million pictures, too. We all pretend we're sisters, because Dianne honestly looks young enough. The lines get longer as the day goes on, but we don't care. I just wish I could go on some of the rollercoasters, like Splash Mountain, it's another one of my favorite rides. I don't want to do anything to potentially hurt Cheese Puff, though, so I don't.

At around three, we begin to get tired, so we take a break on a bench. I sigh happily, looking at all the families walking by. Everyone has such bright, excited smiles on their faces. I see why they call it the happiest place in the world. I remember when I was ten and I came here with Mom and Dad and Josie. We had so much fun together. It makes me so sad to think I will never be able to come back here with Dad. I wonder if I'll ever come back with Mom and Josie. Maybe one day...with Cheese Puff, too. What a dream come true that would be.

Then something occurs to me. Will I ever even have the *money* to take Cheese Puff to Disneyland? I'll have to make sure I do, because I want Cheese Puff to one day have as much fun as I'm having right now.

At the end of the day, we go on the Ferris wheel. I love how you get such a great view of everything when you're so high up. The people look like ants and the bright lights and colors from the rides look so beautiful as it's getting dark, so they really show up. It's a perfect way to end the day.

On the car ride home, I just keep thanking Dianne over and over for taking us. Molly says she wishes she could live in Cinderella's castle. It was so much fun to go with my best friend, we've never done that before. We feel like little kids again.

I rest my head against my seat, tired out. Suddenly, I notice my phone ringing. It's Mom. I feel guilty but I shut the ringer and let it go to voicemail, not wanting to talk to her in front of Dianne and Molly. I don't listen to it until I get home and into bed.

-Voicemail- from 'Mom'

Hi Madison, it's Mom.......I miss you. I wanted to talk to you. I understand if you don't want to, but I would like to soon, if that's alright with you. I'm sorry, I've just been so incredibly busy, with work and all. I've reached an agreement with Leo's parents, and they will be depositing money on a monthly basis into an account we will set up that is for the baby, to be managed by you and me. It will cover things like healthcare costs for the baby, since I don't know if you've worked that out yet, you know, paying for a pediatrician and all. Anyway, all things considered, it's a generous offer and I really hope you'll accept it. Whether you do or not, this account will be set up and the baby can access it when she or he is eighteen. This is one of the things I would like to discuss with you. Please call me back when you can. Hope you're okay. Bye.

Wow. It really sounds like she's coming around, and I'm *so* happy, but I'm also scared to trust it. I worry that when we actually do talk or see each other, we'll start fighting again. The whole account for Cheese Puff and the Schmitzes being involved is too much for me to deal with right now. I guess they can do what they want because they're trying to be legal about the whole thing, but I'm still going to try to not use their money. It's *my* baby.

I feel the stress creeping back, but I don't want it to ruin the perfect day we had. I sigh, I just *really* wish I had someone that I could confide in. I can talk with Molly, but she doesn't get it, really. Dianne isn't my age, so it's hard sometimes, because while she did go through it, she isn't going through it *now*.

I remember the school counselor mentioning that they had teen mom support groups. At the time, I didn't think it was something I would need or want, but right now, I'm curious, so I look it up on the computer. I put "teen mom" into the search bar and a couple of things pop up. I walk over to my computer and search up "teen mom support." I'm surprised by how many links pop up. I click on one of them: "Teen Mom Support Group: TMSG."

The website shows that they have group meetings at the community center, it's just a mile away. They hold meetings on Mondays, Tuesdays, Thursdays, and weekends, from noon to three. Open to anyone, you can just walk in. This sounds almost too good to be true, but I'm definitely going to go.

<>

When I wake up the next morning, I hear the printer going nuts. Dianne must be printing out the manuscript of her book that they're considering turning into a movie ready for when she goes on her business trip later this week. I'm excited for her, and it'll also be fun for Molly and me to have the house to ourselves for a few days.

Before I leave for the support group, I take one hundred dollars that I've saved in tips and put it in my wallet. I'm planning to go get some more maternity clothes once the meeting is over. My stomach is definitely getting bigger, and I have no choice.

I drive to the community center where they have the meetings. It's a quaint house with old brick and lots of ivy on the walls. I remember taking a creative writing class here when I was ten. I remember the dark wood floors and all the different rooms. There's a smell to the wood that I don't remember from before, but it could just be because of the pregnancy, my sense of smell has gotten really strong.

I go into Room 108, which is where the website said to go. Three other girls are already there: one of them who's heavily pregnant and looks a bit older than me, another girl who looks even younger than I am, with a small pregnancy bump, and then a girl who looks pretty young, who doesn't seem to have any sort of bump. Her eyes look puffy, maybe she's been crying. But other than that, she's very pretty, with black hair and striking green eyes. She keeps biting her lip and fidgeting with her nails. None of them are talking to each other. They all stare at me as I enter, and I nervously take a seat on one of the black fold-up chairs. There's a white board in the middle of the room.

We sit there in silence, it's kind of awkward but we're all in our own little worlds, waiting. A woman who looks like she's about my mom's age walks in, she looks very put-together in contrast to the mess of teenagers in the room.

"Hello, everyone, and welcome. For those of you who haven't been here before, my name is Clarice. Everyone here should be either a teen mother or a soon-to-be teen mother." She looks at the clock. "We'll wait another few minutes and then get started."

In the next minute or so, four more girls enter. One is holding an actual newborn baby, who is sleeping, in her arms. I notice she doesn't sit down but stays standing and rocks slowly back and forth, I guess trying to keep the baby asleep. She has dark purple bags under her eyes, oh geez, I'm in for it.

But I truly can't believe how many other teen moms there are. I've never known another teen mom and I guess I just figured I never would.

"Alright, I think that might be everyone. Nice to see some familiar faces. Hello and welcome. As I say at every meeting: it would be most helpful for you to be able to come consistently every week. However, sometimes other things get in the way, and that's okay, just come when you can, you will always be welcome. For those of you who have never been here before, this is a non-judgemental room. A safe place to talk about everything and anything, to help one another. Sharing feelings and experiences is so important in getting through this. I am here to facilitate but I want you to all feel free to talk to each other, and we will have time at the end for free chat. Let's start by telling each other a little bit about ourselves, how far along in our pregnancies we are, and how we're feeling today."

I wait to see who will go first. It sure isn't going to be me. Then the girl with the newborn baby says, really quietly. "Hi everybody, my name's Sara. I'm eighteen. I used to go to Redford High but now I'm doing online school so I can be home with my baby. This is Winter and she's three months old."

"Thank you, Sara," Clarice says kindly. She asks who wants to go next, and then she waits, smiling.

The heavily pregnant girl clears her throat and shyly says, "Hi. My name's Eleanor, but you can call me Ellie for short...I'm nine months pregnant and due in a week...I'm fifteen years old...and I'm, uh, living with my dad now. My mom was really angry and she won't speak to me. My dad is also angry but he's letting me live with him. My school counselor told me to come here."

Clarice nods and smiles kindly. My heart beats faster and I force myself to speak. "Hi, I'm Madison, and I'm six months pregnant. I'm sixteen, and I go to Redford High and I work at a coffee shop to make money for the baby. I'm living with my best friend and her mom, because my mom still needs time to think things through. She's been really angry. My best friend and her mom have been really good to me, her mom was also a teen mom." It all comes out so fast. I take a breath. "So, yeah. I'm here because I just wanted to talk to people that are going through it, too." *There.* I sit down on my chair, relieved that *that's* over.

A few more people share their stories and then the pretty, black-haired girl speaks. "Hi," she says quietly. "I'm Alexa, and I just found out I'm pregnant, and I think I'm three months along, no idea yet, and I'm only *fourteen,* and, well...I'm really scared. I haven't told a soul yet, I Googled this group on the computer because I really need to talk to someone and...and figure out what to do..." She trails off and bursts into tears, and Clarice gets up and hands her a tissue and pats her back. It makes me want to cry too, I feel so bad for her, and I know exactly how she feels. Wow, she's even younger than me, though. That's insane.

I love this group. I wish I'd been doing it the whole time. It's such a relief to hear other people's stories and to know I'm not alone. We are all so different, but we have one huge thing in common.

"Okay, I think that's everyone." Clarice says, "Now, it's time for an exercise. When I point to you, I want you to name one problem associated with teenage pregnancy, and then I will write it on the board. Then we will discuss."

She points to Eleanor. "Um...money," she says quietly. Everyone nods and Clarice writes it down.

Then, she points to me. There are so many that my mind can't land on a single one. "School," I finally say.

She points to Sara, who says, "Living arrangements."

After everyone gives a problem, Clarice talks about each one. We all pipe in at different times. At one point, Clarice asks me to talk about what it's like working at the coffee shop.

I tell them about how much I make, and about the numbers I've been adding up, and I say that I'm trying to find a higher-paying job where I can also bring the baby with me once it's born. It feels both good and weird to be talking about all this personal stuff with strangers.

Clarice also talks about school and how even though teen pregnancy is rare, most schools will make arrangements for babies to be allowed on campus. She also says that depending on our budget, we might be able to pay for daycare, which can be really inexpensive. There's also online school, but I don't think I'll want to do that.

At the end of the meeting, Clarice hands out a list of names of types of jobs that pay $10 or more and that have options of being able to have your baby with you at work. The meeting just flew by, and I can't believe how helpful it was. I really want to be able to come every week, but I know I'll have school and work, and homework on the weekends.

Before I leave, I see Alexa standing by the doorway, blowing her nose. I can relate to the crying all the time, and I feel sorry for her. I go up to her and ask her if she's okay. She shakes her head, crying and blowing her nose. I ask her if she wants to talk and she nods, so I take her outside to a bench and we sit.

She takes a deep breath and then lets it all out, saying, "I just have *so* many questions, I don't even know if I should keep it or not, I think maybe I should just get an abortion, but I don't know if I can, and I'm just scared to death. I have to tell my parents *and* my boyfriend that I'm...pregnant with his *baby.*" She starts crying harder again, heaving sobs, blowing her nose.

I put my arm around her. "I know exactly how you feel right now. I went through the same thing at the beginning." Weirdly, I feel a lot like Dianne right now.

"Sorry for pouring all this out onto you, I haven't been able to talk to anyone."

"It's okay. You can talk to me."

"Thanks." She slowly stops crying, and we just sit together, not speaking for a few minutes. Then she asks, "What did the father of yours say when you told him?"

"He...he left me. We broke up and he's not...he's not involved." I pause. "Wait, who's the father of your baby? Maybe I know him?" I'm curious, because she's only fourteen. That's young. Like, really young. I know I was fourteen when I met Leo, but I never thought of sex or anything like that until I was fifteen.

"I'm in eighth grade, but he's a year older, at the high school. His name's Danny. I didn't know that this would happen, I didn't even *know* what I was doing. Trust me, I know how young I am...oh God, my dad is going to be *so* angry, I'm so scared..." She puts her face into her hands, starting to cry again. Her whole body shudders with sobs.

"I totally get it. My mom was really angry when I told her. It's been so hard, I'm not going to lie to you. But you have to decide what *you* want. Have you been to Planned Parenthood? There's someone there who helped me make a decision. At one point, I thought of going with adoption because I didn't want to have an abortion."

She shakes her head. "I haven't been. I've been scared to do anything, that's why I came to this group, it seemed like the safest thing to do. It might sound crazy, but...I really don't want to have an abortion and I don't want to give this baby up for adoption. I've always wanted to have a baby, just not this way, not now. I'm only *fourteen!*"

I feel like she's telling me the thoughts I had when *I* got pregnant. We're so similar, I can't believe it.

"You're not going to believe this, but I felt exactly the same way. That's why I'm having the baby. And if that's what you choose to do, I can help you through it. This group will help us through it, too, Clarice seems amazing." I pause. "I'm sure everyone in the group feels like this, like we don't feel ready for this. I really don't think we will *ever* feel ready, but you know what? I think it'll be worth it in the end. You need to come up with a plan, though. I would really recommend going to the counselor at Planned Parenthood just to see what she says."

Alexa sort of laughs since the first time I've seen her. "Why do I need a counselor when I've got you?"

I laugh a little, too, and I give her a hug. "It's going to be okay."

Alexa nods, with tears in the corners of her eyes. I don't think I've ever felt so empowered or wise before.

<>

It's Thursday, and Dianne left for Los Angeles. She flew, even though it's less than an hour plane ride. We laughed about the fact that it took longer to drive to Disneyland. We offered to drive her to the airport, but she said she wanted to just chill and that she preferred to take an Uber. Now, Molly and I have the house to ourselves and we're excited. But it's also weird. Is this what it's going to be like when I move out? Having a whole place to myself? Well, the baby will be there, but still...no adults. *Except me. I will have to be the adult.* I guess this is good practice.

"I hate that spring break is already half over," Molly groans.

"I know," I say, and then I smile. "Come see the maternity clothes I bought."

I show her my three new maternity shirts and three new pairs of pants with elastic waistbands. I spent eighty dollars on everything, which was actually a good deal but I hate spending money on anything right now. I just think of it in terms of how many work hours it took to earn the money and how it goes so quickly.

"They're so cute! Mads, you'll look great!" Molly says. Thank God for Molly.

"I got them at this really cute place called 'Mama's Clothes.' The owner was very friendly and she helped me choose everything. I didn't tell her my age, and even though I'm sure she could tell, she was really nice to me."

"That's good."

"Speaking of ages, can you believe you're going to be sixteen next week? I'm so excited for you to get your driver's license!"

I've been looking everywhere for a present for Molly. I found the perfect card, and the perfect present, too. It's a new art set, and a cool funky shirt that I know she'll love. Her birthday is on March 26th, and she's signed up for her driving test that day.

"I know, I hope I pass! By the way, Mom is planning to throw me a Sweet 16. A pretty small one, but I'm inviting Cheryl and some other girls, and I think we're going to 'Salsa' for dinner, and then coming back here and having a sleepover in the living room. The living room will be turned into a slumber party!"

"Oh, nice. My family used to go there all the time to celebrate birthdays."

"Do you not like it? It's really good food."

"No, I do. It *is* good. Sorry, I was just thinking of something else."

It's Molly's favorite Mexican restaurant, and I don't want to say anything but it was Dad's favorite, too. It was actually where we were supposed to go for his birthday dinner. Molly doesn't know, and I don't want to tell her, because I don't want to ruin the mood, she's so excited.

"I can't wait to finally be able to drive!" she squeals. I'm so glad she changed the subject.

"Hey, speaking of which, do you want to go for a drive? I mean, there's not much else to do, since your mom banned parties," I say, and she laughs. "Besides, it'll be good, I can show you what they told me to do, so you can be prepared."

I grab the keys and we get into my car, which is parked on the street. "This is such a cute car, and it was your mom's, right?" she asks, and I nod. "I'm going to have to use my mom's, I don't think she's getting me one. Maybe once her book gets turned into a movie."

We laugh, and after I show Molly what they're going to ask on her driver's test, I tell her about how Leo's parents are going to want to help and be involved and that my mom is working out the details with them. Molly is surprised I am accepting the help as she knows I didn't want to. I try to explain to her that I'm worried about money and not being able to cover all my expenses. I tell her about the support group, how I've learned from it that I need to be responsible and do whatever it takes to take care of Cheese Puff, and she tells me to just do whatever I think is best.

I pull up to a red light, tapping my fingers on the steering wheel and looking around. For once, the sky is clear, not a cloud in sight, and the trees seem even taller than they usually are, they look almost happy as their leaves sway in the mild wind. We're on the street where the pharmacy is, where I got the pregnancy test. It feels like a lifetime ago. And now that I'm obviously keeping Cheese Puff, I wish I would have saved the pregnancy test instead of throwing it away. It would be a cool thing to show Cheese Puff one day.

"Do you think we'll ever move out of Redford?" Molly asks suddenly.

"I don't know," I say. "I mean, *I'm* not."

"Yes, you are. You're going to Boston for Harvard!"

"That's saying I'll get in."

"Still."

I sigh. "I don't think so. I mean, if I get in, I'll obviously be there for school, but after I'm done, I'll probably come home and look for a job *here.*"

"Hate to say it, but I don't think there will be many exciting journalistic jobs here in Redford. Nothing interesting ever happens. Except you getting pregnant."

We laugh. The laughter feels so good. It makes me feel suddenly optimistic. It's so weird, the rollercoaster of emotions that go along with being pregnant. Do all pregnant women feel this way, or just the teenage ones?

Speaking of teen mothers, I got a text from Alexa yesterday just saying hi and thanking me for talking. She's still scared, she doesn't know how she's going to tell her family or Danny, but she told me that she went to Planned Parenthood and, like me, once she saw that heartbeat, she knows she wants to keep her baby. She even went to an adoption agency yesterday, because that was the next thing she was considering, but she told me that she didn't want to do it. She told me that she's due in late September or early October. She has no idea what she's going to do, but she told me she got a job and she's going to figure out how to tell everyone soon. I want to plan to hang out with her. It would be amazing to have a friend who was going through the same thing at the same time. Molly is amazing, though, even though she's not going through it. I don't know how I would be getting through it if I didn't have her.

"Getting through *it.*" It's what everyone says. But what is *it* exactly that we're all getting through? What is that mysterious "it?"

I guess it's just all the hardships that come with being a teen mom. Almost everything in our lives has to change, instantly. I've had to leave behind almost everything that I knew before, and now I have to work a million times harder for everything I need and want, while facing many, *many* problems along the way. Kind of like drilling through a really hard rock. And once we all get through the rock, then maybe, just *maybe,* we get through to the other side, the side where there's hopefully, *finally* some sort of serenity.

All I can do is hope that I get through to that side one day.

23 weeks

❀ Spring
    break ❀

To-Do List

- pick up paycheck on Friday from Roast and Drink

☆ D I S N E Y L A N D ☆

Average
Food Costs
(per week):
$100
↓
$400/
month
+ $200/
month
(baby costs?)
$600
+$1,000
⬤ (rent)
= $1,600/
month
= expenses

360
x 4
1,440
not
enough

2 jobs??

$ $ $

- go to teen mom support
  group (Mondays, Tuesdays,
       Thursdays, + weekends
       from 12-3pm)
- go maternity clothes shopping!!
- call Alexa soon
- look into relaxation
  techniques
- go to Babies R' Us again?
- do research on parenting

☆ work on budget

☆ wrap Molly's birthday present

Cheese Puff

buy:
- new notebooks
- cheese puffs
- look into car
  seats?

☆ find lotion
   for stretch
   marks?
☆ keep eating
   healthy +
   get more
   exercise!!

☆ look into
   birthing classes

* figure out
  baby names
  other than
  "Cheese Puff"!!

173

Chapter 20: Week Twenty-Four

"Your baby is as big as a pomegranate," I read. I never eat those, but I've seen them and they are pretty big! And, according to this website, Cheese Puff is rapidly putting on more weight. *Join the club, Cheese Puff.*

I've been playing *Twinkle, Twinkle, Little Star* and other songs on my phone and holding it next to my stomach. I know Cheese Puff can hear my voice, and I figured that when I sing songs when she or he is actually out of my stomach and into the world, she or he will recognize them and maybe they will remind her or him of being warm and safe in my tummy.

That's one of the fun parts of being pregnant. One of the not-so-fun parts is what's been happening lately, which is that I've been *so* constipated. I read that it's another pregnancy symptom. Literally every single thing that could be wrong with your body is a pregnancy symptom.

Right now, I'm in the car with Dianne and Molly, on the way to Dr. Lippincott's office. Dianne's trip to Los Angeles flew by, and Molly and I had fun at home alone, but we were really happy when Dianne got back. There's something scary about being in a house at night without an adult there, and I'm worried about how it's going to be once I move out, completely alone except for my baby, which honestly makes it more scary, because then I'll have to take care of someone else, too.

Anyway, we picked up Josie to come with us today, because I'm getting a 3D version of the ultrasound, which means I'll be able to see the baby's face up close, and Josie will think it's awesome.

She takes my hand and says, "Thank you for letting me come. I'm so, so, so excited to see the baby!"

"Of course," I say, smiling. "I love it when you come with us."

Just before we drive off, Mom rushes out of the house and gets in the car. "Mom, what are you doing?"

She smiles, almost shyly. "I thought I'd come, too. I took my shift off today."

I'm *so* surprised, but I'm also very happy. Dianne and Mom exchange a glance, and then I realize it was a plan. I wonder who arranged it. I bet it was Dianne, to get us to talk.

"Don't be upset with us," Dianne says, smiling. "This will be great."

"I'm not upset, are you serious? I'm so...I'm so happy!" I immediately start crying a little, I'm just so surprised and excited that she's coming. She takes my hand and smiles at me. She looks like she's getting tears in her eyes, too. This is a really big deal.

At Dr. Lippincott's office, we take up almost the whole waiting room. It's amazing to be here with everybody and we get called in pretty quickly. They do the usual weighing me, taking my blood pressure, and I leave a urine sample. Dr. Lippincott comes in and I introduce her to my mom. I can tell Dr. Lippincott is really happy to see my mom here.

Dr. Lippincott says, "Well, no sugar in your urine, and your weight is normal, it's good to see you putting on some more pounds. Now, this is going to be a 3D ultrasound today. Kind of similar to what you had for your anatomy scan. We should get some good images of the little one." She turns to Mom, smiling. "Mrs. Davis, why don't you come have a seat beside Madison and you can get a good look at your little grandchild."

She moves a stool next to the exam table, beside me, and my mom comes to sit down, looking a little nervous. I think she was surprised to hear the word "grandchild." This might be the first time she's heard that.

Dr. Lippincott rubs the wand on my stomach, and instead of seeing the black-and-white image like always, it's a warm orange-brown tone, and everything looks like its actual shape. It's so cool, and I just love seeing all the different images of the baby.

Mom takes my hand and stares at the screen. She looks fascinated to see the baby. *Her grandchild.* She keeps squeezing my hand. Josie is smiling from ear to ear, and she keeps giggling when Dr. Lippincott points out the different body parts. At one point, it looks like Cheese Puff is waving. We get to see a nice close up of the face, and Dr. Lippincott asks me if I want a picture. I nod, and then she asks my mom if she would like one too, and Mom smiles and says, "Yes, I would. Thank you."

Dr. Lippincott prints them out and hands them to us. Mom stares at hers and she looks like she's about to cry. I'm worried she's about to get upset or angry again, as she realizes the situation all over again: I'm way too young to be having a baby, and she's going to be a grandmother at age forty! But she doesn't get upset, she just quietly tucks the picture into her wallet.

Dr. Lippincott says everything looks good and that the baby and I look healthy. Then she says, "After the twenty-eight week appointment, I start seeing you every two weeks, and once you're thirty-six weeks, we see each other *every* week. And then, well, we all hope you go full term. Lots of teen moms are at risk for a preterm birth, and we want to try to avoid that."

I tell her that I had to buy new shoes because my feet have been swelling, and she says that's normal. Then she says that my sugar levels are okay, but she'd still like to see me eating less sugar, as we want to avoid gestational diabetes, and I promise to stop eating so much of it, because now I'm pretty scared. I haven't been drinking coffee, so to get my energy up, I'll eat a chocolate bar, which I know is bad, but I'll try to stop. I tell her that my main snack is cheese puffs and that I've been calling the baby "Cheese Puff," and everyone laughs. She says that's okay, but to maybe try eating some *real* cheese sometimes instead. That the calcium is good for both me and the baby.

It's kind of weird to have Mom in here with me, listening to everything I'm saying. We're discussing such...intimate medical details about my pregnancy, and Mom hasn't been here for any of it until now. I keep looking over at her, and she has a strange look on her face, not really angry, but kind of uncomfortable. I wonder if this is all too much for her and if this is the last time she will want to come to an appointment or if she'll want to go back to not seeing each other at all again. It makes me sad to think of that so I try to just be happy that she's here right now.

"Also, it's time to start thinking about pediatricians and health insurance," Dr. Lippincott says. "I'm happy to give you some recommendations."

Now I'm nervous, because I realize I hadn't really thought about these things. Mom says that Leo's parents want to pay for the health insurance, but we haven't discussed the details and I don't want to talk about it right now, in front of everyone.

Thankfully, Dr. Lippincott switches to another topic. "Also, I'll be asking you to count your kicks once you enter the seventh month, so that's starting next week, alright? I'll send you home with a print-out paper on how to do that," she says. "Any other questions? Anyone?"

I shake my head, but then to my surprise, Mom says, "I have a question. Do you know if it's a boy or girl?"

Dr. Lippincott smiles and looks at me and says, "I do, actually. But Madison has asked to not reveal the gender, she wants to wait until the baby is born."

Mom nods and gives me a tight-lipped look that's hard to read. I can't tell if she approves or disapproves of my decision to be surprised. "Okay, then, see you at your twenty-eight week appointment! So nice to see everybody!"

I'm so lucky to have Dr. Lippincott as my doctor. She's so cheerful and calm and she doesn't make me feel like I'm making a mistake having the baby. It really helped make things easier today, with Mom here.

Everyone is pretty quiet on the car ride home. Mom sits in the front with Dianne and they talk quietly to each other, but the music is loud and I can't really hear what they're saying. Just as we drop Mom and Josie off, Mom hands me a wrapped package. "Open it when you're home."

"Oh, okay, thanks," I say, wanting to give her a hug and thank her for coming, but she gets out of the car quickly. Josie gives me a hug and says it was one of her "best days ever." She's so sweet, it breaks my heart. Mom waves and calls out to Dianne to thank her for driving and before I know it, she and Josie are gone.

I can't wait to open the package, and I do it as soon as I get home and into my room. "For Madison and the baby. Love, Mom," the little note reads, and inside is a small, square pastel yellow picture frame. Happy tears spring to my eyes. I can't believe she did this. That, and the fact that she came today means she's going to come around, I think, it's just taking some time, that's all. But this is more than I can even ask for right now. The ultrasound picture fits the frame perfectly and I place it on my night table so I can look at it before I go to bed every night. This has been one of the best days ever, just like Josie said.

I take a nap, and when I wake up I feel like I've been asleep for days. I must have been really tired. The first thing I see when I open my eyes is the picture of Cheese Puff in the yellow frame and I remember everything that happened earlier today and it makes me smile.

I realize I'm starving and I haven't eaten since this morning. I'm going to try to eat less sugar and more healthy food, as Dr. Lippincott suggested. Molly and Dianne have gone out somewhere, but Dianne left me some leftover chicken, rice, and vegetables to heat up. While I'm eating, my phone rings and the Caller ID says it's Matthew! I go to answer, but it disconnects and then a text appears from him.

Matthew: Are you there? If so, please meet me at Stonewood Park in 10 minutes.

Oh wow, what could this be? *Maybe he's changed his mind and he's going to not listen to his parents?* I text him back to say I'll be there and then I wolf down the rest of my food, put on my new maternity jeans, one of my cuter maternity shirts, grab my coat, and run out to meet him.

I get to the park, and it's completely quiet. No one's here except for a woman running around the track. I see Matthew behind the tennis courts, he starts walking over to me and we meet up and go to sit on a bench. It's cold out and I wish we had a blanket.

"I'm sorry. I wanted to say that for the last couple of weeks, but my parents grounded me and took away my phone. It's been killing me that I couldn't talk to you."

I look down. "It's been really hard on me, too. I missed you so much and I just wanted to talk to you, but I thought maybe you...I don't know, hated me."

"Madison, no, are you crazy? I could never hate you. I wanted to be with you. I think you're amazing. I'm sorry for all the things my mom said to you. My parents are just so...traditional and strict, and I would never be able to go behind their backs or lie to them. I hope you understand."

I nod and start crying. *What else is new?* I just can't believe how sweet he is, he waited until his being grounded was finished and then he came straight to tell me this. I wish Leo was half as good a person as Matthew is.

Matthew puts his arm around me. "It kills me when you cry." He sighs. "Madison, I wish things were different, but they can't be. Not now, anyway. I just wanted to make sure you knew how much I care about you, and how much I would *want* to help you if I could," he says.

I manage to stop crying and say, "I care about you, too. I mean, just when I was realizing my feelings for you, *this* had to happen."

"I know." He shakes his head. "It's the worst. But maybe it won't be like this forever. Maybe my parents will come around one day, or when we're eighteen and don't have to worry about what our parents think...sorry, that was a stupid thing to say."

"Don't worry about it."

"But I do worry about you. I want you to be okay."

"I *am* okay. And I feel better now that I've seen you and you told me all this."

He pulls me to him and we lock into a kiss. A long kiss that makes my worries float away, into the clouds. I know that this can't happen for us, not now anyway, but I just wish I could stay like this forever.

I eventually pull away because I don't want to get sucked into this again only to have it be taken away, and I know this will be our last kiss for a while, if not forever.

He strokes my cheek. "Maybe one day, okay?"

I nod sadly. I wonder if we really will be together one day, but honestly, I don't know if I'll want to be with a guy who has a family like that. They should have let him keep working at the coffee shop, at least. I'll miss that so much, and him making the latte swirls for me.

Is this what's going to happen to me every time I try to be with someone?

I always dreamed of marrying someone someday, having a little family together, being with someone who made me feel not only loved, but respected. With Leo, it was a stupid high school romance, but now that I'm having a baby, I'm not going to waste my time with another pointless relationship. No, now I want a *real* relationship, one that isn't based on whether or not I'm going to have sex with him. I want someone to look at me someday and think of me as beautiful in every way. That now includes the me that will already have a baby. I want to be with someone who can accept all of it and actually *want* to be with me and my child. To accept my situation and not have to worry about what their parents think, to accept the whole package.

But most importantly, I want to feel like I can be myself with that someone. I want to feel like *me*. I want to feel completely comfortable and unconditionally loved around that person, that mysterious guy who right now is just a dream I have.

I just hope that I actually get to find that person for real one day.

<>

The next day at school, I get called to the office during my free period. Everyone turned to look at me when the librarian called out my name. The usual whispering and laughter took place as I walked across the room. It happens everywhere, all the time, at school now. I hate it, but I've gotten used to it, so it doesn't upset me as much as it used to.

Principal Barnes is at the front desk when I get to the office, and is actually nice to me and asks me how I'm doing. Whenever anyone is kind to me, it makes me want to cry. She tells me that Mrs. Sherman wants to talk to me about something, so I go to her office.

She smiles brightly when I come in and she tells me to sit down and asks me if I want a glass of water, telling me that I should always remember to stay hydrated when pregnant. "I wanted to check in with you and see how you're doing, and also to let you know about an event that is taking place in town that you might be interested in," she says. "It's a focus group for pregnant women and it pays two hundred dollars for you to give your opinion on certain baby products. This isn't that common an event, so I think it would probably be worthwhile for you to register. It's next Tuesday at six p.m." She hands me a piece of paper with all the information.

Wow. Two hundred dollars? I could really, really use that. The only problem is that it's on Molly's birthday and that's right around when her party is starting. I don't think dinner starts till eight, though, so maybe I could do both? I want to make this work.

I thank Mrs. Sherman and tell her I will definitely do it. I ask her if I can come back to talk another time, as I have a lot of studying to do. She's really sweet and she says her door is always open.

Back in the library, I look at the piece of paper. Tuesday at six, in a building pretty close to where the Mexican restaurant for Molly's birthday will be. I make a note on my To-Do list. I will call after school to register. I hope Molly won't be upset that it might overlap a little with her party. I really need the money. I remember she told me everyone was meeting at the restaurant at eight, so that should still give me enough time to get there, if the focus group starts right at six.

At lunch, I decide to tell Molly about it. She thinks it sounds great and she's excited for me that I will make so much money in such a short amount of time. Until I tell her when it is.

"This is the only problem," I say uneasily. "It's the night of your birthday party, but before you say anything, I'll be back in time, I promise. The focus group is at six and I'll either be back at the house to leave with you guys for the dinner, or I can meet you all at the restaurant."

I can see she's a little worried I will be late. But she just says, "It's okay, I understand, you need the money. It's more important than a silly Sweet 16 party."

I can tell she's trying to sound like she doesn't care, but she doesn't sound happy. I'm kind of torn about what to do, but I really do need the money and I will just have to make it work.

After school, I have my shift at Roast and Drink and Johnny tells me he needs to talk to me. I'm worried he's going to fire me, and for a second I think it's because I still can't make good latte swirls, especially now that Matthew is gone. But he just wants to know if I'll continue to work even when I'm more pregnant and then after having the baby. He says, "I'm legally required to give you a bit of maternity leave, but I was just wondering about your plan."

"Oh. Well, I'm due early July, so I'll probably stop working around the end of June. But I need to be honest with you. I really like working here, but after my baby is born, I'm probably going to need to look for a job that pays better, one that I can also bring my baby to. I'm sorry."

He nods. "Yeah, I had a feeling that might be the case. Well, you'll let me know. And you need to give me two weeks notice, okay?"

I nod, feeling a little disappointed. Part of me was hoping that he'd offer me a raise, because it would make everything so much easier. But he didn't, and I know I have to really look for more opportunities to make money. If I had it my way, I wouldn't have to use any of the money I'm supposed to be getting from Leo's parents, but now I'll probably have to.

When I get home after work, Molly and Dianne are talking about Molly's party. Molly says she wants to get red balloons, because she thinks it will go along with the theme of Mexican food, and red is the color of salsa. She's so excited and I can tell it'll be a really big deal if I'm not there on time. Why does this have to be happening on the same night?

The night before Molly's birthday, I stay up late with Dianne and help her hang up party decorations. We are doing a Mexican theme at home with red streamers and balloons and then bringing the balloons to the restaurant. Dianne is upset that I'm staying up late but I really want to help. Dianne tells me Molly told her about the focus group and that she understands I have to do it, and she thinks it's great that Mrs. Sherman told me about it. I tell her I'm worried I'll be late, and she says Molly will understand. I'm not so sure she's right, but I smile and tell her that I hope so.

In the morning, I wake up to the sound of Molly giggling excitedly when she sees the decorations. I come into the kitchen and Dianne is serving up pancakes. She puts a candle in Molly's and we sing happy birthday to her and she makes her first wish of the day and blows out the candles. She thanks her mom for the decorations.

"Madison helped," Dianne mentions.

"Oh, that's so sweet! When did you do it? You must have been up late! Thanks, Maddie!" Then she says excitedly, "I can't believe I'm going to get my license today!"

"Yes! Very exciting! The question is, will I ever sleep again?" We all laugh. Dianne's cell phone timer goes off and she goes to shut it off. "Seven-eighteen a.m. on March 26th! The exact time you were born! I can't believe my little baby is already sixteen!" She goes to hug and kiss Molly. Then, to me, she says, "You'll see how fast the time goes by, Madison. Your little Cheese Puff will be sixteen before you can blink! It's crazy!"

Right now, it feels unimaginable to me to have a teenager. I'm not even ready for a baby. I'll be hardly thirty when Cheese Puff is my age! It just feels very far off in the distance, and I'm glad I don't have to think about it yet.

On the way to school, Molly tells me her appointment at the DMV is at four, so she should be home by around five or six and she'll then be getting ready for her party. I have to leave to be at the focus group by five-thirty. I already feel guilty about not really being able to get ready for her party together.

After school, I get some studying done and then I start to get ready for the focus group, trying to look really nice so I can go straight to the party afterwards. Suddenly, I get a text from Molly.

Molly: I GOT MY LICENSE!! Be home in a few :)

It really sucks, but I can't even wait for her to get home to congratulate her because I have to leave for the focus group. I send her a really nice text congratulating her and telling her that I can't wait to be her passenger.

Once I get to the building where the focus group will take place, I check in and I'm told to wait in a room with several other pregnant women. Of course, I'm the youngest one here and I'm getting stared at. I tap my foot anxiously as I wait. I keep checking my phone. It's nearly six-thirty. Why aren't they starting on time? This is really making me nervous. Wasn't it supposed to start at six? How long do these things take, anyway?

Finally, a woman dressed in a professional-looking suit comes into the room. "I'm so sorry, ladies. The presenters were late and the screen monitor has been going nuts all day. Come with me, please." She leads us down a hallway into a large room with a big conference table, and a big screen at the front. We all take seats.

"Thank you for coming," the woman. "Now, I'm going to hand out these sheets for you to fill out during the presentation. It's easy, just check off which products you would most likely buy, why you would buy them, and answer the other questions on there for each product we show."

Then they finally turn on the presentation. Hopefully, it'll go quickly. The presentation is actually interesting and informative and I'm really glad I came. I can't believe I'm getting paid so much money to do this. They show us a bunch of diapers and wipes and baby shampoo and cribs, all different brands. The only problem is that the monitors keep screwing up and it's taking much longer than it should have. It's almost eight o'clock now and I know I'm going to be late for the party. I can't believe this. But I can't leave or I won't get paid. I really don't know what to do. The restaurant is close-by and the presentation is almost over, so I'll just have to rush to get there and hope I'm not too late and that Molly is having such a good time, she won't be mad.

There are *three* more presentations, and I'm busy filling out the forms when I check my cell phone again and see it's almost *nine*. Oh no, I'm really screwed. This is going way later than I thought it would be. I feel horrible, this is so bad. I quickly text Molly and ask her if she's still at the restaurant, but she says that they're heading home already. I can tell from her cold-sounding text that she's mad.

After the presentations, everyone thanks us, and then we are each handed checks for $200. I don't even care about the money anymore, I'm so worried about how late I am and I'm sure Molly will hate me. *I* hate myself right now.

I rush home, the whole time thinking about how Mom told me to be careful and how I'm really being stupid, driving so fast. I feel like I've made one stupid decision after another. Doing that focus group was way more trouble than it was worth.

I pull up and park in Dianne's garage, scrambling inside, seeing everyone already surrounded around the cake, singing. I rush over, joining in the last phrase of the song.

"...happy birthday to you!" Everyone claps as Molly blows out the candles. I take a look around the room. Cheryl's here, and several other girls that Molly knows pretty well, most of them are from her art class at school.

When we are eating cake, Molly comes up to me and takes me

aside. "I can't believe you. I mean, you said the focus group wouldn't take long," she whispers, her voice filled with hurt.

"I'm so sorry, Molly, I really didn't know it would go so long, they started late, and...I know there's no excuse. I'm really, *really* sorry."

"I can't believe my own best friend wasn't at my Sweet 16. My *best friend!*" She stomps away and then goes back to talking and laughing with the other girls. I can't remember the last time I felt this bad.

After cake, we all sit together on the couch and watch a horror movie. Molly sits as far away from me as she can. We also paint each other's nails, and originally Molly had said she wanted to do mine and I would do hers, but I see now she's doing it with Cheryl instead. When the movie's over, everyone gets into their pajamas and gets ready for presents, and then we'll go to bed after that. I'm so exhausted, I just want to go straight to bed, but I summon up all the energy I have. There's no way I can let Molly know how tired I am. Not now, after I've already upset her so much.

Molly leaves to use the bathroom and I follow her in and shut the door. "Molly, I'm so, so sorry. It's not like I planned for this to happen. The focus group went way later than I thought it would. The waiting time was awful, their monitors were being screwy, it wasn't my fault. I couldn't leave or they wouldn't have given me the money, which was the whole point of doing it in the first place."

Molly glares at me. "So you're saying the money is more important than being at your best friend's birthday party? After all my Mom and I have done for you?"

"I need money for *after* I move out! I'm *so* grateful for everything you two are doing for me! You know that!"

"My mom has been supporting you so much. So have I. The least you could do is show up for my party! I was there for yours!"

"I know, I know, and I'm sorry! And I want to hear about your driver's license, too! How it went, and-"

"Don't even bother asking. I don't care anymore."

"Molly, you know I didn't do this on purpose! I would never! You'll see, I'll make it up to you. I got you a great present! I spent my money I'm saving for the baby on it! Please, can we just-"

"I'm so sorry if you had to spend money to buy your best friend a present. Maddie, I don't care about a present. I wanted your *presence*. But you couldn't give me that. Sure, the other girls are great, but *you* are my best friend, and *you* couldn't even come? I had to share the salsa and chips with *Gwendolyn*! I wanted to share them with *you!*" she says, starting to cry. Then she tries to compose herself. "I want to have a good rest of my birthday party, so I'm going to forget this for now, but if you want to keep on being my best friend, you are going to have to seriously take a look at where your priorities lie."

She storms out of the bathroom, forcing a smile on her face. Someone asks her what's wrong, I guess they heard us. Dianne comes out from the kitchen and tries to give me a reassuring look, but I know she's probably disappointed in me, too. I'm so ashamed.

We sit on pillows on the floor while Molly opens her presents. It's really uncomfortable for me to be sitting like this because of my stomach, but I don't dare complain or move. Molly hardly acknowledges my present, which is a cool shirt and also an art set. I've never felt more horrible in my life. I feel so guilty. Have we ever even fought before? Maybe over little things, but nothing like this. I wish I could make Molly forgive me, but the saddest part is that *I* wouldn't even want to forgive myself if I was her.

I'm fighting to keep my eyes open and I feel like it will never be time to go to bed, but finally, Dianne comes into the room and says it's getting late. We all get in our sleeping bags, and I realize I'm going to be totally uncomfortable. As if reading my mind, Dianne comes over with an extra thick blanket while the others are busy, and she helps me put it under the sleeping bag so I have a bit more padding. I feel so disgusting and awkward, like I need this weird special treatment. Tears clog my eyes and throat.

As everyone is falling asleep, I feel like a total outsider. I really don't belong here, at a Sweet 16, with teenage girls talking about hair and makeup and boys and which nail polish color is the prettiest. No one has even asked me about the pregnancy, and I'm guessing it's because Molly told them not to. They've been nice enough to me, but it really hits me that I don't fit in with these girls anymore. No one wants a pregnant teenager at a slumber party.

I want to sneak into my room and spray some of Dad's shaving cream on my wrist. I can't do it, or people will ask what I'm doing and then they will smell it. I need it so badly right now, though.

Suddenly something occurs to me: I'm actually glad I didn't go to the restaurant. I hadn't really let myself think about it before, but it would have been so hard to be there. *The same restaurant we were supposed to go to the night my dad died in the car accident.* Even though I don't really know whether to believe he's "up there" or wherever, there is a part of me that thinks that it's totally fate that I did the focus group. It's almost better that I wasn't there at the party. I might have started crying, or who knows? I could've ruined Molly's party even more than I did by not going at all. As bad as it is, I feel slightly better thinking about this as I finally fall asleep.

184

☆   ☆   24 weeks   ☆   ☆

● To-Do List
♡♡ ♡ ♡♡

Budget (per month)	-pick up paycheck on Friday from Roast and Drink
Food = $300	-appointment with Dr. Lippincott today! pick Josie up!
Baby = $200	* next appointment: Sunday April 14th 5pm
Other = $100	* eat less sugar!!
+ Rent (estimation = $1,000)	* eat more calcium ☆ look into pediatricians/
	* start counting health insurance
	the kicks next week!! plans
$1,600/ month	♡ ♡ ♡ ☆ seriously work on
TOTAL	budget!!!!
$400/ week	Spring break = over
	BACK TO SCHOOL... buy:
●	-history notes due Monday -cheese puffs!
make $80 each day?	-finish science lab sheet - REAL cheese
	- math problems #30-50 page 410 - new science
NEED A	- English summary chart due Friday notebook
$20/hour job (impossible)	- memorize new French verbs -paper
	- write editorial on how more - pencils
	books should be added to student - CRIB!
	library
	- edit stories from "features" writer
$	- SEND FINAL DRAFT OF NEWSPAPER
$	TO BE PRINTED
$	* Molly's birthday!!!
$	☆ focus group for *
	pregnant women
	Tuesday at 6pm
	☆ BE THERE ON TIME apologize
	FOR MOLLY'S SWEET 16!! to Molly!!
●	

Chapter 21: Week Twenty-Five

"Your baby is as big as an eggplant," I read on my phone. Wow. For some reason, after all the fruits and vegetables it's been compared to, this one seems really big! It's Tuesday, I've had a packed day at school today, I have a lot of homework to finish later, and I'm rushing to get to work all at the same time.

Molly has ignored me for a week. I can't bear it. Every time I enter a room, she leaves it. She leaves before me to go to school so we don't walk together anymore. She's been having her lunch with Cheryl and I don't feel comfortable with her ignoring me, so I don't join them, I've just been eating alone quickly and then going to the library.

On a happier note, I'm already at the beginning of my seventh month! My stomach is really getting bigger now. Even though I'm used to being pregnant now, I'm still amazed that all of this is developing and happening, that my body is just making this human being and I don't feel any of it going on.

The paper that Dr. Lippincott gave me about how to count Cheese Puff's kicks says that at this stage of the pregnancy, I should be feeling the baby move at least ten times per hour. So I'm supposed to count the kicks or movements every few hours to make sure it's happening. I've been doing it in class, at work, then in bed at the end of the day, pretty much everywhere, and Cheese Puff is always kicking. She or he does way more than ten kicks sometimes. So I guess that's a good sign.

I've been moisturizing a lot more, because my stomach is dry and itchy from all the stretching, and I don't like the stretch marks, I hope they go away. I'm still changing for gym in the bathroom, because even though everyone knows now, it's still embarrassing when they stare and start whispering. The other day, I was actually too upset to participate in gym because a few of the girls were making fun of me because my stomach was poking out under my gym shirt. The coach was nice about it, actually, and he told me to just wear my maternity clothes from now on. Dr. Lippincott gave me a note to give to the coach that says I can only do what feels comfortable at this point. I definitely can't do the jumping jacks anymore, my stomach bounces all over and people start laughing, it's so horrible.

After my shift at work, I go home and as I'm getting out of my car, I see Molly leaving, getting into Dianne's car. I can't believe I still haven't gone for a drive with her since she got her license. I wonder if we'll ever get back to being as close as we were before I made the huge mistake about her party. "Molly, wait!" I call out. "Please!"

"What do you want?" she huffs at me.

"I want to sincerely apologize," I walk over to her, and look her straight in the eye. "Please, Molly. I can't tell you how sorry I am. I've been trying, but I guess it's not enough. But people make mistakes. I didn't mean to do it, you know what happened. Please. I mean, you've been mad at me for a *week*. Isn't that enough? I miss you."

Molly stares straight ahead. "You really hurt my feelings. You...you were the main person I wanted there."

"I know. And you're my best friend, too. I've never had another friend as great as you. You've given me so much, and you've helped me with so much." My voice breaks. "I just had no idea the focus group would go as long as it did. I'm really sorry, I really needed the money, but I didn't mean to hurt you at all."

Now Molly is crying a little. "Okay. I believe you. And...I'm sorry, too. I know that you needed the money, and you're going through something really, really hard, and I'm sorry for getting so mad. I mean, we can go get Mexican food together any time."

I laugh and then we hug awkwardly, because I'm so big now, so it's hard to get close enough to hug. It makes us laugh again.

"Besides," she says, "I can't stand giving you the silent treatment when there are so many things I want to talk to you about. Seriously, I'm about to burst. And I really want to take you for a drive already!"

We laugh again and we decide we'll do something fun this weekend, with her driving. I'm so happy that we've *finally* resolved this. It's been really hard and stressful not getting along with her. And all I wanted was for everything to go back to being the way it was with her, and now hopefully it has.

<>

The next day at lunch, Molly and I are sitting in the cafeteria, and a group of girls, the ones that I recognize as the ones who were making fun of me in gym, walk up to us. "You're a sophomore, right?"

I nod and then look away. I know where this is going. "Can you guys just please leave me alone?" I ask.

Another girl smiles slyly. "Who's the father? Did he run off?"

"It's Leo," the other girl says, rolling her eyes. "Do you not pay attention to anything?"

"How do you know it was him? I mean, she could've just been sleeping around."

"Nah. It was Leo. Because they broke up, and it was clearly because of..." She gestures to my stomach. "...this."

"It's none of your business!" Molly yells. "Why do you have to be so mean?"

"Why'd your friend have to be such a slut?"

One of the girls in the group looks like she feels bad. She gives me a sort of apologetic look and then gestures for them to leave. They walk off, snickering, and talking loudly. "I bet she just had sex with him to keep him around."

"But he left anyway." They laugh loudly. Once they're finally gone, I let out a big exhale. I didn't even realize I was holding my breath. Then I glance over to where Leo and his soccer buddies sit. My heart falls through my rib cage and into my stomach. He looks so good, he always does. I hate myself for thinking this but I wish I was still with him. I really do. I'm so, *so* stupid. But I don't think it's the current him I want to be with; I want to be with the old Leo. If we were still together, I bet these girls wouldn't be making fun of me. They'd be scared to, if Leo was defending me.

"Madison," Molly says, noticing me staring. "You really need to stop thinking about him. It's not healthy."

"I know. I know. But I can't help it. He's the *father* of my *baby*," I say, my voice beginning to crack. Oh, no, I really don't want to cry right now.

Molly sees I'm about to cry, and she goes to sit in front of me to block my vision of Leo across the room. I feel like such an idiot, sitting at this cafeteria table with my growing stomach, with Leo laughing it up with his buddies while I'm being humiliated by everyone at school. I know this was my decision to keep Cheese Puff, but it's a *beautiful* thing to have a baby, why can't anyone else realize that? And this happened because Leo and I were *together.* It's not like it was all me!

Thankfully, the bell rings and we all go back to class. I try to focus on school, and there's so much work to do that I manage to forget about all of this for now.

After my awful day at school, I feel like I need a treat. I've been craving the fries from Home's Diner again, so I decide to go there after my shift at work. As I'm sitting in a booth, indulging in the fries, I hear someone call my name. *Oh no, what's this now?* I don't want to deal with anymore bullying today. But when I look up, I see that it's Billy. He was a really close friend of my dad's and I haven't seen him since just after the funeral. I used to see him all the time when Dad was alive. He's a contractor, so he knows how to build things, and he built me my first treehouse. I would force him to have tea parties with me and my dolls and he would play with me and Josie all the time. I called him "Lily" when I was really young, because I couldn't say the "B" sound.

He smiles and I wave, and he comes right over. "Oh, wow, Madison. You've really grown!" he says. "It's so nice to see you!"

I smile back. "Sit with me!"

He says he's just coming to get take-out, but he'll join me for a bit. He slides into the booth, grinning. "Best fries in town, right?"

I nod, so happy to see him. I offer him some fries and he takes one. "So, how have you been doing?" he asks.

"I'm...good. You?"

"Good, good." He hesitates for a second, and then he says softly, "It's been a really long time. I feel bad that we kind of lost touch. I think about you guys a lot. I can't believe it's been, what, three years?"

I nod. "It's crazy. It feels like it was just yesterday, but at the same time, it feels like it was centuries ago."

"You couldn't have put it better. But how are you guys? How's your mom?"

"She's...okay. We're doing better than when you last saw us."

I guess he hasn't noticed my stomach yet. I have a napkin on it and it's kind of hidden in the booth. I could probably get away with not telling him. But part of me wants to tell him because maybe he'll say something like what my father would have said. He's actually the closest person I ever knew to my father, other than my mother.

The waiter comes up and Billy asks if it's okay if he has his take-out order to dine-in instead. I'm so happy that he decided to join me. I feel so safe and comfortable to be with him in our little booth, looking out the window at the street and smelling all the amazing smells from the diner. I really love it here. This is turning out to not be such a bad day after all. I decide to tell him.

"Billy, you know, since you're here, I want to tell you something."

"Oh no, what?" he asks, frowning. "Is everything okay?"

My heart rate speeds up. "Yes, well, no. Well, yes. Okay, so, I'm..."

"What is it?" he asks, frowning again.

"This might seem...crazy, and so sudden to you, but, uh...I'm pregnant."

His mouth drops open and he immediately looks at my stomach. I take the napkin away and it shows everything. He looks totally shocked. "Wow," he says. "I don't even know what to say, I..."

"Yeah. Seven months along. My boyfriend and I...we broke up, though. But I'm managing okay, I'm staying in school. There's, well, a lot to tell you."

He looks so concerned, and there's also that same look of pure disappointment that I've gotten used to seeing on people's faces. I hate that so much, it's one of the worst parts of this whole situation.

I tell him the whole story, including having to move out of the house and not speaking to mom, and he listens to the whole thing without talking. When I finish, he doesn't say anything right away, but then he says, as if reading my mind, "Oh, Madison, I wonder what your *dad* would think about all of this."

"Well, I know he would probably be so disappointed and he'd think I screwed up my whole life," I say, tears starting to form in my eyes.

"No, Madison. That's not what I was thinking. I know you probably think he would be mad or upset, and maybe he would have been just like your mom, when he first found out. But if you really are staying in school and you're even working now, and you have a plan, he would be cheering you on. I know it. I know he would." And then he says, "And I'm not just saying this because I want to make you feel better. Your father was one of a kind. He really was. I'll never have another friend like him, and I miss him every day. You and your mom and Josie...you were his whole world. All he wanted in life was for you to all be happy. He would want that for you now, more than ever."

What he says breaks my heart because he's right. Every word of it. My dad was sweet and warm and strong and happy. He was an amazing father who had to die because some idiot was drunk and went through a stop sign. I'm still *so angry* about it. I haven't really thought about the angry part, but now that we're talking about him, I realize how *angry* I am. No kid should ever have to lose their father that young. I was only thirteen when he died. Then I had to grow up so quickly. It's ironic, because I'm pregnant at such a young age, but I feel like I've been an adult for a while now.

"Thanks, Billy," I say. "You're right. He was amazing." I sigh. "I don't know, I guess I would like to think he'd be proud of me because I'm really trying to do the right thing. I really want to have a career and give this baby a good life. I know it's going to be hard, and if my dad were around, maybe it would've been hard at first, like you said, but then once he came around, *if* he came around, it would be so much better." I look down. "The hardest part for me right now is not being able to talk to my mom. It was so hard to move out, even though Dianne and Molly have been so nice to me. I've really just wanted my mom. I can't have my dad, but now I can't even have my *mom,* either?" I start to cry. "I just wish I could talk to my dad. Just for a minute. Just *sixty seconds*. All I want is to tell him that I'm sorry, and I just want to hear from *him* that he still loves me."

Billy hands me a napkin and I blow my nose. He takes my hand and sighs. "I wish I could give you those sixty seconds with your father, Madison."

The waiter comes with Billy's food and he offers me some of his burger, but I'm too upset to eat now. Billy looks at me sadly. I can tell he doesn't know what to say. But what he said before actually made me feel really good. I'm just feeling emotional, seeing him and talking about my dad.

"Actually, Madison, it's really weird, but I was going through my garage the other day, and I found this scrapbook that your dad was making for you and your sister. I think he was trying to keep it a secret so he asked me to hold onto it for him. He was going to give it to you, he was putting together pictures and things from when you were a baby. It's crazy that I found it just a few days ago, and then I bump into you!" He laughs. "Anyhow, I can drop it off or send it to you."

"Oh, wow. I would love to have that!"

I give him Dianne's address, and then all I can think of for the rest of the dinner is how happy my dad would be to know that Billy and I saw each other. It's really weird that we ran into each other like this. I go to Home's Diner all the time, and Billy does, too, but we haven't seen each other. And now, it happens tonight, when I've had the worst day and it really just makes me wonder if my dad is out there, somewhere, and he somehow made this happen? It's as if my dad is sort of here right now.

I think of the saying that people use when someone is there for them. They call them their "rock." But when I think of my dad, I think of him more like a seatbelt on a roller coaster. No matter what the ride is like, through all the bumps and going up and down, the seat belt holds you in tight. When Billy and I say goodbye, he promises to get me the scrapbook and we say we'll keep in touch. Seeing him and hearing all about my dad makes me feel safe and protected, like the seatbelt is holding me tight.

...October 2012...

"You can't catch me!" I yelled out to my dad as he chased me around the park one day in the middle of the fall season. I remember the weather was so nice and all the leaves were changing colors, and I was excited to get home and take the pumpkins inside from the garden where Dad was growing them.

"Oh, yes, I can!" Dad screamed playfully, and as he chased me, I slipped on some leaves and he grabbed me and carried me over to the grass. "Ha-ha, I'm faster than you think! And I will *always* catch you, Maddie!"

...

191

A few days later, after work, I get home and I find the scrapbook in a package on the porch. On top of it is a note that says, "For Madison. From 'Lily.'" I laugh at the way he wrote his name, knowing he's referring to my old nickname for him. I can't wait to get inside and open it.

I open it slowly, wanting to savor every minute of looking at it. Inside, the first thing I see are two belly button stumps. I wouldn't have known what they were, but Dad labeled them, one was mine and one was Josie's. I can't believe he saved them! Wow! I'll have to do that with Cheese Puff.

There are so many pictures of me alone with Mom and Dad, and then Mom pregnant with Josie, and then all of us together. There are also little bags of wispy blonde hair labeled, "Madison and Josie's first haircuts." It's unbelievable to see this. I can't believe I never saw it before and if I hadn't seen Billy, who knows if I ever would have? I flip through some more pages of baby pictures, and then there's dedicated pages from Mom and Dad to me and Josie. I read Mom's, to me.

Dear Madison, my sweet baby!

Here's a letter to you! Daddy's going to write one right after this, but here's Mommy's! So...what should I talk about? Your cuteness? Your smile you make when you're about to poop? Or, how about how much I love you? I love you so much. Your dad and I are going to give you a great, amazing life, I can promise you that! And one day, you will have a baby of your own, and you will understand how children are the most precious thing in the entire world, and how much I love you and how much I want you to be happy. Oops, you just spit-up! I have to go clean you up, so here's your dad. But I just want to say that I love love love love you!

Tears fall down my face as I look at my dad's entry to me.

Madison (Or Maddie? Or Mads? I guess we'll figure it out!),

Okay, so your mom just went to clean you up. You spit up all the time! You are quite the spit-upper. Sorry, lame dad joke. I've only been a dad for a couple months, so the dad jokes will get better over time, don't you worry! Anyway, I just wanted to say a couple things to my baby! First off: I love you! I know all parents say that, but I really am filled with a love for you that is so intense it feels like my whole heart has been taken over by you! One day, so many lucky people are going to feel that way about you. Friends, best friends, dare I say boyfriends! But anyone who wins your heart over in any way and gets to love you for who you are, that is one lucky person. I'm so excited for your life, to see you grow up, to see how this little cute baby turns into a beautiful woman someday. I love you! My heart is about to explode from it! Ahhh! One day when you have children of your own, you will not only make me a grandfather, but you will understand why I'm a babbling idiot right now over my love for you. I love you sooooooo much! Love forever, Daddy.

I'm now crying so hard that I can't read the words and I'm worried the tears that have fallen onto the page will ruin the ink and so I close the book and get some tissues. I get into bed and stare out the window. It's truly incredible to read their words and it couldn't have come at a better time. With all the bullying at school and everything that's gone on with Matthew and then fighting with Molly, I've just been feeling really emotional and unsure if I made the right decision. But this gives me strength. I think about their love for me, and they were right, I already feel love for Cheese Puff just like they did with me, and I know that love will grow even more once Cheese Puff is born.

Mom, Dad, I think. *I want you to know that I understand what you wanted for me and I know how much you loved me. I won't let you down. I will be happy, I promise, and I will make sure that my life and my baby's life are good. Just you wait, Dad. I'm going to make this work. I'm going to make you proud.*

Then I put my hands on my stomach and stare at the ultrasound picture in Mom's little yellow frame. I wait for a kick, and sure enough I feel one. Then I rub my stomach and say, "Everything *my* parents said to me? I feel the same way about you, my sweet Cheese Puff. We're going to be okay, don't you worry."

← eggplant   7 months !!!

(25 weeks)

To-Do List

- pick up paycheck on Friday from Roast and Drink

Bank
Account
= $2,303.96

- finish English paper
- math homework pages 411-415   APOLOGIZE TO MOLLY!!
- history report due Thursday
- English summary chart due Monday
- cover the science fair   buy:

♡   (ask Janet to interview winner)   - poster board
- edit "arts" section for this   - new highlighters
  week's newspaper edition   - baby items

♡   - French paper 10 pages due   (more clothes)
  Friday   - cheese puffs

♡   - English Shakespeare-themed   - lotion
  narrative due April 17th

♡   - study for math test next week   ♡
                           ♡

$ ☆ look for the scrapbook that
      Billy sent in the mail   ♡

$ - finish editing Janet's stories for the newspaper

$ ☆ start doing kegel
     exercises   ♡
   ☆ look for crib,
    changing table, baby   ♡
    dresser, car seat, yum

$ stroller? yum
    (try to find sales) yum   ♡
   ☆ write out official
    budget   CHEESE PUFFS
             ♡
       ♡   ♡

Chapter 22: Week Twenty-Six

"Your baby is as big as an acorn squash," I read, and I kind of laugh because I have no idea what an acorn squash is, but I'm sure it means that Cheese Puff is getting bigger, which is exciting.

I can officially say that I look really pregnant. My bump has protruded out so far that now when I glance down, my feet are half-covered. And I've been so bloated, which I bet is adding to the size of my stomach. In the morning, it's not as big as at night. By the end of the day, it's huge and I feel really bloated. I'm eating more and trying to do what Dr. Lippincott said, eating more healthy snacks.

My week has gotten off to a good start. It's Monday after school, and I'm at Roast and Drink, working. Johnny is in the back eating some take-out he ordered in. It smells so good, and I'm starving, too, but I have to wait another two hours to go home for dinner. We're allowed to have as many drinks as we want, so I've been having a lot of hot chocolate, but I only add a little of the powder so that it's not too sweet and not too much caffeine from the chocolate. I didn't even know chocolate has caffeine in it until I got pregnant.

The sun is almost completely set outside. It's April, and the days are getting longer, and I love the excitement that's always in the air when it starts to get warmer. I remember being so happy thinking about summer coming and all the outside sports and parties. This year will be so much different, obviously, because I'll be having a baby this summer.

I'm finding it harder on my legs to stand for so long, and I've started leaning on the counter for support when I'm working and it's not busy. It's dinner time, which is usually very slow around here. When I'm moving around and busy serving the customers, I don't notice it as much, but my legs really hurt when I'm just standing around.

My eyes are kind of zoned out and I actually close them for a second, trying to get a quick nap, which is impossible because I'm standing and I don't want to get in trouble. It just feels good to close them for a second. When I open them, I see a customer has come in and is standing in front of me at the counter. And then I realize *it's Mom*. It's been a couple of weeks since she came to my appointment, and we really haven't communicated since then. She looks really tired and she has dark circles under her eyes. But surprisingly, she *smiles,* and then she says, "Hi, Madison. I didn't know if you'd be working tonight, but I thought I would come by and see."

Then I see her trying to glance at my stomach, but the apron covers it. I tell her I'll see if I can take my break now, and thankfully, Johnny comes out and takes over for me and says that I can have my fifteen minute break. I ask Mom if she wants anything and she says just a black coffee, so I get it for her and we go to sit on the bench outside.

"So, how are you doing?" She looks at my stomach again. I move my apron to the side so she can see it.

"It's growing, that's for sure," I say.

"Wow, it is." She frowns. "So now you're...seven months?"

I nod and then say, "Mom, I know it's a weird thing to ask, I mean, when we haven't really even been speaking, but...did you have stretch marks when you were pregnant with me and Josie?"

Mom laughs, and it's such a relief. I was scared she'd get angry. "Well, now that you mention it, I believe I did get stretch marks. They faded over time and now you can't really see them. Why, are you getting some?"

"Yeah. They're kind of a dark red. And they're ugly."

She laughs again. "I know. I hated them too."

I bite my lip, looking down. "Mom, I'm not trying to be rude or anything, but...why did you come here?"

"Well, I...I actually wanted to let you know that I...I think I'm ready. To talk."

I'm so shocked that I can't even say anything for a moment.

"I know we obviously can't talk right now, but I sent you an email before I came here, and I want you to read it when you get back to Dianne's tonight. It has a lot of important things in it that you need to know before we actually talk. I know you have school tomorrow, but I have the afternoon shift off at work, because they're having a meeting. Maybe you could come by at lunch?"

I can't believe this. We're finally going to talk. "Yeah, sure. I'll come then."

"Okay, then." It's a bit awkward for a few seconds, neither of us says anything and we kind of just sit there staring at each other. Then she gets up and says, "You better get back to work. I'll see you tomorrow." She bends down to give me a quick kiss on my forehead, the way she used to kiss me goodnight. Tears instantly come to my eyes as I watch her leave.

I'm so stunned. *Is this for real?* Will we be able to finally get back into each other's lives? Maybe I'll be able to come home? *Oh my God!* I can't wait to get home and read the email!

I'm a bit jittery for the rest of work, I can't wait for my shift to end. I rush home and run to my room, opening my computer to read the email.

To: maddieluvspizza@gmail.com
From: tdavis31@gmail.com

Madison,

First of all, I want to say that I'm really sorry about our fight, and the things I said. I was seriously upset with you. I've worked so hard for you and your sister, for you to have the best lives possible, especially after Dad died. I didn't and don't want to see you throw it all away. I don't think I handled this situation well and I am really truly sorry about that. I didn't know what else to do other than to have somewhat of a break from seeing you, because I didn't want to keep yelling at each other and saying things I would regret. Now that some time has passed and I've thought about things a lot, even spoken to a therapist about how to handle the situation, I'm ready to talk to you.

Second of all, I'm sorry if it was confusing that I was doing things like giving you the car for your birthday and then coming to your party, but then not calling or being around much. I had to give you your car, because I always keep a promise. I know Dad would have wanted you to have it. I often think about what he would say and since he's not here, I'm acting on behalf of both of us. I'm glad I was there for your party, and I'm also glad that I was able to come to your doctor's appointment. But I'm sorry if you've been confused about my bouncing back and forth from us not having communication, to us having scattered interactions. I wish I could have been ready to talk to you sooner. To be honest, I wasn't sure I was ready to talk even now. But, I got a call from Dad's old friend Billy, or as you called him, "Lily" :). He told me all about running into you at Home's Diner and that you updated him on everything. He was really sad about what has happened to our relationship and that you had moved out. We talked about Dad a lot and what he would want, and he pointed out that Dad would be very upset to know this is going on between us. I was going to reach out to you anyway, but after Billy called, I knew I should do it sooner rather than later.

I want you to know that no matter what my opinion is on the situation, and no matter how upsetting it was to hear that my teenage daughter was pregnant, you are still my daughter and I love you more than words can ever say. You will learn this now that you are becoming a parent, that your child will be the most important person in the world to you. As I said, I feel like I failed miserably in the way I handled this situation, and I'm sorry.

But I also want to tell you that I am proud of you for handling things the way you have so far. Dianne keeps me informed about what's going on, and from the way it sounds, you have really shown that you are being responsible. This is not an easy road you've chosen, but since you've committed to being on it, I want you to know that I will do my best to help you, whenever and however I can.

Now, I have to tell you something that might be upsetting to hear. I hope you know, I took a lot of time and consideration and had discussed it with my therapist before I made this decision. It's about my career. As you know, I've been struggling to keep things together since Dad died. It's been hard and I have really not enjoyed the jobs I've been doing, not to mention I'm constantly at one of my three jobs and I never have time to do anything else. So, I've been looking around for other possibilities and things I might be qualified for. There's a publishing company in Santa Barbara that had an opening for an assistant editor. I contacted them, thinking it was a long shot, but I figured I would try. And guess what? They hired me! It will pay a lot more than what I'm making from all my three jobs combined, so I can't afford to not take it. The thing is, it will mean I have to move with Josie to Santa Barbara. I know this is big news and I know it might be very upsetting for you to hear this. So, I want to talk to you about it, in person, but I wanted you to know what was going on, before we spoke. You are welcome, of course, to move with us. I know it might not be something you would want, and Dianne has told me you can stay here with her and Molly as long as you'd like. She has been so kind and generous. Anyway, the option is there and the offer will never expire. You will always be welcome to live with me. I want you to know that. If you choose to stay here, Santa Barbara is only a two-hour drive from Redford, and we can still see each other a lot. Madison, I hope you understand that this is not an opportunity I can pass up. Please come over tomorrow during your lunch period so that we can talk in person. I love you no matter what, and I will always love you, no matter what.

Love,
Mom

I read the email three times over. It doesn't feel real. I'm so happy she took the time to write all of that down, it was nice and long. I can't believe how much she has come around, it's amazing. I bet it's partly because Billy told her we saw each other and talked about what I told him, but I don't care if it's because of him, I'm just so happy that she wants to talk again. But I'm also really sad. She finally wants to make up and get along again and now she's moving away with Josie?!? I know she said that I could come, but I really don't want to leave Redford. Why did this job have to come now? When she's finally ready to be there for me?

I know I should be happy that she's apologizing and wants to be there for me, but I'm really sad. All the hope for things to go completely back to normal has left me. I'm also angry. Even though we've always been a little distant, she used to say that she'd always be there for me. I *needed* her, especially after my dad died and she was never there because she had to work all the time. And even though I understand it, that doesn't change how hard it was to never have her around. I needed her then and I *still* need her, maybe even more than ever. I know that I have Dianne and Molly, and they're amazing, but I need my *mother.*

I can see why she wanted me to read the email and not tell me in person. She probably knew I would freak out and she wouldn't know how to handle it. And maybe she just couldn't say that kind of stuff in person. She's *always* been a little absent in the emotional department. When Dad died, she grieved by herself. She didn't know how to help me or Josie through it. I know it was hard for her to lose her husband, but what about how it was for us to lose our *father?* I'm surprised, but also happy that she says she has gone to a therapist. I wish she had done it back then. I wish she had done a lot of things back then. I want to try to be the kind of mother for Cheese Puff where she or he doesn't wish I had done things a different way, but I guess that's pretty much impossible.

<>

As I walk to school with Molly the next morning, I can't stop yawning. I got no sleep last night, I was just up thinking about everything.

I sigh and shift my backpack higher up on my shoulders. Molly frowns at me, concerned. "You look tired."

"Yeah, I hardly slept last night. I got an email from my mom and she came by the coffee shop. She wants to talk," I say. "Finally."

"Wait, really? Oh my God, that's amazing! So why didn't you sleep?"

"Well, there's big news from her. She got a job offer in Santa Barbara, so she might move away with Josie, and then...I don't know, she says I can come if I want to, but I really don't think I can leave Redford and school, and you, and..."

"Oh, wow. That's huge news. Oh no, are you going to move away?"

199

"I don't know. I really don't think so. But how can I live so far away from them? I mean, I know I'm not living with them right now, but I always thought that would change, or at least we would live near each other even if I get my own place. Now, they're going to be a two-hour drive away? That's crazy!"

Molly is really sweet and she tries to make me feel better the rest of the way to school, but there really isn't anything she can say. I think I will know more about the situation once I speak to Mom.

At lunch, I head over to Mom's, and I knock. It's so weird that I now have to knock to go into my own house. Mom opens the door and tells me I didn't have to knock. It's so weird to be in my house after I haven't been for months. It all smells and looks the same, and I realize how much I miss that smell of...home.

We sit down at the kitchen table where she has set up some lunch for us. I can't remember the last time Mom made me lunch. I forgot how much I love her sandwiches. She makes this really good combination, cucumbers and tomatoes and boiled eggs, with some salt and pepper, which *her* mother used to make for her.

"Your favorite!" Mom says. We smile at each other and then she takes a deep breath and says, "Okay, so you got my email?"

I nod and just jump right in. "Mom, I don't know if I can move to Santa Barbara. I need to stay here, finish high school here...I mean, I'm editor-in-chief of the paper, I'd have to give that up, and I'd miss Molly and the town so much, and I just-"

"I know, honey. I had a feeling you were going to say this. And I feel terrible on the one hand because I don't want to leave you. I feel really badly about it, I really do. But can you understand where I'm coming from? I need this job. I need the money. Maybe I'll eventually move up in the company and even do more of my own writing, and then hopefully I can find a way to move back here and still make a good salary, but for now, this has to be the plan. Do you understand?"

"I understand. I'm just...sad. Even though I haven't been living at home, I miss you a lot. And Josie. It's been really hard. I mean, now we're talking again, and I'm so happy, but now you're going to leave?"

"It's only two hours away, and we'll still see each other. I'll come in, and you can come visit, too. And then once the baby is born, I'll want to see him or her."

"Really?"

She nods, with a sad smile on her face and tears in her eyes. She takes my hand and says, "Madison. I'm really, really sorry." Tears run down her face. "I didn't handle it well. I'm not going to lie, I still wish this hadn't happened. But you are obviously having this baby, and I want to be there for you. You're *my* baby. You always will be. Okay?"

Now, we're both crying. This is all I wanted to hear from her for so long.

"Okay, so we're going to start fresh, okay?" she says, taking a breath. "Can I ask you some questions?"

I nod, and then take another bite of my sandwich and grin. "By the way, before you start, I wanted to say that this is the best sandwich ever. I miss your sandwiches."

We laugh. I used to drive her crazy to make this sandwich all the time. "I wanted to make your favorite, I've missed making them for you." Then she looks serious. "Okay, so tell me...when did you actually...get pregnant?"

I swallow, turning red. "October fourth. It was here. In my bedroom."

"So Leo came over when I was at work?"

I nod and look away. It's really embarrassing to talk about it with her.

She sighs. "Did you use a condom, or did you just-"

"I didn't plan on it happening, and he was...he was saying other girls would do it with him, and I got jealous and scared that he wouldn't want to be my boyfriend anymore. I know how stupid it is, and I've thought about it a lot, I wish I could've..."

"He should never have pressured you into it. That was so wrong of him, and his parents have also agreed that he is just as responsible as you are." She looks down. "I also blame *myself* a lot. For not teaching you better, for not being there, being at work all the time. If I'd been home, this never would have happened."

"Mom, it's not your fault. It's *my* fault, I knew I could've said no. I *did* say no, actually, but then I gave in, because I was so...in love with him. I really liked him." I feel like I'm about to cry again and I don't want to do this now. So I try to change the subject. "I don't really want to talk about Leo or what happened. I want to focus on the baby."

"Okay, let's do that." She smiles a little. "It's funny, I have a memory of you *always* playing 'Mommy' with your dolls. You loved to take care of them, feed them, change their diapers. You took it really seriously. You celebrated their 'birthdays' and wrapped little gifts for them and gave them handmade cards, and everything."

I laugh. "I know. I remember too. The thing is, you know that I always wanted to be a mommy, I...I wanted to be like *you."*

"Oh, Madison. That's sweet, but you know I'm obviously not a perfect mother."

"I understand why you acted the way you did, seriously. I've been trying to imagine how I would feel if Cheese…"

"Cheese Puff?" I nod and we laugh together. "If Cheese Puff came home one day and told me she was pregnant," I continue. "I would be freaking out and who knows what I would do?"

"You know, Madison, it's possible Cheese Puff will be a *boy.*"

She laughs and I laugh too, and it feels so good to be talking and laughing with Mom again. It's been so long since we could talk like this, I can't even remember when the last time was.

I tell her about how I went to Planned Parenthood, the counselor there, the adoption agency, the counselor at school, and my job and my plans to still apply to Harvard, et cetera. She says she's proud of me and very grateful to Dianne. She tells me she was upset about me living with Dianne partly because she worried I would love her more than my own mom. But she also says she can imagine what I've been through and how hard it's been and that she wants to be there for me from now on.

"You're…lucky," I tell her shyly. "You did things the right way. You had Dad. That's…that's what I wanted."

"Maybe you will still have that, honey. Don't give up. As for the financial stuff, Leo's parents are being very generous. They have a lot of money, as you know. They're going to give me the checks every month and I will deposit them into the account for the baby until you are able to take over, probably when you're eighteen. These will stay in effect until the baby is eighteen."

"That's amazing, but I'm really hoping to not need to use their money. I really don't want anything to do with Leo or his family now that he treated me the way he did when he found out."

"Well, we don't have to talk about them right now." Mom smiles. "I have a story for you that's sort of fitting to this situation. So, I used to play piano, you know, I had lessons once a week, and I did recitals all the time. When I was just a little younger than you, I was doing my graduation recital, and I had been so nervous for weeks about messing up, and guess what? I *did* end up messing up on this one phrase. I continued playing, the whole time thinking that it screwed up my whole performance, but…at the end of it, people came up to congratulate me. They said the fact that I handled the mistake with such dignity showed the type of person I was. I got through it and ended up doing a pretty good job. I see a similarity in this situation, even though it's very different. Do you see what I mean?"

"Yeah. Thank you. That's…wow. That story means so much."

"Of course." She looks down. "And I will miss seeing all of it," she says softly, her voice breaking. "I'll miss seeing the rest of your pregnancy, and…I can't believe I already missed so much of it, and now...I'm leaving again."

What she's saying makes me want to cry, it makes me wonder why this job had to come at the time it did, why she had to get the job in the first place. But I know she can't continue working three jobs. The stress is going to overtake her one of these days if she doesn't get just *one* stable job. She even said so herself. And she's right. I hate the fact that she's missed so much.

She shakes her head. "I guess I've come to accept the situation. It's taken some time and some talks with people, like my therapist. But I know I have to accept this and not just accept it, but be happy about it. When we fought, you were right when you said that I've always said that children are the most precious thing. It's true. And I still feel that way. I just didn't want you to have to go through it at such a young age. But now I'm actually excited about it. I mean, there will be a baby here soon, who will be my grandchild. *My grandchild!*"

"I know," I say, smiling, and then I laugh. "Josie's going to be an aunt."

"And I'm going to be a grandmother." She takes my hand. "So many changes. So much to get used to in the last few years, I can't believe it." I nod. Then she says, "Why don't we try to think of this situation with the move now as if you went away to college, just a little earlier? Okay?"

I nod, hugging her again. "That's a great idea. I...I love you."

"I love you too. More than anything. And just so you know, the option of you living with us is always open. No matter what. *You* made *me* a mother, sweetie. You're my first born. And I'm so sorry, again, for our fight and for how I handled everything, for all of it."

"I'm sorry, too."

I wish I didn't have to go back to school, but lunchtime is almost over. I give Mom a hug and she kisses my forehead, and we agree we will talk again soon. I go back to school, passing by some other students who of course see my stomach bouncing up and down, and they start laughing and making comments that I can hear, like, "Look at the elephant coming down the street!"

But I don't care anymore. Right now, I feel lighter than a cloud.

<>

After dinner that night, Molly and I have ice cream and cheese puffs out on the trampoline in her backyard. It's an unusually warm night for early April, and although it's windy, the wind is warm. We are sitting cross-legged, which is getting harder and harder for me to do. We bounce a little on the trampoline and it makes my stomach gently bounce. It's fun and relaxing, and I can feel Cheese Puff's kicks, which makes me think she or he likes it, too. We're also listening to music, on Molly's cell phone.

I tell Molly what happened with Mom and she's really happy for me that we are getting along again, even though she feels bad for me that they are moving. I tell her that Mom said they will visit a lot and so will I.

Then a song by Christina Perri comes on Molly's phone. I love her music, her songs are so inspirational. "This is my favorite song from her!"

"Yes. '*Miles.*' You've only told me a hundred times." Molly laughs.

I love that song so much. I'm just beginning to think of how the words relate to my life now. It's about not counting the miles away from someone, and just counting the I-love-you's (it's in the lyrics). Now it kind of applies to me and my mom.

I decide to take my phone out and send Mom the link to the song. About fifteen minutes later, I get a text back from her.

Mom: Oh, sweetie, you just nearly made me cry! I love that song. That should be our motto song now. Thank you!

I smile and tell Molly what the text says, and then I lie down on the trampoline and start to count Cheese Puff's kicks.

"Maddie, what are you doing?" Molly asks, noticing how quiet I am.

"Counting the baby's kicks."

"Really? That's so cool!" she exclaims, her eyes lighting up. "Can I feel?"

I nod and lift my shirt, and she places her hand in the corner of my stomach, but I move her hand closer to the center, because that's where Cheese Puff kicks most of the time. Sure enough, Cheese Puff gives a big kick and my stomach kind of looks like wave movements. In the moonlight, I can see how big my belly has actually grown.

It makes me sad to think about how I'm already seven months into my pregnancy and Mom wasn't there for any of it, and now she won't be there for the rest of it. I guess I always clung onto *some* hope that everything would go back to normal. That I'd move back in with Mom and Josie and live there, and raise Cheese Puff there, at least for a little while. But nothing is going back to normal. In fact, it's changing more than I ever thought it would.

"Do you think it's a boy or a girl?" Molly asks, continuing to feel my stomach.

"I really can't tell," I say. "It's so crazy that Dr. Lippincott knows but we don't. But I'm glad I'm keeping it a surprise."

"You don't want a boy because you're scared it'll make you think of Leo, right?"

"Honestly, I feel bad saying it, but...yeah. But I don't want people to know I feel that way, so don't tell your mom or anyone, okay? I would just love to have a little girl. But if it's a boy, I know I'll love it, I just hope it doesn't look like Leo. It will make me think of him everytime I look at it."

"Maybe at the beginning, but eventually it will just remind you of itself, I think. All I can say is that the baby will be one cutie, no matter if it's a girl or a boy. I mean, you're so gorgeous and Leo's..." She trails off, unsure if she should continue.

"You can say it," I say softly.

"He's really gorgeous, too."

I throw a cheese puff from my bag to Molly, and she catches it in her mouth and then asks me to throw another, and we laugh and then we have a little contest to see who can catch more, throwing them in the air, they go everywhere. I win. Nothing gets between me and my cheese puffs...in more ways than one.

We finish the bag, and then we lie back down, looking at the stars. Molly's voice gets serious. "You know...I really think you're one of the bravest people I know. I don't think I could live if I wasn't in the same place as my mom. We're so close. It's always just been me and her. I always tell her that if she dies, I want to die, too."

"I know. I felt that way about my dad. I couldn't even imagine life without him."

"Oh God, I'm sorry. I didn't even think about what I was saying. I know you were closer with your dad than you are with your mom."

"Yeah, it's sad, but my mom and I...we were never that close. Not the kind of close like I was with my dad. And now I feel like we could *get* that close, actually, but now she's leaving. But at least she's not leaving because she died in a car accident."

"Yeah. But you'll still see her a lot."

I decide to send a selfie of me and Molly to Mom. I really want to keep up the good vibes that are happening between us right now. A few minutes later, I get a text back from her.

Mom: You look so happy! Give your tummy a big kiss from Grandma, ha-ha. :) See, this technology-communication is working well!

She sends a funny picture of herself, trying to make a duck face. She looks crazy but it makes me laugh. I touch my lips and then put my fingers on my stomach. "That's from Grandma," I say softly to it.

26 weeks

⬤

♡ ♡ ♡   } ← pregnancy belly!

To-Do List

Jan.–Jun.	– pick up paycheck on Friday from Roast and Drink
800	– math homework problems #50–60 page 432
× 6	– English essay informative-style due Monday
4800	– ask Janet to edit her weekly stories + send them
┌ 200 (Dec.)	to me for review + send this week's edition to
$5000	be printed
(about)	– science project due in ☆read Mom's
340	2 weeks email!!
× 4	– do summary on history notes
1360	– complete activities #3 + #4 Santa
	in French packet Barbara??
$6,360	– finish new layout for newspaper!
(this year)	– study for history test ☆meet Mom at
	next week home during my

⬤

lunch period

Spring sale on baby clothes at Babies R' US!

Per month:	
Rent = $1000	
Electric = $80	
Internet = $90	} estimated amounts
Diapers = $50	
Wipes = $15	
Food = $300	
Phone Bill = $50	

buy:
– POSTER BOARD FOR SCIENCE PROJECT!!
– new binder
– college-ruled paper
– cheese puffs

♡ ♡ ♡ ♡ ♡

Expenses =	$$ from
$1,600 /	Leo's parents
month	for savings??
$6,400	
by the end	
of the year	←

CHEESE PUFFS

⬤

emergency fund?

– email Mom + Josie
– gather up résumé

Chapter 23: Week Twenty-Seven

"Your baby is as big as a cabbage," I read on my phone. It's Monday, and yet I'm already exhausted.

Something odd happened the other night. I was eating some really spicy hot chips and I felt this jumping sensation inside my stomach and at first I freaked out, but I asked Dianne and she called Dr. Lippincott. We figured out that little Cheese Puff had the hiccups! The spicy chips brought it on. I'm tempted to do it again, because I love spicy chips, and it was funny, but I hope it wasn't traumatic for Cheese Puff. Molly wants to feel them so she told me to tell her the next time it happens.

I've been gathering up my résumé, partly for Harvard and partly for when I apply for a higher-paying job. But, after working out my budget, I don't think I'll have enough to cover expenses for the rest of the year. I decided I don't want to sell the car Mom bought me. Especially now that Mom and I are talking again. I feel way too bad doing something like that, so I'll have to figure something else out. The rest of this year is going to be pretty rocky, money-wise. After that, I'm going to have a steady budget if I get a job that pays around $17 or $18 per hour. But I know that Leo's parents will be making monthly payments and as much as I hate thinking about using their money, I have to admit that it's good to know it will be there in case of an emergency.

So far, my résumé looks like this:

Madison Davis

Email: maddieluvspizza@gmail.com

Community Service

- Redford Public Library Volunteering (Age 14-15: 2017-2018)
- Homeless Shelter Volunteering (Age 15: 2018)
- "Teach to Use Technology" Volunteering (Age 15: 2018)
- Thanksgiving Food Drive (Age 15: 2018)

Jobs

- "Roast and Drink" Coffee Shop ($12/hour: December 2019-present)

Education Credits

- Principal's Honor Roll since 8th Grade
- 4.1 GPA

Special Experience

- Editor-in-Chief of *The Redford Story* high school's newspaper (2018-present)

Training

- Hands-On Creativity Workshop (Arts, Acting, Improv, Music) in 8th Grade
- Advanced Writing Elective (through 6th-8th grade)
- CPR-Certified by Red Cross
- Red Cross Babysitting Certified

Special Skills

- Soccer, Swimming, Improv/Acting, Writing, Journalism, Advanced French Speaker, Babysitting

I think I have to change my email address to sound more professional, even though I love it. But I hope the résumé is good, even though I don't have a lot of work experience, I do have a lot of volunteer work. I don't know if I used the right format, but I think it will be okay. I researched online what other résumés look like. I'm just going to save it on my computer now, and update it when needed.

So, I can't believe how quickly it's happening, but Mom is leaving with Josie for Santa Barbara tomorrow. I'm waking up early to see them off. I watched Josie running around the playground on Friday during her whole lunch period, because I knew it was the last time I'd be able to. She told me she's really sad that we won't be living in the same city anymore and she wants to FaceTime all the time, and she wants me to come visit. She told Mom she wants to come back on the weekends and visit, too, but they won't have a place to stay because the house is being *sold,* which I can't believe. I didn't even think about the house. *Our* house. *The last place I ever saw Dad.* I can't even think about it or I won't be able to stop crying. Dianne told them they can stay with us if they ever come visit for a weekend, she's so sweet.

I'm walking home from work, snacking on a bag of cheese puffs, just thinking about everything and breathing in the nice, warm air. I really do love this time of year, when the flowers start to bloom. Pink tulips have always been my favorite. When they start blooming, it's like they're opening up and saying hello after being dormant through winter. And the sun starts staying out later, which means summer is close-by.

As I get inside Dianne's house, I hear a lot of voices in the kitchen, and I go in to find Mom and Josie sitting at the table with Dianne. What a nice surprise!

"Hi, guys!" I run up and give them big hugs. "What are you doing here?"

"Dianne invited us for dinner, since it's our last night," Mom says, smiling.

"Oh wow, that's such a great surprise. Thanks, Dianne!" I'm so happy that Mom isn't disappointed or mad at me anymore. I'm not used to it yet, I think I'm still scared she will go back to being angry.

Dianne made spaghetti, which smells delicious, and everyone sits down to eat. "So, what will your new job be like, Teresa?" Dianne asks.

"It sounds like it'll be great. Like a learning experience for me, too, because not only am I working, but I'm also learning more about what gets published."

"That sounds cool!" I say encouragingly.

Then it's quiet until Josie slurps up Dianne's spaghetti and giggles. "How do you make this meat sauce?" she asks, grinning. "It's so yummy."

Dianne smiles at her. "I just add lots of onions and garlic to it. Molly's loved it since she was a baby, and now Madison likes it, too."

It's quiet for a minute. Mom turns to me. "I'm really happy that you've had Dianne all this time." Then she turns to Dianne. "I really can't thank you enough for taking such good care of Madison. I don't know how we can ever repay you, but we will find a way."

Dianne shakes her head, "No repayment necessary, ever. I've honestly been so happy to be able to help. You might know that I was in the same boat myself, about seventeen years ago." She looks at Molly and smiles, and Molly smiles back. Mom watches them, and kind of nods.

"Well, thank you. So, you're a writer, right?" Mom asks.

"Yes. Horror novels." She laughs and then smiles. "Actually, I'm just about to publish my next book."

"I don't know if Madison told you, but I used to do some writing myself."

"No, I didn't know that. What did you write?"

Mom looks insulted and turns to me. "You didn't tell her about my writing, Madison?" I shake my head, not sure why she's so upset. "I guess it's stupid, anyway, I never got anything published and certainly didn't have the success Dianne had." She sounds bitter, and it's starting to get uncomfortable in the room.

"Did you try to get something published? Was it a novel, if you don't mind my asking?" Dianne asks.

"Well, as you know, my husband died kind of suddenly. And, well, right before it happened, I had been in the middle of the final rewrite of a novel. I tried to finish it, but I just...couldn't...bring myself to work on it anymore. I just could never get back into it, initially it was the shock of his death, but then I just associated it with him dying. That probably sounds silly, but..."

"No, no, Teresa, it doesn't sound silly at all. I'm so, so sorry."

Mom nods and looks down. Josie has stopped eating and looks like she wants to leave. She's never wanted to talk about Dad. Every time I brought it up with her after he died, she would just change the subject. I think she was too young at the time to really comprehend it, she was only seven.

"Thank you," Mom says quietly. "And I'm sorry, Dianne...I didn't mean to say anything rude or jealous, or anything. I mean, I shouldn't be mad at you for helping Madison. Thank God she had you."

"I was never trying to step into your place, I was just trying to help."

"I know. Thank you."

It's awkwardly quiet again. Everyone is looking down at their plates. Dianne gets up to clear the table, and Mom helps her. Out of the blue, Josie says, "Did I smell cake when we came in?"

Everyone laughs and the tension goes away. Dianne brings out the chocolate cake that she made as a sort of sending-off cake for Mom and Josie. Josie sticks her finger in the frosting, licking it immediately and saying, "Yum!" and we all start laughing again.

After dessert, Mom says she has to go home and finish packing up. She thanks Dianne again for everything and they hug. I give her and Josie hugs and tell them I'll see them in the morning.

As I'm falling asleep that night, I think about what Mom was saying about her writing and Dad's death. I haven't thought about how hard it would be for her to hear about Dianne being a successful author. And as upset as I am that she's moving away, I realize now how important it is for Mom to take this job. She had a dream once, too, just like I have a dream to be a journalist. Her dream to be a writer got destroyed, and now this might be her chance to start over again.

I think about Dad and what he would want. He always used to say things happened for a reason, and I never really knew what he meant. I still think it makes no sense, like what was the reason he had to die? And why did I have to get pregnant? But maybe me getting pregnant and living with Dianne and Molly has helped Mom figure out that she wants to try again to follow her dream? I fall asleep thinking that maybe Dad was right, and that sometimes the reason is hard to know at first, but then eventually you figure it out.

<>

As the sun rises against a pastel blue and pink sky the next morning, I go to see Mom and Josie off. The furniture they're taking and some suitcases are being driven up to Santa Barbara in a massive U-Haul truck. She sold a lot of stuff, but saved me a few things that I am storing in Dianne's garage, so that I will have some furniture when I move into my own apartment.

I hug Josie, and then she gets in the car. She's crying, we all are. I lean over and give her a kiss on the forehead, like I used to do before she went to sleep, and like Mom used to do with me. I know I used to complain about having to watch Josie all the time, but now I know I'm going to miss it so much.

Mom and I hug, and she tells me she loves me and that we need to FaceTime a lot. She leans down and kisses my belly, totally surprising me. Then she rubs it gently and says, "Hi, Cheese Puff, it's your grandma. I will make sure to be here when you are born, so try to wait for me, okay?" She gets up from bending down, and we are both laughing and crying at the same time.

Josie and I keep waving to each other as the car drives off, until it's only a dot in the distance. I don't remember the last time I was this sad. It feels even worse than Dad's death. I feel guilty for thinking that, because I know it's different and they're alive and we can still visit and see each other. I think about Mom patting my stomach and talking to Cheese Puff, and it makes me feel better, I can't believe she did that.

I'm happy to go to school and to not have to think about them leaving. It's a bright, sunny day and I walk with Molly and she's really sweet, trying to make me feel better about them leaving.

Since Molly eats with Cheryl at lunch and I finally don't have any homework to finish, I'm actually able to attend a meeting at that teen mom support group, and Alexa is there, too. We get paired up for the partners activity, where we're supposed to share a hard thing that's happened to us lately. I tell Alexa about Mom leaving with Josie. She says her parents are divorced and she hardly ever sees her mom, because she moved to Pennsylvania, which I didn't know.

Then I check the time on my phone, and it's time to drive back to school. I wish I could just stay and talk with Alexa, but I have my science presentation on chemical energy next period, and I have to be there. Once I'm back at school, I heave my giant poster board all the way to my science class.

"Alright, class, settle down," Mrs. Grant drones in a monotone. It's so obvious she hates teaching. I've never understood why some people become teachers, especially high school ones, when it seems so obvious they don't like kids. Then again, maybe they used to like kids until they became teachers. I wonder what she thinks of me being a pregnant teen. She's always been nice to me, all the teachers have. None of them have made me feel bad about this. It's just the kids who have been mean. I could never be a teacher. High school is a pretty traumatic experience, and I would never have any desire to come back after I graduate.

"Hey! Settle down!" Mrs. Grant yells when the kids don't listen. "Today, Madison Davis is up first for her chemical energy review presentation."

The class gets suddenly quiet when I go to the front and set up my poster and gather my notecards. I can hear some snickers and whispers and comments. I wish I could make my stomach disappear for times like this.

I try to ignore everyone and I start my presentation. "Chemical energy is the energy that is stored in chemical compounds' bonds, and the energy is released when a chemical reaction takes place."

There are giggles. Lots of them. "Oh, this is bad," I hear a kid say.

My cheeks heat up, but I continue. "Once this chemical energy has been released from a substance, the substance transforms into an entirely new substance."

Full-on laughter. Now people are looking at my stomach. I look down, fumbling around a little, going to my next notecard.

"Chemical energy is the most used type of energy in the world, used in foods, wood, things like that." Then a girl whispers something to her boyfriend, and he bursts out laughing, and the whole room follows.

I feel sick. Mrs. Grant tries to get everyone to settle down, I can tell she feels bad for me. I just keep going. "Bonds in between the atoms in food break or loosen, and new compounds are created when a chemical reaction takes place. This reaction produces energy that keeps us warm, helps us move, and helps us grow up and out."

I cringe when I say that and sure enough, everyone bursts out laughing again. I feel like crying, and Mrs. Grant slams a ruler on her desk and yells, "Does the whole class want detention after school today?" She looks at me encouragingly. "Continue, Madison."

I finish my presentation and then quickly sit down. I'm so embarrassed, I can't even look up. I know I've gotten used to all the teasing and bullying, but today is a hard enough day with Mom and Josie leaving. I really didn't need this.

<>

That night, I have trouble sleeping. I come out to the living room at around eleven and I go to get a piece of cheese and some milk. Ever since Dr. Lippincott mentioned calcium being good for me and the baby, I've been trying to have it every day. I go into the living room, where Dianne is watching the news. "Madison, you're awake? It's so late."

"I couldn't sleep." I sit down and watch with her for a few minutes. At a commercial, I say, "Dianne, I had no idea that you were calling Mom with updates about me this whole time. When she told me that you did, I was really surprised."

"Oh, Madison, I'm sorry, I hope you're not upset. I just thought it was important for her to know what was going on. As a mother myself, I know how I would feel if Molly was the one who moved out."

"No, no, that's not it, I'm not upset. I'm really grateful, actually. I think what you did was really sweet, and it makes me feel good to know that Mom still knew how I was...even if we weren't talking."

"Thank you, Madison," she says. Then she looks at me and smiles. "It's interesting...it just occurred to me how much you've changed from the scared little girl that showed up at my door when you first found out you were pregnant."

"I have?"

"Oh, yeah." She chuckles. "Well, of course, having a baby and becoming a parent kind of forces you to change, doesn't it?"

I nod. "Definitely."

"Sometimes...things happen for a reason. We don't always know what that is."

It's so weird she says that, it's exactly what Dad used to say.

"I mean, when you look at me, for example, I don't know if I would've become such a successful author if I hadn't been a teenage mom. It sounds ironic, because you'd think that being a teen mom would make things like a successful career almost impossible. But it worked the opposite for me. Having a baby at that age was a great motivator for me.

I didn't party my way through high school like the other kids, because once I got pregnant I had to be responsible, to work hard, to prove myself. Molly made me shape up, she made me smarter, she made me more mature. I can tell Cheese Puff is that kind of motivator for you, too."

"Yeah, I think you're right." I grin. "I think it's funny, by the way, since that appointment where I told Dr. Lippincott about calling the baby 'Cheese Puff,' everyone is calling it that now. It's going to be hard to come up with a real name."

We laugh and I rub my stomach. Suddenly, there are a bunch of kicks and Dianne asks to feel. Sure enough, she feels a few huge kicks.

"Ah, I loved those kicks. Molly was always a very active kicker. I used to pretend that my uterus was a trampoline, and she was going *boing boing boing* inside there." She laughs. "The kicks were my favorite part of being pregnant."

"They're mine, too," I say, my heart filled with love for my sweet Cheese Puff. It's so funny as I look at my stomach, it reminds me of when I was around six years old and I would shove pillows under my shirt when I was playing "mommy" and pretend to be pregnant. It's still hard to believe I actually have a real baby in there. I think again about how Dad used to say everything happens for a reason, and now how Dianne said it tonight. I wonder what the reason for Cheese Puff is. I guess only time will tell.

27 weeks!

♡

Cheese Puff has the hiccups! ♡

To-Do List

- pick up paycheck on Friday from Roast and Drink
- buy maternity clothes for warmer weather
- FINISH RÉSUMÉ!!
- research Harvard more?
- do math homework problems on pages 532-535
- finish English writing assignment
- study for French test on Friday
- practice science presentation!!
- ask "sports" writer to cover football game
- edit my stories for this week's newspaper edition
- finish English classwork!
- do research for history report
- write project review science paper (due Friday)
- go to teen mom support group more!!
- call Mom + Josie soon!

nearly $2,000 for housing costs + $1,000 for other costs * try to save $1,000/ year?

Savings Account = $432.65

(save more!!)

$ $ $

☆ meet Mom + Josie at the house at 5am to say goodbye

buy:
- Cheese puffs
- flash cards
- new shampoo, conditioner, lotion
- new bottle of prenatal vitamins

☆ look for community service opportunities

☆ look up more lullabies to sing to Cheese puff!

☆ think of more baby names
☆ birthing classes?
☆ find things to sell + ways to make more $$$

me + Cheese Puff

go see Ms. Sherman again?

Chapter 24: Week Twenty-Eight

"Your baby is as big as a head of lettuce," I read online. I'm in the car with Dianne and Molly, on the way to Dr. Lippincott for my appointment.

I'm a little stressed, because I have a lot to do later tonight. There's an event at school that they have once a year, where the editor-in-chief and her or his assistant share their best stories and talk about what it's like to be on the school newspaper. It's tomorrow night and I'm doing it with Janet. It's officially named the "Young Journalists' Convention," it's a big event, and I'm excited.

I'm now starting my last trimester of pregnancy, the third trimester, and I've been getting nervous, reading about babies who come early instead of on their due date. I hope Cheese Puff comes on time, or late, because then I'll have more time to get everything together, like my budget. Since I decided to not sell the car, I have to find another way to make money, and I have to look for an affordable apartment to rent, preferably before Cheese Puff is born. I don't even know how to buy furniture. I wish they taught things like this in school, things that are useful, instead of how to calculate the surface area of a triangle.

I wish I could join a childbirth class, but the problem is that I have school when they take place, so I'll have to wait until it's summer, which is cutting it close to my due date. But there's nothing I can do, I have to go to school! And I wish I had more time for things like baby education classes and also the teen mom support group, which I really want to go back to. A voice inside of me says, *If you think you don't have time for things like this now, just wait until after the baby is born.* Oh, boy. Or girl, ha-ha.

I read that Cheese Puff is able to dream now! I wonder if we share the same dreams? My bump is really getting to be more like a mountain now, so she or he is for sure getting bigger. The weight from my stomach is making my legs ache and tingle, and Dianne gave me a heating pad to use at night before I fall asleep, which helps.

At this appointment, Dr. Lippincott tells me everything looks good, thank God. She asks about the kicks and I tell her I can't even keep up with the counting because there are so many, and she laughs and says that's very good. She also says it's important to eat more iron from now on, because babies absorb the majority of their iron during the third trimester. So now I have to remember to have foods that have a lot of iron, as well as the calcium foods. My next appointment will be in two weeks, when I will be in my thirtieth week of pregnancy, wow.

Taking Dr. Lippincott's suggestion, Dianne makes steak for dinner, since it's rich with iron. It's so delicious, I need to learn how to cook like her. After dinner, I go to my room and gather up my best stories from the past few years and submit them to Janet, who will submit them to Marcia, who is running the journalist event.

Since we still aren't completely ready for it, at school the next day, Janet and I meet in the newspaper office to discuss plans for the event, along with Peyton, who's our best 'features' writer and editor. I assemble my printed stories and lay them out on the table, organizing them by the dates of the editions they were in. They are the one I wrote about the prom, the Spread Kindness Week one, and the science fair story. I smile as I think of when I wrote those. I just love writing for the newspaper, I want to do it for the rest of my life. It would be so cool if I could get an internship at the New York Times someday.

We gather our stories, submit them to Marcia to review and turn into a presentation, and then we finally get a break to actually eat some lunch. Out of the blue, Janet asks me if I'm planning on coming to school next year.

"Of course I am," I say, getting annoyed. "I'm planning on *graduating.*"

"Well, that's surprising," she mutters. I wish I could fire her as my assistant, but it's against the rules of the school. Anyone from the school is allowed to be on the newspaper, but I just can't stand her.

I eat quickly and then go to the library where I work on a rough draft of a budget that I made last night. Rent and all the utility and electric costs are going to add up to around $1,200 a month, since I'm aiming to find an apartment for around $1,000 per month or cheaper, and I also researched Redford's average utility costs. Since I'm probably getting only a one-bedroom, one-bathroom apartment, it shouldn't cost that much. There's something called a "studio" apartment, which is basically all one room. It's a few hundred dollars cheaper, but I'm worried it will be too small and I'm hoping I won't have to get one. At least I know it's an option.

I add up the costs of diapers and wipes and things like that, and it's around $70 or $100 a month. I think food will add up to $300 a month, and now I will also have to pay for my Internet, because while my mom is still paying my phone bill, I'm going to have to install internet in my apartment so I can do my homework, and that bill is around $50 a month. By the end of this year, my expenses will be around $6,400 and I will have around $6,360, which isn't enough to cover all my expenses plus the savings I'll need to put away. I'm going to have to figure out something to make up for my savings and how to pay the rest by the end of the year. I really need to find a higher-paying job. If worse comes to worst, I will have to use the money from Leo's parents, but I'm still trying to avoid it and pretend it's not there.

I never realized how much planning and budgeting it takes to have a baby. I always thought everything just sort of gets figured out. But in reality, it takes a *lot* of planning. I also never realized how many expenses there are once you move out. Once I'm in my own apartment, I'm going to have to cover toilet paper, paper towels, groceries, soap, shampoo, toothpaste...all those essentials that I always just *had,* stocked up and right there for me to use, because my mom provided them. Now *I'm* going to have to be the one doing it. It's overwhelming. But I'm trying not to panic and just take things step by step, as they talked about at the teen mom support group.

<>

After work, I quickly go home to change into my outfit for the event and I also grab a bag of cheese puffs to eat, because maybe they'll make me feel less nervous. After quickly scarfing the bag down, I drive to the school, because I don't have time to walk. Dianne and Molly are coming here when it starts. I park and quickly race into the auditorium, panting. It's not easy to rush around when you're pregnant, everything is starting to ache and I get short of breath more easily.

The auditorium isn't large, but it has just enough room for the people that are here, who are the people who run the school and the district, some students, along with some graduates from this school, and some actual real journalists.

After saying hi to Janet and Peyton, a man and two women approach us. One of the women is tall and sleek, with her hair pulled back into a tight ponytail, she looks really put-together. The other woman is shorter and less fashionable.

They introduce themselves to us and they ask what we have to do with the event, so we tell them. The shorter woman smiles at me. "So, Madison, you are editor-in-chief of the school paper?"

I nod and smile, and she says, " I'm Adalynn. I graduated from USC three years ago, I have an internship at the Stanford Daily, and I'm working to become a journalistic reporter. Is that what you are aiming for?"

I try to ignore that they're all staring at my belly. "Yes, but more on the journalism, story-writing, behind-the-scenes area of it all," I answer professionally.

Now I recognize the man as the head of the school district. This is a big deal. My heart rate speeds up as he says, "Madison, have you met Margaret?"

All of a sudden, the name and the way the woman with the ponytail looks makes me realize who she is. It's Margaret Miller! She's a famous reporter around here, and she has her own talk show.

"Oh, no, I haven't, it's so nice to meet you, Ms. Miller, right?"

She nods and hands me her hand to shake, but she doesn't smile, she just stares at my stomach. She asks, "How long have you been editor-in-chief?"

"Since the beginning of my freshman year, so nearly two years now."

"And now you're in your sophomore year?"

I clear my throat. "Yes."

She looks up and stares directly into my eyes. "Well, your principal speaks very highly of you, she says you are one of the best people on the newspaper, and a hard-working EIC. That's short for 'editor-in-chief,' in case you didn't know. In preparation for the event, I read some of your pieces. It seems you have some talent."

"Thank you so much," I feel relieved that she's being nice. I wasn't sure what she was going to say because she was staring so hard at my stomach. "You don't know how much that means to me, coming from you. I watch your show a lot."

I see a hint of a smile on her face for the first time. It's odd that she seems so formal, as she always laughs and jokes on her show.

Then she asks, "Are you planning on attending college?"

Here we go again. This question.

"Yes." I nod with authority, as if I know for sure. "Actually, I'm applying to Harvard."

I hear her start to laugh but she stops herself and gives me a look like she feels sorry for me. I swallow hard so I won't start to cry, I really wasn't prepared for this. I'm relieved as the guy from the district tells her they have to go and he takes her away before she can say anything else. But she made her point. She obviously thinks there's no way I will get into Harvard, as I'm clearly an idiot pregnant teenager. I'm so upset.

I see Molly and Dianne arriving and they come over to me. "Did I just see you talking to Margaret Miller?" Dianne asks, and I nod, trying to force a smile. "That's very good. If you want to become a successful journalist one day, it's great to have her as a contact. She could get you an amazing internship. I hope you made a good impression."

"I hope so, too," I reply nervously.

A little later, Marcia walks up to the stage, and that's my cue. I step up on the stage stairs nervously, as the room draws to a silence. Janet and

Peyton follow, Janet's face looks like she's appearing at a funeral. She's so crazy, if she hates all this so much, why is she even bothering to do it?

I wish Mom was here. She probably would have come, but I didn't want to put pressure on her when she is just getting settled in Santa Barbara. I figured I would just tell her about it after.

There's a microphone set up, and Marcia says into it, "Welcome! So nice to see all of you here! Thank you for showing up to show your support and encouragement for these young journalists-in-the-making!" Everyone claps. "We are now going to have these three talented young ladies each read their three best stories they've worked on, to you."

Everyone claps again. Peyton goes first, then Janet, and then it's my turn. I see people glancing at my stomach and then hear some of the same type of whispering that I've gotten so used to. I take a deep breath and start reading my pieces. At the end of each one, people clap and I see Dianne and Molly smiling at me. There's a huge round of applause when I finish the last one, and then Marcia comes back on stage with Peyton and Janet, and she asks us each to talk a little about the work it takes to run a high school's newspaper. Since I have a speech prepared for this one, I feel pretty confident. I talk about the long hours of researching and writing and editing that goes into it, and then I explain how I became editor-in-chief.

Then it's time for the college part of this. Oh, God, Marcia is going to ask where we're planning on attending college and what we want to study.

She asks me first. "Madison Davis, editor-in-chief, an excellent writer and editor who takes on the task of running a high school's newspaper, where do you plan on going to college, and what do you want to study?"

I swallow down my embarrassment and say into the microphone, "I'm planning on majoring in journalism...at Harvard."

There's *laughter*. I hear it starting in the back, and my cheeks get hot. I see Dianne and Molly near the front, shooting glares at the people laughing. I wish I could just cover my stomach. I've never felt more humiliated. I had been looking forward to this and I didn't even think it would go like this. I'm such an idiot.

I can't really concentrate anymore and I don't even hear Peyton and Janet's answers. Before I know it, I hear Marcia saying, "Well, that will complete our event. Feel free to stay and mingle around. There are refreshments in the hall."

Molly and Dianne rush over to me and give me hugs and tell me they are proud of me. We don't even mention that people were laughing. I see people going up to Janet and Peyton but no one comes up to me. I had thought a ton of people would want to speak to *me,* because I'm the editor-in-chief.

While I'm standing there waiting and Janet's talking to three journalists, she shoots me a smug smile, almost like she's saying I-told-you-so. She's so horrible. I try to think of what it would be like if *she* was the one who was pregnant and *I* was the person who worked with her at the newspaper. I can't even imagine treating her the way she's treated me.

Pretty soon, people start to leave, and Margaret Miller comes up to me, "Could I speak with you in private?" she asks, and I nod and walk off to the corner of the auditorium with her. She has a weird fake-looking smile pasted on her face while she speaks. "I just wanted to tell you that your stories were excellent, and to be honest, I could see myself writing some of them when I was your age. However-"

Totally surprised, I burst out, "Thank you so much, Ms.-"

She cuts me off. "However," she starts again, her smile disappearing. "I don't know how you will be able to manage, being a teenage mother and having such high goals. I'm sure I'm not the first person who has said this to you."

Her words hurt so much, I feel the tears coming no matter what I try to do to stop them. All I can utter is, "Oh. Yeah."

"You seem like a smart girl, which is why I'm confused as to why you would let something like this happen to yourself." Seeing my tears, I guess she feels bad, because she smiles again, but it seems real this time. "Listen, I'm sorry to be so harsh. Nothing's impossible, and I suppose if you really work hard and you have a lot of support, you could still end up where you want to be. You seem like a nice girl. I do wish you the best of luck."

She pats my shoulder and then I watch her walk off. Molly and Dianne come rushing over. They look at me excitedly and ask how it went talking to her. The thing is, I'm not really sure how it went anymore. I was really upset at first, but what she said to me at the end was kind of nice, actually. It gave me *some* hope, and I think she was sort of trying to give me a compliment. Whether she was or wasn't, I'm going to just hang onto that thought. I've realized that letting people's negative comments get to me isn't going to help me achieve anything.

<>

On Saturday, the school is hosting a carnival by the pier at the beach. Every year it's around mid-April, because it's finally warm enough to go to the beach area. Dianne lets Molly drive us in her car. I'm wearing some new maternity jean shorts I bought for when it got warm out, my white maternity shirt which I wear all the time, and some old flip flops. Molly looks really pretty, her hair tied up into a high ponytail, wearing a lacy pink top that makes her look like she's blushing.

"You look really good, Molly. That color really suits you," I say as she pulls to a red light.

"Thanks!" she says, smiling. Her smiling makes me happy. "You look good too, Mads. I love that shirt, even though I've seen it now so many times."

We laugh and she pulls up to a spot on the beach and we walk over to the pier area, where carnival games are set up. There's a whole section we're allowed to go to after five o'clock, with a Ferris wheel and cool swing rides, things like that. I might go on the Ferris wheel, because it's relaxing to be on it right before sunset. It reminds me of when we went to Disneyland, which seems like a hundred years ago.

Dianne gave Molly money for snacks, so she buys some popcorn and we eat it as we go play ring toss and some of the other games. I end up winning a tiny stuffed animal at the pop-the-balloons game, it'll be perfect to give to Cheese Puff.

As it gets closer to sunset, Molly and I get in line for the Ferris wheel. We're excited to ride it together again. The line is pretty long, overflowing with so many kids from school.   Molly says, "I'm going to get us some cotton candy so we can eat it on the Ferris wheel! It'll be fun!"

"Okay, but hurry, the line seems to be going fast."

She nods and runs off. I don't really feel like interacting with anyone from school, so I just browse through my phone as the line inches forward, looking on some pregnancy websites to see the symptoms I'll be experiencing in the coming weeks. After about ten minutes, I'm almost at the front, and Molly still isn't back. This isn't good. If you don't have a partner, they just pair you up with someone else who doesn't have a partner. I look around anxiously for Molly, and there's no sign of her.

Suddenly it's my turn. The woman looks at me expectantly and when I hesitate she says, "Are you going or not?"

"My friend isn't back yet," I say.

"Well either get on yourself or you have to go to the back of the line," she says. *But I've waited so long!* And I really don't want to even have to walk past all the kids from my school in the tight line to go to the back. I can just picture my stomach rubbing up against them. I look around for Molly one last time and I don't see her, so I just get on the ride. Just when I'm thinking she's going to let me ride alone, she opens the gate and another person who is alone gets on. Oh my God, it's *Leo*.

As soon as we notice each other, we both move to get off, but it's too late, she slams the door shut and the ride starts to move.

This is insane. *How did this happen?* I can't believe he isn't with anyone. I know why *I'm* not, but what's *his* reason? Isn't he here with that girl? Dina? A million thoughts go through my mind, and I don't know what to say.

I stare at him and he scowls, says, "Oh, great. This is just great," and then he just looks away, out the little window.

What's even worse is that we went on this exact Ferris wheel together at *last* year's carnival. We had the best time, laughing and trying to swing the cart, and then kissing at the top, just kissing and kissing.

"Where's Dina?" I choke out.

"With her friends," he says gruffly, not looking at me.

I look down at my stomach. I notice he's totally avoiding looking at it, or me. As the ride goes on, I close my eyes and I can't stop the tears that start to fall. It's so painful to see him and be this close to him. What are the chances he and I would end up on this ride together? I'm so mad at Molly, even though it's not her fault.

Then Cheese Puff starts to kick. A lot. It's like she or he can sense something. For a moment, I want to ask Leo if he wants to feel the baby, but I clear the thought away. He'll probably never even touch the baby. *His* baby.

He just continues to look out his side and I try to stare ahead and not look at him, but I can't help but glance at his legs, they're so muscular, from soccer. I glance over at his hair, that messy golden brown hair that I used to run my fingers through. Then I look at his light green eyes that used to look so sweet, but now just look mean. But still, he's gorgeous.

I can't believe myself, but *I still can't help thinking about how cute he is.* It's baffling to me how I can find him attractive in any way after what he's done to me, but I realize that I still love him. I'm such an *idiot.* How can I still love someone who's hurt me so much?

We finally reach the top and there's a beautiful view of the sunset. The sky is gorgeous, a mix of blues, oranges, pinks, purples, and yellows. The sun is just about to set over the ocean. This is exactly the point where we kissed last year when we were here together.

I try to focus on something else. There are mountains in the distance, but they remind me of Leo, too. We used to hike around there, especially during the summer, and we would watch the sunset from the top. He was superstitious and he thought that if we didn't stay to watch the sunset after we hiked, then something bad would happen on the way down. I remember thinking it was cute at the time.

My lip is shaking so intensely that I feel like I'm about to burst. I inhale and exhale, trying to calm down, realizing I've hardly breathed since I stepped on the Ferris wheel. Our cart hangs in the air, teetering a little, almost like it's taunting us, forcing us to watch the pretty sunset together.

"Stop staring at me," he says gruffly under his breath.

I wish I could go back to the night that Leo and I had sex and ask him what he would do if I got pregnant. I even remember asking him to use protection, but he said we'd be "careful," whatever the hell that meant. I still can't believe that I lost my virginity to someone like him. I'm so ashamed. I can't believe his baby is inside me. It's made of him, too, not just me. I have to carry something that has a part of Leo in it.

I know that I could confront him right now. I could really let him have it. It's not like he doesn't deserve it, it's just that I've never been great at confrontation. I can never stand up for myself, I'm such a wimp. I turn away and just pray the ride ends soon.

The Ferris wheel lurches forward, and we start to go down, thank God. When we *finally* get to the ground, we both rush out of the cart, and some of the kids from school that notice we were on it together start whispering and laughing. Leo pushes through the crowd, like he can't wait to get away from me. My whole body is shaking as I fight back tears and go to find Molly.

She's standing at the back of the crowd, looking for me, with two sticks of cotton candy in her hands, one blue and one pink. She smiles and asks me which one I want and I say I don't care.

She frowns. "Oh no, Mads, what's wrong?" she asks. "I'm sorry it took so long, it wasn't even a long line, they were just slow!"

"I want to go home," I say as I feel the tears starting to come.

"Maddie, what's wrong? Did something happen?"

I know that if I say it now, I'll end up bawling in front of everyone. "I'll tell you in the car," I say, and she realizes I'm serious and we walk back to her mom's car. We get in and sit there, she asks me which cotton candy I want, and I say I'm not hungry, I'm too upset to eat. So she holds onto both of them, just staring at me, waiting for me to tell her what's wrong, and finally I say, "I had to go on the Ferris wheel with *Leo*."

"What?! Oh my God, Madison, are you kidding me?!?"

I shake my head and start bawling, as I tell her what happened. She apologizes over and over for not getting back in time. She hugs me and I tell her that it wasn't her fault, what were the chances of me having to go on the ride with Leo? We laugh at how crazy it is, and it feels good to cry and laugh and just let it all out.

She asks me if I want the cotton candy now, and I nod, smiling. "Which one do you want?" she asks me.

"Pink."

Molly laughs. "Of course you do."

Not understanding what she means, I say, "But if you want the pink, I can have the blue. They taste the same, anyway."

She shakes her head and points to my stomach. "No, I just meant because you want Cheese Puff to be a girl."

"Oh, right!" I laugh as she hands me the pink one. Then we sit and practically inhale the cotton candy, the fluffy sugar is so good.

We watch the sky get darker and the lights from the carnival get brighter. From a distance, we can hear people laughing and screaming on the rides. I look at the Ferris wheel, just turning around and around. So many things happen on that Ferris wheel, and no one ever knows, and it just keeps going around and around. Last year, I was so in love with Leo and we were kissing at the top. So many other teenagers have probably done the same thing. *But most of them don't end up in my situation*, I think.

Molly says she's thirsty from all the sugar, but we forgot to bring water, and I'm thirsty, too. Dr. Lippincott wouldn't be very happy about that, she wants me to keep my fluids up because it's important to not get dehydrated when you're pregnant. Molly and I leave to go home, excited to get some water.

I don't think I needed to have a great time at this carnival. Just sitting in the car with Molly, eating cotton candy, that was actually more fun in the end.

And I don't need Leo to be happy. He was only part of my life for a short amount of time, just a year and a half, while I'll have my Cheese Puff for the rest of my life.

As if she or he can hear my thoughts, Cheese Puff gives me a huge kick that actually makes my seatbelt jump. Molly notices and laughs, and then she turns up the radio, and the song I love by Christina Perri, *Miles*, comes on. I close my eyes and try to relax, enjoying the song and pushing all the negative thoughts away.

28 weeks

To-Do List

- pick up paycheck on Friday from Roast and Drink
- appointment with Dr. Lippincott today 5pm
- get budget together
☆ eat more iron!!

☆ get ready for Young Journalists' Convention!!
- ask Marcia about stage directions
- gather best 3 stories (the one about prom, "Spread kindness week" one, science fair one?)
- meet Janet + Peyton in newspaper office to prepare
- send stories to Marcia
- finish French essay (double-spaced)
- study for history test on Wednesday
- do chemistry equations on page 150
- math homework: pages 450-452
- ask Janet to cover the school carnival + edit the story

☆ School carnival on Saturday!

- do more research on Harvard?
- work on savings plan + budget!
- call Alexa!

buy:
- cheese puffs
STOP SPENDING!!

☆ hang up Cheese Puff's ultrasound pictures

☆ buy summer maternity clothes

13
x 4
52
x 5
260
x 4
$1,040
rent, no expenses (possibly?)
$13/hour?

ask Leo's parents about $$?

SAVE $$
SAVE $$
SAVE $$

Cheese Puff

cotton candy!

Chapter 25: Week Twenty-Nine

"Your baby is as big as a head of cauliflower," I read online. I'm pretty much eight months pregnant. Something I didn't know was that when you get pregnant, they count how many weeks you are from the first day of your last period. So, it ends up that there are forty weeks of pregnancy, which is ten months, not nine. The first month, it's not like you're actually pregnant, but it's counted because it's part of your cycle.

So, long story short, I still have two months left to go. It's so crazy to think I've gotten this far, and I really feel like the time has flown by. But at the same time, it's also been dragging along. I really can't wait to not be pregnant anymore and to have my old body back. I also can't wait to meet Cheese Puff.

I feel like the kicks are stronger this week, maybe because it's getting more cramped in there. I really think this is the only part of being pregnant that I will miss. I like the feeling that Cheese Puff is somehow communicating with me, and also it means that she or he is healthy.

I've been thinking a lot about these stories I've read about women who try so hard to have a baby, they want it so badly, and then they either can't get pregnant or they have a miscarriage, or something bad happens. I know the timing isn't what is supposed to happen, but I still feel very lucky. It also makes me feel kind of guilty.

I've become better friends with Alexa, and we FaceTime and show each other our stomachs. It's really cool how she looks up to me because I'm a bit older, and also further along in the pregnancy than she is. I'm only able to get to the support group once in a while, but she goes every week and she tells me what they say.

Right now, it's Sunday morning, April 21st to be exact, and I'm just being lazy and staying in bed. Just as I am trying to decide whether to get up for breakfast or go back to sleep, my phone buzzes and it's an incoming FaceTime call from Josie.

"Hi, Josie!" I say happily.

"Hi, Maddie!" she says with a huge smile on her face. She's always so excited to see me, and I feel the same way. I miss her so much. I see she's in her new room. It looks like her walls are light blue, and all of her furniture is hot pink. It's a weird contrast, hot pink against light blue. It makes me want to laugh.

"What's going on?"

"Well, it's going okay. I like my new school, everyone's pretty nice.

Mom's been working all week and so she's sleeping late today. It's really nice out here, I can't wait for you to come visit. Oh, and I finally unpacked my room!"

"That's awesome, Josie! Why don't you show me around it?"

She shows me her new bed and dresser, and then the paint swatches. She's going to paint her room pink instead of light blue, and I smile approvingly. I wish I was there to help. She also tells me they are getting a small blow-up mattress so that I can stay over whenever I want.

"Did you get more ultrasound pictures?" she asks.

"Yeah, just got some and I'll send them to you, okay?"

She nods and then smiles. "Hey, guess what. In June, I'll be eleven, so you will only be five years older than me, not six!" It's so cute how she says this every year.

"Yes, you will," I say, playing along like I always do. I really hope I can be there or she can be here for her birthday. I don't know if she even realizes how much she's helped me get through this pregnancy, just by being so innocent and excited.

"Josie," I say suddenly. "Thank you."

"For what?"

"For being there for me even after I nearly screwed my life up."

She frowns. "How does a baby screw your life up?"

"Well...for one thing, I'm really young to be having one."

She shrugs. "I think that's a good thing. And you're going to be an amazing mommy, Maddie."

I love her innocent way of looking at things. We talk for a little longer and then she says she's going to wake up Mom because she wants breakfast. We say goodbye after I tell her to tell Mom I say hi and that I'll send ultrasound pictures later, and then we tell each other we love each other, and that we'll do it again soon.

We hang up and when the screen goes black, I see my reflection. Do I look like a mom? It's funny, I don't even know how old I look anymore. I don't feel like a teenager, but I don't feel like an adult, either. In some ways, I had to already grow up and be like a mother to Josie. I've had some practice with her, and so if she says I will be an amazing mommy, I believe her.

<>

Later that day, I send the pictures to Josie and Mom and Mom calls me to tell me to say they are cute and she also wants to talk to me about what's going on with Leo's parents. *Ugh.* She says she spoke to Leo's mom and that Leo's parents are getting a little frustrated with me, because they know I'm not planning on using any of the money that they've been depositing into the account. They think I'm being "difficult and ignorant," according to Mom. She says I'm also being rude. I tell her I will think about it, but I know that I'm only going to use that money if I'm desperate. Mom says she wants me to talk to the school counselor again, she thinks I need to keep up with it until at least the baby is born, so the next day, I go see Mrs. Sherman during my lunch period.

"Hello, Madison," she says, smiling. "Good to see you in here. I've been thinking about you, and I was going to reach out if I didn't hear from you."

"Thanks. It's good to see you, too."

"So, how have you been doing?"

"Good, kind of."

"What's the 'kind of'?" she asks kindly, smiling a little.

I sigh. "Something that's been nagging me is that I'm...well, I'm still being really reluctant about accepting child support from the father's parents. They want to know their grandchild, you know, be involved and visit her or him, and I'm fine with that, I guess, it's just...I'm a little reluctant about the whole money thing. Having them help me with money, with child support, all that."

"Why do you think that you're feeling this way?"

It's hard for me to put it into words, but I try. "Well...I think that..." It suddenly comes to me. "I feel like I have to prove that I can do it myself to other people. So, if I accept help from others, then it's like I'm...I'm giving up. I'm admitting defeat."

"Why do you feel that you have to prove yourself to others?"

"Because..." I trail off, embarrassed to say the words, even though it's obvious. "Because I'm a teen mom! And I just feel like everyone is judging me, and trying to prove I can't do it. I'm going to be constantly trying to prove myself to others, throughout my entire life. No one will see me as a good mother, they'll just see the fact that I was fifteen when I got pregnant and they'll assume I'm stupid. That fact will never go away."

"I see what you're saying, and I understand how you would feel this way. You aren't the first pregnant teenager, and you won't be the last. Believe it or not, I've seen and heard of kids *younger* than you who got pregnant."

"I know. I met one in this teenage pregnancy support group I went to. But she's really nice, and we're friends now."

"That's good, and I'm glad you're doing a support group." She looks right at me. "Let me tell you something, Madison. You are already ahead of the game in that I see how you are taking your responsibility very seriously. Things like you doing the support group and reaching out to me show me that. You are clearly growing up much faster than what you or anyone else would have planned for you. You chose a difficult path, but you are showing a kind of optimism and integrity about it that isn't always the case. I have no doubt that you will be able to make this work, if you keep putting your mind to it and focus." She smiles. "However, it wouldn't be a terrible thing to accept some help from Leo's parents. After all, he's fifty percent responsible and they are doing the right thing, and they are actually legally required to do so, in this situation. No one would judge you for accepting what is rightfully yours to begin with."

"You should hear how people make fun of me," I say, shaking my head. "It would be worse, I think, if they found out that I was taking money from Leo's parents."

"First of all, I doubt it will become the kind of thing everyone knows about. Also, I can imagine how it must feel to have the kids making fun of you. You've made it through this far, and you are obviously stronger than you think. One thing you need to realize is that no one's opinion or judgement is more important than your own. You're aware of what a big deal this is and how hard it will be. You don't need anyone else to tell you, right?"

I nod and then sigh. "They're so mean, though. And the thing is, they're right."

"And you feel you need to prove them wrong?" she asks, and I nod again. "You don't have to prove anything to anyone but you and the baby. I'm not supposed to give you advice, just suggestions. My *suggestion* is that you accept the help. You're still going to have to do a lot of work to make your dreams come true."

She's right, and it feels like a relief to hear her say all of this. We talk a bit longer, and then I tell her I'm going to try to talk to Leo's mom in person. I thank her and then the bell rings and it's time to go back to class.

At work, I go over all the things I want to say to Mrs. Schmitz in my head, and when I get home, I call her and ask her to come over. I tell Molly and Dianne she's coming and they ask me if I want them to be there and I say no, so they say they will go out and give us some privacy, but they will be close-by if I need them.

When Mrs. Schmitz arrives, I ask her if she wants to sit in the living room and she says okay. I notice she keeps trying to sneak glances at my stomach and she's trying not to let me see her doing it. We sit down, me on the couch, and her in a chair across from me.

"So, how have you been?" she asks eventually.

"I'm okay, thanks. The reason I asked you over is because I just wanted to talk to you about the whole...child support thing. My mom says you are hoping I will use the money, but I haven't wanted to. I wanted to tell you why."

"Alright, then," she says, folding her arms and looking at me expectantly.

"I know you're trying to give me some money for the baby to cover healthcare and costs I can't afford and stuff like that. I was really hoping to not use it because when Leo told me he didn't want anything to do with me and the baby, I realized I would have to do everything on my own. I didn't know that you and Mr. Schmitz were going to want to be involved, I just assumed that because *Leo* hates me and doesn't want anything to do with me or the baby, you guys wouldn't either."

"Listen, Madison. We are not pleased with Leo's behavior, you know that. And it's no secret that we were *all* hoping you would terminate the pregnancy early on. But since you decided to keep it, we want to have involvement with what will be our grandchild. You can't deny us that. If you tried to do that, Mr. Schmitz is a lawyer and he would see to it that you didn't get away with it."

I take a deep breath. "I know, and I don't want to do that. My mom explained everything to me. Anyway, what I wanted to say was...thank you. I'm going to try to accept the help now. I'm working really hard to afford things for the baby, but I can see that I will need help. So, thank you."

Mrs. Schmitz takes a deep breath and then actually smiles. "Well, this is something I didn't expect to hear from you today. I can't tell you how happy I am about this. Thank you, Madison."

She actually looks like she's going to cry, I can't believe it. I guess I hadn't really thought about how this whole thing was affecting Leo's parents. I just assumed that they were like him: jerks.

"You should know that Leo will become responsible for contributing money once he turns eighteen," she says. "We have already discussed this with him, and we're encouraging him to have some involvement with child support. He can be difficult, and he really shouldn't have to deal with this kind of responsibility at his age, but I'm sure you already know that."

I think about what she's saying, and I guess this gives him even more reason to hate me. I remember Mom saying something at the beginning of all this about Leo having to pay eventually, not just Leo's parents since it's *Leo's* baby, but I just sort of forgot about it, and I want to keep it that way.

"We will have to work out a visitation schedule, but we can do that another time. I actually have to be somewhere now." She gets up and I get up and walk her to the door, and then she turns to me and says, "Thank you, Madison. This wasn't what I expected." She looks down at my stomach, and this time she doesn't hide that she is looking.

"Do you want to feel the baby kicking?" I ask softly. Cheese Puff is kicking like crazy right now.

"Really?" She looks shocked that I asked, and then she smiles and it looks like she is going to cry again. I move a bit closer to her and she reaches out her hand hesitantly and then lightly touches my stomach. Sure enough, Cheese Puff kicks.

"I felt that!" she says. She actually starts tearing up now. "I had forgotten about this from when I was pregnant with Leo, it was so long ago." I smile, nodding, and she smiles back. "I'm happy you seem to be taking good care of yourself and the baby. Take care, okay? Let us know if you need anything. I keep in touch with your mother, but it would be nice to hear from *you* sometimes."

Then she walks out the door. I stare after her, and my brain is just fuzzy from all that's just happened.

I text Molly and tell her that she left, and I say that she and Dianne can come back if they want. So they do, and they ask me a million questions and I tell them what happened. They say I made the right decision. Then I text Mom and tell her everything, and she says too that what I did was smart.

Later that night, I count the baby's kicks in bed. I do my usual rubbing my stomach and singing some songs. Then I say, "Cheese Puff, I just want you to know that...I'm looking out for the best life for you. Everything I do, I now think about how it will affect *you*. I'm working out different situations and all of that, and I just...I want you to always be protected and loved by the right people, forever."

It's still so crazy to realize that *I'm* going to be the one in charge of parenting and raising Cheese Puff. I will be the one making the rules and making the choices for us, just like Mom did, just like all parents do. It's kind of overwhelming. But I feel like accepting the Schmitzes' help was the right thing to do. Mom was right, as usual. Going to Mrs. Sherman helped, too, and I feel like a weight has been lifted now that I've spoken to Mrs. Schmitz and accepted the help.

And I've also realized that my love for Cheese Puff is always going to overpower how I feel about anything. Even if I didn't want to go to others for help, I did it for my Cheese Puff. I'm putting Cheese Puff first, even ahead of myself. And that's the way it's always going to be.

29 weeks!
11 weeks
away!!

To-Do List

*figure
out average
monthly
groceries
costs?

SAVE!!
(try for
$100/
month?)

- pick up paycheck on Friday from Roast and Drink
- finish English narrative
- math homework: pages 460-468
- 3-page science lab report due Thursday   buy:
- French notes due Friday   - cheese
- history assignment due Monday   puffs!
- read chapters 10-12 for English   - new pencils
- edit newspaper staff's stories for   - baby blankets
  this week's edition   - diapers
- ask Janet to interview librarian for   - wipes
  cover on the library   - toys
- write article on donation opportunities   - baby books

- work on budget!   ☆ go see Ms. Sherman
  $ $ $ at lunch

- send Janet the new story structure layout
- finish French essay
- study for math   ☆ call Mrs. Schmitz and
  quiz next week   ask her to come over tonight
- do English study   - keep in touch about child
  questions #40-50   support
- study for French   - talk to Mom about it
  test on Monday
                              ☆ sale on breast pumps
                                at Babies R' Us next week
                                (research breastfeeding)

CHEESE
PUFFS   yum
           yum
           yum

Chapter 26: Week Thirty

"Your baby is as big as a bunch of broccoli," I read online as I walk on this sunny Sunday morning over to my house. I'm going over to say a final goodbye to it, as it's being sold. Later today, I'm having a yard sale for the furniture in Dianne's garage that Mom kept for me. It's really nice stuff, but I don't need all of it, and I'll save the money for it and buy a few cheaper things, which will still be good enough. I figure I'll keep the couch she gave me, because those are always expensive. I don't know yet if I'm going to have a TV, as I don't think I have enough money for one, and I probably won't have a lot of time to sit around and watch TV anyway. I'm selling the dining table and chairs that she left me, and I will just get a couple of cheap wooden stools that I can put up against a counter. It'll save me space and it won't cost a lot.

My stomach looks pretty big now, and my breasts are really tender this week. I think the milk is starting to get produced. I've been reading about breastfeeding, and I hope I'll be able to do it, because it will save me a lot of money and it's supposed to be the best thing for Cheese Puff, and for me, too.

I have to pee all the time now. I counted yesterday and I peed a total of nineteen times. My feet are still swelling and pressing against my shoes, which is a little uncomfortable. I'm wearing flip-flops almost all the time now, which is perfect, since it's getting pretty warm out.

My heartburn returned at night, and it got so bad I couldn't fall asleep on Friday. I've been trying to drink a lot of water and not eat too fast. Chewing gum and taking deep breaths helps, too.

As I get to my old house, I see the "FOR SALE" sign on the lawn. It makes me want to start bawling, but I try to just stay calm. I use my key, thinking this will probably be the last time I'm allowed to because Mom said that once the real estate person takes over, they won't want us to go in there anymore. I sigh as I walk inside. It looks totally weird, all empty, like nothing was ever here.

I go upstairs to my bedroom and I realize I haven't been inside of it since the fight with Mom, when I moved out. Everything looks so different because there's no furniture. I look at the light blue walls and I remember how much I loved that they matched my bedspread.

My *bedspread*.

Where I conceived the baby sitting in my stomach.

...October 4th, 2018...

Leo and I kissed our way up the stairs and then quietly went into my bedroom, where we went over to the bed. We were trying to be quiet so Josie wouldn't wake up. My heart was thumping like crazy because I'd never been alone in my bedroom with him like this.

He pulled my red tank top over my head, and I stared down at myself, embarrassed at my ratty sports bra. But then he took off his shirt, and I did take a look at his amazingly defined muscles. I remember looking at my bedspread and thinking about how I had had it since I was a little girl and now I was kissing Leo on it. He actually made a comment that it was very girly and I laughed, but inside I felt a little uneasy about being on my bed with him.

As we continued to kiss, he ran his fingers through my hair. It felt really good, but then he started moving his hand down until he was at the opening of my sweatpants. He stopped kissing me for a second and smiled, then pulled down the sweatpants, taking them off, so I was just in my underwear.

"Leo," I said. "I don't think we should-"

"Oh, come on, Madison. You know you want to do this, too."

"We can't...I mean, Josie's in the next room over," I said, like it was an excuse, but really, *I* didn't feel ready. Sure, sometimes I pictured what it would be like to do it with him, and it was always a really nice fantasy, but what I felt comfortable with was just kissing and fooling around a little, that was all.

"She's asleep," he said, tracing his finger along my collarbone. I tugged up my sweatpants and pulled my tank top back over my head and stared right into his eyes, hoping he would understand.

"Leo, I just don't feel ready right now. We haven't even really...*talked* about it," I said, trying to laugh a little. I was hoping he would understand, but instead he just looked pissed.

...

I shake my head, clearing the memory away.

Looking around my bedroom now, it feels like a whole different era. I try to remember how I used to think and what it was like just being a regular kid in here. The thing is, after Dad died, I didn't feel like a regular kid, anyway.

I run my fingers along the walls now, looking out the window for what will be the last time. Then I go into every room and say goodbye. It's really sad going into Mom and Dad's room. And the kitchen is the hardest room to say goodbye to, because that's the last place I ever saw Dad alive. It was his birthday morning and I was leaving for school, and he was leaving for work, and he gave me a big kiss and hug and said that he was excited for his birthday dinner. We were planning to get the ice cream that they set on fire with this special candle that made a cool layer of fried batter on top.

Thinking about these things makes me want to get out of here, so I quickly go to the front door and just turn around one last time and say, "Goodbye, house."

I cry the whole walk back to Dianne and Molly's, and I'm happy I decided to walk, because it probably wouldn't have been safe to drive, because I can't really see well when I cry like this.

When I get back to their house, Dianne and Molly are setting up for the garage sale. They're selling some of their own stuff, as well but it's really sweet that they're helping me sell the furniture I don't want. Yesterday, we went around the neighborhood, putting up flyers.

I'm surprised by the amount of people who come by and buy things. They're priced really cheaply, so they are getting a good deal.

A father who I recognize as a regular from the coffee shop comes by, and he has his three little boys with him. They are hyper kids and he's having trouble controlling them. Watching them makes me think about what I would do if Cheese Puff was hyper. Thank God I'm only having one. One of the boys knocks into the box of Josie's old toys, spilling them everywhere.

"I'm so sorry," the man says. "They can be so obnoxious."

I nod and start bending down to pick them up, and he helps me. I see him notice that I'm pregnant. I'm sure he doesn't recognize me from the coffee shop, and my apron still covers my stomach so he wouldn't have known I was pregnant even if he did remember seeing me there. I wait for him to make a comment, but he doesn't. He tells his oldest son to help me pick them up and then goes to look around.

A few minutes later, he comes back and says, "I'm interested in the dining room table. It's priced for $75, is that correct?"

I nod and he goes back to examine it again. For a moment, I have second thoughts about selling it. So many memories of my family sitting around that table. It's pretty big, though, and I'm worried I won't be able to fit it in whatever apartment I get.

"It's in good shape," he says, admiring it.

"It's a really good table. My mom moved away so we don't need it anymore."

He looks confused, looking over at Dianne, and he says, "Oh, I thought that was your mom."

"No, that's my friend's mom. I'm living with them right now. I'm selling some of my own things, like this table, but a lot of this is theirs."

He looks back and forth between Dianne and Molly and me, then looks at my stomach again. I brace myself for a judgemental comment, but all he says is, "When's the baby due?"

"July."

He smiles and says, "So, this is your table?"

I nod. He takes out his wallet and hands me a hundred-dollar bill. I go to give him the twenty-five dollars change and he tells me to keep it.

"I think it's worth more," he says, and something in his eyes...*really* reminds me of my dad. I blink, trying to push back tears.

I thank him and he smiles and asks another customer if he can help him get it in his truck. I watch as they get it in the back, tie it down, then he and his boys drive off. He waves to me, and I wave back, smiling. I'm so happy that it's going to a nice family.

Eventually, I sell everything except for a couple of Josie's old toys, but Dianne tells me to just save those for Cheese Puff to play with. Dianne and Molly are happy that they sold a lot of stuff, too. We only have a few things left, and we decide to close it down around two o'clock. We have a late lunch and then I count my money. Wow, I made a little over three hundred dollars. I check my bank account online and calculate how much I'll have now, and it equals $3,911.87.

It makes me really happy to see this amount, I've been saving a lot. Then I think of Leo's parents. Mom told me they worked out a final plan and they will be depositing money into an account every month. For now, Mom is going to handle it, and I will be allowed to use it when I'm eighteen. If there's a month that I can't cover all of my expenses, or whenever I have a doctor's bill, I'll let Mom know and send the bills to her so that we can use the child support from Leo's parents to cover it.

Later that afternoon, Dianne and Molly take me to my appointment with Dr. Lippincott. In the waiting room, I calculate the remaining visits until my due date. There's this one, and then six more appointments, so seven in total. I look at the other pregnant women in the waiting room. They all look like they are in their twenties or thirties. I'm used to the looks I get from the other mothers, at this point. I can only imagine how it will be once I actually have Cheese Puff. People will probably think I'm her or his babysitter.

After the ultrasound, we talk about the baby's movements and I tell her I'm worried Cheese Puff is going to break through my stomach, which makes her laugh. She tells me again that it's really important to drink a lot of water now because there is less room in my uterus and I need to keep my amniotic fluid up. She says it would be bad to get dehydrated. I have to remember to keep water with me, at all times.

My next appointment will be May twelfth, and I'll be thirty-two weeks! Dianne says that's the weekend that her brother Ian is coming, and that he'll be here till the beginning of August. I remember her telling us about it when we went to Slurp, the ramen place, that night. It seemed so far away at the time. I really can't believe how fast the time is going. Molly is so excited for her uncle to come, and even though I'm a bit worried about how it will be to have him in the house, I'm happy for Molly, because she never gets to see him except for the summer, and she really loves him.

As if she's reading my mind, Dianne says to me. "And Madison, he knows about you, so I can assure you that he won't judge you or anything. He's not like that, at all. You'll see." It sounds reassuring, but I'm still worried. Also, it will be more crowded in the house and they all belong there more than I do. As much as I've been avoiding thinking about it, I *really* have to start looking for an apartment.

At dinner that night, Dianne tells us that she won't be home after school tomorrow, because she has to go to her editor's office and get the final manuscript of her book together.

"That's okay, Mom," Molly says. "I'll just be here doing homework."

"Molly, why don't you go out, too? I notice you've been staying home a lot," I say.

"Well, I don't really have anyone else to go out with. Cheryl's busy all the time, I don't have a boyfriend, so…"

"Honey, what about that hip hop club at school?" Dianne asks.

"No, I didn't get in on time and it's full."

"Are there any other clubs you could sign up for?"

"I don't like anything except art and photography and that stuff, but those clubs are full, too. I guess I applied too late for things this year."

"Why don't you do some community service?" Dianne offers. "I read in the school newspaper that having it on your résumé is very important for college to accept you one day."

"Wait," I say. "I think *I* wrote that article."

We laugh, and Molly agrees to look for some opportunities. I wish *I* had time to do some community service, but I'm just so busy all the time.

It's really so nice sitting around the table, talking and figuring things like this out. We used to do it when Dad was alive, but after he died, Mom and Josie and I hardly had dinners together anymore, because of Mom's hectic work schedule. I wonder if I had gone with Mom and Josie to Santa Barbara, if we'd be having sit-down dinners again, because now she has a not-so-crazy work schedule. It makes my heart hurt to think of Mom and Josie having dinner and talking together without me, but it was my choice to not join them, so I have to deal with it.

We clear the table and then I go to get my nightly dose of cheese puffs and I realize that I don't have many bags left. Dianne puts them on the grocery list and we laugh. I try to imagine how many bags of them I've gone through since being pregnant. It's probably in the hundreds range.

After dinner, I finish up the last of my French homework and then take a shower. I put lotion on while my skin is still wet, it really helps with the itching and the stretch marks, and it also smells really good. It's a jasmine cream and I wonder if Cheese Puff can smell it through my skin. I think the smell will always remind me of being pregnant.

Thinking about smells makes me think of my dad's shaving cream. It's his birthday tomorrow, and I planned to put some on my wrist and wear it all day so I can pretend he's there. It's too hard to think about the fact that it's also his death day. He would have been turning forty.

Once in bed, I toss and turn, unable to fall asleep even though my eyes are heavy and it's eleven at night. My stomach is getting more and more uncomfortable, and as much as I love the kicks, they are making it harder to sleep every night. I wish I had that first-trimester fatigue so that I could just slip off to sleep easily.

I sigh and get out of bed, then put on a jacket over my pajamas and quietly leave the house, not wanting to wake Dianne and Molly. The neighborhood looks so different at night, and I love the quietness and the dim street lights. I walk along, looking at the tall trees against the dark night sky, which has a ton of twinkling stars. It's pretty warm out and it almost feels like summer will be coming soon. That thought stresses me out, because I am so not ready for Cheese Puff yet.

I love May, it's one of my favorite times of year. The weather is perfect, much better than when my birthday is, in February. It's funny, lately I've been doing this thing where I calculate backwards from someone's birthday to when they were probably conceived. Counting back from my birthday, my parents probably conceived me in May. I wonder if Cheese Puff will like that she or he was conceived in October. But this thought makes me think of Leo, and I don't want to think about him right now. I want to relax on this walk, and hopefully be able to go to sleep when I get back.

My mind really won't stop tonight, it just jumps from one thought to the other, but the walk does help, and eventually I go back home and get into bed. I decide to put Dad's shaving cream on my wrist now, just a little bit.

Forty years ago today, he was about to be born. Because he was born, I could be born. Because of that, Cheese Puff is going to be able to be born. And if Dad hadn't died, maybe Cheese Puff would never have happened.

Dad always said, *"There's a reason for everything."* I don't know what the reason for Cheese Puff is, but I do know that I would rather have Dad back than be pregnant right now. I feel guilty thinking that, and I rub my stomach and try to count the kicks. Cheese Puff is pretty quiet right now, and there are no kicks to count. If Cheese Puff is sleeping, then I'd better sleep, too. I guess "sleep when the baby sleeps" applies to when you're pregnant, too.

<>

When I wake up in the morning, I see there's a text from Mom saying she's coming into town with Josie tonight, and she wants to have dinner together to celebrate Dad's birthday. She suggested we go to the Mexican place, Salsa, but I really don't want to. I suggest Home's Diner, instead, and she agrees. I'm surprised she would want to go to the place he was supposed to go to his birthday dinner with us.

I spray a little more shaving cream on my wrist, rubbing it in and then taking a deep inhale. I'll keep smelling it throughout the day. I have a couple of tests at school today, and I promise myself to do extra well, in honor of Dad.

At school, I really try to tune out all the usual whispers and stares. These people are just not worth the time of day. They have no idea what I've gone through or what my life has been like since my dad died.

Alexa actually texts me, she remembered that I told her that he died on April 29th and that it was his birthday. And Molly has been nice, as always, and we have lunch together today. She asks if I'm doing okay, she remembered about Dad, too.

"I was...at the funeral, remember?" she asks, biting her lip as if she's unsure whether or not she should have said that. I remember Dianne sent us some meals and people sent baskets of food. I still have no idea why people do that after someone dies.

Thinking of this makes me remember that whole time, the days after he died and before the funeral. The perfect word to describe it all was: *hell*. Everyone was just crying all the time. Either that, or it was like we were frozen and had no emotion. We ate nothing except for food from this take-out place that sells submarine sandwiches that I never order from anymore, because it just reminds me of that horrible week. Mom didn't even sleep in her room, she slept on the couch. I overheard her telling one of her friends on the phone that she couldn't stand to be in their bedroom.

She had to plan the funeral without the help of any family, because her parents have been dead for a while and she doesn't have any siblings. I kept hearing her on the phone making funeral plans and talking to her friends about it.

The funeral was held four days after he died, at a church on the outskirts of Redford. I made a speech, and I honestly don't know how I did it. The cemetery where they buried him is a place I never want to go to again. I know some people go to visit the headstone as some sort of way to remember the person who's dead, but I'm definitely not one of those people. It's not Dad; it's just a headstone. I've tried to block it all out, it's such a painful memory.

...May 2016...

I walked up to the front to make my speech and I didn't have the guts to look up, except for one second. I had to take a few deep breaths before I started, I didn't want to cry in front of everyone. I just kept my eyes fixed on the paper where my speech was written. I could hear people sniffling and crying.

"It feels so awful that there aren't even enough words to describe the pain that my mom and my little sister Josie and I are feeling right now. Dad was amazing. He was strong and kind and he had the best sense of humor. He always said our family was the most important thing in the world to him. And I...I can't believe he's gone. I remember looking into his hazel eyes and feeling like everything would be okay, no matter what. We had an inside joke that if we were falling off a cliff, if we looked into each other's eyes, we would forget what was happening. I would give anything to be able to look into his eyes right now. I loved him so much and I'm...I'm going to miss him for the rest of my life..." Then I started crying and I had to stop.

As I walked back to Mom and Josie, I could see they were bawling, too. People came up and tried to comfort us. But none of it mattered.

...

"So is that okay for tomorrow night, Mads?" Molly asks.

I realize she's been talking and I haven't heard her, too busy remembering these horrible memories. "Sorry, I was thinking about something...for what?" I ask. "What are we doing tomorrow night?"

"Going to see the venue where my mom is launching her book. She said that she booked it last week and she wants to show it to us."

"Oh, of course I'll come."

"It won't be too much for you?" she asks worriedly. "I mean, I know

241

that today is probably already so hard for you, and then seeing a place about a book launching, knowing your mom never finished her book-"

"No, it's fine. I want to come."

Molly gives me a hug and says, "Thank you. And I'm so sorry about your dad, I think about it a lot but I never want to bring it up, because I...don't want to upset you."

As she says this, I realize how amazing of a friend Molly has been throughout all of this. She's been there for me through everything. Sure, we've fought, but she hasn't faltered for one moment. She's stood up for me, she's been strong when I couldn't be, she's let me move into her house, she's let me take the spotlight and attention when it comes to Dianne. She's never talked behind my back. She would drop everything for me. I don't know what I would do without her.

I hug her back and say, "Thank you, Molly. For everything. I mean it. Really."

She smiles and then she sniffs around and says, "What's that smell?" I sniff around the air and try to see what she's referring to. "It smells like shaving cream or something."

I just shrug and hope she doesn't realize it's coming from my wrist. I feel like if I say it out loud to someone, it won't work anymore to make me feel like Dad is there.

The rest of the day is kind of a mix of sadness and also excitement because I know I'm going to see Mom and Josie later. After work, I drive over to meet them at Home's Diner. When I get there, I see that Mom and Joise already have a booth. They wave when they see me and Josie runs over and gives me a big hug. Mom comes to hug me, too, and we all walk back to the booth together. Before we sit, they both ask to feel my stomach, and they say they can't believe how big it's getting.

After we order, Mom looks like she's about to cry. "He would've been forty," she says. *"Forty years old."* She sniffles. "Forty was always our lucky number. Because...we met in the English class we had together in college, and the classroom number was forty, and so we always considered it good luck to see that number." She starts crying for real. "And we made a plan for our fortieth birthdays...we said that we were going to share it *together,* we were going to order exactly forty mini cupcakes from our favorite bakery. I guess it's never going to happen now..."

I pass her a tissue from the little dispenser on the table, now feeling like *I'm* about to cry. Then suddenly, an idea strikes my mind. "Why don't we order forty mini cupcakes for dessert *now?*"

Mom laughs through her tears. "That's crazy. They can't serve us that many."

"Okay, fine, how about four?" I ask, laughing a bit, and she agrees, so we ask the waitress to bring us four chocolate cupcakes for dessert. It's actually perfect, because it's as if there's one for Dad, too. Mom brought a birthday candle and matches, and she puts the candle in what would have been Dad's cupcake.

Mom goes to light the candle, but then I joke that I'm going to be a mom soon, so *I'm* going to have to know how to light a match. Mom is a little hesitant but then she agrees, and she shows me how to do it. It's harder than it looks!

Once it's lit, Mom says, "He would've loved this." She says we should all make a wish and then blow it out together. Josie and I nod in agreement, and then we all close our eyes, making wishes for Dad.

I hope you know how much I love you and how much I miss you. I hope that somehow I can still make you proud of me. I wish more than anything that you were still here, but since that's impossible, maybe you are somewhere watching over us. Happy Birthday, Daddy.

<>

After the cupcakes, we sit and talk for a little while. Then Mom says she wants to show us something and she says she will drive us somewhere and then come back and get my car after. She ends up driving us by the house. As we're approaching, I see it: a huge "SOLD" sign. *Wow.* She tells us that the house sold just a couple days ago. She stops in front of it, and we all just sit there staring at it. It's such weird timing that it sold right around Dad's birthday. Maybe it's a sign that he would want Mom to be doing what she's doing, in Santa Barbara, pursuing a career in the writing world again.

Afterwards, Mom drives me back to my car. It's sad saying bye to them, but we had such a good time together and I realized that we really can still see each other a lot, even though they're two hours away. I can go there, or they can come here.

We really did a nice job of celebrating Dad's birthday together. It feels better, now that time has passed. I still miss him so much, but that horrible pain isn't really there anymore. We haven't been able to talk about him that much since he died, but tonight we were sharing stories and bringing up memories and it made us laugh and smile, which is something I never thought would happen. It really felt like he was there with us.

I drive back to Dianne and Molly's, but I feel like I need to walk a bit, so I park the car a few blocks away from their house and I start walking. I decide to call Alexa, because I never returned her sweet text that she sent me this morning.

She's happy to hear from me, since I couldn't make it to the last teen mom group meeting, and we both want to catch up on what's going on. I tell her about the house being sold. She tells me that she moved four times during her childhood, so she totally gets how it feels.

Then I ask her how everything has been going with her dad and the baby's father, and she tells me that her dad just couldn't handle it and they were fighting all the time, so she decided to leave and now she's living with Danny, the baby's father, and his family. They don't really know how anything's going to work yet, they're not going to live with his parents forever, but Alexa is going to high school next year, and they're trying to figure out how to rotate days caring for the baby when the time comes. It's horrible to admit this, but I feel a huge pang of jealousy. She's so lucky that she's actually still with the baby's father. If only Leo could be more like Danny.

We talk a bit more about how we're feeling, the pregnancy symptoms we're experiencing, et cetera. Even though I'm jealous about her situation, it still makes me happy to talk to her.

When I get home, I can barely wait to go to bed. But it figures that now, when I'm tired, Cheese Puff starts kicking like crazy. It's like I'm sharing a body with someone else. I feel bad getting annoyed, and so I say, "I love your kicks, baby." As if encouraged by my words, Cheese Puff kicks more, and I see a little outline of its foot against my stomach, and I smile, because *I grew that foot.* "Your foot is adorable."

I decide to sing, thinking it might help her or him calm down and go to sleep. I sing *Twinkle, Twinkle, Little Star,* which is what Dad used to sing to me and Josie before bed, when we were little. It seems to work, and I'm not sure who falls asleep first; me or Cheese Puff.

♡ ☆ <u>30 weeks</u>!! ♡ 10 weeks left!

● ♡ ♡

To-Do List

- pick up paycheck on Friday from Roast and Drink

Diapers = - go to old house for final goodbye

$10/pack - DO YARD SALE!! ☆ appointment

Wipes = keep / sell with Dr.

$7/pack - couch - dining table $75 ♡ Lippincott

$17/week - bed + chairs $20 each today 5pm

x 4 - dresser - bookshelf $30 ♡

$68/ - desk - TV stand $30 buy:

month - nightstand - Josie's old toys ♡ - cheese puffs (of course)

Bank Account - deposit money from yard sale - crib?

= $3,911.87 into bank - gum

$ $ $ - study for French test tomorrow!

● - memorize English vocabulary ☆ dinner with

- finish English essay questions Mom + Josie

- do English worksheet at Home's

BUDGET!! - assemble new layout for this week's Diner tonight

newspaper edition after work

♡ - write article on "too much homework"

- ask Janet to edit "entertainment" articles for

this week's edition

♡ - do math review worksheet ☆ go to Dianne's

book launch

HAPPY venue tomorrow

♡ BIRTHDAY night

DAD

♡ - start going for nightly

walks again

● - call Alexa again soon

← Cheese Puff

sleeping

Chapter 27: Week Thirty-One

"Your baby is as big as a coconut," I read online. *Do I really only have nine weeks left of pregnancy?* That's crazy. I'm trying to not get too nervous, but I'm thinking about the actual labor more and more. I don't know how I will be able to stand the pain. I've read online about how bad it is, and I really hope I can get an epidural. I also worry that I won't know I'm in labor. I've been getting more and more of the squeezing things that are called Braxton Hicks. I've gotten used to them, but they still kind of freak me out. I find that when Cheese Puff is more active, it brings them on more.

I've also been doing something with Cheese Puff that's kind of funny. I can tell when she or he is sleeping, because there's no movement for a while. So, I get something sweet to eat or drink, like a muffin or a mug of hot chocolate or orange juice, and within a few minutes, Cheese Puff starts moving like crazy again. I try not to do it too often, because I'm trying to not have too much sweet food, but I can't help it sometimes, it's so much fun.

Dianne took me car seat shopping last week, and I found a really good one for one hundred dollars. Dianne is going to teach me how to install it in the car, and she said we should do it a few times so I'm really sure I know how to do it. I know it's really important that it's installed properly so that it's safe for Cheese Puff.

I've been in a pretty good mood lately. May is my favorite month, and I've been taking a lot of walks and enjoying the warm weather, but today's been a pretty stressful day. I have tons of papers to write since the school year is almost over, and there were what felt like a million customers at work today. I like it when it's busy because the time goes by faster, but I guess I'm just getting tired more easily than before.

It's so nice to finally be able to relax and have dinner with Dianne and Molly. Dianne made fish for dinner, which she only makes once in a while. I never used to like fish, and I hated it when my mom used to make it, but Dianne uses some spices or something that tastes really good, and I like it now. She also serves it with garlic bread, which I love.

Dianne looks at me seriously as I start eating. "Is your hospital bag packed?"

I laugh nervously. "I know, I know, I need to do it, and I *will* pack it! I'm not going into labor for nine weeks, hopefully! There's time!"

"Cheese Puff might think otherwise."

"Yeah, I don't think Cheese Puff has a calendar in there," Molly adds, and we all burst out laughing, and the stress from my day starts to disappear.

We finish dinner, and I go to my room to finish a science assignment. Then I take a shower, call Mom and Josie to say goodnight, and then I *finally* get into bed and get ready to count the kicks and snuggle into my pillows and blankets, but all of a sudden I get really nauseated. Worse nausea than I even had at the beginning of the pregnancy. I think it must be my imagination, or just a weird moment that'll pass, but it doesn't. I drink some water that I keep on my nightstand, but it doesn't help.

I start getting really anxious, which makes the nausea worse. I get up to walk around the room, thinking that might help, but it actually makes it worse and now I'm dizzy, and all of a sudden I know I'm going to throw up, so I run to the bathroom and throw up a ton, a lot of the food that we had at dinner is still in my stomach, I guess. Dianne comes rushing in because she could hear me, and she asks what's wrong.

I start crying, my teeth shaking from fear and the acidic taste lingering in my mouth. I don't feel any better, even though I just threw up, and that usually made me feel better, whenever I had morning sickness.

"I don't know! What's wrong?" I ask, crying harder. "What's wrong with me? I'm really nauseous and...and I feel like I need to keep throwing up. I'm...I'm going to throw up again." And so I throw up again, into the toilet. Dianne holds my hair back.

Then Molly comes rushing in to see what's wrong. She sees me throwing up into the toilet and Dianne holding my hair and she starts freaking out, asking what it is. Dianne says that sometimes this can happen with pregnancy, even though it's not the traditional morning sickness. She ties my hair back and hands me a washcloth to wipe my face. Then she helps me back to bed and goes to get a large bowl to keep with me so if it happens again, I don't have to get out of bed.

About twenty minutes later, I end up vomiting into the bowl. It happens *again* ten minutes later. I'm feeling worse and worse and now it feels like I'm going to have *diarrhea.* I run to the bathroom and I have diarrhea and then I get up to throw up at the same time. This is *hell.* I don't remember if I've ever felt worse. I'm shaking and I can't even drink water now, because it just makes me throw up again.

Dianne now looks really worried, and says she wants me to see a doctor. It's so late, and all the doctor's offices are closed, so she calls Dr. Lippincott's after-hours line and we wait for her to call back. I throw up again while we're waiting. Dr. Lippincott calls and Dianne tells her what's happening, and she says she isn't sure it's related to the pregnancy, and that we should go to the emergency room because I might be getting dehydrated.

I try to swallow down my fear. *What could be wrong? What have I done wrong?* My heart races, only making the nausea worse. Molly says she wants to come, even though Dianne said she could stay home. They get dressed but I stay in my pajamas, I feel too weak to get dressed, just moving around makes me want to throw up. Dianne brings a bowl in the car in case I throw up again. She opens the windows, and the fresh, cold night air makes me feel a little better. I hold the bowl really close to my face because it comes on so suddenly, and I don't want to throw up on Dianne's car.

I ask Dianne what she thinks it could be. "I don't know," she says, swiftly making a left to the hospital. "You could have the stomach flu, or it could be food poisoning, but when you're pregnant, food poisoning is *not* something you want to have, trust me. It could be dangerous."

Now I'm even more worried than I was before.

We pull up to the hospital, and after they do my vitals, they take me in pretty quickly. They make me change into a gown, and as I'm changing, I end up having to throw up again and I can't get to the bowl in time, so I end up throwing up on the floor. The nurse comes in and helps me into the bed, handing me a weird blue bag that she says is for throwing up into. The doctor comes in and asks what happened, and after I tell him, he tells the nurse to start an IV and give me fluids, and he orders some blood tests. I'm really scared at this point and I ask him what's wrong. He says not to worry and they're going to find out and help me.

I'm scared about how this might be affecting Cheese Puff, I haven't felt any movement for a while. Then again, I've been so busy throwing up and worrying about my own symptoms, I don't know if I would have noticed the kicks.

I really don't like getting an IV, but the nurse does it gently and it doesn't hurt that much. She says the fluids should help, and she puts blankets on me because I'm shivering. She says I have a bit of a fever, and they will give me something to help with that, too. Then she puts a few of the vomit bags on my bed beside me.

Scared tears run down my face. I want my mom. I ask Dianne to call her to tell her what's going on, and so she leaves to call her, then comes back a few minutes later and says she told her and that Mom is concerned and wants her to keep her updated. She asked if she should drive in, but Dianne told her not yet, that everything will hopefully be okay soon. Molly sits next to me, holding my hand, and Dianne asks the nurse for a cold washcloth, and she puts it on my forehead.

I throw up a couple of more times before the doctor comes back in. He says that the blood tests show that I most likely have food poisoning. He says we have to rule out something called "listeria," which could lead to permanent neurological problems with the baby's brain. I haven't had any deli meats or soft cheeses, as right at the beginning, Dr. Lippincott told me not to eat those things. He says it's probably not the case, but we need to make sure. He asks what I've eaten in the last twenty-four to forty-eight hours and I tell him. Dianne gets really upset and she says she thinks it might be the fish. But the doctor says that even if it was the fish, it will hopefully just work its way through my system and I won't need to have antibiotics or anything.

I tell him I'm feeling a little less nauseous and I don't feel like I'm going to have diarrhea, I'm just really tired. He says to rest a bit, and even fall asleep if I can, and that the fluids should help. He says it's really important to get me rehydrated, not just for myself, but also for the baby. He says that babies are aquatic creatures and they need to have their amniotic fluid kept up, so it's important to drink lots of fluids. I tell him that Dr. Lippincott tells me this all the time and that I'm very careful about it. He nods and then tells the nurse to do something called a "non-stress test" on the baby. He explains that they do this to make sure the baby is doing okay, and it won't hurt.

The nurse wraps something that's almost like a stretchy seat belt around my stomach, and then she connects it to a monitor. As soon as she connects it, we see these waves on the screen and she says that it's the baby's heartbeat and that it's steady and strong. Thank God. I was so worried about how this could be affecting Cheese Puff, I thought something might be wrong, but now I want to cry, I'm so happy that everything is okay. The nurse pats my shoulder and tells me to relax and try to sleep, and then she leaves.

"Madison, I'm so sorry," Dianne says to me. "I bet it was the fish. I'm always very careful with fish, but every once in a while, you can get a bad piece in it. I'm so sorry, I feel terrible."

"Dianne, you don't have to apologize, seriously, we don't even know if it was the fish." Just then, Mom calls and Dianne tells her what's going on. She asks to speak to me, and we talk for a few minutes and I tell her I'm really okay and that she shouldn't worry. Then Dr. Lippincott calls Dianne and she answers and gives her the update.

The nurse comes back in with a little white pill and says it's a nausea medication that will help with the nausea. She says just to let it dissolve under my tongue, and I do. Then I get really tired. She said that it can make you tired, and that I should sleep if I can, that sleep is good for me to get right now.

Molly holds my hand and Dianne strokes my arms as I lean back in the hospital bed, my eyes starting to get even heavier than they were before. I fall asleep the second I close them. I literally couldn't keep them open if I tried.

<>

When I wake up, I see sunlight streaming through the windows. I remember where I am when I see the hospital environment. Molly's not here, but Dianne is stretched out on the small couch in the corner of the room. She sees me wake up and she comes over to ask how I am. Other than feeling tired, I'm okay. No more nausea, in fact, I feel hungry. Dianne tells me that they kept me overnight just to monitor me, and that Molly wanted to stay, but she sent her home to get some rest for school.

Soon after, the doctor comes in, and I tell him that I'm feeling a lot better. He says they gave me two bags of IV fluids during the night, so I'm nice and hydrated and I don't have a fever anymore. I haven't thrown up since before I fell asleep last night, and he says I can go home. As long as I feel better, I can start eating plain foods. I'm getting really hungry and I feel like pigging out, which he laughs at and says is good to hear, but he says to go slow and eat dry toast, bananas, apples, that sort of thing.

Once I'm home, Dianne gets me into my bed with a glass of ginger ale and a piece of dry toast on my nightstand, and she leaves my window open so I can get some fresh air. I thank her and thank her over and over again, and when she leaves, I eat the toast and drink the ginger ale, and then I fall asleep again.

When Molly gets home from school, she comes into my room and asks how I'm feeling. She looks almost scared to see me, but she smiles when I say I'm feeling better and I'm not throwing up at all anymore. She tells me she picked up my homework assignments from school and she puts them on my desk.

I really need to start studying for finals. I should also start trying to build up my community service for my résumé. I know that Molly does a lot of it, and now that I'm feeling better, I really want to start focusing on getting organized, too. I go online to look up local community service opportunities, and it says there are some opportunities on the library's website. There's something that looks like fun, and also relaxing: reading to children for "Bedtime Story-Time" between six p.m. and eight p.m. I could probably take a half shift at Roast and Drink, and go to the library at around seven. It will also be good practice for Cheese Puff. And it counts on my résumé, which is great, so I sign up for it.

Later at night, after a dinner of clear chicken broth and dry toast with sliced bananas to go easy on my stomach, I get ready for bed. As much as I hated being sick, it was good for one reason; I was able to get some sleep! Maybe it was the pill they gave me, but it was the first time I've been able to sleep well in a while. Between Cheese Puff's kicking and me having to get up to pee every half hour or so, I can never get a good night's sleep. My back hurts and I just can't find a comfortable position anymore. I remember reading that having sleep problems is your body's way of getting you ready for when the baby is born, because you won't be getting much sleep anymore after that.

I seriously wonder how the earth got so populated, even *over*-populated, with how hard it all is to bring even *one* life into this world.

<>

The next night at seven, I'm at the library, reading "Goodnight, Moon" to a group of kids with their blankets and teddy bears, sitting with their parents. I love our public library, it's a really modern building and the room we are in is a little children's reading area sectioned off from the rest of the library. It is nice and quiet and there are thick dark blue drapes covering the library's windows and a soft carpet where the kids and their parents sit in front of me while I read to them. I find it relaxing, and I can't wait to do this with Cheese Puff. It's also really good to know that this is building up my community service hours to help me get into Harvard.

Five books and thirty minutes later, my hour is done and some of the parents come up to thank me. They're so welcoming, it's really nice. As I'm leaving, I see a girl wiping down some of the craft tables in the corner of the room. I notice her belly first, as it's obvious she is pregnant, and then I realize it's Alexa!

I go over to her. "Alexa!"

"Oh, hey!" she says brightly. "I'm just doing some community service. You, too?"

I nod. "Yeah, I just did the reading circle. You should try it, it's so much fun."

"Good idea. Actually, I'm just finished now."

"Me, too."

We get our backpacks that we left at the front and sign out and leave. It's so nice and warm out, I love that the nights are getting warmer. We both take out our waters and take sips, and then laugh because we know we're trying to stay hydrated because we're supposed to for the baby.

We decide to go to Sweet Cream Ice Cream, as it's a few doors away.

"So, how are you doing?" I ask her.

"Good, actually. I mean, aside from still having the morning sickness, which is all-day sickness, so I don't know why they call it that." She laughs. "But I have more energy than before, and Danny and I have been thinking of baby names. It's our new favorite game to play, who can come up with the best one."

"That's so great," I say, trying to block out the jealousy, and then feeling guilty for even having the jealous feelings in the first place. "What names are you thinking of?"

"For a boy, I like really strong names, like Richard or something. But if it's a girl, I want to name her something after 'Jewel,' like maybe Julia. It was my grandma's name, and I always told her I'd name my daughter, if I had one, after her."

"That's so sweet."

"What about you?"

"I don't know. I mean, I've thought of names, but none of them feel right. I feel like I'll just look at it and know. But that might not work, because all babies pretty much look the same, so..."

"Well, there's always Cheese Puff, right?"

We giggle. I'm actually so used to calling it Cheese Puff, I wonder if I will even be able to get used to another name.

We enter the shop and I get my usual bubble gum, and she gets mint chocolate chip, and then we go to sit down. I don't think I ever appreciated ice cream as much until I got pregnant. Something about the coolness and sweetness together.

"I don't think I've ever asked you, what is your actual due date?" I ask her.

"First of October. When is yours?"

"July fourth."

"Oh, wow, the Fourth of July!"

"Yeah, I guess this year I'll be partying it up in the hospital room instead of watching fireworks! Assuming the baby comes on its due date, which they say only happens five percent of the time," I say, and we laugh again. Then I get quieter, pausing before I ask, "So...what about Danny's parents? Are they...supportive?"

"Well, of course. I'm living with them. And yeah, I mean, they're kind of...cold to me sometimes, and we don't really talk much, but at least they're letting me live with them. To be honest, sometimes it's weird with *Danny,* too. We're not so attached to each other anymore, we're just focused on the baby. It's really awkward sometimes. I cry a lot, and I don't want him to know I'm crying, so I...I go into the shower and do it."

"I can relate to the crying, believe me. I feel like that's all I ever do.

But at least Danny is staying with you. Leo wants nothing to do with me, and I guess he'll...well, he'll never know the baby."

"Oh my gosh, I totally get it. How could I be so insensitive and say that it's hard for me when it's even harder for you?"

"No, that's not it, trust me I know how hard it is for you, too, it's just...you should be really happy that the father's staying with you."

"But sometimes I'm worried he'll just leave me," she says, looking down. "I mean, there are times when he doesn't even talk to me and says it's because he's busy with school, but...I know he's really not. It doesn't feel like he's my boyfriend anymore, and I have no clue how he will act once the baby is born. I mean, we're so young. We would never have ended up being together if I hadn't gotten pregnant. He told me his parents thought we were way too young to get married, but they also think we're too young to have a baby. It's so crazy. Also, they want him to get a job, and they're at least happy that *I* have one, but he says he's too busy doing basketball practice."

"If he leaves you, which I don't think he will, but if he does, you'll be okay, because you're so strong. Seriously, I'm sixteen and you're fourteen, and yet I feel like we're the same age. You're so mature."

"Well, now I kind of have to be. I don't think of myself as a kid anymore."

"Me neither. I mean...we can't really be kids anymore." Alexa looks sad and I know how she feels. It's so good to be able to talk to someone who really understands how I'm feeling. It's weird, we have only known each other for a short time, but it feels a lot longer.

I say to her, "I think you're going to be a great mom, no matter what. So many people think 'teen mom' automatically means 'bad mom,' and I'm sure that does happen a lot, but it doesn't have to happen to us."

"Well, thank you. You're going to be a great mom, too."

"It's weird, isn't it?" I ask her, laughing a bit. "That we're just kids ourselves, but now we're going to be having kids?"

"I'm kind of excited, though," she says, smiling. "To have someone that belongs to me, someone to take care of, someone to watch over and be worried about."

Hearing her say that, I remember how worried I was when I was in the hospital, just a couple days ago. And the thing is, I wasn't worried about *myself*; the whole time, I was just worried about my Cheese Puff. I tell Alexa what happened and she looks horrified, but I tell her that I'm definitely okay now.

We both want another scoop of ice cream, but we decide not to, because we've already eaten our weight in it, and so I offer to drive her home. On the way, we both keep giggling because the babies are kicking and moving around a lot from the sugary ice cream. I'm so happy that Alexa's in my life. And I'm really going to try to stop being jealous about her situation. I think that it's so hard for *all* teen moms, no matter the circumstances.

← coconut

31 weeks

← little cheese puff

To-Do List

- pick up paycheck on Friday from Roast and Drink $$$
- finish science worksheet + memorize vocab terms
- recruit writers for new "recipes" section of the newspaper
- start studying for finals!
  (science, French, math, history, English)
- get a note excusing me from the PE mile run

☆ ask Molly to pick up my homework

☆ call Mom + tell her I'm okay

- ask Janet to send this week's newspaper edition to be printed ASAP
- history paper due Monday (5 pages)
- math homework: #60-80 on page 480
- read English chapters 13-16
- English character chart due Friday
- 10-page French paper due Thursday
- write a cover on the upcoming school fundraisers for newspaper

☆ Bedtime Story-Time community service at the library from 6-8pm (go at 7pm?)

☆ tell Johnny I'm taking a half-shift at Roast and Drink

290
x 4
——
960

☆ pack hospital bag soon

☆ learn how to install car seat into the car

← me throwing up EWW

buy:
- cheese puffs
- crib!!
- flash cards

$ work on budget $
(not stable)

☆ research labor + delivery + epidurals

* call Alexa Soon!

Chapter 28: Week Thirty-Two

"Your baby is as big as a cantaloupe," I read online, as I'm on my way to Dr. Lippincott's office for my appointment. Wow, a cantaloupe is pretty big, but it makes sense; my stomach grew a *lot* this week, it feels like it's doubled in size. The other day, I absentmindedly reached over for one of my old shirts, but when I put it on, I couldn't get it to go down over my stomach. All my old shirts look like workout bras on me now.

Also, last Saturday, as I was sitting on my bed adding up my tips from the coffee shop, it suddenly felt wet inside my bra. It turns out I'm leaking colostrum now, just a little bit, but I can't believe how cool it is. I bought some nursing pads, and I'm wearing them all the time now.

I've also been having these *really* vivid dreams. I'm always able to remember them, they seem so real. One was where I accidentally left the baby at the park and then I had to call the police, but they came and arrested me, it was horrible. Then, in another one, I couldn't stop spinning while I was holding Cheese Puff, and then I dropped her (it was a "her" in the dream). I read that a lot of women say they experience more vivid dreams when they're pregnant.

I also read that even though it would be early, if Cheese Puff was born now, the chances of survival for her or him are pretty good, because the organs are fully developed this week. I don't want to go into labor early, though, because I need all the time that I can get to get ready.

After my appointment with Dr. Lippincott, we are going straight to the airport to pick up Dianne's brother Ian for the summer. He's coming in from the University of Iowa. Dianne told me they have a great writing program and that he's mainly interested in poetry, which I think is kind of unusual for a guy. It made me think about Matthew and how he liked learning about Shakespeare and wanted to write plays. I miss Matthew a lot. We still talk a little at school, but it's nothing like what it used to be. I thought we could've at least stayed friends, but I guess we're both busy, and since we can't be boyfriend and girlfriend, it's almost harder to try to be friends.

Anyway, Molly's really excited for her uncle to come, and I'm happy for her, but I've been kind of dreading it. I feel like it'll be weird to have to get to know someone new, and also, he's a *guy*, so I feel like that'll make it much more awkward. Even though Dianne said he wouldn't judge me, I'm worried she's wrong.

At Dr. Lippincott's office, everything goes well. She feels my stomach to make sure Cheese Puff isn't breech, and so far she or he isn't, so hopefully it will stay this way and I won't have to have a c-section.

On the way to the airport, Molly whoops. "Woo-hoo, Ian, here we come!"

Dianne laughs and looks at me in the rear view mirror. I smile and hope she can't tell how nervous I am to have someone who's a stranger to me in the house. "My brother's a fun person. And he's really sweet. When Molly was born, he was only three, but he was so careful with her. It was cute, he would bring her his trucks to play with."

They laugh, and I laugh along, trying to meet their excitement, and then I say, "It's so funny that he's only three years older than Molly and he's your brother, Dianne."

Dianne nods. "Yep, well, that's what happens when your mom has you at a young age and then has another child at a later age, and then *you* have a child at a young age."

"He actually turned nineteen on...well, on April 29th," Molly says. "I didn't want to bring it up at the time, because I know it's the same day as your dad's..."

"Oh, wow. That's so weird," I say. "I mean, what are the chances?"

It's quiet for a minute and then Dianne says, "It's crazy he's already done with his freshman year of college."

"I know!" Molly says. "I remember when he was the age *I* am now, and I was just thirteen. That seems like yesterday."

"Time goes by so quickly," Dianne says. "I'm really happy he stays with us in the summers, otherwise I don't know when we'd see him. I mean, he was only around four when I moved out with Molly, so we never got to grow up together. That's part of the reason he stays with me, instead of with our parents. We feel like we still have so much catching up to do."

"He also comes for *me*, Mom!" Molly says.

Dianne laughs. "Yes, that is true, of course. He also has a great summer job here every year."

"What's his job?" I ask, curious.

"He works as a lifeguard and also a swim instructor for kids at the community center pool. He's been doing it since high school. It pays really well and he's so good with the kids. He teaches babies all the way up to teenagers."

"Yeah, he's an amazing swimmer," Molly says.

"Speaking of jobs, Molly, I wanted to talk to you about *you* getting a job. I know that Madison got a job because she's pregnant, but it's good for kids your age to have a part-time job. It teaches you about responsibility and managing your own money."

"I know, and I actually think it would be fun to work, but I have no idea where."

An idea pops into my head. "How about when I stop working at Roast and Drink, you can apply to fill my spot? I bet Johnny would hire you."

"Really? That would be awesome, Mads!" she exclaims, and then she groans. "It's too bad that we didn't work there at the same time."

"Aw, I know! That would've been so much fun!"

"Madison, have you decided where you're going to apply after you leave Roast and Drink?" Dianne asks me.

"Not yet, but I'm working on it."

"Okay, good. Let me know if you need my help with suggestions, okay?"

"Yes, thank you."

"Almost there! Molly, can you text Ian and tell him we'll meet him at baggage claim?" Dianne says, and Molly nods. "Oh, and by the way, Ian usually stays in the guest room, but since you're there now, Madison, he's going to sleep in my room, on the pull-out couch. It'll be fun, because we can really be like siblings for the summer."

Molly rolls her eyes. "He'll just be up telling you his stupid jokes all night."

Dianne laughs again. "Yeah, he's funny. Or, he likes to think he is."

"Is he smart?" I joke.

"Oh, yes, very. He always got really good grades in school and he's doing well so far in university. It's funny, though, sometimes I think he'd much rather just be traveling around the world than being in school. He's just always wanted to travel, it's one of his biggest dreams. It's part of why he has his job. He wants to save money to go to Europe or somewhere someday."

"He and I have talked about traveling somewhere together when I graduate high school," Molly says. "He's always felt more like an older brother to me than an uncle."

I nod. Molly always seems like she's at her happiest when Ian's around. Maybe it's lonely for Molly, being an only child. I don't know what I'd do without Josie.

I start getting nervous again as we pull up to the airport. I know Dianne and Molly keep telling me not to worry and that Ian won't be judgmental of me, I just can't see how that's true.

The airport is really modern, it's mostly glass walls, with very high ceilings. It's always exciting to come here and listen to the sound of all the planes taking in the background. It's fun to imagine all the interesting places that people are going. There are some really good take-out places to eat while you're waiting for your flight, including this one place that has the best pizza.

We park and then go to wait by the baggage claim. Suddenly, I hear Molly scream, *"Ian!"* She runs to meet him, who's walking quickly towards us. He drops his carry-on and picks her up and swings her around, and they both laugh then come over to me and Dianne. He and Dianne share a big hug, and then he smiles and waves at me. "You're Miranda, right?"

"Madison," Molly quickly corrects.

"Oh my God, *Madison,* sorry, hi," Ian says, shaking my hand. "My sister told me all about you. Nice to meet you."

I shake his hand back, smiling. "Nice to meet you, too."

I look down, feeling really awkward. I can only imagine what she told him. Ian seems nice, though, and his smile is really welcoming. He's more good-looking than I pictured for some reason, with wavy dark brown hair that's a bit messy, but in a good way. He also has the most intense blue eyes I think I've ever seen. Dianne also has blue eyes, but his eyes seem even bluer, maybe it's because he seems to have a tan, and so his eyes really pop out. I'm surprised that he actually looks nineteen, and I realize that for some reason, even though I knew his age, I still pictured an older uncle, just probably because of the word "uncle." But he definitely looks nineteen.

It seems like it takes forever for his luggage to show up on the baggage conveyor belt thing. While he and Molly and Dianne catch up, I feel kind of uncomfortable, so I go to sit on a bench near the entrance. Once they get the bags, they come over to me and I get up and we start walking back to the car in the parking lot. Dianne puts her arm around Ian and tells him how great it is to see him and they start talking about school. I notice he's a few inches taller than Dianne.

As we get into the car, Molly says, ""I'm *sooo* excited, I hope the summer goes by really slow!" We all laugh and Molly sits in the back with me and Ian sits in the front with Dianne. A song Molly and Dianne like comes on the radio and they start singing along, really belting it out. Ian rolls his eyes and shoots me a look and I laugh.

"They love this song," I say.

"Really? It's impossible to tell." He laughs again and turns around to look at me. "So, Dianne tells me your baby's due this summer?"

Well, it had to come up sometime and I'm kind of glad that he's being so direct so we can get this part out of the way, and I can hopefully stop feeling so uncomfortable. "Yeah, I'm eight months now. Due July fourth."

"A fireworks baby, that's fun! Boy or girl?" he asks playfully.

"Haven't found out yet. I'm keeping it a surprise."

"I have a funny theory about finding out the gender on your own."

"Oh, no, not another old wives' tale."

"No, this is actually a soulful one," he says, winking, and it makes me smile. "If you go to the beach and stand there, waiting for the waves, if the waves point in the right direction, it's a boy, but if they point in the left direction, it's a girl."

Wow, that's interesting, it's one I haven't heard before. I was expecting something stupid, like the ones I keep reading and hearing about, but I like this one, it's kind of spiritual. "Okay, fine, that's a pretty cool one," I say.

Then the song *Miles* comes on the radio, and Molly squeals, "Maddie, it's your favorite song! Ian, turn it up!"

"Oh, ha, I like this song, too," he says, and then he turns it up.

"You like Christina Perri?" I ask him. It's funny, I've never met a guy who likes her. Only girls. Leo used to fake-gag when I played the song in front of him.

"I just like the lyrics of this particular song." He cringes. "I know, it's girly, huh?"

Molly and I laugh. This is going so much better than I thought it would. Ian seems really easy to be around, and I can see that he and Dianne are siblings, they have similar personalities, they're fun and also really welcoming.

When we get home, it's dark, and Dianne takes Ian up to her room to unpack and get settled. We have pizza for dinner, and the conversation is mostly about Ian's school, and they also try to figure out different plans for the summer, like when they will go visit their parents together, et cetera.

I felt tired throughout dinner, but once it's time for bed, I'm pretty wired up and I feel like I won't be able to fall asleep right away. It sounds pretty quiet in the house, so I guess everyone went to bed, and I decide to go to the living room to have some cheese puffs. I put a limited amount in a bowl, which is something I've been doing lately, rather than taking the whole bag, so this way I won't eat too many.

I sit on the couch and turn on the TV. An old rerun of *Three's Company* pops up. I'm so happy, I love this show and haven't seen it in a while. My mom had the whole series on DVD and she would watch it sometimes, and she always told me that it was her favorite show when she was a kid.

"Midnight snacks are the best, aren't they?" I suddenly hear, and I almost spill the whole bowl of cheese puffs everywhere. I turn to see Ian standing there. He's now wearing glasses and he's holding a mug of what smells like hot chocolate.

"You just totally scared me," I say, laughing a little, and he says he's sorry, and then asks if it's okay if he joins me. I nod, and he goes to sit on the armchair next to the couch.

"My sister is the queen of hiding good hot chocolate mix, but I always know where to find it," he says, laughing.

"Oh, yeah, I always find chocolate-stained mugs around the house."

He laughs. We watch *Three's Company* for a bit and then at a commercial, he asks, "So, how long have you been living with Dianne and Molly?"

"Since December. When I...when I found out I was...pregnant."

"It's pretty cool."

"What?"

He shrugs. "I don't know. Pregnancy. I'm just in awe of women and how they can actually *make a human being.*"

"Well, um...yeah," I say awkwardly. I want to crawl into a hole.

He turns back to the TV and now I'm feeling really self-conscious. I ask him if he wants some cheese puffs and he takes a few. We watch the end of the episode, and then I say, "Okay, uh, I'm going to bed. Goodnight."

"Okay, I'm going to stay up and watch some more TV. I'm a bit of a night owl. Goodnight, Miranda," he says, smiling.

"Oh, it's Madi-"

"I know, just teasing. Have a good night."

I feel like I'm blushing as I head to my room. I brush my teeth and get into bed. Now I'm more awake than ever. I can't stop thinking about what Ian said about women being able to make a human being. It's true, and it's amazing that he thinks that way, I don't know if other guys feel that way, but Leo obviously doesn't.

I sigh and rub my stomach, feeling Cheese Puff kick, and I smile. "Did you like the cheese puffs?" I say. "You know, one day, I'm going to have you try cheese puffs, and I bet you're going to love them more than anything." I smile, thinking about it, and Cheese Puff starts kicking harder, as if we're having a conversation. "I'm going to miss your kicks when you're born."

<>

The next day at school, I have an appointment with Ms. Sherman at lunch. I've been going to her about every three weeks, and I really like talking to her.

"Nice to see you, Madison," she says. "How have you been?"

I sigh, letting my shoulders relax, going to sit. "I don't know, as it gets closer to when the baby is due, I'm...I'm feeling weird about being excited."

"What do you mean?"

"Like, I know I'm supposed to be hard on myself, but I can't help feeling a little excited to see my baby, but at the same time, I don't feel like I deserve to be happy, because, obviously, this whole thing was a...it was a mistake."

"Madison, it's perfectly normal to feel like this, especially now when it's getting so close to being a reality. But I really implore you to stop thinking about this as a mistake. We know it wasn't planned, but it's not helpful or productive to keep thinking about it as a mistake. You need to move on from that thinking, and start really getting ready. Where are you in the preparations and the plans?"

Unexpected tears come to my eyes. "I'm getting organized and I'm getting ready. It's just that, sometimes I...I don't want to be so strong. I just want to be a kid again. But I mean, now I'm almost a mom, so I have to be strong. I used to be...just a teenager. I didn't have anything to focus on except for my friends, and school, and working towards college, and now...I'm having a *baby*. It's like it's *really* hitting me now."

"Something you probably already know is that life is a series of choices. You make choice after choice after choice. That's what makes your life what it is. It's okay to question your choices, and it's important to express your concerns out loud, to talk to someone like me, or anyone, as long as you get it out. It's also okay to have regrets. The important thing is to also be practical and to stay on track. You know what your goals are, and you need to keep focused on them. You've come a long way from the scared girl that first came in here. You're getting stronger and stronger, whether you realize it or not. It's okay to not do everything perfectly, nobody ever does. You will make more choices in life that you think of as mistakes, but that's how we learn. And sometimes what seems like a mistake at first ends up turning into something good. It's all what we *make* of it, do you understand?"

I nod. She's so wise and I always feel better after talking to her. The rest of the day, my mind keeps going back to what she said about not thinking of it as a mistake. But I also can't help but think about the night that started it all.

...October 4th, 2018...

After I told Leo I wasn't ready to do it, he was upset, and I said I had to go to the bathroom. While I was in there, I was thinking about him being annoyed with me. I didn't want to lose him and I was worried that he'd just break up with me and be with another girl who would want to have sex with him. Still, I didn't feel ready to do it. I was only fifteen, that felt too young to lose my virginity. I wondered how old my mom was when she lost hers, but we never really talked about it.

But I also felt like maybe I should just do it with Leo. I mean, we loved each other, even though we had never said it out loud.

I stared at myself in the bathroom mirror, trying to figure out what to do. I really was afraid of losing Leo, I'd never felt the way I did about any other guy. Besides, I should be flattered that he wanted to do it with me, when he could have any girl he wanted. I decided that I should just do it. The thought of getting pregnant never even crossed my mind, I mean, what were the chances? I remember thinking that we should use protection, but we didn't. Obviously we should have. That was the mistake. It was a *huge* mistake. I honestly didn't think in a million years I would get pregnant on the first time I had sex in my life.

...

Alexa comes by my shift during work. She had promised to come by one night so we could hang out and catch up on my break. She orders a coffee and then I take my break and we sit at one of the tables.

"I know you're not supposed to drink much coffee during pregnancy, but honestly, I'm so tired all the time, I just need it," she says.

"Oh, trust me, I'm like that with cheese puffs. If there was a restriction on them during pregnancy, I'd eat them anyway."

We laugh and then she looks around. "It's cool that you work here. It's nicer than McDonald's, where I work. And at least you don't come home smelling like french fries and burgers, like I do."

"No, but I smell like coffee, and when I take a shower, I swear the water coming off of me turns brown from the grinds that somehow get on my skin."

We laugh again, and I realize she's becoming someone I would consider a good friend, and that makes me happy. She leaves after my break, and just as I'm getting back behind the counter, Ian walks in. *Oh my God, did he know I work here?*

He walks up and says, "Oh, Madison, hi! I didn't know you worked here!"

"Oh, uh, yeah. Hi," I say. He orders a coffee and says he doesn't put anything in it, so I give it to him black, keeping my eyes on the cash register. It feels really awkward, he's just standing there and I can't think of anything to say. I mean, yes, we're living in the same house right now, but I don't really know him. It's easier when Molly and Dianne are around.

"You know, I don't know if Dianne told you, but I work at the community center pool. I'm a lifeguard and swim instructor. They have pregnancy exercise classes a few times a week. Maybe you would like to do something like that? It's a really nice pool."

"Thanks, but there's no way I'm getting into a bathing suit right now."

"Okay, but I don't think you should worry about that, the other women are also pregnant and they seem to really love it. They say it makes them feel lighter. Not that you're heavy, I didn't mean that, I just mean because your stomach is bigger because of the baby...ugh, this really isn't coming out right, sorry."

"It's okay. Please don't worry about it, I know what you mean."

"No, but I mean you really look good. In fact, if it weren't for your stomach, I wouldn't even know you were pregnant. And by the way, I told you, I think it's a *beautiful* thing to be creating a human being."

I kind of nod, not sure how to react. I can tell he feels bad for me, but he means well, he's not a jerk like so many of the people at school.

"Anyway, it looks like fun, so if you change your mind let me know," he says. "I don't teach the class, but I can get you into one of the classes."

"Well, I don't know. Maybe. Thanks for telling me about it."

Another customer comes in and Ian says, "Well, I should get going. Are you having dinner with us? Dianne is making her famous steak with pepper sauce."

"Oh, I'll definitely be there. She's an amazing cook."

"Yep, she really is. Okay, see you later!" he says, and then he flashes one of his big smiles and then leaves.

Eating dinner that night, Ian is full of questions for me and Molly. He wants to know about school, mostly. Then I decide to ask him about *his* school. "What are you majoring in?" I already know the answer, because Molly told me, but I figure it's a good way to keep the conversation going.

"English language and literature. I want to teach, and I'd like to be a professor." Then he puts his hand to the side of his mouth, like he's going to tell a secret, and he kind of whispers, "Really, I'd love to just travel around the world, sitting at cafes everywhere, just *writing* about my experiences."

Dianne laughs. "It's no secret, Ian."

"So maybe you could do something like be a travel writer?" I ask.

He nods. "I've thought of that, believe me. And it's a possibility, for sure."

"Our parents don't think writing is a secure enough profession," Dianne says. "So they're encouraging Ian to be a teacher or something more stable."

"Yes, but it's the double standard, because *you're* allowed to be a writer, no questions asked."

They laugh and Molly smiles, she's been in such a good mood since Ian arrived. "Speaking of writing, Mom, do you know the date for your book launch yet?" she asks.

"Sunday May 26th," Dianne says. "I'm still coordinating things with my publisher, but the cover is all done!"

"I'm sure it'll all be great," I say to her, and she smiles at me.

"I want to read this new book of yours!" Ian says to Dianne, smiling.

"It's a horror novel, like all the others. Not really your jam."

"What's happening with the book that was possibly going to be made into a movie?" Ian asks.

"Haven't really heard anything since the meeting." She sighs. "The life of a writer, as you know, has its ups and downs. That's why I stick to the horror novels, they seem to have a large audience."

We laugh and then Ian turns to me, "So, Molly tells me you're an up-and-coming journalist?"

"Yeah. Right now, I'm writing for my school's newspaper. My goal is to get into Harvard, they have a really good journalism program."

"Could I read one of your stories?"

"I'll send you my best one if you want to give me your email address," I say.

"I'll send *my* email to *you*. What's your email address?"

"It's 'maddieluvspizza@gmail.com.'"

He laughs. "I'm surprised it's not 'maddieluvscheesepuffs'."

Dianne and Molly look confused, and Ian says, "Oh, I caught Madison eating cheese puffs last night when she couldn't sleep."

Molly laughs. "Did she tell you that's what she calls the baby?"

Then Ian laughs. "Cheese Puff? That's funny. I like it."

As if she or he can hear, Cheese Puff gives me a huge kick and I tell everyone and they laugh. It's actually turning out to be much better than I expected, having Ian here.

After dinner, I do some homework and then change into my pajamas. I can't decide if I should go get my nightly snack of cheese puffs. I'm a little worried I'll run into Ian again. Why am I worried, though? He was nice the last time. I guess it's just a bit...awkward, having a stranger around. I mean, I just met him yesterday.

I decide to go to the kitchen, and sure enough, Ian's there. I jump and he says, "Sorry, I guess I've scared you once again. I have that effect on people," and he laughs. Then he asks, "Is this what you're looking for?" and he pulls out the bag of cheese puffs from the pantry and hands them to me.

I laugh. "I just have a few before bed, it helps me get to sleep."

He nods and then says, "No TV tonight?"

I shake my head. "I'm kind of tired. And I have a test at school tomorrow."

While he makes himself another cup of hot chocolate, I eat about ten cheese puffs, and then I say goodnight to him and head to bed. Part of me wanted to change my mind and watch TV with him, but I really do need a good night's sleep tonight.

Getting into bed, I look at the can of Dad's shaving cream, and tonight, for some reason, I feel like I want to put a little on my wrist. I put on a tiny bit and then snuggle into my pillows. Lately, I've been sleeping with two pillows propped up under my head so that my heartburn isn't as bad. I also put one on each side of me so that I can put them in between my legs.

I take a deep inhale of my wrist, and then I think about how weird it is that I decided to put it on tonight. Usually I only want to use it when there's something upsetting me, but tonight, I'm actually in a really good mood. It was really fun at dinner, and it's nice to see Molly and everyone so happy with Ian here. I just feel...good, and I kind of want to have Dad be a part of a *good* moment this time.

← cantaloupe

32 weeks!!
8 weeks left!!!!

To-Do List

- pick up paycheck on Friday from Roast and Drink
- appointment with Dr. Lippincott today at 5pm
- pick up Ian at the airport with Dianne + Molly
- finish French essay ♡
- study for math test on Friday   buy:
- do English "book reflection" sheet   — cheese puffs
- study for history map exam on   — lotion
  Wednesday ♡   — nursing pads
- Science paper due Friday   — nursing bra
- fill out science chart
- history notes due Friday ♡ ☆ get more sleep!
- STUDY FOR FINALS!!   ☆ eat healthier!
- write article on the   ☆ next appointment
  upcoming prom ♡   with Dr. Lippincott:
- edit Janet's stories for   May 26th 5pm
  this week's newspaper ♡ ♡ ♡
  edition
- try a pregnancy exercise   * go see Ms. Sherman
  class at the pool? ♡
* LOOK INTO BIRTHING CLASSES
- work on budget ♡   ♡
- call Alexa soon
- call Mom + Josie soon ♡   ♡
- do more research on
  labor/delivery/epidurals/
  breastfeeding   ← hot
          chocolate

☆ 50% off on diapers
  at Babies R' Us next
  week   CHEESE PUFFS
          ← my
  Cheese Puff

$
$
16
x4 $
64
x5
320
x4
$1,280
(possible)

start
looking
for a
new job!!!

Chapter 29: Week Thirty-Three

"Your baby is as big as a butternut squash," I read. This is my first week of my ninth month of pregnancy, and after this month, I only have to make it through the "tenth" month to go full term. It's funny, I thought I was uncomfortable *before,* but that was nothing compared to how it feels now with my stomach so huge. It's getting harder and harder to walk, and also to get up and down from a sitting or lying down position. Also, my back is hurting more and my legs ache all the time. I see why people always offer seats to pregnant women on the bus and stuff like that. They *need* to sit down. I keep thinking about what Ian said about those pregnancy swim classes and they sound good, but I really don't want to put on a bathing suit the way I look right now, and I don't think I can deal with the looks from the other pregnant women, judging me.

The scary thing is that my stomach is going to get even bigger. I can't even imagine it. The itchiness is so bad, the lotion isn't even really helping anymore. Also, I'm getting less and less sleep, between the horrible heartburn and having to get up to pee all the time because the baby is pressing on my bladder. It's so hard for me to get up to pee that by the time I do it and waddle over to the bathroom, I'm wide awake when I get back to bed, so I can't fall asleep right away. Also, the Braxton Hicks are happening almost all the time, which is freaking me out. Dr. Lippincott says it's not labor until it really starts to hurt, and they don't hurt yet, but everytime they happen, I worry I'm about to go into labor.

I've also really started craving sushi, even though I know I can't have it. Before I got pregnant, my favorite thing to get was a salmon roll with avocado and cucumber. I literally can't wait until I can eat that again. I wonder if it's safe to eat it when you're breastfeeding? I hope so. I can't wait to eat all the foods I haven't been allowed to have, like deli meat.

I know I have to start going to childbirth classes. Dr. Lippincott has recommended them and she says they will help me come up with a birthing plan. Basically, I know the plan. What I want is to have an epidural or whatever they can give me so I don't feel any pain. I really can't even think about it, it's so scary. I've been asking Mom about it, and she said it hurts at first but she had an epidural with both me and Josie, and she said it made all the difference. She wants me to call her the second I think I'm in labor, and she'll drive in right away.

It's Sunday, and Molly and I are going to see a movie and take a break from studying for finals. I decide to take a shower before we leave as my hair is getting a little greasy, I haven't had time to wash it since Thursday. The hot water feels good, and it makes me realize I should try to take one everyday, as it really helps with the back pain. I can't see my feet anymore, my stomach is so big. I love lathering up my stomach, it feels so smooth, and I wonder if Cheese Puff feels like I'm giving her or him a massage.

I drop the soap, and try to bend down to pick it up. It's really hard to bend down and I try to grab the side bar in the shower, but I miss it and end up slipping and crashing down hard onto my wrist.

Oh my God, the pain!!! I'm shocked at how much this hurts and I'm freaking out because I can't even get up. I don't know what to do. I start crying and I call out for Molly. The water is pouring down on me and I'm in so much pain, this is really horrible. What if she just can't hear me? I scream louder, and still nothing.

"CAN SOMEBODY HELP ME?" I yell at the top of my lungs. I'm worried I'm going to faint from the pain when suddenly the bathroom door bursts open, and I see Ian rushing in.

"Madison! What happened? Are you okay?!?" He reaches in to help me and I don't even care that he's seeing me naked, I'm in so much pain and I'm scared and I can't stop crying. He grabs a towel and wraps me in it and helps me out of the shower.

"I fell," I say, trying to talk through the crying. "I'm worried my wrist is broken." He looks at the way I'm holding it and he asks, "Can you move it?", his face knotted up with concern. I try to move it, but I can't, the pain is too severe and it just kind of hangs there. "We should go to the hospital."

He tells me that Dianne and Molly are out doing an errand so he will call an ambulance. He dials 911 and then helps me get dressed. I can't stop crying, the pain is so bad. I know I should be embarrassed that first he saw me naked and now he has to see me crying and screaming, but I don't even care, I just want to not be in this pain. The ambulance comes really quickly and they examine me and say it looks broken, so they take me to the hospital, with Ian sitting in the back with me. I close my eyes and try to shut out the pain.

Once we arrive at the hospital, they take me in right away and after examining me, the doctor sends me for an X-Ray. Ian asks if he's allowed to come with me, and they say it's okay. I can't believe I'm back here again, this hospital. First, Molly was sick from not eating, and then I had my food poisoning, and now this? *How many times am I going to have to be reminded of when my dad died?*

After the X-Ray, they take me into a room and the nurse hands Ian an ice pack and tells him to hold it on my wrist. I can see a huge purple-blue bruise is forming all over my hand and wrist, going up my arm.

Ian calls Dianne and gets her voicemail, so he leaves a message telling her what happened. The nurse comes in and says the doctor said she should give me some painkillers, thank God. She puts an IV in my arm, because she said it will work faster if they do it that way. Ian turns away when they do the IV and I think it's funny that he can't look. I never used to be able to stand needles either, but since getting pregnant, they don't bother me at all anymore.

The painkillers work pretty quickly and I finally feel like I can breathe and be calmer. Ian asks for another ice pack and just keeps holding it on my wrist. He really is so nice. I feel terrible that he had to be the one to take me here. It's all so embarrassing.

As if he's reading my mind, he says, "By the way, don't worry. I didn't...see anything. I mean, I didn't look. I know you're probably worried about that, but please don't be."

I smile and nod, kind of drowsy. The painkillers are making me really tired and I want to close my eyes, but the doctor comes in and tells me that sure enough, it's fractured. He says I'm lucky that it's just a hairline fracture so it won't take as long to heal as a full break, but I will need to wear a cast for about a month. He also says that I need to be really careful because accidents like this happen a lot to women when they are at this stage of pregnancy, because it's harder to move around. Also, apparently your bones become more flexible as your body prepares for birth, so it makes it easier to break something.

I'm so tired, and I feel a little loopy from the pain medicine. My eyes start to close as I hear the doctor tell Ian that the medicine will make me tired and he should let me sleep. They will come in and put on the cast soon.

I hear Ian calling Dianne again to give her an update. I can't tell if I'm awake or dreaming, but I kind of drift in and out and I can see someone come in to straighten my wrist and put on the cast, but it feels distant and it doesn't hurt at all. I try to tell them that I want to take some of the pain medicine home with me, but I don't know if they can hear me.

<>

I open my eyes a little while later and I have no idea where I am until I try to lift my hand and it feels really weird and heavy, and I see a dark blue cast that starts at my thumb and goes to the middle of my forearm. Then I see Dianne sitting in the corner on her phone. I remember what happened and I see that I'm still in the hospital in the little ER room.

Dianne sees I'm awake and comes over to me. "How are you

feeling?" she asks. "Is it hurting?"

"It hurts, but not like it did at first."

"Okay, well, the doctor gave me a prescription for some painkillers and you can take them as needed. They are going to discharge you, they were just letting you sleep. I'm glad you could get some rest. I've spoken with your mom, she was very concerned and she wanted to drive in, but I told her that you're okay, and she wants you to call her when you can. If you want her to come in, though, she will, and she's welcome to stay with us, I can make room."

"Thanks, Dianne, I'll call her." I look around. "Was Ian here?"

"Yes, but he left when I got here. I think he went to run an errand or go to work."

The nurse comes in and asks how I'm doing and then hands Dianne some papers to sign and also some instructions on how to care for the cast. She says they will be taking it off in four weeks. *Four weeks? Oh my God.* Then Dianne helps me get dressed and we leave to go home.

Molly comes to greet me when I get home and she looks really concerned and worried that I'm in pain, but I tell her I'm okay, I'm just still really tired. Dianne helps me get undressed and into bed, and I take a long nap.

When I wake up, the pain is pretty bad again. I try to get up and I realize now it's going to be even more challenging to do anything because I can't use that hand. I can't believe this. As if it wasn't hard enough just being eight months pregnant. *Ugh!*

I call out for Dianne and ask her if I can have more pain meds and she brings me some with a glass of water. She says the doctor told her I should only need these for the first twenty-four to forty-eight hours, and then I should be able to just get by with Tylenol. Then she brings dinner to my room, and Molly and I eat on trays just like we did when I had the bed rest.

I haven't seen Ian, and I wonder if he's avoiding coming home because of what he had to see in the shower. It's *so* embarrassing to think about, me lying there naked with my huge pregnant belly, crying and screaming and unable to get up. Like a big, beached whale. I can't even *think* about it, I'm so humiliated.

I call my mom and give her the updates. She asks me a million questions, I can tell that she's still worried about me, but I tell her that I'm truly fine and that she has nothing to worry about. I think she tells me to be more careful ten times before I hang up. I promise her that I will, and I tell her I love her, and she says she loves me, too.

The pain meds are making me tired and really out of it again. I try to do my homework, but I can't really concentrate. I realize how lucky I am that it wasn't my right hand, though, because at least I can still write. I drift off to sleep with my textbooks on my lap and when I wake up, it's dark in the room and I see the moon out the window. The pain isn't too bad, but I'm really thirsty. I don't want to bug anyone, but I really need some water and the bottle next to my bed is empty. I slowly get up, being really careful not to put any weight on my left hand. It's going to take forever to do anything now.

I go to the kitchen and I can hear the TV on in the living room. I'm sure it's Ian, and I really don't want to see him right now. I quietly get some water and then try to sneak back to my room, but Ian comes out to the hall as I'm creeping my way.

"Madison?" he says, looking concerned. "How are you feeling?"

I can't even look at him, I'm so embarrassed about him seeing me not only naked, but then he had to drive me to the hospital, what a nightmare. "I'm okay, uh, the painkillers help. Um...thank you for..."

"You don't need to thank me. I'm happy that I was there to help you."

I nod and turn to go back to my room. "Madison?" he says, and I stop, but I still can't look at him. "I just want you to know, in case you were feeling, I don't know, worried about it, I didn't really *see* anything when you were in the shower. And you have *nothing* to feel embarrassed about, okay?"

I kind of laugh and say, "Just a whale on the beach, right?"

He comes over to me and lifts my chin. "That's not funny. You're the furthest thing from a whale on the beach. Are you kidding me? You're *pregnant*. Stop it, okay?"

Oh, no, I feel like I'm going to cry. Not now, no. I stop the tears and nod. "Okay. Thanks, Ian, really. Thank you."

"Okay, now let's go into the shower," he says.

I give him a look like he's crazy, and he says, "No, I'm serious. You need to 'get back on the horse.'"

I laugh, but then I say, "I'm not taking a shower right now, Ian."

"I know, I know. But there's a surprise in there for you, so come on."

He takes my hand and leads me to the bathroom, where he pulls back the shower curtain to reveal a little chair that's attached to the bathtub and the wall. I look at him, confused, and he smiles.

"I went to Home Depot today and got this for you. It's perfect, now you can sit down when you shower and you won't have to worry anymore."

I stare at it and then look at him. Now I can't help it, the tears come.

"Oh no, I didn't want to upset you!" he says. "I wanted to do the

271

opposite! I asked my sister and she said it was a good idea. But it's removable if you don't want it…"

"No, I do, I…it's really…" I finally find the words. "It's just so nice of you."

"It was fun to install it, actually. And…now you'll be safe. Anyway, I'll let you get to bed. Goodnight, Madison." He goes to leave.

"Ian?" He turns back, and I say, "Thank you."

He smiles and nods and then he leaves. I brush my teeth and get into bed, realizing I'm actually shaking a little. I just can't believe that he would do that for me. I thought he would want to *avoid* me after seeing me like that, but he was actually doing something to help me even more. *Wow.* I see why Molly and Dianne love him so much.

<>

In the morning, the pain from my wrist is still there, but not as bad. I decide to take Tylenol instead of the painkillers that the doctor prescribed, because they make me tired and a bit loopy, so I would rather save them for nighttime. I have my first two finals today, in science and then in French. I need to be able to think clearly.

"What's going on?" Molly asks as we walk to school together. "You seem like you're in a really good mood, and you're never happy on Monday mornings."

"Yeah, well, maybe it's the painkillers…" I smile and then I say, "Just kidding, I only took regular Tylenol this morning."

"Maddie, you broke your wrist and basically stayed in bed all weekend! I was expecting you to be like a monster this morning!"

"Well, I just think I'm lucky, that it wasn't anything worse, I guess. And…well, your, uh, uncle, he was really nice, did you see what he put in the shower? The seat?"

"Yeah, I saw it. He was so excited that he figured out how to install it." She grins. "I told you that he was nice."

I smile again, and then I realize I really *am* in a good mood, and Molly's right, it *is* weird. I know what it is, but I'm trying not to admit it to myself because I feel like a total idiot. I think I have a crush on Ian. I know it's the most ridiculous thing ever, I mean, he's *Molly's uncle,* and besides there's no way he would ever want to be with someone like me. But I keep hearing a little voice in my head that says, *"He's only three years older,"* and he does keep saying that he thinks pregnancy is a beautiful thing. I have to keep telling that voice to shut up, because I know that he just means it as a general thing, not for a teenager, like me. I'm being ridiculous. He's being nice to me because I'm Molly's friend, and that's all. He feels sorry for me. He saw me like a whale in the shower. There's no way he would ever be attracted to someone like me. I need to forget about this right now, I need to just let it go.

"Nervous for finals?" Molly asks.

I nod. "Are you?" She nods, and we laugh, and then we walk into school and wish each other good luck.

During my science final, I finish it pretty quickly and then just keep checking over my answers. The teacher likes us to stay sitting and keep going over it even if we finish early. My mind keeps drifting to Ian. I try to stop it, but I can't help it. I just keep picturing him sitting with me and holding the ice on my wrist at the hospital. And then he goes out and gets me a shower seat and installs it? And he teaches kids how to swim? I just can't believe how nice he is. And his eyes are so blue and his smile is *so* gorgeous. I love the way his hair looks messy, but he still looks clean and fresh.

I start thinking about how he loves to travel, and how we talked about him possibly becoming a travel writer. All of a sudden, a daydream comes to me.

I'm at the Grand Canyon with Ian, and I'm holding Cheese Puff in a baby carrier, and I look really beautiful, wearing a flowy turquoise dress, and my hair is long and blowing in the wind.

Then we're in Paris, standing on a bridge. Ian's carrying baguettes and French pastries in a bag, and we're kissing as we look at the Eiffel Tower-

Oh my God, stop! Stop, Madison! I realize my eyes were just closed, and I open them to see the teacher staring at me. She must think I'm sleeping or something. I shake my head and go back to checking my exam. Okay, okay, I let myself have a little fun and daydream, but now I need to get back to reality and stop being so crazy. It's really bad to keep thinking the way I am. I'm just setting myself up for rejection. Besides, I think Molly would kill me if she knew how I've been thinking.

<>

Thankfully, Ian isn't there when I get home after work later. Dianne is also out, and Molly is studying in her room. I make myself a sandwich and then I decide to take one more of the painkillers that the doctor prescribed for me. The pain isn't too bad, and Tylenol seems to be good enough, but I still have a couple of these stronger ones left and it'll help me sleep. I don't have any homework due tomorrow, and I'm tired and could use a good night's sleep.

I take the pill with water and then go to get into my pajamas and brush my teeth. In the bathroom mirror, I can see the seat Ian put in the shower for me. It makes me want to cry again. I think maybe I should take a shower, but then I decide it's not a good idea now that I've taken the painkiller and also I don't know if I'm ready to actually take a shower yet, I'm still a little scared, even with the seat.

I get into bed and start counting the kicks. I can feel my mind getting a bit loopy from the medicine again, and I look out the window and start thinking about things like what it'll be like when Cheese Puff is my age and gets a crush on someone. I hope she or he will talk to me about it, because it would be so much fun to have conversations about it. I just let my mind drift and I think of all the fun things I want to do with Cheese Puff, like have ice cream and hot chocolate and cheese puffs. I want to watch the same shows I used to watch with my mom, like *Three's Company.* I wonder if Cheese Puff will like to watch the news and reporters on TV, the same way I always have. Maybe she or he will also want to be a writer or a journalist. Who knows?

Thinking about journalism makes me think about how I told Ian maybe he should be a travel writer. I remember my daydreams from earlier today, and they make me smile. Here I go again, thinking of his cute smile and messy hair. I kind of laugh to myself, the medicine is really making me loopy now, and I don't care if it seems crazy or ridiculous to have a crush on him. I just want to enjoy the feeling right now of liking someone.

I heard him come home a little while ago. I could hear him in the kitchen, and then he must have gone to bed because I could hear him and Dianne talking in her bedroom, even though I couldn't hear what they were saying. It's pretty silent in the house now, so I guess everyone is asleep. I look at the clock, it's almost midnight. *How did the time go by like that?* Wow, I really better not take any more of the painkillers. I can see how people get addicted to them, they make you feel so good. I think that they also make you hungry, and I decide that even though it's a pain to get up, I'm going to go get a quick snack and then go to bed. I'm craving cheese puffs, what else is new? Right now, with the painkillers going through my system, the thought of me loving cheese puffs and calling my baby Cheese Puff makes me laugh so hard.

I really don't want to wake anyone up, so I walk really slowly and as quietly as I can into the kitchen. As I walk over to the pantry, something catches my eye and I see it's a new bag of cheese puffs, already on the kitchen counter. It's weird, I don't remember leaving them out, and I actually realized that I had run out of them and I was going to buy more on my way home from work, but I forgot.

Then I see a little note next to them. It says, *"Looking for these? :) - Ian."*

Oh my God. He didn't do this, did he? I guess he did.

Okay, seriously, how could I *not* have a crush on him? I can't stop smiling as I open the bag and start eating them. I try to limit myself, but I decide to give myself a break tonight, especially when I'm this hungry from the painkillers. Eventually, I force myself to stop eating them and I put them away. I take the note with me back to my room and place it next to my bed on the nightstand, next to Dad's shaving cream and the frame that Mom gave me with Cheese Puff's ultrasound. I don't remember falling asleep, but I'm sure I had a huge smile on my face as I did.

☆ 9 months ☆   33 weeks!!

AAH!!

● ♡ To-Do List ♡

-pick up paycheck on Friday from Roast and Drink
-movie with Molly 12pm 🗑 ← popcorn   buy:
- STUDY FOR FINALS!!   - cheese puffs
  * science + French final tomorrow   - lotion
-figure out layout for this year's   - diaper bag?
 final newspaper edition
-ask Janet to cover "Senior Grad Night"
-write article about the highlights   ☆ pack hospital
 of this school year   bag
-edit all the articles for this
 week's edition!   ☆ get note for
                                             PE

☆ cast comes off
  on June 16th!!!

↑   ┌─────────────┐
cast   ♡   │ Items for   │
                                     │ Cheese Puff's│
                                     │ Nursery: │
♡ -study study study!   ♡   │ - crib   │
  -make birth plan?   │ -changing table│
  -look into birthing classes ASAP   │ - dresser? │
♡ -read cast instruction manual   └─────────────┘
  -study for math + history + English final!!

♡   * School is   ☆ stop taking
        over soon!! *   painkillers!!
                            ☆ get plastic wrap/
♡ -learn how to install the   bags for showering
  car seat into the car!!   with the cast
                            ☆ thank Ian for the
●   ♡   shower seat again?
         ♡   ♡
              ♡   ♡   ♡
                              ♡

Cheese
Puff
♡
  ♡
♡

Chapter 30: Week Thirty-Four

"Your baby is as big as a pineapple," I read, and it makes me laugh, because throughout my whole pregnancy so far, I've basically pictured Cheese Puff looking like each fruit or vegetable that this website compares it to.

The other day, I woke up still feeling a little groggy from the painkillers. As I was getting out of bed, I noticed the note from Ian about the cheese puffs, and it made me remember what he did and I'm happy that it was actually real, and not just a dream. I know he's just trying to be friendly and nice because I'm Molly's friend and I'm going to stop thinking about him in the way that I have been, so it's not awkward around the house. I don't want to have to worry about avoiding him and being weird around him.

We are all in the car together now, driving to Dianne's book launch. Molly and I are in the backseat and Ian is in the front next to Dianne. We're all excited because now her book will be in bookstores. I've never been to an actual book signing for someone I know, and it makes me think of Mom and her book. Maybe someday she'll have one for herself. I hope so.

I actually took a shower this morning. I was a bit scared at first, and Dianne offered to stay in the bathroom with me. She had to help me wrap up the cast in a plastic bag and then she showed me how to get the shower head down, and then I just sat on the seat and used my right hand, and it was really easy, so she left. I told Ian how much the seat helps, and he was happy.

I'm glad that I took a shower, because now I'm not scared anymore, it was actually really relaxing with the seat in there, and it's so much easier with this huge belly now. I scrunched up my hair with a new conditioner that you leave in your hair. Molly got it, and it smells really good and it makes my hair nice and wavy. I'm wearing a new maternity dress that I think actually looks pretty good. It's light blue with tiny yellow flowers, and it's made of a kind of stretchy fabric which flows over my stomach so that it doesn't look too big. I'm wearing my usual sneakers because my feet are swollen and my legs are too sore for any other type of shoe, but I think the sneakers look okay with the dress.

The cast is clunky and ugly, and I feel like it ruins the whole outfit. It's really uncomfortable and I just don't use that hand at all, it just gets in the way of everything. It's also getting really itchy inside, and Dianne gave me a ruler and said she broke her ankle when she was a kid, and she remembers how itchy it gets inside the cast, and you can scratch it by sliding a ruler or something inside. It does help, and at least it's not painful anymore. I can't wait for it to come off, though!

I can't believe it's already almost the end of the school year. I finished all my finals, and I think I did well on them. I know I have an A in all my classes, and a couple of my teachers took me aside and told me they were proud of me for doing so well. I think everyone is a little surprised that I managed to do a good job with my grades and everything, since they expected me to start failing because of my pregnancy, I guess.

School ends on the first of June, and we still have classes even though finals are finished, but it's just light stuff and review and preparation for next year.

Molly has a new thing she's driving me crazy about, and it's that she wants to take "maternity photos" of me, where I'm wearing just my bra and underwear to show off how big my stomach got. She says she was reading up on gifts to give a pregnant woman, and this was one of them. She thinks I'll want them later on in life, and even though I find it kind of embarrassing, I also agree that it's something I'll want later, or maybe even something that Cheese Puff will want to see. I am trying to decide whether or not to wait until the cast comes off. Part of me thinks it'll be funny to have the cast on in the pictures, to one day show Cheese Puff what happened while I was pregnant with her or him.

I finally know how to install the car seat into a car. It was really hard the first time, and Dianne and I had to read the instructions a few times and then we did it over and over to make sure we got it right. She said it's different now than even when Molly was born, and she didn't know how to do it right away, either.

I'm also planning on packing my hospital bag soon, and I made a checklist:

Hospital Bag Checklist

- Fuzzy socks
- Phone and charger
- Lip balm/bottles of water (hydration!)
- Hair bands for ponytails
- Cheese puffs!
- Nursing pads
- Pamphlets on nursing/childbirth/books
- Travel-sized products (shampoo, toothpaste, toothbrush, etc.)

- Flannel pjs
- Going-home outfit for me and Cheese Puff
- Onesie and blankets for Cheese Puff
- Diapers, wipes
- Wallet

I don't know if I'll be in there for just one day, or four or five days, if I need a c-section. I really hope I don't need to have a c-section.

Anyway, I'm really excited for the book launch. Dianne has a lot of interviews and meetings this week, so she gave Molly money for take-out every night, except tonight. I'm looking forward to pigging out with Molly, eating pizza, Chinese food, Indian food, Thai food...yum.

I'm not sure if Ian will be eating with us, too, and in a way, I hope he doesn't. I feel nervous around him now, even though I'm trying to think of him as just Molly's uncle and not a cute guy I have a crush on.

Dianne parks, and we go inside and are told to go to this little "backstage" area. It's a rented-out room in a fancy bookstore, and it looks so nice, with dim lights and servers handing out appetizers on trays. There are people wearing formal dresses and suits, and there are chairs set up in front of the "stage" area. On a stand on its own, next to the stage, there's a copy of Dianne's book, perched on a little frame thing. This is all so cool, and even though Dianne is used to this and has had these before, it's all pretty new to me.

My thoughts can't help but go to my mom, trying to finish her own book and hopefully get it published. Thinking of that makes me have flashes of memory of that horrible day, Dad's birthday, Mom upstairs working on her book, then getting ready for dinner when she got the horrible phone call. Josie's unraveling braids, the hospital...

I wish more than anything in the world that I could go back and *change* something. If only Dad didn't go to work that day. If we had planned a day of fun birthday stuff so that he stayed home. If we planned to meet at the restaurant, and not have him come home first.

...April 2016...

It was the night before Dad's birthday, and I couldn't sleep. We always made a big deal about everyone's birthday in our family, and I was excited to celebrate. I tossed and turned and then thought maybe it would help to have a glass of milk, so I crept downstairs, trying not to wake Josie up, and I saw Mom and Dad cuddling on the couch. They didn't see me, but I stopped and listened to them talking for a minute. Dad was telling Mom how proud he was of her for being almost finished the book. She said she might even finish it on his birthday tomorrow, and he said that would be the best birthday gift, ever. She said he was the most supportive, amazing husband and that all she wanted was to make him and me and Josie proud. And he said that he already was proud. Then they started kissing and I left, feeling really happy and excited for Dad's birthday, and at the possibility of Mom publishing her book.

...

Suddenly, I hear someone talking through a microphone and it jolts me back to reality. The memories are making me feel sweaty and uncomfortable. Ian nudges me and whispers, "What's wrong, does your wrist hurt?"

I don't want to tell him what's really going on, I don't want to ruin Dianne's special moment, so I just nod.

"Did you take Tylenol?" he asks.

"Yeah, don't worry about me. I'm fine."

He smiles. "Okay, good."

Dianne walks on the stage, grinning ear to ear, and she begins her speech. "It is such an honor to be able to publish this book I have worked so hard on. I'm so grateful that horror novels are as popular as they are. When I first started writing, I never intended to be a novelist who just writes horror, and if you knew me, you'd know I'm not a scary person at all." This gets some laughs.

As she continues introducing the book and then reading a chapter from it, my thoughts drift back to my mom. Even if Mom can manage to one day finish and then publish her book, my dad won't be here to see it, and that just makes me so sad. A lump rises to my throat.

I try to concentrate on Dianne's reading, but I guess I must have a weird look on my face, because Ian asks me again if something is wrong. I tell him I'm okay, but why does he keep looking at me? I feel bad, he probably thinks I'm rude for not paying attention to his sister. I try to focus on her reading the chapter.

After she finishes reading, everyone claps, and then the publicist tells people they can purchase a copy or bring their copy up to Dianne and she will sign it. She also points to a table which has been set up with some drinks and desserts. Dianne takes a seat at a table with a pile of her books next to her, and a line starts to form. She starts signing books, talking to each person and smiling the whole time. This is really amazing, and I'm so proud of her.

I go to the dessert table and everything looks good, but I know I have to be careful about eating too much sugar, so I just take one mini chocolate muffin and a vanilla sugar cookie. Molly comes over and starts talking to me, she's so happy and I'm really happy for her. As much as I try not to be, I'm a little distracted. My eyes just keep following wherever Ian goes. I see him walking around, stopping to talk to people, introducing himself as Dianne's brother. A pretty woman who looks like she's around his age comes up and starts talking to him. Is she flirting with him? Of course she is. Who wouldn't? He's so cute.

Molly notices me looking around and she asks if I'm looking for someone. I really don't want her to know what I'm thinking, and so I apologize and just say I like watching the people.

We go to sit on some chairs, as it's hard for me to stand for too long these days. After a few minutes, Ian comes over with a couple of mini cupcakes and stands in front of us. He and Molly start talking about the book and some other stuff, and he pretty much ignores me. *I knew it, he's only being nice to me because I'm Molly's friend.* I don't know what I've been thinking, or secretly hoping. I'm such an idiot. This is actually good, though. Now I don't need to feel nervous around him, when there's no way there would even be a chance he would be interested in me.

Eventually, people start filtering out and Dianne comes over to us and says we can go home now. In the car, we all go on and on about how much fun the event was, and how this book is probably going to be her most popular one yet.

"Well, after all this is over, I'm still going to have to sit down and face the blank page, like any writer," Dianne sighs, and we all laugh. I totally get how she feels. Every time I cover a story for the newspaper, I wonder if I'll ever be able to write anything as great as it, and I get nervous, but then I always manage to write another story.

<>

Later that night, I'm tempted to take another painkiller, because I know they help me sleep really well. I ask Dianne what she thinks, and she tells me if I'm not having a lot of pain, I really shouldn't. She says it's easy to get addicted to pills like that because they make you feel good. She actually comes into my room and takes the bottle away. I'm kind of relieved she does it, because even though it would be so nice to have another good sleep, I definitely don't want to get addicted, and also, even though they say it's safe for Cheese Puff, I don't want to keep taking them in case they are wrong.

Sure enough, I'm not tired, and I'm worried I won't be able to sleep again. The cast makes me even more uncomfortable than just being so pregnant, and I have to arrange my pillows now so that my left arm is propped up, or it starts to hurt a bit. I try to sleep for about a half hour, and then I give up and decide to go have some cheese puffs and a glass of milk. I don't like drinking before bed time because that just means I'll have to get up even more to pee, but milk does seem to help me sleep. Since I was about three years old, my mom would always give it to me when I couldn't sleep.

I slowly go down to the kitchen, trying not to wake anybody up. The house is dark, but on my way to the kitchen, I see Ian in the living room watching TV. Part of me wants to sneak away before he sees me, and part of me wants to go in and talk to him and maybe even watch TV with him again.

I get my portion of cheese puffs that I allow myself, and a glass of milk, and then I come into the living room and Ian smiles and then laughs, seeing the cheese puffs. I laugh too, and then I ask if it's okay if I sit down for a minute.

"Of course!" he says. "You don't need to ask."

I was about to go to the armchair, but he pats the couch next to him, like he's telling me to sit there. I hesitate for a second, then I sit down on the opposite end. He asks me what I want to watch, and I think for a second, then say the news. I haven't been watching it as much lately, and I miss seeing the reporters on CNN. I can tell Ian thinks it's weird I want to watch that, but I explain to him that I've loved watching the news since I was a little kid, and how my parents used to say that I was going to be a journalist. He laughs again. He seems to laugh a lot. *Does he always do that, or just around me?* Maybe he's just a person who laughs a lot no matter who he's with.

After the news, he changes the channels and an episode of *Three's Company* comes on. "Oh, this is the show you like, right?" he asks me.

I nod, and we start watching. "Mr. Furley has always made me laugh so hard," I say as he comes on the screen.

Ian laughs and says, "Yeah, I mean, even those high-waisted pants he wears alone are funny." He smiles, and then he looks at me and pauses the TV. "Hey...I don't want to ask something I shouldn't, but I've just been curious. Dianne says the father of your baby isn't involved. What happened with him, uh, if you don't mind my asking?"

"It's okay." I look away, it's just so embarrassing. "He broke up with me when I told him I was pregnant. I was really upset at first, but I'm okay about it now. I realize we're too young to be having a baby and...well, he just couldn't handle it. It's been hard, but I've had some good people to talk to and people helping me, like Dianne. She's amazing."

"Well, I think your boyfriend is a jerk. I hope you don't mind my saying that."

"I don't mind you saying that. I agree. And he's not my boyfriend anymore."

Then something occurs to me. Maybe Ian has a girlfriend back at college. "What about...you? Do you, uh, do you have a girlfriend?"

"Not a pregnant one." He laughs. "Just kidding, sorry, that was lame." He shrugs. "I don't know, I've been dating people, but not just one person."

My eyes go wide. So he's dating a bunch of people. Then, as if he read my mind, he says, "Oh, I'm not having sex with a lot of people, just going out on dates, you know." He laughs. "TMI, right?"

I laugh, too, kind of relieved to hear that. But I can't believe he doesn't have a girlfriend. *Who wouldn't want to be with him?* Maybe it's him, and he doesn't want to be in a relationship. I want to ask more, but I don't. It makes me happy to hear that there's no girlfriend in the picture, and then I realize I'm starting to think about what I promised myself I wouldn't think about, so I stop and just concentrate on eating my cheese puffs. I look back to the TV, but Ian doesn't unpause it. He just keeps looking at me as if he's trying to figure something out.

"Madison, uh...I also wanted to ask, what was really wrong today? At the book launch? I know it wasn't just your wrist, I mean, you looked...really upset."

I had a feeling he was going to ask me this. I could tell he didn't believe me at the book launch. *Ugh.* Should I tell him? I don't know if I want to get into the whole thing. It's like every second there's another problem with me. Then again, he's so nice, I feel like I *want* to tell him. It's weird, I feel like I want to tell him everything about me, and I want to hear everything about him. Kind of like my friendship with Matthew, but not exactly the same. Maybe because he's older? Nineteen seems a lot older than sixteen.

I take a deep breath and say, "Well, I don't know if Dianne told you, but my mom was also a writer. She...she was writing a book, too, a few years ago. She was actually close to finishing it and she had found an agent who might've been interested in finding someone to publish it. But she stopped writing and never finished it."

"Oh. Why didn't she finish it?"

"Well...um, this is kind of hard to talk about. She stopped writing because my dad..um...he died." It's still almost impossible not to cry when I talk about this and I feel the tears starting to come, but I try to push them back. I swallow and take a deep breath. "He died in a car accident. On his birthday. My mom was working on her book when she found out. We were getting ready to go to his birthday dinner."

I look up and Ian is just staring at me, he looks totally shocked. He sits there staring, and I can tell he has no idea what to say to me. I'm used to this reaction from people once I tell them. I hate it. I always feel like I have to take care of *them* after I tell them about this. Like they can't handle my sad story.

"Madison, I'm so, so sorry. I can't even imagine what that would be like. That...that must have been so hard for you." He shakes his head. "I didn't know...any of that. I see why you were upset at my sister's book thing. I'm so sorry I brought it up, I should learn to keep my big mouth shut."

"No, Ian, you didn't know. Please don't worry about it, it's been a long time, and I'm okay now."

"You didn't look okay at the book launch. I'm really sorry, Madison. You've...you've been through a lot. You're a really strong person."

I can't believe he's saying this to me. It's like he really gets what I've been through. Like he cares about it. The way he's staring at me, like he actually *cares,* makes me blush. I take a big gulp of the milk and then I feel Cheese Puff give me a big kick, and I jump and almost spit out the milk in my mouth.

"Oh no, what?" Ian asks.

I start laughing. It's so funny that in the midst of all this, Cheese Puff is trying to get my attention. "The baby's kicking," I say. "I think it just broke my rib."

He laughs and then looks at my stomach. "Is it still kicking?"

I nod and put my hands on my stomach. "Oh, yeah."

A bit shyly, he asks, "Can I...can I feel?"

I nod, blushing again. He slides over to me on the couch and then he really carefully places his hand on my stomach. His hand feels so warm. Sure enough, Cheese Puff gives me a huge kick and then moves around, and my whole stomach sort of ripples. He smiles and I can feel my heart is beating faster, and I hope he can't tell.

He stares at my stomach, waiting for another kick. There are a few more, and then it stops. "I guess it went to sleep?" he says, and I nod and laugh. Then he looks up at me, and our faces are right next to each other. His eyes are so blue, it's crazy, and I can smell his shampoo, it's like an apple scent or something. Then, suddenly, he kisses me. *Oh my God, is this really happening?*

Before I can even enjoy it, he pulls away. "Oh no, I'm sorry. This is not...um, are you okay?" he asks.

I nod and swallow. I feel my face getting red, and I'm upset, I don't want him to stop kissing me. *But why is he doing it? Is it because he feels sorry for me? What if Dianne and Molly saw?* This is so bad, and I can tell he wishes he didn't do it.

"Madison? Look, I'm sorry, it's probably not the best idea to-"

"It's fine, uh...I need to go. I'm going to bed now, uh, goodnight!" I say, and I try to get out of there as fast as I can, but it's hard to move quickly because of my stomach, and it's so embarrassing.

My heart keeps racing, and I feel like I can't breathe as I finally get into bed. *I can't believe that just happened.* Maybe he *does* like me? No, it's impossible, he did it because I was upset and he just wanted to make me feel better. The only problem is that *I* really like him. I know now for sure that that's what this nervousness has been. I *really* like him.

Oh my God, this is crazy. He's Dianne's brother, and he's Molly's *uncle*! Even if he did like me, this can't happen, right? Oh, God, this is so awful. I haven't even gotten into another relationship, but I already feel hurt again. I have such bad luck with guys, first Leo, then Matthew, and now this. I just can't handle anymore rejection, I can't. I will crack, and I *can't* crack, because I have to be strong for *two* people now. I can't think about this anymore, I need to forget it. I'm sure the kiss didn't mean anything anyway, he for sure just did it because he felt bad for me. I could never be lucky enough to get a guy like Ian. I need to just...forget it.

<>

I wake up totally exhausted. It was one of the worst sleeps I've had in a long time. I must have woken up every fifteen minutes, I swear. Of course now that I actually *have* to get up, I'm finally tired and I wish I could just sleep.

My thirty-four week appointment with Dr. Lippincott was supposed to be yesterday, but Dianne had her book launch, so it was postponed to today. I'm missing my first couple of classes at school, but I'll get a note from Dr. Lippincott. Molly isn't coming this time, she already left for school.

On my way to the kitchen for breakfast, I pass by the living room. I look over at the couch and picture me and Ian sitting there. Then I picture the kiss. *Madison, you have to stop thinking about this.*

In the kitchen, Dianne is finishing making scrambled eggs, and she offers me some. I usually just have cereal these days, but eggs sound good, so I say yes and thank her and she hands me a bowl. Just then, Ian comes in, his hair is wet, he must have showered. Dianne smiles and says, "You already worked out and showered?" He nods and she sighs. "You make me feel like a lazy sloth."

He laughs. "I went for a run, it's so nice out. Summer break rocks."

"I made too many eggs, want some?" she asks, and he says, "Sure, thanks."

I can't even look at him, I'm so embarrassed about last night, and I have no idea how he feels at all. I just focus on my eggs.

"No school, Madison?" he asks me. "I thought Molly left for-"

"Madison has a doctor appointment," Dianne says, and I nod.

"Is everything okay?" Ian asks.

"At this point in the pregnancy, she has these quick check-ups every two weeks with her doctor to make sure everything's okay. I'm sure it is."

"Oh, cool. Do you get to see the baby?"

I nod and say, "She does an ultrasound."

"That must be so cool to see."

"It sure is," Dianne says, smiling.

"Hey, would you guys mind if I come along?" he asks. "I'm not working today and I'm looking for something fun to do."

I look up from my eggs. *Is he serious?* Dianne looks at me, wondering what I'm going to say. "Seriously?" I finally ask.

He nods. "Yeah, I've never seen one before." Dianne laughs. "Oh, I mean, I've seen *babies,* yeah, but not while they're still in the stomach, ha-ha."

Dianne smiles. "Up to you, Madison. It's fine with me."

"Um, yeah, I mean, okay."

"Okay, good!" He gets up and puts his bowl in the dishwasher and Dianne says that we should actually get going. I can't believe this. *Ian is coming with us?* Does he even *remember* what happened last night? Actually, I'm glad he's acting like nothing happened and that he's just being his usual friendly self. It's...easier this way.

On the way there, Dianne and Ian catch up and talk about making plans to see their parents. I'm happy to just listen to the music and tune everything out. I rub my stomach and remind myself that the most important thing is Cheese Puff. I can't get all emotional over some stupid crush that's never going to happen.

Dr. Lippincott is surprised to see Ian when she comes into the exam room. Dianne introduces him and she gives him a big smile. "I can see the resemblance," Dr. Lippincott says, looking at Dianne and then at Ian. I guess they do kind of look alike. Ian's eyes are just a lot bluer.

She asks how my wrist is feeling, and explains that the hospital sent her the report, so she knows what happened. Dianne says it was lucky that Ian was there to help, and I can't even look at Ian's reaction because I'm sure he's picturing me like a whale on the shower floor, even though he said I didn't look like that. Dr. Lippincott says it's very common to break something during pregnancy, especially when your stomach gets bigger and your balance isn't as good.

Dianne and Ian go to sit in the chairs beside me, Ian sits where Molly usually does. It's so weird to have him here. He's being really quiet, and I wonder what he's thinking. Then Dr. Lippincott does the ultrasound and all of a sudden, Ian has a million questions. He wants to know what each part is and he asks Dr. Lippincott to point it out. She is giggling a little and she asks him if he wants to be an obstetrician because he's so curious. It's pretty funny, actually, and it's really cool to have all of Cheese Puff's parts be pointed out.

"And that's about it," Dr. Lippincott says. Then she smiles. "Oh, look, the baby is looking right at us."

"Hi, Cheese Puff!" Ian says, and he waves at the screen. It's so weird, he's acting totally normal, as if nothing happened last night. I guess he just thinks it was a mistake and wants to forget about it.

Dr. Lippincott laughs and says, "I wonder if this will always be the baby's nickname? It has a nice ring to it. Could work for either a boy or a girl."

We laugh and then Ian turns to me. "You sure you don't want to know if it's a boy or girl *now?*"

I shake my head. "No, I want it to be a surprise."

"Aw, come on!" he groans. He turns to Dr. Lippincott conspiratorially. "Just whisper it into my ear."

She laughs. "I'm sorry, I'm not allowed to do that. You'll find out soon enough."

When the ultrasound is done, we go to her office to chat, as usual. Ian doesn't come in, but Dianne does. "I wanted to discuss your birth plan today," Dr. Lippincott says. "Even though there's still some time left, some babies do come early, and you need to be prepared. I can help you fill out these forms right now. Just a few questions...who will your primary support person or people be?"

"Dianne and Molly."

She writes that down. "Anyone else that you will allow or want in the room?"

"My mom and my little sister are going to drive up once I'm in labor."

She asks me a few other questions, like if I'll want an epidural. I reply to that with a strong yes, and she laughs and asks if I'll want skin-to-skin after birth, and I say yes, and then she asks if I'm breastfeeding, and I say yes to that, too.

After we're done with the birth plan, she asks, "Have you been eating healthy? As usual, I would like it if you wouldn't eat so much sugar. You don't have gestational diabetes, but your sugar levels are a little higher than I would like."

I nod, and then my cheeks redden. Sometimes after dinner I'll sneak into the pantry and eat some cookies or something like that. But I'll try to stop doing that, I know it's bad.

We make another appointment for when I'm thirty-six weeks, and then Dianne drives us home. Ian thanks me for letting him come, he says it was so much fun to see the baby and that it's something he's never seen before and it was really cool. It's kind of a relief that he's acting normal, and that way I don't have to even think about last night for one more second.

I go back to school, so happy that I missed gym this morning, even though I'm not really doing any of the exercises anymore, the coach still wants me there, and she has me doing research about sports and things like that.

After school, I have work. It's getting harder and harder to stand around, and Johnny is actually being really nice, he lets me sit on a stool behind the counter when I'm not serving customers. I also told him about Molly and that she wants to step in and take my place after I leave, and he said he would consider it and that she should come by to meet him. It's sad being at work now, because I know I'm going to have to look for something that pays more, but I actually like this job, and thinking about working with Molly would make it even better. It's too bad that I'm going to have to leave soon.

When I get home that night, the house smells amazing. Dianne made her meat sauce, which I love so much. "Dianne, seriously, your cooking is so amazing! Can you please teach me how to cook? Cheese Puff is going to be so deprived!"

She laughs. "You can pop into the kitchen any time, and I'll be happy to teach you how to cook any dish in the world."

I laugh and thank her and then go to my room, and I see Ian coming downstairs. He comes up to me, looking a bit nervous. "We should talk," he says.

Oh no, I really didn't think we were going to have to do this.

He sighs. "I...I just...I don't think I should've kissed you last night. It obviously really weirded you out."

My jaw drops open. "Are you *serious?*"

"Yeah, and I'm sorry," he says. "I should never have done that. I hope you're not mad at me."

I shake my head. "You know, it's really funny, because I've been going around all day thinking that you *forgot* about last night, and I thought you kissed me because you felt *bad* for me, and...so yeah, I'm kind of mad!"

"What?" he asks, seeming completely confused. "What are you

talking about? I didn't kiss you because I felt bad for you, Madison!"

"*Shh!*" I say. "And...seriously?"

"Do I not seem serious?"

"I...I liked it, okay?!" I blurt.

"You did?"

I nod, and I see Ian start to smile, and then suddenly I hear, "Mads! How was your appointment?" I turn around, and it's Molly. *Oh my God, did she hear us?*

"Molly, hi!" I say, plugging in a smile, and Ian leaves, giving Molly a high five on his way out. She looks at him, frowning, and then turns back to me. "What were you guys talking about?"

I shake my head, "Nothing, just...saying hi."

"Oh, okay. Anyway, sorry I couldn't eat with you at lunch today, I offered to help the librarian with organizing books as part of my community service. Anyway, tell me! How was your appointment?"

I take a deep breath, trying to calm myself down. *I can't believe what just happened with Ian.* "Uh, it went...well. Yeah, it went well. It went well."

She gives me a weird look. "Okay...good?"

"Why are you being weird?"

"Why are *you* being weird?"

"Dinner, everyone!" we hear Dianne call.

We all sit down to eat, and I force myself to not look in Ian's direction, because I cannot reveal *anything* in front of Molly and Dianne.

"So," Dianne says, looking at me. "It's good that Dr. Lippincott worked out the birth plan with you today, Madison."

"Yeah," I say.

"*We* should come up with a plan for when the baby comes. We might not know right away if it's real labor or not, but if you think you're having contractions, you need to tell me right away."

"I'm coming with, right?" Molly asks.

"Oh my God, yes, of course!" I say.

Dianne laughs. "I still remember Molly's birth so perfectly. I was watching some stupid sitcom, laughing my head off, and then I thought I peed my pants from laughing so hard, but really, my water broke, so I went and told my parents, who took me to the hospital. My dad didn't want to pay for parking, so he parked three blocks away and made me walk all the way to the hospital, and then I almost gave birth to Molly in the elevator." We all laugh. "But I didn't end up giving birth for around eight hours, I wasn't dilated enough. And then the love of my life was born." Molly smiles happily. "That cry was the sweetest thing I'd ever heard. Dr. Lippincott said you had great lungs."

Molly laughs. "How do you define good lungs?"

"She told me that it's a good sign if babies cry a lot when they're first born, because it shows that their lungs are working the way they're supposed to!"

"And then the crying doesn't become such a good sign when it's the middle of the night and you haven't slept for days, right?" I say, and everyone laughs.

Dianne turns to Ian. "I remember when *you* were born. I was fifteen, and since your nursery was next to my room, I could hear you crying all night. It drove me crazy!"

Ian rolls his eyes. "Hey, don't hold it against me. That was nineteen years ago!"

Despite myself, I laugh, and Ian smiles at me. I quickly look back down to my food. I still don't really understand what's going on because we couldn't finish our conversation, and I really don't want Molly or Dianne to know something's up.

After dinner, I go to my room and do my homework and then do some research about birth classes again. I have to sign up for something for when school ends. I take a shower, which feels really nice and I love the seat Ian put in here.

I get into my pajamas, and I notice that even *they* are getting tight now, and they were supposed to be my last pair that would get me through the rest of the pregnancy. *Ugh.* And I'm starving pretty much all the time now, and I really want to go get a snack and watch TV, but I'm pretty sure Ian will be there, and I don't know if it's a good idea. I'm not sure I even want to talk about what happened anymore. I mean, even if he did want to kiss me, the whole thing is crazy, there's no way this can work.

I decide to leave my room. So what if Ian's there? I can't avoid him for the rest of the summer, and I need to eat something. Sure enough, when I get to the living room, Ian is there on the couch, watching TV. I hesitate to come in and then I actually decide that it's a bad idea, so I go to leave, and he says, "Wait, Madison. Please, come talk to me." He pauses the TV and I come to sit on the armchair. "Listen, I'm sorry, okay? I know this is all...weird, and I don't want it to be."

"I agree," I say quietly.

"Okay, good. So, did you mean what you said about liking the kiss?"

I nod. "Did you mean what you said about not doing it because you felt sorry for me?" He nods. My mind is racing trying to think of what to say, when suddenly he gets up and comes over to me and gives me a kiss. He stops and looks at me and I stare back at him. Then we kiss again. And again. We kiss for a while, and then Ian says softly, "I only want to do what you're comfortable with, okay?"

I nod. "I'm comfortable with this, but...but that's it. Okay?"

"Oh my God, of course, Madison."

We keep kissing, and then we eventually realize that it's one o'clock in the morning. I'm so screwed for tomorrow. I say I have to go to bed, and Ian walks me to my room. We tiptoe, trying to be really quiet so we don't wake up Dianne or Molly.

At my door, Ian says, "That was a fun date, Mads." He winks. "Goodnight!"

I laugh, and he kisses me one more time before he sneaks away.

34 weeks!
6 weeks left!

♡   ♡   🍍 ← pineapple   👶 ♡

To-Do List

- pick up paycheck on Friday from Roast and Drink
- Dianne's book launch = today!!

📖 FINALS = DONE

☆ take maternity photos with Molly?

- write a reflection of this school year for the newspaper
- ask Janet to write "goodbye Seniors" article
- ask "recipes" writer to send her stories on summer recipes ASAP
- edit my story on finals being over
- appointment with Dr. Lippincott this morning
  * get note from her excusing me from my first couple classes
  * EAT LESS SUGAR!!
- buy books on childbirth/breastfeeding
- research childbirth classes
- work on budget!!

- pick electives for next year
- call Mom + Josie soon!
- call Alexa soon!

buy:
- cheese puffs!
- crib??
- crib sheets
- baby blankets
- more diapers + wipes

☆ use checklist to pack hospital bag!

♡ Ian ♡
(talk to Ian??)

☆ buy everything I will need for my hospital bag!!

👶 my Cheese Puff ♡   ♡ ♡ Ian ♡ ♡   CHEESE PUFFS 😋 yum yum yum

Cheese Puff

Chapter 31: Week Thirty-Five

"Your baby is as big as a spaghetti squash," I read online. What kind of vegetable is that? For sure that's one I've never eaten, but I guess it's probably pretty big. My stomach is huge, so big that I can't see my feet at all no matter what I'm doing. I have a dark line forming down from my belly button, and I read that it's called a *linea alba,* and it should fade once I have Cheese Puff.

The cast on my wrist is still really annoying, and I can't wait for it to come off. The only good thing about it is that everytime I look at it, I think of Ian and the way he helped me. In a weird way, I appreciate that I broke my wrist, because it's kind of what got me and Ian together.

There's no school today, because tomorrow is sophomore-year graduation! I'm very excited, though it reminds me that I only have this month and then about one week in July until my due date, so I'm running out of time to get everything together. I'm going to try and really work on my budget tonight, instead of having everything scattered on my crazy To-Do lists.

Speaking of crazy, I'm scared to think of what will happen if Dianne and Molly find out about me and Ian. We talked about what's been going on, and we agreed that we don't want Dianne and Molly to know right now. I told him that I'm not ready for anything more than just what we've been doing, and he said he totally understood. It's kind of fun sneaking around and kissing and holding hands when Dianne and Molly leave the room, or when they're asleep. Today I'm going grocery shopping with him, which should be fun. Dianne said she needed a few things and he offered to get them and I said I needed some stuff, too, but that I would come with him because I didn't know exactly what he needed. Dianne and Molly don't suspect a thing.

Ian drives us in Dianne's car to the grocery store. We leave the windows open, it's really nice out, warm and sunny. It's so nice being driven around by Ian, listening to music in the car. I'm trying to take it slow, but my crush on him is pretty big. I seriously love everything about him already, like how he appreciates the world, the way he smiles, his eyes, the way he talks, how *kind* he is. He's *nothing* like Leo, he doesn't act like him and his looks are pretty much the opposite. I would love to shove Ian in Leo's face and let him see what a good guy acts like.

Now, at a red light, I feel Ian's fingers brush mine lightly, and I curl mine around his. We're holding hands. But now I feel myself getting nervous, and he looks at me.

"What's wrong?" he asks.

I sigh. How am I supposed to tell him that I don't know if I can trust him? That this is how it started with Leo? Holding hands, kissing...what if it's just a repeat?

I can't stand the way I do this. I keep bouncing back between being really excited at the prospect of being with him, and being nervous about it.

I stop myself from thinking and smile at him. "Nothing. This is really nice."

He points to a bicycle a little boy is riding across the street. "I had a bicycle almost exactly the same as that one," he says, laughing. "My mom had to call the police once because I rode so far away from my house that she couldn't find me."

"Why did you do that?" I ask, laughing.

"I remember that I was following an airplane I saw in the sky, and so I was riding as fast as I could. I was only six, but I wanted to go wherever the airplane was going."

I smile, soaking up every minute of him telling me about himself. Leo never talked about things like this. I feel like we never shared anything about our lives.

I'm so annoyed with myself. I *have* to stop comparing Ian to Leo.

Ian helps me out of the car, which is both embarrassing and sweet. It's getting harder and harder for me to get up from a sitting position. He again asks me if I want to sign up for those pregnancy swim classes, but I tell him no.

We walk into the grocery store and start to go up and down the aisles. He takes a broccoli casserole frozen meal out of one of the fridge doors. "How about this? Five dollars and extremely healthy."

I stick out my tongue. "Gross! Who even thought up broccoli casserole?"

"Actually, it's quite delicious," Ian says playfully.

I laugh and then I point to a frozen pizza. "Now this is more like it!"

Ian laughs, too. "You told me you wanted to eat more healthy."

"So you're telling me that *you'd* rather have broccoli casserole for dinner than a frozen pizza?"

"Ha, nope," he says, and then he tosses the pizza in the cart. "Pizza it is!"

It's so much fun shopping with Ian, we just keep joking about the different meals and how ridiculous some of the prices are. He takes my hand a few times, and I notice something; people are looking at me differently. Whenever I've been out in public, people look at me weirdly, for obvious reasons; I'm a pregnant teenager. But now that I'm walking around the store here with Ian...people are *smiling* at us. *Do they think that Ian's the father?* Because this is totally different from any of my other experiences being out in public. A woman even comes up and says, "Such a beautiful couple," and then she asks if she can pat my stomach.

It feels so good to be with Ian, and I don't feel self-conscious anymore about my body right now. He keeps telling me how amazing he thinks it is that I'm creating a whole human being. I really hope this can work, but I worry about what will happen and how Molly and Dianne will react if we keep being together. Molly will either think it's perfect, or she'll be really upset and think it's crazy. I can't even think about Dianne or even my mom's reaction. I don't want to think about any of this, I just want to enjoy my time with Ian.

We go to the snacks aisle and I go to grab a bag of cheese puffs. There are different brands of them, but this store has my favorite. I hate that they're almost five dollars each. I wonder how much I've spent on cheese puffs in the last eight months.

Ian laughs and grabs a mega-sized bag of them. "I say go big or go home," he says, and then he tosses them into the cart. I take them out and say that there's no way I want to have that many around, or it will be harder to control myself. Also, they're so expensive.

"It's more expensive to have to keep coming back and getting a single pack. Anyway, let me get it for you," he says, smiling.

I start to say no and that I can't let him do that, but he shakes his head and leans close to my stomach, pretending to hear Cheese Puff. He says to my stomach, "What's that you're saying? Oh, yeah, you want *cheese puffs*, Cheese Puff? Lots and lots of cheese puffs?" I can't stop laughing, he's being really funny. I love how *playful* he is.

He grins and tucks the pack under his arm and I try to wrestle it away, but he holds onto it strongly, and then all of a sudden, the bag pops open and cheese puffs go flying everywhere! We burst out laughing, then look around, hoping we won't get in trouble. Ian picks one out of my hair and eats it and we laugh even harder. I feel like I'm about to faint, I'm laughing so hard.

Suddenly, a store clerk comes up to us, angry. "Hey! What's with this?!?"

Breathless from all the laughing, Ian says, "Sorry, sir, we'll clean it up right away. Do you have a broom?"

The annoyed clerk gets a broom and then comes back and hands it angrily to Ian, which makes us laugh again. Ian does a little funny dance as he sweeps up the cheese puffs. I place a hand on my stomach, which hurts from laughing so hard, and I can feel Cheese Puff moving around and going crazy in there, like she or he is joining in the fun. *I don't know when the last time I've felt like this was.*

"Hm…these cheese puffs leave a lot of cheese *flakes* on the floor," Ian comments seriously, like it's a great big mystery that he's revealed, and I laugh again.

All of a sudden, I can't believe it but I see Leo coming down the aisle. *Oh my God, since when does he go grocery shopping?*

He stops when he sees me and then looks at Ian and looks back and forth between both of us, like he can't figure out the situation.

"Who's this?" he says to me, while looking at Ian.

I turn red. "It's none of your business, Leo."

Ian looks shocked to hear Leo's name. He realizes who it is and then he says, "I'm Ian. And you are?"

"Leo. She just said it."

"Well, hi, *Leo.* Nice to meet you."

Leo glares at Ian. I feel like I'm going to pass out, this is so awkward. "Where's Dina?" I ask eventually.

He ignores me and turns to Ian, looking him up and down with that gross expression he always has on his face when he sees me. "You know that's my kid in there, right?"

"Leo, seriously? What is your problem?!?" He wants nothing to do with me or the baby, but all of a sudden he's upset to see me with Ian?

Ian moves closer to him and says, "I know all about you. You should be ashamed of yourself. How could you leave this amazing girl? She needed you. Actually, make that *two* people that needed you."

He takes my hand and I see Leo look at it, he stands there staring for a minute, then just shrugs and says, "Have fun," and walks away.

Ian turns to me. "Are you okay?"

I nod, but really, I want to cry. I'm so embarrassed of Leo, and the whole situation. Ian gives me a big hug.

"I really just want to forget about this right now," I say quietly. "We were having so much fun, and he just came along and ruined it. What was he even doing here? I don't remember him ever going grocery shopping when we were…together."

Ian rolls his eyes and says, "He didn't ruin anything. Let's get out of here, though."

He takes another bag of cheese puffs and grins, and I smile and we walk to the front, and Ian insists on paying for everything. I fight with him about it, but he won't let me pay, he says he's saved up enough from his job. He is so sweet. I can't believe I even met him. And Leo *should* be jealous, because he would never have even come close to being as good a guy as Ian.

We drop the groceries back at home, and find a note from Molly that she went to do some errands with her mom, so we decide to go to Home's Diner for lunch. It's pretty empty because it's kind of in between meals, and we get a booth. I squeeze onto the opposite side from Ian. It's so hard to get in and out of spaces like this nowadays.

I can't decide what I want, so Ian goes first and gets a chicken sandwich. Then I order a burger with extra pickles, fries, and a chocolate milkshake, and Ian rolls his eyes. "Madison, didn't your doctor tell you no more sugar?"

"Just today, I swear!"

He says to the waitress, "Make it less sweet, okay?" and she nods and leaves.

"Thanks a lot," I say, pretending to be annoyed, but I'm kind of smiling because it's actually really nice to have someone watching out for me. This is what I pictured it being like with Leo. What a joke.

"Yeah, you *should* be thanking me," Ian says, and then he takes his napkin and places it in front of him. "Alright, so, let's review."

"Review what?"

He pretends to write on the napkin. "We make each other laugh. Check. We have fun together. Check."

I start laughing, he's being so cute. "Come on, help me out here," he says. "We-"

"We can talk about everything."

"Check."

"We..."

"Like each other?"

I nod, looking down shyly. He smiles and says, "Check."

I can't believe this is actually happening. *I like him and he likes me, too? Even though I'm about to have a baby and I'm only sixteen?* It seems too good to be true. I can't trust it, I'm worried I'll get too happy, and then it will be taken away from me.

I suddenly realize that Ian is staring at me, and his face looks serious now. "Listen, I don't want you to feel like I'm pushing you," he says. "I know you said you just like things the way they are. I do, too. I just want you to know that I really like you, and I'm having fun doing whatever it is that we're doing."

I nod and swallow, not sure how to respond, and he says, "You look a little, I don't know...weirded out or something right now. If you want to just be friends, then I understand. I know you have a lot to focus on with the baby coming."

It's so weird to have him actually *care* about my feelings. I feel like I'm going to bawl, he's being so sweet. I can't stop it, and tears start to come.

"Oh no, Madison, I'm sorry, I didn't mean to make you cry. It's fine, this is all too much, I...I get it. Let's just be friends then, if it makes you happier, okay?"

I shake my head. "No, it's not that. I don't want to just be friends. It's just, you're so *nice.*"

He laughs. "I'm not trying to be nice, I'm just saying what I think. What kind of jerks have you been with? Actually, you don't have to answer that. I already know."

"It's not even other people all the time," I say. "A lot of the time it's...well, it's my own insecurities, because, well, teen pregnancy isn't something people approve of, you know?"

He shrugs. "I know. But you made a brave decision. You're a really strong and smart person. You remind me of my sister, in a way. Just because a baby isn't planned doesn't mean it can't turn out okay. Look at Molly. Look at *me.* I mean, you think *I* was planned? Dianne and I are *fifteen* years apart." He grins. "My parents clearly weren't trying to have me."

"Well, yeah, but...I'm glad it happened."

He smiles, and then looks at me, *really* looks at me, like he's looking into my soul or something. "You're so...I don't know, you just seem like such an amazing person. You're so brave to be doing this so young, and you're going to be a great mom. And I really don't want you to think that I'd just take off because you're going to have a baby."

I don't know what to say. He's so sweet, and I wish I could trust it. I need to think about it more, but right now I just want to enjoy being with him. I haven't felt this way about anybody, even Leo.

We finish eating and then Ian says he has to go to work, so we go home. Dianne and Molly are still out when we get there, so we're able to kiss for a little bit, and then he leaves for work.

I go to my room and just sit on the bed and stare out the window. I can't believe what a good time I have with him. This is all so crazy.

I've got to get back to reality. I had decided to set aside some time to *really* work out my budget for until the end of this year. To write a real, official one. I get out a piece of paper and review my old To-Do lists with the math on them, and then I start.

ESTIMATIONS

Rent = $1,000/month
Electric = $80/month
Internet = $90/month

Total (for housing) = $1,170/month

Diapers = $50/month
Wipes = $15/month
Total (baby expenses) = $65/month

Food = $300/month
Phone Bill = $50/month
Total (other expenses) = $350/month

Total Expenses: (about) $1,600 (expenses)/month x 4 (till end of year) = $6,400

$6,360 (total from work) + $2,000 (from Leo's parents) = $8,360

$8,360 - $6,400 (expenses) = SAVINGS: (about) $1,900

If only I could share the apartment with someone. It would cut my housing expenses in half, and I'd be able to put a lot more towards savings, for things like an emergency fund and Cheese Puff's future, which are both obviously so important. I can't think of anyone I could do it with, though. I've thought about asking Alexa, it would be amazing to live with her and be able to help each other out with our babies. She seems like she's going to stay with Danny, though.

I hear Molly and Dianne come in, and then Molly comes into my room and asks, "Do you want to come to dinner with me, Mom, Ian, and my grandparents tonight? We're going to celebrate Mom's book and Ian hasn't spent a lot of time with them yet."

I shake my head. "Thanks, but I think I need to just chill here tonight. Also, you guys should really have some family time alone together."

"Aw, okay, Mads," she says, and then she leaves. Thinking about all of them having dinner together makes me sad. It makes me think about my dad's birthday dinner, which never happened.

... April 2016...

A few hours after Dad died and we got back from the hospital, I sat curled up in my favorite chair in the corner by the stairs. Everything felt frozen, like in the world and also in my mind. I couldn't think at all. I couldn't even cry.

The phone rang, and no one went to get it, and it just kept ringing and ringing. I know it sounds crazy, but I think I was hoping it would be the hospital saying that it was a mistake and he was really still alive. I answered it.

"This is Salsa Restaurant," a male voice said. "I'm calling to confirm your reservation for seven-thirty. Are you still coming? We have a table set up for a birthday celebration?"

...

I shake my head, trying to get rid of the horrible memory. Thinking about this also reminds me of Molly's birthday, how I missed the restaurant and we fought. I have no idea why I'm suddenly thinking about all of this, but I don't want to. I had such a good time with Ian, and I don't want to ruin it.

I try to finish the budget, but now I'm really tired, my back hurts, my feet hurts, my wrist feels stiff and uncomfortable. I get into bed without even changing into my pajamas, just to close my eyes, but I end up taking a long nap.

When I open my eyes, it's dark outside. I force myself to get up and go to the bathroom. I really need a shower. Lately, I try to not look at myself in the mirror, especially when I'm naked. I can't stand the way my body looks right now and I have dark circles under my eyes. I look at my face, and I look so different to myself. I look older, that's for sure. I'm tired, so that's part of it. As scared as I am for the baby to come, I can't wait to not be pregnant anymore.

I also can't wait for the cast to come off. I'm tired of having to wrap it in plastic to take a shower. It's so complicated, and washing with one hand is hard. The seat Ian put in really makes it easier, and I start thinking about him, and it just feels like it's a dream and not reality.

As I dry off and get into my pajamas, I remember that tomorrow's *really* the last day of my sophomore year. I can't believe that I'm halfway through my high school career. It's unbelievable how fast time is moving. I decide that as much as I still need to work on the budget, I need to eat first, and I want to do it before everyone comes home. I don't feel like seeing anyone tonight. I eat a leftover bowl of soup and then I go back to my room to go to bed.

I remember that Alexa texted me earlier, and I didn't get back to her. We've been texting a lot, and it's funny, we don't really go to the support group anymore. I guess we're sort of a support for each other now.

Alexa: Hey! What's going on with Ian? :)

Alexa's actually the only person that I've told about him. I had to tell *someone,* and I figured she'd be the safest one to tell.

Maddie: We went on a lunch date. He made me get a less-sweet chocolate milkshake because my doctor told me to not have lots of sugar :(

Alexa: Aww! That's so sweet!

Maddie: :) I know. I really like him.

Alexa: You've only told me 1,000,000 times.

Maddie: LOL! Sorry!

Alexa: No, it's okay! :) Baby kicking? Mine is!

Maddie: Yes, ha-ha, only I would say Cheese Puff doesn't even kick anymore, it just moves around and my whole stomach feels like it's been taken over by an animal or something. By the way, do you have a nickname for your baby?

Alexa: I've recently started calling mine Gumdrop, ha-ha.

Maddie: Ha-ha!

I think it's so funny that Alexa has a nickname, too. I wonder if all pregnant women have nicknames for their babies. I think my mom once told me that she called me and Josie "Sucker," because we sucked the life out of her, when she was pregnant with us and then when she breastfed us. *Very funny, Mom.*

Then I tell Alexa that I'm going to bed, I'm so tired. She says that she is, too. We stop texting and I decide to spray a tiny bit of dad's shaving cream on my wrist. I feel like I need it after thinking about all those bad memories. I inhale it and think of Dad, and it actually makes me smile. I can picture his face really clearly right now, and how he would probably be happy to know I met someone as nice as Ian. It's weird, I realize that if I hadn't gotten pregnant, then I never would have moved in with Dianne and Molly, and I probably wouldn't have met Ian or spent any time with him.

Well, Dad always said that things happen for a reason. And I think that now, I really believe they do.

<>

I wake up with the sun streaming in my window, and it hits me: it's graduation day! I do my usual struggle to get out of bed and then I decide to put on my most comfortable maternity shirt and oversized jean shorts, knowing it doesn't matter what I wear because they'll put a cap and gown on me, anyway. It's usually only for seniors, the whole cap and gown graduation thing, but at our school, if you wear a yellow cap and gown, you're graduating freshman year, red is for sophomores, green is for juniors, and dark blue, the traditional graduation color, is for seniors.

Molly is already dressed and eating her breakfast when I come into the kitchen. She's really excited for today and we talk about how we can't believe the year is already over, and we're graduating. Dianne and Ian aren't here, but Dianne said she'd see us at school for the ceremony and party. Mom called me a couple days ago and said that she was coming with Josie, too.

The ceremony goes well, the principal makes a speech and then we each come up for them to give us the diploma and move the tassel from one side to the other. I look out and see Mom and Josie in the audience smiling and clapping, and I start to cry.

Afterwards, there's a little party in the main hall and everyone eats snacks and talks to each other. Mom and Josie come rushing over to me and give me big hugs. Josie can't believe how big my stomach is. She's literally bursting with excitement because the baby is going to be coming soon.

Then Dianne, Molly, and Ian come up to us and I introduce Ian to Mom and Josie. Mom says it must be so nice for Molly to have her uncle there. She's smiling at him, and I can tell she thinks he's nice. *She has no idea.*

I leave to go to the bathroom and when I come out, Ian is standing in the hall, waiting for me. "You look cute in red."

I blush. "Thanks." I keep looking around, because I'm so worried someone will see us together, but then I realize they would probably not suspect anything, anyway.

Molly calls out to Ian and asks him to join in some pictures. Then I go back over to Mom and Josie and Mom says, "So I got your report card in the mail! Straight A's! I'm so proud of you, honey."

She kisses me, and I almost start crying again, I just can't believe we're back to getting along and things are *good* again. It took a lot to get to this point, and I only want to keep making her proud.

Mom asks about my cast and I tell her it's coming off soon. She says she feels bad that she wasn't here when it happened. I feel like I want to tell her about Ian and how he took me to the hospital, and then it makes me want to tell her that we are actually boyfriend and girlfriend, but I think the timing isn't right. Also, *are we even boyfriend and girlfriend?* There's no way we can talk about it now, anyway. Everyone is around us, and we spend some time with Dianne and Molly, and Ian watches all of us and just smiles and joins in a bit.

Before I know it, it's time to leave, and Mom and Josie have to get back to Santa Barbara. It's so sad saying goodbye and Josie can barely take her hands off my stomach, she just wants to keep feeling Cheese Puff's movements. I tell her that I'll hopefully see them really soon. We realize that the next time we see each other, Cheese Puff might actually be an *outside* baby, rather than an *inside my stomach* baby. We giggle at the thought. I really hope that I get enough warning that I'm in labor, so they can be there.

<>

Later, after dinner, I go to sit on the porch. The sun is setting so much later now that it's summer, and I love how warm it is. The stars look really bright and it's just a perfect night to sit outside. Mom and I text for a bit and she sends me some pictures she took at the graduation. I *graduated.* I can't believe it. Even after all the bullying and my doubts about whether or not I could do it, I managed to do it.

I think about Dad again. I was only in seventh grade when he died, and now I'm almost in my junior year. I'm moving farther and farther away from him every day, whether I like it or not. If he can't somehow see me now, he only knows the thirteen-year-old me. That was the last version of myself that he saw. It's weird to think about that, and how much different I am now. Dad never knew the me who took care of Josie after he died, or the me who ran my school newspaper, or the me who got pregnant so young.

And there's still so much that he's never going to be there for; he won't ever meet Cheese Puff, he won't ever know what college I get into, he'll never see me become a journalist, he'll never be able to walk me down the aisle someday. He'll never know me as *me,* who I'm really going to grow up to be in this world.

It's not fair. I don't care if he said things happen for a reason, I will never understand why he had to die. Never. But I have to keep it in my heart that maybe he can somehow see me from wherever he is. It gives me a sense of hope, and also a sense of motivation, to think he's out there somewhere. No one obviously knows what happens after you die. The universe is a complete mystery.

Just looking at the gorgeous sunset proves that point. It's so magically beautiful, with the amazing colors and how the clouds glow pink and purple, like someone dusted sparkling golden blush all over the sky. The sun is orange now, and it's just about to go to sleep under the horizon, but it's still peeking out a little.

It's funny, just as I'm thinking this, Mom texts me again and she tells me to look at the sunset, that it's gorgeous tonight. She says that she and Josie are sitting on the porch, and I tell her that I'm sitting on the porch, too. It's like we're watching it together. And maybe Dad is somewhere watching it with us, too.

35 weeks ♡
♡

5 weeks left!
AAH!!

To-Do List

- pick up paycheck on Friday from Roast and Drink
- submit elective sheet for next year

☆ go grocery shopping with Ian

buy:
- cheese puffs
- lotion

Bank Account = $4,603.95

- work out an official budget
- look up places to buy cribs
- sign up for childbirth classes next week

♡
CHEESE PUFFS
♡
♡

Ian + Madison

✳ GRADUATION ✳

Summer time!
WOO HOO !!!

Budget = DONE!
$ YAY!
$ FINALLY!!

- pregnancy swim classes?

Ian Katz
Madison Davis
Madison Katz
Madison Davis - Katz
Mrs. Katz
Mrs. Davis - Katz

- appointment with Dr. Lippincott next week

my little cheese puff

Chapter 32: Week Thirty-Six

"Your baby is as big as a large bunch of kale," I read on the way to Dr. Lippincott's office. My appointments are now going to be every week, after this one. Molly is actually driving Dianne's car and Dianne is in the passenger seat, because she wants to see how Molly's driving is going. Molly is always really careful whenever I've driven with her, and I think Dianne is relieved to see that she's a good and safe driver.

I'm getting more and more stressed about the due date approaching. Even though I've gotten really organized, I still feel like I have so much to do. At least my hospital bag is packed and waiting by the door. I'm using Dad's old duffel bag, the one that I took when I moved in with Dianne and Molly. And tomorrow I'm going to my very first childbirth class, which I'm excited for.

At my appointment with Dr. Lippincott, I tell her what's been going on. I explain how everything hurts now: my legs, my back, my neck, my pelvis, all my joints, and it's so hard to get up and down. My stomach feels like it can't stretch any more or it'll pop. I can't stand it anymore (literally; it's hard to stand up). I say that I'm peeing constantly, and I get up at *least* three times a night now to pee. Each time takes forever, because first I have to kind of roll to one side and push myself up, and it's hard with the cast still on. By the time I get to the bathroom, I'm wide awake from struggling so much, and then I try to get back to sleep, but I can't right away. I'm *so* tired.

She tells me that all of this is normal, and that she sympathizes because women often say the last stage of pregnancy is the hardest. I tell her that someone suggested that I do a pregnancy swim class, and I ask her if that's a good idea. Dianne asks if it was Ian that suggested it, and I nod. She kind of gives me a weird look, and I'm not sure what it means. I'm worried that she and Molly are starting to suspect something. We've been watching TV together pretty much every night, and sometimes we kiss a little or I sit next to him and he has his arm around me. As far as we know, they haven't seen us, but I wonder if they *have* seen us and they just aren't saying anything.

Dr. Lippincott actually says the pregnancy swim classes are a great idea, and that a lot of women find it really nice to be in the water where the water holds their stomach up and they feel like they don't have all that extra weight. I really would like to try it, but I'm just too embarrassed to put a bathing suit on and to be in front of all those people who will judge me.

The rest of the appointment goes well, and she says Cheese Puff is still in a good head-down position and the amount of amniotic fluid is good, so she can tell I'm drinking enough water. She also tells me to make sure I'm eating enough protein because this is the stage where Cheese Puff's brain is developing faster than ever, and protein is important for that.

Molly drives us back home, and on the way, she says, "Okay, Mom, should we tell her now?" *Oh no, tell me what? Oh my God, they know about me and Ian. What do I say? This is bad.*

Dianne nods and turns to me. "So, Madison, we were going to surprise you with a baby shower tomorrow morning."

Oh wow, so that's not what it was. Thank God. I sigh with relief and say, "Oh, guys, you don't have to do that! You've already done so much for me!"

"Don't even think about that," Dianne says. "We're *happy* to do it. The only thing is, we realized you might be upset that it's a surprise. We know how uncomfortable you are, and especially after hearing what you said to Dr. Lippincott about how you've been feeling, we want to make sure you're feeling up to it. Your mom and Josie were going to drive in for it, and we also invited Cheryl, and Molly got the number of that girl you became friends with from the support group, Alexa. Is that okay, or is it too much for you right now?"

"Oh, no, that's so nice, I can't believe you guys planned all of this!" I say. "And yeah, I mean, I don't feel great, but it'll be so nice to see everyone, so yes, I really want to have it. Thank you."

Dianne smiles and says she's excited, and Molly says she can't wait for me to see what they are getting me. They've been so amazing and so generous, and I honestly don't know what I would've done without them.

That night, I tell Ian that I can't stay up and watch TV with him, because I want to try to get more sleep so I can be as rested as possible for the baby shower. Of course, I just lie in bed and I really can't sleep, anyway. I've also noticed that when I *do* sleep lately, my dreams have been really crazy. Like the one I had last night...

I walk into my school. The hallways are empty, and I mean completely empty. Usually the hallways are packed, but there is not one person there, and there aren't even any posters on the walls.

The sounds of my footsteps echo as I enter Ms. Perry's classroom. There's no one in here, just her, standing at the front of the room. Wait. Why am I still in my sophomore year?

I raise my hand and ask, and she yells at me, "WELL, MS. DAVIS, YOU'LL JUST HAVE TO KEEP REPEATING IT UNTIL YOU GET IT RIGHT!"

Then the walls of the classroom close in and I can't breathe.
I hate dreams like that.

<>

Mom and Josie are the first to arrive for the baby shower. We hug and then laugh because they can't even get their arms around me anymore. Everyone arrives and brings little gifts that Dianne puts on a table. I really feel like I don't deserve this, and I'm worried I'm going to cry the whole day because I can't believe how nice everyone is being to me.

Dianne made really yummy sandwiches that we call "party sandwiches," they are really thin and the bread is so soft. She also got cute yellow cupcakes with monkeys on them.

We eat first and then play some games that Dianne says they do at a lot of baby showers, like this weird baby diaper game that's kind of hard to describe.

Then Molly announces, "Presents!" and she makes me sit on the couch and brings the presents to me.

I get some adorable baby clothes from Cheryl, and Alexa got me a funny parenting book that she got at the used bookstore. Josie knit an adorable hat for the baby, and she pointed out that she chose yellow so it could be for either a boy or girl.

Dianne and Molly got me a co-sleeping bassinet and explain that it's for before I move out, I can just secure it in my bed so that Cheese Puff can sleep right next to me.

Then Mom says, "I'll be right back," and she goes outside and then wheels in a crib with a huge bow on it. I'm so happy, because the baby's crib was something I was struggling to find because it was hard to get a good-quality but not too expensive one.

Then she says, "This was yours, Madison," and she takes off the bow and shows me the headboard, "See, most of the little monkeys I painted on it are still there, even though some of them have faded."

My baby crib. I look at all the monkeys and hearts all over it, the ones that Mom painted herself, and that both me and Josie slept in, and I just can't even speak. It means so much to have this. I hug Mom and thank her over and over again.

Everyone starts saying, "Speech! Speech!" and Molly says, "Come on, Madison, time for you to make a speech!" and she giggles.

Between my sobs and crying, I thank everyone and tell them how lucky I am to have them, and how I don't know how I could have done this without all of them being there for me. I don't want anyone to leave, and they stay for a while and talk and it's seriously one of the best times I've had this whole pregnancy.

My first childbirth class is at two o'clock, and I manage to get a quick nap in before I go. Molly has an interview with Johnny at Roast and Drink, and I wish her luck on my way out.

The childbirth class is in a small building near the community center, and I think of Ian on my way there. I'm a little nervous to do this class because I know I'm going to learn about the actual childbirth, and I'm sure a lot of it will be scary.

When I walk in, I see the room has a large TV screen and the floor has a bunch of rugs. There are about eight other women here, sitting on the carpets, and each of them is with a partner. *Oh my God, I'm the only one who came by myself?* This is so embarrassing.

I think about turning around and leaving, but then the instructor calls out, "Hello, are you Madison?" I nod and she shows me a place for me to sit. Then she says, "Is your partner coming?" and I shake my head and say, "He couldn't come today." I don't want to admit that I'm alone, I just can't do it. Not in front of all these happy couples.

"Okay, well, try to have them come with you next week. It doesn't have to be your partner, but it should be someone who will be attending the birth." She turns to the whole room. "Alright, let's get started! There will be six classes in total, and some of you might have your babies before we are done."

I notice some stares because I guess people can tell how young I am. Then again, I have been looking a bit older because of the dark circles under my eyes, and I actually feel like my face has aged since being pregnant. What's interesting is that there are some women who look a lot *older*. Like, too *old* to be having a baby.

The class is really informative, and sure enough, there are a lot of scary parts. She begins holding up various charts of the female's reproductive organs, and she says, "First, your cervix will begin to efface and dilate, which means it will start to thin and open, to prepare for the baby's head to come out. It dilates like this until it is ten centimeters. This can take a while. Usually at some point during this stage or the second stage, your water will break. This means the amniotic sac is draining so your baby can make its way into the world. The contractions will definitely pick up faster and stronger after your water breaks. If your water actually breaks, you'll feel a big, warm, watery gush coming out of you, but sometimes, the water doesn't break and the doctor does it for you."

It all sounds so complicated and overwhelming, and it does make me wish I was here with someone. I should've come with Molly. For a second, my mind goes to Leo, but then I push the thought away right away. I let myself fantasize for a moment about what it would be like if *Ian* was here with me. Maybe I could ask him to come next time.

"Most of you are in your last trimester, so your baby is already settling into its final position, where the head will descend down from the birth canal. The contractions you feel during labor are because your cervix, which is normally closed, is opening, and your uterus is contracting, and so it will hurt, and it will feel painful. But it's a good pain, nothing is wrong. It's a sign that your baby is about to be born. Once you've reached the ten centimeters of dilation that I mentioned, you will begin to push. It's kind of like trying to push out a really hard bowel movement. If you feel the baby's head coming, that means you're close. In the final stage of labor, you'll deliver the placenta."

Then she puts in a video and we all watch as a woman has her baby. There are close ups of the baby's head coming out of the vagina. It's unbelievable to see this. It's all so…real. Some of the people in the room wince, and I feel a little uncomfortable, but it really is cool, seeing the doctor and the mother bring the baby out into the world. We watch as the cute, tiny wrinkly baby starts crying and I can hear a lot of people in the room start crying, including me. The instructor hands out tissues, and I can tell this must happen all the time when she does this class. She tells us that next week, we will be discussing birth plans, medication options, and breathing exercises.

I go home and find Molly watching TV, so I get a snack and then come sit with her on the couch. I can't help but think she would be shocked to know how much I've been sitting on this couch with Ian, and that we had our first kiss here. I really wish I could tell her, it feels so weird to not tell her about it, but I don't even know if it'll last with Ian, and I'm scared at how Molly will react.

I ask her what happened at the interview, and she says Johnny was really nice and he said he'd let her know about the job. She asks how the childbirth class went, and I tell her about it and then I ask her if she could come with me next time. She says she'll come, for sure, and she's actually excited to learn what will happen when I have the baby. She asks to feel my stomach, she loves to feel Cheese Puff moving.

"By the way, Mads, when you move out, you know I'm going to be coming over to see the baby all the time," she says, and I suddenly feel really happy and sad at the same time. A bittersweet feeling. I mean, we've grown so close over this whole experience, and it's going to be really weird to not live with her anymore.

"Trust me, I know you will be," I say, laughing. "Maybe one day we could get our own apartment together."

"That would be so cool!" she says. "Anyway, I really hope that you'll count on me as a babysitter for Cheese Puff."

"Aren't you forgetting that you'll have tons of homework to do?"

"So will you, but *you'll* be taking care of it."

"Oh, trust me, I know," I say dramatically, and we start laughing again.

I watch TV with her for a while, and then it's time for me to go to work. I really wish I could just stay home and go to bed, I'm so tired. I decide to walk because I'm really needing some exercise and I'm hoping it will wake me up.

The shift goes by pretty quickly, and it really helps to have the stool to sit on behind the counter. I've been getting a lot of tips now, too, and I think it's because people see my stomach and they feel like they need to help me or something. I'm sad thinking about leaving Roast and Drink. It feels like everything is going to be coming to an end soon. But I know it's also going to be a huge beginning and a totally different life with a new baby. With my Cheese Puff.

After work, I wish I had driven, because now I'm way too tired to walk. I start walking slowly and then I see a group of girls from my school walking towards me. They are a snarky group that has always made fun of me. I want to cross to the other side of the street, but I'm too tired. They walk right up to me and block my path. They all wear tons of makeup and they're dressed in the latest trendy outfits. One of them who's wearing *braids* says, "Oh, look who it is, the slutty elephant." They all start laughing.

"Just please leave me alone," I say, looking down.

"Poor baby has to work at the coffee shop to make her slut money for the baby."

"I'm *not* a slut."

"Then why are you pregnant, sweetie?" another one of them asks condescendingly. "You're just a stupid girl who threw her life away over *Leo Schmitz.*"

"Shut up," I say, tears welling up in my eyes.

"You hear that?" she asks the eyeliner girl. "The slut wants *us* to shut up."

They laugh even harder. And then another girl whispers in a disgusted tone, "How did Leo even have sex with her? I mean, *look* at her," and they all laugh again.

"It's not even Leo's baby," the girl with the eyeliner says, "Leo said that she was sleeping around on him. So who knows who the father really is?"

"Yeah, I wonder if *she* even knows."

I'm shocked. *Did Leo really tell people that?*

"What?" is all I manage to say.

"That's right, cheater. No wonder he dumped you. Poor Leo."

"Poor *Leo?*" I croak out. *Is he really saying this stuff about me?!?*

"I honestly feel *bad* for her baby. Who the hell would want to grow up with-" the girl motions to me and laughs, "-*her* as a parent?" They all laugh and then walk away.

I wait until they are out of sight and then let the tears I'd been holding back pour out of me. I can't walk anymore, I'm too freaked out and tired. Even though I've been bullied the whole pregnancy, it's *never* been as bad as that. I can't even imagine being mean to anyone that was in my situation. Even if I *thought* some of the things they were saying, I would never hurt someone that way. I don't know if it's true what they said about Leo saying I was cheating on him, but if it is, I can't believe how horrible that is, because it's the biggest lie ever.

I decide to call an Uber, and it comes pretty quickly. When I get home, I head straight to my room. I really don't want to talk to anyone. The words of those girls echo through my head. I realize now how *stupid* I've been, being happy about Ian and thinking anything in my life could be good. I don't even get into my pajamas, I just get into bed and get under the covers and try to block out the world. I bury my head in my pillow and just let it all out, there's no way I could stop it, I just hope that no one can hear me.

After a little while, I hear a knock on my door and then Dianne comes in. "What's the matter, Madison?" she asks, softly pushing a strand of my hair away from my face. "Did something happen?"

I turn to her and in between sobbing and trying to catch my breath, I tell her what happened. She hands me some tissues and rubs my back. "Oh, Madison. I know how bad it can be, believe me, I had my share of it when *I* was pregnant with Molly. Although those girls do sound really extra horrible. I know it's hard. You just have to ignore them."

I know she's trying to help, but for some reason, I start to feel a weird anger towards her. "You don't get it," I mumble. "You clearly *don't* get it."

Her eyes square in on me. "Excuse me?"

"You don't get it," I say. "You're so *happy.* You ended up getting everything you wanted. Even though you were pregnant so young! You ended up with all this...this support from your family, and they didn't move away, and *your* dad is still alive, and you're a really successful author! You act like you and I are the same, that you can understand what I'm going through, but you really don't. You and I are *not* the same!"

Dianne looks absolutely shocked. She stands up and just stares at me, with her mouth open. "After all I've done for you," she finally says.

"Taking you in. Feeding you, taking you to your doctor's appointments, opening my *home* to you. This is how you talk to me now?? I'm so disappointed, Madison. So very disappointed in you."

"YOU AREN'T MY MOTHER, DIANNE!" I suddenly shout. "You don't *get* to be disappointed, because you're *not* my *mother!*" I can't stop myself, I'm just so angry, I'm *so angry*. I'm tired of being pregnant and I'm tired of being bullied, and I *don't want to do this anymore! I don't want to have a baby anymore! Look at my life now, LOOK AT IT!*

"Madison!" Dianne shouts. "What is wrong with you?!"

"Stop telling me that you know what I'm going through. Just stop it! Don't you dare tell me that you know what this is like! Look at your house, Dianne! Look at the pretty yellow front door and the perfect kitchen and family photos, and look at Molly! You guys *never* had to go through anything hard, unlike how *I'll* have to with *my* baby!"

"You have no idea what the hell you are talking about," Dianne says, her eyes fuming now. "How *dare* you invalidate my struggles? You have absolutely no idea what it took to get me and Molly to the place we're at now. I didn't just snap my fingers and make it happen. Not for a second. It was hard and you know it! I have no idea what's gotten into you, but I'm not going to stand for it!"

"Oh, just be quiet, Dianne! You know that *I'll* NEVER have *any* of *my* dreams that I had for *myself!*" I choke on my tears. "So just take Molly and your house and your published books and your perfect little life that you somehow have even though you got pregnant as a teenager and *LEAVE ME ALONE!*"

I cough and blow my nose, choking on the mucus from all the crying and screaming. I realize how bad all of this is, everything I said, I know it's horrible, and I don't even know where it came from, but I couldn't stop myself.

Dianne's face has an expression on it that I've never seen before. She stands there, staring at me, her eyes look so intensely angry, I'm honestly scared. Suddenly, she gets almost a weird smile on her face. "*Get out of my house,*" she says, almost quietly, but with such intensity that I know she means it. "Go live with your mother, or get your own apartment now, I don't really care, but you are no longer welcome here. Goodbye, Madison."

She walks out calmly and closes the door. I hear her talking to Molly in the hall, but I can't hear what they're saying. I lie there, stunned at what just happened. I bawl into my pillow, I can barely breathe, I'm crying so hard.

I don't know how this happened. I know it's all my fault. All the frustration pent up inside of me, all the hardships I have had to face and that I *still* have to face just came exploding out of me. Those girls after work were just the last straw. I can't deal anymore. I also can't trust anyone. Does Molly even *want* to be my friend? Or is she just feeling bad for me? Ian likes me now, or at least that's what he *says,* but will he really like me once I'm straddled with a baby? I'm sure he'll leave me, too. Just like Leo. Just like Mom and Josie. Just like Dad. Everyone leaves. And now *I* have to leave. Obviously I was going to be leaving soon anyway, but Dianne has made it clear I need to leave *now.*

But I can't go out there right now. I'll wait until everyone's asleep. I get Dad's duffel bag that has the stuff I prepared for the hospital in it, and fill it up with some clothes and my toothbrush, my pillow and blanket, and then the pictures on my nightstand and Dad's can of shaving cream. All of this just reminds me of when I was leaving *Mom's* house.

I hear a few quiet knocks on my door, but I don't answer. I'm sure it's Molly, but I'm too ashamed to talk to her right now. Even worse, it could be Ian. There's no way it's Dianne. I wonder if she'll ever talk to me again. I lie on my bed trying to figure out where to go. By midnight, the house is totally quiet and I creep quietly out to my car.

As I turn on the car and drive, I realize I really have nowhere to go. I'm not going to just drive to Santa Barbara, it's too late and I'm tired, and besides, Mom would be so upset with me. I also don't want to be so far from Dr. Lippincott and the hospital. I drive around slowly, mostly just going around the neighborhood, and then I start crying again so I stop the car, thinking about Mom's words to me about being safe. I can't see, I'm crying too hard. It's all the anger and fear and sadness and pain. *Pain.* It strikes me right in the chest. It actually *physically* hurts. Why does Mom have to be so far away? *I need her.* But everyone I care about leaves me. The part that hurts the most with my dad is that it wasn't on purpose. But still, he left. *Everybody leaves. No one stays.*

Dianne and Molly stayed, and look how I repay them. How could I say those things to Dianne? I've never yelled at anyone like that before. *What's wrong with me?* I don't blame her for telling me to leave. I should never have said those things, but I couldn't stop myself. It's like I took all the things that have been hurting me and all the horrible feelings I've had since I got pregnant and then dumped them on her.

I have no idea where I'm going to go. There's no way I can just rent an apartment overnight. There's nowhere for me. Those girls weren't even *wrong.* I mean, other than the part about sleeping around on Leo, they were right. What kind of person lets themself get pregnant at my age? I *must* be a slut. I should never have slept with Leo. I can't believe I've been such an idiot thinking that I could do it, that I could keep the baby and make this work. I don't see how I can anymore.

I'm so sorry, Cheese Puff. I'm so sorry, I'm so sorry, I'm so sorry. I wanted to be a good mother to you, and now we're already homeless.

I cry and cry and I have to use my shirt as a tissue because I forgot to bring any.

My mind races, trying to come up with a place to stay, even just for tonight. *Alexa.* She'll let me stay with her. Or, I guess since she's living with Danny's family, maybe they will, maybe just for tonight. I text her.

Maddie: Alexa? I know this sounds weird and crazy but I need a place to stay. Can I come over for the night?

I wait for a response. There is none. I wait about ten minutes and then I realize she's probably sleeping. It's nearly one in the morning. I'm so tired, I need to figure something out. I can't sleep in the car, I need to go to the bathroom.

I start driving around again and suddenly I realize that I'm near my old street.

I decide to drive by and look at it and when I get there, I see the "SOLD" sign is still on the lawn, but it's completely dark inside and I remember Mom said the new people weren't moving in until the end of the month because they were doing renovations. I remember being upset that they were going to change things in the house, like destroy all of our memories and the way the house was, but now I'm happy. I still have my key! I look at my keychain and there it is: the lavender-colored key that Mom got made for me when I was nine and started walking home by myself from school.

I park on the street and I just pray that they haven't changed the locks yet. Thank God, it opens. I've never been so happy to walk in this door than I am right now. Immediately, the smell of cleaning products overwhelms my nostrils. The first thing I do is use the bathroom downstairs, and luckily there's still some toilet paper. Then I start to look around the house. I go into the kitchen and I see they have taken out all the cupboards, and they are clearly doing the renovations there.

I go upstairs and into what used to be Mom's (and also Dad's, but it's too sad to think about) bedroom. The carpet is still there, but I can see they are going to paint the walls, because there are different colors of paint on the walls, like they're testing them out. A huge lump forms in my throat.

Then I suddenly remember what I did right after Josie was born. I took a pink colored pencil and wrote on the very bottom of the wall near the door "Madison loves Mommy loves Daddy loves Josie." I go up to the spot, praying and wishing that it's still there. It is.

I cry harder, tracing my finger along my handwriting. They'll probably cover it up with paint. I take out my phone and snap a quick picture of it, and then I bring my lips up to the writing and kiss it.

"I miss you, Daddy," I say quietly through my tears. "I miss Mom and Josie, too. I want to go home." I want everything back the way it used to be.

I take out my pillow and blanket that I managed to pack and I lay them on the floor. It's so uncomfortable, but I don't care, I'm so happy that I have a place to sleep, and I'm really tired. I will have to get up early to make sure I'm out before the workers come. I spray a little of Dad's shaving cream on my wrist, and lie there trying to fall asleep, but my mind is still racing.

What was I thinking? That I'd be able to do this? I can't. I just can't. It's too much. And I hate Leo. I hate him so much that I can't even think about it or my head will explode.

Suddenly, a text comes through my phone.

Molly: Mads? Where are you?? I don't know what happened with you and my mom, I heard you guys fighting, but please let me know if you're okay.

Maddie: I'm okay. I'm staying at Alexa's. I just need some time alone.

Molly: Oh. Okay. You're not mad at ME, are you?

Maddie: No, I'm not mad at you. Or your mom, even. I'm just really upset. But I'm okay. I'm really sorry. I can't text right now, but I'll talk to you soon.

I feel bad for lying about where I am, but I don't want her to come here, and I don't want her to worry about me.

I turn off my phone. I can't think anymore, I'm too tired. In fact, I'm beyond tired. I'm beyond exhausted. I'm so pathetic that I can't even come up with better words for how tired I am. I set an alarm for six, just in case, so the workers or cleaners or whoever might be coming won't catch me, and I fall asleep, closing my heavy eyes.

My alarm goes off just as the sun is rising. I am so, *so* tired, but I know I have to get up because the workers will probably be here soon.

I get in my car and look in my mirror and see that my eyes are red and swollen from crying. I'm really hungry and I know I need to eat something, it's not good for me or Cheese Puff to go too long without food. I don't really feel like going anywhere to eat, but all I have is a protein bar that I keep in my glove compartment in the car. I have a few bottles of water in the car, too. I eat the protein bar and drink some water, and then I feel a little better.

I decide to drive to the park and sit on a bench. No one's around, except for a few joggers. It's warm out, the birds are chirping, and the sun is coming up.

Suddenly, I just feel really *lonely*. It just kind of hits me that I'm all alone, and I'm *going* to be all alone. Even once I apologize to Dianne, if she lets me come back, I'll be getting my own apartment and leaving soon anyway. Well, I guess I won't be *totally* alone, because I'll have Cheese Puff, obviously, but I'll be alone in taking care of her or him. I know I knew this the whole time, but I've been around people for so long, it didn't really hit me until now what it will be like to live alone with a baby.

The thought of giving Cheese Puff up for adoption crosses my mind again. I haven't thought about doing that for a long time. I feel guilty even *thinking* about it, but I can't help it. I start thinking about how much easier my life would be if I did it, and how much better a life Cheese Puff would probably have. Things would just go back to normal for me.

Or would they? Even just imagining this makes me start to cry. I know everything makes me cry, but thinking of being separated from Cheese Puff causes a weird deep sadness that hits me in the stomach and the heart, and it feels like it will never, ever get better or go away. It would be something I would have to live with for the rest of my life. I don't think I could bear it. I'm so attached already, I feel the kicks and the movements and I literally can't wait to meet her or him. I love Cheese Puff so much already.

That's the thing. No matter how hard this will be and no matter how scary it is, I know that I just have to make it work. I will find a way. One thing is for sure, and that is even if Cheese Puff doesn't have all the luxuries that some kids do right away, I'm hoping eventually I will be able to make a nice life for her or him. No matter what, Cheese Puff will have one hundred percent of my love. One day, hopefully, I will find someone to be with who will make us a family of three. Or even more. I hope one day I can have another baby with someone I love, who loves me, and Cheese Puff will even have a sibling.

Thinking these thoughts makes me picture Ian. He's been so sweet, but it's impossible to know if it will last. I just wish he could be hugging me right now. Just getting a taste of what it would be like to have someone who really cares and can be there for me made me realize how much I want it.

I go back to the car and take out the can of Dad's shaving cream, and I spray a bit on my wrist. Inhaling the smell makes me feel a little better, and I realize that more than anyone, I just want my dad back. I feel the tears coming again, but I stop them. I don't have any tissues and I really want to try to get myself together.

The protein bar I ate wasn't enough and I need to get something more to eat. This makes me realize that this is where I'd have been for my whole pregnancy if it weren't for Dianne. How could I just bite her head off when it's really just the anger I have at *myself*? I shouldn't be talking the way I did to her because she made it through okay, and I'm scared that *I* won't. She has been nothing but kind to me. I really do need to apologize, but I don't know how.

Home's Diner is the only place I know that's open this early. I drive over there and sit in a corner booth. There's only one other person there, sitting at the counter. The waitress who knows me comes up and smiles and hands me a menu. I decide to get chocolate-chip waffles and hot chocolate. I know it's sugary but right now, I just need something to make me feel better.

I realize my phone has been off since last night, and I turn it on and a bunch of texts pop up. Alexa wrote me early this morning to ask what's going on. I write her a few quick texts back saying I had a fight with Dianne and that I'm okay, but I might need a place to stay tonight. She writes back that she will ask her boyfriend's parents.

There's a text from Ian, too, and I instantly feel my stomach drop, I don't even know what Dianne told him and I'm so ashamed about the whole thing.

Ian: Madison, what's going on? I was out late last night, but when I woke up this morning, Molly told me what happened with you and my sister. Are you okay? I'm worried about you, where are you? Please write back and tell me how you are.

Madison: Hi Ian. Yeah, sorry, it's a bit of a mess, and it's all my fault. I stayed at my friend Alexa's. I'm okay but I just need some time to think. Please don't worry but thank you.

Ian: Okay, but please let me know if there's anything I can do. I want to help. I also want to see you. Let me know if you want to see me. We can meet up somewhere or whatever you want. Call me when you can.

Molly wrote again, too, and asked how I was doing and that she tried to talk to her mom about it, but Dianne didn't want to talk to her. I tell her I'm okay and that I would write later. I need to think.

Boy did I ever screw things up. That's who Madison Davis is, I guess. The girl who just constantly makes mistakes and pushes people away.

What's even more pathetic is that right now, I wish I could at least talk to Leo. Not even as his girlfriend or the person who is having his baby. Just as the baby's *father*. I would actually have been fine with him not being in a relationship with me anymore; maybe we could've co-parented. Then I wouldn't be in this completely alone. But he's a selfish piece of crap, so there's no point in even thinking about it.

It doesn't matter what he is or how he acts, a voice in my head tells me. *He's always going to be Cheese Puff's father, no matter what.* It's true; I will *always* be connected to him now. Through Cheese Puff, who will always have half of his DNA.

I finish eating and pay the bill, and then I just do it. I dial Leo's number. Over the months, I've been tempted to delete his contact, but I just couldn't do it. I know that Leo wants nothing to do with me or Cheese Puff, but what if God forbid one day something horrible happens to Cheese Puff? Am I supposed to tell him? At some point, if we all stay in Redford, they will bump into each other. Will Leo ever even *talk* to his kid?

My call goes straight to voicemail. In a way, I'm relieved, because I realize I don't know what to say. I hang up without leaving a message.

I have nowhere to go and nothing to do until my work shift tonight. I was going to try to go to another support group class, but I don't feel up to it today and I really need to figure out a plan. I just need a few more minutes to chill, and so I pull out my phone again and just start to scroll through my camera roll.

I scroll back, further and further. I pass old pictures of me with Molly, me with Josie, me with Leo, me with Mom. Then I do something I haven't done in ages. I look at the pictures of me and Dad, and the whole family together. I don't know why, but it doesn't make me want to cry this time. I just love seeing his smiling face and all the goofy things we used to do. Seeing who I was before he died and all the pictures before I got pregnant makes me realize how much things have changed, and how different my life is now. I don't feel sad, really. I just feel kind of numb to it right now. I think I'm all cried out.

Then I look at the pictures I've been taking of my stomach since I found out I was pregnant. It's amazing to see the changes. I can't believe I thought my stomach was big when I was only *five* months along. It's insane how much bigger it is now.

The waitress comes and asks me if I want anything else, and it's starting to get busy, so I tell her no thanks and I go to leave. When I get back to the car, I decide to text Molly to see if we can talk and maybe she can help me decide what to do about what happened with her mom. Then I notice there's almost no battery left on my phone. I go to get the charger from my bag and then I realize I didn't bring it. Oh, no! Wasn't I supposed to pack a charger for the hospital, anyway? Why isn't it in my bag? I threw in almost everything else, but I don't even have a charger! Not even a charger! *I can't even charge my freaking phone!*

I'm so *stupid!* How am I ever going to take care of a *baby* if I can't even remember something as important as my freaking phone charger?!? Is there anything that I *don't* screw up?!?

I start sobbing all over again. *How is this my life now?* Those pictures, the way it used to be, I would give anything right now to go back to then. The night Dad died, I wish I could go back and not have it happen. If he was alive, all of this would be so much easier, I just know it. He would be there for me. I'm just so tired of pretending that I can live without him, pretending that it's all okay that he will never see me again and that I'll never see him again, because it's just getting too hard. I want to be his little girl again, but I can't.

I'm never going to just be a little girl again.

I realize that I've been feeling so angry at having to grow up so fast because of being pregnant, but it hits me that I've had to grow up really fast *twice* now. The first time was after Dad died. Even though I missed him and have been so sad, I was able to get on with my life and laugh with friends and be happy again, and I know I can do it again now. I just need to focus and get back on track.

I know what I have to do first. I have to apologize to Dianne, *really* apologize, and tell her how sorry I am. Then I need to *really* get organized, and get back on track. I need to find my own apartment right away, and also a better paying job.

All through my shift at work, I think about what I'm going to say to Dianne. I want to talk to her tonight and I plan to text her after work. I asked another barista if I could borrow her phone charger throughout my shift, and she said yes, so at least I'll have a functioning phone soon.

I'm so tired, and I really hope Dianne forgives me and that I can come back to her house tonight, but just in case, I text Alexa again and she says Danny's parents said it was okay, but just for one night. *Ugh.* I really don't want to have to do that. I could always go back to my old house again, but that feels risky, and it was really uncomfortable sleeping on the floor and it was sad to be there with all the memories.

After I finish my shift, I go to my car and just as I'm about to text Dianne, Molly calls me. When I answer, she starts screaming into the phone. "Mads? Are you there?!?"

"Yes, Molly, what's wrong?!?"

"Why did you lie to me?!? I called Alexa, and she said you weren't even there! Where are you? Tell me the truth this time, Madison!"

I start crying. "I'm sorry, Molly, I...I didn't want to lie to you."

"Mads, if you don't tell me where you are, I'm going to call the police, I mean it."

"Molly, stop it. I'm fine, I'm-"

"Where are you?!? Tell me now!"

"I'm...I'm at Roast and Drink, I just finished my shift."

She hangs up. *Great, now she hates me, too.* I shouldn't have lied to her. I just can't do anything right. I need to fix all of this. *Now.*

I sit in my car, trying to think of what to write to Dianne when suddenly I hear a loud tap on my window, and I turn to see Dianne, Molly, and Ian outside my car. They all have worried looks on their faces.

I roll down the window and Dianne says she wants me to come home so we can talk. Molly and Ian are nodding beside her and saying to just come home and everything will be okay. I start to cry and I agree to meet them at home. I can't believe they came to find me, they really do care. I feel so terrible for what I've put everybody through.

Back at the house, Molly and Ian say they're going to pick up dinner for all of us. As soon as they leave, Dianne jumps right in. "Listen, Madison. I want you to know that no matter what you said to me, I should never have told you to leave. That was wrong of me. As angry as I was, it wasn't safe for me to do that to you, in your condition."

"It's okay, I-"

"I was going to call your mom, but then I thought I better not. I remembered that we have 'Find my Friends' on each other's phones, and I could see that you were at your old house. I figured you were safe and I would let you have some space. I knew you didn't go to Alexa's, but I didn't say anything to Molly, but then she called Alexa and, well, you know what happened after that. I planned to come get you today and was going to meet you after work, even if Molly hadn't called you."

I start to cry. *Again.* "Dianne, I've never felt worse about anything in my life than about the way I talked to you."

"I can imagine."

"I'm sorry. I'm *so* sorry. I didn't mean any of it."

"I can't tell you how horrible what you said made me feel. After all I've done for you. Who has taken you to all your doctor's appointments? Who has taken care of you when you had food poisoning? What about when you broke your wrist? Who has been feeding you breakfast, lunch, and dinner? Who has given you a nice room and house to stay in? Who has comforted you every single time something's wrong? *Me!* That's who! And then you have the nerve to say what you said to me?"

With everything she says, I nod and just cry harder. I feel so terrible, she's right about everything. "I don't know what to say," I say. "You don't understand, I was-"

"Oh, here we go again, with you telling me that I don't understand. You don't realize that I *do* understand." She looks at me squarely. "I'm thirty-four, Madison. I had Molly when I was eighteen. But I got pregnant with her when I was seventeen. And it was just about ten years ago when I was *finally* stable enough to give her the life that she deserves. Do *you* understand how hard I've worked to get here?!?" She scoffs. "I get it more than most people you'll come across."

"Dianne, I know. I didn't mean that you didn't understand, I was just trying to explain that I didn't mean anything I said to you. I was just so full of anger and I was upset and those girls that were bullying me just pushed me over the edge, and I took it out on you. The *last* person I should be doing that to. I am so sorry. Please, please, please, can you *please* just forgive me?"

Dianne hands me a tissue and I blow my nose and try to stop crying. Then, she says, a little more quietly, "I don't want you to leave, okay? I know you don't have anywhere to go, and I don't think it's safe for you or the baby right now. Although I'm still very hurt at what you said to me, I want you to come back here. We can try to move on from this. I appreciate your apology, but it might take some time for me to just go back to the way things used to be. You really hurt me, Madison, whether you meant to or not. But I do understand. And I do get it. Okay?"

I nod. "Thank you. Please, can I...can I just have a hug?"

She gives me a hug, and I cry into her shoulder for a minute. Then she tells me to go take a shower and that Molly and Ian will be back with the food soon.

I go to my room and start unpacking my things, and then I get ready to take a shower. It's such a relief to be back here and to know I don't have to find anywhere to go tonight. I realize again that I really need a plan in place for an apartment of my own. I text Alexa and let her know that I don't need to stay there.

The shower feels so good, and I remember again how sweet Ian is, this seat will always make me think of him. I want to take it to my new apartment, when I find one. I wonder if Dianne will let me. I hope Dianne can really forgive me. She's still so angry and hurt, and I don't blame her. All I can think about now is how *I* would feel if one day someone told me that I "didn't get it." That I didn't understand how hard it was to be a teen mother.

I decide to lie down for a few minutes before Molly and Ian get back with the food. I'm starving, and everything hurts. My stomach, my back, my feet, my head, my legs, and my heart. Most of all, my heart hurts. For all the pain I've had and all the pain I've caused others.

I hope Molly and Ian aren't too mad at me. I need to really make things better with everyone again. I will figure out a way to show them all how much I appreciate all of them. Being away, even for one night, made me realize how important they all are to me. I know that they care, but maybe they're just relieved that I wasn't lying in a ditch somewhere.

I hear the front door open and Molly calls out to me to come down for dinner. Before I get up, I place my hand on my stomach and say quietly, "Cheese Puff. I just wanted to tell you I'm sorry. For everything I've been thinking and how I've been acting since last night. I'm angry at *myself*, not at you, okay baby? You haven't done anything wrong to me or to anyone in your little innocent life so far." I remember what I was thinking earlier. "You will always have one hundred percent of my love, and that's a promise. I will *always* be there for you, and so you'll never feel alone, and *I* won't feel alone anymore because I know I'll have you, too."

36 weeks
4 left!!

♡Ian♡

my Cheese Puff

Summer!!

To-Do List

- pick up paycheck on Friday from Roast and Drink
- appointment with Dr. Lippincott today at 5pm
  * eat more protein

☆baby shower tomorrow!!

buy:
- cheese puffs
- crib!! ✓

- childbirth class at 2pm today
- find a better-paying job soon!

Cheese Puff Kicking

* Send thank-you email to Mom for the crib!

just keep going
keep going
keep going for
Cheese Puff

dead phone

find apartment?

I'm so stupid
I can't even remember a freakin' charger

I'm going to be there for you forever, Cheese Puff

☆appointment with Dr. Lippincott next week

Chapter 33: Week Thirty-Seven

"Your baby is as big as a canary melon," I read online. I can't believe that I only have three weeks left until my due date. It really feels like a countdown now. Every time I have a Braxton-Hicks contraction, I wonder if it's going to turn into real labor.

My heartburn has been awful, like the worst burning and nauseous sensation all over my chest, and Dr. Lippincott said I can chew on these tablets called Gaviscon every two to three hours. They're kind of fizzy, and they help a little.

I've also been having this weird, pink discharge in my underwear, and I did some research about it, and apparently it's my cervix's blood vessels rupturing to get ready for dilation. It sort of scares me, but it also really excites me.

I'm in the car on my way to Dr. Lippincott for my hopefully third-to-last appointment. Dianne is driving and Molly is coming with us, as usual. It's been a little awkward between me and Dianne since the fight. She's being nice and polite, but not as chatty and friendly with me as she used to be. It's kind of...formal. I think it makes Molly uncomfortable. I hate this, all of this, and I wish things could go back to normal. I still feel awful about what I said. It just bothers me that after all the time I've been living with them, it has to end like this, with us not getting along anymore.

Molly and I are getting along, though. I don't think she really understands what happened with me and her mom. She really wants to take those maternity pictures soon, in case Cheese Puff arrives early. We've decided that I'm going to wear a bikini top and shorts, and stand against the blank wall in her bedroom, and we will shine her lamp at me so that my huge stomach creates a silhouette against the wall. It should be really cool, and I love that Molly wants to do this for me.

Things are good with Ian, too. We've been watching TV pretty much every night and eating cheese puffs and kissing. It's been really nice and I still like him a lot, but I'm trying not to let myself feel too much for him because I don't see how we will be able to continue seeing each other after the baby is born. I'm trying to just enjoy it right now and not think about it too much.

Aside from things not being the same with Dianne, she also told us some really huge news just the day after I came home after our fight. The book that she went to Los Angeles for a meeting about *is* going to be made into a movie! I think she's really excited about it, and I'm excited for her.

I'm glad that something good is happening to her after our fight last week.

Dr. Lippincott does an ultrasound, and she warns me that my amniotic fluid looks a little low and she says again that when babies are in your uterus, they are aquatic creatures, and they need for there to be enough fluid. She asks if I've been drinking enough water, and even though I say yes, she tells me to have more. I tell her about the childbirth classes and she's happy to hear that I'm doing them.

After she checks my lower half, she tells me that I've already started something called "effacing," which means my cervix is thinning out in preparation for labor. She tells me there are signs to look out for that could mean I'm in labor. I'm supposed to call her if I see my mucus plug come out. She says the mucus plug forms at the beginning of pregnancy, and it stays at the entrance to the uterus to sort of block anything from coming into the uterus, and it prevents infection. It's amazing, I didn't even know that it was there, protecting Cheese Puff. Dr. Lippincott says that when it comes out, it's a sign that labor is starting, and it will look like a big glob of mucus that might be a mix of brown, red, and clear color. She also wants me to call her if the Braxton Hicks get more painful or start happening all the time. I'm also supposed to call her if it feels like I peed in my pants, or if some "water" suddenly comes out of me. It's actually amniotic fluid and it means the amniotic sac burst. Basically, she wants me to call her if there's anything new that happens or if I'm wondering at all if it could be labor.

Most of what she's telling me we learned in the childbirth classes, but for some reason, hearing Dr. Lippincott say it makes it more real and more scary. "Sometimes my Braxton Hicks *are* a bit painful, actually. How will I know if it's *real* labor?" I ask worriedly.

"Trust me, you'll know," she says. "It'll be very painful, almost like really bad period cramps in the beginning. Your back might hurt, too. Also, even if you change positions or lie down, the Braxton Hicks won't go away. I want you to keep paper and a pen on hand, or just document it in your phone when you have the contractions. That way you can see how close together they are. Once they start being around every five minutes or less, it usually means labor is starting."

I can feel my heart speeding up but I try to seem calm and just nod. She puts her hand on my shoulder and tells me that everything is going to be fine. Molly looks terrified, but then I look at Dianne and she nods and smiles, which is the first time she's smiled at me since the fight.

Ian is working, so Dianne heats up leftover stew for dinner for just me, her, and Molly. We discuss what Dr. Lippincott said a bit more. Dianne wants me to tell her the second I feel anything different. She's being nice, but still not fun and laughing like she used to do with me. I ask her about her book and the movie, and she gets more excited when she starts talking about it. She said her agent is working out if she will be involved with writing the movie, or if they will hire another writer. She wants to be the writer, but she's not sure if they will let her. It's really confusing and complicated, but I think no matter what happens, she will make a lot of money. She really is an inspiration to me, because she really did make a good life for her and Molly, even though she was a teen mom. I tell her how happy I am for her, and she smiles. Things do seem a *little* better between us, thank God.

After dinner, I take a shower and then decide to get into my pajamas and try to go to bed early, but I'm not tired, so I just rest in bed, texting with my mom and also Alexa and I tell them what happened at the appointment. After a little while, I get a text from Ian telling me that Dianne is watching the news in the living room, and Molly is asleep, so maybe he wants to just come up to my room for a bit. I'm still worried that they are going to suspect something, but he says Molly's asleep. So I agree to let him come in, and he sits on the edge of my bed.

"So I was thinking of finally telling Molly and Dianne about us," he says, as if he had just read my mind. I think he's also tired of sneaking around, it's stressful.

He looks into my eyes for an answer. I sigh. "I really want to tell them, but...I'm worried about the timing. And Dianne is still upset about our fight, I think."

"I know. But don't you think the longer we don't tell them, the more upset they'll be? Also, I've been thinking, you never know, maybe they'll be *happy* for us."

"I don't think so. I think it's going to be the opposite."

"So, are you saying we're doing something that's *bad?*" he says, clearly hurt, because his playful smile disappears from his face. "Seriously, Madison?"

"I'm just...I'm not ready," I whisper, and he stares at me, looking really sad. I feel bad, but I'm really worried about their reaction and I just can't have Dianne hating me right now. "Ian, I'm sorry. Maybe soon, okay?"

Suddenly, we hear footsteps and then a knock at my door. Ian jumps up and stands near the door as Molly opens it. I thought she was *sleeping!* "Madison, can we-? Oh, Ian! How come you're in here?"

"Um..." Ian looks at me, and I scramble to think of something and I hold up my water bottle. Ian nods. "Madison, uh, texted me that she needed water and she didn't feel up to getting it. She...thought you were asleep, I guess."

Molly is staring at both of us, and she looks totally weirded out. I nod and plug in a smile. "Yeah!" I say. "Okay, thanks, Ian!"

"Sure, no problem. Bye, guys," he says, and then he leaves quickly. Molly watches him go and then looks at me, "Is something wrong?"

"No, why?"

"I don't know, you're acting...weird."

I notice that Molly has her digital camera in hand. I try to change the subject and say, "So, uh, you want to do the maternity pictures now?"

"Oh, yeah. It's best to do it when it's dark so we get a good silhouette."

"Okay, let me just get dressed and I'll meet you in your room." She leaves and I breathe a sigh of relief. Hopefully, she'll forget Ian was in here. But maybe he's right and we should tell them. It's way too stressful to keep hiding it. Besides, we're hardly able to spend any time together the way it is now, we can't even watch TV together because Dianne is now coming into the living room to watch it, rather than in her bedroom.

I put on one of my bikini tops. It was always a little big on me, and now it fits snugly and actually looks really good because now I have so much cleavage from being pregnant. Then I decide to wear my comfy gray shorts because they won't really show up that much, so the emphasis will be on my stomach.

I go into Molly's room and see she has angled her lamp so the light will go against the wall. She tells me where to stand and then she tells me to try different poses and she starts taking the pictures. At first it's a little awkward, even with Molly who's my best friend. It's just something about my stomach being really bare like that when it's so big. She puts some music on her phone and it helps me get in the photo-taking mood. We laugh because it feels like we imagine a real photo shoot would.

Molly is so sweet to do this, and I can't help thinking I should just tell her about Ian. I mean, would she really be that mad? I don't know. Ian isn't going to want to be with me if I want to keep hiding our relationship. But I just don't want it to be out there yet. It's too...scary. What if we break up? And then everyone feels sorry for me *again*? Ian doesn't understand how scary it is for me to think of telling people.

So why don't you try explaining it to him, Madison? I think to myself.

"Maddie, is something wrong? If you're not having fun anymore, we can stop," Molly says.

"No, it's okay, this is fun," I say, and then I laugh. "But maybe we should look at the pictures to see if they're good."

We sit on her bed and flip through the pictures on her camera. They actually turned out really nice. Molly put a warm filter on them, and they look almost antique.

"Wow, Molly," I breathe. "Thank you!"

"Of course! And you look gorgeous, Mads."

Now I have these amazing pictures forever. I tell Molly that she should seriously consider being a photographer. I know that it's a career she's interested in, because she's very artistic, and it's really actually perfect for her.

When I go back to my room, I see there are a few texts from Ian. At first, he's joking about how Molly walked in, but then he says he really thinks it's time to tell them. I write back and explain what I've been thinking about and why I'm worried, and he's really sweet and says he understands, and we can wait until I feel ready. He really is amazing. He signs off with, "Goodnight and sweet dreams, xoxo," and my heart melts.

I fall asleep pretty easily, but I wake up at three in the morning because I have to pee. I have a new thing I do, which is when I go to pee in the middle of the night, I try to keep my eyes as shut as possible so I won't wake up too much. It figures, tonight I bump into the door, and now I'm wide awake with my arm hurting. *Ugh.*

Once I'm back in bed, I try my hardest to go back to bed, but I can't. My eyes just don't feel tired anymore. The clock ticks away. I try to count Cheese Puff's kicks to relax myself, but it does no good. Ian's filling every corner of my mind.

The thing is, he's right. We need to tell Dianne and Molly. I do agree with him. But I just don't know if I can bring myself to do it yet, and I don't even really know *why.*

I think I know why, actually. I just don't want to admit it. I think it's because I'm really scared that I'll...that I'll keep getting more and more attached to him. I'll want him to stay with me once Cheese Puff is born, and even when he goes back to school. I'll want to keep up the relationship, and then I know myself, I'll start daydreaming about marrying him and having him be like a father to Cheese Puff, and then maybe even us having kids of our own one day. I'm already starting to have little flashes of dreams like that, and I have to keep stopping myself.

I know it's crazy to think like this, we haven't even really been able to fully be together. I just like him *so much,* and he's such an amazing guy in every way. So, I guess I'm scared to tell Dianne and Molly, because then it's really admitting how I feel, and then I'm really going to be hurt if it ends.

I sigh. There's no way I can fall asleep. Now it's almost five in the morning and I'm wide awake, worrying about this. I try to think of other things that are way more relaxing. Like going to the beach. I can't believe school's out and we haven't gone to the beach. Maybe Molly and I can go tomorrow.

I decide to text her, figuring she'll get it in the morning because I know she puts her phone on "Do Not Disturb" when she goes to sleep.

Maddie: Beach day tomorrow? I can't sleep haha.

Surprisingly, she writes back! *Wow, she's up now, too?* That's so weird. I hope I didn't wake her up when I went to the bathroom and bumped into the door.

Molly: It's already tomorrow, haha. I can't sleep, either. Meet me downstairs in five? We can watch the sun come up, it'll be fun! :)

I text her back "yes," and then I get ready and go meet her in the hall. We tip toe downstairs, trying to be as quiet as possible. She leaves a note for Dianne and we decide she should drive. We turn up the music in the car and it feels so weird to be driving in the middle of the night, listening to music on our way to the ocean.

"This is fun," I say. "It's not like I'll be able to go to the beach in the middle of the night once Cheese Puff is born."

"Yeah," Molly laughs.

"Why couldn't *you* sleep?"

"I don't know, I just woke up and I couldn't fall back to sleep."

"Sorry, I bet it was me," I say. "I bumped into the door when I got up to go to the bathroom."

She laughs. "Maybe. I don't know, I just couldn't fall back to sleep, once I started thinking about everything."

"Like what?"

"I just don't feel like I'm doing...anything. I mean, I don't have a boyfriend or a career mindset like you, and I don't really know where I want to go to college. I mean, *you* already know what you want to do and everything."

"Well, you're so amazing at art and photography, I mean, maybe you should try to do something with that?"

"I don't know, maybe. You're just so lucky you know what you want to do."

"Well, I know *what* I want to do, but who knows if I'll be *able* to now, because of the baby. I've been up worrying all night, too."

"About what?"

"Well...you know."

"Yeah, I guess I do."

I sigh. "But really Molly, you don't need to worry. You will find a boyfriend, too. You're so beautiful, and I don't see how anyone *couldn't* love you."

"You're lucky. Because you've already had a guy love you."

"Yeah, right," I scoff. "Except he didn't *love* me. Otherwise he would've stayed with me and the baby."

"Yeah, I guess." She shakes her head and frowns. "Sorry, let's try to just forget everything and have fun at the beach, okay?"

I nod and we listen to music and don't talk anymore. When we get to the beach, we find a parking spot right up next to the sand. There's no one around and we just get out, put our towels down, and sit in the sand. It's so quiet except for the sound of the waves. I was expecting it to be cold, but it's a surprisingly warm night. The sky is still dark blue, but the sun is starting to rise.

"Do you know what I was fighting about with your mom?" I ask Molly tentatively.

She shakes her head. "No idea. I told you, all I heard was yelling."

"Well, I was just upset that night, I took it out on your mom, and...yeah. It was really stupid." I take a deep breath. "I...I told her that she didn't get what I was going through. I said these...these awful things about her having a perfect life even though she got pregnant as a teenager. You know, about you guys living in a nice house, her being a successful author, your whole life in general..."

Molly sighs, "I get why you think we never had to go through anything hard, because the way our life is now, it's really good. I don't remember it, but Mom says when I was a baby and a toddler, it was really, *really* hard. Mom worked as a maid, and sometimes I'd have to come along on the jobs. I do have one memory of being in a house that Mom was cleaning, and I started to drink some floor polish. Mom freaked and we had to go to the hospital and they had to pump my stomach. I have just little bits of memories of it and it was really scary, Mom was screaming and crying and I think she thought I was going to die. When I was better, Mom said it was going to take years to pay off the hospital bills."

Oh my God, that's so awful. I can't believe she never told me this before.

"Oh my God, Molly. I can't believe that, it's...so horrible. I mean, I feel even worse now for what I said to your mom."

"It's okay, you didn't know. I just never really like to talk about that stuff."

"I get it. I'm really sorry you went through that," I say, shaking my head. I never want Cheese Puff to grow up and feel this way. I want to have enough money and a good, secure job, but what if I don't get one? I don't want Cheese Puff to suffer because of me.

"It's okay, seriously, Mads," Molly says. "Don't feel bad about saying what you said to my mom. You didn't know how hard things were."

"Okay, but still, I'm sorry."

"I know."

We sit silently for a little bit, just looking at the horizon. The sky is starting to get lighter and the sun is starting to come up over the hills on the other side, across the road. Suddenly, I realize I can't keep lying to Molly. She's been so open with me about everything, and it just doesn't feel okay anymore to not tell her.

"Molly?"

"Yeah?"

I take a breath. "I'm with Ian."

She turns away from the ocean and stares at me. "What?"

"Ian and I are..." I take another breath. "Ian and I are together."

"Mads, stop it," she says, kind of smiling, she obviously thinks I'm joking, but when she sees my expression, her eyes kind of bug out. "Are you kidding me??" she asks, and for a second I think she's going to be really mad, but then she hops up from her towel and starts dancing around in the sand. "Oh my God, I knew it! I just *knew* it!" she says, and she starts laughing.

"You're not mad?"

"Mad? Why would I be mad? This is great! And I'm not even that surprised!"

"What, seriously? Why not?"

"I don't know, I mean, you two just act a certain way when you're around each other. I kept thinking there was something going on, but then I thought it was my imagination. Oh my God, that's why he was in your room tonight! You said he came to give you water! How long has this been happening? Mads, why didn't you tell me?"

"It hasn't been that long, it kind of started when he helped me when I broke my wrist. So about a month. We...we haven't done much, just kiss, but I...I *really* like him, and he's so sweet to me. I wanted to tell you so badly, but I was worried you'd be mad and I'm terrified of what your mom will think. I've also been worried it's going to end, so I didn't want to say anything."

"It's *amazing!* Mom will be so happy!"

"But Molly, he's your *uncle!*"

"So what? He's only three years older!"

"I know!" I say, and we start squealing together, laughing and laughing, and I feel so euphoric that I told her, so amazing that it's out and that she's *happy* about it. It feels like a huge weight has been lifted, and I can't wait to tell Ian that I told Molly. Maybe she can help me tell Dianne, or Ian can tell her. I hope she has the same reaction.

Without us even realizing it, suddenly, it's light out. The sky is so gorgeous, it looks like when it's sunset. I look at my phone and see it's already six-thirty.

We stay a bit longer and then decide to leave. On the drive home, Molly just keeps talking about me and Ian and asking a million questions. She's smiling from ear to ear. She starts saying things like maybe we'll get married one day, and then I'll be her *aunt,* and we can't stop laughing. I tell her I'm way too scared to think about the future like that, even though it's amazing to dream about it, and she gets it.

Molly says she thinks I should let Ian tell her mom about it, and I agree. When we get home, the house is still quiet, so we creep up to our rooms and go to sleep. I sleep for a few hours and when I wake up, I feel totally weird, realizing everything that happened last night. That was so much fun going to the beach with Molly. I can't believe I told her about Ian. I have to tell him that I told her.

I get dressed and go down to the kitchen and I find Ian sitting at the table eating a sandwich. He tells me Dianne and Molly went out to do some errands.

I decide to tell him right away. "Ian, you were right. I decided to tell Molly and I told her early this morning. She knows about us now."

Ian looks totally surprised, and I'm worried now *he's* going to be upset because I told her without checking with him first. But then he just smiles a huge smile and says, "That's great! What did she say? Was she totally shocked?"

"She wasn't that shocked. She said she had suspected it a few times."

"Like last night with the water?" We both laugh. He takes my hand across the table and smiles at me. "I'm really happy you told her."

I smile back, and then suddenly, my mind just races through everything: him helping me when I broke my wrist, the nights on the couch, grocery shopping, the lunch dates, how much I like him, and before I can stop it, I blurt out, "I love you, Ian."

Oh my God, why did I say that? How stupid am I? I should never have been the one to say it first. I'm such an idiot. I probably just scared him away.

I look away and just freeze. I'm scared to look at him, but then he squeezes my hand and I look up and he says, "I'm really mad at you."

"Oh my God, Ian, I'm sorry, I don't know why I said that. I'm sorry, I-"

"I wanted to be the one to say it first!"

"What do you mean?"

He smiles. "Mads, I love you, too."

Oh my God, is this real? Is this really happening?

Before I can think anymore, he comes over and kisses me. We haven't kissed in a few days, we haven't had any alone time. He smells so good, I love the amazing scent of his apple shampoo. He starts to caress my cheeks and runs his hands through my hair. We kiss for a few minutes and then he says, "Well, at least we don't need to worry about *Molly* seeing us anymore. Now I have to tell my sister."

We agree that he should tell her alone. I don't think it's a good idea for me to be there, in case she freaks. He says he will try to do it later today. We kiss again and then I tell him I'm going to take another nap, I'm still tired from getting up and going to the beach so early.

When I get into bed, I just can't stop thinking about everything that's happened since last night. I've never told a boy that I love them before, and mostly, I've never had a boy tell me that he loved *me* before. I realize how pathetic it is, that I slept with Leo before we ever said those words to each other. But it feels so right with Ian, and it never felt like this with Leo. I'm actually feeling happy and safe right now, and even though I'm still afraid to trust it, I want to hold onto this feeling.

AAH! Huge Stomach!

37 weeks

To-Do List

- pick up paycheck on Friday from Roast and Drink
- appointment with Dr. Lippincott today at 5pm
* Signs of real labor:
  • mucus plug comes out
  • regular contractions that don't go away
  • water breaks
- Start looking for a new job
- start looking for apartments?

♡Ian♡

- tell Molly + Dianne about me + Ian ??

☆ give my notice at Roast and Drink
☆ take maternity pictures with Molly

It's okay, Mommy!

Stressed out

buy:
- cheese puffs
- nursing pads
- lotion
- Gaviscon

☆ research what real contractions feel like

♡ Ian ♡
+
♡ Madison ♡

← beach

☆ I'M GETTING MY CAST OFF NEXT WEEK!! ☆

my Cheese ♡ Puff

- call Mom + Josie soon!
- call Alexa soon!

Chapter 34: Week Thirty-Eight

"Your baby is as big as a mini watermelon," I read on my phone as Dianne drives me to my appointment to *finally* get my cast off. I cannot wait to get it off and not have to deal with it all the time. I don't even remember what it felt like to not have one.

It's June seventeenth, so if I make it to my due date, I'm just about two weeks away from having Cheese Puff. I still can't get it through my head that a baby is going to come out from down there. It doesn't feel like it's really going to happen. I'm scared, but I totally get why the instructor in the childbirth class said that you overcome the fear because you're so desperate to not be this uncomfortable anymore. The only thing I'm still worried about is that I won't know when I'm in labor. I know Dr. Lippincott said I would know, but my Braxton Hicks are stronger and they're happening more often, and sometimes it even hurts in my back, so how do I know that it isn't real labor?

Aside from worrying about being in labor all the time, I feel like a bloated whale, and my breasts are leaking and I'm having diarrhea sometimes. It's hard to move around at all, and it takes forever to get up or down.

The only good thing about having such a crazy huge stomach is that I have been able to do something really funny: I use it as a table. I put my cheese puffs on it, and just eat them right off of my stomach. It's awesome and funny and so convenient.

Last Friday was my last day at Roast and Drink. It's just too hard to work anymore when I'm this uncomfortable, even with the stool to sit on. It was sad to say goodbye to Johnny and to the other employees. The good news is that Johnny gave Molly the job, so she's taking my place and it's like I'll still have a connection there. She's actually there right now, it's her first day, and she's being trained.

I started submitting my résumé to a few places, including a daycare, because they could watch Cheese Puff at the same time, but I'm not committing to anything just yet, because they want someone to start working right away, and I can't until school starts, or at most a week or two before. I think that it's good to try to find out what my options are ahead of time, though.

The biggest thing that's happened in the last few days, though, is that Ian told Dianne about me and him. Unlike Molly, she was completely shocked. He told me that she said she never would have predicted or suspected anything like this, even though she could see that *I* was nervous around *him,* but she thought it was because I was being shy about my pregnancy. Anyway, he said at first she was trying to figure out what the problems would be for us to be together, but then she said the more she thought about it, the age difference was only three years and she actually thought we might be "perfect together." I can't even express how relieved I am that she didn't get mad or freak out. And I'm so happy that Ian and I don't have to hide ourselves anymore.

Disrupting my thoughts, we arrive at the medical building where I'm getting the cast off. We don't have to wait very long, and they take me into a room where the doctor pulls out a little tool that he calls an electric saw, and makes jokes about having too much coffee that morning and hoping he doesn't accidentally cut through my arm. Dianne laughs when she sees my scared expression, but then she comes over and takes my other hand and it comforts me.

The cast comes off easily, and I look at my wrist and it looks weird because it's all wrinkly and still a bit puffy. There's also a weird smell to it that makes me want to throw up. The doctor says this will all go away once I shower and the cast has been off for a day or so. He wants me to still take it easy with that hand and not do sports or anything using that hand for a few more weeks. It's not like I'm doing sports right now, anyway. Taking it easy won't be a problem at all, and I'm just so happy to have my arm free again. But then it occurs to me that if the baby comes early, I'll have trouble lifting it with that hand. *So, Cheese Puff, you better stick to your due date!*

Back at home, I do some more research on jobs and apartments. When Molly gets back from Roast and Drink, she tells me all about it, including that it was harder than she expected. It can be a hard job when it's busy because you have to keep track of so many orders and a lot of customers want special things, like half-decaf, with non-fat oat milk and a touch of cream. Sometimes it was hard to not laugh out loud at the orders, which actually made it fun a lot of the time. Molly goes to take a shower and I warn her that she'll probably see coffee grinds go down the drain, and we laugh. It's really too bad that we didn't get to work there at the same time.

After her shower, she comes back into my room and whispers, "What's going on with Ian?" and starts giggling. I laugh and tell her I haven't seen him because he's been working, but we might watch TV tonight. She wants to join us, and I say it's totally fine, but then she says she thinks she should give us some alone time. She's so sweet that she wants this to work out.

She tells me she has to clean her room because her mom is

complaining it looks like it was "taken over by animals." I offer to help, since I can use both hands easily again. We go into her room and start hanging her clothes up and organizing.

As we clean up, I look at the different shirts I used to borrow from her all the time, including my favorite tank top of hers, the peasant top that looked really pretty on me, and her pastel-colored shirts that fit both of us. They don't fit me anymore, obviously. I'm excited at the thought of getting back to being able to wear cute things like that once I lose the weight from the pregnancy.

I notice that on her bulletin board, which is filled with family pictures, there's a new picture up there, a selfie that we took before we left the beach last week. You can see the sunrise in the background. I loved that morning and I'm happy that Molly put it on her board. I wonder if she thinks of me like a sister now. I mean, this board used to have just her family on it, and now I'm on it. Honestly, I really do feel like a part of the family now. I don't know if that's weird, or if it's mean to Mom and Josie in a way, but it's how I feel. I'm going to be really sad when I move out.

We decide to have a spa night, which we used to do all the time, but we haven't done for a while. We do manicures and pedicures for each other and give each other facials, and we blast music the whole time. It reminds me of when Josie would blast her dance music in her room after school. I miss Josie, and I wish we could have done spa nights, too. Maybe she'll come stay with me sometimes after Cheese Puff is born, and we can do it then.

I love when Molly's happy like this and we get to spend time together. I wonder if I'll ever have time to do anything social like this after Cheese Puff is born. I have a feeling that my schedule almost every day will be going to school, going to work, putting Cheese Puff to bed, and then doing homework.

After I take off my face mask, I stare at myself in the mirror. My hair is halfway down my back now, I haven't cut it since before I got pregnant. Suddenly, I get a really strong urge to just chop it off. Molly goes into her bedroom's bathroom to wash her face mask off, and before she gets back and talks me out of it, I take the scissors from the drawer and cut off the split ends. Then I can't help myself, I just keep cutting. Something about the length of it just makes me feel, I don't know, kind of angry. I think it's because in the back of my mind, I remember Leo saying he likes girls with long hair.

I keep cutting until it's basically at my shoulders. I add a few shorter cuts that will hopefully be nice layers. It feels good to do this, and even though I'm worried it won't look good, I just can't help myself. It'll be easier to manage after Cheese Puff is born, anyway. Long hair is such a pain to take care of.

Molly comes back into the bathroom and looks totally shocked. "Oh my God, Mads, what did you do?"

I smile and flip it back. I actually like the way it looks, it has a nice bounce to it, and it just looks healthier. "I had to do it," I say, giggling. "I just couldn't stop myself. What do you think?"

"Actually, it looks pretty good. You should get a job as a hairdresser!" We laugh.

Later that night, I meet Ian in the living room to watch TV. His hair is still damp from taking a shower, and we kiss and I inhale his apple shampoo, and he runs his hands through my hair. Then he stops for a second and looks at me. "Did you cut your hair?" *Oh no, he hates it.*

I shrug. "I needed a change."

Ian looks pointedly at my stomach. "Cheese Puff coming wasn't a big enough change?" he jokes, and we laugh. "It looks good, though. You look...older."

"Oh no, that's not a compliment."

"No, it is, actually." He grins. "I really like it."

He goes to get snacks for us, and of course he gets me a bowl of cheese puffs. I sit back and place the bowl on my stomach, like I've been doing, and he laughs. We watch a few shows, sitting right beside each other, and he keeps looking at me and we end up kissing a lot. It's a really nice night together, and I try not to think about the fact that we will probably not be able to have too many more of these when Cheese Puff is born.

When I go up to bed, Molly sneaks into my room and whispers, "I spied on you guys for a few minutes. Oh my God, you looked so cute!" and she giggles.

I laugh. "I can't believe you. How come you're up so late?"

She groans. "I got my period. The cramps are keeping me up. You're so lucky, you haven't gotten yours in so long."

"Oh, trust me, when I was worried I was pregnant, all I wanted to get was my period," I say, laughing again.

"Yeah. But you haven't had yours since *last year.* Lucky!"

I haven't really thought about that. It's kind of funny. I haven't had to deal with all that crappy period stuff for a long time. Poor Molly. She gets the worst cramps during hers. Unfortunately, I only have a little while left of having no periods, although I heard that when you're breastfeeding, which I'm going to be doing, it prolongs it a little longer.

As I'm about to fall asleep, a notification pops up on my phone from Zillow, the website where I've been looking for apartments for rent. It says that there's an apartment a few blocks away from the school for $900 a month. The pictures are a bit blurry, but I make an appointment with the realtor to go and see it tomorrow. It's funny how things can go from being so horrible one day, like my fight with Dianne, and then they go to being amazing, like now, being able to be out in the open with Ian, and nobody's mad about it, and I'm getting organized. It's like in the song from *Annie: the sun'll come out tomorrow.*

<>

Unfortunately, the next day when I go to see the apartment, it's not good at all. It's a dingy brown building with hardly any windows, everything is so dirty that it doesn't seem like it will ever be clean, and the floors are stained and hard and cold, which is not at all good for a baby to crawl on. Every single appliance in there looked old, and when I was going to leave, a *cockroach* scattered by my feet. No, I'm not even joking. No *way* am I moving in there.

Once I'm home, I scan Zillow for hours, searching for another possible apartment until my eyes hurt from looking at the screen for so long. Dianne even comes up to help me, putting in keywords like "1-bedroom" and "$1,000 rent," but there's nothing. And there I was, thinking finding an apartment would be easy. I guess I'll look again tomorrow. I wonder if I could put this off until after the baby is born, but I know I'll probably be really tired, recovering from labor and delivery, and obviously I'll be busy with the baby all the time. I really need to find a place so that I can move before school starts.

I decide to take a nap, but then as I shut my computer, I feel a really bad cramp in my lower back. *Ow, that really hurt.* Then I feel another one, just two minutes after. Wait. This feels...weird. *Different. Oh my God, is this it?!?* I wonder if I'm actually going into labor. I'm not due for two weeks, and I haven't even lost my mucus plug yet, but still...*please, no! I'm not ready yet!*

I decide to take a shower and see if it helps, maybe I'm just stressed about the apartment search. But they don't stop, even after I put lotion on my stomach and try to relax. I lie on my bed, just trying to take deep breaths and be calm, but they just keep happening. Sharp, pulling pains that feel like the Braxton Hicks, but stronger. This is exactly what Dr. Lippincott described. It's been at least an hour by now. I can't tell if it's real labor, but Dr. Lippincott did say that I should call her if I'm feeling anything different from what I've been feeling. *I have to go tell Dianne!*

I go downstairs and find her watching TV, and I tell her that I think I'm in labor, that I've been having contractions, and I didn't time them, but I showered and tried to relax, but they're still there. She says she's going to call Dr. Lippincott, and as she does, I stand there, unable to move, just going through contractions and shaking, I'm so scared. Molly and Ian are both out, working.

Dr. Lippincott says that she wants us to come to her office for a quick exam and she says she'll know if she thinks it's time. I text my mom to let her know what's happening, but that I'm not sure she should come in yet. She calls me and asks me to describe what's happening, and she says it does sound like labor and she's getting her and Josie's bags packed, just in case.

Dianne reminds me to take my hospital bag, and we hurry out to the car. *Oh my God. Am I really having my Cheese Puff now?!* Dianne tells me to try to relax, and that she knows it's hard to, but I really should try.

At Dr. Lippincott's office, the nurse puts me in a room right away, but we have to wait for what seems like hours, because Dr. Lippincott is squeezing me in. The nurse hooks me up to that same thing I got when I went to the hospital for food poisoning, it's like a belt that goes around my stomach, and it's connected to the monitor, which shows what I think is the baby's heartbeat. I feel a couple more of those same crampy feelings in my back, and Dianne holds my hand. She says we should probably get my mother to come. I'm excited but scared at the same time. I'm not ready.

Dr. Lippincott comes in, smiling happily, and I instantly feel more calm. She's so amazing, and I realize how lucky I am that she's my doctor through all of this. She examines me and tells me that I'm starting to dilate.

I start to freak out, but she says, "Madison, you need to calm down. Remember what you learned in the childbirth classes. Calm, breathe, calm. You are not in active labor yet. Have you lost your mucus plug yet?"

I shake my head slowly, a little confused, and slightly disappointed. "But...I thought that when you were dilating, you were in labor?"

She smiles. "Many women walk around dilated even by a few centimeters for weeks before they go into active labor. The contractions are getting more intense because your body is really getting ready now. Little Cheese Puff still isn't ready to come out."

I breathe a sigh of relief, and she says, "But Madison, you need to know that this is happening very soon. You need to get ready. Maybe try to get in another childbirth class, okay? Judging by how your cervix looks, I don't think you'll go into labor this week, or even next week. I think you might make it to your due date after all, but you never know. Just use this time to get ready, okay?" She pats my arm reassuringly.

On the way home, I call Mom and tell her what Dr. Lippincott said and she's relieved, but she says she has the bags packed now and ready to go anytime.

When I get home, I lie in bed and gather my thoughts. I'm actually pretty ready. I'm almost done with my childbirth classes, I've gotten all the things Cheese Puff will need in the beginning, I've read every single book about parenting there is, I'm rapidly making plans to get an apartment and a new job, and I've done so much more. I really don't need to freak out.

I don't know why I don't feel ready. Maybe every mom-to-be feels like this. I guess I just still can't get my head around the fact that I'm going to be a *mom*. There's still so many things out there that I don't know. Over these past months, I've had to accumulate so much knowledge on pregnancy and parenting and babies and budgeting and how to do this and how to do that, but I'm only sixteen. The world is still so new to *me,* yet I'm going to be responsible for another life.

Well, it's too late to turn back now. It's really happening. *It's really happening.*

← watermelon

♡ ♡ ♡ ♡
♡ 38 weeks
♡ 2 weeks
♡ left ♡
♡

To-Do List

- submit résumé / applications to jobs
  (look for jobs where I can take
  Cheese Puff with me)
- call Mom + Josie!
- call Alexa!

NO
MORE
CAST

I CUT MY ♡ ♡
HAIR!!!! ♡ ♡
♡
♡ ♡

YAY!!!!

me + Ian

← scissors
chop
chop

buy:
- cheese puffs
- lip balm
- lotion
- nursing pads

☆ go see apartment
at 12pm
horrible

☆ look on Zillow again

☆ make sure I
have everything
I need for
cheese Puff!

- work on breathing exercises
just
breathe

- go to another childbirth class

☆ research what
epidurals are like

← dilating!!!

☆ THINK OF
BABY NAMES

343

Chapter 35: Week Thirty-Nine

"Your baby is as big as a honeydew melon," I see, and it makes me smile. I've been waiting my whole pregnancy to hear that the baby is as big as a melon.

I'm on my way to what will most likely be my second-last appointment with Dr. Lippincott. I'm really going to miss her once this pregnancy is over.

Molly asked me if I wanted her to move into my room with me, once Cheese Puff is born; she wants to help out when she or he is up in the middle of the night. I was so happy that she suggested this and we decided to move her bed into my room now, so that we get used to it. It's actually really cozy to share a room with her. You'd think I'd want to have my own space, but I'm disappointed that I haven't been sharing the room with her this whole time. Ian says he even wants to sleep in our room sometimes when Cheese Puff is born, to help out. I have no idea why they would want to be up in the middle of the night with a screaming baby, but they are really sweet because they want to help. The good thing is that if they can't handle it, they can always go back to their own rooms.

I still think it's cool that Cheese Puff might be born on July fourth. Normally, I get really excited for the Fourth of July. Usually, my mom and Josie and I go to this parking area where you can see the fireworks really well. We would make a big deal out of it and bring folding chairs, popcorn and these sugary drinks, and we would watch the fireworks together. It's going to be really different this year, and I realize the only fireworks I might see are from the pain of giving birth!

Since the contractions started getting more painful last week, I'm even more scared, because I can tell this is nothing compared to what it will actually feel like. There's no way I'll be able to do it without an epidural and pain meds. I don't know how anyone can do natural childbirth. I mean, when I read about it, I think it sounds really nice, but even just with the contractions that I'm *already* having, I know I wouldn't be able to handle anything more than this.

The epidural scares me because of the idea of having a needle in my back. The instructor at the childbirth classes told us the details of how it works and she said it is very safe, but it's still scary, because I read that if they screw it up, you could end up paralyzed. Part of me just wants to try to deal with the pain and do it naturally, and I think about the fact that the world is *over*populated, and if childbirth was that painful, it wouldn't be that way. Then again, the idea of having contractions so bad that people need to numb their lower half makes me think that it *is* that painful.

Ian's been really helpful with calming me down and helping me get to sleep. He's into meditation and he has been teaching me what he knows. He uses his "meditation voice," as he calls it. Basically it's just him droning on about being peaceful in a deep, calm, soothing voice, and I like it.

I didn't think it was possible to be even more uncomfortable, but every day it just gets worse. Literally everything aches, from head to toe. I can't stand still, it hurts my legs and my back too much. I either need to be walking or lying down. Walking is painful, and I would just lie around all day, if I could, but I know I can't, it's not good for me, and I still have too much to do to get ready. I always have a headache, but because when you're pregnant you can't take Advil, I have to take Tylenol, which doesn't always work. This is all part of the reason why I'm excited for Cheese Puff to be born; I won't have to constantly feel this uncomfortable anymore. What they say is true: the fear of having the baby doesn't compare to the need to not be pregnant anymore.

Anyway, the appointment with Dr. Lippincott goes well, and she asks if my contractions have still been as bad as last week, and I say that they kind of come and go and sometimes they aren't painful, just the same Braxton Hicks as before. She says that's normal and it means it's not time yet. She says when it's time for the baby to come, they will not go away, they will just get more consistent and closer together.

She asks me if I have names picked out yet for both girls and boys. It must be so funny to her that she knows what I'm having, but she knows I don't know yet. I tell her that I can't decide on names, and I feel like I won't know until I actually see the baby. She says a lot of parents feel that way. Then she jokes that she isn't sure the name "Cheese Puff" is actually legal for a birth certificate, and we laugh.

<>

It's actually fun having Molly in the room with me. It feels like we are having one of our old sleepovers, and we just stay up talking. I'm in my bed, and she's sitting on the edge of it, and she asks me when I think I'll *actually* go into labor.

"I know that you thought it was labor last week," she says. "But the *real* labor could start any day now, right? Like, right this moment, it could happen?"

I nod, with a terrified look on my face, and we both stare at my stomach. "I can't believe that there's an actual real life baby in there," she says. "The only thing separating it from the world is your stomach. It's so unbelievable."

"Trust me, I know. It's crazy. I can feel all the movements, and then when Cheese Puff comes out, I'll see her or him doing the same movements, but in the actual *world.*"

As if on cue, Cheese Puff starts moving around like crazy. Molly puts her hand on my stomach and we giggle.

Ian knocks and we tell him to come in. "Time for your meditation, Mads?" he says, and smiles as sees us feeling my stomach, and he comes over to feel it, too. This is the one part of pregnancy I'll actually miss. I love feeling Cheese Puff, and I also love that other people like Molly and Ian love to feel it, too.

Then Molly gets into her bed, and I get under my covers and Ian sits next to me, clears his throat dramatically, and starts talking in his calm, low meditation voice. It always takes me a few minutes to get into it, and it cracks me up at first. "Imagine you are as light as a feather, floating down from the top of a cloud all the way to the bottom of the beach."

"Why would a feather be floating down to a beach?" Molly asks.

Ian shushes her and turns back to me and says, "Fine, you are no longer a feather. Now you are on a cloud, you are biting into a chocolate brownie, and-"

"Bubble gum ice cream," I say stubbornly. "I like it more than cakey desserts."

He laughs and continues. "In my girlfriend's case, bubble gum ice cream," he says, and Molly starts singing the kissing-in-a-tree song, and we all start laughing so hard that Ian complains that this isn't going to help me relax, it's just getting me more revved up, so he kisses me goodnight and then leaves.

Once he's gone, Molly groans. "You guys are so cute together, I can't stand it. I'm so happy that this happened, I really can't believe it. You're like my two favorite people in the world. Next to Mom, of course." She laughs and then she sighs. "It makes me sad for *myself,* though. Literally everyone will get a boyfriend before me."

I sigh dreamily. I feel bad because I'm only half-listening to her, I just keep thinking about Ian and how amazing he is.

"Did you even hear what I said?"

"Yes. What?"

She grins mischievously. "You're thinking of Ian?"

"No," I pretend, but then Molly pretends to make out with her pillow, which makes me laugh.

"But I really am happy for you," Molly says. "You deserve to be with someone great. You've been through so much stuff."

"Thanks, Molly," I say softly. "And trust me, you'll also find someone great. You deserve it, too."

We talk a bit longer about guys, and I tell her that I'm still worried it won't work out with Ian, but that I'm trying to just enjoy it for now. She says it'll be hard if we stay together because it will be long-distance most of the time unless we both end up moving back to Redford, and I've been thinking about that, too. Molly thinks we can make it work if we both want to. Before I even get a chance to get too stressed about it, the exhaustion takes over my body, and I fall asleep.

When I wake up, Molly is still sleeping. I look at the clock, it's nearly eleven! I put a maternity sweatshirt on over my nightgown, then quietly go downstairs, not wanting to wake Molly up. I get myself a bagel for breakfast, and when I go to the living room, I see Ian is watching TV and eating a sandwich. He pauses the TV and I come to sit next to him. He leans over to kiss me. "Morning," he says, and he just stares at me, smiling.

I blush. "Why are you looking at me like that?"

He shrugs. "I just like looking at you. And I miss our nights down here together. But I totally understand if you want to spend time with Molly."

"Yeah, but I miss you, too. I'll come down and watch with you tonight, okay?"

He smiles and we kiss, and then I sit back and put the plate on my stomach, the way I've been doing, and we both laugh. I really will miss this "Cheese Puff table."

It's so nice being able to use *both* my hands to eat, I hated that cast so much. I'm never taking for granted having the use of two hands ever again.

Ian says he's working this afternoon, but he's free later if I want to hang out or go for dinner, or something. He asks me what I'm doing the rest of the day and I tell him that I'm not sure yet. I don't want to say anything to anyone, but I've decided I want to visit my old house and see the new family who lives there. I don't know *why* I want to do this, I just guess I want to talk to them. Maybe it's because I'm going to have Cheese Puff soon and I'm feeling sentimental or something? And even though I said goodbye to my house weeks ago, I think it would be nice to visit one more time, even though I don't know how I'll feel about it.

I wait for Ian and Molly to leave for work and then I get dressed, squeeze my swollen feet into my shoes, and drive over there.

As I get to the door, I lose my courage and change my mind, and

I'm about to turn around and walk back down to my car, when the door opens. A woman around Mom's age is there. "Can I help you?" she asks.

I take a breath. "I know it's weird, but my family lived here before you and, well, I'm about to have a baby and I'm feeling sentimental and I'm wondering if...well, I wanted to see it one more time."

I cringe at how weird it sounds, but for some reason, she's really sweet and she smiles and says, "Of course, come on in! We love this place. It's funny, my daughter was asking about the people who lived here before us, and now she can meet you! When is your baby due?"

I laugh. "Any day!"

She laughs, too, and says, "I'm Amanda."

"I'm Madison, nice to meet you."

She leads me inside, and I see that the dining room is where the living room used to be, and the whole house still has a cozy vibe to it, even though it looks totally different. Her husband is in the kitchen flipping pancakes. She introduces me and he smiles and says hello. I picture myself making pancakes there for *Josie*.

A little girl runs past me, wearing sparkly fairy wings. She looks like she's about five years old. I also hear a baby crying and the woman goes to the bassinet in the kitchen, and picks it up.

"Would you like to try my husband's pancakes?" she asks. "He makes them with chocolate chips."

The little girl asks, "Mommy, who is that?"

"It's the girl who used to live here before us, remember you were asking?"

The girl nods and tells me to come sit next to her, and she asks me if I'm a princess. Ha-ha, she's in the princess phase, I remember it so well.

"Well, I have to leave soon, and I don't want to be any trouble to you," I say, but the dad is already putting a plate of pancakes in front of me. "Thank you, this is so nice. It reminds me of when I lived here. We made pancakes a lot, too."

"So, you're expecting?" he asks. "Our little one is just two months now. I'm sure you know this, but get ready for some sleepless nights!" He laughs. "What does your husband do?"

"Oh, well, actually..." I decide to lie. I'm just so sick of telling everyone the same story. "He had to go, uh, join the military, so he's not here that often."

They nod, and they look concerned. "How long did you guys live here for?" Amanda asks.

"About a decade," I say, and then it lands, how long it really was.

"Wow, that's a long time." Amanda smiles. "Hey, so once you finish your pancakes, would you like to go upstairs? You can show me which one was your old room."

I nod and quickly finish the pancakes, thanking her husband, and then I go upstairs with Amanda, who brings the baby. Now that she's holding him, the baby is calm and making cute noises. I can't believe I'm about to have one of these.

"I remember that stage of pregnancy, it wasn't that long ago," Amanda says. "It's so hard at the end, isn't it? Makes the fear of labor go away because all you want is to not be pregnant anymore, right?"

I nod and laugh as I waddle up the staircase, and she leads me to Mom's old room. A large, cream-colored bed sits on the opposite end that my mom's was on.

"This was, uh...our room. Mine and my husband's," I say, and then Amanda leads me to Josie's old room.

I look inside. A wooden crib, white mattress, and blue mobile is right next to the closet, which is open, filled with little baby clothes and diapers, and it's a mess, but a cozy mess. It's so cute, with tall bookshelves, baby toys littering the floor. There's the cutest giraffe wallpaper, too. It's *so* cozy.

I wonder if I'll ever be able to make a cute nursery for Cheese Puff. Well, at least I have a crib. I sigh wistfully. "It's such a beautiful room."

"It took a lot of work," Amanda says, laughing. "So, whose room was this?"

"Oh, it was going to be the baby's, uh, nursery, but we moved, so..." I laugh.

"If you don't mind my asking, why did you move? This place is so great."

"Um, we just felt like a change. Seeing as he had to join the military, and all."

She nods sadly. "It's amazing that he's doing that. He must be so young."

I nod, stifling a laugh, and then she leads me to *my* old room. I'm a little scared to look. I don't like the idea of someone else living in what used to be my room, but I guess I have to accept it.

The first thing I see is that the walls are the same. Light blue with white flowers around the trim of the ceiling. "We thought the walls were so lovely, so we didn't bother to repaint," Amanda says. "This is my little girl's room. She's four years old. Her name is Allison. Whose room was this?"

Allison. I like that name, actually. Maybe that would be good for Cheese Puff? It's funny, I realize I'm about ninety percent sure it's a girl. I don't know why, I just get that feeling.

"Oh, just a guest room," I say, distracted as I look around. A little white bed sits where my bed used to. The whole room looks like my old room, just with different furniture and lots of toys. It makes me happy that it isn't completely different, but it's still weird looking inside of it, especially now that I'm about to have the baby. My mind just goes back to that night with Leo.

...October 4th, 2018...

After thinking for a while, I left the bathroom and came back to the bedroom and said to Leo, "Can we talk about this?"

He sighed. "What's there to talk about? Don't you want me as badly as I want you?"

I looked down, trying to think of something to say. "Leo, I'll...I'll do it, it's just...I really don't feel ready. It doesn't even have anything to do with you. I mean, we're only fifteen, you know?"

"No, not really. Lots of people our age are doing it. Dina Caldwell would have sex with me. She actually told me. But you, you, my girlfriend of over a year, won't do it? Come on, Madison, it'll be good."

Suddenly I felt worried. Dina was a girl who always hung around the community center, which was where Leo taught kids soccer. He was calling her by name, like he already knew her. Was he already hanging out with her? What if he started to like her more than me? What if he went to be with her? All because I wouldn't do it with him?

I felt so dumb all of a sudden. Why was I making such a big deal? He was probably right, lots of people our age were doing it. It would be fine. Leo and I had been together for over a year. I had nothing to worry about. I was just being stupid.

Little did I know that I was actually being smart. But I just didn't have the confidence to really say no.

...

I shake my head to clear the memory, and then I turn to Amanda, smiling. "Thank you so much for letting me in," I say. I see that the baby is getting fussy, and I can tell Amanda wants to go feed her or something. "I'd better get going," I say.

We walk downstairs and I ask her the baby's name. "Oscar," she says.

I laugh, because I thought it was a girl. I remember reading that it's hard to tell the difference at this age, but it's funny I just assumed it was a girl.

She walks me to the front door and says I can come back anytime.

I know I won't come back, but I thank her.

On the way home, I start bawling. I'm not really sad, so I'm not sure why I'm crying. I think they are actually tears of happiness because it's so nice to see a happy family there now. Also, they didn't change my room that much. It makes me feel good, and I know I had to do this, it kind of gave me a sense of moving on, in a weird way.

Once I'm home, I decide to weigh myself. I keep meaning to and then I forget, but I think about the fact that one day Cheese Puff might want to know how much weight I gained before I had her or him, so I want to document it. I'm shocked to see that I weigh 131 pounds. I've gained thirty-three pounds! *Wow.* I wonder how long it will take to lose all that weight.

I feel like taking a nap so I go to my room and collapse onto my bed, I'm so exhausted. When I wake up, orange light is filtering into my window, and I look outside. Wow, I slept for almost four hours. The sun is setting. It's turning the sky a splash of colors, like an artist took her paint palette and swirled all the colors together. It reminds me of the sunset on the night I graduated, and I smile and think of Mom, Dad, and Josie. I'm feeling really sentimental right now after seeing the house. I'm really glad I went.

Dianne orders pizza for dinner, because she says we all deserve a treat, and I'm really happy she seems to be pretty much back to her old self with me now.

After dinner, I tell Ian that I'm truly exhausted, and that I seriously couldn't stay up and watch TV even if I wanted to. He says that I don't have to explain myself, that it's completely okay, and I kiss him gratefully before going upstairs to go to bed early. That's another thing I really like about him; he doesn't get mad at me or pressure me when I don't do things his way. He's *so* different from Leo.

When I get into bed, I go to plug my phone into the charger, but I check it one more time and there's a text from Alexa.

Alexa: Hey! Oh my God, I just realized your due date is so close! How are you feeling? Please make sure you let me know when you're in labor and when you have Cheese Puff! I want to come by the hospital!

Maddie: LOL, of course! You're so sweet!

Alexa: I just can't believe how fast the time has gone by. How far along were you when we met, again?

Maddie: I don't know, around twenty-four weeks, I think?

Alexa: That's insane.

Maddie: Don't I know it. Anyway, I've got to go to bed. You have no idea how tired I am. (But you'll understand when you're at this stage of your pregnancy).

Alexa: Haha, I'm already tired, trust me. Sleep well!

Ugh, here we go again. Even though I'm tired, I just toss and turn and toss and turn, no end in sight. This insomnia is no joke, and I don't know if it's just being uncomfortable or the stress of it all. I wish I could just push Cheese Puff out right now.

I'm still trying to fall asleep an hour later, when Molly comes in and gets into bed. She's super quiet, but then she sees me move and she says, "You're still awake? Didn't you go to bed like an hour ago?"

I sigh and say, "I just can't sleep. I think I'm going to go downstairs and get something to eat."

I struggle to get up and get out of bed, go downstairs to the pantry, grab a new bag of cheese puffs and open it. Then I feel someone tap my shoulder, and I nearly jump out of my skin and some cheese puffs fly in the air. I turn around and I see that it's Ian. He's laughing, because it's like we just recreated the scene in the grocery store. He bends to pick them up and pops them in his mouth. "These really are so good. I don't blame you for being obsessed."

We laugh and he kisses me. "Why are you up?" he asks.

I sigh again. "I can't sleep. I'm just way too uncomfortable, I guess."

"Okay, that's it," he says suddenly. "I'm making this decision for you. Get dressed and bring your bathing suit, we're going to the pool."

"What? Ian, no. I can't."

"Why not?"

"Because I just don't even want to get into a bathing suit. I'm resembling a beached whale right now, okay?"

"I know, I know, you feel self-conscious and you don't want to get into a bathing suit, but it's late now, so this is like the only time that no one except us will be there. I have a key, let's go!"

"I really don't want you to see me in a bathing suit right now, Ian."

"Mads, I think you look *beautiful.* Why don't you get it?"

I shake my head, looking down. But I remember what Dr. Lippincott said about how the pool makes everything feel lighter and women love it at this stage of their pregnancy. "Okay, fine," I say. "But one comment, and we're leaving."

He grins and we agree to meet at the car in five minutes. I go upstairs and tell Molly what I'm doing, and she giggles and says, "That's my uncle for you, always coming up with crazy things to do."

Ian drives my car and we listen to music on the way, which relaxes me a little. Once we get to the pool, we go to the locker rooms and change into our bathing suits. I come out to meet him at the pool, feeling incredibly self-conscious.

"Madison, seriously, I'm not just saying this, you really look beautiful," he says. "Your stomach is really cute." I want to cry, he's just so sweet.

"Alright, cut the lies," I say, laughing. "Let's get in."

So we get in the pool, and the water is pretty warm and I instantly get what all these people are talking about. For the first time in I don't know how long, I feel...weightless. It's like it's as if I'm not even pregnant. I can walk around like I always did. I forgot how this feels.

Ian notices the smile on my face and comes over to kiss me. Then he says, "I told you, didn't I?"

I nod and smile, and he leads me around the pool. I can tell he's obviously a good instructor, because he just leads me so smoothly. I can't remember when I last felt this good. "I feel like an astronaut," I say.

We laugh and move over to the steps where I sit on his lap and we kiss. After a little while, he points to the ceiling. "Look, you can actually see stars," he says. "It's so clear out tonight."

I look up and see the glass windows on the ceiling, and sure enough, you can see all these twinkly lights, the stars. Wow, it's really cool.

"So, don't laugh at me," he says. "But do you know that *Star Light, Star Bright* poem?"

"Oh my God, yes! Why would I laugh at you?"

He laughs and says, "Because, I don't know, it's kind of corny. Anyway, sometimes I like to wish on a star."

"That's so weird, I used to do that with my family. We would say the poem and then at the end, we would make our wish and then say, '*Thank you Star, goodnight'*."

"Let's do it."

"Okay."

He starts and I join in, "*Star light, Star bright, first Star I see tonight, I wish I may, I wish I might...have the wish I wish tonight...*" And then we both close our eyes and make our wishes.

There's so much I want to wish for. But right now, all I really focus on is Ian and wishing that we will stay together. I never want to lose a guy like him. He's the best guy I've ever met and I just want to be with him. When he goes back to college, I want to do the whole long-distance thing, like Molly said, and hopefully one day we can actually live in the same place. I wish for that. And then I make a wish that everything goes okay when I have Cheese Puff. For me to have a safe and amazing delivery. I wish for that more than anything.

"Thank you Star, goodnight," Ian says, and then waits for me.

I finish my wish and then say it, too. *"Thank you Star, goodnight."*

39 WEEKS
1 WEEK LEFT

me + cheese puff

To-Do List
- keep looking for a new job
- go on Zillow to look for an apartment   ♡ Ian ♡
- go over budget

☆ appointment with Dr. Lippincott today at 5pm

my bed   Molly's bed   Come on, Cheese Puff, come out already!!

- call Mom + Josie
- keep doing meditation + breathing exercises!
- make sure hospital bag is ready   ☆ go to my old house?
- figure out how to fill out birth certificate forms   buy:
- figure out how to apply for   - cheese puffs
  Cheese Puff's social security #   - lotion
- go over birth plan
- THINK OF BABY NAMES!! SERIOUSLY!!!
- do more research on breastfeeding/baby care

Cheese Puff is coming so SOON!!!!

Star light, Star bright, first star I see tonight...

☆ ask Ian or Molly or Dianne to give me a massage

354

Chapter 36: Week Forty -- The Big Day

"Your baby is as big as a small pumpkin," I read on my phone. I can't believe I'm forty weeks pregnant. I'm officially, completely full term now. It's unbelievable.

Except, it's July *fifth*. Friday July *fifth*. A day *after* July *fourth*, when I was supposed to have Cheese Puff. I didn't have Cheese Puff on my due date, so technically, Cheese Puff is a late baby. I can't handle it anymore. I really just want to go into labor for real and have the baby, no matter how bad the pain is. I feel like I've been pregnant for one hundred years.

Every single hour, minute, and second of my days are uncomfortable, and I'm not even exaggerating. I never in a million years would have guessed what women go through to create a life. I have such a new appreciation for my mom and all the women in the world now. *Men* don't have to do this. It's *so* unfair.

I felt so exhausted today that literally all I could do was just lay on the couch. It was so amazing to be in the pool with Ian last week, and now I wish I could just stay in the pool until I have the baby. Dianne, Molly, and Ian have been bringing me my food and water to the living room, and just basically taking care of everything I ask for, they're so sweet.

They've been so excited because today was my due date, and I think we all thought I would for sure go into labor today, but now it's midnight, so it's technically July *fifth*. I know, I know, it's only like a *minute* after July fourth, but still, Cheese Puff didn't come on time. I guess she or he won't be in the five percent of babies that are born on their due dates.

I did lose my mucus plug on Wednesday. It was a brown-tinged blob, and it came out in my underwear. It was kind of gross, and at first I freaked out, but then I realized what it was. I thought it meant I would go into labor quickly, and I told Dianne and she called Dr. Lippincott, who said it meant labor was coming soon, but it didn't necessarily mean that it was going to happen right away. She was right. It's been around two days since then, and I still haven't gone into labor.

Honestly, I'm so tired, it took me about ten minutes just to walk upstairs to my bedroom. Ian helped me, and he was making jokes the whole time, saying things like, *"Okay, Grandma, just one more step..."*

Right now, I'm just lying in bed, and everyone is in my room, watching the last of the fireworks from my window. Eventually it's the finale, which is an explosion of fireworks in reds, whites, blues, silvers, and golds.

I watch as the last of them fade from the sky, and Molly sighs. "Well, you didn't have Cheese Puff on the Fourth of July."

I roll my eyes. "Figures. I was so sure I would be-" Suddenly I feel a really strong, sharp, intense Braxton Hick. *Oh my God, is it my imagination or was that really painful?* I wait for it to subside, and then I exhale, realizing I was holding my breath, it felt so bad. I close my eyes and try to fall asleep, but then a few minutes later it happens again. It's a *really* bad crampy feeling in my lower back and lower abdomen. This honestly feels even worse than anything I've ever felt, worse than the Braxton Hicks or the contractions two weeks ago.

"Madison, what's wrong?" Ian asks me.

"I don't know, it's..." I frown. "I think I maybe just had a real contraction."

"Wait, really?!" Molly squeals. "Oh my God, is it happening?!?"

"Just wait a minute," I say, grimacing as I shift positions and turn onto the other side. "Usually when I change positions, it stops them."

But when I turn to the other side, it actually feels *worse*. Molly is staring at me, her eyes are huge and filled with excitement. I hold my breath until the pain subsides. Then I have a few minutes of calm, and it's like nothing happened, and I'm convinced it's just more of the same thing I've been having lately.

But the next one lasts even longer, as if it's pulling me underwater it's so strong, and I squeeze my eyes shut to get through it. I realized that I haven't been documenting the times like Dr. Lippincott told me to, so I don't know how long it is in between, but it feels like it's just every few minutes.

I remember Dr. Lippincott's words: when it's time, the contractions will not go away, they will just get more consistent and closer together. And the childbirth class said that you will know you're in real labor if they should hurt badly enough that it would be hard to walk or talk during them. I try getting up from my bed, but the pain is so bad that I can't. These don't feel at all like the ones I had two weeks ago. These are *really* intense. *Oh my God.*

"You know what, I...I think I actually might be in real labor," I say shakily, and Molly squeals and goes running down the hallway to wake up Dianne.

Ian strokes my hair to calm me down as we wait for Dianne to get ready, and my heart keeps racing and I take a deep breath. "I'm excited *and* scared," I tell Ian.

"You're going to be great," he reassures me.

"Thanks. Just try not to look at me too hard while I'm giving birth."

"You're beautiful no matter what you're doing."

I hug him tightly, and then Dianne comes in and Ian tells her what's happening because I can't even talk, I'm in the middle of another contraction and it's really, *really* painful. Dianne goes to call Dr. Lippincott and she tells me to get ready and to remember my hospital bag, that she thinks it's time.

Ian and Molly help me down the stairs while Dianne gets her stuff together and calls my mom. I'm *really* scared, but it still doesn't overpower the excitement I feel to finally meet this baby that's been growing inside of me, and to not be pregnant anymore. As crazy and scary as my life might be once I have Cheese Puff, nothing will be more uncomfortable or awful than how I feel right now.

We get in the car, and Dianne tells me that my mom is on her way with Josie. I focus on counting the contractions and squeezing Ian's hand in the backseat. Dianne tells me to time the contractions by looking at the time when I have a contraction, and then to write it down in my phone, and then when it ends, I have to see how long before the next one. Ian and Molly help count them, too. Thank God I have them helping me. What would I have done without them?

Josie texts me from Mom's phone and says they are driving in, and she asks me if I'm scared or excited. I write back that I'm a little bit of both. I can't wait for them to get here. I really hope they make it in time.

This could be my last car drive while I'm pregnant, I realize. Then again, it could be a false alarm like it was two weeks ago. It doesn't feel like it's possible for it to be a false alarm because the pain is too bad. Part of me hopes it is, part of me hopes it isn't.

Once we're at the hospital, they tell us to go up to labor and delivery. A nurse comes into my sectioned-off room and immediately hooks me up to the belt that connects to a monitor. They tell me Dr. Lippincott is on her way. Poor Dr. Lippincott, it's nearly half past midnight on a Friday night. I'm sure she's used to this, though.

The monitor is a bit different this time. It shows and measures my contractions. I can see on the monitor when the contraction is starting, and the line starts to go up, and then it eventually reaches its peak and then comes back down, and then the pain eases up. It's terrifying when the line first starts going up, because I have no idea how high it will go and how bad the pain will get. There's also a number showing Cheese Puff's heartbeat. I find comfort in looking at the little heart blinking on the screen, and I try to focus on that. It seems like it's beating really fast, but the nurse says that's what it should be, and that the baby is doing great.

Ian leans over and strokes my arm. "Hey, you're okay?"

I nod, but I realize that even though I took the childbirth classes, I still feel totally unprepared. I can't even remember the breathing exercises, but Molly and Ian remember, so they tell me what to do. It's hard to concentrate, especially when I'm having a contraction, but Dianne says that's when I need to really concentrate on my breaths because that's what will help me stand the pain.

I'm really thirsty and I feel like my mouth is so dry. I want water, but I'm told I'm not allowed to eat or drink anything just in case I have to have a c-section, so they keep bringing me little ice chips. The nurse hooks me up to an IV and says the fluids will keep me hydrated.

Eventually, Dr. Lippincott comes in. It's funny, she doesn't look tired at all, she has a bright smile on her face and she looks excited. She's amazing, and again I realize how lucky I am to have her as my doctor. She studies the monitor for a minute and then examines me. "How often have you been feeling contractions?" she asks.

"Every five to six minutes. I've been writing it down in my phone."

"And I've been writing it down here, too," Ian says, holding up a little notebook and a pen with times written down on them.

I turn to him, smiling. "You didn't have to do that!"

"I'm a great contractions documenter!" he says, and Dr. Lippincott smiles at him.

"Madison, I think you're in labor for real this time," she says to me, and instead of getting excited, my smile instantly disappears and my lip starts shaking.

"Oh my God, really? I'm...I'm scared," I blurt out, and Dr. Lippincott reaches over and pats my hand comfortingly. Dianne and Molly come over and Dianne takes my other hand and holds it tightly.

"That is totally normal, everyone feels this way at this point," Dr. Lippincott says. "Let me take you through what's going to happen step-by-step. First of all, you are three centimeters dilated, so there are still seven more to go. It could take a while for you to progress. For now, all you have to do is fill out your hospital admissions papers, and then we are going to bring you up to get you into a real room. When the pain starts to pick up, let me know if you want your epidural. If you are past seven centimeters dilated and your water hasn't broken yet, then we will break it for you. Start some breathing exercises like you learned at the childbirth classes, okay?"

"She's been doing them," Molly says.

Dr. Lippincott smiles and says she'll be back to recheck me in a little while, and to just stay calm. The nurse comes back and hands me some papers, which I fill out in between contractions.

Admission Form (Maternity Ward)

Your OB Physician's Name: Dr. Rachel Lippincott

Pediatrician's Name (for baby): Dr. Louis Brown

Estimated Date of Delivery: July 4th, 2019

Current Date: July 5th, 2019

Have you been a patient at this hospital before? **Yes** No

Patient Info

Name: Madison Eden Davis

DOB: February 18, 2003

Religious Preference: Christian

Birthplace: St. Redford's Hospital (here)

Marital Status (Married, Single, Divorced, Widow, Separated): In a relationship (but with someone else who isn't the baby's father)

Ethnic Background (African-American, Caucasian, Hispanic, Asian, Other): Caucasian

Maiden Name: Davis

Mother's Maiden Name: Hughes

Street Address/Apt.: 136 Tree Street

City: Redford

State: California

Telephone: (310) 128-0819

I fill out the rest of the sections and sign some consent forms, and then Dianne takes it all out to the nurse. A few minutes later, we all go up to a different room, which the nurse calls an "LDRP," which is a labor, delivery, recovery, and postpartum room. Dianne, Molly, and Ian are with me, and the nurse pushes me in a wheelchair. As I'm in the elevator, I text Mom.

Maddie: Josie, I know Mom is driving, so I'm texting you. Please tell her that Dr. Lippincott confirmed that I'm in labor for real this time!! She said it could still be a while until I actually have the baby, but hurry up and get here!

As we go down the hallway to the room, we pass by a room with a huge glass window, and inside I can see rows of babies, with blue and pink blankets. All these new little lives, I can't believe that Cheese Puff is about to be one of them!

The room is nicer than the temporary room with a curtain that I was in when we first came in. This one has a proper door, not just curtains, and there's lots of room for everyone to sit down. Off to the side, I see a little area with what looks like a glass bassinet and a scale. I read about that, and I guess it must be where they examine the baby. There are hospital signs around, the one where there are a row of faces that go from not painful to very painful, to describe your pain level. Right now, I'd say my pain is around four or five, but I know it will get worse.

Some other machines and monitors are here, too, and then a hospital bed that actually looks comfortable. It's a really nice room and it almost doesn't feel like a hospital, which relieves me.

The nurse hooks me up to the monitor and Cheese Puff's heartbeat comes on again. The nurse hands me a bag and tells me to put my clothes in it and to change into the hospital gown and warm socks that they left on the bed. The socks are bright yellow and they have sticky foot pads. I guess I'm supposed to wear them so I don't slip when I get up, go to pee, et cetera.

Almost as soon as the nurse hooks me up to the monitor, a contraction starts and it's a bad one. Molly rushes over and takes my hand and Ian takes my other one and they tell me to do the breathing exercises. This is really painful already. How am I going to stand it if it gets worse? *When* it gets worse.

When it ends, I feel Cheese Puff moving around like crazy. I wonder how the contractions feel for her or him? Do they hurt? Suddenly, I realize these are the last kicks and movements I'll ever feel from Cheese Puff inside my stomach. It makes me a little sad for a minute, I'll miss them, they were my favorite part of being pregnant.

Dianne says she's going to get coffee and asks if anyone else wants anything. Ian says he would like a coffee, too, and Molly asks for a hot chocolate. *Ugh,* I want to eat something so badly, I'm starving, and I would love a hot chocolate.

"I bet I know what you want, Mads," Ian jokes. "Cheese puffs?"

Everyone laughs. It's funny, but he's right, I would kill for some cheese puffs right now. I can't believe I'm not allowed to eat anything.

Dianne leaves and Molly and Ian sit near my bed and go on their phones. I send out quick texts to Alexa, and also Cheryl and Janet, just to let them know that I'm in labor. No one responds, but it's really late, so it's okay.

But then my fingers linger over the phone screen.

Leo.

All the feelings I used to have for him are completely gone. I don't even hate him that much anymore. I think it changed without me realizing it when I started falling for Ian. I don't care what he does or who he's with anymore. My only question is whether or not I need to tell him about the baby. I should probably let his parents know. I'll ask Mom to tell them.

Maddie: Josie, by the way, can you tell Mom to tell Leo's parents that I'm in labor? Thanks.

Mom: Hi honey! It's Mom, we just stopped to get gas. Yes, I will tell them. Josie and I are on our way and we'll be there really soon, so tell Cheese Puff to wait, haha! We are so excited, and we love you very much. See you soon!

Her text makes me really happy. Dianne comes back with the coffees and hot chocolate, and everyone sits and drinks and looks on their phones. My contractions are still about five minutes apart, and they are staying about the same level of pain. Every time I have one, either Molly or Ian come over and hold my hands and help me with the breathing.

After a little while, Dr. Lippincott comes back. "Okay, Madison," she begins, but I'm in the middle of a contraction and I can't even look at her, I'm squeezing my eyes shut. That was a bad one.

She examines me and then tells me that she wants to give me a drug called Pitocin, because I'm not dilating as quickly as she would like me to, and it will help move things along. She said it will make the contractions feel stronger and that I shouldn't worry, it's a good thing, and it means things are moving along.

The nurse comes in and injects the Pitocin into the IV and nothing happens for about a half hour, but then all of a sudden at around 1:30am, the contractions start coming harder and harder. This is way worse than I thought it was going to be, it's way worse than any of my worst period cramps I've ever had. I try to get through them, one by one, doing the breathing, and counting how long each one lasts, but I'm starting to not be able to stand it. I'm getting all sweaty, and the pain actually makes me a little nauseous.

Dianne calls for the nurse and asks for some cool washcloths, and the nurse brings them in, and Molly takes them and sits next to me and pats them on my forehead. The nurse dims the lights a bit. After she leaves, I have another big contraction, and I really don't know how much more I can stand.

As I breathe through it, Molly asks, "What does it feel like?"

"Well, you know the cramps you get during your period?" I ask, and she nods. "It's like those times a thousand."

She looks scared. Dianne laughs and says it's all normal, and it will be over before I know it. She gives me a few ice chips, and then I begin to feel hot, so I take off my blankets. The one thing that makes me feel calm is staring at the baby's heartbeat on the monitor. I touch my stomach. *It won't be big for much longer,* I think.

The nurse comes in and asks me if I want to have my epidural yet, and I say that I don't think I need it yet. I want to wait until Mom and Josie get here to have it. I close my eyes in between contractions and try to get rest, I'm already so tired.

"You're doing great, sweetie," I hear, and for a second I think it's Mom, but when I open my eyes, I see it's the nurse. Maybe it's the Pitocin, but I feel a little weird, like I'm dizzy, and I'm having a hard time keeping track of the time. The nurse says they gave me a little painkiller along with the Pitocin. She says it's safe for the baby.

I really have to pee and I ask if I'm allowed to do that during labor, and the nurse laughs and says of course I can. She says she would like someone to help me walk to the bathroom and wait for me to come out. Ian volunteers first and he walks me across the room, pushing my IV stand at the same time. When I come out, I say that I want to walk around the room a bit. It actually feels good to stand, it helps distract me from the pain. But eventually I get way too tired, and I go back to lie down.

I start to get so exhausted that I can't even keep my eyes open. I keep dozing off in between contractions and it feels like a long time, but then the pain wakes me up and I look at the clock and realize it's only a few minutes each time.

Suddenly, Mom and Josie walk in and they rush over to me. Josie's hair is in pigtails. *Thank God it's not in braids.* She looks so excited, and she asks if she can feel my stomach one more time. I let her, and then after we talk for a few minutes, Mom tells her it's going to be a while before the baby is born, and that she should try to sleep so that she's awake for it. Josie goes to sit on the armchair and curls up in it and tries to sleep. Mom covers her with one of the blankets that the nurse left on the counter. Then she comes to sit beside me, and she takes my hand.

"I want to hug you, but I can't move, I'm about to have a really bad contraction," I say, looking over to the monitor as the line goes up, and I grimace, taking a deep breath, and thankfully it's a short contraction, and it's over quickly.

Mom smiles and gently pats my forehead. "Trust me, I know what this pain is like. Don't worry, honey, you're doing great."

I thank her, and then Dianne offers to go get Mom some coffee and Josie a hot chocolate. Ian and Molly go with her and leave us alone.

"I saw your doctor in the hall," Mom says. "She said everything is going well." She sighs. "Madison, I just want to say again that I'm sorry. I feel like I've missed so much of your whole experience. I...I just wish things had started out differently."

"It's okay, Mom. I wish that, too. But at least we're here together now."

She nods and smiles, stroking my hair. "You are so strong, Maddie. Dad would have been very proud of you."

"Yeah, I hope he would," I say, looking down.

"Trust me. I know he would. And I know he wouldn't be disappointed in you. I'm so sorry I said that when we fought. I should have never said that. He'd be the opposite. He'd be so proud of you. And *I* am so proud of you." She smiles at me. "And I've learned something about you, something important; you have an underlying optimism. No matter what happens, it's always there, under the surface, and it propels you to get through anything. I know you're going to be such a good mommy, sweetie."

I start to tear up, but then a contraction starts and interrupts it. When it's over, I take Mom's hand and touch it to my warm stomach. She holds my hand and I say, "Thank you so much for coming here. I mean, when we...when we weren't talking, I didn't know if you'd be here, while I was giving birth and everything."

"Well, I would be here no matter what," she says, and then she smiles. "You know, I read this article about there being multiple universes opening up every time you have to make a choice. So right now, there's a version of yourself who's not even here, because you had an abortion, and there's a version of yourself who's here, but you're going to give it up for adoption, and-"

I shake my head, suddenly upset. "Why are you saying-"

She holds up her hand. "Let me finish. *This* version of yourself? I think this one's the best one out there."

I smile as tears fill my eyes. "Wow. Thanks, Mom. That really means a lot."

I start to cry, and she hugs me, I breathe in her smell, I'm so happy that she's here and saying these things to me.

"Mom, there's something I need to tell you," I say suddenly.

Mom looks concerned. "Is something wrong?"

I shake my head. "No, it's a good thing, actually. I mean, I hope you think it's a good thing. I'm...kind of together with...with Ian."

"Ian? Dianne's brother?" I nod. She immediately looks confused and concerned again. "Molly's *uncle?*"

I nod again and smile. "He's only three years older than me and Molly, Mom. He's been so sweet to me, you have no idea."

Mom doesn't say anything, and just when she opens her mouth, Dianne, Molly, and Ian walk back in. Ian hands Mom a coffee and she smiles at him, a bit awkwardly. Dianne and Mom go sit next to each other and catch up, while Molly and Ian come back to sit next to me. I see Mom looking over a few times at Ian, and it's hard to tell what she's thinking. I hope she sees how nice he's being to me.

After what seems like hours, but is really only about an hour, Dr. Lippincott comes in and examines me again. "You're four centimeters dilated now. The Pitocin is working. How are you feeling, are you okay?"

"I'm okay, but the contractions are really bad. When do you think it'll be time to start pushing?" I ask her.

"It's hard to tell right now. You still have six centimeters to go. I'm going to increase the level of Pitocin, and that should help move things along even more. This is a good time for you to try to rest, in between contractions, if you can." She looks at Molly and Ian. "You two are being great. I think maybe now would be a good time to try to curl up in a chair, and do what Madison's sister is doing."

We all look at Josie, who is fast asleep in her chair, and we smile. Molly and Ian go over to their own chairs, and Mom comes back and takes my hand. "I can stay here and just hold your hand. I'm not tired and I want to be here, okay?"

I nod, and Dr. Lippincott smiles and says, "Be back in a little bit."

I try to fall asleep, and I manage to get little bits of sleep in between the contractions, but it really is a kind of torture, because each time I fall asleep, it feels like a second later that I'm woken up with another painful contraction. Maybe I should ask for the epidural now.

I look at the clock on the wall and see that it's now almost four o'clock in the morning. I ask Mom to buzz for the nurse to see if I can have my epidural when suddenly I feel a weird gush of warm water coming out of me, like I just peed all over myself. *Oh my God, it must be my water breaking.*

Mom buzzes for the nurse, and she comes in and says, "Looks like your water broke. Okay, I will clean you up and let Dr. Lippincott know."

While she's changing the sheets, I stand up and Mom helps keep me steady. A really strong contraction comes on, much more painful than any of the other ones have been. I can't even breathe while it's happening.

I start whimpering, and my teeth are shaking as I say to Mom, "I'm scared, Mom. I'm really scared."

Mom runs her hands through my hair. "I know, sweetie. It's okay. This is all normal. Just try to breathe, okay?"

I do try to focus on doing the breathing exercises I learned, but the pain is *awful*. Dr. Lippincott comes in a moment later, smiling. "Great, your water broke! Things will move a lot quicker now, and I can tell they already are." She examines me again and says I'm now six centimeters dilated.

Another contraction starts, and I actually scream. It's even worse than the last one, if that's possible. It wakes up Dianne, Molly, Ian, and Josie. Then things become really hectic all of a sudden. Ian jumps up to give me more ice chips. Dianne keeps checking the monitors while Mom strokes my hair, trying to comfort me, and Molly whispers encouraging words into my ear. Josie stands beside me and keeps asking questions, but I can't answer her, I'm just trying to focus on getting through it. I couldn't pay attention if I tried. This pain is *so bad*. It's nothing like anything I've felt before.

"When should I get the epidural?" I ask Mom, panting.

"I think now that it's this painful, you should get it. I'm surprised you waited this long. I would really get it now, honey."

She buzzes for the nurse, and when she comes in, I practically yell at her that I want my epidural. She leaves quickly to go tell Dr. Lippincott to order it.

It feels like forever while I wait for the nurse or Dr. Lippincott to come back. People keep asking me questions and talking to me, but I can't even listen to them, I'm terrified of the next contraction, and when it happens, it's worse than anything I can even describe. Like my whole body is being taken over by aliens who are torturing me.

When the pain subsides for a second, I can hear a scream next door, and that actually makes me laugh because I know someone else is going through this, too. It's crazy how bad this is. I should have gotten the epidural a while ago. What was I waiting for? *Oh my God, I need it now! Now!*

Mom holds my hand and Ian pats my forehead with the cool washcloth. I notice Mom and Ian looking at each other, and Mom smiles at Ian. Molly is trying to keep Josie occupied, and Dianne is trying to find out when the epidural will be coming.

A few different nurses have been coming in, but the main nurse, Nurse Phillips, comes in to tell me they are working on getting me the epidural as soon as possible and she is increasing the pain meds through the IV, in the meantime. She's really sweet, she's a small redhead with a really comforting smile. I'm glad that no one's treating me differently here just because I'm only sixteen.

This pain is the worst thing I've ever felt in my entire life, and I truly mean that. It feels worse than my fractured wrist. I'm sure it's worse than being run over by a car. Worse than being pricked by a million needles. Worse than being tossed off a cliff and falling. Worse than *anything.* I can't even think of something else that could top this pain. Everyone tries to comfort me, but there's nothing they can do. I'm really sweaty and I'm breathing hard and the pain is getting worse and I know it means I'm progressing, and the thing is, I wanted my labor to be a really nice, memorable thing, but now I don't even care, I just want to *get this baby out.*

Then I start to feel some pressure down there, the pain is starting to feel really tight and pulling, and my back really hurts. It's like someone has a rope tied to my waist and is tightening and tightening it and it doesn't feel like it can get any tighter, but it does. I feel like I'm tied down to the bed, and I can't escape this horrendous pain, it's torture, it pulls me under. I can't help it, I start to scream out. Mom calls the nurse who she says she will call Dr. Lippincott.

Dr. Lippincott comes in about ten minutes later, and checks me. She says I'm eight centimeters dilated now. "Getting close!" she says. "I checked on your epidural and they are going to come in very soon. Sorry it's taking so long, we've had a bunch of emergencies this morning and we're short-staffed."

I nod, but I can't talk, the pain is too bad. I feel like I'm in an alternate universe of pain, I'm just trying to focus on getting through every second. When the contractions stop, I'm okay for a few seconds, but then it starts up again. The clock says it's six o'clock. I can see the sun is starting to come in through the window.

Mom is patting down my head with the washcloth and Ian and Molly are on either side of me, holding my hands. Josie is standing next to Mom, looking really scared. I wonder if she'll ever want to have kids after seeing this. Dianne keeps going to check on the epidural. What seems like hours later, but is really only fifteen minutes, Nurse Phillips comes in and tells me that the anesthesiologist has to do an emergency c-section and it will be a little longer. *Nooo! No! No! This isn't happening! I can't believe I waited so long, I should've had it right away! What was I thinking, trying to be brave and stand this pain?!?!? I can't stand it anymore!*

The nurse leaves, and I start crying. I can't do this anymore, the pain is too bad. Everyone tries to calm me down but I can barely listen to them. Then I see Molly yawn and I can't help myself, I just lose it on her.

"Oh, poor you, *are you tired, Molly?!?*" I yell.

"I'm sorry, no, Mads, I didn't mean to yawn, I-"

"*Try going through labor! And then see how you feel when someone yawns!*"

"I'm sorry, I didn't mean to!" Molly cries.

"Don't worry, Molly, she doesn't mean it, she's just in so much pain," Mom says.

"I do mean it, yes I do!" I shout. "*Everybody stop talking now!*"

Mom pats my head. "Labor is a hard, grueling process. I mean, that's why it's called 'labor.' You're doing great, sweetie, you're-"

"*I said don't talk to me!*" I yell, crying. And then, when the contraction is over, I yell, "I NEED THE EPIDURAL! *Please* ask them to get it for me! PLEASE! NOW!"

Josie starts crying and she asks if I'm going to be okay, and Molly takes her outside for a walk. Ian rushes out to see if he can find the nurse.

"Can I *at least* have something to eat?!? I'm *starving!*" I yell. "I WANT CHEESE PUFFS!" I scream as Ian and Molly and Josie come back and I actually see them trying not to *laugh*. Then Josie starts giggling and everyone bursts out laughing.

Ian comes over to rub my stomach. "Did you hear that, Cheese Puff? Time to come out!"

Everyone laughs again. How *dare* they laugh right now? Do they not know how much pain I'm in?!? Josie just can't stop laughing, and it makes *everyone* keep laughing. Another contraction starts, it's so bad that I don't even have words to describe it, it's just so much tightness and cramping and aching and it pulls me under and I scream, "*I need that epidural or I'm going to die, I mean it!! I mean it!!!*"

Just then, the nurse comes in and hands Mom a fresh washcloth, but I push it away when Mom tries to put it on my head. I beg the nurse for the epidural and ask her what's happening and she says they are almost finished the c-section, and the anesthesiologist will be in shortly.

I start bellowing and crying, thrashing around in my hospital bed. This pain is a thousand times worse than all the discomfort I've gone through during my pregnancy. I would rather be pregnant for a million years than deal with these contractions any longer. I mean it!

Mom and Dianne try to get me to do the breathing exercises, while Ian rubs my feet and Molly and Josie hold my hands. Every minute or so there seems to be another contraction, but I can't keep track of the time. My head is spinning with the pain. I feel like I'm going to pass out, I seriously feel like I'm going to.

Dr. Lippincott comes in and sees how I'm doing and says she's going to check me. "Well, there's good news and not so good news," she says. *Oh God, what now?* "The good news is that you're fully dilated and ready to push. The bad news is that it's too late for an epidural."

Oh my God, it's really happening! It's finally happening! But wait, no! I can't do it without the epidural, I can't handle this pain, no way, no way! No freakin' way!

I start crying and saying that I can't take it and I won't be able to stand the pain, and Mom and Dianne tell me that it will be over soon and that this is the worst of it, but I don't believe them. I just cry and cry. Suddenly, some nurses come into the room and Dr. Lippincott tells me she wants me to wait until the next contraction and then start pushing. She says I should push from my lower half and vagina, not from my chest or my face, I should just focus all my energy down there, and she will count to ten while I push, and then I should stop. She wants me to relax and concentrate on my breathing, she says it will make it easier. *Relax? Concentrate on my breathing? Yeah, right!*

Dr. Lippincott finishes setting up with her nurses and two people waiting by the baby area, ready to take the baby and clean it or whatever they do, and before I know it, the overhead lights turn on and Dr. Lippincott sits on a stool at the foot of my bed, and nurses surround me. Mom holds up one of my legs and Dianne takes the other. Ian and Josie and Molly stand behind me, and Ian keeps patting me with the washcloth.

"Madison, it's going to be okay," Mom says. "You'll get through it, baby. You're almost there, sweetie, you're almost there."

I'm crying and crying and screaming and I can't even believe it's *finally* happening. I'm not even scared at all anymore, I just want to get it out of me *now*.

A contraction starts, and Dr. Lippincott says, "Push!" and she counts to ten. I push and push as hard as I can. Surprisingly, it feels *really* good. Like I'm fighting against the pain of the contraction.

"Okay, that was really good, Madison," Dr. Lippincott says. "Now relax until the next one starts. You're doing great. Just try to push as hard as you can. Pretend you're having a really big bowel movement. You're doing great!"

Almost immediately afterwards, another contraction starts and this time everyone counts down from ten. I push and push as hard as I can. It feels so amazing to push, I'm just hoping this time it'll work.

But, eight pushes later, it doesn't feel so amazing anymore. In fact, it feels even *more* painful now. Dr. Lippincott keeps saying that it means Cheese Puff is getting closer to coming out, I'm getting closer and closer, and she says I'm doing amazing. I don't understand how I'm even surviving this pain, I really don't. I can't believe I couldn't have an epidural, this whole natural childbirth thing is torture like I've never imagined. I honestly feel like I'm going to pass out, but I just keep telling myself that this pain means I'll see Cheese Puff soon, I'll see Cheese Puff soon, I'll see Cheese Puff soon.

Two pushes later, Dr. Lippincott says, "I can see the head! Keep going, Madison! Push! Push harder, push harder!"

Everyone screams, *"Push!"* and I push with everything I've got. It *has* to work this time, it just *has* to!

But it doesn't. It doesn't work. The contraction subsides and now I'm *so* exhausted, just completely drained from the pain. "I need a break!" I cry. "I can't do it! I need to stop! I'm too tired! I need to stop!"

Ian leans down and whispers into my ear. "No. You can do it. You're amazing, Mads, I've never seen anyone be so strong."

"I can't," I cry. "I *can't!*"

Another contraction starts and they all count and cheer me on and Dr. Lippincott yells, "Harder, Madison, it's right there, *push! Push!"*

I scream and push with whatever bit of energy I have left. It feels like I'm about to die, it hurts so much and I scream and yell and cry and pray that this time it works, I just can't do it anymore.

It doesn't work again. And *again.* I'm in a nightmare of torture that won't end. There's so much pressure and stinging and pain that I don't feel like my vagina can stretch any further. It almost feels like it's going numb, I feel like I'm going to pass out. Dr. Lippincott stays down there and tells me that she can feel the baby's head and that it's going to happen any minute. Everyone strokes me and kisses me and tells me I'm doing great. It's all a blur. I know that the harder I push, the sooner this will be over, so I start really focusing every last ounce of energy I can muster up and I direct it all toward my vagina, pushing and screaming as I do it. It hurts so badly that it makes me want to just pass out and give up. But I know I can't. *I have to keep pushing.*

Five excruciating pushes later, I feel something *weird. Really* weird. Like something is...slipping out of me.

"One more push, Madison, only one more push!" Dr. Lippincott exclaims.

One more push. One more push and I get to end this torture and see my beautiful Cheese Puff.

"10!"

Push.

"9!"

Push.

"8!"

Push.

"7!"

Push!

"6!"

Push!!

"5!"

Push!!!

"4!"

Push!!!!

"3!"

Push!!!!

"2!"

Push!!!!!

"1! Push, Madison, push, *PUSH!*"

I scream so loudly that colors dance in front of my eyes. Maybe I'm dead, I don't know, I don't care anymore. My mind goes somewhere else.

... July 2018...

I finally reached the top of the mountain that I was hiking with Leo. The sun was setting quickly, turning the light blue sky orange and pink and yellow and purple, the beautiful orange light from the sun glaring onto the buildings in the distance. *The colors danced in front of my eyes.* And I was laughing because I had finally reached the top of the mountain, and I was *way* ahead of Leo. I sat down to rest and wait for him, looking up at the sky and smiling as the colors of the sunset washed over me.

...

And then I hear the first cry.

Chapter 37: First Week of Life

"It's a boy!" Dr. Lippincott says as she pulls my screaming baby out of my vagina. After all the pushing, it just kind of slips out, and it feels very weird, but the pain goes away and Nurse Phillips places Cheese Puff on my chest. He's crying loudly, and I start to cry, too.

Everyone is saying, "Congratulations!" and "You did it!" and "He's so cute!" But it's all a blur to me. I *hear* their voices, but they just stay in the background.

I stare at it. The baby. My baby. It's so crazy, it was just inside of me and now it's here. It's a boy. A *boy.* I wanted a girl so badly and I didn't want a boy because I was worried it would look like Leo or remind me of Leo or something. But he doesn't look like him. At least not yet. I feel guilty for thinking these thoughts, how can I be having these thoughts as the first things I think about Cheese Puff? *Cheese Puff.* Oh my God, I can't call him "Cheese Puff," he needs a real name now. He's so *real. He. A boy. My boy.* Wow, he's actually *really* cute!

Just as I'm thinking all these things, a nurse takes him aside and Mom cuts the umbilical cord, and Dr. Lippincott is busy doing something, I think I heard her say she's delivering the placenta. Then the nurse tells me she's going to take him to the side, where they will weigh him, measure him, assign him an "Apgar" score, and swaddle him, before I can start cuddling with him and breastfeeding. They take him, and all I do is lie there and cry and cry and cry, waiting for them to bring him back over to me.

Everyone is still gathered around me, and I see now that Mom is crying as she strokes my cheek. Josie is standing over by the baby, watching them clean him, she looks so fascinated. Molly and Ian are still holding my hands, and Dianne is standing next to Mom, smiling. Everyone keeps saying how proud they are of me.

"You did it," Mom says to me, wiping tears away. "You were so brave, Madison." She blows her nose. "I can't believe I'm a grandmother." She shakes her head, sobbing. "Oh, how I wish your dad was here."

I nod, tears running down my face. I can't believe how many emotions I'm feeling right now. I feel like my chest is about to burst. I keep looking over to see what's happening with the baby. *My* baby. *My baby.*

Dr. Lippincott comes up next to me, with a huge smile on her face. "So, you did it, Madison! It wasn't that bad, was it?"

I shake my head, laughing. "Oh yes, it was."

"I know, I'm so sorry about the epidural, that was bad timing, we should have ordered it earlier." I nod, and she pats my shoulder and says, "You did such a great job." Then she says to Mom, "Congratulations to the new grandmother!" Mom smiles and thanks her.

Ian holds my hand and kisses it. "He's so beautiful," he says. "Just like you." Mom and Molly smile at him and nod that they agree. My heart swells with joy, along with a million other things.

Josie rushes back to us, with a huge smile on her face. "I can't believe I'm an auntie!" she exclaims, and everyone laughs.

The nurse brings the baby back and puts him on my chest again. "The baby is 20 inches long, and he weighs 8 pounds and 2 ounces! A very, very healthy and strong little baby boy, born on July 5th at 6:52 in the morning!" she says.

New tears leak out of my eyes. Feeling Cheese Puff's warmth on me just makes me cry harder. I can't believe that my little boy is *here*. Now, he's swaddled and he has a little hat on. He's all clean and he looks peaceful now, his eyes are shut and the eyelids are shiny, like they applied some sort of ointment to them.

I can't stop staring at him. I think he's the most amazing thing in the whole world. He's my *baby*. He's what I *grew*. He is *Cheese Puff*. Oh my God, I did it, I gave birth to Cheese Puff, I actually did it, and no matter what happens, I'll have this baby. And he's *always* going to be *mine*.

Suddenly, his eyes open and he looks at me and lets out a soft cry. It hits me how much this little baby *needs* me. Oh my God, he *needs* me. *I'm his mother. He needs me.* I kiss his forehead. He smells so good and his skin is so unbelievably soft.

Dr. Lippincott tells me that I tore a little, but she stitched it up and that it's normal to have some pain, but they will give me some pain medicine and an ice pack to sit on. She says she will be back later today to check on me, and that I should try to rest when the baby rests. She says to ask Nurse Phillips for anything I need, and she says that Nurse Phillips will also be here to help me urinate for the first time, and to help me pass a bowel movement for the first time. Basically anything I need postpartum or baby-wise, she'll be here. And Dr. Lippincott says that I can call her with any questions that I have before she comes back today. She tells me again that she's so proud of me and happy for all of us, and then she leaves.

Cheese Puff starts to squirm and cry a little, and I see his little lips opening. Oh no, maybe he's hungry! *What do I do? Maybe it's time to breastfeed?* I should latch him on, but I don't really know how, and I honestly don't want to do it in front of everyone. To give us some privacy,

Ian offers to take Josie for a walk, and Molly goes with them. Dianne says she's going to call her parents to let them know that I had the baby, so it's just me and Mom and Nurse Phillips left in the room, which makes me feel more comfortable.

"This is the perfect time to start latching on, seeing as he's hungry," Nurse Phillips says. "So, the first thing to do is to untie the top of your gown."

She unties the bows at the top of my hospital gown, and then I can feel my little boy's skin right against my chest, and it makes me so joyful to hold him this way that a rush of love explodes in my heart.

"Now you're going to lightly touch your nipple to his lips, and wait till he opens his mouth really wide. It's a natural reflex, and once he does that, then just lightly guide your breast into his mouth until you have a good latch. A good latch is where the baby's mouth is covering both your nipple *and* your areola, and you can hear and see a rhythmic suckling. It shouldn't hurt. If it hurts, it means he's not latched on properly."

I attempt to follow her instructions the best that I can. It's hard, though, because he closes his mouth when I try to guide my breast to him, and then he cries more and shakes his little head. Nurse Phillips tells me that I need to comfort him before I try to do it again, and I realize I don't really know how to comfort a baby. *My* mom could always comfort me and Josie. But now *I'm* a mom to someone.

Mom strokes my forehead and tells me not to worry, that I'm doing great, and that I will get the hang of it. She says she felt the same way when I was born.

"Try talking to him," Nurse Phillips suggests. "He heard your voice the whole time he was inside you, so it will comfort him to hear it now."

I try to think of something to say, and then I say, "I love you so much, Cheese Puff," and suddenly, those words make him stop crying, and he looks right up at me again, like he's looking into my soul or something.

"Oh my God, you really do recognize my voice!" I exclaim. I can't believe how natural it's already starting to feel to hold a baby. I've truly never felt this way for anyone. *Everything* has changed. I don't feel as worried or scared or sad as I used to. All I can feel is this crazy strong love and connection to this little being. I wonder if I'll ever get used to the fact that I *made* him. I love him so much already. I silently vow to myself that I will do whatever it takes to protect him and to give him a good life.

"I know you're hungry, so let me feed you now, okay?" I ask gently, and he stops squirming and then I do what Nurse Phillips told me to do, and it works this time. He opens his mouth wide, I put my breast in carefully, and he starts suckling. It feels weird, it doesn't feel like anything is really coming out but a few drops, and Nurse Phillips says this is normal in the beginning, that my real milk will come in a few days. She tells me to feed him on this side for a little while, and then I can switch.

I untuck the swaddle slightly and look at his little head. It's a little odd-shaped, and I ask the nurse why. She tells me that he just squeezed out of my body, so he'll look a little roughed-up for just a couple days, but it's normal and his head is going to be a normal shape.

He doesn't have much hair yet, but I do see a shade of blonde coming in. His eyes are murky and blue, so I don't know what actual color they'll be yet. He's making the cutest little noises as he sucks, and I stroke his soft hair, never wanting to let him go. Now I truly understand when parents say that their kids could never know how much they love them; my little boy will never, ever understand how much I love him already until he has one of his own. I want him to stay as young and innocent and little as he is now, and that makes me cry a little again.

Mom is so great, she keeps stroking my forehead and telling me I'm doing amazing while I feed him, and I'm just so happy that she's here. She keeps tearing up and saying that she wishes my dad was here. I do, too.

Then Nurse Phillips says, "Okay, I'll leave you to it for now! If you have any problems or questions you can always buzz me. You're doing a very good job."

She goes to leave, but then she turns around and asks, "Wait, before I leave, may I just ask if you know what you're going to name him, sweetie? If you don't, it's okay, I will just put your name on his tag."

Oh, no, this is really bad. I knew it was inevitable that I was going to have to name him, but I honestly can't think of a name. I've been calling him "Cheese Puff" for so long, and I really thought he was going to be a girl, anyway.

I look at Mom, and she's smiling and staring at the baby. *Her grandson. Dad's grandson.* Suddenly, a memory flashes through my mind.

...April 2016...

It was family movie night, and we were watching "Thomas the Choo-Choo Train." Josie and I asked Dad if that's who he was named after.

"Now, do I look like a train to you?" Dad asked, joking around, and we all laughed.

...

Thomas. My dad's name was Thomas. *Thomas Davis.*

"Thomas," I say softly, like I'm trying it out. And it sounds so perfect.

Mom's eyes light up and she looks at me and then back at the baby. "Oh, Madison, yes! That would be so nice, naming him after Dad. Are you sure?"

I nod, and we both start crying. It's *so* perfect, I can't believe that I didn't think of it earlier. I know I'll probably call him "Tommy" until he's older, because Thomas sounds a little too grown-up. But Thomas is going on his birth certificate.

"Thomas Davis is his name," I say proudly. "Thomas...Paul Davis." I added the "Paul" for his middle name because it starts with the same letter as "Puff." Tee-hee. Nurse Phillips nods and smiles, and then she leaves to go make the ID tag for him.

Mom strokes my hair. "Madison, Dad would be so, so happy. And so, so proud."

I smile and stroke Tommy's hair, thinking, *Dad, this is your grandson. He's named after you. I know he'd love you so much if you were here. And I know that you love him, too. I hope you can somehow see me and him now.*

I look down at my baby, who finally has a name. *Thomas Paul Davis.* I'm now thinking it's actually better that he's a boy, because I got to name him after Dad. I look at every part of his body, which is so perfect. His little tiny hands and feet, and his soft skin and his tummy, and the cutest little baby face.

I have a son.

"Maddie, I'm sorry to bring this up, but...I'm going to have to let Leo's parents know that he was born," Mom says softly.

I don't want to hear this. I've been trying to block it out and not think about Leo or have any association with him and the baby. I know I can't avoid it, though, and I'm glad that Mom will do it and I don't have to. I nod, and she goes to call them.

I just try to think about Thomas and only Thomas. He lets go of the latch and he seems like he is falling asleep. I switch him to my other breast to see if he wants it, and I help him latch on again. This is easy so far, but I wonder what it will be like when my real milk comes in.

I don't know if I could've gotten a good latch if it weren't for Nurse Phillips' help. But honestly, *all* the nurses here are so nice, and everyone is so helpful. I wish I could stay here, it feels safe that there are lots of people showing me what to do. Mom is going to have to leave soon, but I wish she could stay and help me. Mostly, I'm scared to go home. Then it'll really be *real,* that he's all my responsibility and I will have to do everything for him, like setting up his doctor's appointments, for example. His pediatrician is out of town because it's the Fourth of July holiday weekend, but I'm taking him for his first check-up next week.

Mom comes back and tells me that Leo's mom is happy and she wants to come visit me and the baby in the hospital. Oh boy, it's starting already. Mom says she will work out a schedule with Leo's parents, maybe they will visit once a week, or so. *Ugh.* I really don't believe that I'm going to have to deal with this. I wonder if they will even tell Leo. Anyway, I don't really care. I'm actually happy they will come by, maybe it will be helpful in some way. I really am scared and I don't want to be alone all the time.

I see that Tommy fell asleep on my breast and Mom takes him and puts him in the little bassinet next to my bed. She tells me that I should close my eyes and try to sleep while he's sleeping. I fall asleep pretty much right away, I'm *so* tired.

When I wake up, I see that everyone is back in the room, sitting on chairs, mostly on their phones. It's only been about forty-five minutes, but I must have been in a deep sleep because it feels like a lot longer. I see the nurse tending to Tommy, changing his diaper, and I realize that I don't even know how to do that and I'm going to need her to show me.

I tell everyone what I decided to name the baby and that it's after my dad, and everyone is so happy and says it's perfect. Molly says "Cheese Puff" will just have to be his nickname, and we all laugh.

Mom brings Tommy over and says he seems hungry again, and she shows me how I can put a small blanket over my shoulder so that I can have privacy while I feed him. She stares at Tommy, smiling, and she takes some pictures with her phone. After Tommy finishes one breast, I switch him to the other. It's really amazing to me that I can feed him this way, through my own body.

Mom tells me she has to go back to work and she's really sad about it and she wishes she could stay longer. She asks me if I want her to call in and take a vacation day, but I tell her she should go because I want her to save her vacation days to be able to come see me and Tommy later on, when I'm not in the hospital, and when everyone isn't around. She says she can come back at night, she doesn't mind driving in again. She's being really sweet, I just can't believe how *good* things are between us now. I hope it can stay this way.

She tells Josie they are leaving, and they both kiss Tommy and Mom tears up again. Just as they're about to leave, Mom goes to the corner of the room and brings back a big bag, which I hadn't noticed before. She opens the bag and pulls out a pillow that is shaped like a horseshoe. "I got you a breastfeeding pillow, I think you'll love it," she says. The pillow is so soft and it has pictures of baby animals all over the fabric, it's so nice. I thank her and she helps me put it around my chest and place Tommy on top, and it's so easy now, because I don't have to hold him up myself. It's way easier to feed him with the pillow supporting me.

Then Josie hands me a little bag with a big smile on her face, and I open it up to find tiny knitted chocolate cupcakes with pastel colored frosting. "Did you make these?" I ask her, and she nods, excitedly. "Wow, Josie, you are getting so good at knitting! These are amazing, thank you! I bring her in for a big hug. "Thank you, really. You're already such a great auntie!"

She smiles, and then Mom gives me a big kiss on my forehead and she says, "I'll be back here tonight, okay, Madison?" I tell her that if it's late and she's tired, she shouldn't drive, and she nods but says she will try.

Before she leaves with Josie, she and Dianne hug. It's a long one, too. "Thank you, Dianne, again, for everything. You've been amazing."

"Oh, it was nothing," Dianne says, and we all laugh. "But, you're welcome."

I can tell that Mom means what she's saying. I know she was probably a little jealous about my relationship with Dianne, but it seems like she's gotten over it.

Then Mom turns to Ian, smiling. "It was nice to meet you, Ian."

"Nice to meet you, too, Mrs. Davis."

"Please, call me Teresa."

Then they leave, and Ian comes over just as Tommy finishes eating. He turns away to give me privacy while I take Tommy off my breast, and then he asks if he can hold him. I hand him to him and he takes him, and Dianne shows him how to hold him. Then Tommy starts spitting up on him and everyone scrambles to get something to wipe it up with. Ian laughs, but I'm worried he's grossed out.

Dianne cleans him up, and then Ian sits down and holds Tommy with a little blanket pad thing that the nurse left for us, and Dianne says they are called "burping pads," and we will be going through a lot of them. Tommy falls asleep on Ian's chest and lets out a little soft sigh. Seeing them together makes me want to cry, they look so cute together. I wish that Ian was Tommy's father so badly.

"Wow," Ian breathes. "He really looks like you, Madison."

Molly nods and says, "He's *so* cute, Mads, I can't take it. You made one cute baby."

I laugh. He *is* cute, but he's also red and puffy, and his eyes are wrinkled and covered in ointment. He's still adorable, though, but not that typical cherubic baby image yet. I read that it's normal, though, in the beginning.

Dianne carefully takes Tommy from Ian and puts him in the

bassinet, and tells me that I should try to sleep again, and that I should try to get into the habit of sleeping whenever Tommy sleeps. She says that she's going to leave with Molly and Ian to get some breakfast and some things from the house, but they'll be back later.

After they leave, I close my eyes, and fall asleep right away. I wake up to the sound of Tommy crying and a nurse comes in and takes him out of his bassinet and checks to see if his diaper needs changing. She shows me how to change his diaper and then she hands him to me, and I feed him again. She comments on the breastfeeding pillow and I say that my mom gave it to me. She says they are great, and that I'm lucky to have had so many people here looking out for me. I agree, and I honestly feel like it's too good to be true. I wish everyone could just live together with me and Tommy. I'm still scared to leave here.

It's starting to get uncomfortable, sitting in the hospital bed with all the pressure on my lower body, and I tell her, "Um, my, uh, vagina, it kind of feels really sore."

The nurse smiles knowingly. "I'm going to go get you something called an ice donut. Basically, it's a donut-shaped tube that you sit on, with ice inside. It will help numb the pain, and we can also give you some more painkillers."

"Okay, thank you, that would be great."

She gets it for me and adjusts it under me, and then she leaves and says she will be back with a tray of food for me. I realize how starving I am, I can't wait to eat.

Then my phone rings, and I reach over gently and lift it out of my bag, trying not to wake up Tommy, who's nestled in the crook of my left arm, sleeping peacefully.

Leo's calling. *Why is Leo calling?*

My fingers shaking, I answer the call. "Leo?"

"You had the baby?" he asks in a neutral voice, and I nod, but then I realize he can't see me, and then I say, "Yes. I, uh, I did, it was, uh...a boy."

He scoffs. "Yeah, well, my parents told me. They said you're going to be filling out a birth certificate and they wanted me to have my name on it as the father. I don't want that, so no matter what they said to you, do *not* put my name on it. Okay? It's the *least* you could do, Madison. Bye," he says, and then he hangs up.

I sit there, stunned. I can't believe he just did that. The tears start to come, and I just let it out. I let out all the sadness I've been keeping inside about the fact that Tommy doesn't have a father, and that I'm a single mother at *sixteen years old.*

My crying makes Tommy wake up, and *he* starts to cry. I realize that my feelings will probably affect him, and that's the last thing I want. All I want to do is shield him from this. He's so beautiful, he's so perfect, and Leo is crazy not to want to know him. I will never understand how he can be so mean.

Then, suddenly, I get a text from Leo's mom saying congratulations, and that she's excited to see the baby. I wonder if she knows Leo just called me. She says she's going to come by the hospital with Mr. Schmitz. I really want Mom to be here when they come, so I text back and ask if she can come by at night, and then I text Mom to tell her that she'll be there, too.

I really don't want to have to be dealing with any of these people right now, I just want to focus on Tommy. He fell asleep again, suckling on my breast, and it's so peaceful with him right now. I finally have a second to think, and it just keeps hitting me over and over again that I'm not pregnant anymore, and I will be able to go back to being normal. I will be a mother. I *am* a mother. From now on, I will be doing everything for this new little being. I can't let other people affect that, the same way I couldn't let them affect me when I was pregnant. The most important thing is Tommy.

I think about my own parents, and now I think I know how they must have felt when *I* was born. They were so lucky to have each other. I think about Dad and wonder if he really would be proud of me. I do think that he would be happy to know Tommy is named after him. I take out my phone again and go to my music app, find *Fire and Rain,* and start playing it. I want to feel close to Dad. The song makes the tears come, but they aren't sad, painful tears right now. I just feel emotional, thinking about how Tommy is genetically a part of Dad, and so that means now a part of Dad will always live on.

I think I'm just realizing what the song *Fire and Rain* really means. That sometimes there's fire, great, glorious fire, and sometimes there's rain, miserable, gloomy rain. James Taylor says he's seen both. And so have I. I've seen the good and the bad of everything that's happened since the two lines showed up on the pregnancy test. But my little Tommy definitely outweighs the good side far more than the bad.

I look down at Tommy and I whisper to him, "I love you more than anything I've ever had in the world. But...I didn't *just* fall in love with you. I've loved you for so long," and then I kiss his forehead. I can't get over how good he smells.

Suddenly, I'm exhausted again, just as the nurse comes back with my food. She sees how tired I am and she leaves the food on the tray attached to the bed, and takes Tommy and puts him in the bassinet. She tells me to sleep for a bit and then eat when I wake up. Before I fall asleep,

I ask her how long I'm going to be staying in the hospital, and she says that technically I could go home today, but I can also stay overnight for one night if I want, and I say yes. I really want to stay here as long as possible.

I fall asleep right away, and I actually manage to sleep for two straight hours. Wow, Tommy is already so good, he didn't wake me up! They say that newborn babies need to eat every two to three hours, so I'm happy that Tommy actually let me have the full two hours.

It's dark in my room now, and I see out the window that it is now dark outside, too. I feel so disoriented. Then I look at the bassinet and I see Tommy isn't in there. My heart lurches. *Oh my God, where is he?*

Then I hear giggling and Mom's voice saying, "Looking for something?" and I look over and see Mom sitting on the couch in the corner, holding Tommy and smiling. "I didn't want to wake you, I got here a little while ago and figured that Tommy might sleep a bit longer if he was being held."

"Oh, Mom, thank you."

"Dianne and Molly and Ian are here, too. They took Josie down to the cafeteria to get something to eat."

"Thanks for coming back," I say, smiling.

"Of course, sweetie. And you had one good little baby! The whole time I've been holding him, he hasn't been crying! I think he's getting hungry, though."

Mom brings him to me, and sure enough, he starts doing that thing with his mouth that shows he wants to eat. Holding him and having him breastfeed is such an amazing feeling, it's like I'm really nurturing a life, in a way that I couldn't feel when I was pregnant and he was hidden from me.

Then Mom looks at her phone and tells me that Leo's parents will be here soon. I'm really dreading it, but I'm happy that Mom is here.

After about fifteen minutes of feeding Tommy, I latch him off and try to offer him my other breast. I wonder if he's even getting enough to eat, I don't have any real "milk" yet, just drops. But the nurses have said that my real milk will come in a few days, so I shouldn't worry. Tommy looks fine and happy right now, just sort of lying there in my arms and looking up at me.

"Madison," Mom says, interrupting my thoughts. I look up and see Leo's parents standing in the doorway. They are smiling, but they look nervous. I tense up, and Tommy must sense it, because he starts to cry. I try to soothe him and relax. *It's fine,* I tell myself. *You should be happy that they want to be here.*

They say hi to my mom, and then they come over and smile at me and then stand and stare at Tommy. "He's gorgeous," Mrs. Schmitz says, and I nod, smiling.

"I named him Thomas," I say. "After my dad."

They are silent for a minute, and I can tell that no one knows what to say.

Mrs. Schmitz puts her hand on my shoulder. "That's really nice, Madison. I'm sure your dad would be happy."

"That's a good name. Very strong," Mr. Schmitz adds.

"Thank you," I say.

Everyone is quiet again for a moment. Mrs. Schmitz asks me if it would be okay if they held him, and Mom looks at me, and I nod yes. I hand Tommy very carefully to Mrs. Schmitz and as she takes him in her arms, I see her eyes fill with tears. I watch as they go over to the window, holding him very carefully and cooing at him and rocking him. Seeing this makes me want to cry, for so many reasons. I can't believe Leo isn't here. I don't want him here for *me,* but I don't know, maybe throughout my whole pregnancy I thought that he might come to the hospital to see his *baby.* This is *his son.* But I also feel happy that Tommy is already feeling love from all his grandparents, and the Schmitzes have been really nice, so I don't have anything against *them.* I'm happy that they want to know him. And Tommy seems like he's a really good baby, he hasn't cried at all since they got here.

After about fifteen minutes, Tommy does start crying and Mrs. Schmitz says she thinks he might need a diaper change. She laughs and says it's been many years since she's changed a diaper, and Mom laughs in agreement. Mom takes Tommy from Mrs. Schmitz, and then they say they are going to let me get some rest and they thank me and Mom for letting them come. They say they want to come to see us as often as I will let them, and that we will figure out what works for everyone. They are being so nice, I still can't believe Leo is their son.

Mom gets a diaper from the pile that the nurse left and we change his diaper together, just as the nurse comes in, holding more burping pads and diapers. After his diaper is changed, Tommy seems happy and his eyes close and Mom puts him in the bassinet and tells me I should try to sleep again. She tells me she's going to the cafeteria to join everyone and have something to eat. The nurse tells me she will bring me something to eat when I wake up. Once again, I realize how easy it is here, in the hospital, with everyone helping and having my meals taken care of. I'm really nervous about what it's going to be like to go home. I'm so glad that I'm allowed to stay the night.

<>

The next morning, the nurse brings in the birth certificate forms for me to fill out. It hits me again how much responsibility I now have. I have someone to fill out forms for now, I can't believe it. I love writing down his name, *Thomas Paul Davis*. Mr. Schmitz is right, it *is* a strong name. I'm so happy that he said that. I pause over the area where you're supposed to fill in the father's name. I feel sad for a second that I'm going to leave it blank, but I know it's the only choice I have, since Leo has made it very clear he doesn't want anything to do with Tommy. I look at sweet Tommy, lying in his bassinet, sleeping peacefully, and I realize that it really is Leo's loss. He will never know what he's missing.

Last night, Tommy was up crying a lot, and that's when I learned from the nurses how to give him a bath and how to change his diapers properly when it's poop, which is harder than pee. He had his first poop at three in the morning, and it was really weird because it was sticky and black, and the nurses told me that it's normal and it's called *meconium,* and when I start actively breastfeeding, it'll become green, yellow, orange, sometimes a little brown, and seedy. Also, my milk is starting to come in and my boobs are so hard and painful and swollen. It was easier to get Tommy to latch before, when my boobs weren't feeling like they were about to burst. The nurses all told me that it's completely normal, and that I should just try to stay calm, and it will get easier. They also gave me an ointment to put on my nipples if they get sore.

Also, Dr. Lippincott has already been here this morning to check on me. I told her that I've been bleeding a lot, it feels like I have my period right away again. She said it's not a period, it's something called *lochia,* which is basically the lining of my uterus shedding from all the build-up from being pregnant. It's apparently going to last for several weeks, but it'll get lighter over time. It's both funny and annoying to me; I didn't have a period for nine months, and now it's like I'm having all of those periods *combined.*

Since the pain meds that I got yesterday have been wearing off, it's starting to *really* hurt to sit down. The only comfortable position for me is lying down. Dr. Lippincott said the pain will get a little less every day and that it's less painful than a c-section, so I should be happy. She said that to relieve the pain, I should avoid wearing tight clothing and I should try sitting on ice packs or taking warm baths.

I asked her why my stomach is still so big, it really still looks like I'm still pregnant. She said that it takes a little while for the uterus to shrink back to its normal size. She said I will slowly go back to my old weight, but that I need to not try to diet, and it's important to eat really healthy and well-balanced meals because it will come through in the breast milk for Tommy. She also said that I need to try to eat and sleep whenever Tommy is asleep, so that I can keep my energy up. She wished me good luck going home and said I'll be fine and she can tell I'm already getting the hang of it, but I can call her anytime if I have questions before my postpartum appointment with her next week. She's been so sweet, and I honestly don't know how I would've gotten through this with any other doctor.

I've had another visitor since Leo's parents came by last night: Dad's friend Billy. It was such a surprise, I haven't seen him since running into him at Home's Diner. He told me that Mom called him, and he was so happy that I named Tommy after Dad. He held Tommy for a few minutes, and it made me cry, I felt like a part of Dad was here.

Now I'm going home, which I'm scared about, but I'm honestly also a little excited. Molly and Ian are at work, but Dianne comes to help me get my stuff together and bring Tommy home. She asks me if I'm scared, and I nod, and she says she knows exactly how I feel.

"By the way, Madison," she says. "I know you've been stressing about finding a job and an apartment, and I want you to know you don't need to rush to figure that out right now. This is going to be a big adjustment period for you, and it might take a bit of time to find the right job and the right place for you and Tommy. I don't want you to rush on my behalf, okay? You are welcome to stay with us as long as you need to."

She's amazing. I start to cry, and she gives me a hug. I'm so happy that we are getting along again. A nurse comes in, and I get in a wheelchair and the nurse rolls me out to the elevator, down to the garage, and then over to the car. I go into the back with the baby, sitting in the middle as Dianne puts Tommy in his spot. As we pull out of the garage, I realize this is Tommy's first glimpse of the world. He's wide-awake, his eyes looking out the window, and I want to cry for the millionth time, it's so amazing that his life is just starting and he will be seeing so many things in his life, and *I'm* here at the very beginning.

Once we get home, Tommy starts crying and Dianne says he's probably hungry and needs a diaper change, so she helps me get him and everything else up to my room. She brings him up in the car seat, and she says it will be easier this way to have it with us so we can put him in it when he's sleeping, if I'm not staying in the bedroom with him. I go up the stairs *really* slowly, because I'm still really sore. I look at the set-up. Ian's air mattress is now in here, because he told me that he wants to help when Tommy's up in the middle of the night. The top of the dresser now has a mat on it for me to change Tommy on, and the diapers and wipes are stacked off to the side. My bed now has a smaller bed in the corner next to my pillow, a co-sleeping bassinet for Tommy to sleep in. Dianne stands there, watching me notice everything that she set up. I'm overwhelmed with emotion. She's been so good to me, even at times when I didn't deserve it. I can't stop thanking her.

She insists on changing Tommy's diaper, she says she actually *wants* to do it, because it's been so long since she changed Molly's, and she wants to see if she remembers how to do it. She tells me I should take a shower and she will watch him. So I take a quick shower, change my maxi-pad, put on my robe, and then I can hear Tommy wailing through the bathroom door. I rush out and Dianne is trying to soothe him, but she says she thinks he's hungry. The nurses told me newborns cry for three main reasons: they are either hungry, tired, or they need their diaper changed. Sometimes it can be all three at the same time!

I sit myself down on the bed, stuff the breastfeeding pillow under my chest, and then I lift up my shirt. Tommy starts sucking hungrily the second he's on my breast.

"Good job with the latch!" Dianne says. "It was so hard for me with Molly, but you're doing great."

Then the doorbell rings, and Dianne goes to get it. She comes back into my room with Alexa! I had been texting with her earlier today and updating her on everything. She asked if she could come by, and I said yes. She's so excited to see me, and to meet Tommy. She is still so pregnant, and I know exactly how she's feeling, and I feel so bad for her. It's amazing how good it feels to *not* be pregnant anymore.

She watches me feed him and she asks me a million questions. She wants to know about labor and pushing the baby out and what it was like, and I tell her that I'm not going to sugar-coat it: it's *hell*. I tell her that she should try to get her epidural as soon as they let her, and not to make the same mistake that I did.

When Tommy finishes eating, I latch him off carefully, my nipples are already getting sore and red. Alexa looks scared to even see that. She asks if she can hold Tommy, and I hand him to her carefully. She says it's great practice for her, learning how to hold a baby, and I take his hat off and show her his little tuft of blonde hair. She says he smells so good, and I nod, it's crazy how good a newborn baby smells. I show Alexa his tummy, and we both can't believe how soft his skin is. He still has the little black umbilical cord thing on his belly button, but the nurses told me that it will fall off in the next couple of weeks.

Alexa stays for a little while. Dianne makes us sandwiches and we take turns holding Tommy until he falls asleep, and then I tell Alexa that I need to try to nap, because they say to sleep when the baby sleeps. She says she wants to come visit again soon and we hug goodbye, and I realize how much smaller my stomach already is, especially in comparison to her stomach, she's around seven months along now.

I fall asleep right away and then wake up a couple of hours later to the sound of Tommy crying. He's such a good baby, he really goes for two hour stretches, so I'm able to get some sleep. I check his diaper and see that it needs changing, and then I feed him again. I realize I better get used to this routine, it seems to be all I will be doing for a while. Then again, I realize I also need to find time to get food for myself and do laundry and other things, and I'm a little worried that I won't be able to manage it all.

Molly and Ian are home now, and they knock at my door. I put the blanket over my chest the way Mom showed me, so they can't see Tommy on my boob, then tell them to come in. They are so excited to see Tommy and ask how I'm doing. Molly tells me that they are ordering sushi for dinner, because she knows I've been craving it the whole pregnancy and now I can finally have it. *What am I going to do when I'm not living here anymore and I have to worry about all my meals on my own?* I try to not think about that and remember what Dianne said about me taking my time to get adjusted.

Ian comes over to give me a kiss, and he says he will help in the middle of the night, when Tommy wakes up. Molly says she wants to help, too, and they have a little fight over who gets to do what. I want to laugh. I'll be glad to let them be up changing his diaper and fighting over who gets to do it.

Molly goes downstairs to help Dianne with ordering dinner, and Ian sits on his air mattress and asks me how it's going. Seeing him back here again makes me wonder if things will ever be able to go back to being the way they were before I had Tommy. It's all different now. What's not different is that I still think he's cute and I still want to be with him. I wonder if he still wants to be with me, now that he's seeing me as a mom. *A mom.* He's seen me looking so bad, he will be shocked when he sees how good I can actually look, if I ever lose the baby weight and I start to get some sleep again.

Well, there's nothing I can do about it now, and if he doesn't want to be with me anymore, I will understand, even though I'll be totally sad. Just thinking about all of this makes me sweaty and hot, and the blanket is really uncomfortable. As if he can read my mind, Ian says I don't have to be shy around him, and that he thinks breastfeeding is a really natural and beautiful thing. He says he won't look if I want to take it off and if it makes me more comfortable. I decide to just take it off. I realize that I won't be able to keep this up with the blanket every time I need to breastfeed, anyway. I tell myself not to be self-conscious, that it's a natural thing and that Ian means what he says.

The sushi gets here just as Tommy falls asleep. I put my finger in his mouth to latch him off, and he rolls his head back sleepily. I ask Ian to bring me the car seat from where Dianne left it at the door and he gets it and I put Tommy in it and Ian carries him downstairs for me. I know I'll have to get used to carrying it, but right now it feels really heavy and I still feel weak from everything.

The sushi is the best sushi I've ever had. I just can't believe how good it tastes, I've been waiting so long to have it. I just keep putting more and more on my plate, and everyone laughs. I thank Dianne, and she smiles and says that she totally gets how good it feels to have what you've been craving your whole pregnancy. She said when she was pregnant with Molly, it wasn't sushi, it was any kind of deli meat. She says that she remembers her mom pigging out on deli meat after Ian was born. It's so funny to think about all these mothers not eating what they want during pregnancy, and then pigging out once they're finally allowed.

Tommy starts to cry just as I'm eating, and Molly offers to hold him so I can finish. She's scared to try to change him or anything, but she sings to him and bounces around the room with him. He just keeps screaming louder and louder. *Is he really already hungry? I just fed him!*

I sigh and go over to the living room to latch him on, and he starts sucking so hard that it actually hurts. After a few gulps, he calms down and I stroke his head. Ian comes into the room with my plate and starts feeding me pieces of sushi. He tells me it's too bad we can't balance my plate on my stomach anymore, and we laugh.

"I can't believe just a couple of days ago this whole human being was *inside* you. Like, you were balancing a bowl of cheese puffs on him," Ian says.

I laugh and say, "I know, it's crazy." Then I sigh. "I actually miss feeling him move in me. And I also miss calling him 'Cheese Puff.'"

"That's for sure going to be his nickname."

"Yeah, until he's older, then I'm not sure it's such a good idea," I say, laughing, picturing the kids making fun of him, and boy do I not want that to happen.

"Mads," Ian says quietly. "I just want you to know that...things don't have to change. I mean, now that Tommy's here...my feelings haven't changed. I still want to be with you. I mean, I know you're busy and your attention is focused on Tommy now, but...well, do you still want to be with me?"

I'm so happy to hear him say this, I had been worried about it, and he's so sweet to tell me this. I nod and then lean over to kiss him. "My feelings haven't changed, either," I say softly. We kiss again, and it feels so nice and easy and natural, just sitting here with Tommy and Ian. I really hope things don't change.

After Tommy finishes eating, he immediately falls asleep again. It's eight o'clock and it feels too early to go to bed, but I think about what everyone keeps saying about sleeping when the baby sleeps. I'm really tired and so I tell everyone that I'm going to go to sleep now. Ian helps me bring Tommy upstairs. I hardly have the energy to brush my teeth. I'm *so tired.*

I drowsily walk over to the changing table and take off Tommy's onesie, which immediately wakes him up, and he starts crying as I change his diaper, which now has poop in it. His poops are kind of orange-yellow, and it would freak me out, but the nurses told me that's what poops from breastmilk look like. It doesn't smell at all, which is good. I wipe him clean, and then I carefully fasten the diaper around him. I already feel like I'm getting faster and faster at doing this. I put him in some light yellow footie pajamas, and then swaddle him like the nurses taught me.

He cries the whole time, but then once he's swaddled, it calms him down. Once I place him in his little co-sleeper, he starts crying again. Molly and Ian come over and help me try to calm him down, but his mouth is wide open, screaming, and he squirmed out of the swaddle so his little arms and legs are flailing around. Ian says that maybe it wasn't tight enough and he tries to do it, while I show him how. He does it tighter than I did, and it seems to work for a second, but then he starts screaming again. Molly and Ian have a look of panic on their faces, and I'm worried about them not getting any sleep, I feel really bad.

I feel a huge pang of worry. *What am I going to do now? What does he need now?* I just fed him, and I changed his diaper, and he might be tired, but I don't know how to get him to sleep. I sit on the bed, rocking him and then try to breastfeed him again, but he turns his little head away.

Then I pick him back up upright, really concerned and worried that I'm not a good mom, that I don't know what my baby needs, that something's wrong, and then he lets out a small burp. Oh, shoot, I forgot to burp him after I breastfed. I remember the nurses telling me that gas is painful for their little bellies and to remember to burp him after a feeding. I place him on my shoulder and start patting his back, burping him, and he lets out a huge, ear-rattling baby burp. Spit-up runs down my shoulder, and Ian and Molly explode into laughter, and I can't help but laugh, too, even though I'm exhausted. I have the burp pads they gave me from the hospital, but it's too late for this time. I have to try to get more organized and keep them right next to my bed.

I burp him a few more times and then he totally settles down and closes his eyes, and I put him in his co-sleeping bassinet, right next to me.

Molly gets me another shirt to change into and goes to put the spit-up one in the laundry hamper. I tell her and Ian that I feel guilty that they have to deal with this, but they say that they want to help and it's no big deal to miss a little sleep.

Everyone gets settled, and the room is now so quiet and peaceful. I can smell Tommy's amazing smell right next to me, it's so cute. Thinking of smells makes me think of my dad's shaving cream. I really want to smell it right now, so I quietly take the can off my nightstand and under the covers so Molly and Ian don't hear, I spray a little bit on my wrist, rubbing it in and inhaling it. I love how it makes me feel like Dad is here, and that the feeling hasn't worn off even after all this time that I've been using it.

I look over and see Tommy's eyes are still open, but he's quiet and he doesn't seem like he's about to cry. I start whispering the song, *"Twinkle, twinkle, little star..."* trying to be as quiet as possible, but I guess Molly and Ian hear because they join in. *"How I wonder what you are...up above the world so high...like a diamond in the sky...twinkle, twinkle, little star, how I wonder what you are."*

Then we all say goodnight, and I wait to close my eyes until I see Tommy's little eyes close. As I fall asleep, my mind tells me that I need to count his kicks. It's so weird, it just automatically happens, and I have to remind myself that I don't need to do it anymore. I really miss the feeling of his movements in my stomach. It's hard to even understand that like Ian said, just a couple of days ago, he was *inside* and now he's *outside.* I can't even explain how scared I am to be responsible for this little being. It just keeps hitting me over and over again that *I* am the reason he is in this world and the reason why he has a life. All I know is I will do everything I can to make it a good one.

← Tommy

To-Do List

- ask nurse about how to latch off
- ask nurse about changing diapers?
- apply for Tommy's social security #
- fill out birth certificate forms
- postpartum checkup with Dr. Lippincott next week on July 17th at 11am (♡ Tommy)
- Tommy's first checkup with his pediatrician next week on July 17th at 12:30pm

☆ send Leo's parents + Billy + Alexa thank-you emails for visiting me

☆ work out visitation schedule with Leo's parents

Feeding
- every 2-3 hours
- put finger in Tommy's mouth to latch him off
- apply ointment to my nipples if they get sore
- drain one breast at each feeding?
- keep track of which breast I fed him from last

buy:
- maxi pads
- ice packs
- diapers
- wipes
- burping cloths

Changing Diapers
- poop = green, yellow, orange, brown, seedy
- wipe him really well

☆ Bathing = support Tommy with one hand the whole time

☆ 3 reasons why babies cry:
1) Hungry
2) Tired
3) Need a diaper change/gas

Tommy / me ← our bed

Chapter 38: Second Week of Life

"Are you coming, Madison?" Dianne calls up the stairs as I hurry to change Tommy's diaper. I yell back "Yes!" and my loud voice makes Tommy cry. I have to keep trying to remember to not do things like that. I've noticed that he really responds to how I'm feeling or acting, so if I'm calm, he's calm, and if I'm stressed, he's stressed.

The past week has been just one big blur for me. It's been a continuous cycle of feeding, burping, changing diapers, and trying to rock Tommy to sleep. He's not colicky, at least not yet, thank God, because I've read about how horrible that can be. He does cry a lot, though, but Dianne said it's normal. It's funny, because in a way, watching Josie for three years trained me to be constantly on my toes.

The nurses prepared me, but I was not aware of how much attention newborns really need. Tommy is up all night, he wants to eat every two hours, and then it takes a while to get back to sleep after I've burped and changed him and settled him back down. I'm lucky if I get a few stretches of one hour of sleep, sometimes two. I'm like a zombie, I'm so tired. Molly and Ian are being very helpful, they bring me diapers so I can stay in bed while I change him, and they've been making me sandwiches and bringing me things like water and protein shakes so that I don't have to worry too much about keeping myself fed and hydrated.

Something weird has happened, though: for whatever reason, I haven't been able to even *look* at a bag of cheese puffs since Tommy was born. I don't know if maybe it's because a part of me thinks I'm eating *him,* because I called him that for so long and I find myself still calling him that sometimes, or if it's because it just reminds me of all this discomfort that came with being pregnant. The sight of them makes me sick now. I wonder if I'll ever be able to eat them again.

I cannot explain how sleep-deprived and exhausted I am. I wore the same pajamas for *four days in a row* this week. I probably smelled so bad. Now I totally get it when new moms say they don't have time to shower; we don't.

And I feel really guilty about Molly and Ian and Dianne helping me all the time. They aren't getting much sleep either, and I know this can't continue that long.

During the day, Tommy seems to want to sleep more than he does at night. I've read that this happens, and that their schedule is all off and takes a while to adjust to sleeping at night and being up more during the day.

I think I've already changed a million diapers. I'm so glad that I stocked up before he was born, because this is the first time I'm going out since I had him, and I don't think I could have gone shopping while I was recovering from labor and delivery.

My favorite time with him is in the late afternoon, after he naps, he's really quiet and alert. Sometimes it seems as if he can't focus on my face, but then all of a sudden he does and he cries for me to feed him. I feel like a milk machine, and feeding him takes so long because you have to "drain" both breasts, or else the one you don't do gets too full of milk and it's very painful. Also, I've read that you can get something called a "clogged duct" or "mastitis," which can lead to an infection. I've considered using formula, but it's really expensive, and from everything I've read, it's good and healthy for them to have breastmilk, so I'm going to try to stick with it.

Now I'm getting ready for my first postpartum check-up with Dr. Lippincott. My vagina doesn't feel as sore as it did last week, but it still really hurts to pee and poop, and I'm just generally still weak all over my whole body. I'm still bleeding, just not as heavily, and I've felt contraction-like cramps in my lower abdomen, and it's apparently my uterus contracting as it shrinks back to its normal size. My stomach still looks big, and it hurts and feels swollen in a way. I keep checking my face and it looks a bit thinner, and when I get on the scale, I see I've already lost about fifteen pounds, and eight pounds of that is Cheese Puff. I still can't help calling Tommy "Cheese Puff," I wonder when and if I'll ever stop. Anyway, I gained thirty-three pounds in total during the pregnancy, and so I still have a lot left to lose. I remember Dr. Lippincott said it could take a while, and that I should not try to diet or anything because I need the nutrients for both me and Tommy.

Right after my appointment with Dr. Lippincott, Tommy has his very first pediatrician appointment, with Dr. Louis Brown. When I was working out my health insurance plan with Mom a few weeks ago, he was one of the pediatricians on the list that my insurance will accept and I did some research on him, he sounds really good. Thankfully, until I'm twenty-six, I'm able to still be on my mom's health insurance plan and program and everything, so I don't have to worry about paying for that, I just have to cover pediatrician appointments, and I will probably have to use the child support from Leo's parents.

Speaking of Leo's parents, they have been really nice in not bugging me to see Tommy since the hospital visit. Mrs. Schmitz has texted me and asked for me to send pictures, so I've been doing that. She said she wants to work out a schedule once I'm more settled, and she also said to call her if I need anything. She's really nice, and I see why Mom likes her. I wish Leo was more like his parents.

Ian is working, but Molly comes with me, and Dianne drives all of us to Dr. Lippincott's. Almost the second Dianne starts driving, Tommy falls asleep. I've heard a lot of parents take their babies for drives in the car to get them to go to sleep. I can't help but stroke his little soft cheeks as he sleeps, he's just so cute. I still can't believe that he's mine. I've started to learn what calms him down when he cries; singing to him and also talking to him, probably because I talked to him a lot when he was in my stomach, so my voice must calm him.

It's so weird to be back at Dr. Lippincott's office and not be pregnant. As I walk through the waiting room, I see a few other mothers, with their big bellies, and I feel like it was a million years ago since that was me. When we walk in, they smile at Tommy and look up at all of us, me, Molly, and Dianne, and I can tell they're wondering which of us is the mother, what our relationship is.

This time, I don't have to pee in a cup or have a blood test. They take my blood pressure and then I change into the gown and Dr. Lippincott comes in. I realize I won't be having an ultrasound anymore, and it's just so weird.

Tommy is still asleep in his car seat and Dr. Lippincott is all smiles, looking at him and then at me. She gives all of us a big hug. She really is the nicest doctor.

"So, how have you been feeling, Madison?" she asks.

"Really, really tired. Still sore down there, too, and I'm also still bleeding. And it's also hard for me to, uh...pass a bowel movement?"

"All of that is perfectly normal. It takes a while to make a baby and it takes a while for your body to bounce back after all it's been through. You're doing great. Let me check you."

She examines me and says it is healing nicely but it will still be sore for a little while longer. She presses on my uterus and it hurts a little but she says that's normal for it to still be sore and that it is compressing down to its normal size nicely. She also checks my boobs to make sure they are okay and there are no clogged ducts. There aren't, but she says that if I ever feel extreme tenderness or if there seems to be any redness or inflammation, I should call her. She asks about how the breastfeeding is going, and I tell her that it's not easy but that I really want to keep doing it. She tells me I can always supplement with formula if it's easier, and it's actually good to know that I have that as an option. She says there is a lot of controversy about whether breastfeeding is better than formula and that they shame mothers who don't breastfeed, but that it's wrong to do that and everyone's circumstances are different. She says to do what's easiest for me, as she knows I'm a single teen mom.

I ask when my stomach will go down, even though I already know the answer, and Dr. Lippincott says again that it takes some time and not to rush it and to make sure I'm eating healthy, well-balanced meals.

"Now, how have you been feeling, emotionally?" she asks.

"Just..." I take a deep breath, and then I smile. "So in love with the baby. But I'm a little overwhelmed. Not depressed or anything like that, just...stressed out."

"Again, that's perfectly normal, especially in the first few weeks, when you're getting adjusted. All moms feel this way, not just teenage ones. But I want you to promise me that if you start to feel really anxious all the time, or you have strange thoughts or are feeling very sad, you will call me. Sometimes there's something that happens called 'postpartum depression' and it's pretty common, and also treatable. It doesn't sound like you have it, but you will keep me posted, right?"

I nod. I tell her I have a breathing app that I use on my phone, which tells me to take deep calm breaths and it calms me down and I've also noticed that when I'm calm and I'm doing calm breathing, Tommy is very calm, too. "See? You're a natural," she says, smiling.

She tells me to make another appointment for six weeks from now, and that I can always call or set up an appointment if needed beforehand. She hugs us all goodbye again, and Tommy starts to cry just as we're leaving, so I change his diaper in the exam room and think about how funny it is to be doing that in here. But he's still crying when we get to the car, so we sit in the car for a few minutes while I feed him.

"I still remember *my* postpartum appointment," Dianne says, chuckling. "Molly had quite a big head, and I had a tear all the way to my...well, you know."

Molly laughs. "Sorry, Mom."

"It's okay. You made it up to me by crying all night long. I think you were actually colicky, but I didn't realize it at the time."

"But I was worth it, right, Mom?" Molly says, grinning.

Dianne pretends to be thinking about it, and we all laugh. Tommy falls asleep on my breast, so I latch him off, put him in his car seat, and Dianne drives us a few blocks over to Dr. Brown's office.

His office is on the sixteenth floor and we get in the elevator. There's a couple other women in here, another one with a baby who looks older than Tommy, and a woman who looks like a grandmother. They both stare at me holding Tommy. The grandmother even asks Dianne who's baby it is, and Dianne says matter-of-factly to her that he's mine. I swear I hear the woman gasp. The grandmother says he's cute, but her voice sounds clipped. I look away, embarrassed. I'd better get used to this,

I know it's going to happen a lot.

Thankfully, they get off before we do. Dr. Brown's office is cute, the walls are blue with puffy clouds painted on them and there's little toys in boxes and kids books on bookshelves for the kids. There are other people in the waiting room, one is a woman with a kid who looks about four and another is a couple with what also looks like a newborn baby. *A couple.* That is normal. My situation is not. Am I going to keep thinking these things forever and ever? Comparing myself to other families?

They stare at Tommy, and then the mother asks Dianne how old he is. I think she thinks Dianne's the mother. I want to let her think it this time, I just don't want to deal with it. "Two weeks old," Dianne says. "And yours?"

"Four weeks," the woman says, and we all smile at each other and then they get called in. Tommy is sleeping and Molly keeps saying she thinks he's already gotten bigger, and look how much more of his car seat he fills up.

A few minutes later, we get called in, and Dianne carries Tommy in the car seat, it's still a bit heavy for me. I need to get used to doing it myself, though.

A nurse comes in and tells me to take off his onesie and diaper so she can weigh and measure him. As soon as I undress him, he starts screaming, and when I take the diaper off, he pees straight up and I frantically look for the little washcloth I have learned to use to cover his penis when I change him. The first few times I changed him, he sprayed it in my face and the nurse at the hospital told me that all boys do it and they've been squirted in the eye more times than they can count. I have tried to be prepared for it each time, but this time I completely forgot. Anyway, it's just a little bit of pee, and the nurse laughs and hands me a small towel to wipe myself. I think our reaction to his pee shocked Tommy, and now he's lying there, just staring at us, so the nurse is able to get the measurements. He is nine pounds and 20 and a half inches. Wow, he's already gained weight and grown, it's so crazy how fast babies seem to grow. The nurse says I can put his diaper back on while we wait and that he's adorable, and then she leaves, telling us Dr. Brown will be in soon.

As soon as Dr. Brown walks in, he instantly reminds me of my dad. I'm actually shocked at how much he looks like him. He has the same color hair and eyes, and a really warm, kind smile.

"Ms. Davis?" he says, and I nod. "And who's this little slugger?"

I laugh. "His name's Tommy."

He nods and goes over to Tommy, and starts talking to him, and Tommy just stares up at him. Dr. Brown laughs and says, "It's nice to meet you both."

I smile. "Very nice to meet you too. I've heard that you're a great pediatrician."

He chuckles. "Well, thank you. And I'm sorry that I wasn't able to come by the hospital after he was born, I usually do that for the first visit, but I was away with my family for the Fourth of July weekend." Then he looks at Dianne and Molly and asks, "Is this the proud grandmother and sister?"

Dianne explains who they are and that my mom is out of town. I say she will probably come to another appointment, and that it's a bit of a complicated situation.

"Before we start, I'm just checking, no judgement here, you're only sixteen, is that right?" Dr. Brown asks. I nod, feeling slightly embarrassed. But surprisingly, he smiles. "Well, that's actually good, because his weight is normal, and you made it past your due date, and usually with teen pregnancies, the risks of a low birthweight baby or a preterm birth are higher. So, good job, Ms. Davis."

I'm so relieved to hear him say this and be nice about my age. I smile and say, "Thank you."

He does a whole physical exam on Tommy, feeling his stomach and listening to his chest and looking in his eyes and nose and ears. He does something with his legs and says he's checking his hips. He goes to undo his diaper and check him down there, and I can't believe it, but just as he does it, Tommy pees again and it goes straight up. Dr. Brown shields it with a piece of gauze that he had on the table that I didn't even see, and says, "Gotcha!" and we all laugh. I tell him that I've been using a washcloth, and he says I should get a big pack of gauze, it might be easier. I make a note on my To-Do list.

After the exam, we go to Dr. Brown's office and Dianne holds Tommy while I take notes. "So, the umbilical stump looks like it will fall off within the next week or so," Dr. Brown says. Then he looks at his clipboard. "Based on what the nurse wrote down, he's around a quarter of an inch taller, and he gained a pound, which is very good. Initially they lose weight after they've been born, then they gain it back. Is the breastfeeding going well? You are breastfeeding, correct?"

"Yes, but I never really know how much or when to feed him."

"I always tell mothers to feed on demand. Eventually it will be good to settle into a schedule but it seems like what you are doing now is alright. Try to drain at least one breast at each feeding. Do you know about the foremilk and the hindmilk?"

"Yes, the nurses at the hospital explained it to me. They said the foremilk is like the meal and the hindmilk is like the dessert."

He laughs. "Yes, that's a good way of putting it. The rich calories are at the end of the 'meal,' in the hindmilk, so it's important to make sure Tommy is getting a lot of that." I nod, and then he asks, "And have you been doing tummy time?"

"No, but I've read about it. Should I start it now?"

"Yes, you can start slowly, just a few minutes a couple of times a day. Place him flat on his stomach so that he has to lift his head. He won't like it, no babies do, but it will strengthen his neck and back muscles. Make sure to supervise him while he's doing it, and increase the time a little each day."

I say I'll do that, and then he asks if I've been placing him on his back every time he sleeps, and if I know about SIDS. I nod again and say, "Yes. Every night, wrapped in a swaddle, on his back." I'm terrified of SIDS. During the last few weeks of my pregnancy, I researched horror stories about it, and I was so horrified. I plan to do everything it takes to make sure it never happens to my little Tommy.

"Good. Just remember, no blankets or stuffed animals or pillows until the age of one, but I would wait till even two years old. Just a mattress and the swaddling is good enough to keep him warm, and also studies have shown that it makes the baby feel snug and secure and they are likely to sleep better. You've probably noticed that babies don't really have control of their arms and legs yet, so they can flail all around."

I nod, and then I wince. I've been giving Tommy a stuffed bear to sleep with but I'm taking it out of the crib immediately.

"You seem to have done a lot of good research and I'm really impressed, Ms. Davis," Dr. Brown says. "Believe it or not, mothers much older than you don't know a lot of this stuff when I tell them."

I thank him and then he asks me if I have any questions. I ask about sleep training and he says it's not a good idea to do that until the fourth month. Their stomachs need to be big enough to hold more milk and then go longer between feedings, and it's way too early for that.

Then I ask if it's normal if his poops are orange and seedy, and Dr. Brown laughs. "It's very normal, and it's good to know that it's been consistent and seedy, it's a sign that he's being well-fed and digesting well. Now, one more thing, may I ask if you're planning to circumcise?"

"Oh, yes, I actually completely forgot that I wanted to talk to you about that. Will the doctor who ends up doing it tell me exactly what will happen?" I ask, a little nervous now, even though I was planning on doing it, anyway.

Dr. Brown nods. "Yes, and don't worry, it's a very routine procedure, nothing to worry about."

"Okay, then yes, I want to do it. Do you think we could do it today?"

"Not sure, you will have to set up an appointment. Here is the person I recommend. Dr. Ross," he says, and he hands me a card.

He tells me that I can always call the office if I have any other questions, and then he says goodbye to all of us and pats Tommy on the head lightly, and says that his next appointment is when he turns one month old.

We go back to the car and I call Dr. Ross's office and ask when his soonest available appointment is, and they say that they actually just had a cancellation and I can come in an hour if I want.

Dianne says we can get take-out sandwiches and eat them in the car, so we stop by the little corner deli and Dianne goes in to order pastrami sandwiches for all of us. I'm excited to have deli meat, and even though it's not as big a deal to me as not having sushi, I still missed it when I was pregnant. I change Tommy's diaper and breastfeed him while we wait. Molly keeps talking about how she can't believe that she has a best friend who has a baby. She says she can't wait to have a baby herself one day, and that maybe I'll have another one someday, and we can try to plan them at the same time so they can be friends. She asks how things are going with Ian, and I say that she sees him as much as I do now, and that it's not like it can really be romantic right now but that I hope we can keep being together. She says she thinks he really cares about me, and that she hopes we stay together, too.

Dianne comes back with the sandwiches and I put Tommy back in the carseat so I can eat. He stares at me eating the sandwich, and I tell him it's pastrami and that he'll be getting some in the breastmilk soon. I can't wait until he's older and he can eat stuff like this. There are so many things that I can't wait to do with him.

Then we drive over to Dr. Ross's office, which is just a few blocks away. One of the reasons I like living in Redford is that everything is pretty close to everything else. It's really hard to imagine living in a big city and having to manage a baby and driving far distances all the time.

Inside the waiting room, there's an area with an aquarium, and I take Tommy up to it and point out the colorful fish, and he looks at a big, bug-eyed one, and all of a sudden, he starts screaming. I laugh, but Tommy just screams louder and louder, and so I go sit down with Dianne and Molly, trying to bounce him a little to calm him, but he just starts crying more, so I hold him against my chest so that he can smell me, and that calms him down a little. Dianne tells me that she took Molly to the zoo when she was a couple months old, and she started screaming when she saw the giraffes. That makes me laugh, too.

Five minutes later, they call us back to a room, and Dr. Ross comes in and introduces himself. He explains everything about the procedure and I wince when he describes the part where he cuts Tommy's penis, but he reassures me that Tommy will only feel pain for a second and that he will never remember it. He says this is a controversial subject, and some people choose not to do it, but that a lot of studies have shown that it's good for health reasons. He hands me a pamphlet about it. I tell him that I've done some research, and that I know it's something I want to do for Tommy. It's weird how much is controversial about having a baby, between breastfeeding and circumcision and other things, as if being a teenage mom isn't bad enough.

Dr. Ross hands me some consent forms to sign and then he says the nurse will bring him back in a minute, and then he leaves.

As I'm about to sign, I say to Dianne, "Wait, am I actually allowed to sign for him? You know that I'm still a minor."

"Yep. Your age doesn't matter. He's *your* baby. Your responsibility. I know, it'll take some getting used to, trust me, I get it."

Molly laughs and says it's so interesting to her to watch me with Tommy, and it makes her almost see firsthand what her mom went through with her. But I feel suddenly really scared and vulnerable, like I'm all alone with little Tommy. I have to make *real* decisions for someone else now. I don't even really know how to make certain decisions for *myself*. I wish Mom was here.

I take a few deep breaths and then sign. For a second it crosses my mind that it would be easier if I had a girl, so I wouldn't have to make this decision. I hope Dr. Ross is right and Tommy won't feel too much pain, and that he won't remember it.

The nurse comes to take Tommy, and then she tells me to be ready to breastfeed right away after she brings him back. She says it will help soothe him. We sit and wait. Molly clutches my hand to reassure me. I don't really feel like talking. I'm suddenly really tired and I have a bit of a headache, and it's hurting to be sitting down.

It's really quiet in the waiting room, and then all of a sudden, we hear Tommy crying, and a couple of seconds later they bring him back in. The nurse immediately hands him to me, and I put him on my boob and he starts sucking right away. He has tears running down his cheeks and his face is all red. I feel so horrible that he had to go through that pain, and I realize I'm going to feel this way for the rest of my life, anytime he has to go through anything painful.

But they were right, he immediately calms down with the breastfeeding. It feels amazing that I can comfort him this way. Dr. Ross comes in and says that it went very well and that I can stay and feed him for a bit, and he gives me a manual on how to care for the wound, and that I can give him Tylenol every four to six hours, and then he tells me to call if I have any questions.

As soon as I put him back in his car seat, he starts to cry again and we try to get to the car quickly where I comfort him by feeding him a bit more. Then I put him in his car seat, and as soon as we start driving, he falls asleep again.

He starts crying *again* when we get home, and Dianne carries the car seat up to my room. I take him out carefully so I don't accidentally touch the area that hurts, and I get in bed and feed him some more. Molly says she's going to try to take a nap. I want to take a nap, too. So badly. I'm exhausted from everything, and I feel irritable and really stressed. It's so hard to cart everything around everywhere. I've forgotten how much easier it was to do things before I was pregnant, or even when I was just pregnant. It's so difficult to go out now. Not only do I have to obviously carry Tommy and his car seat, but I also have to carry this huge diaper bag that's stocked with diapers, wipes, extra outfits, a first-aid kit, toys, and even more. For a second, I think it was so much easier just being pregnant, but then I remember how uncomfortable I was and I realize that this is honestly easier.

I give Tommy some Tylenol, using the little dropper from the package, making sure I give him the right amount. It's scary giving him medicine, and I double check that it's the right amount a few times before giving it to him. This is an example of where I wish I had someone with me who I could ask to make sure what I'm doing is right. *Leo should be here,* I think, but then I push the thoughts away. I'm not going to let myself go there for the millionth time.

I decide the easiest way to get him to sleep now is to feed him, and he's not that hungry, but he latches on and it seems to comfort him and he falls asleep pretty quickly. I can't decide which I want more, to sleep or to eat. I'm starving. I go downstairs and grab an apple and just as I'm going back to my room, Ian comes home from work. I tell him that I got Tommy circumcised, and he makes a face and says, "Ouch! I feel his pain. Is he okay?"

I nod and say I'm going up to take a nap, and he gives me a quick kiss and goes into the kitchen while I head up to my room. I realize that I don't even know if Ian is circumcised, but then I remember Dianne telling me and Molly she actually remembers when it happened with Ian, because she was already fifteen.

Before I take my nap, I quickly check my email. I'm dreading seeing how many emails I have, because I haven't checked it since before Tommy was born. There are some emails from my teachers wishing me congratulations, and a bunch of emails from Babies R' Us, because I subscribed to their website for sales they're having and things like that. I know I should get off email and go to sleep, because Tommy will wake up soon and I keep remembering how I'm supposed to sleep while he's sleeping, but one email catches my attention.

To: maddieluvspizza@gmail.com
From: sunshinestreetdaycare@gmail.com

Hello, Madison Davis,
We received your application for the job of "Child Care Assistant." We have scheduled you for an interview on July 18th at four p.m. at our location, Sunshine Street Day Care at 110 North Ridge Avenue. If you cannot make this time, please let us know so we can reschedule. Make sure to bring your résumé. Thank you.

Sincerely,
Sunshine Street Day Care
110 North Ridge Avenue
(310) 907-1231

Oh no, that's tomorrow, and I never confirmed! This was one of the jobs I applied for because I can bring Tommy with me, and it sounded really good.

I write them an email back, confirming, and after I send it, I realize how much I really hope that I get this job. A lot of the other places I applied to didn't even get back to me, and the only other job that could feasibly work is a gardening service, because I *used* to garden with Dad when he was alive, but I don't know how much I could do on my own and they haven't called me in for an interview, anyway. I have a higher chance of getting this job at the daycare because of all the babysitting I've done with Josie, and now that I have my *own* baby, I'm learning even more about how to take care of kids.

I write it down on my To-Do list to make sure I don't forget when to go, and then I also write Molly a text to make sure that she can watch Tommy with Dianne and Ian tomorrow night, when I go.

Molly and Tommy are fast asleep and I finally collapse only my pillow and fall asleep. *Finally, finally, some sleep for me!*

Not even an hour later, Tommy wakes me up from a deep sleep. I'm so stupid, I knew I shouldn't have checked my email. I could've had at least another hour, and now I'm *so tired.* I do the usual feeding him, burping him, changing him, and it takes about forty-five minutes, and then it takes me about a half hour to get back to sleep. I really don't know how mothers do this and get anything else done.

<>

Waking up the next day, I realize that it doesn't even matter if it's morning or the middle of the night, I'm not really "waking up the next day," because I'm waking up every couple of hours, at least. I'm so tired, I would give anything to get more sleep. I'm *so exhausted.*

But the interview is really important, and I don't want to screw it up because I look tired or like I can't handle it. I manage to squeeze in a nap just before ,and then I have a quick cup of coffee and a sandwich and get ready. I still can't fit into my old, nice clothes, so I put on some black stretchy pants, which are the most professional bottoms I can fit into without feeling sore, and a matching black button-down shirt.

Dianne is going to help Molly watch Tommy, and I tell them everything they need to do and Dianne laughs and says not to worry, she remembers what to do, it hasn't been *that* long since she had Molly. I'm so grateful for them.

When I enter the daycare, I swear it smells like animal crackers. I check in with the receptionist, and she calls the person who's doing my interview to let her know I'm here. A stately-looking woman who tells me to call her "Mrs. Samson" comes into the room and tells me to follow her.

On the way to her office, she shows me around a bit. There are multiple rooms with soft-looking curtains separating them, and when I look inside them, there are a bunch of cribs and also mats on the floor, with toys for them to play with. It's such a happy place, it makes me smile.

We get to her office and she signals for me to sit across the desk from her. She has my résumé and application in front of her. "Thank you for coming to this interview, Ms. Davis," she says.

"Of course. Thank you for considering me."

"We take things very seriously at this day care, so this interview is going to be mainly based on questions to see if you would fit in here," she says.

"Alright, I'm ready," I say confidently.

"How well do you deal with kids?"

The way she's talking to me makes me nervous. She's staring right into my eyes, like she's already decided that she doesn't think I can do this job before even interviewing me. I take a breath and tell her, "I absolutely love kids. I have a little sister, and I babysat her for three years straight, along with other kids around my neighborhood. There are a lot of references on my résumé." I smile. "I also have a son of my own. His name is Thomas."

"You have your own child?" She looks at my résumé again. "Aren't you only sixteen? How old is your child?"

My cheeks get hot. "Yes. I'm sixteen. My son is a couple of weeks old, and I-"

"You have a *newborn baby?*"

I nod and say, "I'm very responsible. I told you, I took care of my sister for years while my mom was working, and I'm a quick learner-"

She puts my résumé down and looks directly into my eyes. "Are you applying for this job because it provides a place for people to watch your child while you work?"

I shake my head quickly, even though she's right, that *is* the main reason I wanted to work here. "No, no," I say. "I mean, I need a job, yes, but I've always loved kids and I would be very honored to work here."

Mrs. Samson eyes me again. "I see." She stares at me for a minute, and then she gets an almost amused expression on her face. "Here's a question for you: when an adult comes to pick up a child, what do you do?"

"Well...I would probably ask them to show their ID, but as I'm applying for the job of only an assistant, I don't know if I'd be the one handling that."

She does not look impressed by my answer. *Shoot.* She continues to stare at me with a weird smile. "Are you comfortable changing diapers and cleaning up messes?"

"It's a dirty job but somebody's gotta do it." I laugh. "Sorry, that was a joke. Yes, I'm very comfortable with that."

Her smile disappears. "Could I see proof of your CPR certification and Red Cross babysitting skills?"

Thank God I brought those documents. My hands shaking, I take them out of my purse and hand them to her. She looks them over, squinting like she doesn't believe they're real, and then she places them down and looks at me again. "Tell me why we should hire you, Ms. Davis."

I take a deep breath. "I know a lot about kids from taking care of my sister, and now my baby. I work hard, and everyone knows me to be responsible. In my opinion, I've handled my teenage pregnancy very well. But most importantly, I just *love* kids. So it would be great to work somewhere where I get to be with them all the time."

She squints again, and then *finally* smiles. I smile too, in relief. "Well, Ms. Davis. Thank you for coming in," she says. "We'll get back to you by tomorrow."

I thank her and leave, feeling confused. I really can't tell what she's thinking. I could tell she disapproved of my age and being a new mother, but maybe she will actually think it's a good thing? I can't tell, all I know is that now I'm starting to get nervous, because I really want and need that job.

When I get home, Tommy is sleeping in his carseat in the living room while Dianne works on her computer. She tells me that he slept almost the whole time I was gone. *Figures.* She asks how the interview went, and as soon as I open my mouth, Tommy hears my voice, and he starts crying. I guess he realizes that his food is nearby. I sigh, and Dianne laughs and says this is what it was like with Molly, too, and that eventually the feedings will be stretched more apart and not to worry, things will get easier.

She offers to make me a sandwich and I thank her, thank God for her, I really don't know what I'm going to do when I leave here. I feed Tommy on the couch and he sucks away, hungrily.

Molly comes into the living room and says Tommy was really good, and then she asks me about the interview. I start to cry. I tell her what happened, and I guess it's just the exhaustion and feeling overwhelmed, and it's all just getting to me.

I decide to go upstairs and I ask Dianne to just leave the sandwich in the fridge. I'm really tired, and I want to just feed Tommy, change him, and then go to sleep.

I want to call Mom, I've been texting with her and sending photos, but I really want to see her on FaceTime or at least talk. I'm too tired, though, and I know I need to sleep as soon as Tommy falls asleep this time.

I wake up to Tommy crying and look at the clock, which says seven o'clock. Wow, I managed to get a whole two and a half hour stretch. I actually feel pretty good, it's the longest amount of sleep I've had since I had Tommy. I remember thinking it was hard to sleep when I was *pregnant.*

I start feeding him, and then I hear a knock at the door. It's Ian, and he brought me the sandwich Dianne made. I thank him and gulp it down while I feed Tommy. Ian sits on my desk chair and I tell him what happened with the job interview, and he tells me not to worry, that even if I don't get it, I will find something else. He's so sweet, and I wish I had the time and energy to really spend time with him and do fun things like we used to. I have to start trying to make time, even though I'm just so busy.

After Tommy eats and I burp him and change his diaper, he's still really fussy, and Ian says maybe it's his circumcision bothering him. He gets me the Tylenol and I give Tommy another dose. He spits up a few minutes later, so I have no idea how much he actually ingested. Ian takes him from me and does a really tight swaddle, and then he holds him and we sing to him. Molly comes in and joins in the singing. Eventually,

Tommy calms down. Thank God for their help.

When it's almost nine o'clock, we decide to all try to go to sleep. I feel really guilty when Tommy starts to cry again. It's not fair to them to always have to be up with a crying baby. Maybe I should offer Molly to move back into her room. I can tell both she and Ian don't want to help anymore. I ask Ian if he's sure that he wants to sleep in here tonight, and he says yes, that he wants to help.

It's another night of being up every two hours or less. He woke up at midnight, then again at two, then three, then at four-thirty, then at five forty-five, and now here we are. I'm so tired, I can barely see straight. I take Tommy downstairs so that hopefully Molly and Ian can sleep in. I put him in the car seat and make myself a bagel with cream cheese. He starts crying again, so I put it away and go to feed him on the couch in the living room. I'm starting to feel really irritable. *Will I ever get a moment to myself again? But this is what you wanted, Madison,* I remind myself. *You chose this.*

I must doze off while I'm feeding him, because when I wake up, Tommy's asleep on the breastfeeding pillow, and I can hear Ian, Molly, and Dianne in the kitchen. I crane my neck around to a clock. It's nearly eleven.

I take Tommy off my chest and position him safely in between two pillows on the couch, so that he can sleep comfortably and won't roll off. I go into the kitchen and finish making my bagel, feeling relieved when I take a bite.

"How was the sleeping situation with Tommy tonight?" Ian asks. "Must have been good, I didn't hear him crying all night long!"

"That's because when he'd start to cry I'd bring him downstairs so you guys didn't wake up," I say tiredly.

"You didn't have to do that," Molly says sternly. "We would help. That's why I moved into your room in the first place! So we can help! Right, Ian?"

He nods vehemently. "Of course. I already told her that."

"I don't want you guys to get no sleep because of me. Molly, you should just move back into your room."

"No, Mads, I just get grumpy when I'm tired, but really, I love helping you take care of Tommy," Molly says.

"Me, too!" Ian says. "I love babies, even when they cry."

I cross my arms and say, "Fine. But don't blame me when you get as sleep-deprived as I am."

"Madison, what's wrong?" Ian asks softly.

"She's still upset about the job interview, I think," Molly explains. "Even though I bet she'll get it."

Ian grins. "I'll bet ten dollars that she gets it!"

"Ten dollars? Seriously? *That's* all my and Tommy's future is riding on?"

I know I'm being a jerk right now, but I can't help it. I'm nervous and scared and depressed. I ask Molly if she can watch Tommy so I can shower, and she says yes, and then Ian says he's getting ready to leave for work, and he gives me a kiss. I think they understand that my bad mood is just because I'm tired and irritable.

I take my shower, and then I look at my phone, realizing I haven't checked it since yesterday. There's a voicemail from Mom, she's really concerned because she hasn't heard from me, and she wants me to call her. I call her back right away, and we FaceTime and I tell her what's been going on. She's really sweet and says she wishes she could be there to help me. She offers to let me come to Santa Barbara, and it's really tempting, but I tell her I have to stay here and try to get a job and get settled with an apartment.

Molly brings Tommy into the room and says he needs to be changed, and she's about to do it, but I do it instead, and she says she has to go to work but she can help more later. Dianne is out doing errands. I change Tommy and then he falls asleep. I know I should be trying to sleep, too, but there's just too much to do.

I go on Zillow to look around for apartments, and a notification pops up. It shows that there's a studio apartment for rent that's just a block away from the high school. The address is "429 Aurora Street." The rent is $800 each month, which would be totally okay if I got the job at the daycare. I look at the pictures. It's all one room, with only one room with actual walls, which is the bathroom. My heart deflates. It's a *studio* apartment, and even that is so expensive. At least I prepared to have to pay $1,000 each month. One day, hopefully I will be able to afford much more.

I call the realtor and ask when I can see it, and she makes an appointment for me for Monday. I hope I'll know about the job by then. But wait, didn't Mrs. Samson say that I'd know by *today?* Even if she didn't, I really can't take it any longer. I pick up my phone and call the daycare center.

"Hello, this is Madison Davis," I say to the receptionist. "I came in for an interview yesterday. Just wondering if there's any decision yet? I think Mrs. Samson said that you would let me know by today?"

"Hang on, let me transfer you," she says quickly, and after two minutes of holding music, I hear Mrs. Samson's voice. "Hello, Ms. Davis?"

"Yes, hi."

It's quiet. Before I'm about to check if I've lost connection, she says,

"Madison, you seem like a lovely young woman, but I'm afraid you don't have the level of experience we are looking for. Good luck in your search," and she hangs up.

I sit there, stunned. I knew I wouldn't get it, but I guess I still had hope. I look at Tommy, asleep in his co-sleeper, so innocent and peaceful, he has no idea about any of this. Just looking at him and knowing that I'm responsible for making money for him to have a good life and that I'm already failing is too much for me. I lie face down and bury my head into my pillow and cry my heart out. *What am I going to do now? What if I can never find a job? I should've been more prepared, I should've-*

My thoughts are interrupted by suddenly feeling someone's arms around me. I turn around and see that it's Ian. "What's wrong, Mads?"

"You owe me ten dollars," I say, crying harder.

He frowns. "Oh no, you didn't...get the job?"

I nod and he pulls me into his chest and I just cry and cry. "And I *needed* that job. There's not many more places that I can apply to, I mean, I need to work at a place where they can watch Tommy, I can't afford childcare or daycare, it's not in my budget...I don't know what I'm going to do now. I gave up my old job back at Roast and Drink with my stupid hopes that I'd get a *better* job, and even if I *tried* to get my job back, Molly took my place, and it wouldn't be enough money, anyway, it still just wouldn't work. Nothing's going to work. Everything is falling apart..."

I'm really bawling now, and Ian just holds me, and I think about how amazing he is and how I have no time to even spend with him anymore, and then I cry even harder, thinking he probably won't want to stay with me much longer. I mean, who in their right mind would want to be with someone like me in this situation?

It's weird that Tommy is sleeping through this, and at one point, Ian and I look over at him and start laughing, because he's sleeping through it all. He wakes up constantly, but right now, with all this noise, he sleeps? It's actually so funny, and I start laughing so hard, I can't stop. Ian laughs, too, and we just sit there like two crazy people, laughing.

We kiss and it feels so good, it really calms me down. Then Ian says he has to leave for work. We kiss again, and as he's leaving he says, "It's just one job, Mads. You'll find something, I just know it. Something even better."

He smiles and leaves. Whether he's right or not, the way he says it gives me hope. And right now, hope is exactly what I need.

♡ Tommy = 2 weeks old ♡

To-Do List
- postpartum checkup with Dr. Lippincott today
  ✱ ask about when my stomach will go down
- Tommy's appointment with Dr. Brown after Dr. Lippincott
  ↓

✱ check email

questions to ask!   → on demand
- how much/when to feed him
- when the umbilical stump will fall off
- when/how to sleep train
  → within the next   → 4 months
    week or so   old
✱ Tommy = 9 lbs
          20 1/2 inches

buy:
- pack of gauze   ✱ circumcision
- diapers/wipes   instructions:
- ointment   - ointment +
- bandages   a new bandage
- more Tylenol/   at every diaper change
  syringes   - Tylenol every 4-6 hours
                          if he seems like he's in pain

✱ start doing
tummy time, a
few mins. each
day, supervise,
increase time a
little each day
✱ no blankets/stuffed
animals/pillows
until Tommy is 1
year old, just a
mattress + swaddling

✱ restock diaper
  bag   ♡   ♡   ♡
              ♡

call Mom!

♡   Calm down,   ♡
                                 Mommy!
✱ job interview at "Sunshine   ♡
Street Day Care" 110 North
Ridge Avenue tomorrow   ♡
at 4pm   ✱ go see studio apartment
(bring résumé + CPR   "429 Aurora Street"
certification/Red Cross   on Monday
babysitting skills documents)   (rent = $800/month)

✱ look for more jobs

Chapter 39: Third Week of Life

"It actually looks okay," I say to the real estate agent as I look around the studio apartment. It's in a building complex just a block away from the school, and it's $200 less than what I budgeted for, but I'm nervous about getting it because I still don't have a job. August 22nd is my deadline to be moved into the new place, because it's the first day of school. Even though I knew I had to do this, for some stupid reason I felt that I could wait until *after* I had Tommy, but I should totally have done it *before*.

Dianne is watching Tommy again, which makes it so much easier, but I really feel bad about how much I'm relying on her and Ian and Molly. I know they would never say anything, but I'm sure it's hard for them, and I know I can't do this much longer. Still, the fact that I could go look at this place without having to get the diaper bag organized and lug the car seat and Tommy around is just unbelievable. I feel almost like I'm naked, just being able to drive somewhere and be there by myself. It's a weird feeling. The only annoying thing is that my boobs are starting to leak when I go even an hour without feeding him. I have so much milk, and now I have to wear nursing pads in my bra to absorb the milk. I keep thinking that I need to get home, because I need to be there to feed him.

It was another rough couple of nights, and it didn't help that I was worrying about the job situation. Every time Tommy fell asleep, I was up, and then when I would finally fall asleep, he would wake up. I may have gotten only three or four hours of sleep altogether. I read online that a bedtime routine could help, so I've decided I'm going to start one: at seven o'clock, I will bathe him, then I will read him a children's bedtime book that Mom saved from when *I* was a baby, called *"Goodnight, Moon,"* then I will do a little massage on him with baby lotion, then I'll put him in pajamas, and then I'll breastfeed him until he falls asleep. Since he's only three weeks old, he's still supposed to wake up for a feeding every two to three hours, but this will change once he's around four months and he can go longer in between feedings.

On top of everything else, I think something is wrong with my left breast. It's really red and tender to the touch. I think it might be a clogged duct, which is what the nurses and Dr. Lippincott warned me about. A few times in the middle of the night, Tommy fell asleep while he was on the right breast, and I didn't switch him over to the left, I just let him go to sleep because I was so desperate to try to get back to sleep myself. I remember the nurse said you have to drain the breast completely because

408

the hind milk is very thick and it can get backed up and cause a clogged duct. Now that breast is really huge and painful, and even when Tommy eats, it doesn't go down. I'm going to call Dr. Lippincott after I look at this apartment.

The real estate agent, Celia, shows me around. The more I look, the more I realize that it isn't that great, it's kind of dirty and needs a lot of cleaning. It's all one room, and it's really small. There's a small area for the kitchen, and the bedroom and living room will have to be one room. There's a tiny little bathroom with a small shower, and it has a door so at least there's privacy for that if I have someone over.

I try to work out the space arrangements in my mind. My "bedroom" area would be next to the kitchen, where the tile ends. Tommy's crib would be diagonal from *my* bed, and the couch and coffee table would go in the middle, and that's where I would eat. It'll be cramped, but I've seriously looked all over Zillow, typed in every keyword possible, and there's very slim pickings.

"So what are the costs of this place again?" I ask Celia.

"$1,000 deposit," she says. *Deposit? I didn't even know you needed to leave a deposit. Ugh.* "Then it's $800 each month, plus utilities, which would run around $100 a month, depending on how much water and electricity you use."

I try to picture myself living here for the next two years, before I hopefully go off to Harvard. Maybe if I don't get a job in time, I can use some of the child support from Leo's parents, but I don't want to do that. Maybe I could ask Mom for a loan?

I shake my head. *No, Madison. You are the one who has to make the money. You can't rely on other people. You have to try to get a job as soon as possible.*

"Do you have other people interested in this apartment?" I ask. "Like, how quickly am I going to have to take it if I want it?"

"There are a couple of other people who said they were interested, so I would suggest applying as soon as possible," she says. "We're looking for someone to move in by September 1st."

Seriously? I can't believe anyone who wasn't in my situation would want a place like this, I think to myself.

Celia hands me an application and says that I can scan it and email it to her, and she will send it to the owner of the building to review it. As I'm leaving, she smiles at me and says, "I like you. You seem like a very responsible young woman, even with a baby at your age. Good luck."

I go downstairs and fill out the application in my car before I drive home, because I know that I won't have time once I get back, and Tommy needs to be fed and changed, and it's hard to focus with all that. Then I scan the papers using my phone and send them to Celia.

Then I call Dr. Lippincott and I tell her what's happening, and she asks if it looks red on the skin around it, and I check and it does. She says she wants to prescribe antibiotics to prevent an infection that might be starting. She says they might upset my stomach, so take them with food. *I can't believe this, as if things weren't hard enough.* She tells me to hang in there and that a lot of women get this, but if it gets to be too much, I can stop breastfeeding. That really isn't what I want to do, because it's good for me and Tommy and it saves a lot of money. She tells me she will call in the prescription to the local pharmacy, the one I haven't been to since I was buying the pregnancy test. *Great, another thing to do today.*

When I get home, Tommy is screaming, and Dianne says she's been trying to calm him down, but she thinks he's hungry. I rush to drop everything and sit on the couch and lift my shirt, and he grabs at me and chomps down on my left breast. *Ouch!* It's way too sore, so I immediately switch him to the right one. I tell Dianne about Dr. Lippincott and the antibiotics, and she tells me that she had mastitis because she had a clogged duct that didn't get better, and she ended up getting a fever and she was really sick, so it's good that I'm getting the antibiotics. She says that from now on, I should alternate breasts for each feeding and that way I can fully drain each breast, and my breasts will adapt to this way of feeding. I'm happy to have a plan, because the pain is getting worse and worse.

All I want to do is nap, but I have to go to Babies R' Us to get a few things, and I have to take Tommy with me this time, because Dianne has to run some errands, too.

Of course, Tommy falls asleep while he's eating and so I don't even burp him, I just put him in the car seat and take him to the car. Then I realize that I forgot the diaper bag, so I quickly run in to get it, and I hope it's stocked up. He sleeps the whole car ride, but of course once I get to Babies R' Us, he starts screaming. I change his diaper in the car and burp him and he spits up, so I have to change his clothes. Before I even get in the store, I'm exhausted and sweating and my breast is really hurting now.

I go inside and put the car seat in a shopping cart, and I hope Tommy falls asleep. He cries as I'm walking through the aisles, and I try to go as fast as I can. I want to get a breast pump so that I can store milk and then not worry about feeding him in class. I also need more diapers and wipes, I can't believe how quickly I go through them. I also get some baby shampoo for his baths, and some more Tylenol, because I'm already almost out.

The total is close to a hundred dollars. I can't believe it. *Why does everything have to be so expensive?* I sigh and reach into my wallet, pulling out my debit card, and then the cashier loads my stuff into two shopping bags. I can tell that the cashier feels sorry for me, because Tommy is crying and I have so much to carry. I remember going shopping with my mom when Josie was a baby, and how easy it seemed. I wonder if Mom ever felt like this.

The whole car ride, Tommy keeps crying and crying. I feel so bad that I can't comfort him, but I just want to get everything done and get home. I try to talk over his cries to calm him down, but he just screams louder.

When I pull up in front of the pharmacy, I just get in the back seat and try to feed him again. I really want to give him my left breast, but it just hurts too much. I cannot wait to get the antibiotics, I'm now really worried that I'm getting an infection.

It's so weird to walk into the pharmacy, I haven't been inside since I was here getting the pregnancy test. And now I *have* the baby in my hands. It's so surreal.

I go to the pharmacist's window, and she says I have to wait a few minutes. Thankfully, Tommy is quiet now, but the car seat is heavy so I put it down on the floor. I just linger by the counter, and then suddenly I notice a couple laughing by the candy counter. Oh my God, it's Leo and Dina. I really, *really* don't want to see them.

No such luck, though. Dina sees me and rushes over and I see Leo watching her and then looking in disgust. *Oh no, I just can't handle this right now.*

"Oh my God, so cute! This is your baby? Is it a boy or a girl?" she gushes.

I stammer for a second, looking at Leo, who has turned away. Obviously, he doesn't want me to tell Dina that it's his, and honestly, I don't want to say anything, I just want to get out of here.

Honestly, I feel kind of sorry for her that she's with Leo. Maybe it's a good thing that she never went to our school, because she doesn't know that I had a baby or that it was with Leo. She goes to a school just outside of Redford, a private school or something. She met Leo at the community center, but there are tons of people who go there and I guess the gossip about me didn't go around there.

I take a breath and paste on a smile. "A boy. His name's Thomas, but I call him Tommy," I say.

"*Sooo* cute," Dina says, sighing. Then she turns back to Leo and calls out, "Leo, isn't he cute?"

Leo walks away, pretending to look at something in one of the aisles. Dina looks at me closely, and then realization floods to her face.

"Wait a minute! Madison, right? You worked at Roast and Drink? I used to see you there sometimes, but I didn't know you were pregnant!"

I smile. Dina actually seems really nice. Maybe in an alternate universe where none of this happened, we would've been friends.

"Yes, but actually, I stopped working there. I'm looking for a job where I can make more money, because of, well, because of...him," I say and look at Tommy.

"Have you tried Food Direct? The food delivery service?" Dina asks excitedly. "I work there after school. They're so busy, my manager mentioned that they were looking for people. They pay really well and you get tips. Maybe you should check it out?"

Hm. That's actually something I hadn't thought about, but it might be a really good idea. I could take Tommy in the car with me while I work.

"That sounds great," I say. "But I doubt I'll get an interview."

"I can mention you to my manager. He's looking for someone to hire as soon as possible. Do you want me to?"

I nod. "Thank you, that would actually be really, um, good. Thank you, seriously. It's Dina, right?"

She nods happily and pulls out her phone. "Here, give me your number and I'll text you after I speak to him."

I give her my number, and then she pats Tommy on the head and says how cute he is again and leaves to go look for Leo, just as the pharmacist has my order ready.

Back in the car, I realize that I'm shaking. That was really stressful seeing Leo and Dina, even though Dina was nice. It's funny how the people around Leo are so nice, but he is such a jerk himself. His mother texts me every few days to see how I'm doing, and she and Leo's dad have come by a few times to see Leo. We've worked out a schedule where they usually come by on Sunday afternoons for about an hour. They're always polite and respectful and don't ask a lot of questions, they just want to sit and hold and play with Tommy. One of the times, we did tummy time together and they loved it. They are really nice people, Mom was right. They always ask me if I need anything, but I really don't want to ask for anything from them, they are already giving so much with the payments for Tommy. Mrs. Schmitz has offered to babysit when I have tests or things at school when I can't have Tommy with me, and I said that I would probably say yes to that, and she was happy. It's nuts that Leo is her son. How did he turn out to be so horrible with such a nice mother?

Once I'm home, I take my first dose of the antibiotics right away with a piece of bread and some water. I head up to bed, feed Tommy, burp him, change him, and then get into bed.

As I'm falling asleep, I get a text from the real estate agent telling me that the owner checked out my references and says I'm too young to rent, and they need someone who is an adult to co-sign, which means that she has to pay the rent if I fail to. I didn't even think about this. I call Mom, and when I hear her voice, I start crying. It's just too much to take everything that's going on. I tell her about what's going on with my breasts and the antibiotics, and now the apartment. But she says that she will co-sign, and when she does that, they will rent it to me. I feel guilty, but I also know that I need her help or I won't be able to find any place. Thank God she's willing to help me. I tell her that I will not be asking her to pay anything, and I have enough to cover it on my own. She says she isn't worried about it, and she's proud of me for taking the steps to do all of this. I give her the real estate agent's info and she says she'll call, and I tell her that I'll call her later and send more pictures of Tommy, and then we hang up.

Just before I fall asleep, I get a text from Dina, saying that she talked to her manager and he says that he wants me to come in for an interview tomorrow night at five-thirty. I text Dianne and ask her if she can watch Tommy again, and she texts back that she can and that she's excited about the new job prospect. So am I. I really hope it works out. I fall asleep thinking about how ironic that would be if I get the job all because of Leo's girlfriend.

<>

The interview actually goes really well. My stomach has gone down a lot, and so I'm able to squeeze into one of my old outfits that makes me look sort of professional. The manager is really nice, his name is Mr. Lopez, and he says that they are desperate for new employees because they are really busy and they have expanded the areas they are delivering to.

He tells me that he loves Dina and he would hire anyone she recommends. He looks at my résumé and asks for my driver's license and makes a copy. I tell him that I know my way around town very well. He tells me that he needs to check a few things and will get back to me within the next week. I leave, in disbelief about how *easy* that was. Things are finally looking up. My breast is starting to feel better, too.

Back at home, Tommy is crying, and Molly is with Dianne, trying to sing to him and calm him down. I take him and feed him, and tell them about the potential job. Then I offer Dianne and Molly some money for watching Tommy and they laugh me off, but I'm serious, I feel so guilty.

Tommy falls asleep after a few minutes, so I go upstairs to change him and try to sleep a little. I end up on my phone to catch up with my texts and emails. The real estate agent wrote to say they accepted me now that Mom co-signed. I also have a few sweet texts from Ian, and we tell each other that we miss each other and that hopefully soon we can watch TV again or go for a walk. I text with Mom a bit, and then I crash.

I wake up after what feels like a long time, but I see on the clock that it's only been an hour. It's still early, it's only eight o'clock. I decide to do the bedtime routine. I start with the bath, which Tommy seems to love. I love shampooing his little fluff of hair. He coos softly, and then out of the blue, the belly button stump just falls off. I grab it and place it on the edge of the tub to dry. I want to save it. His belly button looks so cute and fresh now. I feel a bit sad, looking at the stump. It's like that was the last connection to him being inside of me.

Afterwards, I do the lotion and the story, and it's actually really nice. I feel like it relaxes me as much as it relaxes him. I love reading to him, even though I know he can't understand it yet. Still, I read online that it's good to start reading to babies early, because they'll grow up loving books.

Sure enough, he falls asleep, and I put him in his little co-sleeper and then try to go to sleep myself. I want to shower, but I know that I need to take advantage of him falling asleep. I'll shower tomorrow. Ian and Molly aren't here yet and I text them and tell them that if they want to stay in their own rooms tonight, I completely understand and want them to get some sleep. Honestly, I also don't want them to come in and interrupt *my* sleep and wake up Tommy.

As I'm falling asleep, I think about how weird it is that Leo's girlfriend is actually really *nice*. I wasn't expecting that, I just assumed she would be a jerk because she's with Leo. Then again, *I'm* not a jerk and I was with him. Now I actually feel sorry for her, and I hope that she doesn't get hurt the same way I did. I wonder if she'll ever know that Tommy is Leo's baby. He's obviously not changing his mind about wanting nothing to do with Tommy. But honestly? I'm starting to think that it's better this way. I'm happy with it being just me and Tommy. Me and Tommy against the world.

Tommy = 3 weeks old!!!

To-Do List
- look at 429 Aurora Street today (rent = $800/month)
  - * fill out application
- call Dr. Lippincott about my   + $1,000 deposit
  left breast

*alternate breasts at each feeding!!

- go to Babies R' Us ➔ ☆ go to pharmacy to pick
  buy: up antibiotics
  - breast pump   - take them twice a day
  - milk bags for breast pump   for a week with food
  - diapers/wipes
  - shampoo   ☆ start a bedtime routine
  - Tylenol   with Tommy
                              ☆ restock diaper bag
- call Mom

☆ Food Direct interview
  tomorrow at 5:30pm   ➔ call Dina to
  (print out another copy of   thank her for getting
  my résumé)   me the interview

- call real estate agent to
  confirm co-signing
- use child support to put down
  deposit?

☆ schedule Tommy's 1-month check-up

                                   Tommy's
                                   belly
                                   button!!

- look into other jobs in case I don't
  get the job at Food Direct?

415

Chapter 40: Fourth Week of Life -- One Month Old

"Could I speak with Madison Davis, please?" Mr. Lopez asks on the other end of the phone. I'm finally hearing back from Food Direct after about a week. I had given up because I didn't hear anything, and I've been looking into other jobs, but this was the one that I really wanted.

"Yes, this is she," I say.

"Great news! You got the job. There are flexible hours and shifts, and it's sixteen dollars an hour, plus tips. We would like you to start reporting to work on August fifth, training takes about an hour, and then you can start, sound good?"

It's like my mind can't comprehend what he's saying. "Um, what?"

"I'm sorry, couldn't you hear me?" he asks.

I...got the job? I got the job? *I got the job!!*

"Yes, sorry, thank you so much! And yes, it sounds good. So, does this mean that I get to pick my own hours?" I ask excitedly.

"Yes, but typically we would like our employees to work at least twenty hours a week. You can decide how to break it up."

"I can work four hours every weekday. Is it okay if I work from four to eight?" I ask. It doesn't even matter that I won't be getting paid per hour as much as I would like, because I'll get tips. *This is amazing!*

"Yes, that's great. So, please be at our main location for an hour of training at three on Monday August fifth," he says.

"Okay, I'll be there right at three! Thank you, Mr. Lopez, thank you! Goodbye!"

I hang up and jump up and down. Ouch, that hurt, I'm still a bit sore down there. But I got the job! I still can't help but think of how ironic it is that I got the job because of Dina, my ex's girlfriend. Nevertheless, *I got the job!*

"Tommy, did you hear that? Mommy got the job! Mommy got the job!" I sing out, and he squeals, but in an annoyed way. He needs to eat, so I latch him on, grinning ear to ear. I'm so glad that I got this job, because I also officially got the studio apartment! I'm putting my deposit down soon, I collect the keys the week after I start work, and then it's mine. I can move in just in time for school to start.

Ugh. School is starting up again really soon. And I'm going to have to bring Tommy. The last time I saw everyone, I was pregnant, and now I have an actual *baby.* I can already imagine the stares I'm going to get.

I've pretty much finished the antibiotics, and my left breast feels normal again. I'm alternating breasts for feedings now like Dianne suggested, so Tommy drains one breast completely each time, and it's feeling much better.

I can't believe it, but Tommy's already going to be a month old at the end of the week. Tomorrow is his one-month check-up and he's due for vaccines, which I'm not looking forward to. He will squirm and scream, and I hate seeing him in pain, just like with the circumcision, but I know it's what he needs for his well-being. I'm a little nervous, though, because Dianne and Molly aren't coming this time. Molly is working and Dianne has a meeting, and I know that I have to start doing these things on my own now, and I will, but it's a little scary.

The one thing that's really bothering me that I'm trying not to think about is that Ian is leaving to go back to college in a few days. He has to settle into his dorm and be there for his sophomore year orientation and for his prep classes. So we only have a few days left together. I knew this day was coming, and we've talked about how we can still text and FaceTime and he will come visit whenever he can, but things are going to be so sad without him here. When he first told me this, I thought he was breaking up with me, but he said that he wants to do long distance, which makes me so happy, even though I'm still going to miss him so much. In a way, the timing is good, though, because I'm so busy with Tommy that I don't really have time to focus on Ian, and I think that it will get easier as Tommy gets a bit older.

As if he can sense that I'm thinking about him, Ian comes downstairs, kisses me on the forehead, and grins at me. "What?" I ask, blushing. I'm feeding Tommy, and even though I've become less self-conscious about it in front of Ian, it still feels a bit weird, like I'm just sitting there naked in front of him.

"You know I'm leaving in a few days, right?"

I groan. "Don't remind me."

"No, your line is, 'yes, and I'm very sad about it,'" he says, and I laugh and play along, rolling my eyes and saying it.

He grins. "Well, I wanted to take you out for dinner tonight."

"Really? Where?" I ask, surprised. We haven't ever gone out for dinner. I don't even think we've actually ever been on a real "date." How sad is that?

"I think we should go to that new Italian restaurant that opened up a few blocks away," he tells me. "It's called 'Taste in Italy' or something."

"Oh, yeah, that's perfect!" I say excitedly, burping Tommy.

"So then, be ready at seven tonight."

"Okay, yes, I'm excited! Oh, wait I have to find someone to watch-"

"Already checked with Molly and my sister, they're good to

babysit." He smiles. "Okay, see you later, I'm going in for my last work shift. I'm sad to leave the job, actually, it's been fun. Especially the night we went there when you were still pregnant."

"I loved that so much," I say, smiling back. "I'm so glad you talked me into that. Doesn't it seem like it was a hundred years ago?"

He nods, kisses me on the forehead, pats Tommy's head, and leaves.

Then I go upstairs with Tommy, and see Molly scrolling on her computer. "So, you're watching Tommy tonight? Thank you, Molly. I really appreciate it."

"Mom and I are excited," she says, and waves at Tommy, grinning. "He's getting cuter by the minute." I tell her again all the babysitting instructions for Tommy, even though she knows them. She smiles. "Don't worry, I'll make sure he's okay. Can I hold him?" she asks, and I pass him to her. He's fast asleep. *Of course. So he'll be up all night.*

While he naps in his little bed, I scour my closet for something, anything *remotely* nice to wear. My old clothes are still a bit snug on me. I manage to fit into a pair of nice dark jeans, and all I want is to wear my favorite wine-colored top that ties in the back in a criss-cross pattern, but my body is just not working with it right now. If I wore it, it would make me look like I was still pregnant.

I eventually settle on a cute black tank top that hides my stomach fat pretty well, and it won't show milk stains if I leak. I decide to take a nap while Tommy sleeps. I manage to get a couple of hours. After feeding and changing him, I ask Molly to do tummy time with him while I shower. Afterwards, she braids my hair and then blow dries it so it'll be curly with lots of volume later tonight. For a second, I worry about having braids in my hair, but then I tell myself that I'm a *mother* now. I have to be more mature. I can't freak out over a hairstyle anymore.

I guess Molly sees my facial expression but misinterprets it, because she says, "You're sad that he's leaving, huh?" she asks softly.

I decide not to get into the whole thing about the braids and how they remind me of my dad's death. I nod and she says she's sad, too. We both agree that we can't believe how quickly the summer went by.

"What if he meets someone else, you know, at college?" I ask Molly. I'm worried that Ian will find someone better than me. Someone who doesn't have a baby. This has been a fear of mine from the beginning, but it's more real now that he's leaving.

"Trust me, I know Ian, and one thing he isn't is noncommittal. Once he's with you, he's *with* you," she says.

As we talk, poor Tommy is grunting away on the floor, doing his tummy time. I feel so bad for him, but the doctor said he has to do it, and

I know it's building his strength. I cringe everytime he cries and grunts, though.

"So guess what? I got the job at Food Direct, that delivery service for food," I tell her. "Leo's girlfriend actually helped me get it, can you believe that?"

"Um, excuse me, Mads! What? You didn't tell me any of this! Start from the beginning!"

I realize that I haven't even had time to tell her what happened, I'm always so busy with Tommy, and I also didn't know if I would get the job, so I just didn't bother. I tell her all about what happened and then Tommy starts really crying, and it's been long enough so I pick him up and reward him by feeding him. He latches on hungrily, and Molly starts laughing. "Mads, you're such a good mommy, I can't believe it."

I smile, and then she says, "Oh, I keep forgetting to show you this!" and she gets her camera and brings it over. "I was going through my pictures, and there's one that I took one night of you and Ian watching TV. You were eating your cheese puffs, and I thought it was really cute that you had the bowl resting on your stomach. Ian had his arm around you, and you both looked so happy. You didn't see me, I was really quiet."

She shows me the picture, and I can't believe how nice it is. Something about the lighting, it almost looks black and white. It's kind of a shot from the side, but you can see that we both have smiles on our faces, and it just looks so...peaceful.

"Molly, you are seriously an *amazing* photographer," I say. "I really think you could do this for an actual career. I love it."

She grins. "I'm going to print it out for you."

Suddenly, I have a thought. "Can you make it bigger? I want to get a frame and give it to Ian for a going-away gift."

"Oh my God, that's such a good idea. He'll love it!" she exclaims. "I'll definitely do it tomorrow. I have to go to work now, but I'll be home in time to help you get ready for tonight." She winks, and Tommy starts grunting. It's the grunt that he makes when he's pooping. Molly laughs and then leaves.

"Are you pooping?" I squeal at him. He's so adorable, and even though it's all so hard, I just love him so much. It's the kind of love that starts in your chest and then works its way through your whole body, so that it's there forever. It'll never leave. This is a love I get to keep. He won't leave me, not like Dad or Leo. And I will *always* love him, no matter what he does.

Then a thought pops into my head, one I haven't thought of before. *What if Tommy gets a girl pregnant when he's a teenager?*

I have to talk to him when he's old enough to understand. I have to make sure that he knows it wasn't okay to do what I did when I was so young. But I have to make sure that he never thinks of himself as a mistake. It's going to be hard.

I shake my head hopelessly. I'm not ready. I'm *still* not ready to be a mom, even though I am one. I feel like I'm just faking it, and barely doing it right. And the scary thing is that it's easy now, when he's just a baby and only needs a few basic things, but what will I do as it gets harder? I'll have to teach him life lessons, and I haven't exactly set a good example.

I think of Mom and how she must feel knowing that after all the things she did right, I still ended up doing what I did. I know she loves Tommy now, but I'm sure a part of her is still really sad and disappointed that he came about the way he did. She would never say anything to me, but I'm sure that's how she feels.

...October 4th, 2018...

After I decided that I was being stupid and I should just have sex with Leo, I got out of bed and closed my curtains tight, and then we eased back onto my bed. I just prayed and prayed that Josie wouldn't wake up and come into my room. Sometimes she had nightmares, and I had no idea what I'd do if she came in.

"Leo, um, maybe we should use, you know, a condom, if we're going to... do...this?" I said. "Do you...have one?"

"No. It's fine. You won't get pregnant. I swear, I won't let it happen, I know what to do, it's fine. I'll be very careful."

After he said that, I felt a little better. Of course he was right. I told myself to just stop worrying and try to enjoy it. A nagging voice in my head wanted to stop me from doing it, but I blocked that voice out. I remember shutting my eyes tightly while we did it, hoping the pain wouldn't be too bad. Hoping it would make Leo happy and that we'd be closer afterwards. It was kind of painful, but it was over so fast, and I didn't even really know if he actually...finished.

...

I push the memory out of my head. I really, truly don't want to think about it anymore because my regrets make me feel guilty. I love Tommy so much and I don't want to associate him with being a mistake, ever.

As if he senses what I'm thinking, Tommy starts crying. I pick up his rubber duck and sing to him, "Who likes his duck? You do, you do!" He kicks his legs and stops crying, looking at me with interest.

420

"I'm your mommy, yes, I am," I say as I move him to the changing table. He pooped again, I can smell it. He reaches out and grabs my hair and he kicks his little legs as I try and change his diaper.

"Stop that," I say playfully. It's so funny how babies flail about, they really don't have control at this age. Some of his poop flies onto me and I realize I'm going to have to take a shower again. *Ugh.* I really want to nap again before I go out with Ian.

But there's no time for a nap. No one is home to watch Tommy, and I take him into the bathroom with me and put him in his car seat so I can shower again and wash off the poop. He cries and screams the whole time. I try to calm him down afterwards, but he just keeps fussing and it makes me wonder if he actually is colicky. I'm going to tell Molly and Dianne to just try and keep him awake till I'm home so I can do the bedtime routine. Maybe if he goes to bed later, he'll sleep in later, and then I can sleep in with him tomorrow, too. I need more sleep.

He finally calms down while I feed him again. I really understand now why mothers describe themselves as cows or milk machines.

Molly comes home in the middle of it and she starts doing my makeup while I feed him. I urge her to put a lot of concealer under my eyes, and she says that my under eye bags really aren't that bad, but I don't believe her.

She does the rest of my makeup and finishes with a quick swipe of lip gloss. I blott it so it doesn't look too strong, and then I latch off Tommy, who's fallen asleep, making cute little grunting noises. Then I look in the mirror. Molly did an amazing job. My hair is bouncy and curly, and I don't look tired, I look better than I have in months.

I hug Molly and thank her. I get dressed and take one last look in the mirror. Ian told me to meet him outside at six-thirty. I glance at the clock, it's 6:25.

"You're gorgeous!" Molly exclaims. "Now go!" She takes Tommy from me and starts singing to him and rocking him.

"If Tommy needs to eat, there's a bottle in the fridge, I pumped it, it's around three ounces, but he might not drink the whole thing. Tell Dianne this, too, and if *anything* is wrong, anything in the slightest, please just call me, and-"

"Mads, everything's going to be fine. Take this night to have some fun and relax."

When I get downstairs, Dianne is there and she tells me to have a great time and not to worry. She opens the front door for me, and then I see Ian standing there on the porch, waiting for me. He looks so gorgeous, and I realize that I haven't really even *looked* at him in a while.

We start walking down the path to the driveway, and all of a sudden

I see a carriage and horses. No, it's not a dream. It's really one of those old-fashioned carriages drawn by horses that you see in the movies. Redford has a cute place by the park where you can rent them, and the driver will take you anywhere you want to go in town. I remember that Dad took Mom in one once, for one of their anniversaries, but I never thought that *I'd* get to go in one. They're expensive.

I can't even speak, I'm so surprised. I just stare at it and then look at Ian, who's smiling a huge smile. "Are you...are you serious?" I manage to croak out.

He nods and takes my hand, and we start to walk towards it. "I wanted our last night to be special," he says.

My eyes tear up, and then I realize that he just said *our last night.* *Oh no.* I look at him and he laughs. "I don't mean it's our last night forever, but I mean for a while, until we can see each other again. That's all."

He helps me get into the carriage. There's a white satin seat with a blanket, and the driver takes our picture with Ian's phone. I'm speechless, I just can't stop smiling and giggling. Ian laughs too, and tells the driver that we can go.

We start to go, and I hear Dianne and Molly screaming, "Have fun!" and I look at the front door and realize that they've been standing there, Molly holding Tommy, watching the whole thing. They are laughing and waving. They must have known that he was planning this. I'm so surprised that they could keep this secret.

"Ian, I don't even know what to say. This is the nicest thing anyone has ever done for me," I say, cuddling into him, tears welling up in my eyes.

He kisses me. "You deserve it and so much more, Madison," he says. "And by the way, you look gorgeous."

We hold hands and look out at the street, and the people we pass who are walking and in cars turn to look at us. I'm usually the one looking with envy at the people in these carriages. Now, it's me. *Boy, would I love to have Leo see me like this,* I think. Then I push the thought away, I don't want anything negative coming into my head. This is too special.

I snuggle into Ian. "I feel like I haven't *really* seen you for so long," I say.

"Wait, what was your name again?" he asks, pretending to be confused, and I laugh and lie against him with my head on his chest.

He tilts my chin up so we can kiss again, and I just breathe him in. I want this to last forever. I really feel like I'm in a fairy tale.

We pull up to the restaurant, and the driver gets out and helps us out of the carriage. We thank him and Ian pays him, and then we go inside.

"Our reservation is under 'Katz'," he says to the hostess, and she nods and takes us to a beautiful, secluded table for two on the patio, which has flowers and candles everywhere. It's packed, but our table is off to the side and it's kind of private.

"Drinks to start?" a waiter asks, and he hands us menus.

"Water, please," I say, and Ian nods. The waiter walks off briskly.

Ian takes my hand across the table. "How are you feeling?"

"Amazing."

He laughs. "Good. I hope you're not too tired."

"Oh no, do I look tired?" I think of how much concealer Molly put on me, but I guess I still have the dark circles.

"No, not at all. You look great, Mads. I just know you've been getting no sleep." He smiles. "Don't worry, I won't have you back too late tonight."

"I'm not worried at all."

We look at the menus and order, and then I tell him about the new job at Food Direct, and he's happy for me. It feels so good to be with him like this. I fantasize that we're married and out for a date night, and our baby is at home with a babysitter.

"So, we should talk about how we can try to make the long-distance thing work," he says, interrupting my fantasy. "I'm going to come in for Christmas, and possibly for Thanksgiving, too."

"Okay, but just warning you ahead of time, my apartment's hardly big enough for me and Tommy. You can stay with me, and I would love that, but it might be really cramped in there."

"We can see. I can always stay with my sister. We can play it by ear."

I picture the apartment and how small it is, and how there's no way he will want to stay with me. Then I picture his life at college, and how many girls there are there, free and clear with their whole futures ahead of them, not tied down with a baby.

"What's wrong, Mads?" he asks.

I shake my head. "Ian, I hope you're not just doing this because you feel like you *have* to, to avoid making me upset. You know, you don't *have* to be with me."

"What? Why are you saying this, Madison?" he says, confused.

"I don't know, I guess I thought that you would break up with me once I had Tommy. And I wouldn't blame you. I mean, you aren't even twenty, and you shouldn't have to be with someone in this situation...you-"

"I *want* to be with you, though," he says. "Why don't you understand that?"

Now I'm almost annoyed with him. "Is it because you feel sorry for me?" I hate myself for going there, but I can't help it. I need to know the truth.

"What? No! Madison, why would you-?"

"Because you're a nice guy. Everyone says you're so nice, and it's true. So obviously you're too nice to break up with me."

"Madison, why are you doing this? Look around. Would I take you to this restaurant? Would I plan the horse and carriage? Why would I do *any* of it if I was just trying to be *nice?*"

I shake my head and the tears start. "I don't know. I don't *know*. But if you're going to end it, just do it. I can't take any more surprises." I start bawling. Everyone turns to look, the waiter comes and leaves a box of tissues on the table. Ian gets up and comes over to me and hugs me.

"Madison, I'm in *love* with you. Don't you know that by now?"

"Why? *Why are you in love with me?*"

"Do I really have to name every reason?" he sighs, and I look up and we laugh, and he hands me a tissue and I blow my nose. My makeup is for sure ruined, and I'm *so* embarrassed. Why on earth did I do this now, here, at this amazing restaurant, on this amazing night? *What on earth is wrong with me?*

Ian sits back down and says, "Mads, you're one of the sweetest people I've ever met. You're so strong and brave. You care so much about everything, you put your heart into whatever you're doing. You were faced with a huge challenge and look at you now, you're *doing* it. You're an amazing mom to Tommy. You're smart, beautiful...should I keep going?"

I nod and start to smile, and he laughs but then gets serious again. "Listen. I'm trying to look at it from your point of view, okay? I get it. I get why you're feeling the way that you are. But it's really making me feel bad, to be honest. I mean, we've been together for a long time now! Since May! Don't you feel the same way about *me?* Is this some weird plan of *yours* to break up with *me?*"

"No, of course not!" I exclaim. "You're kidding, right? Do you know how upset I'd be if we broke up?" My eyes start filling up again, but this time I manage to control it, I really don't want people to keep looking over. I whisper, "I just want to make sure that you're...happy. That this is what you want."

"It is," he says strongly. "I wouldn't be here if I wasn't committed to this." He shakes his head. "It worries me that you have such low self-esteem. Look in the mirror sometimes, Madison! You're the most gorgeous person, inside and out. You're capable of doing anything. Honestly, I'm the one who should be scared that *I'm* not good enough for you."

"I seriously think you should be locked up in a mental facility," I say, and we both start laughing. I can just imagine what the other people in the restaurant think of us.

Ian laughs again. "You realize that we're 'fighting,' yet we're both telling each other how amazing each other is."

I laugh, feeling lighter. "Let's talk about something else." I grin. "How about we work out a schedule for calling each other? Every Sunday morning, every Friday night, and sometime in the middle of the week? And we'll text all the time, okay?"

"No way, I need to hear from you more!" he says playfully.

Suddenly, as I look at him across the table, just smiling at me, I remember what my dad wrote to me in that scrapbook, about people who will get to know me and love me for *me*. He would've loved Ian.

"You know, my dad would have loved to meet you," I say, smiling.

Ian smiles back. "I would have loved to meet him, too."

Now I feel like I'm going to cry again, but thankfully, the food comes. Italian food is definitely one of my favorites, and this tastes like heaven. At one point, Ian and I reenact that movie *Lady and the Tramp* by slurping the same strand of spaghetti until our lips meet, and we can't stop laughing. I feel like such an idiot for ruining the first part of the dinner. Thank God we were able to get back to having a good night. He really did go to a lot of trouble with the horse and carriage and making a reservation. I know that I have to stop being so insecure, or I'll end up losing him, because I can tell that he's tired of me saying those things.

We have gelato for dessert and then Ian pays and I thank him over and over again and we start to walk home. Ian jokes that the horse and carriage turned into a pumpkin. I'm happy to be walking, it means that we get more time alone together. And it feels amazing to walk now that my back and legs aren't hurting, and I don't have a huge stomach. Ian can actually put his arm around me, and I'm not waddling.

We walk slowly and enjoy the warm summer air. Just before we get back to the house, we stop and kiss for a bit, and I want to take it all in because I know this is probably the last piece of alone time that I'll have with him for a while.

He eventually pulls away from our kiss and grins, reaching into his pocket and handing me a folded piece of paper.

I smile. "What's this?"

"So, you know how I've liked to read poetry since high school?" I nod, and he continues. "Well, I've been working on something of my own. I'm an awful rhymer and I'm still not finished with it, but I wanted to give it to you now, before I leave, so that you have it. It's not perfect, so don't judge, okay?"

He laughs, and I say that I would never judge him, and then I open it and start reading, and my eyes immediately fill up with tears.

Madison Flower
For Mads

The airport.
Planes taking off and landing, people coming and going,
Busy baggage claims and the sounds of suitcases rolling,
Hugs hello and goodbye,
Laughter, tears, and deep sighs.

And suddenly, there she was.
A modest flower, yet born to be seen,
On display, though she didn't want to be,
Still growing into her strength but already so brave,
For all to take notice and watch her behave,
Hard work and determination written all over her,
And sadness. And beauty. Like a fragile but strong flower.

Her outer beauty matched by her inner,
Worried about losing, but only a winner,
Her sweetness and caring so pure and deep you could swim in it,
A mix of innocence and wisdom, her smile is so lit.

Three months that I want to continue forever,
Better than any summer I can remember,
New life begins in every way,
And I wish I could be there for every new, special day.

Time to leave back for the airport, but not leaving in my heart or my mind,
She's the type of person who's hard to find,
Someone who has so much power,
The one-of-a-kind blossoming Madison flower.

I don't even know what to say. This is unbelievable. I truly feel like I'm living in a dream, and he's not real. How did he write something like this for me? How did this even happen that I got so lucky to have a boyfriend like this?

I wrap my arms around him and hug him so tight, I don't ever want to let him go. We just kiss and hug, and I let the tears flow.

Then, when we pull away, he says, "So, I guess you like it?"

"Like it?" I roll my eyes. "No, I don't like it, Ian. I love it. I can't believe you wrote this for me. I'm going to keep it forever."

He kisses me. "So, did I do a good job planning the perfect romantic night?"

"This was one of the most special nights of my life, Ian."

"Well, I'm glad. I love you."

"I love you, too," I say, smiling. I can't believe what an idiot I was at dinner.

As soon as we walk into the house, we hear Tommy screaming and Dianne and Molly trying to calm him down. They both have spit up on their shirts, and I see that they tried to feed him the milk I pumped. I feel so guilty, and I immediately rush over to take him. I sit down on the couch and start feeding him, and he calms down right away. Dianne and Molly laugh and say that he just wanted his mommy. Dianne says that she remembers it being like that with Molly. I thank them and tell them how sorry I am, but they say that it was fine and that they hoped Ian and I had a fun night. We say that we did, we tell them all about it, but we leave out the "fighting" part.

Then everyone goes to bed and I stay downstairs with Tommy, making sure he drains the whole breast. When he's done, I take him upstairs and settle him into his bed. Molly is already fast asleep, and Ian is getting onto his air mattress. I lean down and give him a kiss, and he strokes my hair for a little while, and then I eventually get into my bed. He whispers to me, "Goodnight, my Madison flower," and I feel like crying again. Why does he have to be leaving? Why does everyone I love have to leave?

But he's not leaving, Madison, I tell myself. Think about what he said in his poem.

<>

On Saturday, when we take Ian to the airport, it's rainy. Hot, humid, and pouring rain. *Perfect*. We park and go inside with him and Dianne and Molly say their goodbyes, and he kisses Tommy on his head, and then Dianne holds Tommy as they leave me and Ian alone for a minute. We hug and I wrap my arms around him, holding him so tight. I breathe him in and whisper, "Thank you. For everything."

"Thank *you*, Mads," he says, pulling away from our hug and holding my face in his hands. "I love you so much, and you really need to know that."

"I know it. And I love you, too."

Then I grin and hand him a wrapped gift. He unwraps it and sees the picture that Molly took of us watching TV and eating cheese puffs. It's now in a really nice frame that I found and ordered online.

"Oh my God, I love this!" he exclaims. "But who took the picture? I don't remember-"

I giggle. "Molly took it one night. She was really quiet and snuck up on us. When she showed it to me, I asked her to blow it up, and I got the frame. Do you like it?"

He holds it to his chest and smiles. I smile back. But then I start to tear up and he says, "No, I don't want this to be sad. We're going to see each other very soon."

He looks at the picture again. "This is going right onto the shelf in my dorm. It's so weird to see this, it feels like so long ago. It was when you still liked cheese puffs!"

I laugh. "Yeah, maybe it's a good thing I don't like them anymore."

We kiss again and hug one more time, and then he walks away, rolling his suitcase over to security. He keeps looking back as he walks away, and we wave until he has to go down the hall and we can't see each other anymore.

I cry quietly the whole way home, and I can see my reflection in the window, the rain rolling down mixes with my tears. Molly and Dianne are talking in the front, and Tommy is asleep in his car seat. I look down at my phone, and a text comes through from Ian.

Ian: I'll see you soon, my Madison flower.

I smile and send him a few heart emojis back, and then I look back out the window at the raindrops. I remember a term I once learned in English class: *pathetic fallacy*. *When the weather reflects the mood or what's going on.* I'm really sad, but I'm also really happy. Because even though it was sad to say goodbye, I think of another saying that I've heard over and over again in my life: *Goodbyes are necessary before you can say hello again.*

♡ Tommy = 1 month old !!!! ♡
♡   ♡   ♡

To-Do List

- call Mom + Josie soon   ☆ I GOT THE JOB ☆
- send lanlord the deposit for   Details:
  the apartment   - $16/hour + tips
                       - work from 4-8pm
☆ Tommy's 1-month appointment   every weekday
  tomorrow at 11am   - be at the main
  ✓   location at 3pm on
Questions to ask: ☆ review   August 5th
1. Vaccines?   rental lease
2. Tummy time?   agreement +   ↓
3. How to latch on   SIGN LEASE   call Dina to
   when he's excited?   thank her for
                       ♡   helping me get
☆ date with Ian tonight   .♡   the job
  at 7pm at "Taste in Italy"   ♡
  (find something to wear!!)   buy:
                       - baby books for
- get the picture Molly took of   Tommy
  me + Ian framed for a   - toys for Tommy
  going-away gift for him   little   - nursing pads
- pump more bottles for when   Tommy   - Concealer
  school starts   - parenting books
- get the keys to the apartment   - baby mirror for
  soon   car
- figure out the logistics of   ♡
  going to school + work with   ♡
  Tommy   ♡
        ♡   ♡   ♡
   ♡
♡   ♡   bye Ian...
   ♡   ♡

429

Chapter 41: Fifth Week of Life -- A Month and a Week

"I'm leaving for work!" I call out as I leave the house and get into my car with Tommy, on my way to my first day of work! I'm *so* nervous, but I'm also really excited. I have a feeling I'm going to like this job, and I'm so happy that I get to bring Tommy. It's a beautiful summer afternoon, it's really warm out and kind of humid. It makes me wish that Ian was here, and we could go for a walk together.

It's been so weird and sad and miserable not having him here. When I'm in my room, I keep on turning to say something to him, and then I realize all over again that he isn't here. It's the worst being in the living room, for some reason. I guess it's because that's where we had so many amazing nights, watching TV and eating snacks together. I miss him putting his arm around me, I miss him kissing me.

We've been texting and FaceTiming a lot. He sent me a text this morning, wishing me luck on my first day of work. He sent me a picture of the framed photo of us that I gave him, it's right on the shelf next to his bed. It makes me happy that he put it up in his dorm, and I feel like he wouldn't have done that if he was thinking that he might meet someone else.

I was able to look pretty nice for the job, as I can now finally fit into most of my old clothes. My stomach has gone down a lot, but there's all this extra skin from it being stretched out. Nothing really hurts anymore and there's no more bleeding, except for some light brownish-red spots sometimes.

I got my course list yesterday morning in the mail, along with a list of the supplies I need to get. I keep forgetting that I have to tell the school about my change of address. I'm getting the keys to the studio apartment next week, on Wednesday.

These are the classes I'm taking this year:

Period 1 = AP ENGLISH -- Mr. Flanigan

Period 2 = AP PRE-CALCULUS -- Mrs. Hertz

Period 3 = HONORS JOURNALISM (ADVANCED) -- Ms. Lamont

Period 4 = PHYSICS -- Mr. Williams

Period 5 = FRENCH 4 -- Madame Bisset

Period 6 = FREE PERIOD

Period 7 = AP U.S. HISTORY -- Mrs. Bennett

Ugh. I'm going to have *so* much homework.

These days, I'm mostly in denial that my days of living with Dianne and Molly are numbered. The night before I found out I was pregnant, which was the night before I moved in with Dianne and Molly, I didn't know it was going to be my last night in my *own* family's house. This is different, almost worse, in a way, because I'm just sadly counting down the days.

Once I arrive at the Food Direct headquarters, my trainer, a twenty-something guy, comes up to me, introduces himself as Derek, and then freaks out when he sees I have Tommy with me, sleeping in his car seat. He asks if Mr. Lopez said that it would be okay to bring a baby along.

"I didn't think it would be necessary to bring it up, since it won't interfere with what I'm doing," I say, shrugging.

"So...he has a car seat, which is in the back of your car?" he asks. I nod, and he says that he will have to mention it to Mr. Lopez, and he hopes it won't be an issue. *Great, what if it's a problem? Please, no, don't let it be.*

Derek calls Mr. Lopez, and goes off to the side of the room to talk to him. He comes back and says Mr. Lopez cannot fire me for having a baby, as that would be discrimination, but he isn't happy that I didn't tell him at the interview. He says that I need to make sure I'm being responsible and not distracted with a baby in the car. Also, if I need to make stops to change his diaper or whatever, it will take away from me being as fast as I could be and it might affect my tip. If people complain, he might have to rethink things. *Ugh. Well, at least he's not firing me.* I'll just have to make sure that I'm really careful and efficient. Thank God Tommy is fast asleep. I fed and changed him right before I came and the car ride put him to sleep.

Derek tells me to follow him, and we go into a sort of central office where there are a lot of people coming and going. He hands me a navy blue cap with the words "Food Direct" on them, and a name tag, which already has my name on it and the Food Direct symbol.

He tells me to download the Food Direct app, and I tell him that I already did. Then he explains how it works. "You have to press the button that marks the start of your shift, and during your shift you'll get different orders and different addresses on the app. An order will come in, and then you'll go to the restaurant or take-out place, let's say McDonald's, and go inside and order whatever the order is. For the restaurants, you'll call ahead and then just go in and pick it up. Then you take the food to the address on the order. It's pretty straightforward. When you're done with your shift, press the button that marks the end of your shift. Oh, and no taking breaks, unless it's to stop and use the bathroom somewhere. You'll see that this is a very busy service and you will be delivering pretty consistently until the end of your shift."

I nod and write everything down in my phone so that I have the instructions in case I forget anything. "Mr. Lopez will know if we are slacking off or not doing a good job of getting the order right, et cetera, because people will call in and complain, or we will get bad reviews online."

"Okay, yes, I understand," I say.

"Most of the time, people will tip you. Some people are very generous and some, well, let's just say it makes you want to do something to their food the next time they order. But don't do that. It's not worth it. Other people's generosity will make up for their cheapness. You'll see. Obviously, you get to keep all your tips. Any questions?"

I think for a second, and then I shake my head. "No, but thank you, this was really helpful, and it all makes sense."

"Great," he says, and then he checks his watch. "Your shift starts in ten minutes. So, put on your cap and name tag, go to the bathroom if you have to, log into the app and you're good to go."

I nod and thank him, and he smiles back and wishes me good luck. I use their bathroom and then change Tommy's diaper before I go. He starts to cry a little bit, and I give him one of his rattly toys and it seems to calm him down. I quickly leave and put him in his car seat, then log onto the app and press the button to mark the start of my shift. Almost immediately, an order for McDonald's shows up. That's funny, that was the example Derek used, I guess people really are lazy if they won't even get out and drive to a drive-thru. I drive to the nearest one, and place the order. The whole thing is pretty quick. It smells so good, and I want to get some for myself. I realize that this will probably keep happening, and I need to be prepared with my own food and snacks so that I don't start buying food and spending all the money I'm making.

As I drive, I keep checking in the baby mirror that I got that goes over the rearview mirror so I can make sure that Tommy is okay. He's sleeping again, and that is part of the reason I love this job. He loves to sleep in the car, so it really should be pretty easy. I drive to the address from the order, and run up the driveway to the front door, leaving the window open for Tommy. I keep glancing back to make sure he's okay, and he's fine. When I told Mom about the job, she said I have to always make sure Tommy and the car are within my sight.

A grumpy-looking man opens the door, snatches the bag after confirming his payment online, and closes the door. I just stand there for a moment, even after he's closed the door, dumbfounded. *No "thank you"? No tip? Wow.* I hope Derek was right about other people making up for people like this.

I get back in the car and check my phone and sure enough, there's another order showing up on the app. There isn't a lot of traffic, and I'm able to do things pretty quickly. Tommy is sleeping and this is going so smoothly, I can't believe it. I like driving around, looking at everything, listening to music and smelling delicious food. It's totally different from working at Roast and Drink, but I like it.

After that order, three orders pop up at the same time. *Oh, boy.* One of them, for Italian food, has an address that looks familiar, but first there's a Thai food order and another McDonald's order.

After I finish the McDonald's order, my luck runs out with Tommy. When I get back to the car, he is wailing. *Great.* Now what? I have to work! I'm going to get in trouble if I take care of him. But maybe I can just take a couple minutes. I have the diaper bag with me, and it has a bottle that I pumped inside, just in case this happened. I take five minutes to feed him, and he settles down. I have the next delivery, to the Italian restaurant, in the car, and I'm worried that it's getting cold. I quickly burp Tommy, put him back in his car seat, and then drive to the address on the order. When I look at it again, I see that it's Leo's address. *Oh my God, is this some kind of joke?* But I do remember that his family always orders take-out, I don't think his mom is big on cooking. Oh well, I guess I have no choice, but boy do I not want to do this.

I drive up and park on the street, and then I grab the food and quickly run up to leave it on the front steps. I ring the doorbell and rush back to the car, not wanting a tip or to even see anyone. But it's too late, I hear the front door open, and I turn back and there's Leo.

His face immediately darkens when he sees me, and he kind of scoffs. "So you're working for Food Direct now? You actually listened to Dina?"

"Yeah," I say simply, and point to the food on the doorstep. "There's your food."

He takes the bag and opens it. "It feels cold."

I want to scream at him, *Yeah, because I was busy taking care of your kid!* But I just keep my blank expression on my face, and he just shakes his head in a disgusted way and turns to go inside just as Mrs. Schmitz comes to the door. "Leo, what's taking so...oh, Madison, hi. What are you doing here?"

Leo walks inside, and Mrs. Schmitz gives him a dirty look. I smile and swallow. "Um, I started working at Food Direct," I say. "I just delivered your order."

"Oh, wow, I mean, it's great you're working, you hadn't mentioned it. Do you like it?" she asks.

I nod and say, "It's my first day. I was going to tell you next time I saw you. Tommy's in the car, do you want to see him? Don't worry, I'm very careful and I always have him in my eyesight."

She nods and smiles, and we walk down to the car and she looks in and sees Tommy sleeping. She says how cute he looks, and that he looks like he's grown even since she came by last week.

"Since you're here, do you think I could chat with you for a second?" she asks.

"Okay, but, well, I should really get back to work," I say.

"Alright. I'll call or text you later, I want to try to meet up with you and your mother for lunch before school starts. I'll find out when she's coming in next."

I quickly nod and she thanks me for letting her see Tommy, and then wishes me luck and goes inside. It's so funny how it's not awkward to see her anymore, but with Leo, it's the complete opposite.

Tommy wakes up and starts crying once I get into the car. I look at my phone and see that there are more orders, and I'm getting behind, so I can't tend to him right now.

As I start driving, he gets louder and louder. I have to pull over at the side of the road to call in the next order for pick up, and I actually have to get out of the car so they can hear me, because Tommy is crying so loud.

After I place the order, I go to pick Tommy up and he feels really hot. *Oh no, does he have a fever?* I quickly get the little digital thermometer and some Vaseline that I keep in the diaper bag. Dianne showed me how to take a rectal temperature, because she said that it's the most accurate, and I need to know how for when I'm not sure if he has a fever. Figures it's happening now, in the middle of my first shift, in the middle of the street. I do it gently, and thank God, it shows a normal temperature. She told me anything under 100 degrees Fahrenheit is normal, and it's showing that he's 99 degrees Fahrenheit. But he feels *really* hot. I realize that I'm sweating, too. It *is* really hot out.

Oh my God, I've been leaving him out in this car, in the heat, for a few minutes each time I go to drop the food off. *What was I thinking?* I've read that just a few minutes in a hot car can be long enough for babies to overheat, especially in this summer weather. Just because I've been leaving the window open doesn't mean that he's not overheating.

I start to cry. *I'm a horrible mother.*

Shaking, I get my cold water bottle from my bag and I press it up against his warm skin, just clutching him close to me as hot tears run down my cheeks. "I'm sorry," I croak out. "Sweetie, I'm so sorry..." I cry really hard, right into his soft amazing-smelling skin.

"I didn't mean to hurt you. I know how hot you are, and I'm so sorry, I just got distracted with work, but there's no excuse. I'm so, so sorry, I won't do it again, I'll take you with me everywhere I go, all the time. From now on, whenever I see anyone, whenever anything happens, it doesn't take priority over you. You come first."

He feels like he's cooling off, so I put him back in his car seat and blast the air conditioning as I start driving again. I start doing what's called "narrating," to Tommy, as I read on a parent blog that it's good to talk to your baby as you do things and tell him what you're doing, it helps them learn about the world and learn to eventually talk.

"Look at the blue sky, Tommy," I say softly. "Look at the cars rushing by. There's a yellow one, like Mommy's! And there's the bakery. They sell really delicious cookies there. Before I had you, I'd sneak over there with Auntie Molly on weekends and get the amazing chewy chocolate-chip ones. I can't wait to eat those things with you."

I end up being a little late for a couple of deliveries to stop and tend to Tommy and make sure he's comfortable. I hope I don't get in trouble, but there's nothing I can do. I have to make sure he's okay, and I'm doing the best I can.

Then I get an alert on my phone from the Food Direct app, telling me that my orders have been "temporarily suspended," and then right after I get that alert, I get a text from Mr. Lopez. *Oh no, something's wrong.*

Mr. Lopez: Ms. Davis. We've already received TWO bad reviews from two separate orders saying the food was late and cold. One of them said they saw you tending to your baby in the car. This is unacceptable. I know it's your first day, but this cannot happen.

I'm completely shocked. I can't believe that people would write reviews about this. And yeah, it's only my first day, this isn't good. I wonder who it was. It must have been the last couple of orders after Tommy got fussy. *Oh my God, I bet Leo was one of them. I can't believe it, but I bet one of them was him!*

Maddie: I'm so sorry, Mr. Lopez. This is not like me at all. My son wasn't feeling well, but he's better, and anyway, I know it's not an excuse. I will not be doing that anymore, I will work harder and deliver faster. I'm very sorry and I will show you how reliable I am. Could you please let me access my orders again? It says on my app that they've been "temporarily suspended."

About a minute later, I get another alert on my app that my orders have opened up again. There's four listed. I quickly order all of them and go to deliver them, trying to be as fast as possible without going past the speed limits. I'm feeling really self-discouraged. I'm not doing this whole "working mom" thing very well.

The last of the round of deliveries is Thai food, and it's just on the edge of the town, a bit further out from the city than the others. It takes me about fifteen minutes to get there, and Tommy sleeps the whole time. When I knock at the door, Dina opens it. We both look shocked, and then we start laughing. I tell her that it's my first day, and she actually gives me a hug. *Leo's girlfriend is giving me a hug.*

Then she smiles as she looks at Tommy sleeping in his car seat. Since I'm not leaving him in the car anymore, I'm carrying him up to each doorstep. I wonder how Dina would feel if I told her the truth about who Tommy's father is. I still just can't believe how ironic it is that it's because of Leo's girlfriend that I have this job. And I can't believe how nice she is.

"Hey, do you want to meet at Home's Diner for breakfast at ten tomorrow?" I ask. "Since you helped me get the job, it would be my treat."

"Sure!" she says, and I hand her the food and she gives me a five-dollar tip, which is really generous. Then she looks at Tommy in his car seat and says, "It must be heavy carrying him in that all the time."

I nod and roll my eyes, smiling. "Yes, but at least I get to bring him with me," I say. "Thanks again, by the way. This is really the perfect job for me right now."

"I'm so glad," she says, and then she says how cute Tommy is, and goes inside.

As I get back in my car, I realize I'll probably end up delivering food to tons of people I know, because it's such a small town and everyone uses Food Direct. I used to use it sometimes when Mom was working late and I needed food for me and Josie.

It's eight-thirty by the time I'm home. I'm so exhausted, I feel like someone attached weights to my eyelids. Dianne and Molly are already eating dinner. I rush up over to say hi and hopefully sit down to eat but no such luck, Tommy starts crying. I have to feed him first.

"Guys, um, could you please save me a plate?" I ask.

Molly giggles. "Duh, yeah! We actually ordered Chinese food from Food Direct and we thought we were hoping to get you, but we had someone else as our deliverer."

"Aw, thanks, guys," I say, smiling.

After Tommy eats, he falls asleep and I put him in the car seat so I can eat. I tell Molly and Dianne about the job and they are so sweet and encouraging. I realize again how weird it's going to be when I move out. I'm really sad about it.

I take Tommy upstairs and begin his bedtime routine, talking to him the whole time I bathe him. I coo to him and he squeals back. I love that he talks back to me now, with his own little sounds. It's just adorable.

"I was really...doubting myself today, sweetie. That I wasn't being a good mommy to you. I mean, I should've never left you in the car." I sigh, frustrated. "I know it's hard, I know that all of this is so hard, but it's all because I want you to have the best life possible, because it's what you deserve. Okay?"

It's so quick that I think I must have imagined it, but then he does it again: Tommy smiles. *He smiles! For the first time!* "Tommy, did you smile?" I shriek happily. "Smile again, Tommy!"

He doesn't, but I caught it. I saw his very first smile. "Oh, I'm so proud of you, sweetie!" He gurgles and drool runs down his chin. I giggle and lift him out of the tub.

I dry him off while singing to him, I put his lotion on and his diaper on and I cuddle with him in the bed. Molly comes in a half hour later. He still won't sleep. I rock him gently, trying to get him to sleep because I know we'll be up later.

It's really empty in here now without Ian. Even though Molly is still here, now that Ian is gone, it's just not the same. I miss him so much. I text him while I'm feeding Tommy and I tell him about work, and he tells me about school. I also text with Mom, and she says that she's really proud of me. I send her some pictures of Tommy and update her about Leo's mom and everything that's going on.

Molly falls asleep as I'm feeding Tommy, and hopefully he will go to sleep now, too. I feel a bit wired now, even though I'm exhausted. I just keep thinking about how different my life is now than what it used to be like. On the last summer nights before school started, I would do things like go with Molly to the beach or to parties, or I'd go out with Leo. Or sometimes I'd just stay up really late with a bowl of popcorn and I'd watch movies, completely relaxed, caring about no one but myself for that moment.

I have to admit that I'm sad about losing that fun, carefree part of my teenage life, but I know that I have to face things the way they are and be strong for Tommy. Knowing that I have to be there for him all the time has changed me so much. I feel like I'm a completely different person than I was just a year ago.

I take out Ian's poem from my nightstand drawer and read it again. I love what he wrote, and I feel like I also want to live up to the way he sees me.

Tommy finally falls asleep and I put him in his little bed, and then I take my dad's shaving cream off my nightstand and put a little on my wrist and inhale it. It's amazing to me that it still makes me feel like he's here. I think about Dad and how Tommy is named after him. I wonder if he can see me. *Us.* This was a big day, but I did it. I'm doing it. *We're doing it, me and Tommy.* I hope Dad really can see us, and that he's proud.

<>

In the morning, I blink open my eyes. Molly is still sleeping, and so is Tommy. I yawn and sink back down to my pillow, it's only nine, I don't have to get up yet.

It's really sunny, the sun is streaming through my eyes. I feel like I have some sort of commitment that I'm supposed to get ready for, but I'm too tired. Tommy woke up six times, and while all he needed was to eat or a diaper change, it's still exhausting.

Wait! I have to meet Dina at Home's Diner for breakfast in an hour! *Shoot!* It's going to take forever to get ready with Tommy. I bunch up pillows on the edge of my bed. Tommy hasn't started rolling over yet, but it could happen at any time and so I have to make sure that if he does, he won't fall off the bed.

I go to the bathroom and take my first shower of the week. *Gross.* There never seems to be any time to shower. I still love being in the shower and sitting on the seat that Ian put in for me. It just reminds me of how amazing he is.

I want to blow dry my hair, but I hear Tommy's cries and so I sprint to the bedroom and bring Tommy back in with me while I get ready. I prop him up in his car seat, which I left in here last night. He screams as I dry my hair and I can't do it the whole way, but at least it's not dripping wet.

I try to brush my teeth and wash my face quickly, but then Tommy's cries get so loud that I have to take him downstairs and feed him for a half hour. By the time I'm done, it's a quarter to ten and we're nowhere near ready.

I hustle him upstairs. He's *finally* stopped crying. I change him into a cute yellow onesie and he kicks and flails as I put him in his car seat. Now I'm going to have to install the car seat back into my car.

I change myself into the same dark jeans I wore to the restaurant with Ian, because they are the only pair that my belly fat doesn't overlap over nowadays. I throw on a blue sweatshirt because it's the first thing that comes to my eyes as I search the messy closet floor. I tuck my hair into a quick messy bun. It looks horrible, and I'm just realizing that the light blue sweatshirt was from the dirty pile, but I still hustle myself out the door with Tommy and drive to Home's Diner. Luckily, I find a spot not too far away and I heave the car seat out and walk, struggling with how heavy it is.

I'm so tired already, and I still have a full day ahead of me, and I have to work later on. Why didn't I think this through more? I can't just be making plans like I did with Dina, now that I have a baby.

When I get inside, Dina's already sitting in a booth and she smiles and waves me over. Thankfully, she doesn't look upset that I'm ten minutes late. Instead, she just says that she understands how hard it must be to get ready with a baby. The waiter comes over as I sandwich Tommy's car seat into the booth next to me.

"I'll have the breakfast sandwich with extra bacon and cheddar cheese, please," I say, passing him my menu without looking at it. I'm so hungry.

Then, it occurs to me that an entire hour of working at Food Direct pays me just about the same as the sandwich costs. *Ugh.* Well, at least it pays more than Roast and Drink. And I'm not going to be doing this all the time, but I really felt like I had to thank Dina, because she's the reason I found out about the job in the first place.

Dina orders the same thing, and then she says, "I don't know about you, but whenever I buy something, it always makes me think about how long it took me to earn the money for it."

"Oh my God, you do that, too?" I ask, and we laugh. It feels really good to know that even Dina feels this way, and *she* doesn't have a baby.

Then, she looks over at Tommy and says, "It's so funny, because I've been trying to think of any run-ins we might've had when you were pregnant, but there were none! Seriously, I had *no* idea that you were pregnant."

I laugh. "Well, it makes sense because we're at different schools. Anyway, be glad you didn't, because I looked like a beached whale."

"Oh, I bet you didn't," she says, but she laughs too. Then a weirdly serious look grows on her face. "I actually wanted to ask you something today."

"What?" I ask, taking a gulp of water.

"I don't know, I've just been wondering...why does Leo act so weird around you?"

I cough, nearly choking on my water.

"It's not even just when he's around you, it's...I mean, I was on the phone with him last night, and I told him about you getting the job and being the one to deliver my food and everything, and he was just...weird. I don't know, he always says such negative things about you, but you seem so nice. Did anything ever happen between you guys?"

I have no idea what to do. Clearly, she just doesn't know anything. Being at a different school, I guess that somehow the rumors never made it there. If I tell her everything, who knows how she'll react? Leo would kill me for telling her, but I think he's crazy to think she'd never find out. The problem is that now it's like we're becoming friends, and it really doesn't feel right to keep such a huge secret from her.

"Well, actually..." I begin uneasily. "Yeah, we, uh, dated for a while."

"Oh, God, I'm so sorry, I didn't know. When did you date him?"

"Um, well, about a year ago. We were together for about..." I trail off and shake my head. "Um, listen, there's something you need to know. I'm really sorry that I have to tell you this. It really shouldn't be me telling you this, but I didn't think we'd become friends. I didn't know that I'd like you so much. You're so nice."

She looks really confused, and I almost change my mind, but then I realize that I just have to do it. "Leo is...he's Tommy's father."

She turns white. I don't know if I've ever seen anyone look more shocked. Well, Mom looked that way when she found out I was pregnant.

"Are you *joking? What?*" she says. I nod, and the tears just start flowing and there's nothing I can do to stop them. I tell her pretty much everything, leaving out the details about how it actually happened. I do tell her that I really felt like it was too soon for me, but that Leo pressured me into it, even using her as a way of convincing me to sleep with him. I tell her that he basically said if I didn't do it with him, then she would.

She covers her face with her hands and keeps saying, "Oh my God, Oh my God," over and over again. In the middle of it, Tommy wakes up and starts crying, and I give him the bottle of milk that I pumped, and he calms down. She just stares at him and then she says, "How could he do this? How could he *leave you?* How could he not tell me?? I'm such an *idiot,* I had no idea. I feel like such a...such a fool!"

Then *she* starts crying. We both just cry and blow our noses and people stare at us, I can only imagine what they think is going on. This is really crazy. It feels right, though, for her to know. I am scared for what will happen when Leo finds out, but I don't care, Dina had a right to know.

And I had a right to tell her.

"You don't get it, Madison," Dina says, crying harder. "Leo *lied* to me, he told me he'd never been with anyone else. He said I was his *first.*"

Oh my God. "Dina, I'm so sorry," I say. "I really didn't know whether to tell you or not, but...I feel like you had a right to know. You've been so nice to me."

"Thank you, Madison. You had every right to tell me." She shakes her head. "I can't believe that Leo didn't tell me. I can't believe that all this time, I've been thinking we both lost our virginity to *each other*. That he was this sweet, innocent, amazing guy."

She cries harder. I don't know what to say anymore, I just keep apologizing and she keeps telling me that I don't have anything to be sorry for.

She says she has to go, that she's too upset to eat, and she takes twenty dollars out of her wallet and puts it on the table, saying that no way does she want me to pay for this meal. As she leaves, I beg her to not tell Leo that I was the one who told her. I can barely eat my sandwich, I'm too upset, but I don't want to waste the food, so I eat it quickly and then go to leave, lugging Tommy in his car seat back to the car. As I'm just about to drive off, my phone beeps. *Oh no, it's from Leo.*

Leo: WHY DID YOU TELL HER?!? I HATE YOU!! You just keep ruining my life over and over again! I HATE YOU! STAY OUT OF MY LIFE! DO YOU HEAR ME?!?

A few seconds later, another text comes through, from Dina.

Dina: I had to tell Leo. I'm sorry, I hope you're not mad. Please don't feel bad about telling me. You did me a huge favor. Thank you, Madison.

Just as I'm about to write her back, *another* text comes through. *Oh my God, it's Leo's mom. Now what?*

Mrs. Schmitz: Madison dear, I just spoke with your mother, and she agrees that we should all meet up for lunch before school starts, so please let us know if next Sunday, the 11th, works for lunch at Sandwich. My treat. Looking forward to seeing all of you. Let me know if you need anything.

Tears rush down my cheeks. It's all just too much for me. Everything is *such a mess. It's all a mess.*

Tommy starts to cry, too, just like he always does when I'm upset. I get into the back seat, trying to soothe him. When he was still in my stomach and I was upset, my singing and talking to him always calmed me down, and I think it probably calmed him down, too. So I start to sing, even though it's the last thing I feel like doing.

I sing *Twinkle, Twinkle, Little Star,* and as I do it, I look at the sky and I think about the fact that even though I can't see them right now, the stars are out there, shining brightly, and one day things will be good again. I just know they will. I don't know how, but I have hope that things will get easier someday. The stars are always there, even if you can't see them. Looking down on us. Me and Tommy. Tommy and me.

Little Tommy = 5 weeks old!!

To-Do List

- 1st day of work = Monday (be there at 3pm for training)
- pick up paycheck on Friday from Food Direct
- get the keys to the apartment next Wednesday
- tell the school about my change of address
- get school supplies!!
- call Mom + Josie soon
- call Ian!!

☆ meet Dina tomorrow at Home's Diner at 10am for breakfast

Tommy Smiled!!!!!

☆ meet Mom + Josie + Leo's parents on Sunday for lunch at Sandwich

- call Dina?
- restock diaper bag
- look for sales on baby items!!!

☆ last postpartum appointment with Dr. Lippincott on the Sunday before school starts at 11am

☆ Tommy's 2-month appointment = September 8th 12:30pm

buy:
- bigger clothes for Tommy
- school supplies!!
- bottles for pumping
- butt paste

✳ Twinkle, Twinkle, Little Star ✳

my little Tommy

Chapter 42: Sixth Week of Life -- A Month and a Half

"I'll be home in a few hours!" I call out to Molly and Dianne as I leave to get in my car with Tommy. It's gotten a lot easier to lift him in the car seat, and the muscles in my arm are getting strong. I feel like I get a good workout everyday, just from carrying him around.

It's Sunday August 11th, and Tommy and I are on the way to *Sandwich* for lunch to meet up with my mom, Josie, and Leo's parents. Last week, I called and texted Dina a few times, but she didn't answer or respond. It's obvious that she doesn't want to be friends anymore, and in a way, I guess I don't blame her. She probably sees me as a reminder of Leo, and I see her the same way, so I don't see how we could really have been friends, anyway.

On a happier note, I get the keys to my apartment this Wednesday, and then the place is mine. I'm not actually moving in until two days before school starts, or maybe not even until a day before. It's not ideal, seeing as I wanted to move in at least a week before school starts, but there's just not enough time to get everything together.

Ian has been texting me a lot. We also did FaceTime last night, while Tommy was doing tummy time. It was really nice to see his face. It feels like he's so far away, and I always find myself wanting to spend more time on the calls we have. I'm counting down the days until Thanksgiving, when he's visiting for a week.

I had to spend nearly ten dollars on what's called "butt paste" for Tommy because he's starting to develop diaper rash. The name makes me laugh. I ask Tommy, "Do you want some butt paste?" in a funny voice, and he laughs, too, even though he has no idea what it means. I've been trying to change him more often and not leave him in a wet diaper because that can cause the rashes. I was trying to save money by leaving his diaper on longer, but I know I can't do that, and now I had to buy the butt paste.

I park outside *Sandwich,* and then I remember the time Molly fainted here, I haven't been here since. I hope this lunch goes better than that one did.

As I walk up, I see that everyone is already here, sitting on the patio, which is empty other than all of them. Josie runs over to see Tommy. I laugh, because now she doesn't even hug me first, she only seems to care about Tommy. It's the same with Mom, her eyes are just on

444

him. Mr. and Mrs. Schmitz stand up, and they are also just looking at Tommy, smiling. I don't even really mind that no one's that interested in me anymore, I'm just happy they all love him.

I get Tommy out of his car seat and tell everyone that they have to take turns. I give him to Mom first. She holds him up, looking into his eyes with a big smile on her face, then gives him a big kiss on his tummy, and he smiles. Mom looks at me, her mouth open. "He knows how to smile now?"

I nod, grinning. "He did it last week. I thought I told you?" She shakes her head and I laugh and say that I've been so busy with work, I can't keep track of anything.

"I feel like every time I see him, he's bigger and bigger," Mrs. Schmitz says.

"They grow up so fast," Mom says.

"*Too* fast," Mrs. Schmitz says, and they smile at each other.

Then Mom hands him to Mrs. Schmitz, and Mom finally notices me. "You look great, sweetie! You don't even look that tired."

"You look like a mommy," Josie says, and everyone laughs.

Then the waitress comes to take our orders. She comments on how cute Tommy is, and Mrs. Schmitz jokes, "We all know what *he'd* like to order," and she gestures to my chest. We all laugh again. I still can't believe how Leo has such *nice* parents.

Then Tommy starts to cry, so I take him and he instantly settles down. It makes me so happy that I'm the one he wants. "I know he can't be hungry because I fed him right before I left, and I burped and changed him, too. He's probably just tired," I say.

Everyone catches up for a bit, they ask Josie how her summer has been, and they ask Mom about her job. I can tell that Mom is a little jealous or upset or something, because Leo's mom keeps talking about her visits to see Tommy on Sunday. It really is weird that she sees him more often than my own mom does.

They ask me about school starting, and I tell them that I'm nervous but I think it will be okay. I'm allowed to take Tommy to my classes as long as he doesn't cry, and if he does, I'm going to have to find someone to watch him. The Schmitzes will be watching him some of the time, and I can tell that this makes Mom both happy and sad. "I'm glad that you guys are here for Madison," Mom says to them. "It will help her stay focused on school."

Then Mom turns to me and asks, "How's Ian doing, Maddie?"

"He just left back for college, but we're going to do long-distance."

"Who is Ian?" Mrs. Schmitz asks.

"My boyfriend," I say, and it honestly feels good to tell her. I've wanted to mention it, kind of to show them that just because their son didn't want me doesn't mean that other guys don't.

"Wait a minute, I'm confused...you have a *boyfriend?*"

I nod. "Is something wrong with that?" Mom says pointedly to Mrs. Schmitz.

"Well, yes...it's just, quite frankly, I don't think it's appropriate."

Now it's getting uncomfortable. Leo's parents exchange a look, and Mom says, "If you have something to say, then just say it."

"I mean, the fact that you, Teresa, are letting her *date* someone when she's-"

"Do you really think it's your place to judge what *my* daughter does?" Mom asks.

"Of course I do. She's the parent of my grandchild. She should be-"

"Please don't say what *my* daughter should or shouldn't be doing."

"Maybe if you were around her more, you could monitor her behavior!" Mrs. Schmitz says.

Oh, wow, that was a low blow. I want to get out of here so badly. Sure enough, Tommy picks up on my tension and he starts to cry.

"Let's not do this, okay?" Mom says to Mrs. Schmitz. "Not here, not now. You and I can discuss this another time."

Mrs. Schmitz rolls her eyes. A sudden, strong anger flares up inside of me as I say, "You know, Mrs. Schmitz, I really don't think it's appropriate for you to be saying things like that or judging who I'm with. *Your son* did not want to be with me. And for your information, the guy I'm dating is so much nicer to me than *Leo* ever was! I don't know if you know how much Leo hurt me, or if you know how much I wanted to be with him, but I don't want to sit here any longer and take this...crap!"

"Madison!" Mrs. Schmitz and Mom say at the same time.

Tommy starts crying harder and harder, and I stand up and rock him. "Fine," I say. "I'm sorry for being rude. But you're being really rude, too. I appreciate how you're helping me with money and all that, but you don't understand how much I just wanted to stay with Leo, and if you wish I wasn't with someone else, then maybe you should have raised your son better!"

Mom gets up and comes to put her arm around me. "Madison, come on-"

I wave her away. Then I look right at Leo's parents and say what I've wanted to stay for so long. "I just love the way *Leo* gets off without having to take any responsibility, even though this happened because of something *we* did *together!* And then you act like I'm being inappropriate because I found someone else? For your information, Leo was the first person I'd ever been with, and I don't know if you know this, but he pressured me into it." They look completely stunned, and I just keep going, like a car whose brakes aren't working. "I don't regret it, because I have Tommy from it, but my life is *totally* different now, and I'm sure you know that it *still* isn't going to be easy. But Tommy is here now, and this is *my* life, and I am allowed to be in any relationship that *I* want! I will make sure the person that I'm with is good for Tommy, if that's what you're worried about. And you don't have to worry about Ian, he's the nicest guy I've ever known. He's the *total opposite of your son!*"

Suddenly, I realize that I'm bawling, and Josie has jumped up to hug me. Tommy won't stop screaming, so I just leave. I grab the diaper bag and the car seat, and I just get out of there.

I get into my car and start feeding Tommy. About a minute later, Mom and Josie come out of the restaurant and get in the car with me. Josie looks worried, and Mom says that Leo's parents feel terrible and they want to apologize, but I say that I'm not going back in, that I'll talk to them later. I tell them to go finish their lunch and that I'll be fine, I have to go get school supplies anyway. Mom says she will go try to calm things down with Leo's parents. They sit with me for a few minutes, and then we say goodbye and hug and I tell them that I will try to come up and visit soon, or they can come down again. This wasn't a very good visit with them, we need another one soon.

After they leave, I just sit in the car, feeding Tommy, staring out the window. That was horrible, beyond what I'd ever imagined would happen today, so embarrassing. I'm so glad that there was no one else on the patio. I'm never going back to *Sandwich* again. I feel like that place is just the restaurant of bad luck. The only thing is, I *do* feel better now, after saying all those things. It feels good to let them know what I think, and I feel like they should know *my* side of things, because I have no idea what Leo has told them.

Just as I'm about to drive off, I get a text message from Leo's mom saying that she's sorry and she understands what I'm saying, and she would like to move forward and not fight anymore. I quickly write back and say that I'm sorry too, but that I had to say what I said. Then I put the phone away and start to drive to go get my school supplies. It's really stressing me out that school is starting so soon. I don't feel prepared, and it seems as if they're cracking down on us this year. Plus, the junior SAT's are in the fall, and I'm going to have to really study hard for them. Maybe I should join a study group, though I doubt I'll have time for that.

Once I get to the store, Tommy's still asleep from the car ride, and I just plop his whole car seat into the shopping cart. I'm pretty quick getting everything, as I know which brands I like for pens and pencils and other things I need, and I always get the same ones. It's pretty busy, there's a long line waiting for the cashier. I see a few people looking at me and Tommy, and then it hits me that I don't really get the dirty looks that I used to anymore. I mean, when I was pregnant, I would get all these judgemental looks, but now it seems like people are just looking at Tommy. Some of them even smile at him, and then look at me and keep smiling. Maybe they assume I'm babysitting or something, but they don't seem to get that I'm his mother, or maybe they just don't realize how young I am. Maybe I don't look so young anymore, I get no sleep, so I must look tired and older.

The woman behind me smiles and says, "Is that your little brother?"

I'm about to tell her the truth, but honestly, I just can't take anymore today, so I just say, "Yes, he is, his name's Tommy."

The woman smiles again. "Aw, he's lucky to have such a sweet older sister! I wish my kids got along like this." I shrug and laugh, just happy to not have to get into the whole thing.

Finally, it's my turn, and I pay for my supplies and then take the shopping cart out to my car in the parking lot. It's hard lifting the car seat out of the cart, and trying to do it carefully so that he doesn't wake up. I get him buckled in, and then I unload the bags. This is a time where it would be great to have someone helping me. At least they could return the shopping cart so I don't have to walk all the way back to the entrance of the store and back. I'm so tired.

I think about just leaving the cart at my parking spot, but then I remember how Dad always said he hated it when he saw people do that, and that he thought it was rude to the people who worked there, so I take it back. Just as I click it into the other carts, I hear a loud bang as someone else tries to get one from another row. I look over to see who's making so much noise, and I realize it's Leo. *Are you kidding me??*

I quickly turn away and walk back to the car, I don't even want to say a word to him, but he calls out, "Are you following me or something?"

I turn back around and call out, "Ever heard of a small town?"

"Yeah, sometimes it's *too* small."

"I fully agree," I say, and then I go back to my car and open Tommy's door to check on him. He's sleeping, and I see Leo notice him and then scowl. "So what else in my life are you planning to ruin?" he asks me.

"What?"

"I'm sure you know that Dina broke up with me. Happy with yourself?"

Fury rages through me. "I don't see how I've ruined your life at all. You just go on with everything without a care in the world, not even *acknowledging* that Tommy should be as much your responsibility as he is mine. You should've at least been honest with Dina from the beginning, but it's not my problem. I'm sure you'll find someone else today or tomorrow. That's pretty much what you did with me."

"Whatever," he says, scoffing and turning to leave.

I call out after him. "I can't believe that you told her you never slept with anyone else! What kind of a jerk are you?"

"Oh, just *shut up, Madison,*" Leo says with disgust. "You're just an idiot."

"*I'm* the idiot?" I choke out. "*I'm* the one who carried your child through the whole nine long months, and *I'm* the one who's going to raise your child. And he's amazing, but you'll never know him."

Suddenly, Tommy wakes up and starts crying, and I go to pick him up. I see Leo just staring at us.

"But guess what, Leo? I'm not even upset that you left me anymore, because I met someone a million times better than you, someone who I *love.*"

He scoffs again. "Yeah, right. Who is he? A homeless person? Who else would want to be with someone like you?"

Suddenly, Tommy starts screaming, not crying, *screaming,* and Leo just stares at him with such a look of hate, it's horrifying. I start to choke up. "Do you even remember that my dad *died,* Leo? Do you remember that?"

It's weird, the mean expression sort of drains from his face. He just suddenly looks shocked, like he really *did* forget. "My dad, he was the opposite of you," I say. "He was the most caring, sweet, amazing father in the whole world. He was there for us until the day he died. *Literally.* But not you! Not you! You can't even accept the fact that you *have* a son!"

Suddenly, Leo bursts out screaming, "*But your dad CHOSE to have you! I didn't want this! I didn't CHOOSE this!*"

I just stand there, stunned. It's true. Leo didn't want this, and I didn't have to have Tommy. I could have aborted him or given him up for adoption. It's not the point, though. It's the way Leo handled it. There's just too much to say, and I don't have it in me to fight anymore. Tommy is crying, and I just want to tend to him and feed him.

All I say is, "I guess next time you convince someone to have sex with you, maybe you should at the very least *wear a condom,*" and I get into the car with Tommy and slam the door. Leo stares for a second, then walks away, and I start feeding Tommy, which calms him down immediately. I stroke his sweet cheeks and tell him over and over again how sorry I am.

He finishes eating, and I get ready to drive home when I see Alexa calling me. I answer immediately and say, "Alexa?" I hear her sniff, like she's been crying, and I ask, "What's wrong?"

"I'm at my dad's house. I'm...I'm not at Danny's house anymore."

"Oh, no, Lex, what happened?"

She starts crying so loudly that her words get all jumbled up. "Danny and his parents and I just had the worst fight of my entire life...we're...we're...we're not together anymore, that's all, I just don't even know how it happened, but we haven't been able to agree on anything lately, and he said the most...the most *awful* things to me, and..."

She trails off into another round of sobs, and I instantly feel hit with sadness for her, but also a sense of recognition. "Lex, it's going to be okay," I say.

"No," she says, crying even louder. "No, it's not. My dad might have let me back in the house, but he still hates me, but...the plan was for me to have the baby with *Danny*. To live at his parents' house and raise the baby together!" She starts breathing quickly, almost like she's hyperventilating. "I'm thirty-five weeks pregnant and I've got nothing going for me anymore. I can't do this, I can't-"

"You can do it, Alexa, you're strong," I say, but as I say the words, I feel so defeated and worn out that I wonder if I even sound convincing.

"Look, I'm sorry for ranting to you like this," she says, quieter this time. "I think I'm going to go talk to my dad, and...I'm going to see what to do."

"Okay. That's a good idea, that's really good."

"Madison, what I'm about to say isn't meant to be rude at all, but...you and your baby, you guys are doing fine. But it's all just hit me, you know? I'm...I'm a teenager, having a baby. And that part was bad enough, but now that I'm doing it without the *father,* I...I just don't know if I'm as strong as you."

I'm about to say something else, but she hangs up.

I drive home, millions of thoughts racing through my head about all the horrible things that happened today. I lug Tommy out of the car and bring him into the house, just leaving the school supplies in the car, I'll get them later. When I come in, I see Molly's in the living room, watching TV. She notices the expression on my face and asks me what's wrong. I fill her in about Alexa, but I don't feel like getting into everything else right now.

She asks me if I want to order pizza because her mom is out, and I say yes. Tommy is wide awake and he keeps smiling at Molly. She goes to pick him up and asks if she can hold him for a while. I'm so happy she's here, all I want to do is just chill out and watch TV. We order the pizza and watch a rerun of *Three's Company,* which reminds me of Ian. Tommy is just happy sitting with Molly as she bounces one of his stuffed animals around him. When the episode is over, Tommy starts getting squirmy so I feed him as I tell Molly about the awful lunch, and then the awful run-in with Leo, and she just looks horrified.

Tommy falls asleep just as the pizza comes. Perfect timing, for once. I let him sleep in his car seat, and we eat, and it's so delicious. I realize I never really ate my lunch, and it's like I haven't eaten all day.

"Madison, can I tell you something?" she asks. *Oh no, what now?*

"I mean, I just really want you to know how...proud I am of you. I hope that doesn't sound weird to say because we're the same age. But, I keep thinking about what you've been through." she says. "You're just...the strongest person I know. Even *before* you had Tommy, you were still stronger than anyone, you got through your dad's death and you were so..." She actually starts crying a little now. "You're *so* strong, and every single time something has knocked you down...you've gotten right back up. You don't care what the idiot kids at school think of you. I really...I wish I could be more like you."

Hearing Molly say these things to me makes me cry. I thank her and she hugs me, and I just start bawling so hard that I have to spit out my pizza or else choke. Molly cries harder, too, and then Tommy wakes up and starts crying, and eventually we laugh because it's so funny, all of us are just crying together.

"Molly, do you know what it shows in *you* that you stayed best friends with me after everything?" I say. *"You* are a strong person to stand by someone as messed up as I am."

"Maddie, stop. That's the whole point of what I'm trying to say. You're not messed up. You're more organized and strong than people even a lot older than you. Leo's more of a baby than Tommy is, and you were way too good for him, and so is Tommy. And I'm also so happy that you're with Ian." She grins. "Let's FaceTime him, okay?"

I nod, smiling. We call him on my phone, and it's really fun to do FaceTime with all three of us. Thank God for Molly and Ian. I really don't know what I would do without them. I don't want to say anything to Molly, but I'm really dreading moving out. But then I think about what Molly said, and I realize that her words mean so much to me. I never think of myself as strong, but I guess I am, in a way. Whether I want to be or not, I have no choice, and so I will keep trying to be as strong as I can, not just for Tommy, but also for myself. As horrible as it was standing up to Leo's parents, and then Leo, it felt really, *really* good.

<>

The next morning, I get woken up at ten by Tommy's cries. But when I look over to his co-sleeper, he's not in there. I whip my head around and then I see Molly holding him, trying to shush him as she grabs a diaper. "Molly?"

She looks over at me. "Sorry, I've been trying to keep him quiet since eight so that you could get some sleep. We've been downstairs, but I had to come upstairs with him to get a diaper."

"Oh wow, you are so sweet, thank you!" I exclaim. "This is the most sleep I think I've had in so long!"

All of a sudden, we hear something that sounds like an explosion, and Tommy's face is all red and he grunts and grunts and we hear more explosions. "Oh no, I bet it's a blowout!" I say. Every once in a while, Tommy has such a huge amount of poop that it covers his whole diaper, and it goes all over his legs and butt.

Then the smell wafts out, and Molly says, "Oh my God, that's strong. Shit!" and we burst out laughing as I take him and tell her that she's never done anything bad enough in life to deserve to change this diaper.

Still, she helps me change him. Sure enough, it's all over his legs and it's going up his back. I should probably just bathe him, instead of trying to clean this up with wipes. I hold him up so that Molly can see the whole thing, and she screams a little. We literally can't stop laughing, it's so bad that I have to put Tommy down so I don't drop him. "Someone needs a bath," Molly sing-songs, and we laugh again, and I pick him up and we go to the bathroom together.

Molly helps me run the bath for him, and then I throw the poopy diaper in the garbage, placing the poopy clothes on the floor so that I can put them in the laundry after his bath, and then I put him in the bath, supporting him with my arms. He has the funniest expression on his face, he's almost grinning, like he's pleased with himself. Molly and I are laughing so hard that Molly actually leaves the bathroom, she says if she laughs much more, her stomach muscles are going to explode.

After she leaves, I look at Tommy in the bath, and for the first time since I woke up, I'm not smiling. I look at the dirty clothes on the floor and how I'm going to have to do laundry *again,* but first I have to finish his bath, then feed him, then read to him, play with him, do tummy time, and so on, and who knows when I'll be able to sneak in a quick piece of toast or something for myself? It makes me think about yesterday and running into Leo. I think about my life now, and how I have to move out on my own and pay rent and take care of Tommy and go to school, and I think about Leo and how carefree he is, and his biggest worry is that Dina broke up with him, even though he'll just find another girl to have sex with, and it just makes me so *angry*.

It's been the same way ever since I told him I was pregnant; just an awful cycle of running into him, getting upset, and never feeling like things were ever truly done with him. I need closure. *Real* closure. I remember what Ms. Sherman, the counselor at school, said months ago about writing a letter and how I don't have to send it, but it's good to get the thoughts out and let them go. And I know what I have to do.

After Tommy is out of the bath and dressed, I feed him, play with him, he does his tummy time, and then he gets tired, so I put him down for a nap. The whole time, I'm distracted, composing something in my head. Once he's asleep, I can't wait to get to my pen and paper. I scribble down two pages worth of thoughts I've felt. It's like my hand has a mind of its own. I write and write, and the tears come and I let them pour down my face, and some of them even drop on the paper. It feels so good, just *so good.*

When I'm done, I think about reading it over and maybe editing it a bit, but then I realize that it's not an article for the school paper. This has to be my raw, real feelings for it to do what I need it to do. I quickly put it in an envelope and seal it, before I change my mind.

I grab my phone and send a text.

Maddie: Leo. Meet me at Stonewood Park in 10 minutes. I need to see you. This is the last thing I'll ever ask from you, I swear. Please just meet me there.

Dear God, I hope he listens.

I put Tommy in the baby carrier that Dianne got me, being careful not to wake him, then I grab the envelope and the diaper bag, and walk to the park. I sit on a bench right near the entrance, and wait for Leo. He probably won't even come. Whatever, if he doesn't come, I'll just leave it at his house, but I really don't want his parents to see the letter before he does. I'm sure he won't show it to them, anyway.

I just sit with Tommy, enjoying the sun and all of a sudden, there he is. I'm surprised he came, actually, but I guess me saying that it was the last thing I'll ever ask from him made him curious. And the thing is, no matter how much of a monster he's become, I can't help but see him as the same cute guy I used to know. He's wearing his cutoff jean shorts and his worn-out soccer shirt that he always loved, and he just looks...cute. For so long, it made me mad to see him look good. I always thought, *How can he still look good if we are not together anymore?* But right now, I don't really care. In fact, it makes me happy. I know what I'm about to do with this letter, and then I can let it all go. All the anger and the expectations of him. And I guess knowing this, it makes me *happy* he's cute. Because if Tommy looks like him at all, then Tommy is lucky, because he will be cute. And that's *good* for Tommy. And it doesn't make me scared anymore, like I won't be able to love Tommy if he looks like Leo.

All the things that I've been angry about don't matter anymore, because we'll be *done.* All of my thoughts of him, all of the run-ins, all of the fighting, all of the everything that's been in my head since Leo stopped responding to my texts that horrible day when I told him I was pregnant.

He approaches us and says, "What is it?" and he stays standing, taking little glances at Tommy sleeping but not really looking at him.

I keep my voice low so that I don't wake Tommy. I need to be calm for this. I hand him the letter and say, "I need you to read this."

"What?" he asks, suddenly looking angry. "What is it?"

I just shake my head and hand him the letter. He reluctantly opens it and starts reading it. Then, when he sees how long it is, he sits down on the grass and kind of turns away from me and keeps reading. I watch him read it, and I picture the words that I wrote, in my head.

Leo,

What you said to me yesterday really made me realize something. You didn't choose this, you're right. You chose to have sex with me, but you didn't choose to have a baby, I did. I chose it. And I guess it might seem unfair to you that I could choose to do whatever I wanted and you didn't have a say. Thinking of it from your side, I could see how you would be angry. I get it, I really do.

But what you need to really understand, Leo, is that when you have sex with someone, especially when you're not using protection, you're taking a huge chance that that person could get pregnant. You kept saying it wouldn't happen and I shouldn't worry, but you were wrong.

We all make mistakes, and I guess this is one you will have to live with for the rest of your life. And I feel sorry for you, because you will always see the fact that Tommy was born as a mistake. If you even think about him at all. I realize how lucky I am, because I will *never* think of Tommy as a mistake, even

though sleeping with you when I wasn't ready because you made me think I'd lose you to another girl who *would* sleep with you *was* a mistake. I hate that you did that to me, but more than that, I hate that I was so weak that I gave in to you.

You don't know how many times I wished that after you realized I was going to keep the baby, that you would accept your part of the responsibility. I imagined how it could work with help from our parents, and then eventually being on our own and being a happy family together. It was so hard to let go of that dream. But I'm over it. Completely over it.

We have a baby together, Leo, and it doesn't matter whether you accept it or not. He is made of you just as much as he is made of me. You didn't just leave me; you also left him, which is even worse than you leaving me. He's even starting to look a bit like you, he has your nose, and I think he might even have your lips.

I am not going to let this little boy grow up and not feel loved just because his father didn't want anything to do with him. I have enough love for twenty parents. And *your* parents have been really nice, did you know that? It's hard to believe they could have a kid like you.

But the thing is, whether I like it or not, you will always be an important part of my life, even if it's just my past. I will never want you back, I've given up on that dream. But you were my first boyfriend, my first love. I loved you, Leo. I really did. I loved you so much that I thought about you all the time, even after you left me. But then, I started hating you. Hating you more than I ever thought I was capable of hating anyone.

But now I've made a decision: I don't want to hate you anymore. I actually want to still love you. But not in the way that you think. Just in the way that I can be grateful that because of you, I have the sweetest and cutest little boy in the world. You were a part of giving him to me, and so I have to love you for that.

I am writing this to let you know that we are done. I'm not

going to worry about running into you anymore and having fights with you anymore. I don't care who you're with or what you do. I genuinely hope that you have a good life.

But I am asking you for one thing now, and that is to stay away from me and Tommy. If you see us out somewhere, just don't come up to us. Stay away. Keep your mean thoughts to yourself. I've read stories about these parents who have nothing to do with their kids, and then all of a sudden they show up one day and want to be involved. I am asking you to never, ever do that. It would be horrible for Tommy.

By agreeing to stay away and let us live our lives, it would be the one nice thing you can do for him. This fighting that we have been doing is really horrible for him, and I need to put him first. I do not want to be dealing with you ever again. We have to say goodbye forever. It's dramatic, yes, but it's something that we both need. I'm sorry for anything that I might have done to hurt you. And while I wish that you were sorry for all you've done to me, I know that I can't make you apologize. So I'm just asking you to say goodbye, okay? Goodbye, Leo. I wish you well. Please wish me and Tommy well, too, and then we will be done.

He turns to look at me. I can't really figure out the expression on his face, it's one I've never seen before. He sort of looks at Tommy for a second, I almost feel like he's going to reach out and touch him or something, but then he just looks down, and it's *so weird. He starts to cry. I've never seen him cry before.* He doesn't say anything, he just cries. It's not loud, but it's there. He's crying. I sit there, completely stunned, and he eventually pulls himself together, wipes his nose and his eyes, takes a breath and says, "I wish you guys well." *He actually says it. And he doesn't seem angry anymore. The edge is gone from his voice.* "And yeah, I'm, uh...I'm leaving. I'm...goodbye, Madison."

And then he walks away. I watch him go, and I realize that I'm hoping he will look back one more time, or change his mind, and when he doesn't, the last of my hope for anything with him disappears. Like one of those sand timers that slowly drain the sand, and then eventually, it's all on the other side. The sand is gone. The hope is gone. The anger is gone. It's all completely gone. I'm on the other side.

I get up and walk home with Tommy. In the sunshine. *Like a movie,*

I think. Then I laugh, because I know that my life won't be anything like a movie, where everything gets tied up neatly in a perfect bow and it all works out. But for this one moment, right now, it feels like it could. I may have given up on my dream of Leo, but I'm never, *ever* going to give up on my dreams for myself and for Tommy.

Tommy = 1½ months!!

To-Do List

- pick up paycheck on Friday from Food Direct
- lunch with Mom + Josie + the Schmitzes today
- get the keys to the apartment on Wednesday
- clean the apartment
- order movers?

☆ move into apartment next wednesday

☆ look for present for Dianne + Molly

- last appointment with Dr. Lippincott next week
- call Ian soon!
- call Mom + Josie soon!
- call Alexa again?
- go grocery shopping soon!! (frozen meals, canned soup + food, bulk items, snacks, paper towels, toilet paper, soap, laundry detergent, etc.)

~~Leo~~ goodbye forever

buy:
- SCHOOL SUPPLIES!! (pencils, pens, notebooks, binders, highlighters, erasers)
- diapers/wipes
- more butt paste
- plates + bowls for the apartment
- a microwave for the apartment

☆ get ready for the 1st day of school — Thursday August 22!

☆ school orientation next Sunday

my little Tommy

☆ ask Dr. Brown at Tommy's next appointment about his sleeping/feeding schedule

457

Chapter 43: Seventh Week of Life -- Almost Two Months

"Well, I guess this is it," Dr. Lippincott says, and I nod tearfully. It's my last postpartum appointment. It feels like I've known her for a hundred years. I will never forget how nice she was to me, right from the very beginning, she never judged me, she was just there to help. Dianne is with me for this appointment, she wanted to come to say goodbye, too. Molly had to work, and she was bummed she was going to miss it.

Dr. Lippincott examines me and says that I've healed up really well, and my uterus is pretty much back to its old size, and then we talk for a few minutes. I update her on everything that's going on, how I'm moving in two days, and how weird it's going to be to be on my own with Tommy. I got the keys last Wednesday, and the day after, I went over with Tommy and cleaned the apartment, just mopping and wiping down the appliances. Mom paid for movers to come, and it only took less than an hour to move my bed, dresser, couch, Tommy's crib, and all the other furniture I have. It was really sweet of her to pay for it, and I told her that I would definitely pay her back.

I tell Dr. Lippincott that Tommy has actually (I really don't want to jinx it, but I say it anyway) been sleeping more at night. Instead of waking up every two hours, it's more like every three to four hours. I worry that he's hungry, so I'm trying to wake him up to eat. Dr. Lippincott says she thinks I can just let him sleep, but I make a note in my head to ask his doctor about that. It just goes to show how much I still have to learn about parenting.

At the end of the appointment, Dr. Lippincott gives me a big hug. "Good luck with everything. I have complete confidence in you. Remember, you can call me anytime. I'm still here for you if you need me." She looks at Dianne and smiles. "Keep in touch, okay?"

Dianne nods and gives her a hug. I think about how Dianne had Dr. Lippincott for her doctor when she had Molly, and then I think to myself that maybe one day, I'll have another baby the "right" way, and if I do, I hope that I can come to her again.

We hug one more time, and then she looks over at Tommy and smiles and blows him a kiss as he sleeps in his car seat. "Take care of your mommy, okay?" she says to him, and he grunts in his sleep and we all laugh.

In the car on the way home, Dianne is very quiet and she looks sad, so I ask her what's wrong. "Well, I just wanted to say that I'm really going to be missing you when you leave on Wednesday," she says.

"Really?" I ask, and she nods. I've been so worried that it's been way too long with me staying there throughout my pregnancy, and then Tommy screaming and crying and the whole mess. It's nice to hear that she will miss me, I hope it's true.

"I care about you very much. And Tommy, too. The house will feel kind of...empty without you two. You've become like...a second daughter to me."

I feel like I'm about to cry. "Dianne, I don't even know how to thank you for everything you've done for me. You and Molly have been so amazing. All your support and encouragement, I really truly couldn't have done any of this without you."

We agree that just because I'm moving out doesn't mean that we won't see each other anymore. She says she wants to help whenever she can, and babysit Tommy and have us over for dinner. She asks me about Ian, and I tell her that we've been talking and texting, and she says that she still can't believe we are together but she's happy about it and she hopes it lasts. She says that I couldn't find a guy nicer than her brother, and I agree. Dianne really did change my life, in so many ways. I think about how Dad always said that things happen for a reason. Then Alexa pops into my head, and I realize I haven't heard from her since the other day. I hope she's okay. I make a note in my phone to call her later, and also to call Mom. I miss her and Josie so much.

Once we get home, I change Tommy's diaper and then I get ready for my school's orientation. It's always held the Sunday before school starts, and since we have to pick up our textbooks, they do it at the school library. They also set up booths so that you can sign up for clubs, et cetera. Then the freshmen come to the school for an hour for a tour. Just two years ago, I was one of the freshmen, and now I'm in my second-to-last year of high school, it's crazy.

I change into a pair of my old jeans. They aren't really old, although I keep calling them old. It's just that they were the jeans I wore before I got pregnant, so they're kind of stuck in the "old" era of my life. I think of everything this way now, the "before Tommy" and "after Tommy" stuff. I used to do this after my dad died, too, but eventually I stopped. I wonder if I'll ever stop with *this*.

Now that my stomach has shrunk, I can wear most of my old clothes, and I decide to put on a yellow shirt that I love, because it's so bright and happy, and it makes me look a bit tan. I check the time and realize that I'm going to be late, so I rush out to my car. Thank God Dianne is going to watch Tommy, because I really just don't want to deal with having everyone at school see him until I absolutely have to.

The library is packed with all the kids from school. I see Molly here, too, she came straight from work. I see a group of girls that I used to hang out with before Lulu started spreading the news that I was pregnant. It feels like another lifetime ago, I haven't spoken to any of them in so long. They really weren't true friends. Looking around, I wonder if I'll ever make new friends. It's hard enough to make a good friend, but then to have someone accept me now that I'm a teen mom?

Being around everyone just makes me feel so...*different.* I also feel like I'm much older than them, which is weird. I might be technically defined as a teenager, but I don't feel that way anymore. The thing is, after my dad died, I didn't feel like a kid anymore. I realize that I don't remember when I really felt like the age I was.

Sure enough, just as I pictured, I get a lot of looks and comments from people. They haven't seen me since I was pregnant and my stomach was huge. A few people tell me that I look good, and they can't believe I lost all the weight, and they ask how the baby is and whether it was a boy or girl. Then, of course, there are the mean girls who say things like "I guess the beached whale had her baby." I try to ignore them and just focus on getting out of here as quickly as possible.

I go to the newspaper booth and sign up for another year of being editor-in-chief. I see on the list that Janet's already signed up to be the assistant-editor-in-chief. It's nice that she's not trying to take over my position. Maybe she likes being the assistant because it's less responsibility, I don't know.

I see a bunch of guys at the soccer booth, and I'm sure one of them is Leo, but I don't bother to really look. I just remember the other day and our goodbye, and I don't feel sad or anything anymore, it's really a relief.

I go collect my textbooks, and boy are they heavy. How am I going to carry all this *and* a baby at school? At least I won't have to carry all of it all the time and I can leave some in my locker. I groan as I stuff them into the large bag I brought with me. My arm instantly buckles under the weight, and Molly comes up to me, her arm also dragging under the weight of her books, and we laugh. Then she says, "So I was talking to Cheryl, and we realized that we have to plan our first-day-of-school outfits!"

Every year, we would always get so excited about what we were going to wear for the first day of school, and it was always fun to plan it together. It's funny, but I just don't care about it anymore. Molly is so excited, though, and I don't want to bring her down, so I just smile and nod.

I have to get going, because I have to pick up some groceries. I want to stock up with frozen meals and canned soups and bulk items, like rice and pasta and snacks, and take it all over to the apartment. I also need to remember to get paper towels, toilet paper, and laundry detergent and coins to use for the laundry machines, which are on the first floor of the building. That's another thing I'm going to have to get used to: not having my own free laundry machines. These are the things that are going through my head as I leave the library, hearing everyone laughing and talking about their summers and who their crushes are.

I pick up Tommy from Dianne so that I can bring him to the grocery store with me. I think it'll be cute to have him ride around in the shopping cart, in his car seat. He's very awake at the store, but he's not crying, he's just looking around at everything.

As I cruise down the junk food aisle, I say, "Those are yummy, yummy chips and cookies. Not healthy, though, and they'll make Mommy gain lots of weight." I chuckle. I see a bag of cheese puffs, and I remember the day with Ian when they exploded all over the place, and how much fun we had. I pick up a bag and show it to Tommy, and I say, "These are cheese puffs. That's what I used to call you, do you remember?" and I say the words "cheese puff" a few times to see if he remembers hearing it from when he was in my tummy. He tries to grab them, and he makes his cute little gurgling noises. I decide not to get them, for some reason they still kind of turn me off since having Tommy.

We get to the five-dollar frozen meal aisle, and I take a whole bunch of them. When I pick up a frozen pizza, Tommy stares at it and actually smiles. I grin. "You like the pizza one?" I ask, bringing it right up to his face, and he starts screaming in an excited way. "Is pizza going to be your favorite food?" I squeal to him. "I love pizza, too!" I laugh, this is so fun and so much easier when he's not crying.

Then my phone rings. It's Ian! I answer. "Hi!"

It sounds like there's lots of commotion around him. "Hi!" he says loudly. "Sorry, it's really loud, I'm at my orientation, but I just had to tell you, I was in the cafeteria, and they have cheese puffs for a snack, so I thought of you."

I tell him where I am, and how I just passed through the aisle where the cheese puffs exploded. We laugh and then he says he has to go, but he wants to FaceTime later and he tells me he loves me. I'm really happy to hear this, I've just been feeling really worried lately that he'll find someone else at college. I tell him I love him too, and I can't wait to FaceTime, and then we hang up.

The groceries are expensive, but I tell myself that they should last a little while and it's in my budget. Once we get home, I think about all the stuff I have to do, packing and getting ready to move. I don't want to do any of it. I wish I could just stay here forever, with Dianne and Molly and the nice, big house with the free laundry machines and Dianne's cooking. I'm going to miss all of it so much.

I start to make Tommy do tummy time, but he instantly starts grunting and crying, and I decide to just let him take the day off. Instead, I put him on the bed and lift his shirt and blow into his tummy. I remember seeing Mom do this with Josie when she was a baby and how it made a funny sound. I do it to Tommy, and all of a sudden, he starts *giggling*. I've never seen him do this before! He's actually giggling! Smiling and giggling!

"Tommy's tummy!" I coo. "Is this your tummy, Tommy?" I do it again and he giggles, and I start laughing and I realize that this is so much better than doing tummy time. "See, Tommy? Your tummy can be a fun thing, too. I don't want you to think it's always going to be the horrible *tummy time* that you hate doing."

I know he doesn't understand me, but it makes me suddenly feel very philosophical, like it's symbolic of life. I'm going to have to do a lot of my own "tummy time," but I have to remember to take time to laugh and be happy, just like I'm trying to show Tommy. I have to remember that even though I don't feel like one, I still *am* a teenager, and just because I have more responsibilities than the typical one doesn't mean that I can't still have fun and be happy sometimes. I want to get back to being excited about my first-day-of-school outfits and things like that.

... August 2018...

Last year, a few nights before school started, Molly and I were at my house, in my room, picking outfits to wear for the first day. As I held up a baby blue top, Molly said, "That's so perfect, it'll look so cute on you!"

"Thanks!" I said. "I'm so excited for school. I mean, we're sophomores now!"

"I know, it's crazy!"

"I bet it's going to be a great year," I said wistfully.

Little did I know. *Little did I know.*

...

On Wednesday morning, Molly helps me pack up my car with the last boxes of my clothes. I realize that I really don't have that much stuff, and it only takes two trips there and back to get everything moved. I still can't get my head around the fact that I'm moving to my own apartment.

"I can't believe you're really going," Molly says disbelievingly. "It's going to be so weird not having you and Tommy there." She tears up and so do I, for like the millionth time this week.

"Well, we'll still see each other a ton," I say. "We were practically always together even before I moved in, so-"

"It won't be the same, though," Molly says quietly.

For the last trip, Dianne takes Molly in her own car and we meet at the apartment. Dianne looks around at everything and tells me that I did a really great job. She says that it reminds her of when she moved out with Molly for the first time when she was a baby, but she says she thinks I did a better job. I shake my head and we laugh, and then she takes a wrapped gift out of her purse and hands it to me. "Housewarming gift," she says, and Molly giggles.

I open it to find a little gift pack of pretty, colored mugs, and a pack of Hershey's hot chocolate mix. Then Molly goes into her purse and takes out another little gift and I open it to find a pack of marshmallows. I laugh and thank them and tell them it will remind me of being there with them and having our late-night hot chocolates. I start to cry again, and Dianne hugs me and tells me again that I can come over anytime.

Then I go into the closet and bring out a wrapped gift for them. "Here's something for you guys," I say. "It's not even close to being enough to say thank you for all you've done for me, but, well, I hope you like it."

Dianne lets Molly open it, and when they see it, they both smile and Dianne even looks like *she's* now going to cry. It's a painting of a little house that kind of looks like Dianne's, with a yellow door, and there's pastel letters on the top reading **Home is Where the Heart is.** I got it at this little shop in town where they sell interesting things that are one of a kinds, made from local artists. I used a lot of my savings for it, but it was worth it now that I see that they love it.

I tell them that it made me think of them because even though we won't be in the same home anymore, my heart will be with them. I also think about how this applies to my mom and Josie, too. It makes me feel both sad and happy at the same time.

Dianne gives me a big hug and tells me what a meaningful present it is. Then they have to leave, so I hug Dianne again, crying, and she says, "Madison, please stop acting as if this is goodbye. It's not! You're welcome over anytime, and if you need help with something with Tommy or with you, just let me know. You are *not alone,* okay?"

I nod, tears streaming down my face. Molly joins the hug and cries along with me. Then *Tommy* starts to cry, and we all start laughing. I pick him up to feed him, and they say goodbye to them. As Molly is about to close the door, I say, "Meet you at the front of school tomorrow, Molly Lolly Pop?" She smiles and nods, and then leaves.

After feeding Tommy, I put him down for his nap. I take a look around, and it's all so weird being here and realizing it's only one room. It's *so* small. How am I going to get used to being in such a small, cramped space?

The kitchen is all stocked up with my groceries, and I bought a few plates and bowls and Dianne gave me some extra cutlery that she had. Mom got me a small toaster and I also bought a little microwave, for heating up the frozen meals.

Next to the kitchen is where my desk, dresser, nightstand, and bed are. I still have to unpack my clothes, but thankfully Tommy's area is all set up: his crib and a tiny chest with drawers filled with his stuffed animals and books and diapers and wipes and everything he needs are in the corner. And I had the movers put the couch and TV in the middle of the room, as it was the only place they'd fit. It hits me that it'll be hard to watch TV late at night like I used to, because I won't want to wake Tommy up and his crib and the TV are in the same room.

I never pictured the first place I would live on my own to be this way. Honestly, before I got pregnant, I never even pictured living on my own at all. And a cluttered studio apartment is really kind of depressing, and even *this* is hard to afford. I also should have thought this through better, moving into a place literally the day before school starts. I should have given myself more time to organize everything, but oh well.

I realize that it will be weird to have people come here to visit. It's so small, and I'm kind of embarrassed. Leo's parents will be my first visitors, they are coming on Sunday morning. Leo's mom texted me the other day and said again that she was really sorry about what happened at lunch. She said that they really want to get to know their grandson, and so she doesn't want to argue. I wonder if Leo told her about our meeting at the park and saying goodbye. I would bet all my savings that he didn't.

I unpack the rest of my clothes and everything else that needs to be unpacked, and then I go to work with Tommy. That was another stupid thing I didn't think through. I shouldn't have worked tonight, I should've canceled my shift. I really need some rest before school tomorrow. Then again, this is something I'm going to just have to get used to. Being exhausted and still working, going to school, and taking care of Tommy all at the same time.

As I'm heating up one of the frozen meals in the microwave, I get a call from Alexa. I wrote her the other day, but never heard back and I was getting worried and was going to try again. I quickly answer. "Alexa? Oh my God, hi! Are you-"

"I had the baby," she says, and her voice sounds weird, kind of far away and very emotionless.

My heart stops for a second. A million questions swim around my head. "Oh my God, wow! Wait, but you were only thirty-six weeks along!"

"I know. She came early."

"Oh wow, a *girl*! Alexa, that's amazing! Did you name her yet?"

She doesn't answer my question, she just continues talking in the really weird, distant voice. "She was early. She's been in intensive care, but she'll be okay."

"Yeah, I remember my doctor saying that a lot of teen moms have a higher risk of preterm labor." There's a long pause. I eventually say, "Well, where are you? Are you still at the hospital? Can I come visit you? What are you going to name her?"

Suddenly, I hear what sounds like a cough or sneeze, but then I realize she's crying. She's *bawling*. Bawling so hard that it's hard to understand what she's saying, but I manage to hear most of it. I almost fall to the floor when she tells me that she decided to *give the baby up for adoption. Oh my God.* She says that the second the baby came out of her, she realized that she just couldn't do it.

She says she'd been worried the whole time she was pregnant, and then after the fight with Danny and his family, it was just too much. She says the arrangements have already been made, and she doesn't even think she will say goodbye to her, it's too hard. As she tells me this, all I can picture is Alexa when she was pregnant, all our talks about being mothers, and yes, being scared, but I figured she would still keep the baby just like me. I don't even know what to say. I look over at Tommy sleeping in his crib, and I'm just speechless.

"Madison?" Alexa asks, her voice sounds shaky. "Are you there?"

"I'm here, Lex, I'm...I'm just really shocked." I take a deep breath and try to think of something to say. I can't think of anything. I can hear her crying, and I start to cry, too. "I'm so sorry, Lex," I say. "I don't know what to say. I'm just so sorry. And I'm here for you, anytime you want to talk."

"I know. Thank you," she says. "I'm going to go now. I'll...I'll call you later."

And then she hangs up. I just sit there with the phone in my hand. The microwave is beeping, but I really don't even want to eat anymore. I sit there, staring at Tommy. I can't even *imagine* how I would feel if I had given him up. I couldn't have done it, I would never have gotten over it. I remember when I went to the person at the adoption agency, and I remember her telling me that most teen mothers find it a relief to know that their baby will be raised with another family who really wants them.

It makes sense. But it wasn't the right choice for me. I know that for sure. Just like I bet one day Alexa will think that her choice was the right one for her.

My heart still breaks for her, though, and I feel like I'll never get the sound of her bawling out of my head. I hope she'll be okay. The more I think about it, I think it probably *was* the right choice for her. She can go back to being a regular teenager now. I wonder if we'll still be friends, or if it'll be too hard for her to see me and Tommy.

I need to take advantage of Tommy being asleep, so I take a shower. *My first shower in my new place.* I was able to bring the seat that Ian got me when I broke my wrist, and I just sit on it and let the water pour down on me.

After I get out, I call Mom. She answers and says she's at work and asks if she can call me later. I say sure, and then she asks me if everything's okay. I just say quietly into the phone, "I just wanted to hear your voice." She tells me that she loves me and she'll call me later. Ian and I do a quick Facetime. He says that he wishes he was there with me, and I wish he was, too, but I know he'll come to visit soon.

Later that night, after my shift at work, and after I've put Tommy to bed, I just lie on my bed, looking around at everything. There's my nightstand with the picture of me and Mom, the ultrasound picture, the note from Ian, and the can of Dad's shaving cream. I spray a little shaving cream on my wrist and then take a deep inhale of it.

I look out the window and think, *Dad? Are you out there? I don't know what to believe, but I hope you are. I'm really scared, Dad. I'm...alone. I have Tommy, but that's it. I've never been this alone before. I'm so scared, Dad. I wish you were here.*

I decide to leave the small light over the kitchen stove on. I'm too scared to have it be completely dark. I look around the room, and I realize it's actually good that the place is so small. I would be way too scared to be in a bigger place, with separate rooms and so much space to take care of. This place is perfect. Everything I need is in this room. My eyes get tired, and before I know it, I'm asleep. And I have a weird dream.

I'm sleeping in my bed, but then suddenly, I feel like someone's watching me. I open my eyes, and there's Dad. He's here. Smiling at me. His warm hazel eyes staring right into mine, his familiar comforting smell filling the room. He's alive! Somehow, he's alive, I don't know how, but he is!

I jump out of bed and run to him, throwing my arms around him, crying. "Daddy, you're here! Oh my God, Daddy, how did you-"

He calmly reaches out and touches my hair. "No, sweetie. I'm not alive. But I am here."

Then, suddenly, he starts to disappear. First his arms are gone, and I can't hug him anymore. Then, his legs and then his body. The last thing to disappear is his head. I try to find him but I can't. I call out to him and he says, "I'm still here, Madison. You just can't see me. I can see you. And Tommy. Thank you for naming him after me. You're doing a really good job. I'm so proud of you. I have to go now."

I start to cry in my dream. "Dad, no, please don't go, please stay with me!"

But he doesn't answer, and I cry and cry. But I also feel like he's somehow still here.

<>

The next morning, I wake up and for a second I forget the dream I had, but then when I go to the bathroom and see that my eyes are all swollen and red, it all comes back to me. I must have been crying in my sleep. *Just great.* But, I don't even have time to think about it, because I have to get me and Tommy ready. It's the first day of school!

I laugh when I realize I picked a first-day-of-school outfit for Tommy, but not for myself. I put him in a little giraffe outfit that I got on sale at Babies R' Us. As I get ready, I play music on my phone, and it makes the place feel happier and it puts me in a good mood. After fixing my hair and brushing my teeth, I finally decide on some jeans and a cute top. I'm pretty much back to my weight before I had Tommy, and I think about how if I didn't have to bring him with me to school, then people might even forget I was ever pregnant, and I'd just go back to being a regular teenager again. I think about Alexa and how that will be the case for her soon enough. But I don't think I want it to be the case for me.

Then I decide to do something I've been thinking about, but I wasn't sure if I'd have the nerve. I decide to put my hair in braids. I think it's my way of saying that I'm not going to let my fears control me. I'm going to turn sad memories into happy ones. I look at the picture of me and Mom, where I'm wearing braids, and I show it to Tommy and say, "Look Tommy, that's me, Mommy. And I'm with *my* Mommy. *Your* grandma." He makes his little gurgling sound and smiles, and I just can't get over how cute he is.

As I put him in the baby carrier, I put the tiniest little dab of Dad's shaving cream on his arm, and I inhale deeply. Tears come to my eyes as the dream I had last night flashes through my mind, but I stop it and try to focus on the crazy day I have ahead of me. Right now, I don't know exactly how I'm going to get through it, but even though I'm nervous, I'm also really excited to find out.

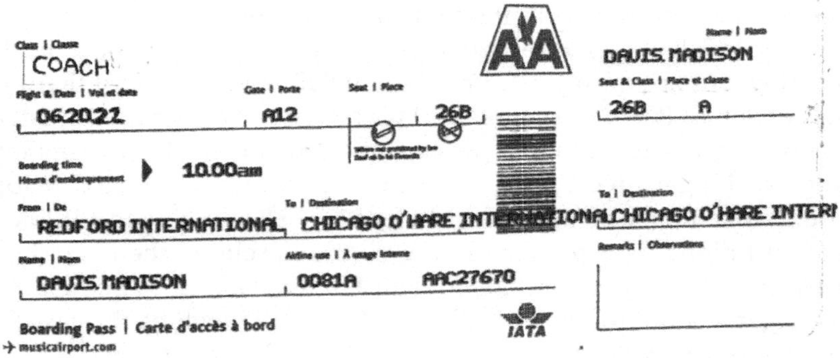

Class | Classe
COACH
Flight & Date | Vol et date
062022
Gate | Porte
A12
Seat | Place
26B
Boarding time
Heure d'embarquement
10.00am
From | De
REDFORD INTERNATIONAL
To | Destination
CHICAGO O'HARE INTERNATIONAL
Name | Nom
DAVIS.MADISON
Airline use | À usage interne
0081A AAC27670
Boarding Pass | Carte d'accès à bord
musicairport.com
IATA
Name | Nom
DAVIS.MADISON
Seat & Class | Place et classe
26B A
To | Destination
CHICAGO O'HARE INTERN
Remarks | Observations

Epilogue

AROUND THREE YEARS LATER

"Passengers and flight attendants, prepare for take-off," the pilot says over the speakers.

Tommy and I are on our way to Chicago. Yes, Chicago. Not Boston, where Harvard is, because I didn't get into Harvard, even after applying for two years in a row. The first time I got the rejection letter, I cried a lot, and I mean, *a lot*. It was devastating, and I decided to take a gap year to just work and make some money and take a few courses at the community college to improve my grades, and hopefully my chances for getting into Harvard when I reapplied. But it didn't work. I got my second rejection letter, and then I knew I had to be realistic, so I said yes to one of the other backup universities I applied to. University of Chicago was my second choice, and I got in there. Besides the fact that they have a good journalism program, I feel like it has meaning to me because my dad was born in Chicago, and he lived there until he was ten.

I still plan to apply to Harvard for my postgraduate college years, and hopefully get my master's in journalism there. In the meantime, I'm excited about Chicago. I did some research and found a small studio apartment in a safe area, near the campus. I've decided that I actually like living in a small space. My place in Redford ended up being perfect for me and Tommy. It was really cozy and not too hard to take care of, and it was sad saying goodbye to it. I'm having my car shipped to Chicago, and I found another job for a food delivery service. I got a reference from Mr. Lopez, and he was actually sad when I quit, because I ended up being one of his most reliable employees, I got a lot of good reviews. I'm really excited to learn my way around a new place, but thank God for Google Maps if it's hard.

So much has happened in the last three years. Tommy is turning three in less than a month. His hair is still blonde, just a little lighter than mine. His smile is adorable, and he's so sweet, the sweetest little boy in the whole world. His eyes ended up being light green, which he got from Leo. Just like that day at the park when I said goodbye to Leo, I feel happy that Tommy has some of Leo's good looks, and there's truly no more sadness or anger in me when I think of Leo.

I've worked harder than I could ever imagine to keep up with school and a job and being a mom. It's been really brutal at times, and I didn't think I could get through it, but so far, I've been able to manage. As hard as it's been, I'm so happy that I've been able to be with Tommy to see him do all his firsts. Take his first steps, say his first words, then learn to go on the potty, it's all so amazing. His first word was "cheese," which I thought was hilarious. His second one was "mama," and I cried tears of happiness when he said it.

I got into a good schedule with Mom and Josie, where they would come down to see me and Tommy every couple weeks, and I would go to them sometimes, too. Mom bought some air mattresses for her and Josie for when they would stay with me, and it was a lot of fun, feeling like we were camping out. I'm going to miss them, and it'll be hard to be in a different state from everyone, but we will still plan for visits during Thanksgiving and Christmas and times like that.

I still miss Dad so much, and I had to buy a new container of his shaving cream when his original one ran out. Tommy likes the smell of it, too, and whenever I put it on, he now says "Grampa," because I've been telling him that it was his grandpa's. It's so sad to know that Tommy will never meet him. He has the same shape of hands as him, and they make me think of Dad every time I look at them. I always tell him stories about Dad, because even though he will never meet him, I want him to know about his grandfather. At bedtime, Tommy prefers to hear the stories about Dad rather than his actual books, and it makes me so happy. I haven't really had another dream like the one I had the first night I moved into the apartment, or at least I haven't had anything where it seemed like he was so real, but I hear his voice in my head all the time, and I try to imagine what he would say to me.

The Schmitzes have actually been really helpful, babysitting Tommy a lot, especially Leo's mom, who I get along with really well now. It's really weird to have such a good relationship with Leo's parents and to never see or hear from *him,* but he's respecting my wishes and staying away like I asked him to do in my letter, and that's the most I can hope for when it comes to Leo.

Alexa and I didn't keep in touch for a long time. She told me that it was too painful to see me or talk to me after she had her baby and gave her up. But then, on Tommy's first birthday, she called me and said she remembered it was his birthday. I was so happy to hear from her, and we got together and caught up on everything. She told me that it took her awhile to get back to being happy and feeling like she could just be a teenager again, but then after a little while, it became like the pregnancy never happened. I often think about the different choices we made, and how different our lives are now because of them. I've come to the conclusion that neither decision was right or wrong, but it was what was best for each of us, at the time.

Even after moving out, I still spent a lot of time at Molly's until she left for NYU last year to major in the arts. Dianne was really sad when she left, and I came over a lot afterwards so that she wouldn't feel alone. I can't even imagine what it will be like if Tommy goes away to university one day. Molly and I talk all the time, and we're of course still best friends. We both plan to move back to Redford one day.

Now I'm nineteen, which I still can't believe. Tommy is talking more and more these days, and it really feels like I have another actual *person* with me all the time, he's really not a baby anymore. It's still unbelievable to me that he was once this little thing that was the size of a cheese puff in my stomach, and now he's this living, breathing boy, who's getting bigger all the time. I know that one day, he will probably have lots of questions. I'm still figuring out what exactly I will tell him, but the most important thing that I'm going to want him to know is that I love him more than I can ever tell him. Until I had him, I never knew that I could love someone as much as I love him. I understand now how my dad must have felt about me, and how much Mom loves me and Josie. When I tell Mom how I can't believe how fast he's growing up, she laughs and says, "I feel the same way about you, Madison."

As hard as it's been, I've been able to learn a *lot* from being a teen mom. One of the main things I've learned and keep learning is that life is all about your choices, from the simplest, like what you want for dinner, to the most complex, like, in my case, whether or not you're going to keep your baby. When I got pregnant, I was presented with three choices: abortion, adoption, or keeping Tommy. And I definitely chose a hard road. I guess I will never know what it would have been like if I had made the other choices, but I really can't imagine my life without Tommy.

Even though I love Tommy, I honestly don't think that I should've had sex as young as I did. I was only fifteen years old, and I really didn't think about the consequences. I also wish that I had waited to lose my virginity until I was older, when I really knew that I loved the person and he loved me back. Sometimes I think about how much more I would probably be able to enjoy Tommy and being a mother if I had waited. There's nothing I can do about it now, so I try not to think about it too much.

Something else I've learned is that it's a *lot* harder than you think it is. It's funny, but when you look at your parents, or at least when *I* did, I thought it seemed easy. Now I know it's not. My parents had each other, or at least they did until Dad died, so that's part of it, but they were also older and they had jobs and they weren't in school. They did things the "right" way, and now I know that even then it was still hard for them. When you're a parent, it feels like every time you learn how to do something, another thing pops up right away, because kids change so much, all the time. It feels like you conquer one problem, and then another two show up. It's like that saying "one step forward, two steps back." There's so much to be done to be a teen mom, and it's really hard to do all of it while you're still growing yourself, and when your emotions get in the way. I've been *so* angry and sad and scared at times, and the worst part of that is trying to not let Tommy see it, which is impossible.

I missed out on so many of the major teenage milestones. I didn't get to party or have a real group of friends, I didn't get to stay out late at night and break curfew, I didn't even get to go to my prom because Tommy was sick with a high fever. Basically, I never had any simple carefree teenage *fun*. Instead, I had to deal with sleepless nights and dirty diapers and cleaning our place and making sure there was food on the table, taking care of Tommy when he was sick, and taking care of him even when *I* was sick. I had to make sure that I kept my job and made money, and at the same time, worry about school and studying and trying to get good enough grades to get into university.

The scariest part is knowing that you can't stop. No matter how hard it gets, you can't just quit. You can't give up, because you're not just giving up on yourself, you're now giving up on another whole person. You actually have to work even *harder* to make things okay. All I can say is that I put my heart and my soul into whatever I was doing for myself or for Tommy. He has been my motivation for all the work I've done.

But I don't want to make it sound like it's all bad and like it has all these problems. There are so many good moments, so many amazing things that I feel so lucky that I get to experience. Watching Tommy grow is the biggest reward. The bigger and stronger he gets, the more I feel like I'm doing something right. The other day, I told Mom that I feel like Tommy and I are growing up together, in a way. She laughed and said, "Madison, I *still* feel like *I'm* growing up. Trust me, it takes a lifetime."

Growing up is like being on an airplane; you can't *feel* yourself traveling through the sky, but before you know it, you are somewhere really far from where you started. There's always going to be turbulence, but there will be times when it's smooth and easy, too. All we can hope for is to have more and more of the times when it's smooth and easy as we try to get it right.

As the plane's engines turn on, a text pings through my phone.

Ian: Have a safe flight, Mads. I love you. Call me when you land :)

And yes...Ian and I are still together. We've been able to see each other quite a bit, considering it's long-distance. We've spent all our breaks together, and we plan to keep doing that. I've had many moments of being insecure and worrying he's going to find someone else, but he still says that he wants me and only me. He's so sweet to Tommy, and Tommy loves him. When Tommy sees him, his whole face lights up and Ian laughs and says he wishes I could look at him that way. He's joking, of course.

I smile and show Tommy the text and Ian's picture that's at the top of the screen. "That's from Eee," I say. Tommy calls Ian "Eee," it's really cute.

The plane starts to move, and suddenly Tommy stops smiling. "Sweetie, what's wrong?" I ask.

"I'm scared, Mama. The pizza plane is moving!" He's calling it the "pizza plane" because the wings have red circles on them, and he told me it looks like pizza. Yep, his favorite food turned out to be pizza, with pepperoni, so far.

I smile at him. "Don't worry, sweetie, the plane is supposed to move," I say, and then I reach into my backpack. "Guess what? I used to have these a lot when *I* was scared. And they always made me feel better."

When we were waiting to get on the plane, I saw cheese puffs at a store in the airport and I bought a bag. I haven't eaten them since I was pregnant, but today, I felt like I should buy a bag and try them again. Now couldn't be a more perfect time.

I open the bag and hand one to Tommy. He smells it, then pops it in his mouth, chews for a second, and then smiles a huge smile and says, "More, Mama, pleeease!" and he kicks his legs, which usually means he's happy.

I smile and give him some more, and then take some for myself. I'm surprised at how much the taste and smell reminds me of being pregnant, and for a second, I feel like I want to throw up, but the feeling passes and I realize how much I've missed them.

The plane starts to take off, and it's a little bumpy, and once we're in the sky, Tommy looks out the window and says, "Look, Mama, the clouds look like them!" and he holds a cheese puff up against the window to show me.

That's my son, alright. I nod, laughing, and he laughs, too, and we zoom forward into the endless blue sky, surrounded by the cheese puff-shaped clouds. Eating our cheese puffs together.

"Ladies and gentlemen," the pilot says over the speaker. "Apologies for the bumpy take-off, but now we've reached cruising altitude. It should be smooth sailing for a little while..."

RUBY MATENKO

About the Author

Ruby Matenko has always been passionate about stories. An avid reader since the age of 4, she is rarely seen without a book in her hand. Ruby's love of characters also led her to pursue acting, which she has been doing professionally since the age of 7. Writing has been a natural evolution of her passion for books and characters. That passion, in combination with her aspirations to become an obstetrician, gave birth to her novel *Cheese Puffs: A Teenage Journey of Grief, Pregnancy, and Hope.* Ruby is an honor-roll student as well as a competitor on her high school tennis and debate teams. Find her on IMDb and on YouTube at her popular channel, rubix cubix.

Made in the USA
Middletown, DE
31 May 2022